DAWN OF RAGNAROK

THE COMPLETE SERIES

The Royal Wizard   Dragonblood   Prince of Deceit

BOOKS BY ALIANNE DONNELLY

BLOOD AND SHADOWS
Blood Moons
Blood Trails
Blood Debts
Blood Hunt

THE REBEL COURT
Catch Me
Dearest Love
Sweetest Kiss
Rebel Heart

DAWN OF RAGNAROK
The Royal Wizard
Dragonblood
Prince of Deceit

THE BEAST
Bastien
The Beast

WOLFEN
Wolfen
Helena

OTHER TITLES
Virtual
Function: L1VE

ALIANNE DONNELLY

DAWN OF RAGNAROK

THE COMPLETE SERIES

The Royal Wizard *Dragonblood* *Prince of Deceit*

THIS IS AN ALIANNE DONNELLY BOOK PUBLISHED BY ALIANNE DONNELLY.
It's not bragging if it's true.

DAWN OF RAGNAROK is a work of fiction. Names, characters, places, and incidents either are the product of the author's imagination or are used fictitiously, and any resemblance to actual persons, living or dead, business establishments, events, or locales is entirely coincidental.

aliannedonnelly.com

ISBN: 978-1-948325-13-4

PUBLISHING HISTORY:

The Royal Wizard - first published March 2013
Dragonblood - first published September 2016
Prince of Deceit - first published December 2020

Published in the United States of America

CONTENTS

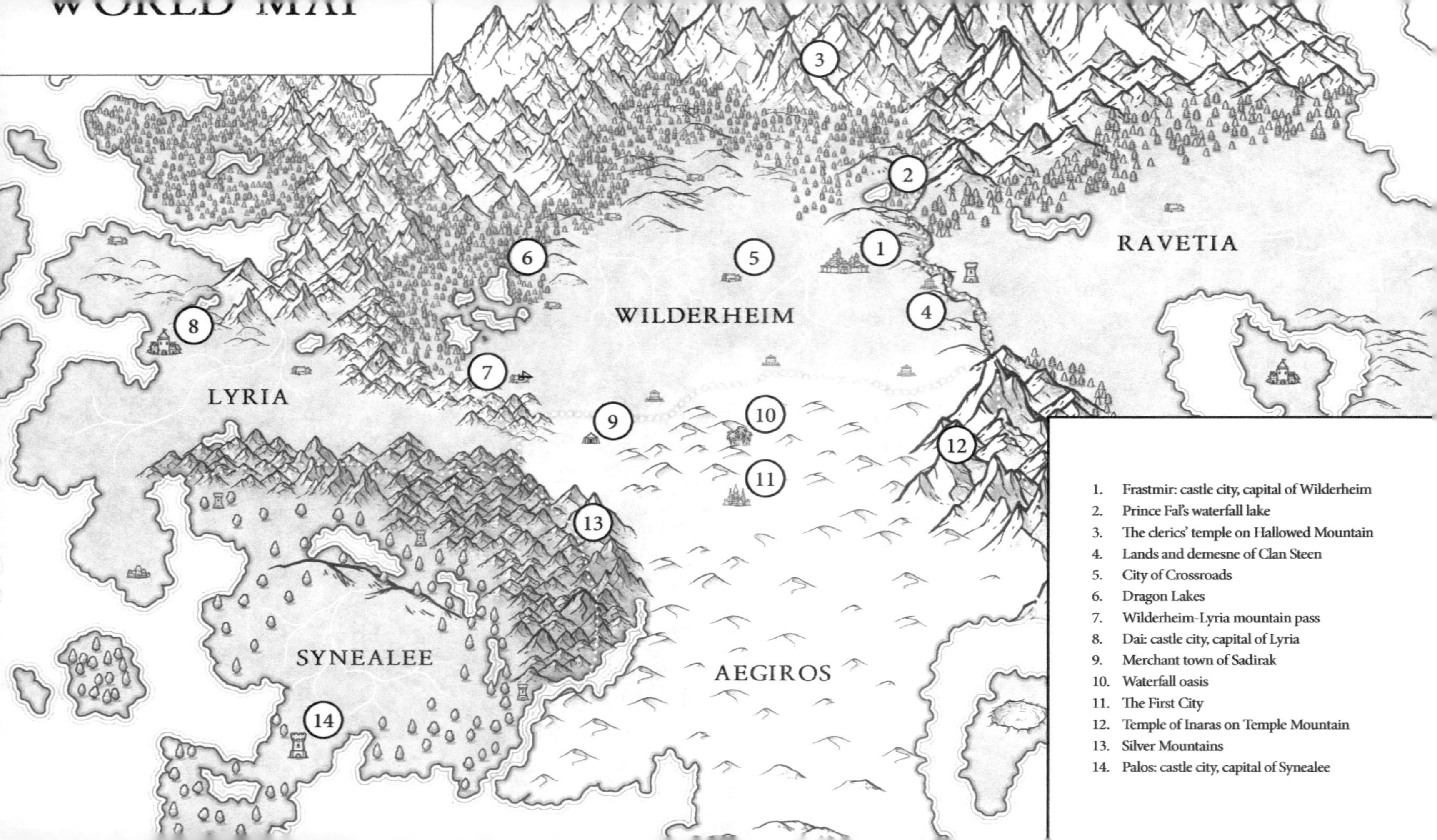
WORLD MAP
RAVETIA
WILDERHEIM
LYRIA
SYNEALEE
AEGIROS
1
2
3
4
5
6
7
8
9
10
11
12
13
14
1. Frastmir: castle city, capital of Wilderheim
2. Prince Fal's waterfall lake
3. The clerics' temple on Hallowed Mountain
4. Lands and demesne of Clan Steen
5. City of Crossroads
6. Dragon Lakes
7. Wilderheim-Lyria mountain pass
8. Dai: castle city, capital of Lyria
9. Merchant town of Sadirak
10. Waterfall oasis
11. The First City
12. Temple of Inaras on Temple Mountain
13. Silver Mountains
14. Palos: castle city, capital of Synealee

THE ROYAL WIZARD

Dreams open the windows through which in our waking hours we seek to see. They are the worlds we create when reality fails to live up to our expectations, and the secret lives we wish we could live. They are the stories we write for ourselves, with no thought of critics or audiences, knowing that, whatever they might be, they will always be well received.

PROLOGUE

Through the Veil of light and shadow, a moment away from time, the great raven's croak announced a coming rift. Each beat of his black wings sent ripples through the air, disturbing a world that wasn't a world and beings therein and not.

Freki, awakened from her slumber, raised her head and growled, making the earth shiver beneath her master's feet. Laying a hand upon the she-wolf's head, Woden, son of Borr, the All-Father and ruler of Asgard, hummed to soothe her ruffled fur. "Muninn," he said, heralding his friend's arrival. Freki huffed and settled her head on her paws, but her watchful eyes traced the raven's flight until he perched on Woden's arm.

Muninn beat his wings, cawing madly to relay his news, and Woden's brow furrowed in concern as he cast his sight inward to remember what he'd forgotten. The past splayed out before him, a vast wilderness he'd traversed many a time, seeking wisdom on paths taken and paths abandoned. He flew across its plains and meadows to the present as it wove into the Web of Becoming.

There, in the subtle weave, a snarl of crossing destinies arose. Woden traced a lifestring, then another, and another, searching for the one to cause such turmoil, a being so central to a future its very life would alter the world to make it converge. He found it in a most unexpected place. In water. A young girl knelt where a cottage used to stand, staring at the driftwood remains of a great flood. She called for her caretaker, wept for the old woman, screamed her sorrow until she could scream no more. And when she rose again and began walking away, the snarl pulled tighter and thrust Woden into another place and time.

Frastmir, the castle seat of King Manfred of Wilderheim. Not precisely the castle itself. A chamber deep beneath, in the earth's embrace, where an old wizard scryed the air, seeking wisdom beyond his time. His visions showed him dozens of futures and for a moment at least, the human with magic flowing in his veins saw in the way of the All-Father. War and peace, a kingdom destroyed, a vain, selfish king demanding livelihoods with an imperious gesture, visions of dark futures, one worse than the next...and through it all, a single path, one precious thread of hope for something better. It meant a great risk to everything he held dear, the king he'd sworn his life to and the prince who would one day take his place.

Nico's old shoulders slumped as he realized what he had to do. For the good of Wilderheim, its king and his only heir, he would have to betray Manfred's trust and place in harm's way the very boy he hoped to save. He would have to send the child prince into war. "Forgive me," he whispered, as he would many times again until Prince Saeran returned to his father's side.

But there! The prince and his following already riding out to Lyria, even as the Aegiran armies gathered to march from the south. *May your horses be swift and your will strong*, the old wizard thought in blessing. He knew what was to come. Saeran's guard would see Aegiran arrows fly before they reached King Halden's keep. Nico sent a prayer to the gods that the prince would pass safely through his uncle's gates.

Woden caught the prayer in his fist and flipped it across his fingers like a coin, sensing through it the prayer's truth. The wizard was old. His body could no longer carry the weight of his mind and soul. Nico had seen three generations of rulers sit the throne of Wilderheim, and he knew he would not see the fourth. But how could the wizard dare leave him without counsel?

He needed to school an apprentice, but not just anyone would do. It had to be someone strong of magic and pure of heart, with a quick mind and wise soul. Someone who would one day stand at the young prince's side and guide his hand to be just and fair. But years, decades of searching for the right person, have yielded nothing, and he was losing hope.

Muninn cawed, shifting the vision sideways, and Woden spotted a familiar face. Perhaps the old wizard's hope was closer at hand than he realized. With a thought, Woden bent the flow of destiny. The snarl of lives groaned beneath the weight of his command, pulling tighter, resisting, until it gave way and a shining thread of power sprang free, aligning the others alongside itself.

A pot broke in the kitchen. The cook screamed and chased the thief outside, but the wily youth escaped with a loaf of bread to fill a painfully empty belly. The wizard noticed and Woden smiled, savoring his reaction. There again, the girl who'd mourned an old woman's death. She was the one. She would change everything. If only the wizard and his king could accept the counsel of a woman.

Another shift and there was the young prince, barely thirteen years old, strapping on armor and climbing the stairs to the battlements. He gravely surveyed the armies before him and directed the archers in their assault. A shout went up too late. Saeran's faithful general grabbed the boy, shielding him with his body as a massive boulder struck the wall. The two of them fell off the battlements into the courtyard while pieces of the castle wall rained down on them.

The boy lived. The general did not. Seeing his friend and protector take his last breath, Saeran closed the general's eyes, and mounted those same stairs back again, calling for the archers to light their arrows.

Years passed in a blink. Lyria had won the war brought to its portals and young prince Saeran stood at king Halden's side, rebuilding what had been destroyed, healing what had been hurt. People looked to him and saw their savior, for it was because of the young prince that his father, King Manfred had sent his armies to aid Lyria. To protect his only son, he had sent Saeran the means to save a kingdom.

And as the prince laid down to rest in Lyria, in a candle-lit chamber deep beneath

King Manfred's hall, the wizard's new apprentice cast a spell. There was more than magic in Nia. Like all things Other, she held power in her soul and so an illusion became real and a stone wall shivered into being, locking her in the dark. "Nico!" she called.

With a gentle chuckle, her mentor appeared beside her. "Easy, child. There is nothing to fear." Waving a hand, he uttered an ancient word and the wall disappeared.

Nia allowed Nico to pull her to her feet. "You couldn't have warned me?"

"I thought I was teaching you an illusion." He led her to the table and pressed a chalice into her hands. "Drink."

She coughed as the watered wine slid down her throat. "That was *not* an illusion."

"The wall should have been nothing but mist, an image to fool others," he said by way of apology. "But you made it real." He beckoned to his chair, and it slid over to him so he could sit next to her. Taking her hands in his, the wizard waited until she was calm enough to meet his gaze.

"I don't know how much time we have left, child," he said, "no one knows that. The gods will do as they will. But this you must remember always. Words hold power. Far more than you will them to, more than you would ever expect. Do not use them foolishly. A word can save a life or destroy it. It can cut as well as any blade. Never underestimate the power you hold. Never give voice to an angry thought. You must learn that all actions have consequences and, once spoken, words can never be taken back."

Nia nodded, wide eyed. Nico would never say so, he knew better, but there was more behind his simple lesson. Something that made Nia feel again like the starving, abandoned child she'd been ten years ago. He was saying good-bye.

Woden sighed and let the vision go. Three futures now lay before the kingdom of Wilderheim, all waiting for two people to make a choice. The All-Father resettled Muninn on the arm of his seat and stroked his beard, deep in thought. What would become of this land where humans mixed with beings Other? What would an Other do, given the power to rule humans?

So engrossed in his musings was he that he almost missed the shadow slip away. Almost.

CHAPTER 1

Midwinter was celebrated by all in Wilderheim, rich or poor. It was an entire week of revelry and good food, a time to forget how cruel and bitter winter could be. The lands were covered with snow, the roads all but impassable, yet in Frastmir and the villages surrounding it, there was nothing but joy in everyone's eyes.

Nia kept pace with Nico's tired gait across the courtyard. She worried he might fall on the uncertain ground. Several maids and hostlers had slipped on icy patches just this morning. Looping her arm through his, she steered him toward a more even part of the walkway.

Nico sighed. "Enough for now, I think," he said wearily.

Nia nodded and walked him over to a bench, sitting down beside him. No one acknowledged them as they passed. Unlike Nia's sloppy shadows, Nico's cloaking spells always worked the way he wanted them to, however long he needed them. In all her time in Frastmir, no one had ever seen her in his company, save disguised as a boy.

"The prince returns tomorrow," she told him.

Nico nodded. "And none too soon."

The young prince had not expected to arrive at his uncle's keep during the first wave of attack. Despite having not yet reached his majority, Saeran and his army had managed to turn the Aegiran forces back and restore peace to Lyria.

But it had not come without a price. Everyone in Frastmir remembered King Manfred's rages as news continued to pour in about the war, the casualties. He'd turned on everyone, but most of all Nico whom he blamed for sending Saeran away.

It had been necessary, Nico would say each time. And then he would show Manfred the vain, cruel, heartless king Saeran would have become had he not left. Saeran needed to see war so he might value peace. He needed to learn the cost of a life and soul so he might never take either for granted. And he needed to prove he could stand against an enemy and defend his people, for Wilderheim was rich in something far more valuable than gold or silver. It was steeped in magic, filled with creatures Other, who lived on the borders of the human realm. Wilderheim, some said, was the closest a human could get to the realm of the gods, a bastion between Otherlands and the world of humans. And as such it could not fall.

King Manfred didn't believe in old wives' tales. Even with a powerful wizard as his advisor he was too human to See. Nia prayed Saeran would show more respect to their gods.

"Are you certain they will accept me?" Nia asked, worrying the edge of her cloak.

Nico chuckled. She'd been asking him the same question for five years, and he'd always answered the same way. This time, however, he spoke slowly, chose his words with care. "The king trusts me."

While there was no uncertainty in what he said, there was caution. Manfred's steadfast trust had been broken the day he realized Nico had sent his only son into war. It had to be earned back, and though Saeran was returning safe and sound, a hero already beloved by his people, whether Manfred's faith in his wizard was also restored was yet to be seen.

"When I tell him you are worthy of this office after I am gone he will accept you without question. Besides, is there any man alive capable of resisting your charms, my child?"

Nia blushed. "My charms, as you know, still need a lot of work, but I doubt I will ever be able to charm anyone to do my bidding."

Her master laughed. "They will do it for the asking."

"I wish you would be serious," she chastised. Even after all her time in study, even at her age of ten and nine, Nico had more faith in her than she had in herself. "What of the prince?" She asked, tracing circles in the snow with her toe.

"What of him?" Nico returned.

Nia sighed as the wind picked up, ruffling her rebellious hair. She brushed it back and readjusted her hood as she spoke. "The king will not be king for much longer, you said so yourself. I will be in the service of Prince Saeran, and I know nothing about him."

Prince Saeran's accomplishments were commendable, but what should she expect from a man raised in war?

"Who is to say he will heed my word when…when you're…" She looked away. Her greatest fear was not for herself but for all of Wilderheim if its ruler and wizard were always at each other's throats. This land thrived because of the balance of justice and magic. If that balance became disturbed, everything would suffer, and that weakness would call to those hungry for its secrets.

Nico patted her hand. "Prince Saeran is a good man. I have sworn to provide counsel to the rulers of this kingdom, and I will bring them someone whose judgment I trust and value more than my own. But by that same token, Nia, I swear to you that I would not bring you to a king unworthy of his crown and your magic."

"You have great faith in him."

"As I do in you."

She smiled. "Tell me about him."

Nico sighed. "It has been a long time since I've played games with the young prince. He used to love seeing me weave illusions. I would show him pictures of heroes and horses when he was a child, and he would laugh in delight and say that one day he would grow up to be just like them."

A gust of wind snatched Nia's hood off her head. Pulling her cloak closer around her, she helped Nico to his feet and led him back inside the castle.

"Once," he continued, "there was a great celebration and the castle was filled with foreigners. They came from faraway lands, bearing gifts that dazzled the king and his son. The prince walked among them, looking at everything and asking hundreds of questions about them until the merchants became unsettled, fearing the prince's displeasure. Then an old woman with a veil hiding her face beckoned to him and placed a simple wooden box in his hands. 'What is it?' he asked. The woman waved her hands over the box and opened it. It was empty. The prince laughed and thanked her, then returned to his seat at his father's side."

Nia frowned. "I don't understand. What was the box for?"

Nico chuckled as he lowered himself into a chair before the hearth. A fire sprang to life and he sighed in pleasure as its steady warmth seeped into his old bones. "It was only a box. But as she waved her hands over it, she slipped a colorful stone into his hand. Saeran spent the rest of the night trying to learn the trick."

"I assume there is lesson to be learned from this story," Nia encouraged. She filled a basin with hot water and placed it on the floor for Nico to soak his aching feet.

"The lesson is, child, if you keep searching for answers about the obvious, you will miss the true treasure. There is no point to worrying about the prince's reaction to you. What you should be worrying about is what sort of king he'll make."

The way he looked at her as he said it, Nia knew he'd seen that very fear in her mind. Rather than confirm her insecurities, she said with confidence, "A good one."

Nico raised a brow in question.

"He will have me to advise him, will he not?" She grinned with forced humor.

Startled by her answer, Nico laughed, shaking his head at her impudence. His apprentice had grown into a unique woman. Though she hid beneath her cloak most days, she was beautiful as few women were. She had the easy charm and playfulness of a child, yet her mind was as ancient as his own. She worried, at times too much, about things that rarely plagued even the king himself. Nia had become like a daughter to Nico, and she was more than worthy to serve as Saeran's advisor.

But would the prince be worthy of her advice?

Nico had glanced into the future, and what he'd seen troubled him.

Nia poured wine into two goblets and gave one to Nico. "It's strong. I think this should be a day of celebration."

"Wisely said," Nico praised, bringing the goblet to his thirsty lips. He ached. In body as well as mind. For Nia's sake he'd stayed longer than he should have. He wanted to be there to present her at court as his successor. Nia shouldn't have to face that on her own. But the effort was taking a toll on him. It wouldn't be long now.

Glancing at his apprentice, he felt at peace. Not because his worries left him, but because Nia exuded serenity. She was the calm in a raging storm. She would do the same for the prince and help him lead the kingdom. Nico had chosen well when he'd brought her under his care. At the age of nine, small and starved, an orphan with no recollection of where she'd come from, she'd proven herself capable of much more than either of them had anticipated.

“They’ve not yet hung the mistletoe,” he remarked absently.

“They will do it before the prince’s arrival,” Nia told him. “Would you like to see?” As with any ritual, the hanging of mistletoe would be a celebration all on its own.

Nico shook his head. “Not tonight,” he said, closing his eyes to hide his sorrow. “I think I will rest awhile before the prince’s banquet.” Before he would present Nia. As much as it pained him, he could not wait any longer. After tomorrow, Nia would no longer be his charge and he would no longer be needed.

Nia kissed his brow. “Sleep now,” she said, covering him with a blanket. “I will wake you when the time comes.”

«»·◇·«»

“Stable the horses,” the cloaked rider said, and without waiting to see his orders obeyed, he ran up the stairs into the great hall. The guards changing shifts grew wide eyed when they beheld him. He smiled in greeting and held a finger to his lips to silence them.

It was good to come in from the cold. The sun had set not long ago, but when it did it took all warmth and comfort with it. Stripping his gloves and cloak, he paused by a hearth to warm his hands. The journey had wearied him. He glanced at the chair nearby, wanting nothing more than to rest awhile, but he knew he’d be asleep the moment he sat down and there was important business to attend to.

Shaking off the winter’s chill, he continued on his path, up the stairway and to the royal wing. A long hallway stood dark before him, all the torches extinguished for the night, but he could see well enough by the light of the moon. He traced the tapestries with a reverent hand as he passed, recalling fond memories of hiding behind them. The servants always pretended they couldn’t see his feet poking out.

At the very end was a set of double doors. The guards who stood watch before them during times of war and unrest were gone, no longer needed now that peace had been restored. He grasped the handles and shoved the portals open.

As he’d suspected, the chamber was lit with candles and the king himself paced before the hearth, tugging at his beard.

“What weighty business troubles your mind, my king, to furrow your brow this late at night?” he asked, deepening his voice and biting back a grin.

King Manfred started and spun around to stare at him, but the moment recognition dawned, the ruler of Wilderheim rushed forward to embrace him. “My son,” he cried. “My boy!”

Ceremonies were for kings. There would be time enough for them tomorrow and the next day, and the next. After ten years, this was all Saeran had wanted. To embrace his father without crowds of witnesses watching their every move and gesture.

“I’m home,” he said as his father wept with joy.

CHAPTER 2

It was late. Nia was exhausted, but she couldn't sleep.

Tomorrow the prince would arrive and Nico would present her at court as his apprentice. He would expect her to stand tall before them and be worthy.

Worry gnawed at her.

What if they turned her away or shunned her? Women, as all mothers, shared a connection with the earth, and female witches with gifts of foresight, truthsense and the like were common enough. But it was rare for any woman to carry raw magic like Nia did, let alone so much of it.

She would have to prove herself, if the king deigned to allow it. If even one of her spells went awry…

Nia set aside the scroll she'd been studying and took another tome from the shelves. Yawning, she read spell after spell, committing it to memory. She wiggled her fingers, playing with magic while she read. Not enough to work the spells, only enough to create sparks in the palm of her hand. It helped her concentrate. The ancient language was no longer a mystery to her. The words were clear, and she understood their meaning no matter what dialect they were in.

To learn magic is the same as learning anything else, Nico's voice guided her, *You need only open your whole self to it. Open your mind and let the words in. Their meaning will follow.*

She immersed herself in her studies, allowing nothing else to distract her. She read the spells and repeated them to herself, letting her voice echo softly all around her. Once she knew she'd not forget one incantation, she moved on to the next one, and the next.

She shifted in her seat when it became uncomfortable; stood to walk back and forth. The words came faster and faster as she chanted with her eyes closed, her concentration absolute.

Then, all of a sudden, a strong wind whirled around her, raising her hair and making her cloak billow. Just as quickly, it was over. Nia opened her eyes to total darkness and sighed, listening for the sound of all her scrolls and parchments fluttering to the floor. But she couldn't hear the rustle parchment. All she heard was the walls whispering in rushed words she couldn't quite catch.

At the very least, their voices assured her she was still inside the castle. Scowling, she clicked her teeth together, trying to remember what incantation she'd been saying to make all the torches and candles go out.

It made no sense. Recalling the symbols in the scrolls, she tried to match them to the words she'd chanted. She couldn't. The spell she'd chanted wasn't the one she'd read. One small mistake in pronunciation and something like this happened. "Bah," she whispered. This was precisely what she was trying to avoid!

Something stirred in the darkness, and she turned her head toward the sound. Had she conjured something else besides the wind?

It stirred again and this time, Nia was certain she heard cloth swishing.

"Who's there?" a male voice demanded and Nia started. The man sparked a flame on one of the candles and brought it around to look at her. Without thinking Nia blew lightly and the candle across the room went out.

But it had been enough for her to see she was no longer in her study and for the man to catch a glimpse of her. She was in someone's bedchamber!

"I wish Father had told me he was sending someone to me," the man said, a grin in his voice. "I would have been better prepared."

Nia drew back a step. *What?*

He was moving again. He'd risen from bed and was coming toward her in the darkness. His step was somewhat unsure, but he seemed to know which way to go. Nia had no such advantage. She didn't know where she was, or what was around her, and she didn't dare conjure light. It would make it too easy for him to find her.

Closing her eyes, even though it was dark in the chamber, she tried to create an incantation to take her back. Nico had said something about reversal spells a fortnight ago, but she couldn't remember his exact instructions. Frantic words slipped over her lips in a hushed whisper. A transportation spell needed words to be voiced, not thought. Nia needed a place to appear and a way to get there, and neither of those would help if she didn't know where she was in the first place!

He must have followed her voice, for she suddenly sensed he was in front of her, so close her nose almost touched his chest. His breath stirred the hair at the top of her head and she could hear his heartbeat. Gasping, she took a step back, but encountered a wall. The contact threw her off balance. Nia began to tip to one side, her hands flailing for something to grasp on to.

The man caught her waist and turned her so she was trapped between the wall at her back and him.

"Release me," she hissed, funneling a small thread of magic into her voice to charm his compliance. It didn't work.

"My, aren't you in a temper," he said with a chuckle. "Not to worry, my girl, I'll take good care of you." As his lips brushed her temple, his hands slid up from her waist until they were level with her breasts.

Nia slapped his hands away and shoved as hard as she could at his chest. It didn't make him fall back as she'd intended, but he did move to give her room. She sensed he only did it to humor her, which only frustrated her further. Anger made her magic boil, and she gritted her teeth to keep it contained. "Don't touch me."

Silence answered her. Nia felt the moment he sensed a threat like a charge in the air. His alarm, however muted, sparked her own, and she felt along the wall, moving sideways to get away from him while racking her brain for something to help her get out of here.

What came to her was nothing so structured as a spell. It was a sloppy invisibility cloak she'd used as a child. It never lasted long, and it took more magic and concentration than she'd had back then, but it was something. Reaching deep inside her, she called up her magic and drew darkness and silence around her.

Completely cloaked, she moved another step to the side and winced when her hand struck a rickety table. The water jug and wash basin on top of it rattled together and in a blink the man was in front of her again, caging her in. "If you aren't here to warm my bed, girl, then why are you here?" His hand braced on the wall next to her head, but it was his other hand that worried her for in it he held a dagger which scraped along the stone wall, making her cringe. Her cloak dissipated.

"By mistake," she said hoping the man didn't decide to stab that dagger into her heart. Nia could hurt him if she needed to, she could even kill him if he forced her hand. Magic filled her palms, ready to be used, but caution kept her still.

"Mistake," he repeated, his deep voice strained, as if he was trying to hold back laughter. "You came to the prince's bed chamber by mistake? And how, pray tell, did you manage to appear here without me hearing you enter?"

"What prince?"

"This prince," he replied. "Son of King Manfred of Frastmir, heir to the throne of Wilderheim. Are there so many princes around you need clarification?"

"The prince is not due to return until tomorrow. You're lying to me."

He leaned in closer. "Are you certain of that?"

Scowling, Nia quickly cast her senses down through the walls into the earth to orient herself. She went two stories down and through the underground study before she touched packed earth and bedrock. She found the leylines running north and south and determined she was in the south wing of the castle. The royal wing, where only the king, his heir, and visiting nobility slept. Flowing back to the chamber, she followed the floor stones out into the hallway and traced it left and right. Not far to the left, she felt a different song. Wood. A great wooden portal which could only be the king's bedchamber.

Oh, no.

"P-prince Saeran?" she asked weakly. Who else would be sleeping in the prince's bedchamber?

"Who are you?" he demanded. "Did you come through the window? Where are the ropes? Who helped you?" The tip of the dagger ran up the crease in her cloak to her neck. "Why are you here, little bird?"

"It was an accident. Please, I mean you no harm," she implored reaching out. She didn't need to touch the dagger to make the blade disappear; she could work the spell through him.

He breathed in deeper when her fingers curled into his night shirt. The blade was gone. He wouldn't see it disappear in the darkness, but he might feel the weapon's balance change. "So you're not here to warm my bed," he said, "but you want to. Is that it?"

Nia sputtered.

"If I were you, I'd choose my words wisely."

"Release me," she told him.

"And if I do not?"

"Then…then I will…" She would what? He was the royal heir, the future king to whom she was supposed to be swearing her fealty tomorrow. What could she do? Maim him? Enchant him? Turn him into a bumbling idiot? "I'll turn you into a toad," she finally said and winced.

He chuckled. "A witchling, then? Turn me into a toad, you say?" She felt his lips by her ear as he whispered, "I'm fairly certain they jail people for that."

They would do more than jail her if anyone found out. "Don't make me do this," Nia said, willing him to step back and release her.

Instead he leaned in even closer, his nose to her neck and inhaled. "I can make you relent. I can make you want me."

At her wits' end, Nia did what she had to. "And I can make you regret this for the rest of your life." She shouted three words, hoping they were the right ones. There was no flash, no great boom of magic, only silence. Nia reached out but encountered only air where the prince had stood. "Prince Saeran?"

Nothing.

With a thought, she conjured light and looked around. The chamber was grand and worthy of a prince, but it was cold in its opulence. He had yet to make it his home again. "Prince Saeran?"

Croak.

Nia looked down and her light flared brighter as relief washed over her. She hadn't killed him!

There at her feet was a bewildered toad, staring at his hands, his eyes wide and mouth open. Then he looked up at her. He croaked and jumped, landing on his side and rolling onto his back. His wild struggle to right himself made Nia wince. He kicked his legs and made a sound no natural toad would make. It might have been a panicked scream.

Taking pity on him, Nia picked the creature up and brought him to her face so they were at an equal level. "I did warn you," she said. "No, don't struggle, you will hurt yourself. I will turn you back but you have to stay still, or I cannot release you."

The kicking continued. He even tried to bite her, not realizing toads had no teeth. The clamp of his soft mouth over her fingers was little more than a tickle but when his long tongue shot out at her face, he almost struck her eye.

"All right," she said, holding him a little farther to evade his continued attacks and spoke the words to reverse her spell. The air shifted, her light flickered, and the toad grew and transformed back into a man, which left Nia holding his face. Any doubt she may have had as to his true identity disappeared when she recognized him by the light of her magic. Dread settled in her belly. *Gods protect me.* She'd turned the crown prince into a toad!

Saeran blinked his eyes rapidly, panting as his heart fluttered in his chest. His feet tingled and his arms and legs were shaky. But at least he had feet. And legs, and arms! Saeran pushed away from the accursed witch and immediately tripped over his own feet. He hit the floor hard, but the pain was nothing to him while his heart tried to beat its way out of his chest. He stared at the witch with his eyes open so wide he thought they might fall right out of his head, but he dared not blink even once for fear of what she might do to him next.

There was still light in the room, little orbs of it floating in the air between them like giant fireflies. Breathing hard to keep from fainting like a girl, he stared at the woman, truly seeing her for the first time.

She wasn't very tall, but she carried herself with the air of someone much bigger and nobler than her dress would let on. He'd caught the merest glimpse of her before his candle went out earlier, but now that he saw her Saeran had no doubt she was powerful. He could see it in her eyes.

"Are you all right?" she asked, wringing her hands together.

"All right? I..." That was when he saw his dagger. Or rather, the hilt of it because the blade was gone. His favorite dagger! The one gifted to him by King Halden, which he kept at his side all the time and beneath his pillow when he slept. It was ruined. And it was her fault! "You changed me into a toad!"

"You thought I was a whore!" she returned with righteous indignation.

"Who the bloody hell are you?"

She took a deep breath and absently waved a hand. All the torches and candles in the room flared to life. "Ah!" When she took a step toward him, he scrambled back, grabbing the ruined dagger hilt and waving it at her. "Stay away from me!"

She stopped, looking unsure. "I am Nia," she said, bowing at the waist like a knight. "Nico's apprentice."

The wizard's name stirred a memory, but as awake as he was at the moment, Saeran was still exhausted from the journey. He'd only gotten to bed moments before this stranger appeared, having spent long hours talking to his father. "My father did mention something about an apprentice," he said, trying to recall his exact words. "He did not say it was a woman." But he had said he'd never met the apprentice himself.

Nia blushed, appearing much younger than she had when he'd seen her through the eyes of a toad. "He doesn't know, Highness. I am to be presented at court tomorrow."

In the silence that followed, Saeran's mouth quirked. "He doesn't know?" Sitting there on the floor of his bed chamber, dressed in nothing but his night shirt while a cloaked woman with hair like sunshine caught in gold looked at him as if she expected him to shout for the guards and have her beheaded, Saeran's dagger hand lowered. Of all the things he'd imagined coming home to, this had to be the most ridiculous.

As the panic he'd felt slowly melted into irrational hilarity, he imagined this Nia appearing before him and his father tomorrow and suddenly he couldn't contain his mirth. The chuckle turned into a laugh, and when she looked at him as if he'd lost his mind it got worse. “Gods, I can’t wait to see his face!” He fell back, lying spread eagle, laughing until he couldn’t breathe. “Ahahahahagirlhahahahahwizardahahahah…”

If anyone saw him in that moment, they would think him mad. Every time he tried to stop, he would look at the girl and start all over again. His sides began to hurt and his eyes watered, which only made him laugh harder.

Finally he struggled to raise himself off the ground, his insides still tickling, but he tried hard to make himself stop. He grinned at Nico’s chosen apprentice and had the satisfaction of seeing her completely confused, which he would wager his future crown didn’t happen often.

She drew back when he approached, another spell no doubt on the tip of her tongue. He liked her already.

“Calm yourself, Nia,” he said, his grin turning crooked, “I know better than to make you angry twice. Who knows what you would turn me into next?”

After an uncertain moment, Nia returned his smile. “I was considering, a caterpillar. Or some other kind of worm.”

Saeran chuckled. “I could not have asked for a more fitting advisor.”

“Nia,” Nico’s familiar disembodied voice whispered through the chamber, and Nia’s smile fell away.

“I must go.”

“No, wait!” But she was already gone, dissolved into mist and then nothing at all.

Saeran sighed, disappointed.

She’d turned him into a toad. He smiled. The woman had courage. He needed that. Someone who wouldn’t be afraid to tell him the truth, no matter how unpleasant. He’d spent too much time in a place where no one could afford to be above another. To come back here, where even as a child no one had ever told him anything but what they thought he’d wanted to hear was something of a disappointment. How was Saeran to trust someone who couldn’t look him in the eye?

But Nia was already proving herself different. Even unsure of herself in the presence of the royal heir, she hadn’t hesitated to put him in his place. Curious that it ended up being at her feet. Even more curious was that while she’d bowed to him, he’d wanted to bow to her in return.

Nico would not have groomed a fool, let alone presented one at court as his successor. If he had enough faith in a female to have her take his place, it meant she had to be not only powerful but learned as well. The wizard Saeran knew would have made certain his successor was everything he himself had been. He would have taught Nia all he knew and groomed her to put the welfare of the kingdom before anything else.

Saeran had no doubt Nico’s faith in her would be justified, and that intrigued him immensely. He would have kept her here with him until morning had she not disappeared. He wanted to talk to her, get to know the woman who would be his right hand when he took the throne.

During the hours he’d talked to his father, the king had informed him of his decision to step down in a few months’ time. The years he’d been away had taken their toll on his father. The once proud king was now tired, eager to relinquish his crown and all its responsibilities. With Saeran returned healthy and hale, he wanted nothing more than to be a father to his son.

Saeran would be king before he'd even had time to reacquaint himself with his kingdom, and he would need Nia more than she realized if he was to justify Manfred's faith in him.

There would be argument, but Saeran didn't care. He couldn't wait to stand up in front of the assembly tomorrow and thumb his nose at tradition and all those old goats on Father's advisory council by accepting her as his.

CHAPTER 3

Nia spent the day avoiding Nico. Since she couldn't go outside and the study was too obvious, she hid inside her room, locked and warded so he couldn't get in. Of course, that wouldn't stop him if he was really determined; he'd taught her those wards, after all. But at least he respected her wishes and left her alone. The king no doubt kept him busy, seeing as the prince arrived ahead of schedule. The entire castle was talking about it. Not just the servants, but the walls as well. Nia was mortified. If the walls knew, then Nico definitely already knew.

Nia moaned and hid her face in her pillow. "How am I supposed to face any of them?"

The walls laughed at her.

At noon, Nico knocked on her door.

"I don't want to see anyone!"

"Very well," Nico said. "Stay there if you wish, but do not be late for the ceremony. Your dress robes are ready."

When she was certain he'd left, Nia cautiously opened the door and looked at the garments hanging there as if a person stood in them. "You are not dress robes," she said.

The garment shoulders raised in a shrug.

Nia rolled her eyes and stepped back, allowing the clothes to walk in.

These were the clothes that took months to be decided on? She supposed it could be worse. As a wizard, Nia had no rank. She wasn't a commoner so she could not wear the dresses they wore, nor was she a noble to wear gowns and jewels. Instead, Nico decreed a wizard should dress so no one would see her as one of them, but everyone would know to come to her when needed. Nia would wear a pair of breeches, a blouse and a long jerkin. The breeches were wide for modesty but while the jerkin was long, it would mold to her figure, leaving no doubt in anyone's mind that she was female.

Nia had spent the last ten years dressing like a boy, and modesty wasn't something she'd spent too much time thinking about. What worried her more was that people would be looking at her and really seeing *her*. Their eyes wouldn't glance off her to look at something else, and at the king's right hand on the dais she would be the center of attention right along with him. Come what may, there would be no more hiding from anyone.

Nia touched the clothes, and they flew away from her, pointing at the bath tub before laying neatly out on her bed, ready to be donned. Nia considered running away. She could fly out the window and be long gone by the time they came to summon her.

But she couldn't do that. Nico had saved her life. He was the only family she had and the only one who hadn't turned her away. She owed him more than she could ever repay, if she lived to be a hundred years old. This had always been the price for his hospitality, friendship and tutelage, and Nia had accepted it knowing this day would come.

All too soon the bell tolled for the evening meal. It was time for Nia to get ready. She washed in the tub, scrubbing her skin until it was pink and rinsing her hair with flower-steeped water. With a thought, she dried herself and dressed and then paced the room trying to come up with an excuse not to go down to meet her mentor.

But when Nico summoned her, he gave her no choice but to obey, and she appeared at his side in front of the great hall. The doors were closed, but the sound of revelry still reached them. So many people. From all over the kingdom and beyond.

They had come here tonight to welcome the prince back home, but they would also be there to witness her presentation. Laughter rang clear over the strains of music. The jugglers were performing in the corners, she knew, but the center of the room was for dancing. There would be long tables lining the walls, laden with food and so many torches and candelabras that it would seem like daylight.

Nia knew exactly how it looked. She'd seen the preparations of the great feast.

Movement in the corner of her vision had her spinning to face the tapestries. She just caught sight of something small before it ran off again. Nia followed its mad flight to the main castle door.

There, standing in shadow, was a whole family of them. Wispy creatures, childlike in stature, their overlarge eyes the color of gemstones. They watched her and whispered, and the vines growing out of their heads like hair spread wildly around them as if for cover.

"Seedlings," Nico said. "They've come to see you take the crown."

"What crown? I'm a wizard, not a queen."

"To them that is precisely what you are. Their rulers and guardians will look to you when there is need, not Saeran. They will seek your magic. Humans cannot see creatures Other unless they make themselves seen. They have their own kingdoms and lands within Wilderheim and they rarely concern themselves with human affairs unless something we do encroaches on their well being. When it does, we…you will be their intermediary."

Nia's eyes widened. "You never told me this!"

"I never expected I would need to," he said and while she recognized the truth in his word, she also heard there was something he was holding back. "They never appeared to me. Not in all my years. This is a great honor, Nia."

The seedlings blinked their big eyes and melted into the walls. But they opened Nia's Sight to all the rest. Everywhere she looked creatures large and small appeared for just a moment and then hid from her once more. Tall, regal Sidhe glided in pools of torchlight, away from the shadows. Winged creatures perched in the rafters, their talons digging grooves into the wood. Animal spirits with wise eyes roamed the hallways, watching her with suspicion. Shadowy forms moved across the floors, horned things with tails like snakes. They hissed words she couldn't understand, but the sound of it sent chills up her spine.

"There are so many." There one moment, gone the next. In an instant the hall was empty again, and Nia was so terrified she couldn't move. "I don't think I can do this," she managed to say. "I cannot be the royal wizard. Please don't make me do this."

"You can and you must," Nico insisted. "Now look at me. There's a lass. Help will never be far for someone like you, Nia. You have friends and allies all around you. All you need to do is call out to them, and they will come to your aid. But you must do this."

"It is too much."

"It will never be less. Only more."

Nia shook her head, looking at the seal on the great hall door to give herself something else to focus on. "You should be in there. Your place is by the king's side." Something had to be wrong. The prince must have told his father who she was, what she'd done.

She would walk into the great hall with Nico and kneel before the king, and then he would rise from his throne and point a finger at her. The guards would rush forward to seize her, and she'd be dragged to the edge of Frastmir to the waiting noose. They would hang her and leave her there to be devoured by wild thing.

"You worry for nothing, child. All will be well, wait and see."

The music quieted suddenly and Nia froze with a gasp. "Why have they stopped?"

"The king is making a speech, no doubt." Nico rose to his feet and came to her, pulling her to the side. "We will have our turn soon enough. But first…" he nodded toward the staircase.

Nia followed his gaze just as prince Saeran hurried down the steps, still working on the fastenings of his jerkin. He spared her a brief glance, his gray eyes twinkling as he passed them. The timing was impeccable. Saeran never slowed in his step, yet he reached the door just in time to walk through it as the guards on the inside opened the great portals.

A cheer went up in his honor and Nia watched with her mentor as Saeran made his regal way to the dais where his father sat waiting. The crowds parted at his approach, smiling faces following his progress with affection.

On the dais, Saeran leaned over the king to say something in his ear and then faced the people and nodded his thanks. He would make a speech of his own before seating himself to his father's right.

The great door closed, shutting out the sight of it and Nia strained to catch something of what was said. She needed to know. He could be calling for the guards this very moment. She stood there for untold moments, oblivious to everything but the silence in her mind. It was as if the castle was holding its breath in anticipation.

Then Nico took her hand and squeezed, bringing her attention back to him.

"Take a breath," he said, letting go of her hand. He turned her to face the door just as it opened and added, "Walk."

The crowd was silent. Not a word was uttered as Nico strode toward the dais with the help of his staff. Nia wanted to help him, to provide a shoulder for him to lean on, but she sensed this was the way he wanted it to be.

She did not look at anyone as she walked, keeping her gaze on a point at the foot of the dais. Any lower and she would look meek. Any higher and she would see the prince.

At last they reached the dais. Blood roared in Nia's ears as both she and Nico lowered themselves to one knee before the king.

"Rise, old friend," the king said before they knelt completely. "It is no good for men of our age to kneel to anyone." There was warmth and friendship in his voice, their strife buried now that Saeran was home safe and sound.

While Nico stood, Nia remained where she was. She was not to raise her gaze until Nico called her. Her palms were moist and her mouth dry. What was the pledge she was supposed to make? What were the words? She couldn't remember! Her throat became tight, but she willed herself not to lose control. If she was to be banished, flogged, or killed, Nia would submit with whatever dignity she possessed.

"My liege," Nico was saying, "Accept my humble welcome to prince Saeran and my deepest commendation for the aid you both have rendered to our Lyrian neighbors."

"We thank you," the king said formally. There was a pause in which Nia held her breath. When next he spoke, the king sounded hesitant. "What news have you, Nico?"

"Most honored great king," Nico started. It was almost time. They had practiced this endlessly in the past week. Nia knew she had to do this, but it frightened her. What if the king refused Nico's choice?

Oblivious to her rising panic, her mentor continued speaking, his voice strained, but strong. "All things come to an end, but with each end there is a new beginning. I have served your family for many years, and it has been the honor of my life to stand guard over Wilderheim and its kings. But I fear I can no longer, in good conscience, uphold my oath to you, nor swear another to your successor. I am old, my body weak. The time has come for me to retire from your service. Tonight I bring before you the one whom I have chosen to take my place and perform my duties from now on. I present to you my apprentice."

Those were the words. Nia took a breath and stood, taking the two steps that would bring her to Nico's left. Her entire body shivered as she raised her chin and looked up. She made certain her eyes revealed nothing of her apprehension.

A low hum went through the crowd, but the king waved his hand and all fell silent at once. He studied Nia for a moment and then transferred his gaze to his aged wizard. "A woman," he said with a note of question in his tone. "This is the one you would have replace you, Nico?"

Nico half nodded, half bowed in answer. "She is, my liege. Nia is in every way equal to the task and will serve you as faithfully as I have."

A spark jumped from one of the torches behind the king. It floated like a feather through the air, and as it did, Nia noticed it had a shape: long, pointed ears, crackling wings, and long insect-like arms and legs. The spark perched on Saeran's shoulder and gazed at his profile for a moment before it whispered something in his ear. Nia didn't hear what it said, she doubted anyone but Nico noticed. Saeran himself showed no sign of being aware of the creature.

More of them separated from the torch flames, circling King Manfred's head.

"You are certain of this?" Manfred asked.

The sparks crackled as if in argument with each other and then, before Nico could say a word, Saeran spoke up. "Father," he said, rising from his seat to join the king. As he did, the sparks flared and burned out. Nothing remained of them, not even ash. "You know Nico's judgment to be beyond reproach. Has he not proven that countless times over the years? In your service, and your father's, and his father's before that?"

Manfred grunted his reply, eyeing Nico with something very close to reproach.

Saeran took the noise as agreement and said, "Then why do you question his decision now?" There was no disrespect in his tone, only mild curiosity and perhaps a little mischief.

The king turned to him, an imposing, though aged figure. "You have known the wizard all your life. Do not let friendship cloud your judgment in this, son. The apprentice will serve you in the future. It will be your choices she will guide."

Saeran nodded. "I understand, Father. That is precisely what compels me to speak. Should not I be the one to approve or disapprove of Nico's choice?"

Whatever secret message those words contained, they did not please the king. Nia could see him weighing a difficult decision in his mind as he studied his son, and she knew just what he was thinking. Saeran had been a boy when he left, but he'd returned a man. As much as Manfred wanted to treat him as his son, he had to show him the same respect he would expect from everyone in the kingdom. If he humiliated Saeran now by taking away a choice that was rightfully his, it would look as if his own father had no faith in his ability to lead, and Saeran would spend his entire rule defending his claim to the throne of Wilderheim.

If the smile Saeran was biting back was anything to judge by, the prince knew quite well that he'd left his father no choice but to agree.

Manfred's mouth quirked, but he schooled his features, appearing to contemplate the situation. "I am not sure you are ready for such a choice," he said, eyeing Nia. She dropped her gaze just enough to not look into his eyes. "It's one thing to turn away a raging army of marauders, but quite another to resist the charms of a beautiful woman."

The assembly chuckled, making Nia blush. But when she dared a glance at Saeran she saw that he did not appreciate his father's insinuations. His handsome features became hard as stone, but he tempered his voice when he said, "Though I am young, I would think I have acquired enough sense by now to hear words of wisdom, no matter who speaks them. We look to our fathers to make us strong, but we have our mothers to make us wise. No woman should have to use her charms simply to make herself heard. And having grown up without a mother, I would be a fool to turn away a woman's counsel now."

There was silence after his speech. Saeran's mother died not long after his birth, and some said the king never recovered from the loss. He never took another woman to wife, and he cleaved to his son all the more because Saeran was all he had left of the woman he loved. It was the reason why Manfred lashed out against Nico with such vicious anger for sending his only son away, to his death for all he knew.

Everyone in the great hall knew the story and their pity for both king and his son was a palpable thing. But as Nia looked around at the Others hiding among Manfred's court, she saw something else. Pride. Acceptance.

At last, the king sighed. "Very well, Saeran. Since it is your choice to be made, let it be thus: The apprentice shall be yours to accept or not. Should you accept her, she will speak her oath to you, not me, and you alone shall live with your decision from this moment on."

Another hum went through the crowd, and Nia glanced nervously at Nico.

He remained calm, nodding his own acceptance of the king's decree and bowed to the prince. "I present to you, then, Prince Saeran, my apprentice, Nia."

Nia prepared herself for the harsh words she knew she deserved.

Saeran, however, merely looked at her for a moment, his lips tight as if he was trying not to smile. Then he spoke. "A man would be either witless or a toad to disregard the wisdom of his elders. Since I am neither witless, nor a toad"—he winked at Nia—"I receive your apprentice, Nico, with full confidence in both you and her."

Nia almost fainted.

"Come forth, Nia, and make your pledge."

Her tongue darted out to moisten her dry lips. She glanced at Nico as she came forward, kneeling on the first step of the dais.

"No," the prince said suddenly and her heart sank. But he continued speaking in a milder voice. "Rise," he told her. "I would have you say the words to my face, not to my feet."

Terrified, Nia's mind raced in all directions, blanketing the great hall and bringing back thoughts she ought not hear. She felt the shock of everyone there. She felt Nico's pride in her and Saeran like the warmth of sunshine, and Saeran's solemn dignity as he stood before her, waiting for her to rise and speak.

She felt the king stand from his seat, but he stopped himself from interfering. There was admiration in his mind as he stood witness to the ceremony. He even glanced at Nico, wondering if the wizard thought him a lesser man than his son, for he had adhered to tradition when Nico had given his pledge. An old man already, Nico had struggled to rise once he'd knelt.

Nia took a breath as she rose to her feet, pulling back inside herself. She searched for the words and spoke them with all the confidence she could find. "I swear my life to your service, my liege," she said. "My wisdom and magic are yours. I swear to advise you as best I can, for the good of the king and kingdom. I swear to defend your life with my own and serve you faithfully for as long as need be, until death or longer."

Saeran nodded acceptance. "I honor an oath with another," he said. "Truth for truth, loyalty for loyalty, sword for spell. From this day forth, your place shall be at my side, as my right hand. Until death or longer." Then, though the ceremony was almost over, all the necessary words spoken, he added, "And you shall kneel to no one more."

He grasped her shoulders, as was custom, and sealed the pledge with a kiss on each of her cheeks. "I thought you'd have me beheaded," she whispered at the first kiss.

"Ribbit," he replied at the second.

Once he stepped back, Nico approached and turned her to face him. "I have raised a magnificent wizard," he said, affection shining in his eyes. "No father could hope for a better daughter. Nor wizard a better apprentice." He pressed a kiss to her forehead and then moved his hands in the air between them, conjuring a robe. When it came into being, it floated in the air, billowing on an invisible current of magic. He settled it over her shoulders, closing the clasp at her throat. "I shall miss you, child," Nico whispered and then released her. "Now go take your place."

She nodded and woodenly walked up the stairs to stand behind the prince's seat. From there, she watched Nico bow once more to the king and prince and walk away. As he retreated to the great door, Nia balled her hands into fists, refusing to let the tears fall. She would not cry out, or run after him. This was the way it had to be.

As the door closed behind Nico, the Others disappeared and Nia's hands slowly uncurled. Who would take care of him now? Who would support him over the icy patches? Who would warm water for him to soak his feet? Who would make his tea?

For the rest of the night, Nia was not alive. She watched the banquet with vacant eyes, listened with deaf ears as the musicians played, and the king and his son conversed. She nodded when she ought, spoke when it was required, yet in her heart, she searched for Nico.

He was gone.

CHAPTER 4

The next day King Manfred announced he would be stepping down and relinquishing rule of Wilderheim to his son.

The news was unexpected, and Manfred, with Saeran and Nia at his side, spent the day assuring the nobles that Saeran was, indeed, ready and worthy of taking the throne.

"But he is just a boy!"

"Barely a score of years to his name!"

While the king tried as he might to tell them all again about his son's great deeds and Saeran vowed all those things kings always vowed, Nia wanted to make herself deaf to escape all the noise, which kept getting worse the longer they talked. No platitudes would ever be enough to appease these people because their outrage had nothing to do with Saeran's age or Manfred's wishes. With Saeran just returned, they hadn't had time to assure themselves of his favors. And they would do all they could to stall until those favors could be secured as Manfred's had been when he'd taken the throne upon his father's death. And with each moment the king tolerated their insolence, the nobles grew bolder, louder and even more insolent.

When she couldn't stand it any longer, Nia strode forward. "Quiet," she said, and all the noise stopped. The nobles still bickered, but nothing came out of their mouths.

"Thank the gods." Saeran sighed, not realizing everyone could still hear him.

Manfred was not amused. He glowered at both Nia and Saeran. "These are your people," he said. "Will you ignore them this easily when you take the throne?"

"No," Saeran replied. "But neither will I condone rebellious drivel that serves no purpose other than to fill the hall with noise. I am your son and heir. No one should be questioning my claim to the throne. Has such blatant bait to treason become accepted among your court since I last sat by your side?"

Nia smiled, watching the nobles' mouths stop moving. "Well, they heard that last part, if nothing else," she told the king and his son. "And as words go, it seems those were the only ones truly necessary." Nia returned to her place behind Saeran and took apart her spell. When the two royals only stared at her, she nudged her chin to urge them to face their people. "They're waiting."

Saeran raised an eyebrow at his father, grinning smugly.

Manfred harrumphed and, keeping his laugh in check, Saeran faced the nobles.

He didn't need to say another word. One after the other, they all dropped to one knee before him.

The following weeks passed with excruciating slowness as the preparations began for Prince Saeran's coronation. King Manfred wanted everyone worth noting to attend the celebration. It was to take place in the spring, when the snow thawed and the roads were safe to travel.

Nia went through the motions, spoke when spoken to, but her mind was elsewhere. She missed Nico terribly. The study seemed so empty without him there. The servants had moved her belongings to his old chambers, one floor beneath the royal bedchambers, but Nia refused to sleep there. What if he came back one day? In her heart she knew he was gone, but magical things happened every day. Nico could find his youth again, and when he returned, he would need his own bed.

But no one had seen the wizard since he'd walked out of the great hall. Worried for his well being, the king had sent messengers in all directions, looking for him. He'd meant to reward Nico for all his years in the king's service and never got the chance. If Nico was still alive, he was hiding somehow, from everyone including Nia because even scrying for him proved useless.

She had little time to stare into water with the coronation keeping her occupied. While the prince prepared with his father and all those in charge of orchestrating the celebration, Nia met with guards and cooks, maids and servants, everyone who had a function to perform in the castle. She spoke with them at length, learning about them and their trades. She enjoyed the conversations for the simple reason that she missed having someone to talk to.

They seemed to like her well enough. After she helped the butcher's sick daughter and resolved a dispute between the milliner and baker, showing her willingness to aid commoners and merchants as well as nobles and kings, the townspeople embraced her as one of their own. And the more time she spent with them, the more at ease she began to feel. While she was in town, trading stories and jests, she didn't have to be anyone but who she was. The Others didn't show themselves anymore and soon she forgot there was more to being a wizard than standing by the king's side all day long.

As winter continued, Nia acquired more work. There were more oaths and rituals to learn. As the royal wizard, she would be the one to place the crown on Prince Saeran's head. It was a great honor, usually bestowed upon someone much older, but she wasn't worried. The only one with the power to dismiss her now was the prince, but instead he seemed to have already gotten into the habit of asking her thoughts even after he'd spoken to his advisory council.

One day, when a great winter storm blew in, keeping everyone in their houses and in front of their hearths, Saeran summoned her to the meeting room. "I want to see my kingdom," he said.

"I am sure after the coronation there will be a procession planned—"

"No, Nia. I have been gone for ten years. I want to see what's become of Wilderheim. I need you to show me what the others won't say."

Nia bowed. "As you wish." She knew of only one way to show him what he wanted to see. Closing her eyes, she drew on her magic and started writing in the air. The runes etched in light floated in a circle between them until she drew the last. Then the circle solidified and in its center an image took shape.

Saeran came closer, gazing at the castle as if from a great height. "This here, what is it? I don't remember it being there before."

"It's an armory, Highness. Your father commissioned enough weapons to arm several battalions should they be needed. He also reinforced Castle Frastmir's defenses. Here, here, and here, you see? That is for oil. The channels run through the walls to pour out around the perimeter."

"He expected me to fail."

"At first, perhaps. You were only a child, Highness. No one expected you to take command as you did, let alone lead Lyria to victory."

His eyes darkened at the memory. "Halden couldn't do it. Have you ever been to Lyria, Nia?"

"No, Highness."

"It's beautiful. The entire kingdom is a work of art. People journey there from all over the world. They have the greatest masters of music, art and poetry. It's a place of peace and knowledge, meant to be open to those who seek it. They didn't stand a chance against Aegiros. Halden is a great king, but he's no warrior. All he knew to do was close the gates, and I thank the gods he had at least that much presence of mind."

"Why didn't the guard take command? Why did you?"

"Halden's queen was expecting their first child, and he was not about to leave her side for even a moment. With them unable to do anything, I was next in line. My father forced the issue when he gave his order. Three thousand Wilderheim soldiers came to aid Lyria because of me, but only on the condition that they follow no one's orders but mine under the threat of death to their families. He never meant for me to lead them. He only wanted to make sure no one would use me to bring down a kingdom—his or Halden's. The soldiers were to protect me even at the cost of their lives. Many of them did.

"I would not have survived without them. They were the ones drawing up battle plans and leading the troops. Until the Aegirans were turned back, all I did was learn from them, issue the orders they themselves came up with, and watch them die carrying them out."

"It must have been terrible."

"Yes," he said at length. "It was. Can you show me our borders?"

Nia turned back to her window spell and altered the view. For the rest of the day and half the night, she showed Saeran his kingdom and told him everything that happened and changed since he left. The prince proved to be an attentive student, genuinely curious about everything and concerned with the welfare of his people. While he made sure Wilderheim was properly guarded and defended, he also asked about the crops, the forests and game, the merchants and their trade routes.

When she told him the roads had been neglected, he took a quill and parchment and began writing down what needed to be done. Widerheim didn't have a mountain of gold and jewels in its coffers, but it had skilled stone masons and a young wizard willing to lend her magic to the task.

By the time she finished explaining about the cycles of flood and drought along one of the major rivers, Nia was exhausted and Saeran looked to be no better. The candles had almost burned down. They'd go out soon, leaving only the hearth fire to light the chamber.

"Nia," Saeran said.

"Hmm?"

He smiled at her, and she noticed the window spell had quietly dissolved, leaving individual symbols floating through the air between them. She must have dozed off. "It's late," the prince said. "You should get some sleep."

She nodded and rose from her seat, wincing at the pins and needles assaulting her legs. "Good night, Highness."

"Good morning, Nia."

⋘ »·◇·« ⋙

Saeran sat irreverently across a chair, only half listening as the master of ceremonies explained the coronation rituals for the hundredth time. He gazed out the window which overlooked the courtyard. This far up, he could scarcely see its edge, but instead he saw over the castle wall. The fields stretched in that direction, all of them covered with snow. The sky was dark with heavy clouds. One storm may have passed but another was brewing in the distance. It wouldn't be long before it reached them.

He shouldn't be here. These meetings served no purpose other than make him restless. The council never discussed anything of import. All they did was give him lists to approve. Supply lists, food lists, lists of entertainers, lists of dignitaries, and lists of complaints. All centered around the coronation. Why couldn't he simply take the crown now and move on? Why did everything have to have celebrations and feasts and revelries attached to it? A celebration for his return. One for his coronation. Another for his father, in remembrance of his reign. When did it end?

When was he supposed to do his duties as king? Or was this what his father had done all these years behind closed door? No, he wouldn't believe that.

Saeran had yet to set a foot outside. If not for Nia, he would have no inkling of what Wilderheim truly looked like. He was slowly going mad trapped in here. His entire body hummed with the need to do something. Roll around in the snow like a child or ride for hours on end.

"Your Highness? Your Highness."

Saeran looked at the master askance. There was a map of the castle on the table and several little flags dotted it. This meeting was to plan where the guests would be housed. Celebrations of this magnitude sometimes lasted a month, perhaps more. It would not do to place a crown prince next to an impoverished noble. The prince looked over the map and then back up at the master.

The man attempted a brittle smile, his voice tense with strained patience. "Would you care to finish the thought?"

The thought. What had he been talking about? There were so many thoughts and sayings the master fancied. Sometimes he had entire speeches composed of proverbs. He could have been talking about any number of them, one more useless than the other, but he stood on the ceremony of uttering them because it seemed to be his purpose in this room.

Saeran dropped his feet to the floor, straightening in his seat to stall for time.

"I am sure he would," the king's voice intruded on the tense silence, "if he had any idea what the beginning was." He stood in the doorway, his eyes bright with amusement.

The master bowed so low his forehead almost touched his knees. "Your Majesty, what an unexpected surprise."

King Manfred smiled. "Enough for today I think, Master Samson. We would not want the prince's head to explode. Where would he wear the crown?"

Saeran almost jumped out of his seat. He tensed in anticipation, ready to kiss his father for freeing him from the clutches of this goblin. Yet he waited for his father's words. He was not free to leave until the king said so. At least that was how it should have been. In truth, the king indulged his son perhaps a little too much.

"Oh, but your Majesty!" Samson sputtered, his rounded cheeks turning red. He was one of the more well-fed masters, those the king retained out of deference to their long service. As soon as the crown was his, Saeran would compensate them handsomely for their service and send them on their way. It was time for fresher minds. "There is still so much to review," he was saying, but the king waved his words aside.

"Later," he said with royal finality.

Master Samson bowed. "As you command, my liege," he muttered and made his exit as if the king had delivered a great affront. Or perhaps it was Saeran who'd done that.

He rose from his seat, heaving a great sigh of relief. "I will never be able to thank you enough, Father."

The king chuckled. "I remember my days before I got my crown. I thought perhaps you might need some help."

Saeran grinned sheepishly. "You were not wrong."

"Off with you, then. Go do something I would not approve of. And if anyone tries to stop you, tell them you are the king's heir."

Saeran was out the door almost before he'd finished speaking. Shaking his head, Manfred took the seat his son had left and gazed at the castle's map. Things were progressing even better than he had expected. His brother had not lied to him about Saeran. The boy had a gift for making people love him, a gift a king could not do without. He was more than able to rule this kingdom, and already he had little need for a father's advice.

Though Manfred still had doubts about the new wizard, he'd seen her shoulder her duties with as much dedication as Saeran carried his. Nico had trusted her, and she was already proving worthy of Manfred's trust. Saeran was well met by her.

Ah, he missed his old friend now. All his messengers have returned empty handed. There was no trace of the wizard since the day he'd presented his apprentice. It seemed as if Nico had disappeared into thin air.

Manfred couldn't say he begrudged Nico his peace. Not after the way he'd treated him these past few years. He only hoped Nico would forgive him a father's devotion. It seemed to Manfred that the wizard's final decision had been as wise as his very first, and each one in between. Nico had trained a successor and trusted her enough that he had not stayed to oversee her conduct or meddle in her decisions.

Now Manfred would have to do the same. Saeran was a clever, eager boy, a king already before the crown was even his, but each time he made a decision on Manfred's behalf, he looked to his father for confirmation and support. He had all the makings of a great leader, but he also had love and respect for his father. Manfred worried that as long as he was by Saeran's side, his son would spend his days looking over his shoulder for approval.

If he wanted Saeran to thrive, and Wilderheim to accept him, Manfred could not remain a shadow over his son's reign.

Perhaps it was time for him to pay a visit to his brother, one long overdue. Ten years, in fact. Ten years in which Halden had weathered a war, fathered three children and good as raised Manfred's own. Now that Saeran was here to sit the throne, Manfred was free to see for himself how Halden was faring. They had much to talk about.

After the coronation, he would make the arrangements. He might not disappear as completely as Nico had, but he would give his son the chance to show what he is capable of.

CHAPTER 5

Nia watched with apprehension as three servants scaled up a tall ladder to hang a banner above the archway. They were arguing and gesturing wildly, the one on the bottom jumping up and down, throwing the ladder off balance. Not one of them seemed to notice what they were doing. It would only be a matter of time before the ladder tipped away from the wall.

She moved closer, preparing to stop them from falling such a distance, should it be needed. Opening and closing her hands, she waited, watching the top of the ladder as it shuddered and shifted ominously.

"Good morning."

Nia jumped and turned, almost butting her head against Saeran's. The prince smiled, his gray eyes twinkling in his handsome face, a lock of dark blond hair falling over his forehead. "Good morning, Highness," she replied. "I thought you were meeting with the masters."

He flashed a quick grin. "Come with me." Without waiting for an answer, he turned and walked away.

"I…" she started, glancing at the ladder. The prince took precedence. Sighing, she turned to follow him and winced as she heard the servants give a shout and crash to the ground behind her. Nia shook her head and hurried to catch up with him. "Where are we going?"

Saeran stopped inside the stables, looking around in indecision. "You there," he pointed to one of the hostlers, "saddle two horses. I and the royal wizard are going for a ride."

Nia glared at him. "His name is Micah," she scolded as the man scrambled to obey.

Color stained the prince's cheeks. "Forgive me," he said. "I have not yet learned everyone's names. Many of them are new to me."

When the hostler led two readied horses to them, Saeran nodded and gave him a coin. "Thank you, Micah. You do fast work. That is always appreciated."

Micah's eyes grew wide at the praise, and he bowed away at once.

"Now then," Saeran said, swinging up into the saddle with ease. "Shall we?"

Nia swallowed hard and cautiously approached the huge gray stallion. "Hello," she said with a tentative smile. "I am Nia. Please don't throw me off."

The animal snorted a laugh. *Nico has neglected his duties to you, child.*

Nia's smile turned sad. "He did the best he could."

"What was that?"

"Nothing, Highness."

"Mount up, then," he urged. "I intend for this to be a long ride."

The stallion snickered. *You will come to despise chairs. Hop up then. No good to keep the princeling waiting.*

Nia did as she was told, following the horse's directions to mount. She'd seen others do it many a time, but it was a different matter to have to do it herself. It only took her three tries to find her seat. Nia was proud of herself.

Hold on now, he said at the same time as Saeran shouted, "Let's go!"

The first jolt would have had her flying through the air, had her mount, Satardust was his name, not kicked out with his hind legs to set her upright once more. Before she could even draw a full breath, they were out in the open, galloping across the frozen fields.

Hold on with your legs and lean forward, Stardust advised. *See how the princeling rides?*

Nia took a chance and looked to her left. Saeran rode beside her, moving in rhythm with his mount's gallop. Nia mirrored his pose, grinning as the new position gave her much more balance and control.

They rode for a long time until the wind chill made Nia's face go numb, and her legs became so sore she didn't know how much longer she could keep her seat. When the castle was so far in the distance they could barely see it and they approached the forest's edge, Saeran slowed their pace and then stopped to catch his breath. His eyes were feverish, his face alight.

He dismounted at once, lifting his face to the sky. "This kingship will be the death of me," he muttered.

Nia grinned and swung her leg over to dismount as well.

Careful, Stardust urged, but it was too late. Her knee buckled and she yelped, tumbling to the ground. With her foot still caught in the stirrup, she gazed up at Stardust with her mouth hanging open. "That hurt!"

Saeran peeked at her from behind her mount. "Nia?" He came to her and freed her foot from the stirrup, holding his hand out to help her up. When her legs still refused to support her, he laughed and slid an arm beneath her shoulders to brace her against his side. "You should have told me you do not ride."

"Your Highness?"

"Yes?"

"I am afraid I don't ride."

"Thank you for telling me. Perhaps I should have a carriage prepared instead."

She returned his easy smile with an awkward one of her own. Her rump felt numb and her legs were wobbly. As mortifying as it was to be so helpless, it was made a thousand times worse by Saeran's helping her. But though she could have restored her sapping strength in moments, she didn't. It didn't occur to her while Saeran had his arm around her and was smiling the way he was. Nia forgot she was a wizard, and his vassal. For that small moment in time, she was nothing more than Nia.

Stardust suddenly tossed his head with a snort and paced sideways right into them.

The other stallion backed away from the forest's edge, both animals' eyes wide. Saeran frowned. "What in Thor's name…"

He ascertained her balance before he released her. Grasping onto his mount's reins, he settled the beast with a soft touch and then drew his long dagger, returning to Nia. "Handsome does not spook easily," he told her. "There is something there."

Fangs, Handsome said, *and claws.*

"It's an animal," Nia translated, taking a couple of uncertain steps toward the trees. "Put that away."

"What are you doing?" Saeran hissed. "Get back here. Get behind me."

She looked over her shoulder at him. "Behind you?" she repeated, puzzled. "I am supposed to protect you, Highness."

"Nia, stop," he said.

She didn't listen. Not even when something rustled a short distance off. The prince swore and came to her instead. Nia could feel him at her back, his blade shining next to her. She put her hand over his on the handle and made him lower it.

Neither of them wore gloves and the touch of her warm hand on his cold one jolted Saeran. He didn't know what to do first. The horses needed calming before they panicked and trampled them to death, or ran off and left them here. It would take a day to get back to the castle on foot. The snow came up to Saeran's knee in the shallow parts.

But he couldn't leave Nia unprotected. She had no armor or weapons, and when she lowered to her knees in the snow, he was certain she'd lost her mind. "What are you doing?" he demanded. Brandishing his dagger, wishing he'd taken his sword instead, he waited for the beast to appear.

"Come forward, brother," Nia called out. "You will not be harmed."

"Must you?" Saeran growled at her.

"I must," she returned, her gaze never leaving the trees.

A massive gray wolf stumbled out of the shadows, easily half the size of a draft horse. No wonder the animals panicked. Handsome reared and Saeran had to duck to escape his hooves. He expected to be trampled, but then Stardust slammed into Handsome from the side, somehow subduing the mount and moving him out of the way at the same time.

Saeran didn't know what was going on, but he turned his attention back to the bigger threat. The one with a maw large enough to crush a man's skull in a single bite.

But something was wrong. The wolf was licking his snout again and again, his legs stumbling over each other. If Saeran didn't know better he'd say the beast was drunk. He moved forward raising his blade. "Get back, Nia."

"Put that away," she told him again, never taking her eyes off the wolf. "He couldn't harm us if he wanted to."

As if to agree with her, the beast whined, almost falling over with the next step. Nia held out her hands in a sort of welcome, and to Saeran's utter shock the wolf came to her, ears flat. The beast sat down as soon as he was within reach, shivering and huffing as the whines continued.

"Tell me what ails you, brother," Nia said, and if he hadn't seen it with his own eyes Saeran never would have believed. The wolf was weeping.

At a loss for words, he lowered his blade and watched as woman and beast stared at each other. The wolf licked his snout and shivered, and his front legs were bowed as if he could barely support himself.

Nia sucked in a sharp breath. "Will you allow me to look into your mind?" she asked.

Another soft whine.

Nia placed her hands on either side of the wolf's head and looked into his eyes. "He has been poisoned," she said for Saeran's benefit. "He ate from a carcass left in the woods. It's…killing him. I can't…I…" Nia released the wolf and circled her arms around him for a moment. "I am sorry, brother. Will you let me take your pain away?"

The wolf lied down with his head in Nia's lap, one of his paws reaching for her hand. Tears in her eyes, Nia grasped his paw and placed her other hand over his eyes. "Sleep," she whispered. "I will see to it your pack does not suffer as you have. Be at peace."

The great beast closed his eyes with a sigh and Saeran watched his chest rise and fall while Nia stroked his fur. It didn't take long. Within moments the wolf became still, expiring quietly beneath the wizard's touch.

For a while, Nia sat there, cradling his head, as her tears slid down her cheeks. She mourned him as she would a true brother. Saeran was amazed at her compassion. Kneeling in the snow beside her, he touched her shoulder.

As if awakened from a dream, she looked at him with fire burning in her blue eyes and said, "Huntsmen did this."

She brushed off his touch and moved the wolf off her lap, pushing to her feet.

All at once, the sky became dark with storm clouds. Thunder rolled in the distance as she walked into the woods, and Saeran pushed to his feet to follow.

"Nia!" he called after her. Anger trailed in her wake, so thick it choked him. A terrible wind picked up, lashing at her robes, but the branches that hindered Saeran's progress bent out of her way to allow her passage. Within moments they reached a clearing. By then the sun was gone and the forest was pitch black, yet somehow he could still see her. She almost glowed in the darkness, drawing his eye, his only guiding star in the unnatural night.

Nia reached her hands to the sky and lifted her face to it. Saeran felt magic wind around her like a cloak, twisting around her arms. She spoke a series of words, reached higher.

When the rustling started anew, Saeran raised his blade. They were surrounded by the sound of it, and there were too many to fight by himself. "Nia," he tried again, but she didn't answer.

To his left something exploded out of the bushes. Saeran turned, dagger at the ready, but what landed at his feet was a piece of meat. Dozens more came flying out, all of them piling together around them.

When the last of the carcasses fell, Nia lowered her arms and faced him, her eyes sparking with terrible light. "Your huntsmen did this," she told him, furious red lights flashing around her. "They were all around, in every corner of the wood. Just tossed on the ground for any beast to feed on and die." She gritted her teeth as tears slid down her cheeks. "The poison tore through their bodies and it took days."

Rage simmered in his veins. He saw from Nia's reaction that she could see it in his eyes. "Show me," he said tightly.

Nia weaved her hand through the air between them, drawing on the red light and pulling it in. Mist following her movements until it formed a circle. She said a word of command to make it glow like a torch and in its depths images took shape. Four huntsmen argued in the woods. Saeran knew them. They'd brought in a great boar only yesterday, boasting of the hunt's thrill. Telling him he'd have loved it. In the vision their words were drowned in silence, but their meaning was clear. They had just evaded a pack of wolves. The forest was full of them; they could not step foot past the creek without hearing their howls. But hunting them was forbidden unless they attacked livestock, and that had not happened in too many years to count. For the safety of Frastmir and its inhabitants, they proclaimed loftily, something had to be done.

If there were fewer wolves, they mused, there would be more game for them to hunt, more mouths to be fed with such bounty. In truth, they thought only of the people. But disobeying the order to spare the beasts was punishable by a lashing and imprisonment. Two of them had wives and children to feed, one was courting a shopkeeper's daughter, and the last was quite sought after by the tavern wenches. None of them could chance being caught.

They looked from one to the other, each weighing his comrades and all alighting on the same idea at once.

All it took was a wild boar or two, a vial of poison, and a sad shake of the head when the palace guards asked after the day's trophies. No one had to know.

With a swirl of black smoke, the vision changed and Saeran found himself in the castle, looking at the huntsmen's drunken faces. Their beards were greasy with food and their hands filled with meat. One took a bite from a succulent pig's leg and threw the rest to the dogs. They fought over it viciously, tearing into each other as much as the meat, and the huntsmen laughed, entertained by this. "Enough," Saeran ground out, unable to watch anymore. "I've seen enough."

The images faded back into mist and then disappeared. As they did, the carcasses all around him burst into flames. The smoke they emitted reeked of pain and death as the poison burned off. That was Nia's doing. She was a distance off, staring into the dark forest, her back to him. The lights were gone, her magic darkened once again.

"They will pay for this," he said, joining her on the other side of the pyre. She wouldn't face him.

"There are still others out there," she said weakly. "Many more, and all suffering the same." Her hands were clenched at her sides and somehow he knew she'd felt the wolf's pain. Just as she felt the pain of the others now.

"Can you help them?"

Nia shook her head and he could see it break her heart to say the words. “Not from this far away. They are too weak to come to me and it would take too long to find them.” She swayed on her feet and Saeran caught her, sitting down in the snow with her. “Nico would have known what to do,” she sobbed.

Saeran pulled her closer, but though she allowed the touch, she didn’t lean on him. “I swear to you I will see them hanged.”

When the fires died down, Nia stood, wiping her sleeve across her wet face. “We have to go back,” She said, pushing to her feet. “We’ll freeze out here.” She waited for him to stand and then turned in the direction they had to walk in.

“Wait,” Saeran said. He went to a raspberry bush and ducked under it, pulling out a large piece of wood. “I saw this earlier,” he told her, handing it to her. It was curiously even from one end to a large, twisted knot at the other. “You’ll need it. Even Nico had one.”

Nia curled her fingers around the wood and tested its balance. It fit into her hand. Saeran couldn’t see any obvious weaknesses; it would be sturdy enough to lean her weight on and with some work, a fine staff, indeed. “Thank you, Highness,” she said, managing a small smile.

They returned to the castle in silence, and said not a word to anyone about what they had seen, but Saeran knew something needed to be done. And when he met her gaze in front of the great hall, a moment before going his own way and leaving her to hers, seeing the pain still there, he knew he would be the one to do it.

CHAPTER 6

Nia would not leave her chambers again until the day of the coronation. It was not by choice. The spell she'd worked that night drained her so completely that when she returned to the castle, the staff proved to be invaluable. It would take some time for her to recover both physically and magically.

What happened outside her study doors, however, did not escape her. Nia could feel the walls shiver with whispers. Rumors of things she would not have believed—had she not expected them.

The walls gossiped to her of the prince. How he'd marched through the castle courtyard, bearing a heavy beast in his arms, a small group of guards following close behind. How he'd kicked down the door on the huntsmen's cottage, tossed the furry heap at their feet and demanded, "Is this your work?"

How the huntsmen had stared in fright at the prince's countenance, unsure of which answer would bring his wrath down upon their heads. Ah, but the prince needed no answer, for he knew it already.

The walls described how he made the four men tie each other's hands and lead each other outside the castle. And then it was the earth itself who whispered to her of Saeran's angry words. "Were I to be fair, I would give you that selfsame poison to drink and watch you writhe in pain. And you would drink it again, for each animal that died from it, shaking in agony."

The huntsmen, the earth told her, shuddered and fell to their knees begging for mercy, but the prince had none to spare them, for he knew they'd had none for the beasts.

And so, a great oak groaned, the four huntsmen were hanged from his branches, dancing in the wind.

Such was the prince's justice.

But then the breeze slipped through a crack into her study, hissing a secret in her ears. For as the prince had stood before the men preparing to be hung, as he'd watched them weep and pray, he'd whispered it to the winds: "For Nia."

"Enough," Nia told the walls, the earth, and the breeze. "No more rumors. No more death or secrets." And she closed her eyes, willing herself not to dream when sleep claimed her.

Dreams found her anyway, childish memories grown into a nightmare to haunt her day and night. She sat in her tree, telling it all her woes. Eirwen was being cruel again. She'd heard a merchant caravan passing not far from their cottage and Nia wanted so desperately to see them, but Eirwen refused to let her. It was too dangerous, she said. They had no business with those people, she said.

But she could hide, Nia argued. They wouldn't even know she was there!

Eirwen would hear none of it. One day Nia would understand. Eirwen had promised she would keep Nia safe.

In her anger, Nia screamed at the old woman, ugly words she'd never meant to say and, ashamed of herself, she ran here. But then it got dark, too dangerous to walk through the forest on her own. Instead, Nia fell asleep in that tree and dreamed of singing. She sang to a river and its waters rose up to her, tendrils of it caressing her cheek like a mother's touch. Then more of it rose, reaching to her, cradling her, answering her voice with a melody of its own. A song of home to drown out Eirwen's cry…

Nia started awake, then again when she saw Saeran right next to her.

She sat up on her pallet. "Your Highness!"

"Wizard," he replied. "Why do you sleep under the castle when there are dozens of much nicer places you could rest your head?" He looked around the dark room. He wouldn't see more than shadow, the large table and the overflowing bookshelves behind the archway. No point wasting candlelight when all she did was sleep.

Nia struggled off the pallet, her legs unsteady. She was fully dressed but felt raw and exposed with Saeran watching her. No one but she and Nico ever stepped foot in the underground study. "What are you doing here?"

Saeran caught her elbows to steady her as he led her to sit at the table. He was smiling, and she couldn't fathom what might have amused him. "Calm yourself," he said, "I am the prince, remember? I can go wherever I please."

Nia sparked the torches with a thought and a small burst of magic. They flared to life, filling the chamber with light until she could see him clearly. He looked worn, tired. His clothes were disheveled as if he'd slept in them, and though he smiled, it was a weary smile.

"What princely business brings you to my private study?" she asked, glancing at the pitcher of water some distance away. She was so thirsty her lips stuck together, but the pitcher was too far. If she tried to call to it with her magic still so weak, it would fall and shatter halfway to the table.

"At first," the prince said, following her gaze, "I looked for you in Nico's old chambers." He left her to retrieve the pitcher and poured her a goblet of water. "But it looked as if no one had stepped foot in it in months. Then…" He handed her the goblet and resumed his seat. "I inquired among the maids where the wizard was housed, and they pointed me to another chamber, across from Nico's. But that one looked the same, so I asked, very politely, where my royal wizard might be found, and they pointed to the ground."

"Hmm." Nia drank from the goblet, feeling her strength return a little more with each sip.

Seeing she would not speak, Saeran grinned. "And so I found my way here to give you something and found you sleeping. I knocked, mind you. And called your name. Several times. You did not move at all, so I came closer to find you were barely breathing. Naturally, I became worried. But you looked so peaceful I was loath to wake you.

Instead I decided to wait for you to awaken on your own."

Nia blushed. It was a wizard's sleep she'd slept, something a body forced on the mind when one's strength was depleted. For a wizard to drain herself of magic completely meant death. To restore herself, Nia needed rest and time. She would not have awakened, even if he'd tried to rouse her. "And how long have you waited?" she asked, dreading his answer.

Saeran shrugged. "Not long. Half a day, perhaps."

Nia choked. "Half a day?"

The prince's good humor faded. His eyes grew serious and his lips compressed into a tight line. "I want you to teach me," he said. "Every spell an incantation you know, I need to learn. What happened with the huntsmen can never happen again. They could have poisoned the streams and killed us all."

She stared at him agog. "You want me to teach you magic?"

Saeran nodded.

"I…I'm not sure I can." Rather, she wasn't sure it was wise to try. True, no one knew what they were capable of until they attempted it. Magic could be found in the oddest places and many went through their entire lives changing the world in subtle ways without being aware of it. But there were also those hungry for power which would forever be denied to them. What if Saeran didn't have any magic in him, no matter how much he wanted it? What if he blamed her?

"You can try," he said.

He was in earnest! Nia shifted in her seat, wincing at the ache in her back. Could she defy a royal order if he gave it? "You mentioned you've brought me something," she said, stalling for time. "It wouldn't by any chance happen to be food, would it?"

Saeran grinned. "Wait here. I will call for a tray."

Nia sighed when he left the study, looking around for guidance. "Nico," she whispered, "what have you gotten me into?" She fancied she could almost hear him laugh at her in gentle mockery.

The prince returned, placing a stack of parchment on the table. "We begin now."

"Wait, I have not said yes."

"I told the runner to bring two trays. I am starving. We can eat here, can we not?" he asked, reaching for the pitcher again to pour himself some water.

"Yes, but I—"

"Yes is spoken. You may begin your instruction." He sat down facing her like an eager school boy, waiting for her to speak.

Nia glared at him. "Very well. We begin."

"Excellent!" Saeran nodded. "What do I do first?"

"You close your mouth and listen."

"What—"

"Shh!"

He quieted.

"Listen until you hear everything. Every movement of the air as you breathe, every beat of your heart, the hum of the candle flame, the chatter of mice…everything."

Saeran shifted to find a more comfortable position and strained his ears to listen. "I hear nothing."

"You are not listening hard enough. Concentrate. It helps if you close your eyes." She closed her own to demonstrate. "Put everything from your mind but the sounds, and listen not only with your ears, but with your heart."

Saeran breathed in deeply and held his breath, counting heartbeats. He could hear them getting louder, but only because they were thrumming in his head now. Expelling the air from his lungs in an explosive sigh, Saeran shook himself and tried again. He drummed his fingers on the table—that he could hear. He tapped his foot. Also a sound his keen ears were able to pick up. Besides that, he heard nothing. "This is boring. When can I work a spell?"

"When you learn to hear what is around you," she said without opening her eyes. "A thing will tell you how it wants to be changed. It will know your intent and help you achieve it. A pitcher will know when you want it to float next to the table instead of sitting on it. It will do as you command. But a flower will not obey a command to grow if it knows your only intent is to pluck it."

There was wisdom in her words. She sat unmoving, composed, but still at ease. Saeran's backside was starting to ache from sitting on the hard chair, yet Nia didn't show any discomfort at all. Her control over herself was astounding.

She knew what to do and was the only one who could teach him. He would have to learn on her terms and trust she would lead him true. Saeran closed his eyes again and quieted his mind. For a long time, nothing happened. He heard nothing but his own breathing, felt nothing but his weight sinking into the chair.

But then it began to change. Slowly, he began feeling lighter, almost floating. His hands felt warm, his head swam. The flicker of torchlight cast shadows on his eyelids, and he followed the movement as if he could see the real flames dancing.

Suddenly he heard them. Two torches, then three, and then all of them. They were singing! Not in the sense of a human voice, but it was a melody nonetheless. They sang in the direction of the book shelves, as if performing for them, and Saeran's awareness floated toward the dark alcove. The scrolls and tomes there whispered. He could hear words so ancient and powerful they sent a chill up his spine, and he knew such knowledge in the wrong hands could destroy with impunity.

Wary of it, Saeran withdrew.

He pictured Nia in his mind, sitting in front of him, regal as any queen, and suddenly he heard her breath as he did his own. He heard her heart beat like a drum to the rhythm of life all around him.

Saeran opened his eyes, amazed when the sounds didn't dull. He saw Nia there, and she was so beautiful it pained him. She hadn't moved, sitting quietly with her eyes closed. Saeran had faced armies, felt warriors' souls leave their bodies and seen peace at last in their dying eyes. He'd met with great kings, masters of every trade, wizards and holy men; sought their knowledge and wisdom. Nia's silence was more profound than anything those men had ever taught him. Her serenity seeped into his bones and made him feel as if no ill or plight could touch him as long as she was there.

He leaned toward her, captivated by this strange, beautiful dream, and reached out to touch her. His fingers brushed through her hair, and the golden strands chimed for him a harmony of countless strings. Nia tensed. But she didn't move. Saeran felt like a master musician, playing the silken strands to yield a melody that shamed the most accomplished bards.

The music all around him grew louder to compliment his movements. He did it again, savoring the sound as clear as crystal, and then he leaned closer still and touched his mouth to hers.

The song quieted. His ears became deaf to everything but the beat of his heart, thumping in perfect unison to hers. He kissed her softly, reverently, and Nia yielded to him with a sigh that shivered through his soul.

In that moment, Saeran sensed everything stop and wished it could stay that way forever. Shrouded in silence, hidden in the depths of time itself, Nia looped her arms around his neck and he pulled her closer still. The table was gone. They floated together in a warm current of air that folded around them like a blanket.

They had no anchor to latch on to except each other. Saeran held Nia so tightly he could feel her heartbeat against his chest, yet it still wasn't enough. He needed more. Her heart set the rhythm of his. Saeran wanted inside her skin, to touch her soul and bind it to his.

Sounds began to intrude. Someone was approaching.

A sharp knock at the door rang out in deafening echoes, jolting Saeran and Nia out of the trance and they fell to the ground several feet apart.

Nia stared at the prince, frozen in shock, unable to look away. Her heart was racing so fast she couldn't catch her breath. Saeran seemed similarly incapacitated. He looked as if he wished to say something, but couldn't find his voice. And neither of them dared to blink.

The knock came again.

"Enter," Saeran managed to say, pushing to his feet. The last contact broken, Nia exhaled at last.

The servant opened the heavy door and entered, stopping just inside, his mouth agape. The table was overturned and the chairs lay in broken heaps against the walls opposite each other. Candlesticks were strewn all over the floor among piles of parchment and scrolls, the tapestries half torn off the walls. It looked as if a storm had raged through the study, catching the prince and his wizard in its path.

"I…" Liam began but never finished. He offered the large tray instead. "Food."

"Thank you," Saeran said, reaching for the goblet at his feet but the pitcher he sought was shattered by the book shelves. "You may set it down on the floor there."

Liam looked concerned. "You Highness, I could send for maids to straighten up—"

"That won't be necessary," Nia said, grateful to have found her voice. She rose and tried her best to smooth her hair back. "Thank you, Liam. That will be all."

Doubtful but obedient, Liam set the tray down, bowed and retreated to the safety of the castle above.

There was silence for long moments after he was gone. Nia didn't trust herself to look at Saeran, but she felt his gaze on her the entire time. The he swallowed hard and said, "Time really stopped. I did not dream it, did I?"

Nia nodded. "Time stopped."

"Was that supposed to happen?"

Nia met his gaze uncertainly. "I don't know," she admitted.

Saeran looked away, searching through the mess on the floor. He retrieved the bundle and came toward her.

Nia shrank away, making him stop in his tracks. "I came to give you this," he said, placing the bundle on what used to be her pallet. "It did not seem right to leave it lying in the woods. I burned the rest." Then he turned on his heels and left, closing the door behind him with a gentle click.

Only when he was gone did Nia move again. She took the bundle and carefully untied the cloth.

Inside was the wolf's pelt.

CHAPTER 7

"Something is bothering you."

Saeran looked away from the window at his father. "What?"

"I said something is bothering you," Manfred repeated. "And before the crown has even touched your head. This does not put my mind at ease about leaving, son."

"Oh. It's nothing, really." He looked back out at the children playing in the wet, melting snow. "Only…time."

"Time?"

"Yes, time. It comes, it goes. Never stops. Have you ever thought about time, Father?"

"I don't believe I have. Time, you say?"

Warming to the subject, Saeran came to the table covered with long sheets of cloth. "Is this the whole of time or only a part of it? Is there an end to time? Where is the beginning? Does it move from past to present, or is it still and we are the ones who move? And what if it stops?" He crumpled the fabric together. "Does anyone else notice?" He looked to his father for an answer. "What do you think?"

"I…"

"Because if all of time stopped, nothing should have moved." He wasn't certain anything had moved. But everything had. There hadn't been a single thing in Nia's study that hadn't shifted, flown, fallen or shattered. How had that happened? The lack of answers maddened him, especially when he couldn't ask the one person who might have the answers.

But would she? Nia had looked just as stunned that day. Then again, a wizard probably encountered stranger things every day. She would have already forgotten about it. No doubt. Put it right out of her mind.

How could she? Time had stopped! Or they had stopped. Or the world had, or… something. He'd kissed other girls before, and that had never happened. And one or two of them had been witches.

"Well, I see you are otherwise engaged. I will leave you to it, then."

And that kiss! What had he been thinking? Why for the love of Freya had he stopped?

He couldn't be thinking this way. It was exactly the sort of thing his father had accused him of being too weak to resist. "When are you set to depart?" he asked Manfred. "Father?"

The king was gone.

Saeran frowned and followed him out into the hall, watching his beloved father hurry away as fast as dignifiedly possible. Shaking his head, Saeran returned to his window.

Spring was coming. Soon all the snow would be gone and everything would be green again. The ceremony was to take place in a fortnight, and the dignitaries from other lands were already on their way. Halden wouldn't be among them. News had reached Frastmir that his youngest child had the fever. Less than a year old, the boy probably hadn't lasted long enough for the message to arrive.

Another reason for Manfred to go to his brother. As soon as Saeran had the crown on his head and the burden of a kingdom on his shoulders, his father would be gone and there would be only him and Nia to look after Wilderheim. People would bow and come to him with their concerns and disputes, expecting him to know what was best and what was needed. He would never again walk through the villages without an escort, and people would forever see him as only a king.

Saeran didn't know why that suddenly seemed like such a bad thing. Everyone wanted to be king, or at the very least noble. He smiled, watching a little girl scoop snow and water into her hand and dump it down the back of a boy's neck. All he'd ever wanted was to be at peace. After so many years of destruction and death, just peace.

Perhaps with Nia at his side, he might finally find it.

↞ »·◇·« ↠

The ceremony was a short affair. No grand speeches or oaths. It consisted of presenting the new king and Nia's placing the crown upon his head. To make up for the lack, Manfred had commanded a feast to be held afterward in celebration of all good things.

The grand hall was filled to the brim like a giant treasure chest of jewels, and Nia didn't know where to look first. Colors swirled all around her as jugglers, performers, flame breathers, dancers, and guests moved about. There was soft cloth everywhere, covering the walls and ceilings like a tent, and it billowed in the breeze coming in through the topmost windows, giving the illusion that everything moved.

Wine flowed freely and there was food aplenty. The tables were laden and bards played in honor of the newly crowned king. Important guests had come from all over the kingdom and beyond to witness the coronation. Two kings had come, allies of King Manfred, to witness the occasion, bringing with them their entire courts. Those who had no room in the castle took up residence with wealthy nobles in the realm. Knights set up tents in the outer bailey, leaving the inner courtyard open for fairs and more revelry.

In the chaos of merry making, rules seemed to be forgotten. Nobles mingled with commoners, men took liberties behind the cover of columns and tapestries, queens drank their fill with no regard to decorum, even allowing touches that should not have been allowed. No one seemed to mind.

Nia rose from her seat at the crowded table to find a more open spot from which to view the festivities. She found refuge in a dark corner and cast a spell to shield it and herself from sight. Safe inside her hiding place, she could see everything without being part of it.

Faces paraded before her, carefree and joyous, paying no heed to anything but their own revelry. Several times a juggler passed in front of her, or a flame breather displayed his art. Nia admired their skill. Their discipline was astonishing.

Saeran himself seemed to be everywhere at once. Several people have already commented within her hearing how unseemly it was for a king to be so restless. It was tradition for the king to sit his throne and observe the revelry, not walk about and be part of it.

Saeran happened to overhear one such comment. He turned to the man who'd spoken and raised a brow. "If you think you can sit that throne all night, take it. I will find myself a more comfortable seat."

Nia eyed the royal seat and had to agree. It was made of black metal, its back and armrests covered with grooves and thick knot work which formed the symbols of Wilderheim. There was a thin cushion on it, but it looked no more comfortable than the rest of the throne. No wonder Saeran refused to sit on it.

Having settled that, Saeran turned to move on. He was three paces from her when he stopped and looked around, frowning. He couldn't see her. Nor hear her, quiet as she was. Her spell was perfect. Nia had spent weeks making certain of it.

Saeran tipped his head and stepped back, looking at the wall on either side of her.

"Is something wrong, your Majesty?"

Saeran took the noble by the arm and pulled him closer. "Lord Dunbar, look at this. What do you see?"

The portly man wiggled his ruddy moustache. "Nothing, your Majesty."

"You see the wall, do you not?"

Dunbar squinted. "Yes, your Majesty."

"Then you do not see nothing."

"Yes, your Majesty. I mean, no, your Majesty. Is everything all right, your Majesty?"

Saeran grinned and Nia scowled at him. "Thank you, Dunbar. You have confirmed what I thought. There is nothing here to be seen."

The celebration went on and on, even after the king and his father took their leave of the festivities. When the noise rose to an unbearable pitch, Nia left as well. She wasn't yet ready to sleep and instead went out to the courtyard. The moon was full in the clear night sky. She lifted her face to it and breathed of the spring air. All around her everything was returning to life. The night had music of its own, and Nia could almost dance to it.

Countless stars twinkled and winked at her. They called to her, beckoned her closer. *Come fly with us,* they said, and Nia was tempted. But she knew better than to succumb to that temptation. Those who dared to fly up to the stars never returned. Some scrolls said it was because the night sky was the gateway to Valhalla, others that such beauty and splendor was unbearable and it burned the poor creature to ashes.

Yet there were stories of a wizard so pure of heart that he was accepted among the stars and became one of them. But when he began to miss his beloved, the stars returned him to the ground and he brought a piece of one with him, to gift the one he loved.

"Can you command the moon closer?"

Nia smiled, without turning to face the new king. "Of course. What sort of wizard would I be if I could not? But simply because a thing can be done does not mean it should be done."

"A flower will not bloom simply to be plucked," he quoted in passing.

Nia gaped at him and then laughed. "What are you wearing?"

Saeran grinned. Now lying on the bench, he inspected his tattered sleeve and breeches torn off at one calf. He looked absolutely bedraggled. "A disguise," he told. "Someone should have told you, child, I am the king. The only way to do anything without being noticed is to wear a disguise."

"My sincerest sympathies, your Majesty," she said. "And yet…" Without warning she pushed him off the bench to the ground. "If you insist on dressing as a commoner, you'd best get used to being treated as one." Then she regally seated herself on the bench he'd vacated.

Saeran pulled on her hair in retaliation as he sat next to her from the other side.

"I smell sheep's dung," she noted absently.

"It is part of the disguise," he replied in kind.

"I'm sure."

After a moment of easy silence, Saeran shifted with a wince. "I would like to continue my lessons."

Nia nodded. "You have practiced on your own." He had somehow known where she was hiding in the banquet hall. "You notice things now that not many others do."

Saeran shrugged. "Well, I notice the obvious. When a hall full of people shifts to leave a sizable portion of empty space, one tends to wonder why." Nia pushed at him, but the grin he gave her faded too quickly. "I tried to…the time. I could not make it stop again."

Nia didn't look at him. "Neither could I." Though she doubted her methods were the same as his. She wasn't as oblivious as she might sometimes appear. There were several maids and ladies tittering to others about the young king's robust spirit. While she'd searched her books and scrolls for the smallest hint to explain what had happened, Saeran had gone around kissing strange women, and Nia did not like it. Not at all.

But that was neither here nor there. Unknown magic was unpredictable. Something like this could happen again, trap them in time somehow, and what if they never got out?

She drew her knee onto the bench to face him. As she did so, she changed. Her robes disappeared, replaced by a simple peasant's dress, her hair pleated itself into a rope to hang down her back and shoes melted from her feet. "I tried to find an explanation in the scrolls. There isn't one. Any reference to time always says the same. It cannot, and should not, be tampered with."

"Then how do you explain what happened?"

"I don't," she said, frustrated at her own shortcoming. "I can't."

"Perhaps we should try to do it again."

"Again? I don't even know how we did it the first time."

We kissed. Neither of them said it. The knowledge was simply there.

"We cannot," she said, straightening in her seat again.

Saeran swung his leg over to straddle the bench and face her. "Why? Keep in mind, Nia, you speak to a man from a royal lineage. A king. And I do not like being denied."

"In your place, I would start getting used to it. I am not here for your amusement. If that is what you want, there is a bevy of willing bodies for you to seek out. I hear you have already given some a try. I am sure they would welcome you back with open arms."

Saeran reached out to her face, but a small blue spark burned his fingers, her way of refusing his touch. Saeran pulled back with a huff. "Nia, face me."

She didn't move.

"Please," he said.

Nia hesitated, but as much as she felt like a spurned lover, she wasn't. Saeran was her king and she'd sworn to serve him. A tantrum was not acceptable behavior from a wizard. Once she had convinced herself of this, she turned only her face toward him.

"You misunderstand my intentions. A bevy of willing bodies? That is not what I want. Not from you."

"Then what do you want?"

"I want you to look at me and see a man, not a king. I want you to laugh with me and talk with me, to be my companion and friend."

He shouldn't be saying such things. There had to be balance between justice and magic. Her duty was not only to the king, but to all of Wilderheim, and Nia had to be able to put the needs of the kingdom above Saeran's if it came to that. Her heart was not hers to share.

"I need your magic, Nia," he said, "but I also need you. Let me be your friend. Let me hold you when you need to be held. Like that day in the woods." He reached out again. "Let me kiss you—"

"Why?" Nia cried. He had to know this couldn't be! He would have to take a wife soon, a princess or noble who would give him more land and wealth, make him a stronger king and give him heirs. Saeran had far more obligations as king than he knew, and no matter how sincerely he looked into her eyes now, Nia had no place in his future, except as a wizard.

"Because," he said fiercely, cupping her face in his hands, "the first time we kissed time stopped. That has to mean something."

Humans ever lived at the whim of the gods. They toyed with lives, gambled for destinies. They could be unrepentantly cruel or generous beyond one's wildest dreams. But one never knew which of the two would be their lot.

Nia had felt something when Saeran kissed her. Something too powerful to be imagined and too subtle to be the result of a spell. Time had stopped, and she had a sinking feeling it wouldn't have if anyone but Saeran had kissed her.

How was she supposed to explain that?

She wasn't. The kingdom had to come first. As much as she wanted to believe Saeran cared for her, a deep sense of unease held her back. Something was coming and she wasn't sure either of them was truly prepared for it. Saeran would need a wizard at his side, a weapon and a tool. Not a friend. Not a lovesick girl dreaming of a star she would never be allowed to touch.

When he leaned closer, Nia covered his hands with hers and pulled them away. Stroking his cheek, trying to ignore that bewildered, hurt look in his eyes, she pressed a chaste kiss to his lips. "May Woden smile upon your reign, your Majesty. May you never have the need to go to war again, and may your kingdom love you and prosper. Let Freyr send you a woman to love and cherish and give you heirs. For it can never be me."

Rising to her feet, Nia became the royal wizard once again, her robes flowing around her and her hair shining silver in the moonlight. Her gait was fluid as she walked away, carried by magic when her step faltered.

"What about my lessons?" Saeran called after her.

"Tomorrow," she replied, not trusting herself to face him again. "In the glen."

CHAPTER 8

Nia returned to her study, never so grateful to have a sturdy door between her and the rest of the world. The torches were cold, but two dozen candles burned bright to illuminate the space. In the past, this must have been a prison, perhaps even a torture chamber. There were still metal rings embedded in the stone walls from which shackles could be hung. The archway had hinges on one side and a hole on the other where the cage door would have locked.

Instead of thieves or murderers, it now held ancient words scribed on parchment spelled to withstand the test of time. Instead of torture implements, there was a makeshift washstand, a small altar to the gods, and a table with but two chairs to it and its surface reserved only for manuscripts and tomes.

Nia had done what she could to set everything back to rights. She'd managed to repair many of the things that had been broken, but some she'd had to replace. There was a proper bed where her simple pallet used to be and a wooden chest to hold her few belongings.

She ought to be sleeping in her chamber in the castle, but she liked it here better. It was familiar. Safe. Nico's presence was still here, a comfort to her always. The sneaky old man had left a part of himself behind. Everywhere she looked, in small cracks and crevices, Nico had stored away pockets of his magic. Perhaps nothing more than raw magic, perhaps some secret message left just for her. Nia didn't want to disturb them to find out. As long as they were here, Nia could pretend he was only a call away.

She yawned, weary of the day, already dreading tomorrow. She had hoped Saeran would give up on this quest for magic after what happened last time. Instead it only seemed to have made him more eager. "Why does he do this?" she asked aloud, frowning.

For you, the walls returned from all sides. Scowling, she poured water into her crystal scrying bowl and set it on the table. "Not for me," she said. "Do you know why?"

For you, the walls insisted.

She'd show them. Gazing deep into the bowl, she let her will sink into the water, seeking the future. "You'll see. He does not…he cannot…"

As images began to form, her words trailed away. Instead of an older king, she saw the boy Saeran had been years ago. He was sitting at a long table with king Halden and a number of Wilderheim's soldiers at one end. At the other sat warriors of another kind. They had shirts made of dark red cloth, and leather armor shaped like scales. They were dark skinned and black haired, in contrast to Saeran and Halden's fair northern complexion. These had to be Aegirans.

Between the two groups was a window to another place. Nia couldn't see into it, but she could hear the voices speaking from inside it. "You threaten us at your own peril, Farraj. You are beaten. Accept your failure with honor."

"There is no honor in failure!" The one called Farraj snapped. "We will come. Many more. You have magic men, we bring our own. You hide in your stone houses. Where we come from, stone crumbles into sand. Nothing will stop us!"

His warriors shouted their agreement, some reaching for the curved swords strapped to their sides. There were only a handful, the ones sent back to demand recompense for the men they'd lost in the fight. It was customary in the desert lands of Aegiros for the winning side to appease the conquered with a tribute to bury the bad blood between them. Nico had made Nia learn this early on, while the war still raged. Life was precious, and no matter how foolishly lost, it had to be repaid. To deny the Aegirans this was a great affront to them, fueling their rage at having been defeated.

"You raze our cities and expect payment in return?" Manfred demanded. "By the gods, I have never been so insulted in my life! Bring your armies, Farraj. We will water our fields with their blood!"

Halden paled as the Aegirans began shouting angrily, shoving away from the table, readying to fight.

"Wait," Saeran said. No one heard him so he stood and shouted it again. "Wait! There is another way."

"Saeran, sit down," Manfred ordered, but the prince would not be silenced.

Instead of listening to his father, he looked to the guard sitting at his left, a man wearing a bloody bandage over one eye. Whatever he saw in the man's face made Saeran's shoulders droop with a sigh. "There is a way to resolve this. Life for a life, that is what you want, Farraj, is it not?"

"*Rah!*"

Saeran held up his hands. "Then have mine."

"No!" Halden and Manfred shouted at the same time. Halden was on his feet in an instant, trying to push the boy behind him.

"When there is no wheat to pay the life price," Saeran said, "A marriage can be brokered between the clans to ensure peace."

"Saeran, stop!"

But he didn't. "I can never leave Wilderheim," he said. "But if you will accept, I will marry a daughter of Aegiros as a symbol of peace between our kingdoms."

Farraj stroked his beard, staring at the prince. His tribesmen whispered harsh words in his ear, clearly unhappy he was even considering Saeran's proposal. He heard them, one and all, nodded to each in turn, but when he faced Saeran again, it was his word alone that mattered.

Manfred was rambling, saying the boy had no authority to speak on behalf of Wilderheim or Lyria. His frantic arguments only served to convince the foreigner of Saeran's importance. That the prince hadn't dropped his gaze from Farraj's didn't help matters, either.

Farraj twitched his head to the side, indicating for Saeran to meet him halfway. Each with four men behind them, the two met in the middle of the room. The Aegiran official was tall among his people, but at sixteen, Saeran was almost of a height with him. "You are correct," Farraj said. "A marriage can end fighting. We call this *ramesh feh*. My *shansher* has two daughters. The older promised to another. You marry younger. Pay bride price. There will be peace."

"Consider carefully, Highness," the guard advised, but they both knew there was little more to consider. As prince and heir to the crown of Wilderheim, Saeran would have eventually had to make a politically advantageous marriage. Now would be as good a time as any. Aegiros was a kingdom of tribes bound by custom and each had a sort of king, called *shansher*. To marry one's daughter was equivalent to marrying a northern princess. Saeran would gain not only peace, but a powerful ally as well.

"I understand what I am doing," Saeran replied. To Farraj he said, "No more will die."

"No more." The foreigner held out his hand.

Saeran stared into his eyes for a moment longer, making Farraj's mouth twitch with amusement. When they clasped forearms, the deal was struck. Farraj touched a hand to his heart, then his forehead. He bowed to Saeran and his company before all of them walked out of the room without another word.

Nia dissolved the vision with a wordless cry, stumbling away from the table.

For you. For you. For you, the walls chanted over and over.

Nia slapped her hands over her ears. "Stop it!"

For you. For you. For you.

Torches flared to brilliant light, burning higher and brighter than they should. The flames licked the ceiling slithering in her direction, adding their voices to the walls.

"Enough!" Furious tears blurred her vision. Her magic pulsed inside her skin, leaking from her hands, creating bursts of light and heat.

For you. For you…

Nia screamed.

The study plunged into blessed dark silence. With all the flames extinguished and the walls turned mute, nothing else dared intrude on her solitude.

Left to herself, Nia found her bed by touch, laid down upon it, and buried her face in her pillow to weep in peace.

≪ »·◇·« ≫

There were duties Saeran had to perform as king, yet all seemed to have been forgotten. Guests still celebrated, masters oversaw the servants, his father was busy packing for his travels, and Saeran was free to do as he pleased. He went to the glen.

When Nia arrived, he wanted to be ready. She'd been right last night. Saeran's future was already set. He didn't know why he'd said what he had, but was grateful Nia hadn't taken his words to heart. Perhaps the wine had gone to his head.

Today, however, was a new beginning. He'd prove to her that he was a good student and he'd make her forget about any foolish thing he may have blurted out in the heat of the moment. Saeran was resolved. He would make this work somehow. No matter how enchanting Nia might be, no matter how seductive the thought of kissing her again might become, he would be steadfast and true to his goal. She would never have reason to regret taking him on as her student.

Thusly decided, he climbed an apple tree up to the third branch and settled in to wait.

A sparrow flew circles around his head. It lighted on a higher branch and stared at him, tilting its head first to one side then the other before it opened its beak and made a shrill sound.

Saeran grinned and held out his hand, delighted when the bird perched on his finger. "Hello."

The sparrow chirped.

"What brings you to my tree on this fine day?"

The bird chirped again, this time with enough gusto to ruffle his feathers.

"I see you've made a friend up there."

Saeran grinned down at Nia. She was dressed in her usual robes, but today she'd draped the wolf's pelt over her shoulders for warmth. The head of it rested on her shoulder as an old friend. He was glad she wore it. A wizard he was not, but even he could sense its proper place was not mounted on a wall or tossed over a chair. No, that wolf was meant for Nia.

"He just came to me," he told her studying the sparrow now nesting in the palm of his hand. "You are a he, are you not?"

Nia chuckled. "Come down from there, the both of you. We have much to do today."

The bird abandoned him and landed on Nia's shoulder. Saeran shook his head. "Does all of nature obey your every whim?" He jumped to the ground, falling into step with Nia as she walked farther away from prying eyes.

"As much as the whole kingdom obeys yours, I would think." She lowered herself to sit on a fallen log.

"Such a powerful ally," Saeran mused. "I am glad you stand with me and not against me." He sat on the ground facing her. "You may begin your instruction, master."

Nia attempted a smile. It was feeble. Something weighed on her mind, and by the look of it, it wasn't good. "I've had to think long and hard about the wisdom of continuing your lessons."

"That does not bode well."

"I have decided to carry on only as long as it does not interfere with your rule and my ability to aid you."

"Nia," Saeran said softly, "the only thing that could interfere with my rule is your absence." He may have spoken foolishly last night, but he realized now he'd meant what he said. Saeran couldn't be king on his own. The restrictions were too great, the responsibilities too heavy for any one person to shoulder. Without Nia, he'd make himself mad with the games and intrigues of court. Seven noble houses already vied for his favor. Saeran didn't know what they would ultimately want, but he knew if they had their way, those nobles would manipulate everything and everyone in order to make themselves indispensible to him.

He'd seen it happen in Halden's court, the way this master or that had only to mention his displeasure at a roving tribe making camp on his lands to have the king order them immediately removed and jailed, without reason other than appeasing a man who called himself friend. Saeran had no stomach for it. He needed Nia to keep him sane.

"I am here to advise and teach you," she said. "A wizard is meant to be her king's aide. But nothing more."

"And if that is not enough?" The words were spoken before he could stop them. He didn't regret them, though he knew he should.

Nia shook her head. "No. I…"

"Nia—"

She abruptly pushed to her feet and paced around the log to the other side. "You have already learned to listen; now I will teach you to understand what you hear." She petted the sparrow gently. "Thank you for agreeing to help me." It chirped in answer. To Saeran, she said, "Listen as you already know, but listen for meaning."

Saeran met her gaze, but hers skittered away. She wouldn't look him in the eye again. Something had frightened her. Had he done this? Saeran sighed. "I hope one day we have enough trust between us for you to tell me when something weighs on you."

She said nothing.

The sparrow began to sing then, forcing Saeran's mind to the task she set him. There was a certain pattern to the chirps and trills, but no meaning that he could discern. What was he saying?

"Don't force it," Nia said. "Calm your mind and let the meaning come to you."

Saeran closed his eyes and relaxed, concentrating on nothing but the sparrow's song. He listened and simply enjoyed. After a while, a slow smile spread across his face, and he chuckled as the melody began to make sense. The sparrow wasn't singing, he was complaining! His nest was too far and his mate too fickle, his offspring perhaps not his own. He bemoaned the lack of food and the long winter cold that hurt his joints. This was an old bird as bitter as any man made grumpy by his age.

Saeran opened his eyes and looked at the bird with what he hoped was more sympathy than humor. "I am sorry for your plight, friend."

The sparrow chirped grumpily at him. *Let me not catch you near my nest, sonny. I'll peck that grin off your face, king or no!*

Nia thanked the sparrow before he could get more agitated and gave him a handful of seeds to eat while she turned her attention to Saeran. "Well done," she praised. "You learn quickly."

"Will I understand all animals now?"

Nia smiled. "If they wish to allow it, yes. If you work hard and practice often, you might even learn to understand the earth and the wind. The earth and anything of it never lies. Only humans can do that. You can trust the wind to tell you of coming riders. The earth will tell you when it is tired and cannot yield crops."

"What of fire?"

"Fire is born and dies too quickly to know anything of use. But fire can sing as well as any songbird. It can lull you to sleep or roar a warning if someone intrudes when your back is turned."

"Then I shall never be without one."

Nia hugged the wolf skin closer around her. "Perhaps we should continue indoors. The next lesson is scrying."

They walked back side by side in companionable silence. If the wind sensed his heart yearning, it did not say a word. If the earth felt the weight of his step, it held its silence.

And if his hand brushed Nia's, lingering, he chose to pretend it meant nothing.

CHAPTER 9

Within the fortnight, Manfred bid his son farewell and set out on his journey. It was a long ride to Lyria, and the caravan was prepared for anything, but Manfred planned to take shelter in an inn whenever they could. Nia asked the gods for blessing on their behalf that history might not repeat itself. She prayed Manfred's journey was easy and that he arrived in good health and high spirits in his brother's home.

"I expect weekly reports," he told Nia before he left. "And leave nothing out, girl. I may not be king anymore, but I am still Saeran's father."

"Yes, Majesty."

"And you," he said to Saeran. "You grew up too fast, my boy. But you grew up well. Fret none, I will be back in a few months. We will have all the time in the world then." Manfred embraced his son, adding a quiet warning for his ears only. Nia still overheard. "Be careful," he said.

"Yes, Father."

With the old king on his way, Saeran didn't hesitate to put Nia and himself to work, and she was surprised to find that what she'd told him weeks ago was still fresh in his mind. Saeran personally met with cooks, butchers, huntsmen, milliners, merchants, and travelers to learn what winter had wrought on Wilderheim. Only when he'd made certain no one would go to bed hungry in his kingdom did he turn his attention to everything else. He held court, consulted with guards and sentries, met with the masters and the nobles, heard complaints, carried out judgments, sent messages and received them.

Nia was present for all of it. Saeran called on her to sense truths and falsehoods, to see to it his orders were obeyed, and to advise. And once the day was done, the two of them met alone in a room Saeran had turned into a makeshift library where she taught him magic deep into the night.

Saeran proved to be a quick study. Once he caught on to the makings of a spell, he didn't need it explained to him a second time. Nia taught him the rhythm of nature, how everything, from the smallest fly to the largest bear, had a place in the order of things. Often by observing a malady in one aspect of nature, one discovered the cause somewhere else. She taught him how to find leylines in the earth and follow them to points of convergence. Castle Frastmir stood on one of these points. Here, the earth lent its strength to everything and magic wrought on these grounds was more potent and powerful than anywhere else.

Nia enjoyed teaching when her student was so attentive. But more than that, she enjoyed his company, which was very ill advised. Saeran made her smile and laugh. He seemed to know when she got hungry or tired before she noticed it herself. At times she would say something exactly the way Nico had said it to her and for a moment she could think of nothing except how much she missed him. Whenever her sentence faltered, Saeran noticed. He took her hand in his and reminisced with her about the old wizard until she no longer felt so alone.

But when it came time to say good night and she returned to her cavernous study and her lonesome bed, the feeling returned. It was only then that Nia could let herself acknowledge how much she ached inside. Every night Saeran burrowed deeper into her heart, and every morning she found it more difficult to cast him out, something she had to do if she hoped to get through the day. Very soon she feared there would be no denying him any longer.

Weeks passed quickly this way until Saeran announced he wanted to reform the advisory council before the spring equinox. There were seven members on the council, old men rewarded handsomely for their years of service, who've come to enjoy the privilege of the king's audience too much. They no longer served the kingdom's interests but their own, and Saeran wanted to be rid of them. Having made the announcement without consulting her, he'd put Nia in the awful position of having to defend the king's decree while at the same time pacifying those who would be asked to return to their family lands.

If he thought this would relieve him of an unwanted burden, he was mistaken. The council was necessary, since no man, not king or wizard, could do everything on his own. Not only that, but since he'd appointed Nia to take care of the old council, he was forced to handpick the new members by himself. Nia would, of course, have to give her approval of each one he chose, but the most difficult task of sorting through the eager crowds of learned individuals was up to the king. Especially since she made her excuses every time he called her to the proceedings.

Nia didn't feel guilty about that at all.

"It is impossible, Nia!" he complained one night, dropping his head to the table with a thud. "They are coming from everywhere like locusts! Charlatans, each and every one of them! I cannot trust the ones who come forward, and I cannot find the ones I would trust. You have to help me." He slid out of his chair to the floor and knee walked to her side of the table. Grasping her hand, he looked into her eyes and begged, "Please, please. Save me from their wretchedness. It is your duty to protect your king."

Nia was laughing too hard to answer.

Saeran grinned. "Or at the very least distract me for a while."

"Now that I can do."

"Thank you," he cried with heartfelt gratitude. "What is tonight's lesson?"

"Scrying."

His head thudded to the table again.

"You wanted to learn," she reminded him.

"Can you not teach me something else?"

"Hearing the wind tell you there is an army at your door will not help you if you cannot see how big the army is. Why must you continue to fight me on this?"

"Because it amuses me to see your brow pucker every time I do."

Nia set the scrying bowl in front of him hard enough to splash water into his lap. "It is easy to listen to what is already there. To conjure something from nothing takes focus, strength of will. You must want something enough to will it into a vision." Raising a pert eyebrow at him, she asked, "Is there nothing you want, my king, now that you have everything?"

Saeran gazed at her so long her good humor waned and her face grew warm. Without a word, he lowered his head to stare deep into the bowl.

"Look beyond the water and the vessel," she guided. "They are only a window to what you seek. Hold the thought of what you wish to see in your mind, let it sink into the bowl and guide you to the vision."

Nia let her voice trail off into silence. This time was different from all the other nights he'd attempted to See. This time she felt his will as if he was working a spell without words. The intensity of it grew, filling him, leaking out of him without direction. Nia couldn't sense what it was, but she could lay a hand on his shoulder and look into the bowl with him. Thus connected, she Saw his vision without altering it.

She saw herself. Her own nightmare playing out before her just beneath the water's surface. Eirwen's face was as wrinkled as she remembered. The old woman, her caretaker, stood by the fire, listening to Nia shout. She didn't say a word, merely stood there. And then the waters came.

Her fault. Nia dreamed of water, and water tore apart the life she'd known. Eirwen was dead. Their cottage gone. Nia was alone in the forest, with nowhere to go, no one to look after her. Nine years old.

She saw herself walk away, seek out the merchants passing by. She'd hidden from their sight but followed them into the village. And another after that. Until they led her to Frastmir. By then she'd been half starved, half asleep on her feet. Hiding took more strength than she possessed. The shadows slipped from her grasp as she was stealing a loaf of bread from the baker's kitchen.

Nia's hand slipped from Saeran's shoulder. He caught it and held on as the vision continued. Nico stopped the bread thief, searched her soul and saw something there that Nia never knew. He never told her. She saw him taking her in, teaching her, giving her a home again. She saw herself smile, laugh, fall asleep in safety and comfort, but wake up screaming in the night.

Saeran squeezed her hand tighter when she tried to pull away.

The water showed her the night Saeran pledged himself to the Aegiran girl he didn't even know. Nia hadn't known it then, but the king had, as had Nico. That was the night he'd taught her how to make lights dance and cast shadows. He'd sat at the table and watched her play with them and laugh, as if her joy was the only good thing there was.

Nia saw her first meeting with Saeran, the day in the woods, their first kiss. She saw this very moment, with Saeran clutching her hand as an anchor for the vision, and her looking over his shoulder. Then another vision began to form: a dark foggy image, the shape of a man and woman in a passionate embrace, and Nia couldn't bear to see more.

With a wordless cry she knocked the bowl off the table, breaking the spell, and Saeran's hold on her. Shaken, she went to the window and braced her hands against its ledge, breathing deeply of the night air.

"I am sorry," Saeran said behind her. "You never told me where you came from. I just wanted to see."

"I came from nothing," she told him numbly. "I am no one."

"Are you angry with me?"

Nia shook her head. "No." He'd only done what she told him to do. There was nothing to fault him for. Saeran was not responsible for her past.

When he laid a hand on her shoulder, she allowed him to turn her around. "Then why do you weep?" he asked, brushing her tears away.

Nia had no answer to give him. He didn't demand one from her. Instead he drew her into his arms and held her until her tears dried. She watched the moon rise bright from behind the tree line. Its light brushed the fields and villages in silent affection. The wolves would be out to play tonight, she could feel them gathering. As the first howls rose up to the sky, Nia pulled away from Saeran. It was time to say good night. She gathered her scrying bowl and crystals and half bowed to Saeran, taking her leave.

"Nia," he said as she was passing through the door. "You are not no one."

Nia closed the door behind her without saying a word

CHAPTER 10

Saeran stared into the bowl of water, willing images of his father to appear. He'd been sitting there since dusk trying to practice his scrying to look in on the old man. His entire body felt cramped, his legs completely numb. Still, after all this time, there was nothing in the bowl but water. He was beginning to think Nia did something to make him see things when she taught him to scry. It was the only lesson she had to repeat almost daily, and he still couldn't do it on his own.

The one time he'd managed to catch a vision, he could hardly believe his eyes. He'd have thought it a fluke, an illusion, were it not for Nia's tears. She broke his heart that night. And he hadn't seen a vision since. Instead he did this. Sat at the water bowl for hours on end, wondering if Nia was already asleep. If she was waking up from nightmares alone in that cursed tomb of a study.

Frustrated and sore, his head pounding without mercy, Saeran shoved the bowl aside. He pushed to his feet, nearly falling back down when his knees gave out. It took long moments for feeling to return to his lower extremities, and then it felt like he was standing on needles. Saeran hobbled with as much dignity as a king could muster to the bed and sat on the edge, sighing.

Tomorrow was another day. More royal decrees and more disputes to settle. He'd have to get the new council together and present it to Nia. Again. She'd turned half of his chosen candidates away and restored three of the old members, including Allon, whom Saeran could hardly stand on a good day.

Nia had her reasons. Something about respecting tradition and wisdom guiding youth. He didn't care about why she did it. What he cared about was that the ones he'd most wanted were where he wanted them. Saeran grinned. No one but Nia had met the new council members yet. He couldn't wait to present them. One by one, he would buck every antiquated tradition his father had upheld out of laziness. When Manfred returned, Wilderheim would be a much different place.

It was too quiet. Today he'd had Nia open a window to Manfred so they could talk. He hadn't realized how long they were at it until the window began to close in on itself as Nia's strength flagged. She'd been forced to beg off from their daily lessons. It was the thing he looked forward to the most each day and he missed it. He missed Nia.

She'd taught him so much already. If he had to, Saeran could cloak himself from the sight of others. He could create an illusion of himself for a short time; he could even speak and have the air carry his words to a single person alone in a crowded chamber. He understood all things now, and they spoke to him often, telling him so much more about his own kingdom than he could ever hear from his sentries and advisors. Yet no one knew of this, save Nia.

When they were alone, Saeran was no longer a king. He was simply Saeran, a man and nothing more. But when he sat his throne, Nia proved invaluable to him. She saw things he would have missed, gave him sound advice when he needed it, and her presence alone calmed him. If he let himself, Saeran could love the wizard with her sad eyes and quick wit. But that would only bring pain to them both. Saeran had sealed his fate six years ago, and there was no going back. He'd done what he had to for the good of two kingdoms, and he prayed the gods showed him mercy enough that he never had to regret that choice.

Saeran stretched out on the bed. Nothing stirred this late at night. The windows were open, but the air outside was still, with nary a breeze to whisper in his ear. The fire in the hearth was dying down, taking its song with it. Saeran was completely alone, cocooned in silence.

It bothered him. He closed his eyes and thought of what he wanted most in that moment. "Nia," he said out loud as she'd taught him.

All at once, there was a gust of wind and she was there.

Saeran jerked upright on the bed. She was naked. Her hair pinned up, her hand holding a washcloth to her shoulder. Her back was to him, and for an instant Saeran wondered if he'd fallen asleep. He had dreamed of her so often he couldn't be sure.

But then her hand stilled and her head lifted to look around. She gasped, then growled furiously, and the sheets were pulled out from beneath him. They draped around her to conceal the expanse of skin, and Saeran nearly snatched them back again. When she was covered, Nia turned to spear him with an icy glare. "When I told you you could summon me at will, I did not mean for you to do it on a whim!"

"Forgive me, I did not realize..." He couldn't stop staring. Nia was before the hearth and the dying light was still strong enough to shine through the sheets, outlining her form as a shadow.

"Close your eyes," she commanded and his eyelids obeyed. But Saeran could still see her in his mind, so close he could reach out and touch her. Gods, but he wanted to!

There was rustling, and when he could open his eyes again, she was clad in her robes; her feet bare, her face blushing. "Here," she said, tossing the sheets at him. They hit him in the face and he grinned as he pushed them away.

"Ah, Nia," he cajoled, standing off the bed. "Don't be cross with me. I had no way of knowing you would be bathing when I called you." He reached out to pull the pins out of her hair, letting it cascade down her back and over her shoulders. "And it is your fault for not expecting this could happen when you taught me how to will you into my presence."

Her glare didn't lessen, but her lips were pale and she shivered.

"The floor is cold," he said. Reaching around her shoulders and beneath her knees, Saeran picked her up against his chest. "You will catch a chill."

The flames in the hearth blazed higher as her temper rose, but Nia was too tired to do anything other than ask, "What are you doing?"

Saeran sat her on his bed as if it was perfectly acceptable for her to be there, nearly naked in the king's bedchamber. "Seeing to it you don't die of cold and leave me without counsel," he answered, covering her bare feet with a thick blanket. "And making up for summoning you away from your bath."

"Why did you summon me?" she asked, her eyes narrowing in suspicion. She shouldn't have. Almost halfway closed, her eyelids became even heavier. Her head was already swimming. She couldn't keep this up much longer. The spell she'd done for Saeran and Manfred hadn't been difficult in its making, but in its perpetuation. There was no flare of magic and then a moment to restore herself. To keep such a window open, Nia had to channel her magic into it in an even, continuous stream. It had wearied her more than she realized. She'd been moments from bedding down when Saeran summoned her.

"I couldn't sleep and I hoped you would keep me company for a while."

"It has been a long day, Saeran, I will not be much of a conversationalist." Beltaine was almost upon them, and there were preparations that needed to be done. Nia had to rise before dawn tomorrow to oversee the villagers' efforts, and to perform some of her own spells and ritual. For many, Beltaine night would be one of celebration, and they would care for little more than that. But for those many to enjoy it, a few had to work very hard in the days prior.

Saeran caressed her cheek. "You are tired."

"Yes. Send me back." She shouldn't be here. But her mind wasn't focused enough for her to transport herself back to her own bed. If she tried magic, she might end up in a wall. And walking barefoot through the castle at night left her exposed not only to attack but also gossip.

Saeran cupped her face and kissed her eyes closed. "Don't worry, Nia. There is no need for you to stand the king's guard tonight. I will keep you safe."

Nia felt the world shift as he pushed down on her shoulders to make her lie back. Her eyes refused to open; she was half asleep already. "Send me back, Saeran," she asked him, consciousness fading. "You know how."

"No," he whispered in answer, and then there was darkness.

CHAPTER 11

The breeze woke her, sighing her name. *Niaaa.*

She opened her eyes and sat up with a start. It was day, by the brightness of the sun she judged it to be nearing noon. She'd slept half the day away in the king's bed, and there was a tiny creature with a limp hat and a beaked nose almost as big as his head perched on the pillow next to her, watching her with curious brown eyes. Mortified, Nia fought the coverings to get out from beneath them. By the time she looked back, the gnome was gone.

Gods, what had possessed Saeran? Anyone could have come in here while she slept, and she didn't want to think about how the people would have mocked her for it.

Nia, I need you, the breeze said in Saeran's voice. Of course, Saeran didn't dare summon her as he had last night, he wouldn't want her to appear in the great hall half clad and sleeping.

With a thought Nia transported herself to her study. The candles had burned down with no one to tend them and it was pitch black. Summoning light, she stripped her robe and dressed in her usual clothes. There was no time to do more than splash cold water on her face and drag a comb through her hair. Mornings were when Saeran held court and heard petitions, and it was part of Nia's duty to oversee the proceedings should she be needed. She was late!

When the walls called her name, echoing each other, Nia moaned her frustration, took up her staff and disappeared, reappearing outside the great hall.

She opened the door with a wave of her hand and hastened toward Saeran. There was a crowd gathered, and several men knelt before the dais, facing the king. They were knights by the look of them, but Nia didn't recognize their crests. They must have come from far outside of Wilderheim, and by the tense set of their shoulders she could tell they've been waiting for quite a while.

Nia sent Saeran a meek look of apology. It wasn't like her to neglect her duties, as he well knew. He shouldn't have let her sleep so long. But when his mouth twitched in answer, she realized he'd done it on purpose. Nia scowled. She'd get him for that later.

"The royal wizard and advisor," Saeran announced, his voice carrying to the farthest corner of the great hall.

Nobles bowed and nodded their greetings. Nia kept her gaze on the wall in front of her, debating whether it would be more effective to summon an army of fire ants into Saeran's boots or pour sticky honey in his hair. Neither was good enough. This offense was too great to be tolerated. She'd toss him into the stream and make everything he ate taste like old fish. Yes, that ought to do it.

One of the men kneeling before the king glanced up as her robes brushed his shoulder in passing, and once he looked, his gaze snared. Nia could feel the weight of it on her before she turned to face them. He was first in his company to dare raise his head. He was not the last.

Nia spared him a glance but didn't return his open regard. Her magic reached across the great hall to take measure of the crowd.

She sensed curiosity about the knights among the gathering, one the king didn't seem to share. Saeran's agitation chafed against her mind like bristling fur. "These men are travelers from Synealee by the Sea," he said for Nia's benefit.

Nia glanced at him, surprised at his harsh tone. She'd never heard him speak that way, not even in the face of insult. Saeran didn't anger easily, but it was clear something had upset him.

"They ask for shelter and our assistance in their quest."

Nia addressed the knights. "I have seen Synealee. You have come quite a distance from the land of eternal summer. What is it you seek this far north?"

The one in the middle looked askance at the king. "Your Majesty," he said uncertainly, "surely this is a matter to be discussed among men."

"Sir Frederick duChamp," the king said by way of introduction, turning his head toward Nia without looking away from the knights. "He speaks for this lot."

Nia nodded to the knight. He was the elder of this company, a man whose pride kept his shoulders back despite his gray hair and weathered face. The simple clasp securing his cape was a circle wreath with a hand brandishing a sword in its center. They all wore a similar symbol, but his was the only one etched in gold.

"The wizard is my right hand," Saeran told the knight, daring him to argue. "You will show her the same deference you show me."

"Answer to a woman, by the grace of god inferior in every way?" Sir Frederick said, his face turning red.

"Tread carefully, knight," Saeran said. It was the only warning he would give.

Rather than leash his tongue, the knight stood. "Boys, we have come to the wrong place! The king's woman rules this land; we should have gone to her instead!" As the onlookers hummed in displeasure, Sir Frederick turned on Nia. "And where would we have found her, I wonder? In the king's bed, perhaps?"

Saeran rose from his throne, and all those with sense backed away from the dais and the man who had just incurred the king's wrath.

Nia stood her ground and held the knight's gaze without saying a word.

"Do you please him well, *wizard*?"

Rather than roar his fury, Saeran quietly dared, "One more word."

Sir Frederick sneered. "Harm a hair on my head and you will have the armies of Synealee descending on you to avenge me."

It was the worst thing he could have said. The guards filed in, arms raised, but they looked to Nia and Saeran for orders. Both shook their heads to keep them back.

All of the knights were on their feet now, trying to reason with their companion.

He would hear none of it. Shrugging off their hands, ignoring their warnings, he toed the very edge of the first step. "We came to you out of courtesy, not need," Frederick declared. "This insult will not be borne. I will not yield to a boy's fancy, nor woman's whim!"

Saeran drew his dagger, but Nia stayed his hand. She brushed past him, her robes pushing him back. The gathering retreated more with every step she took, all but the foolish knight who thought himself above a king. Nia descended three steps and looked Sir Frederick in the eye to see his soul.

She wasn't gentle, and she didn't hold back. Arrowing through the haze of red temper, she found his pride and fear. Deeper still, she followed a path of determination to the heart of him, where all that he was and would ever be resided. There she found his quest, a dream of touching godhood in its purest form.

His obsession with a lone god's son, neither human nor divine, but both at once made no sense to Nia. This man worshipped what she could only call a wizard, yet he scoffed in the face of another. He sought a holy object with the power to grant eternal life. Nia had never heard of such a thing. To find it would mean great honor to him and all his descendants, a blessing he hoped to prove he deserved. Only one whose soul was worthy, blessed by his god, would be allowed to touch it, and he desperately wanted to be such a man. To fail in this meant an eternity of fiery torment at the hands of demons, but to have come this far gave him hope and made him believe he was their better.

Baffled, Nia left where Frederick was headed and sought where he'd come from. The knights didn't move while she searched him; she didn't allow them such freedom. They stood frozen, watching, waiting for her judgment while Frederick shivered before her, wide eyed, terrified of being found out.

"He lies," Nia declared. "A reckless old fool. They have no supplies left and the journey has drained them. This one is an outcast from his own lands. The others hold allegiance to no one. They seek a treasure far to the north where even our own people rarely venture. Their legends led them here, and they require a guide to go the rest of the way."

Nia released him and raised her head high as everyone present sighed in unison. Saeran issued the signal to bring the guards closer, but it was her honor the knight had impugned and she would be the one to pass judgment over him for his insolence.

Free of her spell, Sir Frederick clutched his chest as his aging heart shuddered and slowed. As with the poisoned wolf, Nia felt the knight's pain as if it was her own. She schooled herself not to show it.

"Foolish old man," she said, keeping her voice soft. "Your god has no power to protect you here. This is Woden's realm, and his children do not take kindly to such insult."

Sir Frederick dropped to one knee, sputtering, dying. Nia descended two more steps and held her hand out over his form huddling at her feet. Closing her eyes, she droned a hum and then gave it words: a healing spell which drew on the earth's nurturing magic to mend the flesh of man. It wasn't a forceful order, but rather a prayer, a petition. The earth, as all living things, could choose whether to obey. The knight stilled, breathed in deep, then straightened and stood, his eyes wide. He had finally run out of words.

"I saved your life this day," she told him. "Think twice before you slander me again." Turning away from him, she returned to her place at the king's side. "They are no threat to us, my liege. The treasure, if there is one, has value for them alone. The sooner we help them find it, the sooner they'll leave."

"What of him?" Saeran asked, indicating Frederick with a nod.

The knight still staring at her traced a cross over his chest and knelt, bowing his head. "Bless my soul," he said reverently. "Forgive me for not recognizing the great Lady of the Lake. My life is yours if you ask it."

Nia and Saeran looked at each other, equally confused.

"Lady of the Lake," the rest of them echoed, kneeling along with him, and once again those present hummed with gossip.

Saeran despised gossip, yet he always seemed to find himself in the midst of it, its subject or its audience. By tomorrow, some great fable about Nia would be making its way across Frastmir and this time he would have no explanation for what she'd wrought. Who were these knights, casting judgment one moment and then prostrating themselves the next? What utter drivel would the nobles invent about what they'd seen?

Saeran didn't like this sudden shift, didn't trust it in the least. He found himself wary of them. They were fervent in their beliefs, fanatic in their quest for what they themselves had admitted might not even be there. Such steadfast faith could be a powerful thing.

Even now, though he showed humility to Nia by kneeling, Frederick still raised his head to gaze upon her with unnerving reverence, and Saeran knew without question Nia would rather be anywhere in that moment than standing there before him.

He looks at you as if he sees a goddess given form, Saeran thought, willing the words to her. He didn't expect her to hear him, but she answered all the same.

More fool he. A goddess would pluck his eyes out for daring to meet her gaze.

Her disgruntled voice in his mind soothed Saeran.

But then he noticed the knight at the far right of the company who, much like Frederick, didn't have the sense to drop his gaze. This one was different. There was something very familiar in his eyes. Saeran had worn that selfsame look many a time when Nia either didn't notice or chose not to see. Saeran's fingers curled tighter around the dagger he hadn't yet sheathed.

Nia stepped closer but said nothing. Saeran held their lives in his hand. Knowing she would stand by him no matter the judgment made it harder to choose but easier to carry the burden of choice. Saeran leaned to the side a little to brush shoulders with her. She reciprocated, elbowing his dagger arm. Scowling, he sheathed the blade and resumed his seat.

"Beltaine comes in two days' time," he said. "There will be no talk of quests until it passes. For now I will choose to overlook the affront you've caused. Have a care, I will not tolerate another."

"We understand," one of them said. "Our thanks, your Majesty."

Saeran waved the guards to lead them out and clear the great hall. The court session was over. "I do not trust those men," he told Nia when they were all gone. "Keep away from them."

"As you command, your Majesty," she replied.

He looked up at her where she stood. "I mean it, Nia."

"Why do they bother you so?"

Saeran thought of the way the younger knight gazed at Nia and dread settled in his bones. He couldn't shake the feeling that somehow, someway, these knights would rob him of something precious. The maddening sense of portent hovered just out of reach, as visions always did each time he sought them.

"You are the one with magic Sight. What does it tell you?"

Nia tilted her head and looked off into the distance, no doubt seeing many things Saeran would never glimpse. "It tells me we are nearing a fork in the path."

Saeran reached for her hand and squeezed it tight. Whichever path the gods chose for him, he would walk it with Nia by his side. Or not at all.

CHAPTER 12

Sir Frederick was pacing. He'd smoothed his shaggy hair six times since he'd come out to the courtyard, and it still wasn't tidy enough to him. If he didn't stop, he would smooth what little hair he had left right off his head. Arnaud shifted in his seat, made nervous by his fussing. Frederick must have seen dozens of pagan ceremonies in his life, he ought to be used to the sights.

Ah, but this one would be attended by the Lady of the Lake, and that was no ordinary thing.

The night the royal wizard had healed him, Frederick had told them all what he had seen. He described the lady Nia without the human mask he said she wore. He said he'd seen her shining from within, draped in a glittering pearlescent gown. He'd seen her beneath the surface of a deep lake, with fish and water nymphs paying her homage. But as she was in King Saeran's court, Frederick said she'd also been out of place in the lake. Honored and revered, yet somehow greater than the nymphs around her. One of them, but separate. Her eyes, he'd said, had been like that of a doe, not a fish. A creature of land as much as water, and both at the same time.

Did she have the sword of kings, they all asked. Frederick hadn't seen one in his vision. Did she say anything of the cup, they asked next. Hanging his head, he again answered no.

What was Arnaud to make of that? If it was a vision from God, it was one that seemed to serve no purpose. If it was the workings of evil, why would it have healed Frederick when it could have so easily killed him instead? The wizard didn't lack for acolytes, and there was no service a wandering group of knights could render to one like her, so what reason could she have for deceiving them with a false vision?

Arnaud's faith in God was unshakable. He'd seen the face of his Savior and would do whatever He commanded to see it again when his life in this world came to an end. His faith in Frederick's vision was far less. They'd all been exhausted by their journey here, pride alone keeping them on their feet before the pagan king and his wizard. What Frederick had seen could have been nothing but a dream. Arnaud would not be swayed to believe otherwise unless he saw evidence of it for himself.

Tapping his foot, he chose to leave his companions to stroll about, lest he begin to pace as well. He'd heard talk in the village about this so-called festival. Despite the mystery surrounding the ritual itself, it seemed to him the rest of this day's importance lay in the fervid coupling these people seemed to look forward to with more than a little impatience.

When he'd come out to check on his mount this morning, he'd found a young maid already being chased by the hostler in the stables. Arnaud had made a hasty retreat into his sanctuary for prayer. *God give me strength to remain true.*

He was tempted, increasingly so as the sun dipped lower and torches were lit, casting shadows all around. Wickedness lurked in those shadows, wearing the face of innocence. Temptation dressed in revealing gowns, smiling with open invitation. So many beautiful wenches brushed past him with ill concealed intent that he was hard pressed not to avail himself of one of them. Yet each time he came close to succumbing to such sweet temptation, he closed his eyes and saw the golden one. The lady who'd swept into the great hall on a summer breeze and faced them with sunshine in her hair and lightning in her gaze. Sir Frederick's Lady of the Lake.

Arnaud had never seen her equal. In beauty, poise and bearing, she surpassed any queen he'd ever glimpsed, and he was ashamed to admit, if only to himself, that he was smitten. His weakness in the face of a pagan sorceress reminded him of his pitiful humanity. No matter how he strived to be pure of thought, devoted to his God and his quest alone, lady Nia had become a constant spectre in his mind, beguiling him, tempting him. He ought to hate her for it, yet everywhere he went, people loved her and sang praise enough to make a martyr blush. She was a healer among them, in every possible way. She mended bodies and minds, reconciled friendships, birthed children and cared for the old. She was their priestess and midwife, advisor and confidant.

Whether she was the Lady of the Lake the legends spoke of was irrelevant. Here, in this enchanted land, the wizard was a legend in her own right. And she was the true ruler of these people, Arnaud knew, for the king was no more immune to her beauty than the rest of them. She would guide his hand with a single word or gesture.

A child pushed through the crowd and barreled into him in his haste, dropping a handful of polished stones. "No!" he cried, diving for them, heedless of the feet so close to stomping him to death. The boy's dark eyes were wide and brimming with tears, and his wee hands shook as he gathered the stones.

Arnaud knelt to aid him. "There now," he said, keeping his voice soft. "What's this? Tears on such a happy day?"

The child looked up at him, wiping a ragged sleeve under his nose. He did his best not to cry. "They're a gift to the gods," he said, "and I almost lost 'em." His chin wobbled, but he squared his bony shoulders and pushed to his feet. "They're for lady Nia," he finished grandly, opening his hand to show Arnaud his collection.

"They are lovely," he said, "Perhaps too lovely for the wizard. You should save these for your mother."

The boy shook his head. "Every 'un gives something to the gods. But me Ma says the gods are far and hard of hearin' a wee one as me. 'Tis why the wizard is here. She's their ears and voice. She hears our prayers and tells 'em to the gods an' they listen. She sings to 'em, ye see." He glanced down at the precious pile of pebbles. "She'll pray for me Da to return. An' he'll listen an' come back to us, I know it."

Arnaud looked after the boy as he hurried away once more. "The poor child," an old woman said, following his gaze. She was dressed in gray, save for the red and yellow ribbons in her white hair. "His father died last winter. Attacked by a poisoned bear. That was before the wizard rid the woods of the poison. And before the king rid the kingdom of them what put it there." She shook her head sadly. "The boy's right to pray to the wizard. But even she can't bring back his Da."

Arnaud pushed to his feet and bid the woman farewell. If the lady Nia was worthy of such honor and praise, then perhaps she was worthy of such offerings. He would find her a bloom, the most beautiful one around. And only Arnaud would know it was meant for her alone.

≪ »·◇·« ≫

Tonight the Veil would thin. What was unseen could easily become visible if one was willing to look hard enough. It was Nia's duty to keep the dark spirits away until the light of dawn. She would be the voice of Wilderheim as well as the gods and Others.

She had been dreading this night for a long time, since the moment the Others had appeared for her presentation at King Manfred's court. Everyone would expect her to know what to do, but how could she? Nico hadn't taught her what he himself had never known. The Others had never appeared to him. They seemed to be around Nia constantly. Even when she couldn't see them she felt their presence. They've been roaming the castle since dawn, more of them now as night approached.

Nia retreated to her study, hoping the wards would keep them away. They didn't. The great dire wolves she'd seen at her presentation paced the underground chamber as she bathed, making her extremely nervous. They tilted their heads at the walls, growled at the books and scrolls, but it was when they approached the wolf skin Saeran had given her that Nia wished she could disappear.

In her panic, she felt magic gather and pool in her chest, a precursor to her disappearing and reappearing somewhere else, but no matter how frightened she became when those feral glowing eyes turned on her, she stayed put as if her magic had suddenly become inert, a dead weight on her heart.

One of the pair, the larger, darker male shifted so close his nose touched hers. Nia closed her eyes. "I tried," she said.

You failed, his voice growled inside her head.

"I know."

And now you keep his pelt as a trophy.

Nia shrank from his terrible anger. "No, as a reminder. So I never forget that death is inevitable, but mercy is a gift."

He snarled and suddenly her bath was gone and she stood naked before him. With the female stalking behind her and the male baring his massive fangs before her, Nia had no way of retreat, but she didn't want one.

"You led him to me, didn't you?"

The dire wolf's hackles rose, making him even bigger.

"Why didn't you heal him yourself? He was one of yours. He must have called out to you, in agony, dying. Why didn't you help him?"

He snapped his jaws a hair's breadth from her face, his breath burning her. *You dare question me!*

"Yes!" she snapped. "You led one of your children on a useless chase after a human who could never hope to do what you could have so easily, had you wanted to. You let him suffer, and for what? To test me?"

His hackles smoothed down and he tilted his head at Nia to an almost impossible angle. The female woofed behind her and the two met eyes. They circled her until their positions were reversed and now the female stood before Nia, lowering to meet her gaze. Her eyes were wild, but also kind. Her gaze hypnotized Nia, made her feel tired. Her legs weakened and she lowered to her knees. *We are Other,* the female said, and her voice echoed with the sound of countless pups calling to her with infinite affection. *We can walk among humans, but we are not them.*

Before Nia's eyes, the dire wolf shifted, her great body dissolving like a vision into that of a tall, slender human woman. Her long hair was gray, her eyes golden like the moon she revered, and though she looked human enough, Nia sensed the shape for what it was, a beautiful mask for the wolf beneath her skin. *Who are you, child?* she asked, revealing teeth too sharp to be human.

The male dire wolf came around to his mate, and she stroked his fur with a graceful hand. He nuzzled into her touch, sitting by her side so close she became half engulfed in his fur. Nia was envious of the love they obviously shared for each other, something she could never have.

"I am the royal wizard," she answered. "My duty is to stand as Wilderheim does, between humans and the gods, and the Others. I walk the path of inbetween, and I know I walk it alone."

The wolf's smile was menacing, her words rough. *You know nothing. Learn.*

Nia frowned. "Learn what?"

The male dire wolf huffed and nudged her shoulder hard enough to knock her off balance. *Learn,* he ordered, and then both of them were gone. In their absence, the wolf pelt seemed to watch her from its place on her bed.

Shaken, Nia rose to her feet and donned her robes against the chamber's chill. It was almost time for her to make an appearance outside.

CHAPTER 13

Torches were lit all at once when the sun kissed the western tree line, flooding the courtyard with blazing light. It was magic as much as fire; hundreds of hearts beating together in the same wish for children and a healthy harvest later in the year. Saeran could almost see their prayers shimmering interspersed with torchlight, floating among the sparks thrown by bonfires. It was a beautiful sight to behold.

Every house was decorated with vibrant flags and ribbons to celebrate the beginning of summer, every man woman and child dressed in their finest. The music was loud, the laughter even louder, but through it all the breeze teased him with secrets of things unseen. The Others were walking among them tonight. Saeran strained to catch a glimpse of even one, but he saw nothing.

He weaved amidst the crowds, searching for anything that was out of place. The courtyard was a melee of dancers and revelers, the great hall open to everyone on this holy night, for all were equal before the gods. Instead of formal feasts, everyone would go to the altar on the hill where offerings to the gods would be made.

Nia would lead the procession. She would weave spells around her to make sparkling lights follow in her wake and her white robes would glitter in the dying light with a magic of their own. There would be flowers in her hair and a golden mask covering her eyes and nose. She would be the embodiment of the goddess Frigga.

They come, they gather, the breeze whispered. *They come to see...*

"What?" Saeran asked.

See, the breeze repeated, swirling around him once and then streaming toward the castle. *See...*

Saeran walked in the direction of the wind. He focused his intention as Nia had taught him, willed it into a vision to See the Others among his people. It took him long moments to realize he was following a leyline, and when he saw what it was leading him to, the young king almost dropped to his knees.

In an instant, all became quiet and the crowds parted to create a passage. They bowed deeply as Nia passed, paying homage to her and the goddess of fertility she embodied. Saeran forgot to breathe. She glided along the uneven ground on bare feet, her step silent but for the tinkling of tiny bells that none could see. It was an illusion, the king told himself, but couldn't be certain.

See...

He saw.

He kept his features calm, falling in step behind her; the first in the procession. It was his right as king. The breeze wafted over him, bringing with it the scent of her. She was summer. She was sunshine and flowers, rainstorms and life.

As they passed the outer gate, a cheer went up and the music and revelry resumed, following in their wake. Nia never faltered. She led the way to the hill, oblivious to everything else. When she reached the altar, she turned to face the crowds and raised her arms above her head, speaking to the heavens and the setting sun. She called for blessings upon the land and all who lived on it, asking for a bountiful harvest and happiness for couples young and old.

When she finished speaking, she rounded the altar and passed her hands over it. Then the villagers came forward, placing their small offerings onto the slab of stone. They brought wreaths of wild flowers, pieces of fruit, if they had any, or puppets made of hay, ribbons and cloth. They brought what they could spare to please the gods, laying it before Nia and speaking soft prayers as if she truly was the goddess who looked after them.

Nia accepted the gifts formally, thanking each person and blessing them as they passed. The offerings would be left on the altar for the gods to do with as they pleased. No one was allowed to take from them, lest they incur their wrath.

The foreigners came forward at the end, each taking part in the ceremony as they would. Sir Frederick gave a silken handkerchief, saying a prayer of thanks to both the gods and Nia herself. He bowed deeply to her as he stepped away and Nia nodded to him in acknowledgement. The rest of the knights followed suit, one bringing a piece of bread, another a carved wooden horse, the third a piece of chain mail, and the last a single red bloom. She nodded in thanks and blessed all of them as well.

Finally it was the king's turn and, for him, Nia rounded the altar once more to face him without barrier. The king had no tribute to give. It was tradition for him to show respect to the gods by proving his humility.

Saeran stepped forward, grateful the ritual required no words. His mouth was too dry for him to speak. The fires sang out with the wind, even the sky added its voice to the chorus. He bowed his head before Nia and knelt. The crowd echoed with a prayer for the king, that he might find a wife soon and sire offspring, and their voices made the earth shudder beneath him.

Nia touched a hand to his chin, urging him to look up. When he did, she leaned down and kissed him, as was custom. Saeran balled his hands into fits, fighting the urge to pull her to him and kiss her the way he wanted to. He was drunk with the scent of her, the feel of her lips so chaste against his.

Too soon, she withdrew. In the darkness, only he could see the hesitation in her movements as she straightened and he wished the others would disappear. "Rise, King Saeran," she said, her voice ringing out over the hill. "May your reign be prosperous for all the years to come."

He obeyed, but he couldn't make his feet move him from the spot. For a moment they merely stared at each other, caught in an instant of pure magic. It pulsated in the air around them like a heartbeat, making it difficult to breathe.

Another cheer went up, startling them both, and Saeran forced himself to walk away. The bonfire would burn all through the night, and few would leave before the sun rose again to light their way home.

Nia faced the altar and once more raised her arms above her head, her own tribute and offering. She removed the flowers from her hair and placed them on the altar, saying a soft prayer. Then she turned in a circle thrice and dissolved into mist, disappearing from sight.

When she reappeared next to Saeran, her golden mask was gone. Instead of white robes, she wore the blue ones she'd received at her presentation and the wolf skin over it. She watched the celebrations with a smile on her face, though it seemed a disguise for something else lurking beneath her carefully composed mask of calm.

Only those too young or too old stayed to the side; the rest danced around the fire in celebration. The foreigners, Saeran noted, did not dance either. But while four of them watched the revelers, the fifth's eyes searched through the crowd until they settled on Nia. It was the selfsame knight who had gazed at her in the great hall, the same one who'd presented her with a red bloom and placed it so close to her hand. Arnaud was infatuated with the wizard, and he'd scarce seen her once since he'd arrived.

Lady Brigit spun out of the circle and caught Saeran's hands. "A dance for the fire spirits, your Majesty?" She pulled him into the throng before he could answer, obliging him to dance. She held him so close he was tripping over her skirts, but Brigit only laughed. Saeran suspected the lady had sampled the mead one too many times. It loosened her tongue enough to say, "A finer king Wilderheim has never had! Maidens are praying for you tonight, that you will choose a wife and make her queen, but each of them wants you for herself."

It was nothing he hadn't heard before, but tonight the flattery only served to remind him that he'd already chosen.

Brigit grabbed his waist and spun them around. She leaned in and said, "If you choose me—"

Saeran didn't hear the end of it because the seamstress sisters, Finna and Maeve, pulled him away, chattering one over the other. He danced around the fire thrice, and each time he thought he was free someone pulled him back into the jig. Saeran heard Nia squeal. The woodsman, Dahl, had picked her up one-armed to dance her around. Like Saeran, she was passed from one to the next, but unlike him, she seemed to enjoy it. The fire illuminated her laughing face as she spun and hopped directly across from him.

Then, out of the corner of his eye, Saeran saw the knight Arnaud step into the fray, following Nia. She was in Hundr's arms now, but before Arnaud could join them, Hundr passed Nia to Geir and away from the knight. Geir lifted Nia by her waist to spin her around while Saeran found himself with the shy Dagmar in his arms. He smiled at her briefly, but his attention was on Nia and the knight following after her from Geir to Konall, to old Sigmarr, and back to Geir.

"Your Majesty!" Brigit called, but Hundr pulled her away as Elsa replaced Dagmar.

Maeve caught the knight's hand, but he shook her off and continued around the circle after Nia like a bloodhound after a scent. Saeran turned Svana around to go the opposite way. Hundr with Brigit danced quicker than the rest, past him and halfway around the circle in a few steps. And just as Nia spun away from Tannir, as Saeran was preparing to switch partners yet again, Brigit stuck her foot out and tripped Nia in the direction of the blazing bonfire. Saeran let go of Svana with gasp and made a grab for Nia as she tipped forward, arms flailing to stop herself.

He caught hold of her sleeve and pulled her upright into his arms just in time, and when her gaze met his, Saeran went deaf and blind to the world. *Nia.*

She shivered as if she'd heard him speak her name. She couldn't have. Only in the deepest, most secret corner of his heart would he ever dare to say it that way, with the whole of his soul calling out in anguished longing to the mate it could not reach.

"Lady Nia," Arnaud said close enough to startle him.

Saeran felt his mouth pull into a snarl. With Nia in his arms, he spun out of the circle of dancers. Darkness pulled around them and a facsimile of them broke off to continue in the current of dancers. The darkness was his; the illusion Nia's. Taking her hand in his, he pulled her into the woods, far from prying eyes.

He took them so far the massive bonfire was little more than a flicker, but not so far he couldn't hear the revelers anymore. Only then did he release the shadows around them. "Wait, Saeran—"

He crowded Nia against the trunk of a tree.

"This is not real," she said in a rush, "It's Beltaine. It's affecting all of us."

"No, Nia, this is us." His mouth descended on hers before she could say anything else. Too long denied, Saeran gorged himself on the taste of her. He couldn't pull away and wished with everything he was that he could stop time just once more, have this much of her at least. As if she'd whispered it in his ear, Saeran felt the same wish in Nia.

She kissed him back, her fingers grasping at his shoulders to hold him close. A strange fervor had them in its hold, demanding they give in to its power. Nia let go of everything. She willed the mischievous sprites away, ignored the shadows that weaved between the trees, watching her, waiting. If this was another test, it was the cruelest one yet. Out here, she couldn't hold back from Saeran, not even knowing it might destroy her. She yielded to her king, giving herself this one moment because there would not, could not, be another. Nia opened her mind and soul to feel everything around her breathe. The entire forest and all that lived within it leaned and bent toward them, flooding her senses and making her body sing under Saeran's touch.

She wrapped her arms around him to hold him close and everything else sighed away, leaving nothing but Nia and Saeran. Their feet left the forest floor and this time, she embraced it. Saeran's hands searched for the fastenings of her robes, slipping inside while the garment fell away. She wore nothing underneath, and his hands slid over her skin, caressing molding, teasing. She moaned, the sound muffled by his kisses.

It was dangerous to feel this way, but she couldn't stop it. With no more than a gesture, Saeran's jerkin and shirt disappeared. Her breasts flattened against his bare chest and she shivered, bringing her leg forward to hook her ankle around his calf.

Skin to skin, she could feel Saeran's mind and soul open, and she couldn't help falling into both. Joined with him this way they shared thought and sensation, feeling with each other, for each other, in a dizzying cycle. Saeran's heart beat fast and hard and Nia's matched it. Blood roared in her ears, yet she could still hear his every breath and all the words he didn't speak. She reveled in the moment, committed every detail to memory. He kissed her, touched her, gave her all of himself, and she sensed his determination to show her with his body what he couldn't tell her in words—that she was his and no one else would ever lay claim to her.

It broke her heart.

Saeran shuddered. "Don't," he whispered. "Don't hurt." But when she looked into his eyes, she could see the same pain reflected back at her. Saeran cupped her cheek, drawing breath to say what was shining in his heart. Nia kissed him, stealing the words from his lips. Words held power and once spoken, they could never be taken back.

Nia caressed his shoulders and back, her nails scoring lightly before she looped her arms around him to bring him to her heart. With one swift motion, Saeran buried himself inside her and she cried out against his shoulder as he tore through virgin flesh.

Saeran moved slowly, taking his time to bring her pleasure to take away the pain. His thrusts were deep and sure, so deep that she no longer knew where he ended and she began. She felt their souls twine together like sheens of mist over the moors and in a single moment of perfect ecstasy the mists pulled tighter, binding her to Saeran in some elemental way.

As the feeling faded, her awareness of Saeran did too, and within moments she was alone in her mind, as if none of it had happened. They descended back to earth on a current of magic, in a tangle of limbs she didn't want to leave. Saeran held Nia to him as if afraid she would disappear. They were so close when one inhaled, the other exhaled, as if they breathed for each other, their hearts beating in unison. "Beautiful Nia," Saeran said. "Be my queen, beloved. Sit by my side forever."

His words cut her to the quick, and Nia squeezed her eyes shut. Too far. They went too far. Saeran had not been meant to be hers this night. They'd stolen a moment from time, but that was all they could ever have. She knew what had to be said, though her heart broke to say it. "No," she whispered and a part of her died.

Saeran didn't push her away, knowing as well as she that he asked the impossible. Instead, he tightened his hold on her, giving her awhile longer to pretend. As long as he held her, nothing else mattered except that she was his and he belonged to her.

They stayed there until morning light. Cushioned by the soft forest grass, covered by the blanket Nia wove from the plants around them, they didn't stir and no creature intruded.

When at last sunlight tickled her eyelids and teased her awake, she cursed the light of day. Saeran slept soundly in her arms, her head nestled against his heart, but he woke when he felt her move. He smiled at her and kissed her, squeezed her closer as he stretched.

But his smile died away too quickly. “They will be looking for us,” he said.

Nia nodded and slowly rose, calling for her clothing. Everything fell down from the branches above with a shower of leaves that caressed her sensitive skin. She dressed in silence, trying to ignore the cry in her heart. She had known what would happen if she got too close to the king, but she'd done it anyway. It was her own fault, and she would have to live with the consequences.

When she faced Saeran again, he was dressed, his jaw set and his eyes hard with regret. She held her hand out to him and he came to her, pulling her into his arms. For a moment, she basked in his strength and warmth. For a moment too long she remained in his embrace, wishing.

She couldn't make herself move away; her very soul protested it. And so Nia did the only thing she could. “Good morning, my king,” she told him before squeezing her eyes shut and sending Saeran to his bedchamber alone.

Left holding nothing but air, Nia stood there until she could breathe again. It was almost noon when she summoned her staff and walked. She wandered the forest without aim or direction until she came to a lake hidden by thick foliage. There, she shed her clothes and stepped inside, wishing the lake could cleanse the grief from her soul.

“Where are you?” she demanded.

Silence answered her. The sprites who'd pulled her and Saeran away from the dancers last night didn't appear, but she didn't expect them to. Their mischief was finished; they had no reason to come back again.

Furious, she drew magic from so deep inside she felt it tug on her heart. “Show yourselves!” she commanded, trying to force her will on the Others. “Gods damn you, you don't know what you have done!”

Nothing stirred, not even the wind.

Nia dropped to her knees in the lake with the water up to her chest and lowered her head until her nose almost touched it. As light played over the rippling surface, images appeared. What should have been. Nia and Saeran leaving the circle in opposite directions to stand watch over the people until morning. Nia leading them all back to the castle as the sun came up and bidding Saeran a good morning by the great hall. They would have parted as friends and everything would have been all right.

Instead the wood sprites had interfered and made the drunken Brigit trip Nia right into Saeran. With the Veil so thin, magic had saturated the earth and air, and everyone capable of sensing it had been drunk on its heady power. Even by the light of day Nia still felt the effects of what the sprites had done and knew there would be no easy way back. Saeran would never be satisfied with only friendship now; she'd sensed it in his heart last night and was even more certain of it today. He would defy everything and everyone for her.

The lake rippled again, and in the light-play over its surface she saw Aegirans gathering in force. If Saeran refused the bride he'd sworn himself to they would stop at nothing to tear him and Wilderheim apart. To the last they would fight and die to avenge such an unforgivable betrayal.

Nia's tears dropped silently into the lake, marring the vision.

The water embraced her. It warmed to her and grieved with her. *Have hope,* it said.

"There is no hope, there never was."

Always hope, it replied. If only she could believe it.

Nia didn't return to the castle until she was certain she could hold her cloak of shadows and hide from everyone, including the king. Avoiding the great hall, she went to her study instead, finding what little solace there was in her tomes and scrolls.

She picked up one after the other, gazing at the words without seeing them, no matter how hard she tried to make out their meaning. Food held no taste and wine burned like acid as it slid down her throat.

She dared not sleep that night, afraid of what she might dream. When morning found her the next day, Nia's eyes stung from the tears she'd locked inside. Her jaw ached from clenching her teeth against the pain, and her body was cramped from sitting huddled on the floor.

How she wished her mentor was there to counsel her. She needed his advice, his shoulder to lean on. "Nico," she whispered brokenly. "Why did you not warn me?"

For the first time, not even the remnants of his power in the walls could console her. Heartbroken, she let the tears come.

CHAPTER 14

The council of advisors met in its entirety for the first time in Saeran's presence. Nia should have been there, but she hadn't deigned to appear, just as she hadn't for the last three court sessions. She would not be called, summoned, or brought before him. She was avoiding him, and Saeran had no idea why.

The sun had set long ago, his fire was dying down, and he still couldn't sleep. Pacing his chambers, he tried yet again to summon his wayward wizard. Closing his eyes, he imagined her there with him and willed it to be so. It didn't work.

Cursing, he poured water into the scrying bowl and concentrated to conjure a vision of her in its depths. Instead of Nia's golden hair he saw a dirt road and a caravan of wagons traveling north. Dark skinned men and women dressed in colorful draping attire walked on either side of a closed carriage and armed guards surrounded it from all sides, sharp eyes on alert for any threat.

Saeran swiped the bowl off the table, his heart thudding in his chest. No, it couldn't be. It was too soon. He raked a shaky hand through his hair, looking out the window, but the breeze blowing in from the south only confirmed his vision. They were close. What few lights still flickered in cottages were going out one by one as the kingdom settled in for the night, but he could almost make out a lighted camp far beyond the towns, and all he wanted to do was disappear.

Storming out of his chambers he ran to the staircase and down to the empty great hall. The guards woke from their half slumber and stood to attention as he passed, but he ignored them. He traced the path he'd walked a dozen times today, out into the courtyard, to the small door and the stairway down to Nia's underground study. Where he would have stopped and turned back before, he shoved the door open and marched down there heedless of what he would find. If she was hurt or afraid, he could soothe her, but he couldn't go on this way anymore.

"Nia!" He threw open the door at the bottom of the stairway without knocking.

Nia looked up from the scroll she was writing on, and it was all Saeran could do not to sweep her into his arms then and there. Passionate words locked in his throat, foolish words.

"Yes?" she said.

Saeran started for her but hit an invisible wall halfway there. "Nia?"

"Your Majesty."

He frowned. "What is this? Release me."

"It is a ward," she said. "You are free to move anywhere on that side of it."

"Is this a test…or another lesson?" His entire being ached to touch her. Why would she deny him?

"No. The magic lessons have become a detriment to both of us. I will not be continuing your instruction." Dipping her quill in ink, she bent over her scroll again.

Her careless dismissal shocked him, but if Nia wanted to play, so be it. Saeran placed his hands on the ward and traced it left and right, searching for an edge. The cursed thing was a perfect circle surrounding her with no way in that he could discern.

Oh, but she'd taught him well. Magic was little more than will and determination. He had an endless supply of both where she was concerned. Saeran closed his eyes and listened to the ward humming its own melody. There was a pattern to it, and if he could disrupt it, he knew he could get through. He hummed until he matched the tone and felt it shiver beneath his touch. Smiling a little, he altered the tune and the wall rippled, weakening.

He pushed a hand through, ready to pass completely, but then something changed. The wall bowed inward and solidified again, shoving him away as it flexed back to its original shape. Saeran slammed his fist into it in frustration. "Nia, let me through. Please."

"If there is anything you require of me you have only to say so," she said without looking at him.

"I want you," he said. The caravan had stopped for the night. They had at least a day before the Aegiran princess arrived. He could marry Nia before then and break the arrangement with Aegiros. It would mean war, but he had fought against them before. He knew their weaknesses and no matter how many Aegiran soldiers marched into Wilderheim, with Nia at his side they could beat them back.

Her quill disappeared from her hand and she blew lightly on the scroll to dry the ink. "No, that will not be possible." She rolled up the parchment and carefully tied it off with a black ribbon.

Saeran shuddered. Nia had taught him the code for the library. The ribbon on each tome and scroll indicated the potency of what it held. Blue and green were constructive spells, descriptions of herbs and healing incantations, spells to mend what was broken. Red were battle spells for war and defense. Black was reserved for the deadliest, most dangerous of spells, the ones that meddled with dark forces and could destroy a target as easily as the wizard herself. In all the months he'd known Nia, she had never even touched a black-bound scroll.

"I love you," he said to her back as she placed the scroll back in its place.

"You are under a spell," she replied. "It will fade in time. I told you Beltaine affected everyone this way. You did not listen."

"Beltaine was one night, Nia. What I feel for you goes back a lot farther than that."

She sighed with impatience. "I do not have time for this. If I don't transcribe these scrolls the spells will fade forever. The Others have been roaming Wilderheim since the day I was presented. They have been meddling with everyone, not just you. Believe me when I say they will get bored sooner or later and this will pass. Now please leave me to my work."

Saeran drew back. "Then you don't—"

"Love you? I am your wizard. I cannot love you."

"No, I will not believe that." He'd felt her soul Beltaine night; part of it was still with him as part of his had to be with her. Everything she was saying felt wrong. This wall between them, her distance, the dispassionate tone she spoke with, it all reeked of deception.

A heavy black-bound tome thudded to the table. "You try my patience, Saeran. Why do you think you latched on to me? What possible reason could there be for a king to fall in love with his wizard?"

"You are—"

"I am not for you," she said. "Don't you see? It's a jest. This is what they do to amuse themselves; play with people's emotions and watch them implode. What better entertainment could there be than a handsome, powerful young king yearning for the one woman he can never have?"

"Stop it! If I have done something, hurt you in some way, tell me. Let me make amends, but don't push me away. This is not you."

"Oh, but it is," she countered, pulling on the ends of the black ribbon to untie it. "You just refused to see it. Well, I am done hiding. Take a good look, Majesty. This is the wizard you chose to stand by your side."

"You are trying to provoke me," he said to himself as much as her. It was working. Anger boiled low in his gut, a hot swirl of it pulling him in. He resisted, holding on to what they had because whether Nia admitted it or not, it was real.

"I am trying to make you leave! Why are you still here? There is nothing here for you."

Saeran slammed his hands on the ward. He knew he couldn't beat his way through, but what else could he do? Give up? Never. Changing tactics, he stepped back, let his hands drop to his sides. "We were friends. Was that a spell too?"

"Yes," she said. But she'd hesitated.

It was enough to bring Saeran to the wall again. "Nia, please let me through."

Her expression shuttered and he lost hope. "I have work to do and so do you. We crossed the line. It was a mistake, and I will not be making it a second time. Besides, I quite like that dark haired soldier Geir. I don't plan to take up with a man anytime soon, but when I do, it will probably be him."

Saeran's anger burned hotter. "Then he is a dead man."

Nia raised her head again, her eyes shining with fury. "You will not touch him," she said and he felt the charm slither into his core, commanding his action.

He struck the ward with all his might. "Why do you insist on making me hate you!"

"Leave!"

"I will not!" he roared back.

Nia opened the tome and a low rumble started beneath his feet, spreading outward until the walls shuddered and squealed. Rubble rained down on him and Saeran backed away from the ward, staring at Nia in astonishment.

"You will," she warned, her eyes pale like glacier ice. "Or I will bring the castle down around your ears."

For the first time Saeran saw the true extent of her magic and felt cold beneath her stare. He believed Nia would do as she threatened without hesitation. She might come to regret it, but by then it would be too late. Saeran couldn't reconcile this version of her with the lover he'd held in his arms all through Beltaine night, thanking the gods for bringing her to him. This Nia was a stranger, cold, unfeeling, and dangerous.

Seeing him hesitate, she lowered her gaze to the tome and murmured strange words that chilled Saeran to his soul.

"Stop," he said, disappointment numbing the raw ache in his heart.

Nia looked up and raised an eyebrow in question.

"I am done with you." The words sounded hollow, fitting, coming from the empty shell he'd suddenly become. Saeran dropped his gaze to escape the sight of her with that cursed tome and made himself turn away.

The ground shivered beneath his step, the disturbance following him across the chamber. Nia waited for Saeran to walk out the door and close it carefully behind him. She counted his footsteps up the staircase until he was out in the courtyard and away from her door. Only then did she release the earth to settle. She pushed to her feet and had to grab hold of a bookcase to stay on them. Her legs had cramped hiding there and her knees felt weak. When she made it out of the library, she regarded her doppelganger and shuddered at the ice spreading through her eyes.

Her, but for the kindness of an old wizard.

Nia raised a hand to dismantle the illusion and was shocked to see how badly it shook. Turning it over, she gazed at the lines in the palm of her hand. There lay the destiny she had never been able to decipher, glowing as if to remind her there were things she could never avoid, no matter how hard she tried. It didn't matter which paths she took when all of them eventually led to the same place. She'd chosen poorly and caused unnecessary pain to Saeran as well as herself. And now here she stood, the same way she would have stood regardless of what she'd done or not done. Alone.

Nia closed her eyes and took a measured breath. When she opened them again, she moved quickly to touch the doppelganger illusion and watched herself fall apart, cracking into thousands of thousands of pieces which fell and scattered all over the floor. Like ice, the pieces melted into the ground, leaving no trace of their presence behind. The room warmed by slow degrees but Nia didn't feel it. She picked up the tome and the ribbon which bound it. In her hands, the length of silk faded to blue and she carefully retied it around the tome and carried it back to its resting place in the library.

For once, the walls of her study were silent. She was glad.

CHAPTER 15

"They have progressed," Sir Frederick noted, watching the two young knights battling with wooden swords. There was pride in his voice and a little sadness as well. Their youth reminded him of his own age. "Their skill grows daily."

Arnaud glanced at them briefly before returning his gaze to the forest line. The treasure lay that way, and he was as eager to continue on their journey, as he was reluctant. "Alec still needs to gain more courage and Jonah's footing is wrong. Practice will correct that. Let us pray it will not be needed."

"If it is," Lucca said, "they will do what needs be done." He was carving something out of a piece of wood again, his own form of worship. Lucca was not like the rest of them. He believed in God, but having lost his wife and three children in a fire, he no longer spoke of Him as the Savior. He never entered hallowed ground and rarely had Arnaud heard him utter a prayer or sing a song. The man often got a look in his eyes that worried Arnaud. It was as if this quest was one of revenge for Lucca, not salvation. What he hoped to find or prove, none of them knew, and he would not say. They've all learned it was best not to ask.

The young knights locked their swords and grunted, trying to push each other back. They were covered with dust and Arnaud wondered when he'd last gotten as dirty in practice. It seemed like a lifetime ago that he'd been forced to draw his sword. Perhaps it was the long journey that had dulled the memory of past battles. Or perhaps it was this place. He could feel something here with every step he took. Magic or the Divine, he could not tell, but he hoped it was the latter. This far north, perhaps they were closer to God than they had thought.

Perhaps it would help Lucca find his way back into His grace.

"Come, then," Frederick said, pushing to his feet. "Enough, you two. The king has commanded our audience today. Set yourselves to rights."

Arnaud stood. "Today?"

"That is what I said, boy. The king is as good as his word. Beltaine has passed. We are to be on our way soon."

"Beltaine was three days ago," he argued. "Surely the festivities take longer than this."

Frederick stopped and turned to him, his faded eyes narrowed. "The day we came here you urged me to ride through. You said you would as soon bed down with the Devil than share a meal with these heathens. What's changed?"

"A certain fair haired witch caught his eye, isn't that right, Saint Arnaud?" Lucca mocked, as he had since the night Arnaud had spent chasing after her. Days later his face still turned ruddy to recall it. There had to be magic in this land to make him lose his head like that.

Arnaud shifted his weight from foot to foot. "Nothing has changed," he said, not believing himself. "I only worry about the sort of guide his Majesty will deem to give us. Last night all of Frastmir was drunker than sailors in port. What good will they be today?"

Frederick shrugged with uncharacteristic nonchalance. "It is not for us to decide. I am certain the king will choose well."

Lucca grunted. "You did not have so much faith in his judgment a few days ago. The witch must have spelled you both."

Frederick glared at him but said, "Mayhap." Was he beginning to doubt his own vision? "Or mayhap God has chosen to answer my prayers and take away my doubt."

"What about…" Arnaud began, afraid to finish. It needed to be said. He tried again. "What about last night?"

The old man's composure faltered, and even Lucca shifted uneasily. "Saints, I thought I dreamt it."

"The whole castle shook, Frederick. Are you not curious why?"

"No," he answered, turning his back on Arnaud. His gait was slow and uneven. His knees always gave him trouble if he sat still too long.

"Cheer up, man," Jonah said with a grin, slapping Arnaud on the back and urging him to follow Frederick. "Soon the dust of this cursed odd place will be behind us, and you will need not think on it more."

Arnaud whistled to Alec and went inside. Thinking was all he seemed to be doing of late. It didn't sit well with a simple knight. All kinds of new ideas now distracted him from his devotion to God and his mission, and though he knew it to be wrong, he couldn't stop his mind from wandering where it ought not go.

⋘ ››·◇·‹‹ ⋙

For the second time, the knights knelt before the dais in the great hall. Their eyes no longer downcast, they waited for King Saeran to make his decree.

Nia walked toward the dais with her head high, ignoring the Others who filled the great hall instead of Saeran's court. They always gathered when there was a spectacle to be seen and Nia was beginning to resent it. She didn't spare Saeran a glance when she ascended the steps to take her place, and he didn't seem to care. It was just as well.

"My lady," one of the knights said to her, and she looked at him in surprise. Arnaud was his name. "Is aught amiss?" he asked.

She would have expected the question from Saeran. But not today.

"You will address me when you speak," Saeran said before she could answer the knight.

Startled, Arnaud bowed his head. "My apologies, your Majesty."

"I have summoned you here to grant you passage through my lands."

Nia straightened as the earth whispered to her of a nearing caravan. "Riders approach," she said to Saeran, but he ignored her.

"And because certain duties are about to render me beyond reach, I do this now, whilst I still can."

Nia frowned. The earth spoke to her of exotic places of sun and sand, where water was scarce and strange animals roamed. It sang songs so strange to Nia's ears, yet the melody was as beautiful as a thousand songbirds taking flight.

Aegiros. Nia bit her tongue to distract herself from the arrows of pain stabbing at her heart. Saeran's intended bride was coming to claim her crown.

"Wizard," Saeran called, as if she was standing on the other side of the great hall, instead of right next to his throne. "Stand by these knights and face me."

The chamber echoed with silent hisses and growls, the Others voicing their displeasure. It made Nia's head throb and her face heat with embarrassment.

Even the knights started, all and one at the insult Saeran had just delivered, degrading his right hand to the level of a peasant. It was cruel but not completely unexpected. She'd hurt him and now he wanted to hurt her back. The malicious gleam in his eyes told Nia she'd done it so well Saeran had no idea the pain he felt was hers as well. He never would, if she had any say.

Nia complied, taking the insult in stride. She would not disobey the king. Descending the steps to the bottom, she faced Saeran with her head high, eager for this humiliation to be over with. The caravan would be arriving soon. And they were expected. The Others knew it, too. Several of them loped, slithered, or simply disappeared to see the new queen arrive. But the rest stayed behind to watch Nia.

She cast a question out to them: *Why are you here?*

The Sidhe dressed in flowing gowns and robes came closer, so near she could make out the diamonds inlaid in their pearlescent skin. *What will you do?* the silver haired female asked without her mouth moving. *When the river forks and jagged rocks await you down each path, which will you choose to brave?*

Humans have their laws of honor, the male said. *We follow our hearts—that is our justice. What will you do? We wish to see.*

We wish to see who you are, the female added.

"The time has come for me to take a wife and ensure a line of succession," Saeran said and both Sidhe turned their heads to look at him.

From the other side of her, the dark male dire wolf stalked out of the crowd, head canted low. He moved just behind her, his fur bristling against her skin and the Sidhe retreated as if afraid of him. *Have you learned?* He growled in her ear.

"Under different circumstances I would be choosing from among our noble maidens the one most fitting to stand by my side." He looked at her as he said it and Nia flinched. He'd dressed in his most intricate clothes, the cloak dyed a stunning shade of blue and a thick bear skin over his shoulders. A heavy chain hung about his neck, the crown he seldom wore resting on his head. For all the splendor, he could not hide the shadows beneath his eyes. His hair was shaggy and the beginnings of a beard made his handsome face look gaunt and his gray eyes even paler. Saeran looked every bit the king he was and every bit as miserable. The sight of him pained her twice over, for she knew the cause of his despair.

He has, the dire wolf said and moved away, back to his mate. His tail struck the backs of Nia's legs and she was grateful for the staff which kept her from falling to her knees.

"Happily, I have no need of it, as I have chosen my intended bride years ago. Knights, you may be the first to hear the news. I will be taking my chosen to wife within a week." His gaze settled on Nia again, expectant. "Wizard, what think you of this?"

Nia bowed her head. "A wise decision, Majesty," she answered in a hollow formal tone. "That very same bride now approaches in the caravan, does she not?" She spoke without a wince or flinch, without any indication that she felt anything at all. Saeran's very soul rebelled at making the proclamation, and Nia stood there as if she didn't know. And there were Others around them, Saeran could feel it. Their presence set him on edge, made him feel as if he were being judged without knowing what he'd done.

"Indeed," he replied, silently damning all of them, including Nia. Did she not care in the least? Seeing she wouldn't stop this nonsense, Saeran drew himself up and made himself the king he was. "I wish to inform my father at once. The wedding will not take place until he is here to witness it. Knights, you may choose to remain for the happy occasion."

"Majesty," Nia spoke before any of the knights could say a word. "Allow me to congratulate you on this happy occasion."

"I thank you," he said.

"And as it appears that you shall be indisposed for some time to come, it is my duty to aid you and relieve you of some of your responsibilities, this company of travelers among them."

Unease made Saeran shift in his seat. "What are you saying?"

"I will facilitate a communication to King Manfred about the arrival of your bride that he may join you and give his blessing. And then I will accompany Sir Frederick and his knights north and serve as their guide."

Saeran's eyes narrowed. "Leave us," he commanded the knights.

They picked themselves up and wisely retreated, but in their absence, the great hall felt even more crowded. Magic throbbed in the air, pushing on his mind, demanding all his secrets. He resisted, but in the effort something changed. Saeran could see currents of multicolored lights flowing left and right, whispers passing among the Others. Though they hid themselves, they could not hide their magic.

Nia stood her ground, her gaze steady on some point beyond him as if none of it mattered one way or another, including him. The king forced his muscles to unclench enough to allow him to speak. "You think to abandon your post?"

"I am confident that you will not require my counsel for the time being. The journey ahead of these men is not a short one, but with my aid, we can all be back before a fortnight has passed."

She was not asking him. The wizard was telling him she was leaving, in a way that dared him to argue. He couldn't believe the months he'd known her to be a lie, yet here she stood as if none of it had happened. She'd deceived him then, or she was deceiving him now and how could he have a wizard he didn't trust giving him counsel?

How could he have anyone but Nia at his side?

Trumpets blared, announcing the caravan's approach and Nia flinched, light flaring out of her skin briefly before she pulled it back and Saeran's eyes widened. She was hiding. He made himself push his emotions aside and truly look at her. He had never seen Nia as anything but composed in the great hall, ever the calm, steady strength at his back. Now she was tense, her posture rigid. She clutched her staff in a white-knuckled hold and her wolf pelt was gone. She looked tired, haunted and lost.

She looked as if she would rather be anywhere but here, and Saeran didn't have the heart to force her to stay. "So be it," he said and it felt right, though he could barely admit it to himself. "You leave by sunset."

⋘ »·◇·« ⋙

With the exception of last night, holding the window open for Saeran to tell his father he was getting married to the Aegiran girl was the most excruciating thing Nia had ever endured. Manfred knew the moment he saw his son that something was amiss, but he attributed it to the impending ceremony. No one wanted Saeran to marry the girl: not Manfred, not Halden, and certainly not Saeran, that was obvious.

He would do it because it was his duty, and because Nia gave him no other choice. By the time she let go of the spell she was exhausted and she still had to prepare for the journey into the most inhospitable land known to man. There was a reason why no one ever ventured far beyond Wilderheim's northern border. Nothing lived there but creatures humans ought not tangle with.

Saeran sat forward in his chair, staring at the ground by her feet. His fists were clenched tight enough to shake the slightest bit, and she had to stop herself from reaching out to him. Rubbing her tired eyes, she rose from her seat and turned for the door.

"Don't go," he said. It was so soft Nia half thought she'd imagined it.

She turned back to face him. "I must." There was no other way. She could tolerate being in the shadows, she could stand his anger or indifference, but she could not stand there and watch Saeran take a wife. When he did, Nia needed to be as far away as possible.

He smiled bitterly. "I remember when you spoke your oath to me; I believed every word you said. *As long as need be, until death or longer.* Do you know, I believe it still? I just never realized the one thing you would not be able to save me from is myself."

One more time, Nia focused her Sight to scry the air and looked into the future, seeking any way to avoid this. What she saw was war. Hundreds of horses trampling fields, sowing salt in their wake and setting crops aflame. Swords clashing, magic burning through the night, and blood. So much blood. Death and disaster waited down every path she chose. An arrow through the chest. A blade across the neck. Poison in a chalice of wine. Treachery and deceit. She flinched each time she saw Saeran meet his end. Frastmir would burn to the ground one way or another, unless Nia did what she already knew had to be done. There was no other way. "This is the way it has to be."

Saeran nodded, his eyes bleak. "I suppose it is."

She was at the door when his voice stopped her a second time.

"I know you will not want to," he said. "But come back to me anyway."

Close to sunset the gates opened to admit the caravan. Over twenty riders entered, followed by a great tent-like carriage and an entourage of another twenty people on foot. Nia and the knights watched their progress from the stables. Their horses ready and their supplies packed, they came outside, to join the curious crowds in the courtyard.

A single wind instrument played in the tent-carriage, its melody sounding their soft fanfare. These were desert people. They wore long robes and cloth wound about their heads, their horses' reigns adorned with tufts of ribbons and cords. The women were draped in robes from neck to foot and they wore veils to cover their hair and face. Nothing but their hands showed. An odd way to dress, Nia thought, but then they must be thinking the same about the northerners.

Wondering what Saeran would think of this, Nia glanced up at the catle windows. She could just make out his shadow in one of them. But he didn't seem to be looking at the caravan. As soon as she caught sight of him, he stepped away from the window and out of sight.

No good to be leaving in pain, Stardust told her, gently butting his nose against her shoulder.

"I know," she replied. "But it would be even worse if I stayed."

The caravan stopped and the men dismounted as Nia swung into her own saddle and made ready to ride out. As she nudged Stardust forward, a bright glitter caught her eye. One of the men in the entourage was not a southerner. He dressed in robes, yes, but he wore no cloth around his head, and his hair was as fair as her own. About his neck hung a pendant. It was a glittering black stone as big as her palm, set in pale gold. Curious, Nia tried to get a better look, but with so many people milling in the courtyard, it was of no use. She gave up for the moment, shaking her head at her own silliness.

But when they passed close by, the pendant once more caught her eye as the man bowed. Her gaze became unfocused as she watched the pendant sway back and forth and in the haze, she saw a vision. No longer in the courtyard, she watched the dream unfold before her.

There were two women, the older teaching the younger her craft. She was a midwife, well liked and respected in her village. But soon, the vision showed her, the younger woman surpassed her mentor and fearing the old woman was no longer trustworthy, the villagers turned from her, to her apprentice.

The old midwife ran on stiff legs to a great rock that served as an altar and dropped to her aged knees. With her arms raised above her head, she beseeched the gods. She cried to the heavens, invoked incantations she had no knowledge of, shouted for all the gods she could name until one of them answered.

Lightning struck the altar, frightening her into fleeing for her life, but when she found her courage again and cautiously returned, she discovered a jewel. Taking it into her bony hands, she turned it to the light and Nia saw through her eyes the wicked gleam of Loki's gaze in the depths of that black crystal.

In the next blink Nia was in the young apprentice's cottage. The woman was asleep in her bed, wearing the pendant around her neck, a treasured gift from her mentor. The gleam of a knife by candlelight was the only thing to betray the old midwife before she plunged the blade into the sleeping woman's chest. The apprentice died quietly, with no one the wiser and her murderer retrieved her gods given trinket with shaking hands. As soon as she put it on, her posture straightened and she sighed, walking away with an easy step. Too easy for one so old.

Stardust jolted her and Nia blinked, finding herself the object of a curiously knowing gaze as the man with the pendant grinned at her. Before she could approach him, Stardust took off, leading the way out of the castle.

CHAPTER 16

The first stretch of the path north was easy enough. They rode hard to make headway before the sun dipped low. The wide, well used dirt road wound through the forest for miles until it ended abruptly as if whoever traversed it suddenly decided they'd gone far enough and turned back the way they'd come. Beyond this point, there was nothing but trees.

Nia would have ridden on, but the knights grew wary of riding in the dark of night. The moon wasn't bright enough to touch the forest floor and lighting torches would only blind them to the shadows. They made camp under a giant oak and lit a small fire to stave off the chill of night. Once everything was done, they retreated together for prayer, leaving Nia alone to stare into the flames. Shapes danced within them, slender, sensuous waifs moving to the music of the night. Fire sprites.

They danced and they beckoned to her, smiling when she refused to join their play. "What do you want?" she asked, tired of being made a source of amusement.

The sprites laughed, making the fire crackle and spark.

Nia blew on the flames, banishing the sprites in lieu of a vision. Scrying flames was different than air or water, the images obscured by ash and smoke. It was also more difficult because fire touched Spirit and Soul. Asking something of the flames meant opening oneself to them, and more often than not, the fire pointed in two different directions. One leading to the object sought, the other to the one most desired, without revealing which was which. It was as close to deceit as an element could get and even then it was self-deceit which sent a petitioner the wrong way. Some desires ran so deep a person was not always aware of them.

"What do you see?"

Nia blinked through the flames at Lucca. She thought he'd gone to pray with the others. "I seek guidance to the treasure you are after," she said.

"And?"

Nia gazed into the fire. From opposite sides two hands raised a chalice in a salute. One silver, inlaid with blood red stones and engraved with runes, the other gold with elaborate silver filigree depicting a winged man with horns and a tail. Both were reaching toward her, a choice between the two. It could mean any number of things and with her heart still bleeding over Saeran, it probably had to do with her choice to leave rather than stand by his side as she'd sworn to do. Red stones for her aching heart, wings to symbolize the freedom of flight. "I see two cups raised in offering."

Lucca smiled somewhat sadly. "Our legends say there is a cup which once held the blood of our savior. It is said this cup is one of judgment. To those who serve god without question, it has the power to grant salvation. But those who serve only themselves get cast into damnation."

"Do you believe this?"

"No. Man was given thought in order to question everything, even god."

"But you just said only those who do not question will have salvation."

He grinned. "Yes, well, not everyone interprets the words as I do."

Curious, Nia studied the knight who spoke so little but said so much. "You are not here for the treasure of eternal life, are you?"

"And you are not here to lead us to it, are you?"

"Why else would I be here?"

"Why indeed?" Lucca stoked the fire. "Perhaps to run away from something? Or someone?"

A twig snapped, announcing the return of the others and Nia was grateful for the interruption. For the rest of the night, Alec played a thin wood whistle to entertain them and Nia stared into the flames, seeking guidance.

But every time she asked her silent question, only the two cups raised in answer.

↞ »·◇·« ↠

The moment he lost sight of Nia and her company of knights Saeran felt hollow. He welcomed the Aegirans in the great hall as was his duty, meeting his intended for the first time and receiving the wedding gifts they'd brought with them, all while silently wishing he was anyone but himself. A small army had accompanied the girl here, many of whom would stay behind to ensure her well being and comfort.

Farraj, Saeran was relieved to learn, would return to his *shansher* as soon as the deed was done. He liked the man well enough, but he didn't want him to linger. A warrior whose honor bound him as surely as any of Nia's spells, Farraj would give his life to protect those he served and Saeran could see how he doted on his princess. Should Farraj ever suspect Saeran of wrongdoing against her, he had no doubt he would find himself without a head.

To marry her at all felt wrong when his heart belonged to another. No, he did not want Farraj to stay long enough to discover that.

The girl's name was Mari and there was never a moment when she was not surrounded by handmaidens, all cloaked and veiled to hide everything but their eyes. Saeran could not pick her out of a crowd if he tried. And they would remain estranged this way until their wedding night.

Saeran spoke the words, acknowledged the oath he'd taken years ago and sealed the pledge with another to ensure the Aegirans' good will. He could not look away from the girl's eyes. They were so very young.

When all the ceremonies of greeting were finished, the Aegirans were led to their chambers to rest after a long journey and Saeran escaped into the glen. His chest ached with each breath he took and all he wanted to do was mount a horse and ride as fast as he could out of the castle, away from the life of a king. Anywhere but here.

"Your father is not here."

Saeran felt the earth tremble at Farraj's footsteps but he could not face the man. "He rides this way as we speak," he replied. The moment Manfred had heard the news, he'd ordered a carriage. If he changed the horses often and never stopped for the night as he intended, he would be here in two days time.

"It is good to see you well."

"And you, Farraj."

"Now noble talk over. We speak as men."

The words felt like an order, compelling Saeran to turn and face the southerner. "Say your peace."

In the years since the war, Farraj had changed. He'd acquired new scars in battle, and adornments to mark his victories. His hair was longer, graying on one side, but his eyes were as shrewd as Saeran remembered. "Where we come from the women are treasured."

"They are bartered with," Saeran said, instantly regretting his words.

Farraj drew himself up, but chose to overlook the insult. "They are protected and given to worthy men who can keep them safe. It is not so here. Mari is not strong like your women. She has lived only with other women and never known a man."

Knowing he would be the one to change that made Saeran want to turn back time, undo the foolish deal he'd struck and take his chances down another path. "I expected as much," he said with difficulty. "You have my word I will treat her gently."

"She can never know you do not want her as wife."

Taken aback, Saeran could only stare.

"In Aegiros she would have been one of a noble's many wives, but cherished. Here she will be lonely queen. But her children kings and queens after her. For her it will be enough. But she cannot know she is reason for another's heart pain. It would bring too much sadness for her to bear. Better she believe you will not love her than that you cannot. I ask this for favor. For Mari."

Saeran blanched. "How did you know?"

Smiling a little, Farraj laid a hand on his shoulder. "I look in your eyes and see the woman you want. She is in your soul, and she is not my *idrah* Mari."

"I will honor our agreement. I will be true to Mari."

Farraj grunted. "This I know," he said, stepping back. "You are man of honor. It is not an easy thing to be. Many winters ago, when you offered a life for a life, I knew then you would regret it. You bargained bravely for your people, young king. Bravely, but foolishly. For life of another you gave up your heart. A heart without life will sleep until it breathes again. But what is life without heart?" The Aegiran wise man touched a hand to his chest then to his mouth, and finally his forehead and he bowed at the waist. He returned to the castle, leaving Saeran alone in the dark glen.

CHAPTER 17

They made camp in the forest on the third night. The knights gathered wood for a fire and Nia lit it for them before she walked away, needing the comfort of solitude. It was difficult to find in a place where everything was alive and singing. Dozens of voices spoke to her, asking questions she didn't want to dwell on and giving her advice she had no wish to hear. Well meaning creatures, they were, and their presence infuriated her. How dare they broach the subject when they had no knowledge of what they were saying?

The trees wanted to know why she was here when her place was at Saeran's side. The sparrows told her to go back and speak to him. The earth hummed to her that the woman he was to wed was not his true intended; that she did not belong. And the brook she crossed sang to her that it knew her heart and knew that it was no longer inside her.

With each new voice her anger rose. It was easier to confront than the pain. Nia had chosen this path. It had been her choice to teach Saeran and learn his heart in the process. Her choice to share her evenings with him, countless witching hours when sitting in silence next to him began to feel like the most wonderful thing in the world. She could have turned Saeran away countless times; could have refused him Beltaine night, but she hadn't. And so it was her own fault she was here when he was miles away, wedding a southerner out of obligation.

You did not have to turn him away from your embrace, the earth whispered and the words stabbed at Nia.

She'd had no other choice. Not turn him away? Nia shivered. The king's happiness might mean the world to her, but it would have mattered little to a kingdom torn apart.

No, Saeran had chosen this fate long ago, as had she. Wilderheim had to come first.

That she'd done what was right for the greater good, however, meant little when her soul howled in anguish at the crescent moon.

Knowing it was a mistake but unable to help herself, Nia weaved her hand through the air to conjure the castle. Just one peek, she told herself. A brief glance at Saeran and then she would put him out of her mind and finish what she'd started.

Light followed her movements, creating a window, and in its depths she saw the throne and Saeran seated upon it. He was somber as he watched the celebration in honor of his bride, but his gaze strayed often to the woman at his side.

A child. She was draped in colorful silks, the bottom of her face covered with a transparent veil. Her eyes were beautiful. Dark and exotic, both innocent and sensual. She was a beauty, to be sure. And Saeran had noticed it as well. When he turned to gaze at her, his eyes became dream hazed and a small smile pulled on his mouth.

Nia turned away with a whimper. She let the spell dissolve and sank to a fallen tree trunk, burying her face in her hands. She couldn't breathe; didn't trust herself to release the air in her lungs, lest it take her voice with it. If she cried now, she would never stop.

It was done. Saeran was married. He had his queen just as Nia had wished for him the night of his coronation. She would sit by his side, guide his hand, and ease the burden of ruling a kingdom. She would be his friend and hold him when he needed to be held, kiss him when he came to her each night. She would give him heirs unlike any Wilderheim has ever seen.

It's as it should be, she told herself. *My place was always in the shadow.* Hugging the wolf skin closer around her she lifted her gaze to the stars. Not for the first time she wondered what Nico would have wanted her to do. But then her thoughts turned dark, wondering why the old wizard had even brought her to the castle, made her face things she'd never wanted to see, and then abandoned her when she needed him most. He must have foreseen this as a possibility.

In the shadows, a dark form stirred. It was Lucca. This morning when she'd greeted each of the knights he'd coldly informed her that he was not truly a knight and that he did not wish to be addressed by the title. She'd heard him cry out in his sleep the night before and knew he suffered his own nightmares which made him surly in the mornings. But whatever he dreamed, he never told her and she never asked.

Now, a fair way from the camp fire and the rest of their company, he kept his distance, hiding in shadows rather than stepping into the light of the moon. He addressed her from that darkness as if its embrace was the only reason he could speak the words at all. "I know your pain," he said, his voice so hollow it called to her, and she reached out unbidden to his mind. "It is the pain of loss, same as mine."

His memories rose like mist in her mind, pulling her into his past without being invited. She saw a child suffering with fever, his worried mother sitting by his bedside while Lucca hunted like a madman for a healer, a priest, a witch, anyone who could help his dying son. She saw a kindly old priest enter the house in his absence to console the mother and light a candle by the child's bedside, saying a prayer for his recovery. Then the priest left. Exhausted, the praying mother fell asleep on her knees. The candle tumbled, sparked a flame in the thresh and within moments the entire house was ablaze.

"They tell you it will pass," Lucca said, banishing her back into herself. "They tell you to give yourself to god and let him take the pain away. It is all a lie, wizard. Pain like that never goes away. And it only becomes worse with time."

"Among my people we believe our loved ones await us beyond death," she said.

"Your gods are not mine. The one I worshiped took my wife and children from me because I loved them more than him." His harsh tone made her flinch. "You cannot imagine the hatred I hold for him, and for that he will keep me from them forever."

Nia's heart broke for him. This was the torment he lived with day and night, mourning his family, cursing his god. Lucca had lost everything, and in his despair the pain had become all he had. It was overwhelming, the kind of grief that scarred the soul. It went beyond her ability to heal and she wasn't fool enough to try. "I am sorry," she whispered.

Heavy rustling footsteps put an end to their conversation. Lucca retreated deeper into the night and then disappeared all together.

"Lady Nia."

Nia did not face Arnaud. "I told you not to call me a lady. I am not noble."

"You are something," he said coming closer. Lowering himself next to her, he plucked a sleeping flower to toy with. "May I ask you a question?"

"You may not."

"Why have you decided to join us? It is because of the king, is it not?" He pulled on the flower, forcing it open and tearing off its petals. Nia's hand twitched every time she heard the delicate rip. Still raw from Lucca's memories, it aggravated her much more than it would have under normal circumstances. Where she felt an odd kinship with Lucca, Arnaud's presence was forceful, bothersome. She wanted him gone. "Matters of the heart are—"

"None of your affair," she snapped. "My reasons for coming with you are my own and you have no need to guess at them. Rest assured, I will get you to your treasure, and I will lead you back again. But my obligation to you goes no further than…" She never finished the sentence. Her skin prickled and the wolf pelt's hackles rose as if he was still alive and scented danger.

Power was in the air; not her own. It controlled the wind and made it spy. She stretched her senses to find the source but it was beyond her boundaries. Its magic tasted different than her own or anything Other she had thus far encountered. It made her shudder, for she knew that this grand display was only a hint of its true potential.

"What is it?" Arnaud rose to his feet, hand on his sword, looking for an enemy to slay.

"Hush for a moment," Nia told him and knelt on the ground to bury her hands in the earth. It was a stronger medium than the air, and through it she would be able to reach farther. Closing her eyes, she concentrated, using the power's scent to track it as a predator. She separated herself from her body and streaked across the forest floor with incredible speed. She felt nothing in this state, not grief or pain, not love, anger or regret. Only the freedom of flight. Nothing restrained her, and if she wanted to she could disperse to eternity and never return. It was a temptation Nia forced herself to resist. She had her target and she was getting closer.

The earth was cold, covered with ice and it sped her progress. She was vaguely aware of what was around her. A field of snow and ice, a sparse forest and in its depths a cave. This was where the spy dwelled, hidden away from the world where no one would think to look for him. She slowed as she neared the cave, her limits stretched as far as they could go. If she went too far she wouldn't be able to return to herself.

Nia pushed a little more. It hurt to move, but she put it from her mind and approached the cave. There was light. A fire burned in the back, but the light of magic was much brighter. So bright it blinded her, though she had no eyes. She reached for it and just managed to brush the core.

Pain exploded in her physical body, merciless talons ripping into her mind so deep she screamed. Her essence pulled back with such a rush that it knocked her back against a tree. And still she screamed, trapped in the clutches of a being she couldn't identify. It probed her, searched her mind and soul with cold efficiency, leaving no secret undiscovered. Nia burned. Her blood was on fire, scorching her from the inside, yet her skin was freezing from the Other's touch.

At last, it touched upon something that made it still. For a moment, lucidity returned to her. Instead of the forest, she was suddenly in her study beneath Castle Frastmir. The chamber was tossed around as if after a great storm. And then her gaze fell upon Saeran. Nia squeezed her eyes shut, refusing to allow the creature tearing through her to see with her eyes. It was useless; it was in her memories, not her body, and it saw everything as clearly as she remembered it.

For a terrible moment, all she could do was breathe and hear it breathe with her, inside her.

Then, all at once her torturer released her from its clutches and disappeared. Nia fell to the forest floor as many footsteps rushed toward her. She heard the knights, their voices so far away she couldn't make out their words. They touched her, but she felt nothing.

And then everything went dark.

She awoke by the camp fire, her entire body aching as if she'd been stomped to dust by Stardust's hooves. Arnaud and the others stood over her, all of them wearing identical expressions of fear and concern.

One of them, she wasn't sure which, helped her sit up. The simple motion brought her so much agony she almost cast up the meager contents of her stomach. The remnants of that strange power still lingered inside her. She felt seared with it, branded. Her hands were stiff and she couldn't hold the cup Arnaud handed her. She saw their mouths move, knew they were talking to her, but couldn't make any sense of their words past the ringing in her ears.

It didn't matter. Such immense power had a source. It was a territorial being, dangerously intelligent and cunning. It relished its seclusion and didn't tolerate any trespasses on its land.

It knew who they were and where they had come from.

They were heading right for it and the creature knew.

It was waiting for them.

CHAPTER 18

Wilderheim would never suspect the sacrifice Saeran had made for the safety of his people. Manfred had known the day his son shook hands with the Aegiran delegate that one day he would have to stand by and watch the boy's heart break. It was a thousand times worse than he'd ever imagined now that Saeran sat next to his young queen, and Manfred would give anything to spare him this; to give Saeran what he'd had with his mother.

Manfred had come riding in with two hundred of Halden's finest soldiers to tell Saeran he had only to say a word and he would have two armies at his back to defend Wilderheim and its king. But his son would hear none of it. With Manfred at his side, he'd wed the southern girl at once and fulfilled the foolish bargain he never should have struck. Now he sat his throne with her at his side, watching over the feast but Manfred knew he wasn't seeing any of it.

"A fine pair they make," one of the border lords begrudged. There were many who shared his disgruntlement that the king had chosen a foreigner over one of their daughters.

Manfred motioned to one of the servers. "Where is the wizard?"

"She's gone, my lord," the serving girl said, blushing. "She rode out days ago with a company of knights."

"For what purpose?" What could be more important than this? And how dare she abandon Saeran when he needs her the most? If anyone could have put a stop to it, the wizard Nia could have done it.

"No one knows, my lord. All's I know is that the night before she left the castle shook as if the very earth was set to swallow it whole! And she looked none too pleased to be leavin', her and his Majesty."

Manfred closed his eyes and sighed, dismissing the girl with a wave. He should have known. Reaching for his chalice, he drank deeply of the honey mead, but it did nothing to sweeten the bitter taste in his mouth.

"Hail King Saeran and Queen Mari!" someone shouted and dozens of voices echoed the toast.

"Hail the king and queen! Huzzah! Huzzah! Huzzah!"

Saeran met eyes with him and Manfred fisted his hands against the urge to give an ill advised order. Instead he rose from his seat and climbed the stairs to the dais and his son. "You spoke to her before she left," he said for Saeran's ear alone.

The boy nodded.

"Did she tell you anything of use?" He knew the way of wizards all too well. Nico had spoken in riddles so often Manfred still gritted his teeth to remember it. He could only imagine his apprentice was likewise disinclined to reveal what she thought his son was not prepared to know.

"She said this must be so."

"And you believe her?"

Saeran looked away, his jaw set. "She is the stronger one," he said after a while. "Regardless of the king's happiness, Wilderheim must hold. One of us had to put the kingdom first, and three days ago it would not have been me. Yes, Father, I believe my wizard spoke the truth, though I wish to the gods it was not so. With all my heart I believe it."

Then there was little hope for either of them.

Manfred sighed and bid his son good night, feeling every one of his many years in his bones as he descended the stairs and retreated to his chambers to rest. Of all the many wishes he'd held for Saeran in his heart since the day of his birth, none were greater than that he grow up hale and strong and find someone to make him as happy as Rhys had made him. Now he wondered whether he'd called down some sort of curse upon him instead.

Better that Saeran never know that kind of happiness existed than live the rest of his days with it just beyond his reach. Better that he never know love than ever pine after one that could never be matched.

For if ever a woman lived to make his son lose his heart and soul in love, the wizard Nia was she.

⋘ ››·◇·‹‹ ⋙

The music was overwhelming. Three different groups of musicians played three different songs, several of them plucking tunes Saeran had never heard before. The entire kingdom was rejoicing, celebrating his marriage to the Southern princess. Saeran sat his throne as tense as a statue, feeling the same way he had the first time he'd seen the Aegirans on the other side of the battlefield. Cornered.

He wanted to howl his anguish, willing to make an utter fool of himself because maybe, just maybe the sound of his heart breaking would carry far enough for Nia to hear, loud enough to call her back to him. But what could he do once she was here?

The princess, his queen now, had barely moved since she'd sat next to him. She was a beauty to be sure. At ten and five she was a vision in silks, no matter that he couldn't see more than her eyes. Dark skinned, with raven hair that reached almost to her knees, Queen Mari watched the feast through wide, exotic eyes. Those eyes held magic as hot as the desert sun.

If only it scorched Saeran as it seemed to burn all his nobles. Old lechers, the lot of them.

He tapped his foot to a particular rhythm, straining his ears for the breeze. It was difficult enough to concentrate with music blaring and everyone shouting congratulations his way, but everything seemed more difficult without Nia close by. She must have witched him somehow, made him see and hear things that were never there when she was absent.

There lay true magic. Not in the eyes of Mari, but in the presence of Nia. She wore power like a lady wore a cloak, yet she rarely called on it. Magic came to her, eager to do her bidding, eager to be touched by her and to touch her in return.

Eager for her as Saeran was desperate.

A breeze tickled his neck and he sat up straighter. *What news?* he asked it, hoping to catch word of his wizard and her companions.

The breeze wavered with silent laughter and tickled him once more. *I bring news from the south,* it said, *and your wizard treads not here.*

Frustrated, he sat back once more. He needed to walk out into the night and question the trees, the earth. Anything at all. There'd been no word of her since she rode into the woods. No one had seen her or the knights pass through a single village. No one could tell him where she was, whether she was safe. Saeran didn't trust a single one of those knights; he never should have sent Nia out with them.

He needed his wizard back.

In her absence, Saeran had nowhere to turn but to Mari. "Does this please you?" he asked, striving for at least the appearance of civility.

She blinked her dark eyes at him as she slowly deciphered his words. Someone had taught her his language, but she still had much to learn. At last she nodded.

Saeran returned the gesture and turned his attention back to the revelry. She'd not said a word to him yet. It annoyed him, her silence, more than the musicians, and more than the nobles. He missed Nia's prickly tongue. Never had that woman lacked for something to say, whether to anger him, amuse him, or teach him. She'd have risked her neck to speak out of turn rather than hold her silence when the stakes were high.

The timid creature next to him now was her exact opposite. If she had strength in her, any spirit at all, Saeran couldn't see it.

With Nia, he'd felt it. From miles away he'd felt it.

Now all he felt was a void where she'd once stood, keeping watch over him and his reign. His trusted advisor and beloved friend. Friend, for he could never now call her by a name more dear.

Clenching his hands into fists on his knees, Saeran forced his thoughts away from the wizard. He had a wife now. A queen. He should be among his nobles, dancing and rejoicing with them. But though his feet ached to move, it wasn't to dance. Though his gaze was watchful, it wasn't to take in the spectacles. And though his ears were sharp, he didn't care for the bard's ballad. Despite his best intentions, Saeran couldn't help but search for what he knew he would not find.

His nose tickled and for a moment he thought he smelled summer blooms. *Nia.* He had but to think her name and all of a sudden the music of a thousand hearts beating at once made his own beat faster. Colors seemed brighter somehow, everything more beautiful, and he felt as if she was there, causing this change in him. His frown gave way at the fanciful thought, imagining things he knew could never be.

In his mind, he was well and truly wed—to the woman who'd taught him to hear the wind sing through trees. And when he glanced to the honored seat to his left, it was a golden haired nymph he saw sitting there, proud and regal, draped in robes instead of silks, with a wolf skin hugging her shoulders. She wore no gold, or adornments, but for that. He saw her red lips curve into a smile and his own curved in answer.

And then, as quickly as it had come, the feeling was gone, as was his wizard. In her rightful place now sat a southern girl of ten and five, no doubt petrified at being wed to a northern king.

Saeran pushed to his feet to leave, not realizing his mistake until the music stopped. There was only one thing he could say, the thing they all expected to hear. "It is time for us to retire." He choked on the words. As tradition dictated, he bowed to his young queen and offered his hand. He told himself he didn't see her glance uncertainly at the guards who had accompanied her here. He told himself he didn't feel her hand flinch when his fingers closed around hers.

And later, when he left her chambers, he told himself he didn't hear her weeping softly in her bed.

Nothing would compel him to sleep after that. Saeran could not close his eyes to escape knowing he would have to open them in the morning and return to the same world he'd left tonight. It would break him all over again. The briefest moment of hope for relief could make any torment that much worse.

Instead, he slipped outside into the glen. All was still in the castle now to give the king and queen their privacy, but he could hear laughter and dancing carrying on in the town of Frastmir.

Taking a knee, he caressed the ground. *Tell me, mother earth who birthed us all,* he beseeched, *tell me of my wizard.*

The earth sighed beneath his touch. *The wizard's wish is stronger than yours, king Saeran. She bid me hold my peace.*

Stunned, Saeran recalled Nia's lessons about charms and commands. The larger or older a thing was, the more difficult it was to command; a sapling was easier to bend than a full grown tree. Sometimes charms worked better than spelled commands, but even so there were few who would ever try to move a mountain, let alone succeed. Yet somehow Nia had compelled the vastness of earth itself to keep her secrets. He couldn't fathom it.

A cold wind made his shirt billow and he shivered at its touch. *Have you any news, wicked breeze? Have you news of my Nia?*

It swept by him again, playing with his hair and trailing between his fingers when he held his hand up to it. *I do indeed,* it hissed, twining around him like a cat asking to be petted.

Tell me, then.

The wizard travels north, the wind told him, sweeping once more into his hair and making him shiver with cold. *She travels with armored knights, seeking treasure.*

Saeran rolled his eyes. *This I already know. Tell me…* He hesitated, unsure of what he would hear. *What is she doing now?*

A moment's rest in the air silenced the north wind and he feared he'd missed his chance. Saeran wondered if his summoning spell would work. Could he simply call Nia to him as he had before?

No. If she'd charmed the earth into silence, she wouldn't come to him for the asking. He could shout himself hoarse and Nia would not appear. She was well and truly gone.

But just as he was about to lose hope, the wind returned, sweeping past him with renewed strength and chill. It rushed at him with such force he nearly fell off his feet and it spoke to him four simple words:

She screams in pain.

CHAPTER 19

The first snow began to fall on the twelfth day. Arnaud pulled the hood of his cape over his head and watched the wizard ride out front to scout their way. They should have reached their destination by now, yet she kept leading them farther north.

It was getting colder by the day, the landscape more and more barren. Where before they'd hunted for their dinner to ration supplies, there was now little game to be found. Lucca and Alec had returned empty handed the night before and Arnaud himself had had no luck this morning. If something didn't change, they would freeze or starve long before they ever made it back. If they made it back.

The wizard returned to confer with Frederick and Lucca. Arnaud might have savored the sight not long ago. Now chills ran down his spine, and they had nothing to do with the snow.

Arnaud had faced armies before. He'd felt the blade of a sword kiss his neck, moments away from death but for the grace of God. He'd brought lawbreakers and sinners to justice, looked in the eyes of monsters wearing a human mask, and never felt a twinge of fear for he'd always had God on his side.

The night he'd so foolishly sought the wizard alone, he'd felt his Savior abandon him. Demons had been out to play that night. They'd clawed their way inside the wizard, and Arnaud could still feel their taint lingering. He felt it each time she rode near, whenever she looked his way. The ice in her gaze now frightened him.

And no one else seemed to see it.

"What do you think they are talking about?" Alec asked.

"Planning the easiest path, no doubt," he replied, but the way Frederick frowned, shaking his head, he couldn't be sure.

Lucca separated from the group to come to the rest of them. "We camp here," he said.

"It is midday!" Jonah protested.

Lucca glared at the young man. "Dismount and make camp," he ordered.

"What's happened?" Arnaud asked.

"Nia says there is a squall awaiting us not far ahead. We need to wait it out before we can ride on."

"We have our winter gear," Alec argued. "We have ridden through storms before."

Lucca shook his head. "Not like this. We cannot risk it."

"Especially when not even our guide knows where we are going," Arnaud added with venom.

Lucca speared him with a hard look. “You two, do as you are told. Arnaud, a word.”

Arnaud dismounted and followed Lucca a fair distance off. Though the land was slowly turning white, the blanket of snow was not thick enough to cushion his step and frozen grass and foliage crunched beneath his boots.

“Something is bothering you,” Lucca said.

“I—”

“I do not care what it is. Look around you, Arnaud. This is as far from what we know as we have ever been, and if we cannot work together this land will kill us.”

“I put in my fair share,” Arnaud snarled.

“Then do it without questioning every step of the way,” Lucca snarled and stalked off.

Angered more than he had ever been before, Arnaud returned to his mount to retrieve his pack. As he tossed it to the ground, the hairs on the back of his neck stood on end and he turned around to see the wizard watching him. He shuddered. Taking his crossbow from his pack, Arnaud went east to hunt for their midday meal. Anything to put some distance between him and the wizard.

He didn't return to camp until the growing darkness forced him to the warmth of their fire. His hands were empty. The snow had begun to fall in earnest, hiding any tracks there might have been. Even creatures of the air were sparse here; he hadn't seen a single bird in days.

Someone had unrolled his pallet and unpacked his winter gear. Arnaud nodded his thanks to Jonah and Alec, knowing that Lucca and Frederick would not have bothered, deeply engrossed as they were in their conversation with the wizard.

“No luck?” Alec asked, handing him a little piece of stale bread and cheese. Jonah had the flask of wine, which had days ago been refilled with water.

“Nothing moving out there,” Arnaud told them. “It's as if the animals know to hide from us.”

Jonah breathed on his hands and rubbed them together for warmth. He took out his whistle and held it up. “Shall I play?”

“Not tonight,” Arnaud said. “Get some rest. We will all need it for the days to come.” And pulling the furs around him up to his ears, he bedded down to sleep.

When morning came, they didn't wait for first meal. Frederick gave the order to mount up, and he and the wizard took the lead going north. Ever farther north. Arnaud kept his complaints to himself. He filed in rank beside Lucca and held his peace.

They rode over even ground for a while before heading up an incline. Arnaud's mount wasn't as well shoed as the others. He hesitated and fell behind the rest, struggling up that hill. Arnaud picked his way with care, mindful that if they lost a horse now it would mean trouble. Better that he fall behind now than rush and meet his Maker too soon. The others wouldn't leave him; he would take his time now and catch up with them on the other side.

But before they could crest the hill and head down, the front riders pulled to a stop not far ahead. “What is going on?” he called. “Why have we stopped?”

No one answered him.

Arnaud spurred his mount to join them and stopped as they had, lining the cliff. Breath left him at the sight. The valley at his feet was frozen, everything covered in a thick layer of glistening ice. The trees, the ground, even the animals stopped forever in their tracks stood there as if encased in glass.

Frederick crossed himself. "God have mercy, this could have been us."

"It was not God who made us stop," Jonah returned. "You saved our lives, Nia."

Arnaud was speechless. His mount fidgeted, but the reins slipped from his numb fingers when he tried to subdue him. Saints, he could see the animals' eyes wide with fear, their mouths open to scream. Deer, rabbits, squirrels, they all must have sought shelter here. As sheltered as the valley was, it would have been warmer than the rest of the forest before that squall swept right through it.

Arnaud looked at the wizard to find her watching him in return, and he felt no gratitude, only deeper unease.

Lucca dismounted and drew his sword. "Take what you can," he said. "It may be all we will have to sustain us from this point on."

↞ »·◇·« ↠

"He says the orchard is infested with mice."

Saeran looked up from the report at Kvaran. "Mice?"

"Yes, your Majesty." The man looked left and right at the other advisors, but none of them spoke while he addressed the king. "They are destroying the flowers, and Robert says if it continues there will not be any apples left come harvest time."

"But *mice*?" Saeran repeated. "Can mice even climb trees?"

"I do not know, your Majesty."

He groaned and rubbed his aching forehead. Half the day gone and they hadn't even touched on two thirds of the issues the council of advisors had brought before him. He'd never known so many things could go wrong at the same time. The apple harvest was being destroyed, the bears were breaking bee hives to get to their honey, the huntsmen had their hands full with too many wild boar which were digging up all the mushrooms and root vegetables to take care of the bears. The weather was dry, forcing farmers to carry water in pails to keep their crops from dying, and though the lake was filled with fish, the fisherman couldn't catch anything because his nets fell apart every time they touched water.

And Nia had only been gone a fortnight.

Saeran had given orders to be informed the moment she and the knights were spotted returning. It should be any day now, thank Woden. He didn't think he could handle this much longer.

"Your Majesty?"

"Yes, what is it, Liam?"

The servant bowed. "Forgive the interruption. I've been sent by her Majesty to inquire whether your business is finished."

Did it bloody look finished? "Tell her no."

"Yes, your Majesty."

"Wait," he said. "What does she want?"

"I do not know, your Majesty. Shall I inquire?"

He frowned. "No. No, that will not be necessary." He'd told Mari many times if the matter was urgent she could interrupt him no matter what he was doing. But though she nodded each time he told her, she always sent someone else to ask for him and never insisted on his presence. He could only assume it wasn't important.

After Liam left, Saeran turned back to his council. "Send word to the farmers that anyone handy with a bow or spear is free to hunt as many boar as they can slay until further notice. Anything they kill is theirs to do with as they please. That ought to free up the huntsmen to take care of the bears and save our honey, as well as compensate the farmers for the drought. Call together the carpenter guild to come up with a faster way to bring water to the fields and send someone to investigate the mysterious, tree climbing mice."

"What of the fishing nets?" Allon inquired, snickering beneath his moustache.

Saeran closed his eyes and focused to hear the earth speak. It was exhausting this far up and he rarely used the trick, but at times like these, he trusted the earth far more than his own messengers. People lied to achieve their ends. The earth did not. What it told him made Saeran raise an eyebrow. "The fisherman's wife is a weaver?"

Kvaran consulted the scribed message before him. "I believe so, your Majesty."

"Send the midwife Kata to talk to them both. She is almost as good a peacemaker as Nia."

Kvaran frowned. "Why do they need a peacemaker?"

"Because if I heard correctly, the fisherman Neal has been eyeing the weaver Sidda's apprentice, Maeve. And if Sidda found out, I would not put it past the woman to take apart all her husband's nets in retaliation."

While many of them chuckled, Allon asked, "Where might his Majesty have heard such a thing?"

Saeran, in no mood to explain himself, made a grandiose gesture. "The wind told me." Not a lie.

The old advisor harrumphed.

"Enough for today," Saeran ordered. "I will trust you to take care of the rest. You may go, and have someone send for general Orri." He wanted to know how the Aegirans were getting along with his troops. Most of the ones who'd stayed for Mari were trained warriors. At least two guarded her day and night, but the rest were housed in Saeran's army barracks. In times of peace the building was mostly empty, but whenever new soldiers joined, they slept there while they trained.

Happily, Orri reported only a few disagreements, all of which have already been taken care of. Good. One less thing to worry about. After hearing the report on the soldiers and making sure all was in order, Saeran dismissed the general and took the first moment of quiet he'd had all day to stand up and stretch.

He went to the window and looked out across the courtyard to the northern woods. Nia was in there somewhere, hopefully already on her way back. Not a moment went by when Saeran didn't miss her. He dreamed about her nightly and cursed the light of day that stole her from him every morning.

Someone knocked and Saeran sighed. "Enter," he said because he had no other choice.

When no one spoke, he turned around to see Mari come in with a covered tray. She set it down on the table and waved him over with a slight bow-nod she always did whenever they met. The first few days he could not make her meet his gaze for longer than a moment. But as time passed, she became more at ease in his presence and Saeran found he didn't resent her as he thought he would. Mari was a kind girl. She spoke little, embarrassed by her difficulty forming their words, but she listened intently whenever he spoke and he found himself talking to her more and more each day.

It didn't make him miss Nia any less.

"What is this?"

Mari uncovered the tray. She'd brought him a hearty meal and a pitcher of wine and seeing it, Saeran realized he hadn't eaten a thing all day. "Thank you," he said.

Mari bow-nodded again.

"Will you not join me?"

She shook her head and touched her stomach, indicating she didn't feel well. From what he'd managed to get out of her and her people, northern food was much different from what they were used to back in Aegiros, and it didn't always sit well with them. Saeran understood. He'd instructed the cooks to do their best to prepare simple dishes and use the ingredients the Aegirans brought with them as gifts to ease the transition.

"Are you feeling all right?" Since she insisted on wearing her veil whenever she was outside of her chamber, he couldn't tell from her face.

Mari bow-nodded and touched her stomach again. Then she did something he'd never seen her do. She reached up and untied one side of her veil to reveal her face. She was smiling. "Magic-woman tell me I have child."

CHAPTER 20

The great hall was bursting with people and Nia, caught in the midst of them, couldn't find her way out. Everything around her was spinning madly out of control. People's faces blurred together, but she recognized them all.

There was the new queen, her lovely face uncovered and smiling in the sun.

There was Saeran, staring moodily out the window in the royal study.

Nico, no more than a shadow, danced all around her, just out of reach. She tried to speak, to call to him, but no sound would come out.

The familiar faces disappeared into the crowd and colorful gowns blinded her for a moment. This was a celebration of some sort, but the faces were grotesque masks of malice, not joy. They had fangs filling their mouths, monstrous grimaces contorting their features.

The jesters and jugglers came so close to her she could feel their rancid breaths on her face, yet her feet would not move. She had no body here and no way to leave.

The crowd shifted, and from its depths emerged a man. His golden hair was shorn much shorter than was common, and his gentle face was clean shaven like a boy's. But his eyes were ancient. They were the eyes of an old man. He approached her with fluid steps and, though she couldn't hear him humming, she felt the impact of his silent melody. It moved through her in waves, making her sway.

The black crystal was in his hands. He held it out to her and she couldn't take her eyes off it. So beautiful and unusual. It looked to be incredibly heavy, but not because of the stone's weight. That pendant glittering so enticingly in his open palm held ancient magics. Countless separate energies swirled inside, each singing a different tune, yet each a mere imitation of the true wielder's power.

He came closer and Nia reached out, though she had no arms.

A silent scream shuddered through her and broke the spell, allowing her to look away. The sorcerer shouted his fury, but her attention was now on the queen. She leaned over the body of a man, her frame shaking with heartfelt sobs.

Somehow, Nia floated closer. Only the man's hand was showing, but she recognized the ring on it at once. It was the royal seal of Wilderheim. The crowd rushed at her again, taking her along, away from Saeran and his queen. She was carried on the current of countless people until she couldn't tell up from down.

And then the creature made its presence known.

"Nia," it hissed…

"Wizard, wake up!"

She jerked awake and reacted on instinct, shoving with all her might and not a little amount of magic at the man leaning over her, shaking her shoulders.

Arnaud went flying and landed several feet away, his breath knocked out of him.

She didn't apologize. Since her contact with the creature, she'd had terrible nightmares every night. Though she remembered little of them when she awoke, the feeling of dread remained long after the dreams faded.

Nia had made her wishes clear. She slept away from the camp they set up each night and told them she was not to be disturbed. The only way she would make sense of these things was if she could do so in her sleep.

Rising from her pallet, she winced at the ache in her shoulder.

There was snow everywhere. It was their constant companion this far north, the air so cold all the knights had donned their thick woolens and animal skins for protection. Nia still wore only her cloak and wolf skin. It was all the warmth she required.

With a thought she dried her clothes, wet and frozen from sleeping on the snow-covered ground, and stretched out her spine.

Straightening her cloak around her, she took up her staff. Arnaud was on his feet again, though his breath was still uneven. He had a look on his face that told her he was cursing himself a thousand kinds of fool for trying to wake her. "It is late," she told him. "We need to be on our way."

More than a month since they'd left the castle. At least ten more days until they reached Sir Frederick's coveted treasure. This journey was stretching much longer than she'd anticipated. It was, in part, because of her dreams. She slept late and wasted daylight so none of them could cover as much ground as they wanted. But there was no help for it. It wasn't only that she needed the sleep. Once she fell into those dreams, she became trapped in them and couldn't tell how much time has passed. Her mind became so absorbed in the scenes that it took her longer and longer to relinquish the unsolvable mystery and return to the waking world.

Nia feared there might come a day when she wouldn't wake at all. It was as if a sickness had taken hold of her, and she knew nothing of its source to fashion a cure. It was placing all of them in danger.

The land was so silent she could hear her heart beat like a drum as she led the way back to the camp. The absence of animals unnerved her. It had been weeks since she'd heard a bird's song or a predator's soft whisper. Even the earth sounded different here, its voice sharper and colder than Nia was used to.

Her feet buried in the snow as she walked, making her shiver, but she continued on, longing for the surety of Stardust's company.

"You were screaming," Arnaud said and coughed as he caught up to her. "We heard you in the camp."

"I was perfectly all right," she said, though her shaky voice left something to be desired. She wasn't all right. Something was draining her in a frightening way. It felt as if she was using her own essence to work spells without realizing it. Not only did it leave her weak in body, she found it harder each morning to simply cleanse herself.

And it was getting worse the closer they got to their destination. If she was left completely drained by the time they got there, the lot of them would be left defenseless against whatever was waiting for them.

But that wasn't all of it. Her magic was tied to her soul, her essence. It could replenish itself if she used too much, but if it drained out of her completely, it would take her life force with it.

Arnaud caught her arm, pulling her to a stop. "Enough of this," he said. "I don't know what is happening to you, and I no longer care. But you have a duty to us that will not be so easily dismissed. We all know something is awry. If you are ill, all of us are in danger, and you need to tell us."

"Arnaud," Lucca said, his voice hard. "Release her."

"You know I am right!" His hold on her arm tightened.

Lucca drew a long dagger from his belt loop. "You are in a temper. You are not thinking clearly."

Arnaud stared at the blade a moment, and Nia almost feared the two would come to blows. The others were already on their feet, keeping their distance, but ready to step in should they be needed. "What is this?" Arnaud said. "Are you all so blind that you do not see what is happening?" He shoved her toward Lucca. "Whatever happened to her back there, it has left a mark. Can you not feel it? The evil has tainted her. She is not the same wizard who rode out with us."

Lucca's knuckles turned white, clutching the dagger.

"I am well enough to lead you where you need to go," she grated, stepping in front of Lucca to get between him and Arnaud. "But be warned, Sir Arnaud, if you touch me again, you will regret it."

"You will walk today," Lucca told Arnaud. "It seems to me you have a need for exercise to clear your mind. Were I you, I would use the time to reflect." Sheathing his dagger, he turned his back on the man. "Mount up," he told the rest of them. "We have a long way ahead of us."

When their company rode out, Nia took the lead. Lucca was behind her, and behind him rode Jonah and Alec. Frederick took up the rear with Arnaud's mount, keeping pace with the unhorsed knight to lecture him. Such was their arrangement for the next three days.

There was no path here to follow. No animal tracks to mark the white snow. The trees were bare of not only leaves, but sometimes entire branches. The absence of life was worrying. What happened here? Why did nothing live in these woods?

"There was truth to his words," Lucca said, coming up to her right. "We have all noticed something is not right with you."

"I am well," she returned, keeping her eyes on the ground in front of Stardust.

"You mistake me. I did not say I believed you have made a pact with the devil. But there is something troubling you. Gravely, if your sleep is so disturbed."

"Be careful, Lucca," she told him. "Any more of such kind words and a lass might think you care." A sharp breeze laughed at her. It pierced through her clothing, stabbing into her body until she had to suppress a shiver.

Lucca smiled. "You are an extraordinary woman. If I did not know your heart to be engaged elsewhere, I might come to care." He held his hand up to silence her when she would have spoken. "I know, I know. No need for your lovely voice to carry harsh words. I will leave you in peace. But you should know, Lady Nia, that we do not take something for nothing. You have provided us with direction, and for that we are grateful. In return, we are honor bound to protect you against whatever lies ahead. We will do it, whether you want us to or not."

Nia would have told him there was no protecting anyone from what lay ahead, but he'd already slowed to fall back and give her space. She considered telling them something, preparing them for the possibility that they might all die, but in the end thought better of it. If she was being overcautious, there was no need for them to fret. And if she wasn't, there was no reason for them to fret and tire themselves needlessly. If they were to die, better it be a surprise.

Knowing one's end didn't make the remaining days any sweeter. Rather, it killed a man before he was even dead.

They passed through nine days of snow. Nine days of battling the wind and knocking ice from their belongings. Nine days of absolute misery during which a fire once lit had to be shielded and watched over the entire time to burn. If Nia so much as glanced away from those flames, let her concentration slip for an instant, the fire went out. It took effort and energy to keep a flame burning. It took even more to get one started when everything was too wet and frozen to catch the flame.

As cold as she and the knights were, the horses were colder. They had no woolens to keep them warm, and the more skittish of them could not be cajoled closer to the fire for anything. They'd already lost two to this bitter winter, and they all had to walk the rest of the mounts to spare them as long as possible. When they made camp for the night, humans and animals slept huddled together, sharing what warmth they could.

Their food had run out, and melting snow for water took hours in this weather. Arnaud and Jonah had taken to praying whenever they stood still, seeming to derive some strength or courage from ritual. Even Frederick and Alec joined them every so often. Lucca alone refused to say the words, warming himself instead with memories of his wife and children. Whenever the wind died down a little, he sought Nia out to speak to. He told her stories of his past for his own comfort and allowed her to lean on him when the weight of her staff became too much of a burden to carry.

It was more often than not now that Nia needed to lean on something or someone. She'd stopped sleeping because she was needed to keep the fire burning at night. It was just as well; it kept her from her nightmares and whatever was casting them over her. But the effort was taking a terrible toll. Already she was stretching her powers thin. Keeping everyone and herself warm took precedence, and so she'd stopped casting a glamour over herself. The knights could now see how badly she was faring.

It wasn't only her magic that was draining, it was her body as well. Her legs were always weak, and though she didn't want to, she was forced to lean on Stardust to stay on her feet in the harsh winds. They ought to have turned back days ago, but none of them would hear of it. Whatever it was they sought, it was more important than their lives. And she'd pledged to lead the way. So long as they had the will to continue, she had to as well.

On the tenth day, the storm finally died down. They made camp at the foot of a slight hill which provided at least some shelter from the wind. The fire needed only wood to keep burning that night, but Nia kept watch over it nonetheless. Several times she caught herself casting her will into the fire to bring up a vision. She was too weak to complete it, but the intention kept resurfacing, as if it was a habit she couldn't rid herself of. Those dancing flames kept singing their lullabies, making her yearn for her home, her bed.

She missed Saeran. There were times now when her mind recalled memories of him without Nia having any say in it. She would pat Stardust's neck and feel Saeran's hand squeezing hers. She would sit before the fire at night and feel his arms around her. Nia couldn't be sure if it was her imaginings or something entirely different, but she felt as though Saeran was there with her, hiding in illusions. His presence comforted Nia for a short while, but then she remembered everything that happened before she left, and since, and she was left aching and weary, tempted to lay her head in the snow and simply sleep.

Sleep until this wretched winter passed. And if it never did, then so be it.

Staring into those flames, she didn't notice when night turned to day. Lucca's hand on her shoulder startled her out of her trance and she struggled to her feet to help them ready to move on again. For all her good intentions, she couldn't make her body obey. It was all she could do not to fall back down once she'd stood.

The knights did everything on their own, telling her to mount Stardust and wait. Even Stardust agreed with them, butting his nose against her back until she nearly fell over. Nia couldn't argue after that, so she did as she was told.

After hours of riding at a steady pace, Stardust halted at the edge of a clearing. *I go no farther,* he said, ears back.

Nia swallowed past the lump in her throat, her gaze fixed on the cliff face before them. It towered up to the sky, a dark barren rock face rising from a level clearing big enough to hold an army. Even the wind didn't blow here.

This was it.

She dismounted, taking care to find her balance before she let go of Stardust's saddle. She felt weak and what little magic she had left, she was using to stay on her feet. Her body shivered in the cold she could no longer keep away and the wolf skin hugged itself tighter around her. Nia was grateful for that little comfort.

The knights tied their horses.

"We are here," Sir Frederick said, his eyes feverish as he looked for something that clearly wasn't there to find. "Where is it?"

Nia listened. The effort made her head pound, but she had to know what was around her.

There.

In the shadows of a deep cave it stood still. It waited to see what they would do, ready to strike, should they be so foolish as to approach. "This is madness," she managed to say.

"This is what we came here for," Sir Frederick countered, moving forward.

"No!" Nia caught his arm. Bracing herself, she spoke the words she knew would spell all of their dooms. Death waited for them where the knights expected to find treasures untold. Death by means no mortal could imagine. "I will go first."

Sir Frederick hesitated, but half bowed in ascent and backed away from the edge to allow her passage.

Nia took a step into the clearing, carefully placing her foot to make as little noise as possible. She fell through, knee deep into the snow. The beast did not stir. Shaking, dizzy, she took another step and almost collapsed.

Come back, Nia, Stardust pleaded, sensing her weakness.

She couldn't reply.

Instead, she focused all her energy on wading through the snow. Nia felt the knights following her, and she knew they worried. She heard Lucca swear under his breath each time her knees buckled in the deep snow.

It became shallower the closer they got to the rock face and Nia would have sighed in relief if she didn't know something far worse was waiting for them there.

At last, she reached the cliff. It hummed with power, its own as well as something else's. The knights lined up on either side of her, their weapons drawn. They treated her now as what she was, a deathly ill woman, shaking and hunched over, her hair frozen and her face bloodless. Nevertheless, they didn't say a word. As the warriors they were, their eyes didn't linger on her, but searched for enemies to slay.

Not much energy left in her. No more time to waste.

Reaching out with one shaking hand, Nia touched the jagged rock.

All at once, a terrible roar shattered the wall before them, the earth shuddered and shook. Boulders rained down on them, and they fell to their knees for cover as the beast in the cave rushed out of the darkness.

Nia couldn't defend herself, much less the knights; couldn't even shield herself from the horrendous sound. She felt, rather than saw, one of the knights being lifted off the ground and tossed carelessly back toward the tree line. Two more met the same fate, and then the beast reached for Nia. It lifted her up by the shoulders so high she couldn't tell how far off the ground she was. She dared not look.

But then the beast stilled and became quiet, and Nia opened her eyes to behold Saeran's beloved face just beneath hers.

She fainted.

CHAPTER 21

A fortnight had come and gone. It's been almost a month since Nia and the knights had ridden out, and still there was no sign of them. Saeran had sent a trio of soldiers north to where the road ended, marking the border of his kingdom. They'd returned with no news whatsoever. He was beginning to worry, and he wasn't the only one.

Nia's absence had been noted and was much remarked upon in all circles. Some were saying the wizard had abandoned him and took it as a bad omen for his reign. Without confirmation, rumors had begun to spread, one more outlandish than the next. The wizard had died. She'd run off to join the knights' order. She was battling monsters in the north. She'd been abducted into the Otherlands, never to return.

It was the last which bothered Saeran because of all of them, it was the most believable.

Something had changed.

His people grew discontent, the elements spoke to him less and less. It had been days since he'd heard even the wind speak of Nia. It was as if she had disappeared from the face of the earth, and in her absence Saeran saw how important a wizard truly was to the wellbeing of Wilderheim. Without her to interpret the weather, the winds, the changing seasons, Saeran felt blind and dumb, at a loss as to what needed to be done.

But it was worse than that.

At some point, even his mind turned against him. Where not long ago he went to sleep each night eager to see his wizard in dreams, now he dreaded the time when he had to close his eyes. Nightmares tormented him, dark portents of disaster and death. He saw it everywhere he turned, even in himself. For days now he'd dreamed of everyone he knew dying in some horrible way, yet there seemed to be no rhyme or reason to any of it.

Wary without knowing why, Saeran had ordered Manfred away for his own safety. His father had protested, of course. Now that Mari was with child, he'd wanted to stay for both of them and the birth of his grandson or granddaughter.

But the more insistent he'd been, the more nervous Saeran had felt until he'd put his foot down and ordered a contingent of soldiers to pack up his father's belongings and escort him back to Lyria. The sense of dread only left him when his messenger returned with news that the company was well beyond the mountain pass, and his sudden relief assured him that he'd done the right thing. One life, at least, he could save.

But what to do about the rest of them, including his own?

Half crazed with worry, Saeran struggled for control, but it proved elusive. With a foul curse he made a circuit around the chamber before falling back into his path from window to door and back while his advisors watched him as if he had lost his mind.

Saeran's step slowed, and his gaze snared on the floor, refusing to be moved as his latest nightmare came back to haunt him in his waking hours. His vision blurred until he could see it unfold in his mind's eye and he shuddered, unable to call out, unable to escape the sights.

He saw his queen lying dead in a pool of blood, his own hands covered with it. Shock held his body still, but his hands refused to stop shaking. When at last he looked up, he saw Nia, doubled over in tremendous pain. He felt with her, his own body contorting, muscles locking until he couldn't draw a breath. Terror made ice of his blood, but he kept looking at her, fighting his fate and trying to reach her, touch her. Help her, though he himself was dying.

"Majesty?"

The tentative voice brought him back to the present, and Saeran found himself staring at his own shaking hands. Gods, this had to end. He had to get Nia back. If for no other reason, than to ensure that she was safe. If he could just see her, even from a distance…

"Majesty."

A little stronger this time. Despite his torturous thoughts Saeran felt a smile pulling on the corner of his mouth. He glanced at the frail-looking girl with her cloud of unruly russet hair and made an effort to soften his gaze. "Yes, Braith?"

She blushed scarlet to be addressed directly. "Has our business been concluded?"

Her impatience charmed him. Braith would be a hellion as soon as she found the courage to speak her mind more often. Saeran almost looked forward to it. He would enjoy the presence of more confident women among his advisors. The only trick would be to find them. Braith sneaked a glance at the window. No doubt she was eager to get out and join her cousins in their mischief. Saeran decided to be merciful. "It has," he answered her, dismissing them all with a wave of his hand.

He sighed as he watched the oldest shuffle their feet out the door and stroked his beard. Something important was about to happen. He needed to be prepared, and it was damned difficult to prepare for something without knowing what it was.

"If only I could talk to Nia," he said aloud.

Call, the walls replied.

"Do you think I have not tried?" Oh, how he'd tried.

Soulcall, they said.

"What?"

Soulcall.

Saeran shook his head and scowled.

He wished he could speak to Mari; truly speak to her. But unlike Braith, his queen wasn't so eager to demand her voice. She rarely held his gaze for longer than a moment, and though she has learned his language well, she refused to say more than a handful of words whenever she was required to speak. To get her to say that much was a task in and of itself.

"Pregnant," he said, still baffled by the news. Four different midwives and a witch had confirmed Mari's news and the chambermaid told him his queen had asked for a witch to visit her every day since the wedding to see whether she'd conceived. He wasn't sure what to think about that.

She was a mystery, his queen. Saeran had been mistaken to think her weak. On the contrary, there was strength and courage running deep inside her, and he was beginning to admire her for it. True, she didn't speak much, but in her silence she heard and observed so much more than anyone else he knew, besides Nia. She could sit by his side when he held court, listen to the petitioners speak and see into the heart of their dilemma. Saeran could tell by the way she tilted her head whenever she'd heard enough to make up her mind, and her decision, when he managed to drag it out of her, was always wise and just. It was the getting her to voice it to anyone but him in anything above a whisper that was the problem.

"Easier to talk to walls. At least you answer."

Call.

"Even if you are somewhat flat."

Perhaps it would help if he told Mari about his nightmares. He would risk frightening her, but a show of trust might inspire the same in her. And if she still couldn't bring herself to speak to him, he could at least be safe in the knowledge that she wouldn't repeat what he said. "It is as good a plan as any." And it would give him something to do besides sit around and wait for the gods to strike him their blow.

Rubbing a weary hand over his brow he set out in search of her.

He hadn't gone five steps outside the chamber when someone called to him. Saeran turned to acknowledge the magician who had accompanied Mari's caravan and stayed when the rest had departed. It baffled Saeran how a born northerner could end up so far from his homeland. Jasper was such a man. Though his skin was now darkened by the hot Southern sun, his hair still gleamed gold, and his eyes were sharp and blue.

Cold eyes, he had. No matter how much he smiled, he could never disguise that. Saeran was uneasy beneath his direct gaze. He could sense Jasper was not all together sane, but he'd thought better of mentioning it.

Now, the man bowed. "Forgive the intrusion, Majesty," he said politely, but something dark lurked behind his too easy smile.

"Be quick about it, whatever it is," Saeran said, impatient to find Mari.

"Of course, Majesty," Jasper said, rummaging in his pockets with well practiced haste. "I have overheard the maids speak of a wizard."

His tone put Saeran on guard. "And what have you heard?"

"Nothing of import, I am sure," Jasper replied with an easy shrug. "But they mentioned, too, your Majesty's interest in magic tricks, and it so happens that I am in possession of a rather clever one. I thought your Majesty would appreciate it."

Saeran tapped his foot as the boy continued to search for his trinket, but curiosity kept him from dismissing Jasper. Truth be told, he missed talk of magic and spells.

Saeran continued to practice what lessons Nia had imparted on him, though it was never the same without her.

At last, Jasper pulled a chain out of his pocket and Saeran watched as the dark, shining stone pendant settled on its loop, swinging enticingly back and forth. Back and forth. So beautiful and dark, Saeran felt as if he was falling into it. Back and forth. Back…and forth…

"Merely a first step," Jasper was saying, but Saeran was too distracted to follow his words. Something cold and ravenous dwelled in the depths of that stone. He couldn't see it, but he could feel it. It swam in circles, trapped by the pendant, enraged and distraught that it could not get out.

Then Saeran felt its gaze snare on him. It stopped and stared, singing a tune to lure him closer, even as invisible bands slithered around him and pulled taut.

"You see, I need to find the wizard. She hides better than most I have come across, but she cannot hide her love for you."

Saeran swayed forward, as the dark chill of magic spread around him, and, of its own accord, his hand reached out to the black stone, so shiny it seemed like ice.

"She will come back for you," Jasper said with malicious determination, all pretense of innocence gone. All at once he sounded far older than he looked, and for an instant, fear gripped Saeran and he fought against the binds, a last ditch effort to free himself. It was too late. His call for help never made it past his lips. "Oh, aye, she will come. And when she does, I will be waiting."

At those terrible words, Saeran's vision went dark and then he was falling through emptiness with barbed spikes stabbing into him, turning his blood to ice…

⋘ ››·◇·‹‹ ⋙

Nia woke slowly, fighting her way through layers of fog to find that her body was warm and languid, cushioned by something much softer than her mattress roll. It shocked her how difficult it was just to open her eyes and keep them that way. She could not move more, no matter how much she wanted to.

Before her, a fire burned merrily in a stone hearth built into an almost smooth wall. Bright banners covered the walls around it like tapestries to keep out the chill, and there were furs strewn about the floor to protect bare feet. She was lying on a nest of pillows, covered with several of those furs.

Had she dreamed it all?

No. Nia still felt echoes of the pain she'd endured to get here, and her essence was barely glowing—a reminder of how close she'd come to dying. She made an effort to rise, but even raising her head proved to be too much. Too much effort. Too much pain. A helpless sound escaped her before she could prevent it. Her mouth was parched and her eyes felt dry.

Strong arms came around her to help her sit up. The man they belonged to was a shadow against the fire's light, something she thought was very deliberate. He retrieved a goblet and held it to her lips, and that was when she noticed his hand. It was covered with scales that shimmered in the firelight, his nails more like thick claws.

Nia struggled to raise her arm to push him away, surprised to find his skin was warm to the touch. Rough, as if he wore armored gloves, but warm as any human flesh. Nia was shivering even with the many furs covering her, but this creature, whatever he was, seemed comfortable enough.

He growled and twitched his hand to get away from hers, then pressed the cup to her lips again and tipped it, giving her no choice but to drink or have its contents spill all over her. The tepid herbal brew choked her at first, but she made herself swallow more, recognizing its power. Three gulps later she felt her strength returning, and after four she felt overheated and had to wrestle several of the furs off her just to breathe.

When the creature decided she'd had enough, the goblet disappeared behind him and he sat back on his haunches, studying her. "You are strong," he said, his voice as deep as it was menacing. Nia got the impression that this was a whisper for him, his way of tempering his presence. She was grateful. "Most would not have taken more than a sip."

"Where are the others?" she rasped, then coughed.

"Asleep," he answered, "as they have been for the greater part of a month. I thought it best to keep them that way until you were well enough to mediate." Then he leaned closer and she could almost make out his features. "Understand me, wizard, if one more raises arms against me, I will burn them all."

"They fought you?" She struggled to comprehend, but her mind wouldn't work properly.

"Thinking they were defending you, no doubt," the almost-man said, sounding amused. "I will admit I was a bit gruff when you arrived."

"A bit," she agreed. Squinting in the dark chamber, she tried again to make out his features. "Who…what are you?"

Though he'd not moved much since he'd sat, Nia somehow felt him grow still. "You don't know?"

Nia shook her head. "I have never seen anyone like you."

There was silence as she felt him study her and Nia caught herself reaching for the furs to hide. Though she couldn't see his eyes, his gaze felt piercing sharp, as if he could see inside her skin into her soul and found her lacking.

But when he answered, there was no distain in his voice, only something she might have called surprise. "I am a dragon."

CHAPTER 22

Nia's head swam as the light in the room intensified, aided by magic, to reveal the dragon as well as his dwelling. He looked so much like Saeran, but there were also marked differences. His hands were scattered with scales, his fingertips clawed. Though he was tall for a human, he seemed uncomfortable in his own skin, as if it didn't quite fit. And why would it? He was, after all, a dragon.

His hair was black, reflecting many colors when light touched it. The strands fell below his shoulders, but couldn't disguise the smooth horns growing out of his temples. He had glowing silver eyes, slitted like a reptile's, and even his features seemed sharp, hard somehow, as if his skin was stretched taut over stone.

He allowed her to study him without comment, and didn't speak even when her gaze slipped past him to glance at the chamber. But it wasn't exactly a chamber. Though there was furniture aplenty, they were still in a cave. The dragon had made it as comfortable as possible, but at the border where the burrow ended and cave tunnel began, all luxury stopped. Nia could make out the sleeping outlines of the knights in the darkened corridor. They slept on the cold, hard ground, with nothing but blankets to warm them. The dragon's hospitality, it seemed, didn't stretch that far.

As if reading her mind, he spoke again in a deep gravelly voice that made her think he was growling, "Their comfort was not my concern." He pronounced the words carefully, as if unused to the need to form them.

"Then why am I not among them?" Nia asked, not certain she wished to know the answer. From what little she had read about dragons, they were very few and very solitary creatures. But although they despised crowds of people, singular companions, usually chosen for their charm, or wit, were almost a necessity to them. Nia had read stories of maidens choosing to remain with a dragon and giving up everything else. If that was what he wanted from her, Nia might have to fight him to leave.

"You are a wizard," the dragon replied with an elegant shrug, his ancient eyes taking in everything about her. "Wizards are kin to dragons, in the same way wolves are kin to foxes."

"Does that mean you are only being polite?"

He nodded.

Nia shook her head. "You are lying."

The dragon's mouth quirked, but he didn't smile. She wasn't certain he could. "I will admit there were other reasons for keeping you alive."

A knight stirred in the tunnel, drawing Nia's gaze. "Wake them," she said, before she could temper the order into a plea.

The dragon didn't seem to mind. "Not yet. I expect they might give me trouble for what is about to come." He studied them for a moment longer before shaking his head. "Fools," he scoffed. "They risk their lives for something they cannot even use." When he looked at her again, Nia felt him probing her mind. "You do not know what they seek. But how could you? They themselves have never seen it."

Nia pushed off one more layer of furs. Her strength was returning quickly, but even with the dragon's help it would be awhile yet before she was back to herself. It worried her. How long had they already been gone? She thought of Saeran alone in the castle, then remembered he wasn't alone anymore, and never would be again. She cast her worries aside and settled. Nia was in no rush to get back.

"What is your name?" she asked, then winced when he raised a mocking eyebrow. Names held power over their bearers. To name a thing meant to have control over it. Of course he wouldn't tell her. "What do I call you?" she asked instead.

Rather than answer, the dragon reached behind him. When he faced her again, he held a wooden chalice. "Behold, your knights' coveted prize. One of man's most wondrous inventions."

"What is it?"

"A cup."

"What does it do?"

The dragon huffed with impatience. "It holds drink," he retorted.

Nia gaped. "That's it? That is what we have almost died trying to find?" She'd seen little more than ideas in their minds when she'd searched for their treasure. Nothing but myths and legends, stories of miracles and great power to those who found it. "We came all this way for a cup?"

Before her anger could manifest in the air, the dragon waved his hand down, forcing her power into submission. "They came here for the cup. A cup which is useless without something to drink from it, though they would not believe even me, should I decide to tell them. You, Lady Nia, are here for the drink itself."

Leaving her to ponder that mysterious proclamation, he rose and walked to a table near the far wall. He made no sound at all as he walked, making Nia wonder whether he was there at all, and his long, reptilian tail swished left and right in his wake. Taking up a pitcher, the dragon man returned to his seat before her and poured deep red wine into the wooden cup.

"At least tell me it's the magic one. The one they said once held the blood of…I forgot his name."

Again, that almost smirk. "Humans," he said as he set the pitcher aside and placed the cup before her. "Always twisting everything to serve their own purpose." He uncurled the fingers of his right hand and pressed a black claw into its center, drawing blood. He allowed three drops to fall into the wine before the wound closed and the wine boiled and sizzled, giving off black smoke.

Nia swallowed with difficulty, but accepted the cup when he held it out to her. Staring into the dark liquid, she imagined she could see shadows in its depths. "It will hurt," she said, knowing it was true.

"You have and will yet endure far worse," he replied. This was a gift, as well as a test. She knew nothing about the magical properties of dragon's blood, something she was sure dragons kept a close secret. Combined with her own magical essence it could do any number of things: permanently alter her physical being or even mark her soul. If she drank, it would mean submitting fully to the dragon's will. Blood bonds created a link between beings, allowing the stronger to control the weaker if he so desired.

If she refused it, he might simply move on to another topic of conversation, or he might burn her to ash where she sat. There was no telling what mysterious thoughts compelled a creature so old and powerful to give up three full drops of his blood for a lowly, human.

"You wished for answers. They are in the wine. Drink."

She took a bracing breath before bringing the cup to her lips. Her hands shook, but she made certain not to spill a single drop. The wine flowed smoothly down the back of her throat, leaving warmth in its wake, a mere taste of what was to come.

She'd no sooner handed the cup back to him than fire exploded in her belly, sending tendrils out into her blood to scorch her from the inside out. Nia doubled over, unable to draw breath to cry out. Her tears turned to steam before they could be shed, and the inferno inside her kept growing, burning, changing her. Her muscles locked until she couldn't move, but that wasn't the worst of it.

When the fire reached her mind, she choked on a scream as her vision went black and the shadows she'd thought to have seen in the wine took shape. Dozens, hundreds of images flew at her, too fast for her to understand, but they ingrained themselves among her own memories, as if she herself had lived them.

There were thousands of years the dragon had given her—his years, his memories. In them, she saw a beautiful, fair haired woman. She laughed as she spun around a pyre, looking back at the dragon many times with so much emotion in her gaze that even the mighty dragon's heart squeezed in his chest. Nia felt his love for her.

But in an instant, the strength of that love turned to agony as she saw through his eyes the beautiful, dark haired child held in his big, rough hands. Only memories of the child's mother remained, and each brought with it equal measures of pleasure and pain. All he had left was his daughter, his beloved's final gift to him. And he adored that child more than his own life. The girl grew up and ventured into the world, and met a man Nia recognized, though he was still young and full of all the joy he'd lost when his queen died in childbirth.

And then it was the widowed king who stared at a child in his arms, his beloved wife far and gone. The boy opened his big gray eyes and uttered soft coos, mourning his mother as his father did.

The dragon caught her against him when she would have collapsed. "Saeran," she whispered, fighting for breath and shivering as the fire slowly died down inside her. "He's your grandson." It all made sense now. His thirst for spells and magic, his aptitude at both—it was in his blood. Why had she never questioned it before?

"Humans," the dragon said, his voice thick with emotion, "cannot carry our seed. A dragon's life essence is too powerful to be contained in a human vessel, too ravenous. It needs magic to feed on and in its absence, it drains its mother's life."

"It takes dragonblood to birth dragonblood," Nia said, beginning to make sense of what he'd shown her. She could feel the effects of the drink. Her essence was brighter than before, and more volatile as well. Nia would never again be as she'd been before. Dragon's blood was now a part of her.

Why hadn't the dragon changed his beloved mate this way?

She already knew the answer. By the time he'd realized the danger, it had been too late. She would have risked her child, and had refused to do that. The dragon had been helpless to change her mind, forced to live out her remaining days with the constant knowledge that each hour was one closer to losing her. The mere thought that he could save her, but she wouldn't allow it for the sake of their child had driven him mad time and again, and when his daughter was born, and he felt his mate slip away into eternal sleep, the little girl's gentle presence had been the only thing preventing him from becoming a monster.

"But Saeran's mother—"

"Was only half dragon," he said. "She would have lived for a while, in agony, had she survived the birth. No one can live for long with only half their being."

Nia's arms crept around him. She wanted to offer some comfort, but there was nothing she could do or say that would take away the torment he carried. "What do you want me to do?" she said, knowing he hadn't done this to her without good reason.

His hold on her tightened for an instant before he pulled away and resumed his seat. Now, when she looked into his silver eyes, she could see his love's shadow dancing in their depths. His mate was always with him, if only in his mind. And he could never forget, never leave it all behind. "Look after my grandson," he said at last. "He needs you more than he will ever admit, even to himself."

Nia hesitated. "I will stand as his advisor," she said. "I have sworn that much and will stand by my oath."

The dragon cast her a look full of sympathy. "He needs far more than your counsel, Nia. And you do as well."

"The kingdom must come first," she insisted. The future of Saeran's rule was only as stable as his people's trust that the hand of their king was guided by one outside the hierarchy, who would judge fairly for not having anything to gain from another's loss. If they betrayed that, if she ceased to be neutral to his reign, there would be war. It would take so little to incite a battle, merely the suspicion that Saeran was unfaithful to his Aegiran queen.

"Nia," the dragon said, his voice echoed with another—Nico's. Her heart fluttered in her chest at her mentor's familiar rasp, even while she knew it was nothing but a dragon's trick. "Saeran rules with his heart. If it breaks, his kingdom will as well."

"Nia?" Lucca's voice sounded from the tunnel, an unwelcome reminder that soon she would have to return and face her king again. The dragon held her gaze, refusing to release her, weighing her soul and judging her strength.

"Do not fear this," he told her as the others began to rise. "He needs your strength to lean on, as you need his. You are well-matched, Nialei of the Streams. It is only your fear of love that hold you back. Let go. Leap and he will catch you."

"He is wed," Nia told him, her voice harder than she'd intended.

The look in the dragon's eyes revealed what he would not voice.

Not for long.

CHAPTER 23

There were clouds in the sky again, as there have been most days since she'd arrived. The sun tried valiantly to reach out to all those beneath its bright majesty, but was thwarted time and again by those cursed clouds. The sometimes harsh winds snatched away any warmth that might descend upon the earth, and with each step she took, Mari's entire body jarred at the impact with hard packed earth and stone. Travelling north from her homeland, she'd seen rivers so powerful their waters were forever white with foam and lakes so vast it would take a day to walk around them. Everything in the north was green and wet, cold and hard; it was a wonder the people here managed to survive in such a bleak place. This world simply did not feel right.

Mari gazed out the window, ensconced in an abandoned tower room from which she could see over the fields and forests to the mountains in the distance, their peaks brilliant white in a stray patch of sunlight. She told herself to ignore the draft and the ever present chill in her body, despite being cocooned in layers and layers of cloth. Lifting her unveiled face to the sky she strove to ignore the wind's bite.

She missed her homeland. Her eyes longed for the glistening gold sea of sand that stretched far and wide. Her skin yearned for the loving touch of the searing desert sun, and her ears, so sorely abused these past weeks, wished for nothing more than the absolute silence of a clear, moonlit night. But her heart, treacherous beast that it was, longed for something else.

Mari settled onto a hard bench, taking care not to lean against the cold stone wall at her back, and sighed softly, her gaze turning inward. Down a long, winding staircase, at the heart of this monstrous castle, the king slept fitfully in his grand bed. His brow glistened with sweat, though his skin was icy and his lips pale. He tossed and turned, crying out in fevered dreams, his mind as tormented as his body.

And he would not wake.

Mari had tried everything, every remedy she had ever learned from the women of her tribe, every foul smelling herb these northerners favored. But she knew nothing of his illnesses and could not help him, save to hold his hand.

The healers had come and gone. So had the priests. They spoke amongst each other quietly, as though they didn't mean for her to hear. In that way they were far worse than the men of her tribe who, in the absence of her royal father, treated her as though she didn't exist. As brazen and heedless as Aegiran men were with their words, so these pale-skinned northerners were secretive. They would not speak to her, lest their gaze was lowered as hers had used to be all the time, and Mari knew that they did this to spare her. For the truth was that they knew no more about King Saeran's illness than she, and they could no more advise her but to tell her to "cleave to him." Mari surmised it meant she should keep him company, hold his hand.

As a dutiful wife, she had sat by his side for days and days, at first in silence and then speaking to him, secretly relieved when he seemed to quiet at the sound of her voice. But then the illness had taken a turn for the worse, racking his body with horrible shaking fits which had sent many a maid fleeing.

And he had called out. Not for Mari. No, not for his wife who'd sat by his side and tended him, fed him broth, even held council with his advisors there in the sick room. Not for the woman who'd never before known anything but obedience yet was now expected to rule a kingdom until he recovered—if he recovered.

No, the fever stricken king had called for Nia, his voice tormented, as if his soul needed hers to be whole. At first Mari had understood, having heard of the great wizard who served as the king's advisor. A female advisor. The news had been so wondrous upon hearing that Mari could scarcely believe it. From what the others have told her, the wizard was so powerful she could appear out of thin air, from miles away, if the right person were but to call her name. She could heal almost any illness or injury, in people, animals, or the earth itself. Mari could almost believe this woman to be myth. How could any person, leastwise a woman, hold so much power?

She reminded herself to breathe as she once again pondered the amazing tales she'd heard. It was no wonder King Saeran called out to her; he had to know, even in this state, that Nia would be able to heal him.

But, of course, that was not why he called for her. Mari had not seen the wizard with her own eyes, but she knew her to be a beauty, one who walked tall, certain of her place among these people as their elder, despite being very young still. She knew, though people have tried to keep it from her, that there was a powerful bond between the advisor and her king. Only a fool would fail to see how each of the king's cries for her now echoed with soul rending grief—one that Mari recognized to be the result of cursed love.

It was why she cowered here, unable to stand hearing it any longer. Each time he called Nia's name, Mari cursed it, aching in her heart, her treacherous heart, to hear him call for her instead. It was not her place to want, she knew, but how could she not, when at every turn the king showed her kindness; strove time and again to convince her she was among a different people here. She was their queen now and ought not look down in front of anyone. He wanted her to speak her mind and seemed to truly wish to hear her thoughts, as if they were important to him.

He wanted her friendship, but no more. For in his heart he longed for his Nia the same way she longed for him. It was precisely why she kept silent, for it was futile to try for something Mari could never have. She would only gain his pity in the end, and, indeed, they were both to be pitied.

Mari's hand settled on her stomach and she sighed again, feeling a new life stirring within her. It seemed her midwife's fertility charm had worked its magic. Part of her rejoiced at the thought of cradling her child in her arms. But the other part of her died slowly to remember that its father would love it far more than her. King Saeran would welcome the babe, an heir to the throne and his own flesh and blood, but there would forever be only one woman queen to his heart, and Mari was not her. It was this cursed land that made her feel this way. In the desert she would have thought nothing of being one of a man's many wives. Why, then, did it pain her to be the only wife of a good man, a lofty station by anyone's standards, without his love?

The door creaked loudly in the cavernous room, and Mari jumped to her feet, fumbling with her veil to cover her face once more. Her heart raced with dread, and she prayed that it wasn't one of the healers come to bring her news of her husband's death. But it was Jasper's face that appeared when the door opened, his smile stretching across his stone face, a grotesque imitation of true happiness. "My queen," he said in greeting, though he did not bow, holding her gaze, expecting her to submit to him.

His presence, in the past so eerie and daunting, now angered her, and she straightened her shoulders to meet his empty gaze with confidence. His brows rose in surprise, though his smile never faltered. "I have come searching for you," he said, his voice at once smooth and sticky, like a camel's spit. "They told me his Majesty is not improving. I thought I would try to bring cheer with a trick or two." He spoke her language, as well as a native, but on his tongue the beautiful words sounded sullied.

Mari was in no mood to tolerate his presence. When he reached into his pocket for one of his "tricks," she stifled the urge to scream and brushed past him as grandly as she had seen King Saeran do so often. "I was just on my way to my husband's side," she told him, evading his touch as he reached out to stop her. "Find someone else to entertain with your play."

She felt a cold shiver run up her spine and knew he was watching her leave. Why had he stayed behind? The entire caravan, save her personal guard and hand maidens, had departed the very day after her wedding, yet Jasper refused to follow them. Mari supposed it was King Saeran's unfailing hospitality that made Jasper think he could stay as long as he wished. She would give him the moon's cycle to leave on his own. If he did not, she would have him removed. It was, like as not, his very presence that prevented the king from healing as he should.

A sharp pain stabbed through her belly and up to her chest. She had to stop and brace herself against the wall to stay on her feet. Cold sweat broke out on her brow and fear shivered through her, for her child as well as herself. But within moments the pain was gone and she could once more stand unaided.

Casting an apprehensive look behind her, she was glad that Jasper was nowhere in sight, but not willing to take the chance she hurried down the stairwell and to her king's bed chamber. There, at least, she felt safer.

But there, instead of fear, sorrow weighed on her ever more until she could do nothing other than what the healers had advised. Sit by him and hold his hand.

≪ »·◇·« ≫

By the time the knights joined them the painful effects of the dragon's blood had passed and Nia shoved off the rest of the animal furs in deference to the heat burning within her. Her cheeks warmed and her limbs strengthened until she felt sure she could run for miles without rest. The feeling of power was at once intoxicating and frightening. One little slip and she could do a lot of damage. It was as if she was nine again, just awakening her power and all that came with it. Only this time, she had no mentor to teach her how to control it.

"It is the wine," the dragon told her, ignoring the knights completely. "With my blood it weakened your guards. It will pass."

Nia believed him.

"What happened?" Lucca asked, the only one of his company not staring all around them. He reached out to her, but the dragon caught his hand, his eyes glowing with menace. "Do not touch her," he warned.

Nia was grateful for the intervention. Her skin felt unbearably sensitive, and she had a feeling that if she were to touch someone, she would not be able to stop the flood of knowledge from overwhelming her. Even at a distance she could feel the knights' confusion, their worry and anxiety. When Lucca spoke, his voice echoed in her mind as if she was hearing it twice. Nia had no doubt that with his touch he would unwittingly share every thought, sight, emotion and sensation.

"Nia," the knight said. "Are you well?"

"Much better," she replied with a nod, glancing at the dragon. *I know your name now,* she thought in surprise. He'd gifted her with his memories as well as his strength. And in the process left himself vulnerable to her.

His mouth quirked the slightest bit. *So you do.* There wasn't even a hint of worry in his mind-voice. *But do you know how to use it?*

"Can you travel?" Lucca questioned, still looking as if he wanted to reach out to her, but the dragon's closeness kept him wary.

"Yes, I can," Nia said, confident in her physical ability to ride, but unsure if she was ready to return to Saeran's side. To step into shadow once more and watch him smile at his queen the way she'd seen him do before, to become a spectre over their reign as she was bound to do—no, she wasn't keen on riding back to Frastmir with all haste. But for her king, she would.

"Then we should be on our way at once."

The dragon eyed him curiously. "You will not claim your treasure?"

Sir Frederick's gaze snared on the dragon, and Nia heard his breath catch. "So you do have it, then," he said in awe.

The dragon nodded and produced the cup he'd given Nia to drink from. When she would have expected their faces to fall in disappointment, their eyes grew wide with wonder. They knelt before dragon and cup, whispering a prayer and bowing their heads. She could see Lucca's jaw clench, and his eyes shimmer with unshed tears. He knelt with the others, bowing his head, but did not speak the prayer.

Behold, the dragon said inside her mind, *the power of a lone god's dominion. Willing or not they bow to him, not even knowing what he is.*

Can you help him? Nia asked on Lucca's behalf. His grief was so strong she was suffocating with it. How could he live each day with such a burden?

The dragon eyed her a moment, then transferred his sharp gaze to the knight in question. When he handed the cup to Sir Frederick and the knights huddled around it, each wanting to touch the sacred object, Lucca stayed behind, watching them. He was angry with them for their devotion to what he considered a cruel monster, yet at the same time envious of their unshakable faith. The dragon laid a scaly hand on his shoulder and coaxed the man to meet his gaze.

Nia didn't know what transpired in those silent moments when the two simply stared at each other, but after a while, Lucca's shoulders collapsed and he broke into wretched sobs.

Grief shared is grief lessened, the dragon said, his voice strange. Of all of them, he understood the best what Lucca had lost. And while he couldn't return those lives to him, he could at least help him heal. *A lesson you have yet to learn, child.*

Long after he'd composed himself as best he could, Lucca and the dragon remained removed from the rest of the company, deep in conversation. Nia didn't intrude. Instead, she kept the others engaged, asking questions of their god and telling stories she'd heard since childhood. A full night and day passed unnoticed in the dragon's den until, once more exhausted, the knights fell asleep.

While they slept, Nia pondered the strength of their faith. It baffled her. They spoke reverently of a god all good and noble, one who was everywhere, knew everything, and loved everything. He could work miracles, he was the creator of all, yet he didn't scorn those who turned their backs on him. Sins could be forgiven, enemies could be destroyed, and kingdoms could be saved with his power and his power alone.

They held fast to such silly beliefs, even while they had no proof. Save the cup. She held it again, now that it was empty, and felt none of the power that had thrummed into her hand while it was filled with wine and no more than three drops of the dragon's blood.

When she asked the dragon if their lone god could truly exist, he'd not given her an answer. Her people lived every day with the reminder of the gods who ruled them. Kind gods, fickle gods, gods who reveled in toying with people's lives. Gods who feasted on war, drenching the earth in blood. Gods who could bring a man back from the dead, grant him immortality and divine strength. Though one had never ventured into Wilderheim, stories of berserkers traveled to them from far and wide on the wings of messenger birds; on the wind itself. Beautiful maidens in shining armor walked the battlefields, choosing from among the fallen only the strongest, bravest, to take their place of honor in Valhalla.

To these knights, stories of her gods had seemed as strange as their god seemed to her. Perhaps it didn't matter what one believed in, but that they believed. Having someone to revere, or even fear, kept a person humble.

In the morning, when she walked out of the cave with the dragon and told him this, all he said was, "The mind feels what it needs to." Puzzled twice over, she tried to come up with her own answer as he led her over the frozen field to a sturdy stable she didn't remember having seen before. Inside the mounts happily chewed on clumps of hay, clean and warm, though they fidgeted when the dragon approached.

"You wish to ask me something," the dragon man said.

"Do you not already know what it is?" Nia asked, surprised.

He shook his head, gazing into the mount's eyes. "You grow strong with my blood. I can only get impressions now, unless you allow me entrance to your mind."

He seemed completely unperturbed about that. An ancient and powerful being, a dragon, had given her a weapon against him without batting an eyelash, and even now showed not a hint of unease, as if the mere fact that she was who she was should keep her from using it against him. How could he trust her so?

Or was it that Nia was so weak and puny that she posed no threat to him at all, even with the added strength of his own blood? That seemed far more likely and she nodded to herself, satisfied with her own conclusion for the moment.

"Ask already, I grow impatient."

"I wanted to see your true form."

He faced her then, something akin to surprise on his handsome face. "You have seen it. In my memories."

"But only through your own eyes and we never see ourselves as we truly are," she said pragmatically.

The dragon's mouth quirked. "Perhaps another time," he said. And before she could reply, he made his manner brisk and nodded to the horses. "I have procured mounts to replace the ones you have lost. You should start getting ready. They will not let me near them and the sun is rising. It is time you kept your promise."

CHAPTER 24

On a good night, the king slept undisturbed, lying still as death, his chest barely rising and falling with breath. On a good night, the priests and magic men and women lit black candles in his bedchamber, surrounded his bed and chanted prayers in ancient tongues, terrifying Mari and making her wish she had never come to this cursed place. Tonight wasn't a good night.

King Saeran screamed as if his soul was being torn out of him and Mari started awake from her slumber. She must have slept longer than she thought. The fire had died down to embers and she was chilled to the bone. Heart pounding, Mari rose from her hard seat by the hearth and went to her dying husband.

Saeran tossed and flailed on the bed, screaming louder than anything she'd ever heard from him. She caught his arm, but he shook her off so violently she fell to the floor. From there she watched her husband scratch at his neck and chest, still screaming. Helpless sobs tore out of her and she covered her ears to block out his cries, but it didn't help.

Guards and healers rushed in and took hold of Saeran's limbs to subdue him. They called his name, tried to tell him to stop, that he was safe, that they would get him well again, but the more they spoke, the more he thrashed and Mari couldn't stand it.

"Stop it," she whispered. Then louder, "Stop it. Stop it! *Stop!*"

Saeran's body bowed off the bed on a blood curling bellow: "*Niaaa!!*" The fire blazed to renewed life, and Mari screamed in fright. The guards and healers fell away from Saeran and she gasped. He was glowing. The fire didn't simply illuminate his sickly pale skin, it was inside him, burning beneath the surface like a lantern.

Saeran collapsed back onto the bed and the fire dimmed, in the hearth and inside him. Muttering prayers, calling on all the gods they could name, the healers approached him carefully and touched his skin.

Mari became light headed and sucked in a breath. She'd forgotten to do that. "Is he dead?" she demanded.

The healers looked to each other and shook their heads with sorrow. "No change," they proclaimed.

No change? Were they blind? Saeran had glowed!

Becoming aware of the noises behind her, Mari turned to see the servants spying through the open door. "Out," Mari commanded, picking herself up off the floor. "All of you out!"

The guards took charge, herding everyone back as the healers made their exit. The hallway cleared slowly, but just before the last healer closed the door, Mari saw Jasper standing there, smirking at her.

Shuddering, she quickly barred the door from the inside and backed away from it, all the way to Saeran's bed. There, she fell to her knees and prostrated herself, praying and begging her gods to have mercy; bargaining with them to demand whatever price they would of her, but spare the king she loved.

She cried and sobbed, pleaded and made promises she wasn't certain she could keep. She even prayed for Nia to return, for if anyone knew how to help him, the wizard was she. And when she finally ran out of words and tears, she became aware of noises coming from the bed. Whispers, harsh and broken.

Mari stood up and faced Saeran, watched his parched lips move to form the words, but she couldn't make them out. Drawing closer, she leaned in to put her ear almost at his mouth.

"...kissed you...time stopped...love you, Nia. Please...until death or longer."

Mari's heart broke at his words and she clutched her chest to soothe a pain almost too great to bear.

She kissed his brow, caressed his icy cheek and pulled the covers up to his chest. Feeling fragile as an eggshell, she went back to the hearth and stoked the fire until it blazed. It was for him more than Mari; the cold no longer bothered her. Nothing did anymore.

The maids had brought trays of food for them both. All of it sat untouched by the door, as it had all day long because Mari was too unsettled to eat a thing. She retrieved a bowl of broth and set it near the fire to warm while she adjusted the pillows beneath Saeran's head to raise him up a little.

Then she sat next to him and patiently fed him a spoonful at a time until he'd take no more. He must have been hungry. By the time she was finished, most of the broth was gone and very little had spilled. Mari cleaned Saeran up, settled him back on the bed and laid down next to him. She knew now what needed to be done.

Tomorrow she would write a message to her father. Saeran had fulfilled his duty to the *shansher*, and there was no more need to keep up this pretense. Whether he lived or not, there was no place for Mari in his heart or his kingdom. She didn't blame him; how could she? Saeran had been nothing but kind to her. But it wasn't enough. Her father would understand. He was a proud man, but not a heartless one.

He would take her in even if, by returning, she brought shame to the family. Mari could make her father see why she had to come back, but to everyone else she would forever be the abandoned wife, a cast out, pitied or reviled, never to marry again. Perhaps it was for the best. Mari didn't want another husband. All she wanted was a little tent of her own, far from prying eyes and wagging tongues, to live out her life in peace. She would fulfill her own duty to Saeran. She would stay by his side and nurse him until she gave birth to the child who would one day become a king or queen after him.

But once Mari was fit to travel, she would go back home where she belonged.

CHAPTER 25

Ten days after they rode out, the company of travelers came to the edge between the dragon's territory and the rest of the world, a clear line of demarcation across the land. It was at this border that the snow gave way to green grass in such a way that trees straddling it were half green and half barren. Nia spared it a brief glance as they crossed, noting absently that the transition hadn't seemed so sharp going the other way.

They rode at a slow, steady pace, rarely stopping for food or sleep. The knights might be in a hurry to return home as heroes now that they'd found their coveted cup, but Nia felt no such compulsion. Her mind was weighed with thoughts of what she had discovered. There was so much she had to tell Saeran, and knowing he wouldn't want to hear any of it made her as reluctant to return as the idea of meeting his young queen.

It hurt. More than it should, far more than the dragon's ordeal, the surety that her voice, no matter how needful, might fall on deaf ears hurt worse than any physical pain. Saeran was angry with her for having refused him and would turn to his queen for the advice Nia ought to give. The king knew his people, but Nia knew his lands.

She sighed. Fighting a battle with herself was useless. Of course she had a place at his side; she was a wizard. Nico had not chosen her for nothing. She was meant to advise the king and aid him, no matter how stubborn he was.

Nia held her hand out before her and gathered magic into her palm. Aided by the dragon's blood and her own emotion, the pool of light was red with a mixture of love and anger. It came to her so easily now she had to be careful not to draw too much. She watched the surface move like a lake, glistening pure. Curling her fingers, she tipped her hand sideways and let the power pour out. It laid a path in the air alongside her like a trail of fireflies.

When the last drop fell, she swirled her hand and the ribbon of red light curled in on itself to form a circle that kept spinning, following her progress down the little used forest path. She touched the bottom edge with a fingertip, pulling on it to alter the circle's shape. The dip she created filled up and formed a bubble. Then the bubble changed, sharpening at the edges into a five-sided disc, a pendant for the chain. When at last Nia was satisfied that all five sides were equal, she blew on the pendant, searing the shape of a dragon in flight into its surface.

Holding her hand out to her creation she whispered an ancient word of protection into its depths and sealed it. The finished pendant and chain dropped into her hand, formed in pure silver. Nia lifted it to the light to inspect her handiwork. The chain was heavy, as befitted something so elemental. As for the pendant, the dragon had ruby eyes and each visible fang was a diamond chip. The play of light over him gave the dragon an illusion of motion, as if he truly lived and the fire he breathed changed color like oil in water. It stayed warm to the touch, even after the rest of the pendant had cooled in the chill air.

The pendant was a work of art, mesmerizing and entrancing. A powerful tool. It could be used for any number of things, acting as protection, defense, enchantment, and warning. Whoever looked upon it would know at once that its wearer was not to be trifled with. It could be used to channel energy or create a living shield that could withstand any magical assault, except, perhaps, a true dragon's.

And to what purpose will you use this tool? The dragon's voice in her mind was unexpected but soft, unlike his earlier, painful trips into her thoughts.

I will give it to someone worthy of it, she replied. Stardust tossed his head, as if he felt the dragon's presence and didn't like it. She patted his neck to soothe him.

The dragon was silent for a moment. *It has been a long while since anyone has trapped dragon essence in an object,* he mused. *Even the little you used could be turned against you by one like me.*

You sound almost worried about me, she said, smiling to herself.

I worry for myself, he said and she got an image of his scowl. *If anyone harms you through it, I will have to intervene. Then everyone will know where to find me. I do not like this plan, not one bit.*

Then I will simply have to be more cautious when choosing its keeper.

Give it to Saeran. He'll wear it as well as anyone. And it will serve him well. Especially now.

Nia stilled at the odd comment. *What do you mean?* But she could already feel the dragon withdrawing. He would not answer her.

Sir Frederick rode up beside her. "My lady," he said politely, nodding a bow. "Perhaps we should stop for the night. The shadows grow long and the men are tired."

Though they rode slowly, they rode almost without cease. Nia couldn't feel her legs anymore and knew that as soon as she dismounted, she'd crumple to the ground. She looked at the other knights, noting the shadows beneath their eyes and the set expressions that hid any weakness they might feel. They were strong men, and brave. Perhaps they ought to stop.

But the worry she'd begun to feel would not leave her. Something was very wrong if the dragon felt the need to warn her of it. They were still three days' ride away from the nearest village, and from there two more to Frastmir. Did it matter?

Nia pulled Stardust to a halt. There was a small clearing sheltered by a rocky cliff. The wood was dry and the grass soft. This was a good place to rest for the night. Sensing her weariness, Stardust took her all the way to a tree so that she might use it to steady herself when she dismounted. "Thank you, my friend," she told him.

Sir Arnaud caught Stardust's reins as she dismounted, saying, "I'll care for the mounts."

Nia, holding on to the tree to keep upright, could only nod ascent.

By the time she could stand unaided, the others had gathered wood and tended the mounts. They only waited for her to join them and light the fire. The provisions the dragon had given them were laid out and ready to eat and Nia's mouth watered for the bountiful offering.

But she was too weary of sitting to join the others. Instead she lit a fire for them, took up her staff and an apple and went for a stroll to stretch her legs.

The dragon's words wouldn't leave her. Could Saeran be in trouble? Needing to get away, Nia had closed herself off from him completely, rendering even his calling spells useless. He could not have reached her, save by a messenger, and he would not have known where to send one. She'd left him completely stranded, without counsel or aid.

Regret stabbed at her, and she lifted the magical veil she'd cast over herself the day they rode out.

All at once her blood turned to ice. Saeran's calling tolled like a massive bell inside her, amplified each time it had fallen on deaf ears. It wrenched her out of time and space in a mad swirl of colors and darkness. Red for danger. Blue for cold. Black for oblivion.

Saeran was dying. She felt it as she spun end over end in a void where not even her voice would carry its frantic call. When she started falling, she braced herself, but even so her cloak tangled around her and she fell in a heap on the cold stone floor of Saeran's bed chamber.

A soft gasp. Hurried footsteps. Then delicate hands grasped her arm to help her stand. Nia was disoriented and dizzy and the entire chamber, with its dozens of candle flames dancing, spun and dipped around her. And all the while her heart thudded in her chest for herself as well as Saeran. Even with her hearing focused on the sound, his heartbeat was almost too weak to find and his breaths came too slow, too far apart.

"You come," the woman said in a heavily accented voice. The girl, the queen, was holding her upright. "Finally you come."

Nia made every effort to steady herself and slow her heartbeat. She wanted to ask what was wrong with Saeran, but her jaw was clenched against a wave of nausea.

The queen told her without being asked. "He fell ill with fever, but is not fever." When she couldn't think of the right words, she began speaking in frenzied sentences in her own tongue. Nia understood her perfectly. "He's cold as ice. We cannot warm him, and he will not wake. He called for you!" The accusation rang with despair and the small hands on her arms clenched as if to shake her. "He called all the time, and you would not come. You are supposed to help him! So help!"

Nia took a deep breath and reached out to something, anything, to steady herself. Her staff lay by the window, too far to reach. She didn't need it. The queen helped her to the bed and she sat heavily on the soft mattress. Next to her, Saeran didn't move. His breaths were shallow, and each was a sigh—her name. Tears stung her eyes. How many times had he called out to her and met with emptiness?

You know what to do, the dragon said in her mind, his voice banishing the dizziness.

At last, Nia was able to look up without the world spinning around her.

Her gaze fell onto the queen's young face. The girl was beautiful, with dark skin and big round eyes. She wasn't wearing a veil and her thick, raven hair fell to her hips, plaited through with golden adornments. She looked as if she'd been crying for days and hadn't slept for weeks. Her lips were bloodless and dry, not a good sign, especially with the babe in her womb already crying out for nourishment.

Nia's heart sank for the girl, and the child. She couldn't help either. "Eat something," she said.

The queen drew back in surprise at hearing her native tongue. "I cannot leave him," she said. "He needs me." In the small moment of silence that followed her words, Nia was pulled into the girl's thoughts and memories, and she came to understand how much Queen Mari had changed in the months since her arrival. The shy, fearful young maiden was gone. In her place was a true queen. She stood tall now, when before she had cowered. She spoke up, when she hadn't in the past, and she had ruled the kingdom during Saeran's illness. She'd done it well. So well, in fact, that nobody, save those closest to him, knew that Saeran was ill, maybe dying.

The queen squared her shoulders with steely resolve. "He needs you more. You will make him better."

Nia wasn't so certain.

But when the queen made her exit, she had no choice.

CHAPTER 26

The door closed. Nia shook all over, too scared to look at Saeran; scared she would see only a withered shell of the strong man she knew. Scared she wouldn't be able to heal him. Even now, listening to everything around her, she knew this was nothing she had ever seen before. The candles sang their sorrowful melodies.The walls mourned the dying king. The wolf's pelt pulled tighter around her, as if in encouragement.

Steeling herself against the stab of pain she knew was to come she turned her eyes on Saeran and sucked in a sharp breath at the sight of him. His hair was soaked with sweat, his eyes swollen and red, closed and still. He looked frozen, his skin pale and his lips blue. His beard had been shaven, revealing a gaunt face once so handsome. Blanket upon blanket covered him from the neck down, but she knew what they hid; a skeleton covered with skin.

"Saeran," Nia whispered, unable to believe this was the man she loved. She laid a shaking hand on his brow and gasped at how cold he was.

The noble king breathed in a true breath, his brows twitching as if he sensed her presence. Even his heart answered the touch, beating a little stronger.

Nia bit back her tears, struggling to her feet so she could examine him. She drew all but one blanket down to his waist, feeding magic to the hearth fire when he started shivering. Then she laid a hand on his chest and closed her eyes, Seeing with her essence into his.

Breath left her when she found the source of his illness. He was ensorcelled! A ball of sinister darkness, like a coiled spider's web glowed in his core, sending out tendrils that stretched into his entire body. It was in his heart and his mind, racking his body with pain and his thoughts with terror. He was too weak already to fight it much longer.

Nia drew back and opened her eyes. The spell was a powerful one, borne of several essences entwined together. How could that be? Who could wish such a thing on the king? And how could Nia have missed it?

It was too strong now, too deeply embedded in Saeran for her to draw it out. She would kill him in the process.

You know what to do, the dragon repeated, his voice revealing an uneasiness that frightened her.

The pendant won't be enough to banish this, she replied.

But it will allow me entrance.

Nia squared her shoulders, pulling the pendant from her pocket.

You do not hesitate? Even knowing what you will need to do, what it will do to you?

She lifted Saeran's head so she could put the chain around him. *I will keep him with me. Do what you must.* When the chain was in place, she removed the blankets, leaving him in nothing but his night shirt and the pendant. He hissed when she opened his shirt and placed the pendant in the center of his chest over the infection, his icy skin turning red around it as if burned.

Are you ready?

Nia took a deep breath, laying one hand over Saeran's brow, the other over the pendant. She closed her eyes and drew on all the magic she possessed, the dragon's power, and the light of her very soul. She held nothing back, pouring it all into Saeran to entwine her essence with his as tightly as she could, surrounding him. The cold, dark taint inside him made her shiver but instead of pulling back, Nia held on tighter, determined not to let him slip away. She nodded when she was done, knowing the dragon would see.

My blood will protect you, but not completely.

Do it now.

Very well, the dragon said after a small pause. *Do not let go.*

She felt the first wave of heat like a tendril of smoke winding around her and Saeran. It was no stronger than the heat of a hearth fire, but already Saeran bucked and she winced. The smoke twined around them until it created a cocoon from which the infection couldn't escape. Nia's hands shook, but she planted her feet and refused to move.

In the next instant, fire blasted the cocoon, blue and hotter than anything even Nia could conjure. It came rushing in through the smoke and became trapped inside it, just as Nia and Saeran were. Both screamed, and Saeran arched on the bed, every muscle in his body tight. His soul bucked, tried to escape her hold, but she wouldn't let it. He screamed and raged against her hold, begged and pleaded to be released from the scorching flames. Nia hardened her heart against his cries and held on.

And all the while the infection squealed like a living thing, burning like embers in a dying flame. Its tendrils pulled back into the mass at its core, giving it strength, and the fire intensified, determined to scorch every last bit of it.

Nia felt her flesh burning, giving way, but she would never show a sign of this torment on the outside, just like Saeran. Already his body was filling out, reclaiming the strength the infection had leeched from him. In a pained spasm, his hand shot to cover hers on his chest. She thought he might try to pull it away, but his fingers curled around hers, his magic mixing with hers, and he held on to her, gaining more strength and courage as the infection grew weaker and smaller.

The fire swirled around them, inside them in a vortex of blinding heat that drowned out their cries with its roar. The infection sparked and lashed out, trying to find another place to hide, to seed and grow anew. There was nowhere to hide.

Do not fight it, the dragon told her. *Give yourself up to the fire or it will burn you alive.*

Nia opened her watering eyes to squint through the flames at Saeran. His eyes were like mirrors, reflecting the blue fire, and for a moment she recognized in them that which had always been part of him—dragonblood. She managed a small nod and saw him grit his teeth. He squeezed her hand, then closed his eyes and did as the dragon had told them. Nia followed suit. She let the fire in, let it do with her as it pleased. The white hot flame cut off her cry, burned her tears away before they could fall. It embedded itself in her core, the place where the dragon's blood had merged with her life's essence.

But instead of searing her, it fed her strength. The burn turned to warmth, the transition so sharp that it weakened her and her knees almost buckled beneath her. She'd felt this before with the dragon's blood, knew what she had to do, but Saeran hesitated, refusing to accept it completely. It trapped the flame in his body, but outside of his soul, and it could do nothing but burn him. It was killing him as surely as the infection, and Saeran was frozen in uncertainty.

Let it in! she wanted to tell him, but couldn't make herself heard. Saeran was beyond hearing anything. He clutched her hand, fighting the terrible draw pulling him away from her, but it wasn't enough. He was slipping.

Nia cried out. She climbed onto the bed to kneel next to Saeran. *Please. Please do not fight me.* Then she leaned over him and pressed her lips to his, forcing the fire that had become part of her into him through a kiss. The door it opened was small, but it was enough. She felt Saeran gasp against her lips as the flame bonded with him completely. As if awakened from deep slumber, his own fire flared and joined the dragon's, and together they burned brighter, hotter, searing the infection until nothing remained but ash, and then not even that.

The dragon pulled back as soon as it was safe to do so, leaving Nia and Saeran shaken and cold without the fire's heat, but safe. Nia sat on her heels to keep from falling on top of Saeran. Head swimming, eyelids heavy, she was moments away from passing out.

Faint voices intruded, guards and healers entering the chamber. Though her eyes were open, she couldn't make sense of what she was seeing. There were only colors and lights dancing before her, making her dizzy and tired.

Something brushed her cheek. Someone said her name.

Strong arms closed around her and then everything went black.

Nia collapsed against Saeran and for a moment the shock of waking up to see her there turned into blind panic that the fever had passed from him to her. But Saeran felt her breath puff against his skin, heard her heart beat.

He clutched Nia to him, his heart thudding in his chest as it hadn't done in weeks. His limbs were weak, his body still stinging with the memory of fire, but there were no scars on his skin. He felt stronger than he ever had in his life, and knew it had little to do with the fire the dragon had lent him. How Nia had managed to find a dragon, let alone persuade him to help Saeran, he would never know and, at the moment, didn't care. She was back in his arms, and this time he wasn't letting her go.

His hands were clumsy, but he managed to pull on the ties of her cloak and take it off her shoulders. The wolf skin left her with a caress as if it still lived, and it stayed on the bed when the cloak slid to the floor.

"Your Majesty," one of the healers said, breathless, as if he couldn't believe his king's rapid recovery.

"Leave," Saeran said, surprised at the strength of his own voice.

"But your Majesty—"

"Now."

They left. The door closed again, shutting out the murmurs and grumbles and outlandish rumors being born while the chamber filled with the soft music of candle flames and whispered secrets, a lullaby to ease Nia's slumber.

Saeran smiled down at her sleeping in his arms. He arranged the pillows behind him so he could sit against them, then settled back with his beloved wizard in his lap and laid his cheek against the top of her head. In the morning, he would ask her what happened, where she'd gone, and how she'd gotten back. He would ask about the dragon and her quest, and the chain he now wore about his neck. But for the moment, he was more than happy to simply be. Saeran closed his eyes and, with the dragon's fire still burning inside him, warding away the chill of death, allowed healing sleep to claim him as well.

In his dreams, he soared high above mountains and streams, playing among the sun-warmed clouds. And wherever he flew, though he couldn't see her, he felt Nia at his side.

CHAPTER 27

Mari walked out into the courtyard, wandering toward the kitchens. She had no appetite, but for the child's sake she would eat as the wizard had told her.

The sounds coming from the king's chamber were horrible. It was as if a great thunderstorm had become trapped there. Things were crashing, guards, priests, and healers shouting and running to lend assistance. They didn't yet know their efforts were of less use now than they had been before the wizard returned.

Now that she has, Mari knew precisely why the king adored her so. The wizard was a beauty beyond beauty, and her eyes were ancient with knowledge so profound that mere humans could never grasp it. Mari was a creature of the desert, of hot sands and burning sun. The wizard had been created from air and water, at once mysterious and familiar. Where Mari was a shadow, a ghost, the wizard shone like a star, guiding and brilliant.

How could the queen ever compete with such a creature? She, who had not even been born here, when the wizard seemed part of the land itself. And she was as much part of the king.

The queen steeled herself not to sigh. The king would recover, that much she now believed. And when he did, he'd have the wizard at his side without cease to ensure he would not fall ill again. And Mari would fade into the background, into their shadow, as had always been her fate. It was useless to fight it. She'd been reared to defer to others, why should she have come to believe that would ever change?

She paused beneath the stone archway, in shadows cast by her castle home. Mari didn't envy the wizard her magics. Aegiros had its own magic men and women, and she had seen them struggle for years on end to learn how to channel the will of the gods. They could do much harm before they learned. Many did not survive at all; the terrible power turned on them with such force no one could stop it.

Mari had no magic of her own, but she could sometimes feel it in others. The wizard Nia was far more powerful than any other she had ever met. Yes, the wizard would heal Saeran, of that she had no doubt. But even now, through the din and noise inside his chamber far above, Mari could hear their pained screams, and she shuddered to think about what was happening in there. The wizard was welcome to her gifts. Mari had no desire for them, or the pain that came with them.

Someone fell through an open doorway across the courtyard. Mari started and, remembering she had not veiled herself, shifted deeper into the darkness. But she kept watch in case she was needed. The man on the ground curled in on himself, groaning, then shot straight and arched as if he was a puppet being moved by some greater force. He cried out in pain, echoing the screams within the castle.

Mari was about to go to his aid, but then his fingers curled to claw at the hard packed earth as he thrashed. His body smoked, though Mari could see no flames. The sight frightened her; she recognized the workings of evil spells even from this distance and hid behind the corner. The wail he let out terrified her. It shifted like some demon from the depths of hell, as if several voices cried out from a single being.

And then his appearance began to change, flickering between short-haired youth and a shriveled, gray-haired mass. He was ancient one moment, a woman the next, then a man, his body contorting in ways that made him writhe in agony.

He clawed at his chest and then tore away a chain with a heavy pendant, flinging it aside. But it would not leave him. It slid back toward him until it was in his hand once more, glittering in the night like a black star.

Mari whispered a soft prayer of protection. Whatever the wizard was doing, it was affecting this creature, and there could only be one reason for that.

She ran into the kitchens and closed the door before the man-demon could rise and sight her. Her heart raced and her belly ached with fear. A brave woman would have stayed to discover who had poisoned her king. A strong woman would have confronted him, regardless of the danger to herself. Mari was neither.

Another of those sharp, burning pains stabbed through her, and she collapsed into a chair, fighting the darkness threatening to overwhelm her. Something was wrong with her. The pain in her womb was a bad portent and fear for her unborn child made her shiver.

When the wizard finished with the king, she would ask her aid. Surely, if Nia helped the king, she would help Mari as well. All she wanted was for the child to be safe.

But there was to be no speaking to the royal wizard.

When Mari felt strong enough to stand once more, her gown came away from the chair soaked. The last thing she saw before she fainted was the pool of blood where she had sat a moment ago.

<< »·◇·« >>

Ali al-Hassan, third son of the third son of Melorn the True, loyal warrior of *shansher* Dhakir the Conqueror, and faithful servant and protector of *shensari* Mari of the North could not sleep. He had stood his watch from sunup until sunset, guarding his *shensari* and her husband as was his duty. Now it was his time to rest, yet he could not.

The *shensari* was troubled. She would not rest or eat while her husband lay dying, and it was beginning to take a toll on her. It was no good for her to do this, especially now that she was with child. For her sake Ali wished the king's torment would end, one way or another. No warrior wanted to die in such a way. There was no honor or glory in withering away from disease. A man should die by blade or arrow. In battle, protecting his family, serving his *shansher.*

If the *shensari* would allow, Ali would end the king's life the honorable way. But she loved him and would not hear of it. And so she tended him day and night and prayed for his recovery, while the rest of them guarded day and night and prayed for her well being.

A great noise erupted in the castle. Ali drew his sword but saw no enemy to slay. The noises were like a terrible demon dervish raging inside the castle, striking fear into his soul. He retreated, though he kept a watchful eye for the *shensari*. When he saw her strolling in the courtyard, he was relieved.

Sheathing his sword, he turned the other way toward the stables. No matter that these people were so strange, they bred magnificent horses and cared for them quite well. Their stables were clean and well tended, their horses never wanted for food, and no rider was allowed to mount one without proper gear.

Ali liked horses. They always soothed his troubled mind.

Tonight, even the animals were disturbed by the noise. A small mare snorted in her stall, stomping her hooves and shaking her head. The male next to her kicked back at the wall, his eyes wide with fear. A new mother nosed her little one who cowered against her side, hiding his head beneath her neck. Ali shuddered and stroked a beautiful steed's neck, pretending he did not hear.

But then someone screamed outside, and that he could not ignore. Drawing his sword once more, he ran toward it and burst through the kitchen door to see the *shensari* falling to the ground. "Mari!"

Ali caught her, saw all the blood, and his bones turned cold. He shook her, called her name, but she would not wake. "Help," he called. "Help! Someone!"

No one answered. Ali scooped her body into his arms, terrified at how small and light she was. He carried her outside to where they all slept, bellowing for his comrades. "Hamdan! Bakri! Najjar! *Shensari bahran sephri!*"

They came running, as they'd been trained. Hamdan took one look at the *shensari* and swore a vile oath. "Fetch the midwife," he ordered Najjar. "Bakri, help me."

They cleared one of the beds and laid their mistress upon it. Hamdan lit candles for light and Bakri gathered linens and rags. None of them would dare touch her skin; to see her face bare was bad enough. But Ali was most worried about how pale she was, how bloodless her lips. She had been cold in his arms before and now she would not stir at all.

When Najjar returned with the midwife and Mari's hand maiden, the men left the room and let them tend her.

"Who did this?" Hamdan demanded.

"I saw no one," Ali answered, though he wasn't certain himself. His main concern had been the *shensari*. He had not searched for whoever might have harmed her.

"Could it be the babe?" Bakri said. "My sister lost a child once. I was the one who found her. It was much the same as the *shensari*, but Sibaal was awake, and she was in great pain."

They stood in silence awhile. Ali did not know what to say. If it was as Bakri said, then the *shensari* was blessed to have fainted rather than endure such pain. But that she would not wake worried him.

The midwife, Wurud, came out then. Her gaze was downcast and she would not look at any of them.

"What is it, woman? Speak!"

"It is not good."

"What do we do?"

Wurud looked at Ali, met his gaze, and he could see tears in her eyes. "Pray," she said.

Ali met eyes with Hamdan and saw the same helpless anger in him as well. There had to be a villain to slay for this. Ali intended to find him.

With a curt nod, he stalked back to the kitchen where he'd left his sword. The sight of his *shensari*'s blood on the floor made him sick to his soul, but he steeled himself. He was a warrior. He would do what he did best. Kill the enemy.

He was headed for the opposite door when it opened and a man stumbled in. He looked as if he'd gone through a great battle, barely keeping his feet under him. Gasping for breath, he reached for a chair but seeing the blood on it thought better of sitting. "Is the bitch dead?" he rasped, his voice almost unrecognizable.

But Ali knew this man. Or thought he did. "You? You did this?"

The man harrumphed and groaned. "Then she lives. Pity."

Incensed, Ali roared his rage at him, brandishing his sword.

The man only laughed.

Ali charged him, ready to take his head but with a wave of his hand, the man sent him flying back. And still he laughed.

Ali got back to his feet, his sword arm shaking. What witchery was this? He came forward a second time, intent on the demon despite his fear. For his *shensari*, he would do this. He would kill the demon and avenge her.

Laughing harder, the man pointed a finger and Ali's sword clattered to the ground. Baffled, Ali looked down at the weapon and then at the hand which used to hold it. It was gone, his wrist turned to ash. And the ash was spreading up his arm.

Gods help me, he prayed, watching his other arm disintegrate. There was no pain, only fear, and the feeling of his self falling apart, body and soul. When he fell to the ground, desperate prayers slipped past his lips, useless whispers no one would ever hear. No one would ever know who he was or how he'd died.

His last prayer was for his *shensari*, that she wake and heal, and live a happy…

CHAPTER 28

Nia woke to Saeran's call. She opened her eyes, though they wanted to stay closed, and rose to her elbows. She was in Nico's study. How she got there, she didn't know, nor how much time had passed since she'd collapsed. Her head pounded and every bone in her body ached. Her legs would not support her and without her staff, she had to brace herself against the walls and table to stay on her feet.

Someone had dressed her in a night gown. She didn't care. With a swirl of her hand she hoped to conjure clothes, but nothing happened and the action only made her sway more. She leaned precariously to the side and took the blanket that had covered her, draping it over her shoulders for warmth. There was no time to waste. Saeran's call came again, stronger than the first one, which had somehow managed to wake her from a wizard's sleep.

It gave her strength enough to make her way to the staircase, but she was forced to crawl up to the courtyard. She was winded and shivering by the time she made it there. *What is happening?* she thought to the dragon, but was too weak to reach him. There was no answer.

"Micah," she called softly, willing her voice to carry to the stables. That much, it seemed, she could manage. The boy came out frowning, looking around for the person who had disturbed him from his duties. When he spotted Nia, sitting against the wall, his eyes widened and he came running.

"What's happened?" he asked, helping her up and then holding her up when she couldn't stand on her own.

"Don't know," she said. "Need to get to the king."

"Aye, then, at once," Micah said with a nod and turned toward the royal chambers. "Would you have me carry you?" he asked when her dragging feet snared on a stair.

Nia shook her head. "Dignity, my friend," she told him, attempting a smile. "I would like to keep what little I have left." Her words were slurring. She didn't have the strength to speak with her usual authority.

"You turned the castle upside down night before last. Brought a dying king back to roarin' life. There's much dignity to be flaunted."

The assurance made her feel little better. A full day and night she'd been unconscious, and should have stayed that way longer to heal completely. Her chest still ached from the dragon's fire, and the memory of it made her skin sting and burn. It was too much too soon. Whatever Saeran wanted of her, she was sure she wouldn't be able to grant. Not in this state. And knowing he wouldn't have summoned her for any trifling matter, she dreaded what awaited her.

There was a crowd gathered before the queen's bedchamber. Nia planted her feet, stopping Micah's progress. Every healer she knew was standing before her, chanting and praying, looking at her with both hope and defeat. She smelled incense burning inside, heard the walls whispering, but couldn't make sense of any of it.

She didn't need them to know what the matter was.

Two armed Aegiran warriors guarded the door and between them, a woman draped in all white, a veil hiding her entire face.

Nia squeezed her eyes shut as sorrow overwhelmed her.

"You are weak still," the healer Padraig said as he approached. "We can aid you in this."

She shook her head weakly. "It will not help."

The man's eyes flickered to the queen's chamber door and then back to her and he paled. Bowing his head, he returned to the others and told them something that made everyone quiet. They turned to Nia, expecting something she could not give them. Miracles, perhaps, or an explanation. But they could plainly see she was at death's door herself. What the dragon had wrought to heal Saeran would have destroyed her had his blood not been in her veins. As it was, it had nearly done her in, and she had a long ways to go to recover her strength and magic.

The queen would not last long enough for that.

"Nia."

She looked up at Saeran. The king stood in the doorway of his wife's chambers, looking pale and tired, but otherwise hale. His hands were clenched at his sides and his eyes, more than anything, revealed his soul's struggle. He didn't want to ask this of her, but he had no other choice.

He didn't yet know.

The Aegirans made way for Saeran as he came to Nia and took over for Micah, helping her the rest of the way into the queen's bedchamber. "She's fallen ill. I think…I think it was because of me."

Nia took in the queen's still form, lying in the middle of a bed that dwarfed her already small frame. She looked so young and serene, so close to slipping away. "Your illness did not cause this," she said with difficulty. Her eyes stung, though she could not shed a tear.

"Then, you can help her?" She could tell Saeran struggled to keep his voice even. He might not love his queen, but he cared for her very much. She was under his protection and had ruled in his absence. The affection he held for her was obvious.

Though it broke her heart, she shook her head, no. She could not voice the word.

"Are you too weak? The healers can aid you. They can lend you their strength. If you can heal her, then you must!"

"Saeran, I cannot," she whispered, unable to look at him. "Nothing I could do would save her."

"Why?" he demanded. "The healers said she is…bleeding. What is wrong with her?"

Nia's shivers became too much and she fell against him, unable to support herself any longer. Saeran helped her to a chair and then knelt before her, catching her hands in his. "You can help her, I know you can," he said, and every word he spoke was a dagger in her soul. "You are the greatest wizard I have ever heard of. What could be wrong with her that you cannot heal?"

Nia looked at the bed once more. *I am sorry,* she whispered to the queen, hoping the girl would hear her, though she was too far gone already. The girl was too young. Her body too weak to care for the essence of a dragon, no matter how far removed. The child demanded too much that the queen could not provide. It was draining her.

"She is dying."

The words, spoken on a whisper, shuddered through the chambers, silencing the walls.

A log split in the hearth, startling them both, but neither said a word.

The Aegiran guards stepped into the chamber with the woman, Mari's midwife, chanting a quiet dirge for her mistress. They couldn't have heard Nia's quiet admission, but only a fool would need to hear the words to see the truth of them.

Saeran was such a fool. Against everything telling him otherwise, he'd hoped Nia could work just one more miracle. He could see in her eyes now how wrong he had been, and his face grew cold, all the blood drained out of it. He let go of her hands and forced himself to his feet; locked his knees when he would have fallen to them again. Back to Mari's bedside he went, where he'd sat for an entire day, watching her breathe. Strange, he could feel vibrant life inside her, even as he was watching her die. "She did this for me," he said. "I do not remember much, but I remember she was with me."

"I should have been here," Nia said.

"Hamdan told me one of their own is missing. A man named Ali. He disappeared the night she fell ill." The night Nia had returned to save his life.

"Are you blaming him?" she asked them, but the Aegirans didn't know her and would not answer.

Saeran shook his head, surprised that his voice was so steady; that he could speak at all. "They think someone or something hurt Mari, and that Ali died trying to protect her. But no one knows anything for certain. There were no witnesses."

"Your Majesty," Padraig said, braving his way between the warriors into the chamber. "What will you ask of us?"

Saeran didn't know what to say.

"Help me up," Nia said. With Padraig's help she came to Saeran and held out her hand. "I don't know what this might do, if anything. But I am willing to try if you are."

The midwife fell silent and rushed forward. "What will you do?" she demanded, the first sentence Saeran had heard her speak.

"Whatever I can," Nia replied, but her eyes were on Saeran. Because she was too weak to do anything, but Saeran wasn't.

He took her hand without hesitation.

The midwife hurried around the bed to the other side and took Mari's hand in hers as the warriors came closer. "I will feel what you do," she warned. "If harm comes to my *shensari,* there will be retribution."

Nia nodded her understanding and then looked to Saeran. "Do not let go," she said, closing her eyes.

Saeran felt a tug on his heart, Nia drawing strength out of him, through herself, and into Mari. Her hand was over Mari's belly and her unborn child, and for a moment he could almost feel it. That tiny spark of life was so bright it stunned him. So strong, eager for all that life had to offer. As Saeran's strength poured into it, it grew brighter, stronger, and he heard a cry worthy of a warrior in his mind.

But even as he did, Saeran felt himself grow weaker. He swayed on his feet, almost let go of Nia's hand, but she held him fast, drew a little more on his strength.

With a gasp, Mari opened her eyes.

The warriors cried out, rushing forward to witness the miracle for themselves.

"Gods all bless," Padraig whispered, reaching for the queen, but without his support, Nia's legs gave out and her hand slipped from Mari.

Saeran felt the connection break, watched his wife and queen blink twice at the ceiling and then release the breath she'd taken and close her eyes. He felt her soul fade away, and the child's followed. He knew when the midwife wailed her grief, falling to her knees by Mari's side that his queen was gone.

Saeran collapsed on the floor next to Nia.

"It would have taken…that," she said, struggling to form the words and he knew they were all listening, all but the poor, heartbroken midwife lost in her grief. "Constantly, all the days until the child's birth…just to keep her heart beating. I am sorry, Saeran. I'm so sorry. I could not have saved her."

Saeran pushed to his shaky legs. "Padraig," he said, his voice hoarse. "Assist the wizard to her chambers. And have…have the priests take care of the queen."

"No," one of the warriors growled. "We will tend to the *shensari*. She is one of ours. We will look after her."

Padraig looked to Saeran, and he nodded his ascent.

He didn't know how he managed to walk to his chambers; wasn't aware of anything going on around him. People spoke, but he heard no words, only the buzz of their voices. They touched him, but he could not feel their hands. The door slammed shut, closing him away from everything out there, and then his world plunged into total silence and he was alone.

Completely and utterly alone.

CHAPTER 29

The funeral pyre burned higher than the tallest trees, but the smoke curling up toward the sky was white. Pure, as the queen had been. Her personal guard, three strong men who had not uttered a word since she died now roared their grief as they beat their chests. They had seen the queen born, had stood guard over her from that moment until she'd breathed her last. She'd been more than a queen to them. The three guards mourned Mari as if she'd been family. No longer did they refer to her by the formal title of *shensari*. If they spoke of her at all, she was always *idrah* Mari. Dear one, beloved.

One after the other, each unsheathed his sharp, curved blade and pulled it across his cheek, drawing blood. It was a sign of great devotion and grief. They stood so close to the flames their skin was beginning to turn hot, yet they would not move until the last embers were cold. This was their final duty to their queen. They would take her ashes back to their homeland and scatter them across the vast desert planes so she might always feel the sun on her face and the hot sand beneath her feet.

There was to be no feast this day. Though it was custom here to celebrate when a person returned to their ancestors, the Aegirans practiced the opposite and would be offended if they saw the kingdom rejoice at the queen's death.

Nia watched everything from where she would not be in the way. In Nico's study, she felt safe from reproach, but not guilt. Whenever her window spell showed her Saeran, standing still and silent at the edge of the gathering, she could think of nothing but the look on his face when she'd told him the queen would die.

He had not argued, cajoled, or threatened. He'd simply looked into Nia's eyes and read the truth of her words there. Then he'd turned away from her and gone to the queen's bedside to sit with her and hold her hand so she might pass peacefully. He'd not said a word to her when the queen died. He'd not even looked at her again.

And so Nia had returned here and mourned the queen by herself, in too much pain to sleep again.

She had not slept the wizard's sleep yet, though it weighed on her every waking moment. She was still weak, only capable of working the most basic of spells. Nia would not risk Saeran's safety now. When she was in the wizard's sleep, she couldn't perceive the world, nor react to it, more vulnerable than anyone else. And now that she knew someone wished Saeran harm, she couldn't take the chance they would strike again while she was helpless to stop them. It would mean a much longer recovery, but what choice did Nia have?

The gathering was breaking up. The villagers descended from the hill, slowly returning to their homes, the healers and priests following after one last prayer. The knights, now returned from their quest, came after them, once again asking about the wizard. They wished to thank her, but Nia was in no shape to see them. They would leave on the morrow and, having found what they'd sought, never again cast their gazes north.

Saeran was the last to turn away. His face showed no emotion, but his step was heavy as he followed the path toward the castle, leaving the Aegirans behind.

Nia watched his progress until he reached the castle's gate. When she was sure he was safe within, she turned away from the window and let it dissolve into firefly sparks to scatter into every corner of the chamber. Nico's magic still lingered here, and Nia now thought he'd left it to make sure she was never weakened completely.

She had yet to draw on any of it. Its presence was a comfort she didn't want to relinquish, and as soon as she absorbed one pocket, she knew it would be gone forever. Nia might never call on that power now. She needed the reminder of her mentor, however faint. *I am tired, Nico,* she thought, wishing he could hear her.

The door groaned open, admitting the king. He paused just inside, hesitating. Then he closed the door behind him and joined her at the table. Though they sat opposite each other, neither of them moved or looked up, and the silence stretched on while they seemed suspended in time. There was some comfort in that. They could still be in the same room this way without feeling the need to escape. She'd feared otherwise.

"Did you know?" Saeran finally asked, his voice soft and unsteady. "When you sensed her caravan approaching, did you know then?"

"I knew there was a chance..." Words failed her. Would he even believe her? Suddenly the whole idea of looking into the future disgusted her. "Chances, probabilities, that is all the future is. There are always risks. But they change with every blink. A thing so small as pausing to greet a friend could change the rest of a man's life." Nia splayed her hands on the surface of the table, tracing a groove. "There was a chance she would meet with disaster. There was also a chance that the rest of us would. I didn't...I didn't know it was a certainty until it was too late."

He gave a slight nod, but made no other move, still staring at the floor. "Why did the dragon help me?"

"You are his grandson," she told him without skirting it. "Dragonblood is in your veins. That is why you can master spells more easily than others. Magic is part of you."

Something flickered in his eyes. "Then why did he not help Mari?"

Nia drew a bracing breath. This was what she'd been dreading. "Mari would have died in childbirth, had she survived this. You would have had an heir, but lost your queen."

"Why? Why is that a certainty? Stop hedging, wizard, and tell me!" His hands curled into angry fists, but he still would not look at her, as if he wanted to spare her his wrath. He was not angry at her, she realized, but at himself.

"Mari was too young," she said with difficulty, "far too young and unprepared for any child. She had been weakening for weeks because her body could not sustain both her and the babe, and she tired herself out more caring for you."

"So it is my fault."

"No! Saeran, she loved you. I…would have done the same."

Saeran shoved to his feet, making her flinch. "Go on," he demanded. "Tell me the rest, I know there is more. With you, there always is."

Nia clasped her hands together. "Human vessels cannot carry dragonblood," she said. Not knowing how to temper her words, she repeated to Saeran what the dragon had said to her. "Dragon essence, no matter how diluted is too powerful. It needs magic to feed on, and in its absence, it drains its mother's life to save its own. If Mari had survived this, the birth would have killed her."

"Enough," he rasped, plunging his fingers into his hair as he paced around the chamber like a caged animal. His chest rose and fell in harsh breaths, and his jaw was clenched so tightly she could hear his teeth grind against each other.

When he came back to the table he lashed out and sent the water pitcher flying with an angry swipe. It flew end over end, but though it stopped at the wall upside down, it neither fell, nor spilled its contents. It was not Nia's doing.

"Why would my father not warn me of this?" he asked, staring at it. That, more than anything Nia said, proved the truth of what she was telling him.

"He did not know," Nia answered. "Your mother never told him. She was half dragon and must have hoped it would give her strength enough to survive. She died before she could tell anyone."

The pitcher fell and Saeran's head lowered. "You are telling me I cannot take another wife. I can never have heirs without sacrificing the woman's life." He was no fool. Though he wished he could argue, to call Nia a liar, he felt the truth of what she told him. Something had changed him, though whether it was the cursed illness or the dragon's fire Saeran couldn't tell. But whatever it was, it awakened a fire inside him he'd never felt before. The bright, shining flame gave him strength as he'd never known and enhanced his senses beyond anything Nia had ever taught him.

He no longer strained to hear the elements or summon a vision; they came to him for the asking. When he slept, he dreamed visions so sweet he was loath to open his eyes in the morning. Saeran had only to think of what he needed and it appeared before him as if summoned and earlier, standing witness to Mari's funeral, he thought he'd glimpsed white shadows moving among the crowd. The Others had been in attendance. While he embraced the changes within him, they also sometimes frightened him.

And so he understood what Nia was telling him, and it nearly killed him. He mourned Mari as a friend and companion. She hadn't deserved to die at all, let alone because of him—and no matter what Nia said, it was his fault and his alone. From the moment he made the pact to end the war, to the moment he took her to wife and gave her a child, all his fault. Each and every one of the choices leading to her demise had been his and he would have to live with that for the rest of his life. He ached and missed Mari.

But he had never felt for her what he did for Nia.

The wizard was the very beat of his heart. She was why Saeran lived.

But if there had been boundaries between them before, they'd been nothing compared to this. He'd rather die than risk her life.

When Nia didn't answer, a memory suddenly struck him and he turned rigid with fear. Beltaine night. Saeran forced himself to face her, though everything in him resisted broaching the subject. "You would," he said, then had to clear his throat to continue. "You would know if you were with child, would you not?"

Nia blinked up at him as if the thought had never occurred to her. She nodded. "I can control that. Prevent myself from conceiving."

Relief made him sway dizzily and he took a chair, closer to her this time. Her eyes were bright and her posture slumped. "I can see how weak you are." And he knew it was because she wouldn't sleep, though she desperately needed it.

"I am well enough," she replied, but the smile she attempted only made her condition that much more obvious.

"Sleep, Nia," he told her. He didn't like seeing her vulnerable this way. He'd give her his strength, the way she'd tried to give it to Mari, taking none for herself, but Saeran knew without asking that she wouldn't let him. He knew because the walls grumbled to him day and night about the magic she poured into them for protection. Someone had tried to kill the king, and the last thing she would do was take from him and leave him vulnerable.

"Can't leave you unguarded," she said, rubbing her forehead. "The spell that was cast on you was no trifling matter. If there is another attack while I am sleeping, I will not be able to protect you."

Hazy memories of a glittering object and incoherent words floated across his mind. It would make sense that someone had enchanted him. Saeran had always been strong and healthy. He'd not have succumbed to an illness so easily. But the healing Nia and his dragon grandfather had performed had wiped away any memory he had of his attacker.

Saeran tugged on the silver chain around his neck to pull the dragon pendant out from beneath his shirt. He wore it next to his skin now, sensing its power as he could his own. "This might do a passing fair job of it," he told her.

Nia smiled a little and reached out to trace the dragon's image. "It likes you."

Saeran caught her hand and brought her palm to his lips. "Sleep, Nia. I need you strong if I am to rule forever and without heir." The ease with which he spoke the words gave him pause. How quickly he'd given up a future with a wife at his side and children bouncing on his knees.

But he realized he didn't regret the loss. He still had Nia. Until death or longer. The words bound them both better than any marriage ceremony devised by man or god. He had Nia by his side now. Nothing mattered more.

Nia frowned, gazing at the swinging pendant, and he felt it grow hot enough to warm the chain it hung from. She looked entranced by it, her shoulders slumping a little more. "I am a wizard," she mumbled.

"Yes, the greatest wizard Wilderheim has ever seen. And the prettiest. Now let's get you to bed."

"Of the Streams, he said."

"Who said, sweet?"

"The dragon." She struggled to raise her gaze to look him in the eye. "He knew things even I don't. He said *of the Streams.* I was not…paying attention…" Her eyes closed, but she shook her head to wake herself up again.

Losing patience with his stubborn wizard, Saeran picked her up, tucking her against his chest. "Enough of this, Nia. You will sleep whether you want to or not. I order you to sleep. And I am king." He felt her smile against him and his own lips twitched in answer.

"Can't let you walk about alone," she murmured sleepily.

"Then I will just have to stay close to you."

"I could send you away."

He laughed as he laid her on the bed. "Try it."

And she did. But either he'd grown too strong for her to command, or she was too weak to force him away.

Saeran grinned at her attempts to banish him and pulled the covers over her. "Give up?"

Nia scowled. "Stubborn royals." He felt her magic flare again, creating a bubble that expanded until it melted into the walls. Once the guards were raised, added to the ones already in place, he doubted he would be getting out again until she took them down.

Saeran couldn't say it bothered him overly much. He kissed her on the brow. "Sweet dreams, Nia."

She sighed, already fast asleep.

CHAPTER 30

There were shadows, and within them pools of darkness so thick they could hold portals to other worlds. It was through these secret, sacred doorways that a pale, red haired creature chose to travel. He was not one for fanfares or great processions. No, he preferred to remain unobserved when he watched the seeds of his mischief bloom and bear fruit. He uncurled his long bony fingers to watch the lines on his hands change yet again.

Destiny for ones like him worked in odd ways. Nothing was ever set in stone; no eternal pathway lay ready to be walked for always. Only those with an end got the pleasure of reaching it. He cocked his head to the side, black eyes narrowing when the pendulum of his fate swung wildly to settle in an unexpected way.

Merely by appearing here, he'd changed his destiny. His temporary destiny. The darkness that had been spelled out in the center of his palm, the centuries of pain and destruction, the end of all things he'd been foretold to cause were suddenly gone. In their place now lay mist. Balance. A point from which he could move either way.

The legendary Trickster found this new turn of events unnerving. Crossroads and convergences could be distorted, but when there was a clear, straight path, he had nothing to play with. Left to his own devices this way, he usually chose to cause more mischief. It didn't suit him to have a reputation for doing good deeds when plagued with indecision. Faced with such a decision, and the choice he always made, his destiny tended to change instantly, just for the intent of a dark deed, plunging him right back into that blackness he found so reassuring.

It failed to do so now. Instead of dwelling on it, a tiresome thing to do, he stepped out of the doorway and into shadow, casting his wild black eyes about the room. It was plain, unless one possessed the ability to see through illusions. Nothing plain would do for his ambitious sorcerer. His ego was big enough to rival a god, and that his pride and vanity were so wholly undeserved made the Trickster chuckle in delight.

Great golden and silver shields covered the walls to act as mirrors. They reflected the lights of a hundred candle flames, only three of which would be visible through the illusion's cover. The floor, hard packed earth, was covered with animal skins that overlapped each other so that the sorcerer's toes might never touch the ground. His grand bed was bigger even than a king's, with posts reaching the ceiling and heavy velvet drapes hanging from the top as canopy.

"I can feel your presence, Ancient One," the man himself said from that bed, and even his voice sounded different without the glamour he cast on himself. "*It* feels your presence." It was a good one, the glamour. It even made him feel young. But beneath that polish he was an old man already. The power he held so tightly was too much for him to bear, though it was contained for the moment, it still drained his years away and he was far too drunken with it to care. His skin was withered like an autumn leaf, scarred from the pox and boils he could not treat, his teeth were rotted, and what was left of his hair was pure white and matted from lack of washing.

It was the height of rudeness for a creature so low to address a deity in such a way. And Loki didn't take kindly to it. The Trickster narrowed his eyes at the pathetic pile of bones and decided to put the withered prune back in his place.

The heavy bed frame shook and shuddered, a mere hint of what he could do, but it would be enough to get his point across. The mattress lifted toward the ceiling so quickly the sorcerer had no time to draw breath for a scream. He did scream later, all the way down, when Loki let the mattress drop, slightly out of place and balance, just enough to jar the sorcerer until he began sliding off the side. So far off the floor, the fall might have proven fatal. A shame his grip was still sturdy.

Deprived of his opportunity to spy, Loki stepped out of the shadow and into the flood of candlelight. He rushed the bed, coming nose-to-nose with the cantankerous wretch, brushing away the meager spell the sorcerer spat at him. "Manners, mortal," he hissed and then disappeared as quickly as he had appeared, removing himself to the other side of the room.

The sorcerer clutched his chest and wheezed. Even from so far away, Loki could hear his heart thundering, and it amused him enough that his temper dissolved like a snowflake in the sun.

He should have known the stone would reveal him. He squinted at it from a distance. A fine piece of creation, he wasn't too modest to admit. A work of genius. It drained the wearer of his magic without draining him at all. What got sucked into the black ice crystal was a mirror image of the power, just as potent, but forever trapped in the pendant. It had to be touched to release its magics and became so bonded with the wearer that it would forever find its way to him, eager to share what it held, and absorb more.

A ravenous wee thing, it was. Always wanting more.

The sorcerer sputtered, attempting to cast yet another spell. All it took was for Loki to toss a small windstorm about himself to make the fool fall silent. With wide eyes the sorcerer watched him, that precious little gem clutched in his gnarled hand. It was the same look he might give to a ravenous beast that had him cornered. Good.

Loki was used to such reactions. He made no attempt to use a glamour to hide his true appearance, saw no reason to do so. He was, after all, a god. Why should those who look upon him not see it? He knew full well that he exuded energy so potent it made lesser creatures shrink back in fear. His appearance was as it should be; at once beautiful, and dangerous and terrible. His hair was as pure copper, shining and sharp, his war braids merely proclaiming him that much more of a threat. His skin was pale, nigh sickly, but magnificent to behold, and his charcoal black eyes were opaque, without the wet gleam of human eyes, or the whites.

Perhaps his teeth were a little sharp as well, too often displayed in a wicked toothy grin. That very same grin he wore now. “I see you were not expecting me,” he said with mock disappointment and clucked his tongue in censure.

“What would you want of me?” the withered sorcerer rasped and coughed, surprised that his glamour was faltering. One gnarled, shaking hand reached for the goblet of wine by his bedside. Half of the liquid sloshed over the sides as he brought it to his pale lips and drank greedily. When he was finished, he let the goblet tumble from his grasp, spilling what remained.

“It has been a very long century since the day I deigned to answer an old woman's prayer,” Loki said, holding the sorcerer's gaze. He enjoyed the man's squirming. “One hundred years of waiting and watching from afar as one after the other powerful mages destroyed each other and then themselves in the name of grandeur.”

With a careless shrug, he wandered around the room to examine its contents more closely. “A very boring century. You see, my creation was so beautiful and self-sustaining that it no longer needed me to move it along. It wrought its deeds very well without me. I am…displeased.”

Another wheeze. But this time, his brows lowered defensively. He would fight Loki for the trinket, should he think it necessary.

Loki smiled at the sorcerer's reflection in one of his shields. Its shape offended him. Perfectly round and ordered, perfectly shined and centered on the wall. With a thought, he warped the metal, crumpling it like a piece of parchment, the sound sharp music to his ears. When it was nothing but a jagged ball, he straightened out half of it and stepped back to survey his handiwork. Better. “And so I have decided that it might be time to intervene and have a little fun of my own.”

“You want to reclaim it?” The mere thought of losing it made the sorcerer clutch his precious pendant to his chest.

“Perhaps,” Loki said with a thoughtful look. “I have not yet decided.”

“Let me keep it awhile longer,” the sorcerer said, as if his very life depended on the trinket. The sad truth was, by now it probably did. “Let me claim the wizard's power, and then you can have it.”

The crumpled shield went flying off the wall at the sorcerer. With a loud gasp, the sorcerer threw up a barrier to deflect the warped metal and send it slashing into the opposite wall. It became buried there. “It is not your place to barter!”

The sorcerer cowered. What Loki wouldn't give for someone with a solid backbone. “Forgive me, I meant no disrespect.” He pushed up to kneel on the bed. “I meant only to suggest an alternative. If you would but consider, it might prove engaging.”

An attempt at the royal wizard's powers? Intriguing.

But pointless.

“Forget the wizard,” Loki said. “She will never yield her power and far too many forces stand guard over her.” Something he disliked greatly was being told he could not play with a shiny new toy.

“I can do it,” the sorcerer insisted. He was far too weak to make it to his feet to stand, though he did try. And fail. "I can get her power and take it from the stone for myself."

Loki laughed, an ugly sound that resonated in the bright, bright room, and the remaining shields crumpled where they hung. The black crystal sparked with a sinister light in answer, sensing its creator, calling out to him like a long lost favored pet wanting to return.

The sorcerer's ire rose and his face gained some color, though it failed to fully express his feelings. "I can use it to restore myself and live forever."

And again, he spoke out of place! Loki was losing his patience with this puny man. This time, when he made the mattress fly, he dumped the sorcerer off it. When he would have moved, the furs came to life, curling limbs and claws around him to hold him down. Loki took his time crossing the chamber, giving the sorcerer an opportunity to remember his place. He put one foot on the man's chest, lightly, just enough to make it near impossible for him to draw a breath. From the night stand he summoned a trio of sharp, gleaming daggers. He leveled one at the sorcerer's eye, one at his throat, and one at his hand, still clutching the pendant.

"If I gave you a choice," he said thoughtfully, "which would you want part with, your sight, your voice, or your hand with the toy in it?"

The sorcerer was turning blue.

"Indulge me, if you will. I am curious about how that mind of yours works. If I take away your sight, you will have an excuse for your insolence. How are you to know whom you are speaking to when you cannot see them? If I take your tongue, you will no longer say anything insolent. You will not say anything at all. But if I take your toy,"—he drew the blade over the inside of the sorcerer's wrist—"you will no longer have reason to believe you can be insolent."

The sorcerer freed one hand and grasped onto Loki's ankle, pulling with all the might he possessed to save himself. Even with the pendant aiding him, he could not budge Loki an inch.

The Trickster leaned a little more weight on that foot, feeling the boundary past which bones would break. He skirted it closely, but did not cross. Instead, he leaned down to meet the mortal's gaze, letting him see the vast, swirling darkness in his eyes. "Speak to me once more in that tone of voice, and I will give you the immortality you crave. I will give you forever to regret your words."

By the time he removed himself again to the other side of the room, the sorcerer was in his bed, on a righted mattress, coughing wretchedly. "I can do it," he said between ragged breaths.

Of course, there was no possibility of that. The other gods would never allow it. Not that it would ever get so far. Daughter of a demigod and a water sprite, Lady Nialei of the Streams would never yield without a fight. And now, with the dragon's blood, she might even be powerful enough to not only stop the sorcerer, but destroy him as well.

The sorcerer would burn like tinder in the face of her terrible wrath, never knowing how he had failed, still trying to capture that fire inside the stone—in himself, the fool.

But watching him try and fail might prove entertaining. And if the fight came to sway overwhelmingly in the wizard's favor, he could always step in and make it a little more equal. No one had ever said he could not meddle in a mortal's affairs. That it would affect the Lady was simply a tragic coincidence.

It was bad politics to anger everyone around him. Like them or not, he still had to live with all those other gods. If he defied them, they'd become insufferable, and there weren't enough hiding places in all the dimensions to avoid them for long enough. Better to keep them content. For the moment.

This little rebellion would undoubtedly feel quite satisfying once it was under way. And he was certain that as soon as he left the sorcerer, his destiny would once more turn dark. How could it not?

The sorcerer watched him, scarce breathing. He was still, save for the shaking of his hands and lips. It seemed the older humans got, the more difficult it was for them to not move.

Loki held out his hand. The stone tore out of the sorcerer's grasp, and he cried out in helpless anger. It came to the Trickster, rubbing over his palm as if to appease him. He had but to think about wishing it and it opened to him, displaying all the pretty shinies it held within.

Powers and magics no single being should ever possess. Nearly all of what humanity had to offer bottled in a small black crystal, neutral as long as its wearer remained so. They never did. From their influence, the magics were turning dark and evil.

Though Loki was ever one to cause mischief, this darkness in the power made him uneasy. It warped his creation, changing the design and slowly forming a hole. It was not yet finished, he could see. It only waited for that one last bolt to crash through the warp and leave the crystal open wide.

So this was how the sorcerer hoped to become immortal. Once again, the fool didn't realize what he dealt with. Black ice could hold not only magics, but traits as well. Thoughts and feelings, hopes and dreams. Perfect imitations of the wielders' true souls. So many lay within that they would overwhelm the sorcerer, make him crazed. The shock would strip him of his control and the powers would destroy him.

Win or lose, the sorcerer was already dead.

But if the powers held within the stone drained into him instead, his body would not be a strong enough prison for them. They would burst out of him and, dark as they were, wreak havoc on the human world. *Woden would not like that,* Loki thought with a dejected sigh. The god king would know the stone's origins and hold Loki responsible, even though he'd not interfered a single time since the pendant had come to life for the old woman.

And that meant that his choices had just been whittled away to only one. He closed his fist around the pendant, searing it shut for the moment. It would not hold for very long, the warp in the structure was weakening it already. When he tossed it back to the sorcerer, happy tears sprang up in the old man's eyes.

"I knew it," he said.

"Knew what?" Not that he cared.

“I knew I was right,” the sorcerer cried. “You’d not have returned the stone to me if I was to fail. There is too much at risk.” He cackled madly, crawling on hands and knees back to the center of the bed to curl into a ball with the pendant clutched to his chest again.

Loki watched him rejoice for a while, allowed him to gain more and more confidence in himself, and begin celebrating the grand victory he imagined in his future. He built the sorcerer’s hope into a firm belief. Before he shattered it. “You forget who it is you are speaking to.”

Silence descended upon the garishly appointed chamber as the sorcerer realized his fate was no more certain than the outcome of a coin toss. His face turned gray, his eyes opened wider, and a small wailing sound escaped him. Doubt. Fear. He would carry them next to his ailing heart for a day or two, as he carried the crystal, but soon both would fade, conquered by his greed.

Satisfied for the moment, the Trickster melted back into shadow, back through the portal to await the grand battle.

CHAPTER 31

Nia dreamed of walking through a beautiful forest. The sky was bright blue above her, the grass soft and warm beneath her bare feet. Woodland creatures watched her from all around, their large, curious eyes unblinking. Nia smiled at them, sent them her greetings, but they didn't respond. Thinking nothing of it, she continued on her path and came to a footbridge across a forest stream.

There, her step slowed. It was a plain enough bridge, three flat, even planks laid side by side across the stream. Nothing to cause alarm. Yet she felt the tension in the earth as it waited. The stream glistened like magic, singing songs she could almost understand. It called to her, beckoned her closer. But the sight of the bridge held her back.

It didn't belong. Whatever it was, it ought not be here.

But, though she knew this, Nia couldn't stop herself from stepping closer. The grass hugged her feet, the blades sliced skin, but the sting was soothed by morning dew. Another step closer. Close enough to see the grooves in the wood.

Close enough to see the planks had rooted themselves into the bank as though still alive. As she studied it, puzzled by this unnatural magic, the roots groaned and strained. The ground bulged and then broke apart as a long, thick root tore out with enough force to snap like a whip.

It lashed back again and Nia jumped aside, but she wasn't quick enough and the tip cut her skirt open across one thigh. Blood marred her white skin and the roots groaned again, laughing.

One after the next, the bridge planks tore out of their moorings across the stream and stood on end before her. They melted together into a solid pillar, and then what used to be the center plank collapsed in on itself, pulling the others around it to form a frame. The center plank twisted tighter, became darker. So dark it was like black glass, reflecting the world back to Nia, but she couldn't see herself in its surface.

The stream sang louder, a warning this time. It went unheeded. Her gaze on the crystal in front of her, Nia came closer. The forest hissed, creatures crying out; she heard them fighting to come to her. She thought about releasing them, but the idea was as fleeting as a rare southern breeze.

Another step. Reaching out to touch the beautiful, dark thing, wondering at its secrets.

The root whip snapped again, lashing at her wrist and around it, squeezing like a sharp vise. It snatched Nia forward off her feet and into the air. She cried out at the searing pain, tears stinging her eyes. Yet she was still unable to look away from the crystal, searching for her reflection, desperate to see it and…there! An image began to form.

The stream roared; she heard its fury uncoil from deep underground and the crystal's pull intensified. She could almost make out her face.

The stream exploded into the air and broke the root binding her in half.

It jarred her out of the enchantment and Nia fell to the ground, scrambling away. The forest creatures swarmed her, big and small, hackles up and teeth barred at the black glass and the bridge. The stream battered the crystal without mercy. It fought back, growing in size, but the bigger it became, the harder the water beat at it until it began to break apart under the onslaught. It screamed like a wild thing, and the animals gathered closer around Nia, pushing her away from it.

Nia shuddered. It sounded human. Human, and filled with dark rage. This was no ordinary dream.

The stream didn't let up until the crystal reverted back to wood and broke apart into small pieces to be washed away. As it did, the root still twined around her wrist withered and fell away, turning to dust.

Nia opened her eyes and gasped for breath. She was in her own bed, the stillness of earth telling her the world had not yet awakened to morning. Hands shaking, she brushed her hair away from her face and felt wetness smear across her cheek. She frowned and summoned light.

The skin of her wrist was chafed bloody.

≪ »·◇·« ≫

The sorcerer screamed his rage at the crystal and hurled it across the chamber. It struck the earthen pitcher and shattered it to dust. He tore the warped silver disc off the wall, slammed it on the floor and then stomped on it again and again until his foot slipped and he fell.

The furs weren't thick enough to temper his fall, and a bone in his leg snapped like a twig. In his fury, it mended in an instant, but the pain remained and enraged him further. He struggled to his feet, gasping, and hobbled back to the bed. By the time he sat, the crystal was slithering like a snake back into his hand.

He stared at it while he caught his breath. It was a thing. It didn't think or feel. But staring into its depths, the sorcerer admired its imitation of regret.

And then it sang.

In the first few months after he acquired it, that song used to terrify him. Haunting, sinister strains, like those of a reed whistle, would fill the night, bringing him nightmares of demons wearing human skin. They tore into each other, fed on their own innards and drank their own blood. He would wake up in a sweat, screaming and weeping like a child afraid of the dark. But no matter how many times he took it into his head to get rid of the crystal, he could never make his fingers uncurl from around its chain.

It owned him, not the other way around.

But in return for his service, it gave him the world. It showed him the mysteries of the south, the beauties of the west, the treasures of the east and the magics of the north.

Then why, with all its power and cunning, could it not bring him the gods damned wizard?

Thrice now it had failed, and the sorcerer was beginning to think the Trickster had spoken true. Each time he set a trap for her, something snatched her right out of his grasp.

"Why?" he asked the crystal. "Why can't you bring her to me? You want her as much as I do, I can feel it." The stone was ever ravenous for power, and the wizard had so much she all but shone with it. Never had he encountered one so strong.

He wanted her. Oh, yes, he wanted her very much. If he possessed such power he would no longer have need of this pathetic human shell. He could create a new one, in any form he fancied. He could change faces as he did clothes. He could be truly immortal; walk among the Others who hid from his sight.

The wizard is no fool, the stone whispered, not in words but thoughts and ideas the sorcerer understood. *She will not yield easily.*

"Then help me!" he screamed at it. "Tell me what to do!"

She will not surrender her mind. You must draw her out where she is most vulnerable.

"Yes," he said, thinking fast. "I understand. I do." The wizard was human and as any other human, her biggest weakness was her fragile body. If he wanted to bring her to her knees, he'd have to do it himself. "You always lead me true," he crooned, cuddling the stone to his chest as he laid down to sleep. He would have his wizard.

And as a treat, he would have the privilege of feeling the life drain out of her body.

CHAPTER 32

It was the first time in four months that Nia made it up the stairs from Nico's study on her own. Bright sunlight blinded her in the courtyard, the autumn sky clear blue and the air crisp. She turned her face up to the sun's warmth, listening to the earth and the trees begin preparing for their winter sleep. Summers were short this far north. Already the leaves were turning brilliant shades of red and yellow.

The harvest was being gathered; the people sang as they worked. The earth had given them enough to fill their stores; there would be no empty stomachs this winter.

Nia thanked the earth and sent a little wave of power into the ground to replenish the fields. It was a simple spell, one she'd done many times before. The power would lay sleeping with the earth, grow on its own until spring and then awaken to nourish everything in the kingdom.

She wished she could ride out across the fields to see for herself how everything was faring.

Alas, as the royal wizard, her first duty was to the king. The only reason she'd even made her way above ground was because Saeran was meeting with his advisors yet again and required her presence. Though she had her suspicions that he'd only asked her to attend to make sure she would breathe fresh air again.

Sometimes she wondered who was looking after whom.

Nia smiled at the stable hand who'd called a greeting to her. Time to see to her duties. She inhaled deeply one more time and then turned toward the king's council room. The way wasn't long, but it was arduous. The halls were filled with people, servants and guests, all preparing for Samhain. Nia would have to lead a procession to the altar again to thank the gods for a bountiful harvest. The celebration afterward would be no smaller than Beltaine night.

There was a faire in the village, with merchants from all over the kingdom and farther come to display their wares. Though the queen's passing had saddened many, she had only been among them for a very short time. What the people mourned more was their king's loss. The news of Saeran's illness and recovery was slowly spreading throughout the kingdom, though no one but those closest to him would ever know the full truth it.

Nia doubted anyone else would believe it if they knew.

She nodded to the guards at the top of the stairway. There were more of them throughout the castle, keeping an eye on the king. They had strict orders to come for her if they saw or heard anything suspicious. She knew Saeran chafed to be so closely watched, but until she could be sure the threat to him has passed, he would have to endure it.

Once she mounted the stairs, there were no more crowds. The doors were all closed, all but the one to the council room, where she could hear men speaking.

Nia frowned and slowed her step.

"There will not be another queen," Saeran was saying, his voice strained, as if he'd said it several times already.

"But Sire," one of the advisors argued, "the realm will need an heir. It will tear itself apart if you should die without one!"

Saeran hadn't told them the reason for his decision. Who would believe him? Even with a powerful wizard at his side, performing magic in plain sight, no one would take talk of dragons seriously. Until she'd met one herself, Nia had thought them to be no more than legend, and she had Others shadowing her step almost every day.

"Was it the fever?" a timid voice asked. "We thought, all of us, that the wizard healed his Majesty."

"She did," Saeran said tightly. "That is not the reason."

"Then what is?" the first advisor demanded.

Nia pulled her shoulders back and entered the study. "Mind your tone, advisor Allon," she told the old man swathed in purple robes.

Allon was one of two advisors Nia had asked Saeran not to replace. He was old and pampered and often forgot his place, but he remembered a time most of them had forgotten, if they'd lived through it at all. His wisdom on the council was worth these brief spurts of insubordination.

At least that was what she told herself.

"You have heard of this, I assume," he said, his face turning ruddy. "His Majesty has decided not to take another wife. What do you make of it?"

Nia met Saeran's gaze. "It is not my place to question a royal decree," she told Allon without looking at him. "Nor is it yours."

"That is precisely your place! You are the only one he will listen to." His words fell silent at the sharp warning look she cast him. He blushed deeper and straightened in his seat, adopting a more measured tone when he spoke again. "What I mean is King Saeran has no siblings to provide a line of succession. If he dies heirless, the royal line will die with him. There are several noble houses eager enough to see one of theirs sit the throne that would go to war. If there is no one to take his Majesty's place, the kingdom will be torn apart. You know this is so."

"There is also the matter of the Aegirans to consider," Kvaran added.

Saeran drew himself up. "What do you mean?"

"The marriage was a bond of peace between Wilderheim and Aegiros. That bond is now broken. Queen Mari, may she be at peace, died in the land of the people who nearly destroyed an entire tribe."

"And what would you have had us do? Bow down to the Aegirans?"

Kvaran steepled his fingers. "I am simply trying to point out that the circumstances of her death are not clear, and the wizard's involvement might sow seeds of suspicion.

Should they decide that Queen Mari's death was deliberate, the tribe will retaliate."

There was silence after he finished speaking. It was a possibility Nia hadn't considered.

Only the midwife who'd held Mari's hand as she died knew what Nia had done. She was the only one who could tell Mari's family the truth of her death; that they'd done all they could to save her. But would they hear her? And if they did, would they believe her?

A woman in Aegiros was expected to hold her tongue and defer to the men of her tribe: warriors, men whose only purpose in life was to fight for their *shansher* and conquer in his name.

As a people who revered bloodlines as much as the royals of the north, the Aegirans might forgive Saeran for taking another wife directly after Mari's death, but they would never forgive the murder of one of their own, one entrusted to Saeran as a symbol of peace.

Braith, the young girl with wild red hair, cleared her throat. "Perhaps Lady Nia could look into the future?" she suggested.

"No," Saeran said at once. "Whatever she sees there will not affect my decision. If an heir is all you concern yourselves with, I will be sure to appoint a successor before breath has left my body. I may not have siblings, but there are cousins aplenty, King Halden's children, any of whom would do right by Wilderheim, should it come to that."

The advisors spoke up, one and all, except for Braith.

"That is final," Saeran said, silencing them.

Everyone looked to Nia. They expected words of wisdom when she had none to give. She and Saeran alone understood why this had to be so, and Saeran didn't want them to know; therefore, Nia couldn't tell them. Instead, she made her way to his side, taking her place as his right hand without a word. None were needed.

The advisors didn't take it well, but they held their peace. "Be at ease," she told them. "Should the unlikely happen and leave the kingdom without a ruler, it will pass to King Halden's heirs. His Majesty has learned much from his uncle, as I am sure, have his cousins, all of them honorable men and women who owe Wilderheim their lives. That debt alone will compel them to do right by us."

You complicate things far too much, the dragon said, amusement and exasperation lacing his words.

"Let us move on," Saeran said. "What of the Samhain preparations?"

Braith was the one to answer, and Nia smiled to herself. It was about time there were more women telling the king what to do. She sent the thought to Saeran, and he shifted in his seat, subtly elbowing her in retaliation. She hid her grin behind a delicate cough as Braith spoke.

By the time the advisors left, the plans for Samhain were set, the harvest cataloged, news relayed and official correspondences dictated. Saeran leaned back in his seat and rubbed his face. He looked tired, understandably so. "They will not let up on this," she warned him.

Saeran chuckled without humor. "They are more concerned about royal lines than I am."

"Perhaps one of them ought to be king. Or queen." She took a seat, still weak, though gaining strength every day.

Saeran's eyes twinkled. "Perhaps I should name Braith as my successor."

Nia grinned. "I have always said every kingdom needed a woman's touch."

He made a rough noise. "That is the last thing a kingdom needs."

Nia laughed.

Saeran smiled. "And how do you fare, my lady?"

"Well enough, my lord."

So many words remained unspoken between them, words that couldn't be voiced. Not now; perhaps not ever. They lay heavy on Nia's heart, making her feel ancient with sorrow.

What pained her more, Saeran seemed to see it, and his own smile dimmed in response.

"Come," he said, rising. "We will take a walk."

She took his offered hand and let him lead her down to the gardens. After being in the warm study for so long, the cold air chilled her, but she breathed in and accepted it. It was merely another part of life. Sometimes people had to get cold to appreciate the warmth of a hearth fire.

She walked beside her king in silence, enjoying every breeze. All around them life was thriving. Animals scrambled about, making stores for the winter, preparing their nests and burrows. Soon snow would cover everything, erasing memories of a year gone by. The land would start anew, without the burdens humans carried with them.

Sometimes she envied that.

Close to the edge of the forest, the gardens were empty. No one ventured here since the flowers have begun to wilt. The path led past a tall hedge, sculpted into a wall onto an open field. In the summer it was covered in wild flowers and herbs that midwives used to brew their teas and remedies. There was a stream running through the meadow. Its waters were clear enough to drink, and the stones lining its bed were polished by sand and time.

By the banks lay logs to serve as seats. They were nigh invisible in the tall grass, but those who knew where to look would always find them.

Many a noble had sat here with their beloved and spoke vows of everlasting love. They did so hoping there was magic in this place to grant them a long and happy life together.

Rarely did such vows hold true.

Saeran led them to one of the logs and pulled Nia onto his lap when he took his seat. He embraced her tightly. "I miss you," he said, breathing a sigh into her shoulder.

"I'm right here." They shouldn't be like this, but Nia didn't move away. Instead of leaving his embrace she weaved an illusion around them. In case someone happened by, they'd see the king perching on the log and Nia sitting by the creek, playing with the waves.

"Not always."

"No one can spend every moment of every day with another person," she told him, half smiling at this strange conversation.

"You could. But you won't." He caught her hand in his, tracing her palm, and then twining his fingers between hers. "I offered you the crown once and you refused. Would I risk the same disaster to offer it again?"

"I can't, Saeran." Though all she wanted to do was stay with him this way forever, she couldn't ignore the feeling of disaster looming ahead.

"Why?" he asked roughly, and this time the dragon echoed him, puzzled.

CHAPTER 33

Do not tell me you still harbor a mortal's fears, Lady Nia.

Nia left Saeran's lap and took her illusion's place at the creek, blending into it until they matched. The illusion turned into mist and blew away on a breeze. *Will you be spying on me for the rest of my days now, Dragon? Simply because you can?*

You are my window to my grandson, he said. *It is my only amusement in this place. Though I cannot see why you frustrate the poor boy so.*

Saeran was silent, his features tense, waiting for her to speak. It was clear he'd like nothing better than to say more, but it was a moment's passion that would pass as soon as he remembered why he ought not wed again.

I cannot speak to him with you in my head! I do not need you to take his side in this.

But you do, the dragon replied. Then, after a pause, his tone changed. *Child, do you still not know who you are?*

Nia shut him out of her mind. "Someone's coming," she said softly, sending her words to Saeran alone.

Within moments the intruder came into view on the path from the castle. Saeran pushed to his feet and his jaw tensed when he saw the slight man with gleaming blond hair and an empty smile. His instant dislike was obvious and put Nia on guard. *Is something wrong?*

There is something about him, Saeran replied. *Something not right, but I cannot remember what.*

Jasper, the northerner from Aegiros who had accompanied Queen Mari here, had not departed with the others. Not even after the queen had met her end. This land might be his home, but the castle wasn't.

Nia came to stand by Saeran as Jasper approached.

He bowed deeply to them both, that same smile still plastered on his face. He spoke, but Nia didn't hear his words. She stared at his face, which seemed out of place to her. She looked at him again with a dragon's gaze and saw an illusion. It was powerful, carefully constructed, and very detailed, but an illusion nonetheless. What worried her was that she couldn't see through it to what lay beneath.

Nia blinked, trying to adjust her focus, and her gaze snared on something lying hidden in the man's pocket. Her senses returned to it each time she thought to look away. It was at once smooth and sticky, like a perfect little trap. Nia could feel the cold seeping out of it and shivered, but she couldn't look away. Behind her, the creek screamed. Beneath her, the earth shuddered. Her vision clouded over, and in the dark mist she remembered the nightmare from which she'd awakened bleeding, a scream caught in her throat.

The ground shuddered again, hard enough to throw them all off balance. Saeran caught Nia against him, breaking her concentration, and she shifted her sight back to normal so she could once again see Jasper's false face. Dark laughter, sharp as a blade, sliced through the autumn air.

"Nia?" Saeran's said, but she didn't answer him.

She searched with her senses for the threat she could feel saturating the air, careful to avoid the trap, but found no one; no one was around them, except for the man hiding in illusion. The dragon was restless, wherever he was, trying time and again to reach her, to speak to her, but she wouldn't let him.

"Are you well, my lady?" Jasper asked, his voice polite, but beneath it she could hear the edge of glee.

Nia found her feet again and faced him. "I do not know who you are, but I know what you are doing. You have outstayed your welcome. Leave, or I will make you."

The king frowned. She could already feel questions burning inside him. He would ask them later, but for now he didn't say a word.

Jasper's eyes turned assessing. His smile returned, this time with a calculating edge to it, as he looked Nia over. "My apologies," he said, backing up a single step. "I had not realized my presence offended. If the lady wishes me out of her sight, I can oblige. But surely, your Majesty, banishment is too harsh an order in this case." There was a lilting note to the end of his statement, as if he was asking, not saying it outright, and Nia caught the faintest slither of compulsion. It infuriated her that he would dare. But before she could do anything about it, Saeran spoke.

"You waste your charms on us," Saeran said with difficulty, as if he had to fight to speak the words, but speak them he did. "I agree with the wizard in this. Your queen is gone, and you have no more reason to stay. You have until the day after Samhain to depart."

Nia winced. Samhain was in two day's time. A reasonable stretch, by anyone's standards, yet Nia couldn't shake the feeling that it was precisely what Jasper had wanted. Not to prevent himself being banished, only to postpone it a little while.

Jasper bowed. "As my liege commands." Before he left, he spoke his last. "I regret that I have caused you any kind of discomfort. Please, allow me to make amends. I am a fair hand with magic tricks. Perhaps I could provide entertainment for the Samhain feast." His gaze encompassed them both, and Nia felt another push of compulsion.

The wolf skin at her back moved, hackles rising until it made her own tickle. She suppressed an uncomfortable shudder. "No," she said at the same time as Saeran decreed, "I will permit it."

Jasper's glee followed him like invisible smoke back to the castle and out of sight.

Saeran rubbed his chest over the dragon pendant. "It's burning," he said. "I suppose that means I have made the wrong choice."

Nialei of the Streams.

Nia flinched at hearing the words whispered on the wind. She turned toward the source, back to the creek. *Niaaa…*

Drawn to the dancing waves that shimmered in the sunlight, Nia went back to the bank and knelt there, taking off her cloak. The wolf skin remained, refusing to be discarded like a garment. It hugged her shoulders instead.

"What is it?" Saeran asked, coming to kneel by her side.

On the other side of the stream, shapes shimmered into being. Glowing mist swirled around a gathering of Others of all shapes and sizes. Nia recognized the Sidhe and the dire wolves among them, but there were so many others, too. Creatures she'd never seen before, beautiful and terrifying, childlike and ancient, creatures of air, water and fire, earth and pure magic, all gathered there together, watching.

"Gods," Saeran breathed, "look at them all."

"You can see them?"

He nodded. "Why are they here?"

Have you learned? the female dire wolf asked.

What will you do? the Sidhe inquired.

"I think they are here for me."

"What? Why?"

Nia closed her eyes and felt the dragon nudge her mind. "I think it is time to find out who I am," she said, opening her mind again to the dragon. She let him in, but didn't let him speak. The creek looked fuller, eager somehow. Nia placed her hands flat over the stream, just close enough to feel its cold, but out of reach of the water itself. Closing her eyes, she concentrated for a moment and then cupped her hands. They cut into the stream without touching it, and a perfect ball of water separated from the rest, hovering a hair's breadth above her skin, nestled in her hands.

It was still moving, swirling 'round and 'round, still a creek, even caught in her hands. Nia had read about water creatures. They didn't understand words, didn't use them. They communicated with their minds and bodies. These creatures had powerful voices and didn't use them unless there was no other way. Their songs could kill as easily as bring a thing back to life.

Nia searched her memories as far back as she could go, looking for a spell. There had to be one and it had to have been there since she'd been a child. What she found was a dream, and in it a melody.

Nia hummed to the ball of water in her hands. The song echoed, a double voice so strange it couldn't be human, yet it was hers. How could it not be?

Do not tell me you still harbor a human's fears, the dragon had said to her.

The ball of water quivered to be struck by her voice, but it was not a defensive movement. It was dancing to her tune, responding in motion when it could not in voice. It swirled faster and faster, until it resembled a ball of yarn. A single ribbon detached and stretched up from the ball, creating a small vortex.

It grew and splashed outward, straining against her hold. Nia released it to float just above the surface of the stream and sat back to watch it, still singing, letting her instincts guide her when the memory faded away.

At last, Nia ran out of notes to voice and the vortex as big as her now collapsed, leaving in its place a creature so strange, and so beautiful, that Nia could only stare.

The female was shaped almost like a human, but her fingers were webbed and her ears were tiny. She had gills on the sides of her neck and brilliant scales scattered down from her neck all over her body. Her hair was not hair at all, but some sort of water plants. Her eyes were enormous in her face, the color of stars and emeralds, and her eyelids closed sideways, not up and down. She had only two small slits where a nose ought to be, and her lips were full and feminine. When she opened her mouth to draw breath, Nia could see a row of tiny, sharp teeth.

Nia pushed to her feet and bowed to the creature, recognizing royalty when she saw it. She nudged Saeran to do the same.

The female blinked a couple of times, and then Nia's mind filled with images, sent to her on a sigh. She saw a beautiful castle made of shells and pearls, crystals and flowers, deep beneath the water. Creatures like this one swam all around, playing and laughing, singing together to help fish and plants grow. They were the guardians of the world's waters. She was showing Nia where she'd come from, a way of introduction.

When Nia acknowledged this, the images changed to show another female, this one with eyes more white than green. She was floating serene by the edge of a lake but a dark cloud of blood was spreading around her body. She was dying. With her last breath, she sent a shrill call into the air, a summons.

An impossibly tall man came running out of the forest. He had antlers growing from his head, and hair like spun gold. He wore only a pair of tattered pants and his skin was darkened from the sun. Drawings and symbols covered his chest and arms, patterns that changed as he approached the female in the water.

His sapphire eyes were filled with pain at the sight of her. He dropped to his knees at the edge of the lake and caught the water sprite's face in his hands, searching her eyes.

The female brought forth a bundle of water plants and handed it to him with shaking hands. He nodded to her silent pleas, tears of blood running down his beautiful face as the sprite closed her eyes, sinking beneath the surface of the lake where she dissolved into the element which had birthed her.

The male unwrapped the bundle to expose a naked babe, a little girl with eyes almost as bright as his own.

His daughter.

Nia.

But she was too small, too fragile to stay with him. His people were a powerful lot who reveled in contest and battle. Though it broke his heart, he took the child to an old woman who lived at the edge of his forest. Nia's eyes welled with tears as Eirwen took the child into her care, but she made her father swear on the love he held for his water sprite that he would never approach the girl.

Understanding passed between them. Halflings were extremely unstable. Born with human bodies, for that was a shape easily adoptable by all Others, they could change as they grew to favor either of their parents, or both. It all depended on who raised them.

Had Nia stayed with the water sprites, she might well have become one herself. But more likely, she would have drowned in their world before developing the ability to breathe under water.

She could not have survived with her father, either. In his demesne she would have been less than half the size of other children, weak and disadvantaged, easy fodder for everyone to prove their dominance by fighting her into submission.

No, her only hope for survival was to stay human, but she could only do that if she never knew Others existed.

The male gave his word and swore to look after her from a distance..

The old woman nodded, and by the time she raised her gaze again, he was gone.

Nia was shaking by the time her vision cleared, and she could see the water sprite again. The female's eyes were sad. She'd waited a long time to be summoned to show Nia these things. A long time to carry so many memories not her own. She reached out a webbed hand, caressing Nia's hair without touching it.

Water creatures and land creatures rarely mated. Nia's mother had died giving birth to her because she'd been forced to do it near the surface to make sure Nia survived. And to keep her away from her father's people, Eirwen had taken Nia far away, to a no man's land between Wilderheim and its western neighbor Ravetia, where she would never hear anyone speak of magic or Otherlands.

Nia remembered little of her time there. Only that they'd traveled from village to village for years until Eirwen had been too old to go any farther. By the time Nia's magic flared in her sleep and took Eirwen's life, Nia had been on the border of King Manfred's realm, and she'd made it all the way to Frastmir on her own, only to be found by Nico.

Saeran caught her hand in his and held on, his presence warming her cold insides.

You were brought here for a reason, the dragon said. *Do not fear it, there is no need.*

The water sprite tilted her head to hear another's voice. She blinked and sent her greetings through Nia.

The dragon responded with assurances that she was relieved of her burden. He would look after the pair from now on.

The sprite nodded and looked at Nia again. What might have been a smile transformed her face for a moment, before she twirled around and changed into water, splashing back into the creek.

Had it not been for Saeran's arms coming around her, Nia would have fallen to the ground.

CHAPTER 34

Nia spent the next day in her chambers. Not of her own will. She had yet to sleep a wizard's sleep since the healing she'd channeled for Saeran and Mari, and the summons of the water sprite had undone what progress she'd made.

She thought about her father. If he'd ever been around, even at a distance, would she have sensed him? Nia couldn't remember if she ever had. She couldn't even be sure of what he was. He could be a wood sprite, an animal spirit, or anything in between or beyond. Far too many creatures dwelled in this world to know them all, especially when most never revealed themselves to humans.

The only thing she was now certain of was that she was not human. That was what Nico had seen in her the day he'd caught her stealing from the castle kitchens. That was why the Others let her see them—she was one of them. An Other at the right hand of a human king. Or as human as a dragon's descendant could be. Nia chuckled. What a pair they made, Halflings governing a human realm, and no one the wiser. But Wilderheim had always been a kingdom of Others as much as humans, and if Nico could have done it, she could do no less than prove worthy of his faith in her ability to do the same.

Nico. She sighed. Another mystery. Her mentor had served three generations of kings, prolonging his life as much as his human body would allow. Toward the end, Nia had felt the toll it had taken on him. Through practice and sheer force of will, Nico's essence had grown to make up for his withering body. For her sake he'd waited longer than was wise, but now, at least, Nia knew what had happened to him.

For all his power, Nico had been human. With age and wisdom, his soul had begun to outgrow its vessel, dissolving it completely as soon as Nia had taken his place. No one had seen her mentor since then because his bodily form no longer existed but, as with the pockets of magic he'd left behind in his study, his soul was still whole.

By her estimates, Nico had been nearly a hundred years old when he'd disappeared. What did that mean for Nia? How long would she walk this world? The thought of centuries passing her by, everyone she knew growing old and dying while she endured unchanging filled her with sadness.

The ancient ones grow weary of life after a while, the dragon told her. *Some have been known to go mad without an anchor to the world.*

An anchor like a loved one, Nia guessed.

The dragon didn't answer. He didn't have to; he'd given her his memories.

A sudden shiver ran down her spine. There were shadows in her chamber that ought not be there. Her senses sharpened, her Sight shifted, and she could see that the darkness had mass. "Show yourself," she said, feeding what little magic she had into the command.

The sharp laughter she'd heard in the gardens the day before cut through the air again, severing the spell mid-stream as if it were a piece of string. "You dare command a god, Halfling?" said a voice from the darkness. It was like nothing she'd ever heard before. "The audacity of it is…intriguing."

"Who are you?"

"Cannot say," he said easily. "I can be many things or nothing at all." His tone turned conspiratorial as the dark shadow floated closer to her. "I choose to be nothing, you see, because nothing is allowed to interfere."

Nia smiled a quick, sharp smirk. "I know you."

"I expected nothing less."

"Why are you here?"

"To spy."

"And what have you discovered?"

He chuckled, the shadow quivering to mirror the sound. The more she heard him, the less his voice bothered her. "What kind of spy would I be to divulge all my secrets?"

"But they are not your secrets. They are mine. Hence there is no harm in telling me." She enjoyed verbal sparring and sensed that he, too, was reluctant to abandon this little amusement. As the dragon had said, the ancient ones grew weary of life.

"A secret is only a secret so long as it remains hidden. A secret, once uncovered, is nothing more than gossip. Boring. I do not waste my time with such things."

"I thought gods had nothing but time."

"Yet we still know how to make better use of it than you who have so little. Humans." There was a sound, like a hiss, and then he breathed, "Ah, but you are not so insignificant as that, are you, Halfling?"

Nia adopted as innocent an expression as she could, struggling not to laugh. "I am no more significant than a shadow in a dark chamber."

"And we both know what monsters those shadows hide."

"A monster is only a monster so long as it is fearsome. A monster, once accepted, is nothing more than an oddity. Do you think me odd?"

Another chuckle, and with it, the shadow drew back until she almost thought it would reveal its owner. "Most definitely odd. In the way a flame is, enclosed in a watery cocoon. Oddly strange and unnatural. Especially when the flame can reach out and bite the unwary sorcerer."

"And what of the cool watery well within a fortress of fire?"

"Stranger still," he groused. "A strange world indeed it is we find ourselves in, where the well protects the fire and the fire nurtures the well. You weaken yourself needlessly with your sentimental spells. The balance keeps tipping, the clock is ticking, and the sorcerer is not tripping over his own feet the way you are. It spoils my fun."

"Sage advice," she said dryly.

The shadow rushed her, and a face emerged so close to her that all she could see was a pair of opaque black eyes in a grayish pale face, with coppery hair to frame them. "Have a care, Halfling. Your infinite protectors will not be around forever, and I can make your existence quite unpleasant if I choose to."

Nia nodded in wordless ascent, not trusting herself to speak. She kept respectfully docile, but would not drop her gaze from the Trickster's. He smiled at that, though the expression never reached his eyes. Empty eyes, he had. Empty and endless, dark and dangerous. "I have not met one such as you. Even the sorcerer quivers at the sight of me. Yet here you are, with little over a score of years to you, looking at me as nothing but another…oddity."

"Why are you here?" she asked again, softly.

The Trickster's thin mouth contorted. "The amulet is flawed beyond repair. It will not heed my call, and any magic used on it is sucked in to warp it further. The jest goes too far, and I cannot involve myself beyond this point. I risk much by simply being here, conversing with you, Halfling."

"Are you asking for my help?" Nia strove hard to conceal her surprise, but it showed regardless.

"Much as I loath to," the Trickster replied. "Rid this world of the thing, and in return I shall tell you where to find your sire."

Nia's breath left her. "Why should I trust you? I could be walking into a death trap."

"You will be," he said. "But if it will ease your weary mind, I vow on Woden's lifeblood that I will keep to our bargain. And if you do as I say, and precisely as I say, then all will end as it should."

"And how is it that all this should end?"

"With the amulet gone, its evil destroyed and me beyond suspicion."

How like a god to see only his own ends. "What will happen to this kingdom and its people?"

"They are not my concern, hence they will not be affected."

"And me?"

"You have little enough to lose, and even less to fear. Is your life so full that you fear leaving it behind?"

She swallowed. "Yes."

The Trickster studied her for a moment, and what he found seemed to unsettle him, but he regained his composure quickly. "Then you might yet survive the trials to come."

CHAPTER 35

The music began well before sunset. Though she couldn't see it from Nico's study, Nia knew there were people on the castle green already singing and dancing to their hearts' delight. Nia didn't share in their revelry. Her mind was burdened with weighty thoughts, her soul weary of this weakness.

The Trickster's plan troubled her. She'd sensed no falsehood from him, but having never spoken to a god before, Nia couldn't be certain of anything. Whether he spoke the truth, or whether he chose to change his mind didn't matter. What he asked of her would endanger not only her life tonight but everyone else's as well.

For the third time since noon, Nia made a circle with her hand to trace one in light. Just as with her last two tries, the circle blazed white hot and then cleared in the center to show gray mist. The future remained hidden, veiled by some force or another, though she had an idea about whom to blame. It wouldn't amuse the great Trickster to have her know precisely how to play this grand game of his.

Frustrated, Nia swiped her hand to dissolve the circle and then brushed her hair back, clutching it in her fists until the tension snapped a few strands. *I may lose this game,* she thought, something akin to fear coiling in her belly, tying her into knots.

She pushed to her feet slowly and made certain everything was in order. The books and scrolls were all arranged on their shelves, no parchment out of place. The table was clean, a single candlestick gracing its center. The pitcher and chalices stood on a tray in the corner, covered by an old piece of cloth so as not to gather dust. She'd asked the servants to take the bed and all her personal belongings out and back to the chamber she ought to be sleeping in. Nothing more remained here except all the knowledge Nico had gathered over his very long life. And if she never returned, the one burning candle would stay lit to guard it all until someone worthy of it came to claim this place. Forever, if need be.

Nia ran her hand over the grooves of the table, tracing a pattern. She would miss this place. This library was her sanctuary and training ground. The stone was scarred in places, marked by spells gone awry, the domed ceiling black with ash and soot from countless days and nights spent down here by nothing but the light of a hundred candles.

Every chink and groove had a story to tell, and the pockets of magic Nico had left behind shone bright from within, without shining at all. They held his essence like a page in history, proof that he had walked these halls and left an impression on an entire kingdom. There would be more such pockets here, and everywhere in the castle within the hour—hers.

With a few whispered words, Nia sealed the library nook so no one but the king would know it was ever there. A small smile pulled on the corner of her mouth to remember the very first time she'd worked the spell. She'd sealed herself inside that small space with what should have been an illusion. Bitter sweet memories of the past. She had to remember them; remind herself she still had much to live for.

Her mask this eve was a simple one made of leather and dyed to resemble tree bark. It would cover her face so only her mouth and chin would show. She tied it in place and gathered all the charms she'd made the day before. One of them attached to the top of the mask, another hung on a chain at her breast. She put on bracelets wreathed with night blooming flowers and rings made of water reeds and magic. Two more stone charms would fit into small pockets in the seam of her cloak and there was a protection spell written on the sole of each of her shoes, as well as on her staff. It wouldn't be enough, but it was all she could have.

She couldn't make such protections for any of the people present tonight. If the sorcerer suspected anything, the entire game would shift and not in Nia's favor. All she could do was hope that he would be intent on her and no one else.

That was her hope and prayer.

Nia searched the shadows for movement. She hadn't seen any Others in a while. "If you are here, I ask that you grant me one wish. Keep those present from harm. You need not involve yourselves with the sorcerer, but all those people filling the castle tonight are innocent. They will be helpless against him. Please…" She sighed. It was no use to beg someone who wasn't there.

Her cloak and staff waited for her by the door. With one last look around, she clasped the cloak around her neck and lifted the hood to hide her hair. The wolf skin pulled tighter around her back and she grasped her staff. She would need it in a moment or two, just to climb the stairs.

Nia hesitated only a moment before she closed her eyes and envisioned the core of her magic. In her mind's eye, it was a glittering ball of bright light. Slowly, carefully, she melted that ball into the consistency of smoke and let it seep out of her body, shivering at the heat it created. For a moment, her mortal shell glowed like a star in the night as tendrils of brilliant magic curled up and around her, filling the air with sparks like fireflies.

She directed them with her mind to coat the walls of the study and seep into the stone. Once the chamber was saturated with as much as it could hold, Nia sent her power up through the castle, filling strategic places where it would shield the most people from any attack. The king's bedchambers, his study, the great hall, the kitchens and the stables soaked up her magic eagerly.

There wasn't much left by the time she was certain the castle would be safe. Whatever else she could spare without killing herself she gave to the earth to ensure bountiful harvests for years to come.

Drained, tired and weak, she whispered a prayer for luck and left the study, locking the door behind her. Going up the stairs took a while with her knees aching and protesting the strain, but she climbed on until at last she reached the castle green. After locking the second door as well, she made her way to the bonfire to begin the procession up to the gods' altar.

"What's the matter?" Saeran asked, grasping her elbow through her cloak as soon as he caught up with her. His dragon pendant would allow him to see past the illusions she'd woven the night before because it had been made by her and recognized her spells. To all others, Nia looked to be clad in a gown of brilliant green, with autumn leaves and wheat in her hair. She would wear a mask of bronze and bells and chimes would trail in her wake.

"All is in order, my liege," she said. She hadn't told him anything about the Trickster's visit, or his plans for this night. Until it was absolutely necessary, she saw no reason to worry the king. Should something happen to her, Nia had made sure he would be well protected within the walls of his castle. It would have to be enough.

"You do not lie well, wizard," he retorted, aware of the nobles following close behind. Though the music and drumming concealed their conversation, Nia was proud of her student for being careful with his words. "I sensed the magic you sent out. It was too much, especially now when you are so weak. What are you up to?"

"I fulfill my duty to you and your kingdom, Majesty."

"Not at the cost of your wellbeing!" he whispered furiously.

The emotion in his voice gave Nia pause, and she stopped in her tracks to look at him. His eyes were like blue flames, glowing in the night. If anyone saw, he would forever lose a vital advantage. For now, no one knew of his dragonblood, or his aptitude for magic. It was an essential piece of information to keep secret from his enemies, in case he ever had need of it in battle.

Saeran's chest rose and fell with harsh breaths, and his fists were clenched at his sides. This was not good. "Majesty," she said, trying to sound reasonable, "My life was forfeit to your rule the day I made my vow to you and you accepted my place at your side."

Saeran didn't look pleased to have this pointed out to him. He urged her on again. "Keep going before the others notice we have stopped."

"What is the matter with you?" she whispered to him. "Are you regretting your decision now?"

"Father was right," Saeran said, keeping his voice low. "I was not ready to see the wisdom in his doubt back then. Not until it was too late. Had I understood…I never would have allowed you to put yourself in danger to protect me. Not when it should be the king's duty to protect those who serve him; a man's duty to protect those he loves."

"Now you are being silly," Nia told him, but her voice was not as steady as she wanted it to be.

"I know you are up to something," he said, without looking at her. "I know it will be big and, knowing you, probably very dangerous. And I know I cannot stop you." It didn't seem to occur to him that he was walking by her side, when he ought to be following her. In this and all processions, the wizard became the embodiment of a god or goddess, and it was symbolic for everyone, even the king, to follow. Nia knew that a handful of nobles and a couple of advisors had already noticed, though they had said nothing yet.

They were almost at the altar. "You can trust that whatever I do will be for the good of the kingdom."

"That is precisely what I am afraid of."

If she hadn't been so worried herself, Nia would have smiled at that.

Saeran finally took his place behind her as they reached the altar. The procession cheered and the music rose louder. Nia was glad for it. She performed the ceremony, moving her mouth in the right places, though no sound left her lips. She silently thanked the gods for a good harvest, and prayed for protection from bad spirits bent on mischief this night. The revelers were mostly oblivious, caught up in their own celebrations, observing only the necessary prayers for the sake of ritual.

Nia was so drained she could no longer understand the earth, or the breeze. Both hummed and whispered to her, and she sensed their worry but couldn't answer to soothe them. The shadows moved with a mind of their own. There were beings all around them, lured closer out of their hiding places by the sound of celebration. Nia had no way of knowing if they were benevolent or not, and without the ability to see them, she could do nothing to warn the others.

She concluded the rituals with haste and began to lead everyone back to the safety of the castle. The bonfire was lit there tonight because Samhain revelry was always longer and wilder than any other. This way the castle guard could keep an eye on the people and make sure nothing from within or without harmed them.

Nia shed her illusion and joined the dance for a round or two, enough to show the people she was one of them but not more. She couldn't risk losing even more of her strength.

The Trickster had told her very little about what she needed to do. It was his way of making sure she was ready without giving her any kind of advantage. But not even a god could foresee everything. From what he had told her, Nia knew exactly what she would be fighting. She'd seen the pendant born of hate and greed, of a dark prayer on a darker night, to a god who cared little about the fate of mortals. She knew she couldn't use magic on it, because it would only make matters worse.

She couldn't risk having her magic turned against her and had never trained in physical combat. But there were ways to use magic without using it directly. Loki's stone could only absorb powers straight from the wizard directing them at it or through physical touch. Nia planned to do neither.

The king called to his people, catching Nia's eye. There was a warning in his gaze, and his posture was rigid, as it always got when he didn't want to show weakness or fear. He worried, and he should.

Nia came to his side, and the two of them led the nobles back to the great hall. It was ablaze with candlelight. Everything had a golden glow about it, even the lavish feast laid out on three long tables, one that ran alongside the dais and two others at each end to form a U. Many nobles were present for this occasion, some even from the neighboring kingdoms. Saeran wanted to make an impression, and Nia had to admit he had succeeded. The foreigners would think this kingdom strong and bountiful, wanting for nothing.

They would be right. Nia, and Nico before her, had made sure of that.

The guests exclaimed in delight and sighed in awe as the castle bards began a different kind of music. Everyone took their place at their seats and politely waited for the king to make a royal motion before they sat. Nia remained standing behind Saeran's right shoulder to keep everything in sight.

Saeran reached for his fork, hesitated, and then shook his head and rubbed his eyes as if they stung. "Your magic is everywhere," he said, "even in the tables. I will go blind before the night is through if you do not do something about it."

"What would you have me do?"

"Take it back. If it's back where it belongs, it will not make my eyes water where it doesn't."

"I cannot do that," she told him, her heart squeezing at his tactics. Saeran wasn't above dirty tricks when he wanted her to do something for her own good.

He shook his head and ate a little from his plate. A moment later, he stopped again, his fork clattering from his grip as turned to look at her, his face gone pale with horror. "You can't hear me anymore, can you? In your head. I just…gods, Nia, what have you done!" He grabbed her wrist and squeezed hard enough to make her bones scrape together.

"Your Majesty," Jasper's voice carried from the other side of the great hall. "My lords and ladies." He bowed to all sides, but that cold, empty smile never fell from his face. He was puffed up with self-importance, walking on his toes as he came forward, one hand over his heart, the other behind his back. When he was before the king, he bowed again in a mockery of respect and announced, "I have come as summoned to entertain the masses."

CHAPTER 36

There were shadows, and within them the Trickster god paced, a caged beast impatient for the play to begin. The other gods had caught a whiff of his dealings with mortals, and they were searching the worlds for him. So long as he remained in Shadow, he was safe. But so long as he remained there, he could do nothing but stand by and watch. Any interference would draw the others' wrath down upon his head, and he wasn't keen on their punishment, especially when, for once, he didn't plan to cause any harm.

He looked at the palm of his hand again and scowled. The lines had changed, just as he'd predicted they would. Yet, thanks to Fate's sick sense of humor, they'd not changed the way he wanted them to. Curling his fingers into a tight fist, he struck out at the darkness around him. It reverberated like a great, soundless bell, making his bones shudder.

The Trickster was at the edge of his patience, a rare instance in time when he was not in control of whatever trick he'd played. He'd let the jest go on for too long. Loki's shoulders fell in what might have been a sigh. He hated admitting defeat.

A sharp pang of uncomfortable awareness made him tense, and his gaze turned to the great hall. It was filled with Others. Incensed, he rushed the barrier between darkness and light, snarling at the congregation. Did the wizard think to cheat him of his victory? Loki almost laughed. She should have known better than to expect the Others to involve themselves in human affairs.

Tilting his head, the Trickster watched them awhile, wondering at their intentions. Others always wanted to be entertained. But this felt excessive. It felt... What was the word? Deliberate. Yes, that was it. Deliberate. He could tell by their number, the way they moved—or rather not moved—that there was a reason for their presence.

They knew he was here. Perhaps not his true identity or his exact location, but they knew something was here which did not belong. Countless sets of eyes were trained on his Shadow, trying to guess at its secrets. He grinned savagely. They never would. Not even other gods could find him where he now was, a world of his own; a construct of the Trickster's imagination.

Eyes trained on the Others directly before him, Loki stepped away from the barrier. If they interfered with the game, he would wipe their clans from this land and every other.

A commotion broke his stare and brought his attention back to the matter at hand. The ambitious sorcerer was making his entrance. Lofty as ever. To look at him, one might think he was the king. Every gesture, every word from him was a jibe the monarch seated before the dais couldn't possibly misunderstand.

The Trickster's gaze turned to the king. Or perhaps he could, he amended. Perhaps he'd noted other things amiss, such as the bright glow of his beloved wizard's power everywhere, but within her. Perhaps he'd already discovered the state to which she'd brought herself, draining every last drop of her magic from her mortal shell. Perhaps, at this very moment, the king might possibly have other things to fret about than some stranger's manners.

Loki's curious gaze settled on the girl wizard. She leaned on her staff, drained magically and weak physically. There were those who likened magic to a warm cloak of comfort. The wizard had shed hers for the occasion. He wondered how she bore such separation. Did she feel lighter? Or perhaps heavier, weary, without the brace of her power.

The air shifted, though it should not have. Distracted away from his musings, the Trickster glanced over the great hall once more. The noble guests were stirring. They didn't need magic to know something was amiss when a peasant approached a royal gathering without being summoned outright. Some grumbled, some subtly shifted farther from the table, and to his surprise, the Others in attendance drew near, an Other to each noble like guards against bad spirits. Curious.

Loki had no need to look at the king and his wizard to know they were alert. Lady Nia would lean closer to her king's ear to whisper a few words. He would acknowledge with the slightest of nods, hiding his unease very well, circumstances being what they were. He would touch a hand to his chest, to the dragon pendant that lay beneath his shirt, and the muscles in his jaw would bulge and jump, the only outward sign he was displeased with his wizard. She wouldn't notice.

The sorcerer began performing his tricks. He spoke nonsense to ease the nobles' minds while his hands moved to hide the actions of his magic. The Trickster's mouth pulled into a sharp smile at this sight. How utterly frustrating it had to be for the little old young man to try time and again to send his magic out and have it return to him without sticking to anything. He couldn't See. The pendant had not absorbed the power of Sight, or Hearing, and he had not been born with them, so he couldn't See the great hall glowing with the wizard's magic. He couldn't Hear the ancient stone around him laughing at his efforts.

For the smallest instant, his smile skewed in anger, but he smoothed it out quickly. He met the king's gaze as he juggled an illusion of balls, his eyes sparking the same way the crystal at his chest tended to do. The Trickster straightened. The sorcerer was losing patience, and that was when he usually started to make mistakes.

He did not disappoint this time.

His power flowed from him again, sliding down his waist and legs to the floor, like slime with hundreds of hues. It slid and slithered in every direction toward the tables and the nobles sitting behind them.

The Others countered but their magics slid off the spreading mass. They looked at each other and tried again. And again. And once more before they realized it was of no use. Loki smiled. A god's creation, however warped, would ever carry its maker's mark, and there was no creature, human or Other who could counter a god's wish with anything but a god's power.

When they realized this, the Others changed tactics, laying hands, vines, paws or wings on their charges. It wouldn't shield the mortals from the sorcerer's spell, but it would keep them alive until he was finished. Several of the nobles shivered, but none of them moved. Soon the writhing mass of dark magic engulfed them and it was too late for them to try.

The sorcerer tossed the balls high into the air, making them explode in a shower of sparks. It was to disguise the cries of those around him as awe, while his power sealed them to their seats. They were now sufficiently under his spell and wouldn't cry out again unless he allowed it.

But he had been foolish. He'd left the king and his wizard free. Had he bothered to imprison them as well, he would have sensed the protection spells on their persons. The king didn't wear the dragon pendant for decoration, after all. Nor had the wizard stuffed charms and pendants into her clothing for nothing. Clever, clever little cat. She'd known, or gathered, that black ice couldn't draw magic from anything that did not live. She would have warned the king to refrain from casting spells, and she'd drained herself of her own magic to keep it from the sorcerer.

The entertainer let his arms drop to his sides as he sucked in a breath of premature victory. "Now, then," he said, his smile taking on a fragile, vicious edge. "The spectators are stuck to their seats in anticipation. They wait for the players to take their place." He held his hand out toward the king and his wizard. "Come, magicker, let us give them a performance they will not forget."

The foolish king pushed to his feet, sweeping the lady behind him with an arm outstretched. His guests didn't move to stand with him, as propriety dictated, and he finally looked at them. Could he see the Others filling his great hall?

Lady Nia grasped his arm to free herself, but he would not budge. "Stay behind me." He barked the words at her, though his gaze never left the guests. Loki shaped his will and consciousness to See everything through the king's eyes, with his mind.

The monarch was furious. He'd allowed himself to get distracted by the stranger's display, and hadn't noticed the subtle sheen of his power. Nia's magic had blinded him, bright as it was. Now he could see his nobles covered with a multicolored veil and he couldn't free them; Nia had warned him not to. Though she was often foolish with her own life, she had never been with his, and so he had no choice but to trust that she had good reason for keeping him back.

His free hand rubbed over his chest. The pendant burned him. In his mind, he could hear the great dragon shifting restlessly. Saeran could sense him, but he couldn't understand yet.

Nia tried to move past him once more, speaking, though he couldn't hear her through the thundering of his own heart. Loki pitied the king at this crossroad. His royal duty was a double-edged sword in its own right, but his love for the wizard added a third edge, the sharpest. For, as king, he had a need both to protect his people, and to survive to beget an heir. As a man, his being screamed at him to keep his mate safe. But against these forces, he was powerless.

The sorcerer laughed at the look on the king's face. "Still you protect her?"

Thoughts raced through the young king's mind, so many and so fast that Loki didn't bother trying to make sense of them. Memories he couldn't recall itched in his mind, but with each word the sorcerer spoke, the wall around them chipped and cracked a little more.

"You try to hide your love, and it only makes it so much more obvious. I never had to guess whom to use to force the wizard back from her quest."

At this, even the wizard tensed, ceasing her struggles to get free of the king. When his hand on her tightened, hers responded in kind, letting him know she was still there, perfectly safe. For the moment.

Yet, even without her magic, Loki could feel through the king how the air changed around them both. Drained or not, power was in Nia's very blood. She could no more get rid of it than she could live without her heartbeat. The king shivered, and within him the Trickster did as well. The air pulsed with her wrath, a whirlwind built around her and the king, snatching at his robes. With a slight nudge to his consciousness, Loki made Saeran turn to look over his shoulder.

The wizard was as he had never seen her before, and even the king had to suppress the slightest twinge of fear at the sight. Never before had Lady Nia lost her composure this way. Ever the calm lake in the storm, now she was the storm, her hair wild in the wind, her eyes shining like sapphire stars.

The sorcerer grinned, satisfied to have found a weakness. And now he would milk it for all it was worth, to his own peril.

The Trickster sighed, and left the turmoil of the king's mind to watch the battle with his own eyes.

"Nia," King Saeran said softly.

The wizard didn't look at him, but spoke with a voice not her own. "You may use illusions, but do not use them on him directly."

Without further question, the king nodded, and a moment later stepped out from an illusion of himself and took up a place in the shadows opposite Loki. He pulled out his pendant, rubbing the surface to draw strength from it as he worked his spells.

"I lose my patience, woman," the sorcerer said, beckoning. "Come and give me what I want. Or I may just decide to play by myself for a while." One of the noblewomen pushed back from the table, toppling her chair. Clumsy as a puppet on strings, she came around toward the sorcerer, her eyes wild, tears streaming down her face, and her determined Other guardian holding her hand. Her efforts to scream came to naught.

The king's illusion leaned back, as though to say something to the wizard and then sat down to watch.

The sorcerer smiled again. "Have you obtained permission to die?"

Lady Nia stepped through the table, as if it was no more than mist, the wolf skin at her back bristling. “Before this night is through,” she said without emotion, “You will know suffering like no other.”

The noble woman stopped in her approach, quivering with silent sobs.

Eyes blazing with madness, the sorcerer’s smile finally died, his illusion wavering to reveal just a glimpse of what lay beneath. “You do not know the meaning of suffering,” he snarled and the noblewoman fell to the floor in a faint.

In his Shadow, Loki’s smile turned dark. “Let the games begin.”

CHAPTER 37

Nia felt power gathering within her, fueled by her emotions. She was livid, intent on the sorcerer's death as she'd never been on anything before. She couldn't keep the magic at bay, and at the moment she didn't want to. It gave her strength enough to advance on the sorcerer and make her stand.

Jasper's eyes shone black as the crystal he wore. He watched her approach, his anticipation rising in palpable waves, so focused on her that his glamour began to waver over him. He expected to make short work of her, and Nia would use it against him.

Words whispered over her, a warm breeze of magic settling around her like a cape—Saeran's magic. She'd told him to use illusions; it hadn't occurred to her that he would use them on her. The feeling was alien, though not unpleasant. What was he up to? For all that she could feel the spell, sense it taking shape, she couldn't see its result.

Can't think about it now. She curled her hands into fists at her sides, then opened them, sending the tables and those who sat around them sliding across the floor as far as the walls would allow. The tables turned on their sides, spilling food and creating a barrier for the nobles to hide behind, meager though it was against a magical assault. Nia would simply have to keep Jasper occupied fighting her.

Jasper grinned. "That's it," he taunted. "Bare those claws." Power as black as the night pooled in his hand. He grew it into a sloppy sphere and threw it at her with all his might. It shattered on an invisible shield an arm's length from her. Her charms were holding. "Ah," he breathed in understanding. "I am glad. I would have been disappointed if you had let me win so easily."

Another sphere formed, and he launched it, building another straight away. The volley of blows bombarded her shields, weakening them. There was only so much power an inanimate object could absorb. When it wore out, she'd be left defenseless.

Nia didn't give him the satisfaction of seeing any concern on her face. Instead, as the assault continued, she stooped down to run her hand over the smooth stone floor while Saeran's spell slid over her. So that's what it did. She looked up to see herself standing there, hands held out against Jasper's attack. The sorcerer wouldn't have seen her move at all.

Nia caressed the polished boulders, waking her own magic to life. There was plenty of it all around her, though Jasper didn't seem to realize it.

She hummed a soft tune and it filled the chamber, deafening her to everything else. The floor thrummed under her hand, eager to do her bidding. Turning her hand palm up, she made a scooping motion and a dozen boulders the size of a man's torso tore out of the floor to float at eye level all around the sorcerer.

He altered his assault. Each sphere he created split into two, then two again, flying in all directions. Three out of four shots scored their mark, but the stones were unaffected. As a warning, she launched two of them at him as she rose to her feet. The first turned him about with the force of impact. He avoided the other.

Nia stepped out of the illusion of herself, meeting Saeran's gaze long enough for him to nod in encouragement. The sorcerer wouldn't see her. Good. She had a score to settle with him.

Jasper recovered from the hit and gathered power into himself, more and more, until his mortal shell was bending double and his back began cracking under the pressure.

Oh, no. Nia ran forward, pulling more boulders from the floor and raining all of them down on Jasper at the same time with as much force as she could muster.

They never touched him. With a hoarse yell he released all that power at once, an explosion of darkness that shattered her shields and sent her skidding back. What was left of her boulders, dropped harmlessly to the floor.

He was breathing heavily when he faced her again, but though his face was beginning to crack and his eyes were flooded with black, he was still on the offensive.

Nia didn't understand the word he screamed at her, but she felt its vibrations and knew it was bad.

She dived to the floor, rolling away, and continued to roll as he struck the floor with enough force to dig through it like a plow. Saeran's illusion was gone. He could see her now and Nia struggled to keep a meager step ahead of his assault. Not fast enough like this. She took a chance when her hands met the floor, pushing with all her strength and not a small amount of magic to launch herself into the air.

She flew up almost to the ceiling, but Jasper's power followed and pierced the walls too close to Saeran. The attack stopped when he had to catch his breath, just long enough for her to fall back down. She landed on her hands and knees and immediately launched herself at Jasper. This might be the only chance she would get. She wasn't a trained fighter, but she was of a height with him and physically stronger.

But Jasper recovered faster than she could move. Before she could reach him, another shouted word caught her, sending her flying back against the dais steps. Her back carried the impact and her spine screamed in pain. Tears welled in her eyes as she fought to breathe again, but the effort it required was too great and the pain too much.

She couldn't move. Her back was broken, rendering her legs useless and her lungs nearly so. The sorcerer cackled, approaching her on shuffling feet, in no hurry now that his opponent was incapacitated. Nia reached for something to help her drag herself away but her hands slipped on rubble. She was stuck unless…no. She couldn't risk it.

Her body tilted forward as Jasper's magic caught hold of her, slowly pulling her toward him. The agony of it was unbearable. Nia screamed, the sound cut short as her voice broke on a sob. A female Sidhe appeared at her side, her eyes glowing and enchanting. *There is no other way.*

Nia's head swam. She blinked and the Sidhe was gone. But behind Jasper, the male dire wolf paced back and forth, head canted low, watching her and snarling. *Get up,* he growled. *Get up, or they all die with you.* She looked around the great hall; saw the nobles cowering behind the overturned tables, behind a row of Others who were keeping the destroyed floor from buckling beneath them all. They'd heard her.

Move! the dire wolf snapped viciously. *Fight!*

No other way, the Others whispered all around. They were watching her, willing her to do something other than lie there and wait for the sorcerer to get her close enough to finish her off. She had to do it.

If she wanted to survive, she had to call her magic back.

She slid another pace closer to Jasper, toward a massive hole in the floor. He was matching her, moving toward her as she was pulled to him, but he wasn't walking. Instead, his feet hovered off the floor, over thin air where parts of the floor were gone. A waste of power if she'd ever seen one. He was very careless for someone so close to destroying himself.

"Come on, magicker," he said, his voice distorted by many others. "Get up. There's only one way to defeat me, and you know it. Get up and fight me. Get up!"

There was flicker of movement behind him, and then a flash of metal stabbing through his heart. Nia heard the sorcerer groan, a sound not of pain but annoyance. Black magic poured out of the wound instead of blood; she could feel it. It was heavy and sought the floor rather than disperse into the air the way natural magic should.

He clucked his tongue, turning from her to face whoever was behind him. Only one person was still capable of moving on his own, the only one Jasper hadn't enchanted. He grasped Saeran by his shirt and bodily tossed him into the throne. His impact shattered it and the floor beneath it, and Saeran didn't get up again.

Nia screamed louder than she ever had in her life. The sound hurt her ears; made the humans and Others double over in pain and, were he not floating, the sorcerer would have dropped to his knees at the force of it.

The very air shuddered. Like an out of control river, her magic came rushing back into her, all that she'd drained herself of and more, from the great hall and Nico's library; taking his power as well, and Saeran's and some from the Others. It filled her near bursting, forcefully mending injuries and lifting her to her feet, though she'd not commanded it. Her scream ended as she drew a breath.

Without thought or intent, she started moving, step after step, stalking the sorcerer as he backed away from her, wide eyed. She was in a whirlwind that didn't exist, her hair and cloak whipping around her. She was glowing like a lantern as her power leaked out, illuminating the great hall better than the torches she'd extinguished. Nia felt herself on the brink of losing control. If she let go now, she could destroy not only herself and the sorcerer but everything and everyone within miles.

Two of the tables flew at the sorcerer without her conscious command. No more warnings. They flattened him between them, as far as his power would allow. It was still shielding him, though he fueled it now with his own life. It wouldn't last much longer; he had very little physical strength left, depending on magic to sustain him.

The tables shattered as he screamed.

Nia tore out more boulders, hurling them all at once. He had no chance of defending against all of them. Several scored a hit and the sorcerer staggered and fell to his knees, his body broken and his power raging out of control. He gasped big, pained breaths, but still launched another volley of magics at her. She swatted them away without breaking her stride.

By now there was little left of the floor but what pieces there were arranged themselves before her to pave an easy path to her target. The Others were retreating, one by one drawing back from the awful sight of the two of them. The dire wolf was the last to depart, still snarling.

Strange growling words spilled from Jasper's lips, sinking into the ground, making it recoil. He shot at her everything he had. What little part of her mind was still conscious of strategy discerned a pattern to his attack. He never aimed a fatal blow. This was all a studied lure to catch her magic.

At the last moment Nia stopped herself from touching him, physically or magically. Instead, she called to the banners hanging from the walls. They tore themselves to strips and wove together to form ropes that wound around the sorcerer's arms and neck. She used those binds to lift him from the floor as she continued her forward press. He hung before her as she dragged him out of the great hall, out of the castle.

The revelers in the courtyard had dispersed. Only the bonfire remained, burning high and bright. Nia didn't hesitate to send the sorcerer through it. He shouted and screamed; cast burning embers back at her. Nia didn't waste her defenses on such trifling things. She let them sear her face and hair; the burns healed instantly.

Jasper was still ablaze when she pushed him past the castle walls and started up the hill toward the altar. He put the flames out at the cost of his own body. More cracks appeared in the shell of his mortal form, his legs so damaged already they could no longer hold their shape. His limbs shattered, scattering pieces of him over the hill, leaving behind nothing but sloppy, dripping blobs of flesh.

He spat more spells at Nia, though most of them dissipated before they reached her. One or two made her falter, and forced her to heal herself again or risk setting him loose. It was too much. She knew this, felt the strain on her own body. Nia couldn't handle much more of his assault before she, too, began to shatter.

Saeran.

The sorcerer had hurt him. The image of him unmoving in the great hall squared her resolve, and she forced her body to endure. Almost there. Almost at the altar. Her hands were shining like stars at her sides, as were her feet where they peeked out from beneath her robes with each step. The wind howled at her to stop, the earth rose around her feet to slow her, but never quick enough to trap her foot before she lifted it again.

The Others had gathered again, keeping their distance, but watchful. Nia felt their apprehension, but for the safety of their people they would stay and see this through. They would do whatever was necessary to contain this uncontrollable flare of magics. As much harm as those magics could do to the human realm, they could destroy

Otherlands in an instant. It could not be allowed. They would kill Nia if they deemed it necessary, and knowing that gave her the courage to keep going.

Jasper was beginning to look demonic. The watery stumps of his legs had touched at some point and melded together, forming one liquid mass below his waist. His fingers were breaking as he kept trying to bend her will to his, but she had to hear his commands to obey, and Nia was past listening to him.

"Loki," she called into the night when she reached the altar. Her voice was not her own, and in the depths of the forest wild beasts howled in fear.

Fear for her.

Fear of her.

"*Loki!*" She made it a summons, imbuing it with all her will. Her power flared, searing her insides, and she doubled over, briefly loosening her hold on the ropes that held the sorcerer. It was all he needed to break free and drop to the ground. The grass died where he touched it, and the death spread out from him, poisoning the land.

His teeth were gone, his mouth filled with darkness. Though he still had a voice, it growled rather than spoke. He couldn't give his words any shape. One hand clutched the pendant, the source of his powers, as the black liquid he was turning into gathered around it.

And still Nia felt its pull. It could sense her power; called it out. Nia fought to keep her magic reined in, but her control was tenuous at best and she was tired, so tired of resisting. Part of her was curious at this strange toy, wanted to reach out to it. Wanted to kill the sorcerer to possess it.

She found herself drawing closer before a chilling screech in her mind made her fall back again. The dragon's warning had come almost too late. And the sorcerer cackled madly, his cheeks breaking off, taking the lower half of his face with them.

In the absence of a spoken command, his dark power spread out across the earth, killing everything in its path. It was almost close enough to touch her.

The wolf pelt at her back shivered, dragging at her neck as if it could pull her away. Nia couldn't leave. If she didn't stop it, the darkness would cover all the land and everything would die.

She cupped her glowing hands together and gathered light into them. It pooled and then rose, shaping a sphere that grew larger and brighter. In the back of her mind she noticed that the sorcerer had fallen silent. She felt his rapt attention on her, sensed his anticipation and impatience.

The sphere swirled with currents, magic trying to arrange itself so that more could fit into a smaller shape. It became so heavy it almost had a physical form.

Like a crystal ball.

The fanciful thought became a spell and shadows moved across the sphere, forming into shapes. Nia saw the great hall and the people still trapped therein. It fascinated her. Eager to see what else the sphere might reveal, she fed it more power.

The light was so bright it illuminated the ground where she knelt. As the sorcerer spread death, Nia's light brought the earth back to life around her. The light, too, began to spread, overlapping and then banishing Jasper's darkness.

He cackled, staring at the approaching well of power. He was ravenous for it.

Entranced by this thing she had wrought, Nia's attention never wavered from her crystal ball. Curiosity made her deaf and blind to the world outside of it. *What secrets will you show me? What will you teach me?*

Shadows swirled in its depths, and Nia squinted, bringing it closer to her face. She saw a mother giving birth, a mighty dragon circling high in the air, breathing magic fire. She saw a young woman bursting into flames and a young man walking in illusions.

Nia's body began to shake, but she didn't care. Looking deeper she saw demons dancing a horrible dervish in the desert night. A vast army gathering beneath the banner of a blood red cross on a grassy field. Ice slithered up her arms to her heart. Nia didn't mind; she had the cloak and the wolf skin to warm her. And the light spread ever farther.

The wolf pelt whined softly at her ear.

Nia frowned, resenting the distraction.

The crystal was showing her a drop of blood. It splattered on a shining wall of magic and shattered it, erasing the Veil between the human realm and the Otherlands and from that explosion arose a people who would carve a new order into the world.

Oh, to walk among such giants!

Nia's light touched the edge of Jasper's withered form. He screamed with glee, even as the blob of black that was his body began to solidify into rock. As the light moved up to engulf him, the pendant in his hand shimmered with white, shining through the black slime. The sorcerer's laughter died abruptly as rock sealed shut around him and the night became quiet.

Claws sank into Nia's back, fangs bit into her ear. She cried out and almost dropped the crystal ball. Through watering eyes she looked up at the rock that had once been the sorcerer. She cocked her head, puzzled by how this could have come to be, or when it had become day. Everything was so bright, colors so vibrant they blinded her.

The wolf whined again. Nia looked over her shoulder to see the wolf pelt she'd worn restored to life. He tilted his head at her and Nia reciprocated. Hadn't he died? She recalled as much. Yes, poison. She'd felt him leave his mortal shell, yet somehow he was back, flesh and blood, or at least he looked that way. Could it be an illusion?

The wolf shifted uneasily and then lifted his head and howled. Nia looked up. The moon was big and bright, the sky clear and glittering with stars. It was still night.

The wolf whined and barked, got to his feet and jumped forward and back. Nia reached out to pet the beast, only to have him shrink from her touch. Her hands were still glowing. All of her was.

The wolf sniffed the ground, backing away from the spreading light, lifting his paws high as if it bothered him.

And then the ground shuddered and the rock began to crack.

CHAPTER 38

"Foolish girl," Loki hissed in furious whisper, appearing just before her. "Look what you have done. This was precisely what I wanted to prevent!" He snatched the glowing crystal ball out of her hands, making her gasp. "*You doomed all of humanity to make a toy?*" he boomed.

Nia reached out to take it back, but before she could, part of the rock behind Loki crumbled to reveal the shiny black crystal and her hand changed direction. It was too far. *Must get up. Must possess it.*

Loki followed her gaze and straightened an arm out to stop her as she struggled to her feet. He flinched at touching her, but held firm. "Do not go near it," he warned, though he, too, sounded distracted.

Nia couldn't tear her gaze away. It was so shiny. Even from so far away she could see her own reflection in it. And every so often, it breathed! Its breath was as dark as its core. Puffs of black smoke emanated from its depths to disperse in the air. It was alive. And so beautiful and dark. She felt on fire with the light. It filled her, made her shine like the sun and it hurt. She needed that darkness to soothe her.

I might die otherwise.

"It's the magics," Loki said by way of explanation. "This is only the beginning. It will keep weakening until all of them are released."

"Pretty," she said on a sigh, not recognizing her own voice.

"Well, can't have that," Loki said brusquely and whistled. The pendant tore itself out of its cradle and as soon as the last contact was severed, the rock that used to be Jasper crumbled to dust. The pendant floated toward them, still puffing gently, and Nia's eyes opened wider and wider the closer it got. So close she could almost touch it. It felt as if it wanted to come to her. She wanted it to. She reached out to it in welcome, undeterred even when Loki slapped her hand down. Nia tried to shove him out of her way, but she may as well have been pushing at a mountain. The Trickster didn't budge a hair.

He caught the pendant by its chain before she could grasp it and turned to keep it out of her reach. Infuriated, Nia watched through him as he dipped the pendant into her crystal ball. The black stone screeched as it sank into the light. Nia could feel its pain, and it made her angry. She shoved her arm through Loki's body to take it from him, making him yell out, but it was too late. The pendant was fully submerged into the light, and the ball became solid, encasing it forever. Even some of its glow dimmed until she could see the pendant's dark outline in the middle.

It was a strange sight to behold. Nia could still sense the black ice within the orb, but it was getting weaker and weaker, as if the light was slowly destroying the darkness.

Soon, she lost all awareness of it.

Loki yanked at the chain, breaking it off, and growled, "Take your arm back, or you never will again."

Nia shook her head to clear it. What was she doing? She pulled her arm free of him and stepped back. Her entire body was shaking, and she felt as if her skin was stretching, trying in vain to accommodate the power filling her. She would burst with it soon. "Can't hold this much."

Though she wasn't looking at him, she saw Loki glare at her. "I should let you shatter," he said. "If not for you, it never would have gotten this far."

Nia hunched her shoulders, trying to keep together. Just a little longer. It was becoming unbearable. The light made her feel at once heavy and light as a feather. If she managed to hop up into the air, she'd never come back down. But she was too stiff and fragile to make that leap, rooted to the ground like a tree.

Loki tossed the orb into the air and caught it in his other hand. "Then again, if you had not made this little toy, I would have had a much tougher time sealing the damned thing. I suppose that balances things out. And I can't very well leave you as you are. You are as much of a problem now as the black ice was."

"Fix...me," she managed to say, having to shift all of her body just to make her voice work. Nothing was where it was supposed to be anymore. She couldn't feel her heartbeat; couldn't breathe, either, but she didn't seem to need it any longer. That frightened her.

Loki scowled again. "I can't. You did this, you have to undo it. And you can't do it here."

He expected her to solve riddles now? A burst of light escaped her body and she screamed, though no sound came out. She hugged herself to keep from breaking apart. The pressure was too much. It was killing her.

"I said not here," Loki snapped. "Fly up—far up, mind you—and release it there. The stars won't mind. And you had best hurry up. Any longer and you might as well join them."

Up? He meant fly. But how?

When she didn't move, Loki heaved a sigh. "I hope one day you appreciate all this," he said. Turning his face away, he came to her, bending double. She could feel his hands slipping beneath what should be her feet. "Safe journey, Lady Nialei," he said and, with a grunt, launched her into the air.

She flew up fast as a shooting star, just as she'd thought she would. No stopping now. Thousands and thousands of lights sang to her. The stars. The higher she went the better she understood them. They were welcoming her among them, eager to hear stories and to tell their own. Their voices were so beautiful, listening to them felt like coming home.

For a moment she embraced this strange place she was flying through, even let herself enjoy it. There were entire worlds filled with people and creatures she'd never seen before. She could peek into them, watch from afar as they went about their lives;

watch them like players on stage.

And the plays would never end. She knew this. Eternity beckoned to her with all its charms and Nia was curious to see it.

Saeran.

He will not be there.

Her memory returned, shocking her back to what was really happening. Going too far. Nia willed herself to stop.

The stars were puzzled. She only had a little way to go, why was she stopping?

I am sorry, she thought to them. *I cannot stay.*

The stars sang to her to keep going. They wanted to welcome her as a sister, share their world with her. She was almost there, almost home.

Nia stopped listening. There was one thing she had to do before she returned, but she had to return. *Saeran is waiting.* She hesitated for a single moment, just one moment to feel fear and doubt. Then, praying she was doing the right thing, she released all of the light, pouring it out in thick, brilliant white streams. The force of it sent her spinning, and the faster she spun, the faster it drained out of her.

As it dispersed in the sky, the pressure inside her body eased. She could feel herself returning to the way she'd been before. Her heart beat strangely in her chest, but it was beating. Her limbs began to ache, strained and tired, and her lungs expanded, filling with icy cold air. Nia shivered, but it felt wonderful.

She could move with ease again, and her stomach growled for food. Her eyes were stinging with the cold and her mouth felt parched. Wonderful. She laughed into the still night, delighting in the sound of her own familiar voice. It was even better than the stars. She couldn't hear them anymore, and that was as it should be. The smallest hint of regret faded with the anticipation of everything that was yet to come. An entire lifetime she had here. She would fill it with wonders of her own.

At last the streams of light slowed to a trickle, and Nia started descending back to earth. She used just enough magic to slow her fall, and landed softly on the hill, dizzy, but in one piece. Her ears were ringing, and she walked like a drunk as she made her way down the hill to the castle. She had no way of knowing if Jasper's spells died along with him. There might still be terrified people frozen in their seats in the great hall. Or what was left of it.

The villagers who had braved coming out silently moved out of her way. The bon fire in the courtyard had been reduced to glowing embers. Nia didn't know how much time had passed since she'd left the castle, but she was tired enough to guess it was nearing sunrise.

She mounted the stairs and gasped to see what had become of the great hall. The stone floor was all but gone. What remained was a narrow walkway, surrounded by shattered stone and enormous holes. Nia could see straight down to the cellars and there were no pillars to support the walkway, yet somehow it held.

The noble guests were where Jasper had left them. Not because they were enchanted, but because there was nowhere for them to go. Many of them were in tears, all of them looking at her as if she were a demon come to take their souls. She didn't know how to ease their fears. Instead she weaved her hands through the air to move the remaining tables. They created bridges to the walkway so the guests could escape. "They will hold," she assured them.

As soon as one stood, they all were scrambling to get outside, giving her a wide berth. She slowed them just enough to keep them from trampling over each other. What they had seen of the battle would have frightened anyone. Nia didn't expect them to cheer her and write ballads in her honor.

Once the walkway was clear, Nia approached the dais. It looked as horrible as she remembered. The throne was in splinters. Rubble and debris was everywhere, and the floor was sunken where Saeran had landed. He was still there. Nia sank to her knees by his side and carefully turned him to lie on his back.

Noises intruded, robes rustling with hurried footsteps. Now that the danger was over, the royal advisors were coming to ascertain the king's ability to sire heirs. She had no time for them. Saeran's face was bruised and bleeding and the rest of him was in no better shape.

Nia laid her hand on the center of his chest and let the rest of the world fade away. Without closing her eyes she Saw inside the king. His body was battered and broken. He was bleeding, in terrible pain, but he was alive. Barely. The dragon pendant might have saved his life, but it wasn't powerful enough to keep him alive for much longer.

Nia called Light into her grasp, but this time she did it the right way. She called it slowly and let it pass through her and into Saeran. She shaped it into the tools she needed to mend his bones and close his wounds. The light settled like a blanket over tears and cracks, healing them layer by layer. It burned away bruises with gentle heat, warming him where his wounded heart could not. Nia was meticulous in her task, repairing every injury, no matter how small with infinite patience. She took no chances, left nothing to fate.

Some of Saeran's injuries were too severe to heal right away. Broken bones needed time to mend. There, she let the Light seep into him and remain, glowing softly. It would speed the natural process of healing and, though he would be weak for some time to come, he'd be able to move about without splints and crutches.

She looked over her work twice before she returned to herself. Saeran slept. He would wake on the morrow, aching and ravenous, but alive.

Behind her, Braith was the first to speak. "My lady, what is to be done?"

"Have the king taken to his chambers," she replied, surprised at how difficult it was to form the words. She was exhausted again, and this time she wouldn't be able to keep from sinking into a wizard's sleep when she laid her head down. Already the need weighed on her so much she couldn't bring herself to stand. "He will sleep for the time being. See that he has all he needs, but do not disturb him."

"I suppose you will wish us to redecorate the great hall as well."

It was the first time Nia had heard Allon make a jest. She smiled at him. "I insist the floors be inlaid with diamonds."

He returned her smile. “Come then,” he said, holding his hand out to her. “I shall see you to your chambers. It seems to me you are in need of some healing sleep yourself.”

She nodded and allowed him to pick her up. The old man was stronger than he looked. He never once complained, taking her weight easily as he carried her up the stairs to her rooms. “You gave us quite a fright tonight.” He sounded amused.

“I have paid the price for it, as you can see.”

“What should we expect for tomorrow, then?”

When he laid her on the bed, all she could do was sink down and close her eyes. “I will sleep for some days. Do not burry me, old man. I will be very angry if you do.”

He chuckled. “I shall warn the others.”

CHAPTER 39

The snow came up to Saeran's knee, but he didn't mind; didn't feel the cold. He was so tired each step felt impossible. Every time his foot sank into the snow all he wanted to do was sit down and stay there, but he kept going, compelled by some force he couldn't understand toward the dark cave up ahead.

At last he made it out of the snow, into the pitch black tunnel. He knew this place. His feet moved from memory, leading him down into the depths of the mountain without faltering a single time. When he emerged into the cavern, Saeran breathed a sigh of relief. He was home.

Fire pits were carved into the walls like massive torches, illuminating treasure. Giant crystals sparkled in the ceiling, streams of gold were inlaid forever shining in the floors. Shadows played over painted tapestries, making them move as if they were alive, and diamonds the size of his hand glittered in piles all around.

And in the middle lay a massive sleeping dragon, his tail curled around his body, wings folded to his sides. His scales were like shined steel, reflecting firelight, and long black horns adorned his head. His claws were the size of a man's torso and each breath he puffed was black smoke.

Saeran wasn't afraid. "It was you," he said. "You called me here." He remembered the great hall, the battle of magics. He remembered the fear that had gripped him to see Jasper closing in on Nia.

He remembered dying. And the dragon commanding him back to life.

A great, slitted eye opened to look at him. "I thought it was time we met."

≪ »·◇·« ≫

There was a blurry red cloud before him when he opened his eyes. "If the wizard were here, she'd say that was a stupid thing to do." Braith's face slowly came into focus.

"Where is she? What happened?" Saeran's mouth was parched and it was difficult to speak the words, but he managed.

"She is sleeping," Braith told him. "Jasper is gone and the great hall is in ruins. Be glad the castle has not come down on top of us yet." She helped him sit up and brought a chalice to his mouth.

Saeran gulped the water down, and glared at her when she took it away.

"Slowly," she said.

"So you have finally found the courage to order around your king."

The girl blushed and looked away.

His mouth twitched. "Well, don't lose it now, I was beginning to enjoy myself." Braith glared at him, much the way Nia did and Saeran grinned.

"You would not be so cheerful if you knew what has been happening in your kingdom for the last two days."

"Tell me." He winced when she arranged the pillows behind him so he could sit on his own. His entire body pained him, but it was a healing ache. He felt warmth where he knew he'd broken bones. Saeran should be dead now and instead he felt better than ever. Aside from the pangs of hunger and the many twinges in his still healing wounds.

Braith took a chair by his bed. "It was bad," she said. "Those who were able ran at the first sound of trouble. Those who could not…well, they saw everything. Most of them are terrified of the wizard now. She spent so long showing them the gentle, healing side of her magic, none of them realized what she was truly capable of until they saw it for themselves."

"She has done nothing but defend them!"

"As a blade defends the soldier. But he never forgets how easily it can be turned against him if he lets his down his guard. The wizard is a powerful weapon, Majesty, but a weapon nonetheless."

"No, she is much more than that."

Braith lowered her gaze. "Yes. That, too, is quite obvious now. After what happened in the great hall, even those who kept the secret of your illness can't hold their tongues anymore. Rumors are spreading far and wide. About both of you."

"What rumors?"

"That the wizard is not human. That she has enchanted you somehow to gain control of Wilderheim. There are some who say they saw you move like a wraith that night, your eyes glowing like a demon."

Saeran flushed. They weren't far off the mark. He hadn't hesitated when he saw Nia go down. He'd moved, and in the blink of an eye he'd been at the sorcerer's back, a sword he didn't remember reaching for firmly in his grasp. If questioned by one with truthsense, he couldn't honestly say he hadn't used magic that night. Nor could he say he regretted it.

"I am afraid you will have greater issues to contend with when you reclaim your seat than the continuation of your royal line."

"It would seem so."

The foreign emissaries would no doubt be returning to their royal courts with wild tales to tell. Halden would understand but Saeran knew Queen Genevieve of Synealee to be dangerously superstitious and King Gavriil of the western kingdom of Ravetia abhorred all magic. He'd outlawed its practice and anyone even suspected of it faced immediate execution. Both regents would consider Saeran a threat if they believed him to be anything more than ordinary.

And then there was the matter of Aegiros. Saeran didn't want to think about what would happen when this news reached them.

"What will you do?"

Saeran snorted. "What can I do?"

Braith's brow puckered in thought and Saeran crossed his arms, amused despite himself and very much curious to hear what the girl would come up with. "I would not worry about Aegiros yet. Lyria will ally itself with us no matter what, and their armies as well as ours are well trained now, thanks to you and King Manfred.

"The threat of Synealee lies in their faith and superstitions, but their queen is ancient and not quite right in the head, if you ask me. Their lack of organization and forethought will be their weakness. We can exploit it if need be.

"Ravetia would be my biggest concern. King Gavriil is a warmonger, too eager to draw his sword at the smallest provocation. If they choose to take up arms, we will need every able bodied soldier on the front lines to defend Wilderheim."

Saeran gaped at her. Hadn't he just thought the very same thing?

"But with the unrest brewing right here, we will end up fighting a battle on multiple fronts no matter what," Braith continued with a wince. "I think the situation can be salvaged. It will be tricky, but the people love you, and if you meet them halfway with the truth you can regain their trust. We can win favor for Lady Nia back with diplomacy. The post of royal wizard has been created for an emissary for the Otherlands so that there can be peace between us. It has been held by human wizards until now because there has never been an Other willing to live so openly among us, but with Lady Nia here, it is finally as it should be. Now, if we can explain your dragonblood without inciting panic that the Others are taking ov—"

"What did you say?"

Braith's mouth snapped closed and she blushed deep red. "Umm…"

Saeran sat up straighter. "Repeat what you just said."

"A-about the battle on multiple fronts?" She wrung her hands together. "It is something I read in the Histories advisor Allon gave me to study—"

"No, after that. Dragonblood?"

Her eyes grew impossibly wide and she dropped to her knees, grasping his hand in both of hers. "Please, Majesty, forgive me. I did not mean to, it just happens. I swear I will never say a word."

"For all the gods' sake, get up."

As giant tears flooded her eyes, Braith hiccupped and stood, her head bowed. She was shaking with the force of her sobs and trying so hard to be quiet about it.

"Stop it," he said, keeping his voice low so he wouldn't frighten her more.

"I am s-sor-ry."

Saeran rubbed his brow and bit back a sight. "You have done nothing."

"But I—"

"Sit."

She sat.

"Now take a breath, and tell me the truth."

She looked as if she'd rather be anywhere but there in that moment. Saeran knew when someone was trying not to tell him something. He narrowed his eyes at her and

Braith cringed. "M-my ma was a midwife in Ravetia." She said this as if confessing to some crime. "She had a gift with all kinds of herbs and potions. Sometimes, people felt better just for touching her.

"And my gran knew things. She would know what was happening in other villages, and she would tell us when something bad was about to happen, long before it did. But they kept it secret, see? They were afraid for us. When I was old enough to travel, gran brought us all here. The whole family. So we could be safe."

Saeran guessed where this was going, but he let her speak. If Braith stopped now, she might not finish what she'd been about to say.

"It is only a little magic," she said. "Nothing like Lady Nia can do. But all the women in my family have it." She looked up as if to judge his reaction but quickly looked away. "The other advisors do not know. I never told anyone. And then there was so much to do after Samhain they had their hands full with the castle and the villagers, but you were not to be left unattended. Since I am the youngest, they said I ought to stay here, for when you woke up."

Again, she paused. "Braith," he said, "we do not have much time before someone interrupts. Whatever you have to say, say it."

"I know you are descendant of dragons. And that it is why you refuse to take a wife and sire heirs." She flinched, as if she couldn't believe she'd said it. "I can sense the dragonfire in you."

Saeran said nothing. It was most uncomfortable, having this young girl know so much about him. Braith, he imagined, was what Nia must have been like before Nico had taken her under his wing. Untrained, unsure of herself, yet in possession of something no other had. He tried to see Braith as another wizard, not a girl child. He'd appointed her as one of his advisors, after all. It would not do to lose confidence in her now.

"Only dragonblood can carry dragonblood," she said softly. "My gran used to tell us stories." She smiled a little. "I thought they were just that until now."

"Does anyone else know?"

"Oh, no, Majesty. I would never tell." After a pause, she added, "But I think you ought to."

"And give my people more reason to fear?"

"They already do anyway," she argued. "But better a kind, mostly human king they know, than a strange inhuman thing they imagine. And you could wed Lady Nia then. Begging your pardon, Majesty, but after Samhain, no one else will have you."

Saeran laughed. He couldn't help himself. "Is that so?"

Braith nodded.

"Simple as song. Wed the wizard and completely destroy the balance Wilderheim stands on."

"No," she said. "Solidify it."

"Braith…"

"Don't you see? Who would be foolish enough to stand up to a dragon king and his mate? King Gavriil despises magic because he fears it. As a king apart from your wizard, you will always be at odds, an easy target for someone like him. But if you form a united front, he will not dare challenge you. Not with Lyria and the whole of Otherlands at your back."

Saeran gritted his teeth against harsh words. "And Synealee?"

Braith shrugged. "They might try, but they will have to go through Lyria to get to us. King Halden will not be beaten twice, especially not by pampered zealots."

"And what of Aegiros."

Braith's growing winsome smile faded. "I do not know. Queen Mari's death complicates everything where they are concerned. They might care, they might not. There is no way to tell what they will do until they do it. Aegirans do not plan their assaults, they simply carry them out."

"And how do you propose we circumvent the riots in my own kingdom?"

"Do as you have always done. Be the king you have always been and prove to them that the well being of Wilderheim and its people is still your highest priority. I cannot say it will be easy, but you have won them once, it can be done again. You descend from a long line of kings, Majesty, good kings, sometimes foolish kings, but never cruel or heartless. Show them the goodness of your heart and they will love you for it."

Saeran sighed, weary of this. "Which leaves the ever important chore of siring heirs and continuing that long royal bloodline. Tell me, young Braith, what magical solution do you have for that?"

"Lady Nia is Other," she said quickly. "She might—"

"Enough," Saeran snapped. "Thank you, Braith." He'd meant it as a dismissal. His head ached like the devil, and he was in no mood to discuss whether or not his hypothetical dragon spawn would drain the life from Nia as he'd watched it do with Mari. His eyes closed of their own volition and he leaned his head back, half drowsing already.

But Braith didn't leave. "Sire, there is more. I looked in on Lady Nia while you slept."

Saeran cracked one eye open to look at her. "So now you know all of her secrets too?"

Braith stood and arranged a tray of food and the chalice where he could reach them if he wanted to. "I do know what you fear," she told him. "I also know that with her you would not need to."

"She can keep from conceiving, you mean."

She said nothing.

"If you are talking about the Other thing again, don't. I will not risk her life on the possibility that I might be wrong."

"No, that is not what I meant at all."

"Then what?"

Braith wouldn't look at him as she backed away to the door. "Perhaps you should ask her," she said. "Ask her what the dragon did."

Saeran frowned as the door closed behind her. Left with that mysterious pronouncement and no idea what she was talking about, his mind immediately seized on the possibility that there might be even the smallest chance for…something. He rolled his eyes at himself even as sleep began to weigh on him once more. Even if he was willing to believe it, which he wasn't, and even if no one else ever offered their daughter or sister in marriage to him again, which might or might not be true, and even if a marriage between them didn't cause the chaos he knew it would, Nia had already turned him down twice. And he'd thought he'd accepted her decision with grace.

But content as he'd told himself to be with Nia by his side as friend and companion, Saeran's heart had never stopped hoping for more. Nia was part of him; he felt it even now when she was worlds away in wizard's sleep. He felt her heart beating and the world made sense.

Saeran sighed and closed his eyes. He imagined she was there with him, nestled against his side and he smiled, allowing sleep to pull him under.

He dreamed of the dragon flying circles high in the air, breathing fire at the clouds, and a pair of babies swathed in embroidered blankets, looking up at him with big, curious eyes.

CHAPTER 40

Out of total darkness Nia fell into blinding light. She rubbed her eyes and squinted. There were giant orbs floating in the air, their light bouncing off the crystal walls and golden pillars. The chamber was enormous, with a ceiling so high she couldn't even see it and windows big enough to fit a castle through.

"Do you know where you are?"

Nia turned around to face the female Sidhe seated on a delicate white throne.

"Do you know why you are here?" the male beside her asked before she could answer.

"No," Nia said to both questions.

The king of all Sidhe scowled. "I expected better from you by now."

Nia looked around at the hall suddenly filled with faeryfolk. "I was sleeping," she said. "How did I get here?"

"What does that matter?" the queen said. "You were elsewhere, now you are here. What you should be worried about is why you are here and how you will get back."

"If you will get back," the king corrected.

"Why would I not?"

The queen folded her hands together in her lap. "There is a matter of great concern we must discuss. You will not leave until we are satisfied that it is resolved."

"Who do you speak for?" the king asked.

Nia didn't like his arch tone. "Everyone who needs a voice. And you?"

His eyes narrowed and vines burst out of the ground at her feet, twining around her legs and body. Nia kicked and ripped at them but the more she fought, the faster they grew until she couldn't move at all.

"Disrespect will not be tolerated, Halfling."

A mass of black fur hurtled over her head with a vicious snarl. The dire wolf male took a stand between her and the Sidhe and growled, "She is not one of yours."

"Then who does she belong to?" the queen questioned. "The water sprites? She does not look like one. Or her sire's people? Or humans? Or the dragon, perhaps!"

Behind Nia the female dire wolf huffed, and the vines withered at her feet. Nia stepped out of them and faced the royal Sidhe. "I belong to no one—"

"Still you don't know who you are," the queen said.

"—and my people are who I choose them to be."

"Your ignorance grows tiresome."

"Everyone must belong to someone," the Sidhe king decreed.

"Why?" Nia challenged. "Because you decided?"

"Because without someone, you are no one," the queen said.

Even the dire wolves had no defense to offer against that.

"Enough of this. The sorcerer's amulet damaged the Veil between our lands. Humans are passing through where they should not, and our people are becoming stranded in your world. What do you intend to do about it?"

"Me?"

"Yes, you," the king said, rolling his eyes. "The girl without clan, without a name, the nobody standing before royal Sidhe without the sense to kneel. You. The sorcerer came for you, so it is your fault that this has happened."

Nia was speechless. "You want me to repair what gods have created?"

"Are you unequal to the task, she who speaks to gods?"

The dire wolves growled and the female shifted into her human body next to Nia. "You go too far Eilwyn," she said to the Sidhe queen.

"You dare speak my name!"

"You know I will dare much more if you vex me," the female growled.

The Sidhe king stood. At his full height, he was enormous, and pale white shadows moved at his back like gossamer wings. Nia had never seen anything like it. "Remember your place, wolf."

"You would do well to remember yours," the male dire wolf said. "You do not speak for all of us. You only speak the loudest."

"See what she does to us," Eilwyn said, her voice resounding throughout the hall. "Scant moments among us and we turn on each other like humans." She turned to the dire wolves. "And Roukan and Lyall would have us welcome her in our midst."

Accusing stares turned on her from all around. No longer only Sidhe, the hall was now filled with all clans of Others, big and small.

"I do not want to be in your midst," Nia said. "My place is in Wilderheim."

What of the Veil? Nia turned to face the speaker, a male water sprite, looking out from a lake that wasn't there before. *Humans in Otherlands get lost. Humans in our lakes and rivers drown.*

"I don't know how to repair the Veil," Nia said. "But if we agree to a compromise, I can help to mend the rifts."

"Compromise," the Sidhe king said with disgust.

"Sit down, Ruari," Lyall commanded, shedding her human skin in favor of her dire wolf form. "Let the girl speak."

The Sidhe king scoffed, but no one spoke up for him, and with a snarl he sat.

"Go on, Nialei."

It was strange hearing her full name. No longer was she an orphan from the woods, she was Nialei of the Streams. Daughter of a water sprite and…well, she wasn't quite sure what her father was, but what she knew was enough. Squaring her shoulders, she addressed the crowd. "Our legends say the gods wove the Veil from the blood of each clan of Otherlands and gave it the power of illusion. It was never meant to be a gateway to be opened or shut, but a shield to hide the worlds from each other. But they were never truly separate, were they? Not with curious Others passing through whenever they pleased to spy on humans and amuse themselves meddling in their lives."

King Ruari pushed to his feet again, but Nia held up her hand to silence him. "I mean no offense," she said politely. "What I mean to say is that it took all of us to create the Veil, and it will take all of us to mend it. But Otherlands will never again be a mystery to humans, not in Wilderheim, not after everything that's happened. The compromise I propose is that we work together to mend the rifts, all of us, even humans. Because if Others refuse to stay in Otherlands, then humans should not be forced to stay in human lands. Fair is fair, after all. Balance must be kept, yes?"

"How dare you suggest we allow mortals to walk our worlds!" Eilwyn said, outraged.

"How dare *you* assume mortals will continue to fight, bleed, and die to defend your precious worlds without having anything in return?" Nia replied. "It has been thus for centuries. Wilderheim stands bastion to protect *you. Your* worlds and *your* secrets. They are the only ones who still believe in the old legends, and it is that very faith which is keeping the Veil fluid. You know as well as I that the moment the people of Wilderheim stop believing, and wondering, and praying, the Veil will slam shut and no one will pass through it ever again, human or Other."

She paused for breath and chanced a look around. It was a bluff, a wild guess on her part but from the looks of those around her, Nia had guessed right. The Others needed humans as much as humans needed them. Nia swallowed with difficulty, wondering what would happen to those stuck on either side who did not belong. She couldn't be the only Other living among humans. And as fascinated as the Others seemed to be about them, Nia was certain there had to be humans living among Others somewhere as well.

"Those with Sight have always known and will always know there is more to Wilderheim than meets the eye. You cannot hide and expect mortals to fight for what they cannot see."

"They have done it this long," Ruari said with a careless shrug. "Why should they not continue?"

Nia took an angry step before she could stop herself and the ground shuddered beneath her foot. "Because I will not let them."

The Sidhe king and queen leaned toward each other and spoke in whispers a moment. Then Eilwyn stood from her throne and said, "Who will speak for the Halfling?"

The dire wolves stepped up to her without hesitation. "We will," Lyall said.

And us, the water sprite added.

"And us," the fire sprites chimed in.

One after the other the great majority of the Others voiced their support. Nia nodded her thanks to each of them and then turned to the Sidhe, the only ones who had not yet spoken. "And how have you decided?"

Ruari scowled at her and pushed to his feet next to his queen. With a regal nod, he answered for both of them, and then Nia was flying, spinning, dropping away, back into the darkness from which they'd taken her. Back into the wizard's sleep.

CHAPTER 41

Before she awakened fully, Nia felt the presence of another in her chamber. "Trickster," she said, in no mood to spar with him. When she opened her eyes, he perched at the foot of her bed, his black eyes crinkled at the outside edges with mischievous laughter, though his thin mouth betrayed not a hint of humor.

"At last, she wakes," he said, matching her dry tone. "I was beginning to think a dousing with cold water was in order."

Nia sighed and sat up. And immediately frowned. "This is not my room."

"Indeed, it is not," Loki said and disappeared, reappearing again on the sill of a very large window. The drapes were pulled back and Nia had an unobstructed view of the castle grounds, and far beyond to the forests. She could see the road out of Frastmir from here! And the village it led to.

"Where am I?"

The Trickster chuckled, mocking her. "You have been asleep for quite some time now, Halfling. The king has been a busy little bee in your absence. Poking around in his own mind, tasting new magics on his tongue, listening to whispers denied to him for long years. Sniffing out secrets. Always the secrets. Pecking, pecking, pecking away at mysteries best left untouched, if I had any say. It would have been more fun that way."

Ignoring him, Nia slipped out of bed, touching her bare feet to thick bear skins strewn over the floor. She padded to the door and opened it a crack to peer outside. Still in the castle. Near the king's chambers. What was the man up to now?

She closed the door again and leaned against it. "What do you want?" she demanded of Loki.

He scowled at her, as though she'd taken away his plaything for no good reason at all. "I have brought you a stray," he said. With a snap of his fingers, he conjured a wolf. Her wolf. The wolf that had been no more than a pelt hugging her shoulders not so long ago. "He has no place among the living, yet he is not dead."

The creature's eyes did seem different. They were pure white, as if he ought to be blind, yet he seemed to see perfectly. He got up and began pacing around, sniffing everything, fascinated with this and that.

"You don't remember?" Loki said. "I suppose you were a little preoccupied at the time. You brought this poor beast back from the dead. Not completely; his true spirit is free on the other side. This one is, shall we say, a mirror image. His body is not flesh and blood, and thus cannot age or die. His mind remembers everything of his past life, and all that has happened since his death. And he is a very annoying heap of fur! I do not want him in my realm. He is your charge. You take care of him."

The wolf eyed Nia warily, head low, ears pricked forward. He approached her with caution, turning left first, then back toward her, then right again, as if he couldn't decide whether he wanted to get closer or not. Nia kept still, let him make up his mind.

When he finally reached her, he sniffed at her night shirt and her hands, and at long last, his tail began to wag and she felt the rasp of his tongue against her fingers. Nia lowered to her haunches to scratch him behind the ears.

"The sorcerer is gone," Nia said, not looking at the god.

"I am aware."

"We had a deal, Trickster."

"Indeed, we did. I vowed to tell you of your sire if you rid me of the sorcerer."

"Well?" She looked at him.

Loki grinned sharply for a quick instant before smoothing his features out again. "I do not recall specifying when I would tell you, only that I would." Nia scowled and he laughed. "In time, wizard. You have plenty of it. Learn a little patience."

Nia had half a mind to put him to the ceiling and keep him there a good long while. She resisted only because she had no wish to be around him any more than was absolutely necessary.

The wolf rolled onto his back and pawed the air madly, demanding a belly rub.

"Tell me something else, then," she said. "What is this about the king? Tell me of these secrets of yours."

"They are no secrets of mine he has been learning," he said with an easy shrug.

"What do you mean by that? Enough of your games, Trickster. Tell me what it is you want so badly for me to know and leave. I have duties to attend to." And she was famished. Considering how hungry she was, Nia guessed she had to have slept for at least a fortnight.

"The kingling's feet tread far in sleep. He sought a link and found it. Now his grandsire can speak, tho' the king's hearing is weak, and summonses have been sounded."

So Saeran has found a way to speak to the dragon. Did that release her from his presence in her mind? She hadn't felt him since she'd woken. It was a relief to have her thoughts to herself again. But she'd gotten used to the dragon's presence. Even when he'd meddled, he'd at least been someone to talk to.

Not knowing why she did so, Nia reached out to the dragon. She felt his presence instantly, warmth, and kindness, and welcome. "She's awakened," she heard him say, and, realizing he wasn't alone, she withdrew immediately.

"Well, now you have done it," Loki said, rising from the window sill. The afternoon sun reflected off his hair, making it glitter and shine like sharp, polished copper. "They will pour in here in droves now to see to you. A thing I have no wish to be part of, so I shall bid you farewell."

Nia narrowed her eyes at him. "You are hiding something," she accused.

"Always," he replied with another quicksilver grin.

Her mind raced with possibilities. Whatever he was withholding would be of great importance, and he was doing it simply to spite her and amuse himself. "Saeran knows about his grandsire. What else? What other secrets?"

The Trickster's eyes gleamed wickedly. "You will find out soon enough. I would not dream of spoiling the surprise."

"Loki!"

It was too late. He'd disappeared. And while Nia thought she might be able to summon him back, there would be no point to it. He would prove no more obliging than he had thus far.

The wolf came to his paws again, barking at the nothing that remained where Loki had been. It would seem the beast didn't like him any more than Nia did. Then he turned on Nia, or rather, the door behind Nia, and he barked once more, his tail wagging wildly.

With no more time to think or debate the Trickster's riddles, she conjured her robes about her. Her hair pleated itself back as the walls and the floor all but shivered with anticipation. She could feel it in the air, and so could the wolf, if the way he shook himself and grumbled was anything to go by. There were people coming. And she had a very bad feeling that she ought not be found in this room. At the very least she needed to meet them outside in the hall. There, she could think of some reason for her presence.

Needing to escape, she opened the door—

—and walked into Saeran.

They froze, staring at each other for long moments, while the wolf barked and pranced around them and then bounded off to someone else. Nia didn't know where he went. She knew there were others behind Saeran, but all she could see was him. He was dressed in his official kingly garb, his crown heavy upon his brow. His eyes were clear and sharp, with no lingering shadows from his ordeal. He seemed younger, somehow. As if a great burden had lifted from his shoulders. He stood tall and proud, radiating heat and strength in a way that reminded her of his grandsire. Saeran was more dragon than she'd realized.

Nia heard his heart racing in his chest, and her own heart matched the rhythm. The way he was looking at her made heat bloom in her cheeks. She knew she wasn't breathing, but couldn't find a pressing enough reason to inhale.

Then Saeran's mouth pulled into a smile, and then that smile grew bigger, more dazzling as he took her hand and bowed over it, holding her gaze all the while. "Welcome back, my queen," he said, his voice low and full of mystery.

Nia blushed at the endearment aware of the others present. "Majesty," she answered uncertainly.

"It is a shame you did not wake this morning," he said. "We missed your presence at the ceremony."

"Ceremony?" Nia frowned, listening to what the walls could tell her. For once, they were silent, watching everything with rapt curiosity. There was no breeze to speak to her, and if the earth itself knew anything, it wasn't telling. "How long have I been asleep?"

"Nearly three weeks," Saeran said. "We were worried for you at first, but your color improved daily so we waited. But after everything that's happened there were those who believed that we could not wait much longer. Something needed to be done, and so a wedding ceremony was held this morning."

Nia swayed back, and were it not for Saeran's hold on her hand—both her hands—she would have fallen over. Saeran wouldn't be dressed this way for anyone's wedding but his own. "You married?"

That smile remained on his lips as he studied her reaction. Whatever he deduced from it seemed to hearten him, but he frowned as he dropped his gaze. "Sadly, my bride was not yet present, and so I was forced to marry her by proxy." With his head still bowed, he looked up at her, his mouth twitching.

This time, Nia pulled her hands out of his grasp and backed away from him. "You didn't," she whispered as understanding dawned. "Tell me you did not—"

"It is done," the dragon said with his familiar deep voice.

Nia looked to where he stooped by the gleeful wolf, playing with him. He wore dark breeches and a deep red shirt, with a brown leather jerkin. His hair was combed back, but his horns were gone, as was his tail. He looked older as well, though not near old enough to be Saeran's grandsire. There was a sharpness to his gaze when he looked at her, but warmth as well. It was a duality not easily affected by normal people.

Saeran must have summoned him out of his icy isolation, and while he didn't seem unhappy to be there, Nia could tell he wasn't comfortable with his fully human form. His essence was still that of a dragon, and she felt it fill the hallway, though the advisors behind him seemed oblivious to it.

The dragon didn't stop playing with the wolf, but his attention was on Nia. He was waiting, she realized, not for her answer, but for her acceptance. "A proxy still needs to be finalized by the bride's consent."

"It is done," repeated the dragon simply.

"What have you done?" she whispered, her heart beating too fast and her breaths coming too slow. She was beginning to feel light headed.

"What I should have done months ago," Saeran said, following her retreat. He grasped her shoulders firmly and she was glad of the support, even while she pushed against his chest to be released. "Placed you where you belong. At my side. As my queen."

"The people won't accept—"

"We will sort it out."

"Aegiros, and Ravetia…"

"Braith?"

"They will not dare challenge a royal pair as powerful as you, Majesties," Braith answered.

"Your advisors…"

"Gave their unanimous support," Allon said.

"All but shoved me to the altar," Saeran added wryly.

"Heirs?" she ventured. He couldn't possibly have the answer to every question. There were too many! Too much could go wrong, especially now with the Veil damaged and Others looking for an excuse to lash out. There would be fighting, possibly riots, to say nothing of war.

"My decree still stands. Should I die without heirs, the rule of Wilderheim will pass to Halden's children and the two kingdoms will join into one." He softened his tone as he continued. "As to the matter of children, my love, you have yourself told me that it takes dragonblood to birth a dragon. Blood that runs in your veins now. The decision will be yours."

At this last, the advisors hummed unhappily, but they didn't say a word. The dragon, still watching her with his inscrutable eyes, gave the slightest of nods. The wolf now sat beside him, another member of their rapt audience.

Nia shivered beneath the weight of their scrutiny. She was fighting not only them but herself as well. But she couldn't give in to the treacherous part of her that so longed to say yes. Why couldn't they understand? She was trying to keep them all safe! A pair of Others ruling a human kingdom would be disastrous. Her duty was to safeguard Wilderheim. She was trying to protect them! She was…

Lost for her king. And had been since the day they'd first met.

Nia had always known she would never take a lover or become a wife. She'd sworn her fealty to the king, knowing that, for her, such fealty carried a great deal of heart as well. And she'd known what it would mean. A lifetime spent in shadow, dispensing wisdom while keeping to herself. Nia was the royal wizard. She'd accepted her duty as the power behind the king.

Her heart had never been free to give.

"Sweet Nia," Saeran said, drawing her closer, despite her silent protests. "Beloved soul. The beat of my heart. There never was another way." His arms came around her, holding her close. "You were my destiny from the first."

"I am your wizard," she tried, but couldn't voice it with conviction.

Saeran noticed. He smiled again. "You must accept me," he said. Not accept this. He wasn't asking her to rule his kingdom, or bear him sons. He was asking her to let him into her heart. Nothing more.

He didn't know. She'd never told him. Her heart had always been his to begin with. Never free to give, because he'd already held it.

Saeran nuzzled her temple, his voice dropping to a whisper at her ear. "You must," he repeated, and the whole of Nia's being responded to his words. "Because the first time we kissed, time stopped."

When his lips brushed hers, Nia stopped fighting. It was done, had been for a very long time. She simply hadn't allowed herself to admit it. No matter the path chosen, this would always have been her destination because there were some things in this world not even a powerful Halfling Other with dragon's blood in her veins could overcome, nor did she want to. Nico must have known. He would not have brought her here if he hadn't been absolutely certain it was the right thing to do. It gave her the courage to believe that whatever the future held she would weather it as long as she had Saeran by her side.

And so the royal wizard acknowledged the inevitable convergence of two mate souls, accepted her beloved king as her husband, and gladly opened her heart to him, telling him with all of herself what she could not speak in words, lest she break their kiss.

And when time stopped again, she was more than happy to let it.

EPILOGUE

"You doubted me."

Freki surged to her feet. Head low, hackles up, she snarled at the shadow and the figure emerging from its depths. As Muninn took flight and alighted on Loki's shoulder, cocking his head from side to side, Woden breathed a quiet sigh. Here stood the most beautiful Halfling ever born. Beautiful and flawed. "Yes," he replied simply.

Loki's reckless smile skewed, darkness leaking from his empty eyes. "You, who knows all, doubted a future set in eternity?"

"Nothing is ever set, Loki. You should know that better than anyone."

Muninn cawed, unsettled by Loki's growing anger. "I destroyed the stone, did I not?"

"You created it in the first place," Woden reminded him. "And what of the Veil?"

A burst of darkness flared out of Loki. Where it touched, the world changed. Grass coiled like a nest of snakes, pebbles grew spider legs and crawled, jumping onto trees and logs which suddenly groaned like ravenous beasts. "*That was not my doing!*"

"It came about as a direct result of your actions. You will be held accountable."

Loki shouted to the sky, and his new creations screamed with him. Woden fisted his hand and slammed it down on the smooth stone surface of his armrest. A deafening boom made the earth shudder, knocking Loki to his knees and startling Muninn into flight. Everything Loki had brought to unnatural life reverted to its inert form, though it would forever carry his dark taint. Chest heaving with wrath-filled breaths, Loki glared at Woden. He would not stand until Woden allowed it.

The All-Father rose from his seat and looked around, breathing in the serenity of this place. It would not last much longer. Loki's interference had set in motion events which could not be stopped by an act of the divine. The Veil was not only a separation between the human realm and the Otherlands, but also the vessel of divine power. Even now that power bled out of Asgard, dispersing into the aether and very soon it would leech from the gods themselves.

Though he was far removed, Fenrir's howls echoed on the wind. The monster knew his time was nigh. He fought his binds, bit at the delicate ribbon tied about his neck. For now it held. A product of Dwarven magic and skill, it was yet unaffected by the change. But if Nialei and the Others failed to restore the Veil, the ribbon's magic would drain and Fenrir would break free and devour the world as had been foretold.

Loki closed his eyes and smiled to hear the eerie sound. There was something akin to pride in the set of his shoulders. Even subjugated to his knees he showed no humility. "Listen," he whispered. "My son sings to me of freedom. Is it not beautiful? His agony will be your end, All-Father. It's coming, can you feel it?" When he looked at Woden again, his smile was sharp as a blade, promising terrible things.

"Get up," Woden commanded.

Like a puppet on strings, Loki rose to his feet. "You so like your Shadows, Trickster? Good. You will stay in them henceforth."

His black eyes widened. "How long?"

"Until you learn that your actions have consequences. Forever if need be."

"No!" Loki lunged at Woden, but the binding spell held him back. The Shadow from whence he came grew and reached out, wrapping smoky tendrils around the Trickster, drawing him back into its depths. "I'll kill you! All of you!" He screamed ancient words and curses, his voice echoed by Fenrir's rising frenzy. He could feel his father's wrath, as Loki felt his. "*Avenge me, son!*" When the Shadow swallowed him whole, its stain dissipated and peace settled over the land once more.

It took a long time for Fenrir's maddened howls to die down. When they did, mist poured into the clearing, swirling up and taking shape. From its center emerged Frigga, a worried frown marring her brow. "How long will it hold him?"

"Not long enough, I fear."

"Nialei will need time."

"She might not have it."

Frigga nodded. "Then we will have to speed things along."

"Frigga," Woden said, taking her hand in his. "You cannot stop the inevitable."

His beautiful wife smiled. "So you say. But did you not also say that nothing is ever set?" Before he could answer, Frigga turned to mist and blew away.

With a weary groan, Woden settled back in his seat. "Deserted again," he told Freki.

She tilted her head at him and whined.

"What's wrong? What isn't? The Veil is down, Others sit the throne of a human kingdom, magic is spilling everywhere and…" he sighed. "And the worst of it is this is only the beginning. Darkness grows outside of Wilderheim. Can you feel it?"

Freki shook herself out.

Woden nodded and closed his eyes. Unbidden a vision formed in his mind, a portent of both light and dark. The great dragon flew through the air, breathing massive plumes of fire at the clouds. The desert moon rose on a shriek of demons rioting through the night. A vast army gathered beneath the sign of a blood red cross. He opened his eyes and rubbed his aching head. "Whatever you plan to do, my love," he said to the winds whisking her away, "do it fast."

DRAGONBLOOD

For true strength is not contained in the breadth of a shield, or the tip of a sword. It cannot be measured by the reach of an arrow, or the precision of a strike. True strength is strength of spirit, the war cry of a soul standing its ground against the howling winds. It fears neither rain, nor cold, nor lightning—the storm is but an aspect of itself.

PROLOGUE

She was *aseti*. Outcast. She, who'd never caused harm to another, who'd shown her tribe nothing but love and given them all she had. Disowned by her family, stripped of her name, forced to live on the outskirts of their city, and all because she'd been born with something that ought never have belonged to a woman: magic.

They called her a witch, shunned her from their midst. They feared her, and they should. While the Magi relied on spells and rituals, the witch's power came from within, not from the gods. When she called on her magic, it poured out of her heart on a tide of emotions. Outcasts could not work, wed, or bear children; they could only beg and pray the tribesmen would show them kindness. A witch was a blight, a curse upon the tribe, and never allowed near the others. She couldn't even beg, and no one would look upon her for fear the curse would infect their eyes and be reborn in their children.

In all her life, only one had dared to brave such perils and secretly bring an old woman food and water: the *shansher*'s beloved youngest daughter, Mari. For her kindness, the witch had loved Mari like her own flesh and blood, and she'd cursed the *shansher* the day he'd sent Mari to the Northern king. The witch had known the girl was riding to her doom; she'd warned him not to do this, to send another in his daughter's place. He hadn't listened. No one had, because in the eyes of the Imarah tribe, the witch did not exist.

Almost a year had passed since the riders returned with Mari's ashes. Three times the rains had come and gone, while the witch waited for the *shansher* to ride north to avenge his daughter. And in all that time, no one had stood up for her. No one.

How dare they let one of their own disappear this way—a princess, no less! Forgotten, as if she'd been an outcast, herself.

Now, the witch knew they'd never right this wrong. A princess Mari may have been, but she'd still been only a woman. Consumed by hatred for every man in the tribe, the witch couldn't bear to look at any of them, lest she loose a terrible wave of magic and destroy them all where they stood. It wouldn't be a good enough end for them. For what they'd done to Mari, the witch would make them all suffer.

When the sky had turned dark and the sands had cooled, the witch stole a torch and ran into the desert. Countless stars shone above, but the moon was dark tonight, averting its face so that her deeds might go unwitnessed.

The witch looked around to make certain she hadn't been followed. She hadn't. No one cared about her. If she went missing, they'd rejoice to be rid of her. For that, too, the Imarah tribe would pay.

With her toes, she traced a large circle in the sand, deep enough to create a channel.

The black powder came next, sprinkled evenly all around. When fire touched it, the powder would blaze a bright green, an irresistible lure to the *djinn*. And once she'd trapped the *djinn* in the circle, she'd make it do her bidding. It would become the vessel of her wrath.

The witch stepped out of the circle, then raised her torch high, calling on her magic. She'd seen the Magi perform their rituals, summoning the gods' good will, and she mimicked their movements from memory but spoke her own words. Three steps along the left side of the circle, four back to the right. Five to the left, six to the right. At first she whispered the words, then she spoke them, and as she rounded the circle at last, the witch shouted a command into the night, forcing her will into the air, making it congeal as black smoke. When she slammed the torch down into the black powder, green fire flared as high as she was tall, and she stumbled back from its heat.

Gasping for breath, the witch returned, squinting through the fiery veil into the circle. She saw a figure within, heard its rasping sighs on the night breeze. Harsh, foreign words hissed all around; dark groans made her shudder and trace the sign against evil over her chest.

When at last the fire died down, the witch beheld the creature she'd summoned. It was tall and thin with wide shoulders and gangly limbs, its long, black hair plaited back into a thick rope that reached the sands and coiled around its feet. Or rather, where its feet ought to have been. It wore shadows as clothes, and every time the breeze blew, the creature briefly turned to smoke, as if it would dissipate in the wind.

"I am—"

"No one," the creature said. "How dare you summon me, no one?"

"I..." She could not find her voice. The creature's red eyes glowed, following her every move, staring straight through her, into her, and the witch hugged herself for fear of having her soul ripped out of her chest.

The *djinn* laughed; a terrible sound in the night. "No one wishes to be someone. To be seen and feared."

"N-no. I wish—"

"I know what you wish. I can taste your soul, no one." It licked its lips with a long, pointed tongue, and hummed. "It is as bitter as firedust. You wish to see your mistress avenged. But where to begin? With her father who gave her away? Or her mother who gave her such a miserable life?" It floated closer, touching the blackened circle of its prison. "Would you like to see the man who took that miserable life, no one?"

The creature held out its bony hand and, with a harsh command, summoned a blaze into its palm. The flame swirled like a mad thing, twisting and stretching every which way to escape, but the *djinn*'s magic held it in place. "Look upon the face of your enemy. See how happy he is."

The witch looked, gasping at the sight.

There, the castle in the North. There, the fair-haired king sat on the bed, gazing down at a pair of swaddled babies. He looked up at the woman who'd given birth to them and smiled at her with such love, the witch felt tears slide down her wrinkled cheeks. She shook with hate. That love should have been Mari's. Those children should have been hers.

"What will we name them?" the king asked.

"My daughter's name is Liadan," the woman said. "Your son waits for you to name him."

The king peered down at the child, and at length said, "Fal. His name is Fal."

The woman smiled. "Liadan and Fal."

"They're beautiful."

Suddenly, a dark-haired man was there. "They are too much human," he said.

The king and his woman looked at each other, and a grave understanding passed between them. "They are only just born," the woman said, her eyes pleading.

"Yes," the dark-haired one said.

The witch gasped. "What demon is this?"

"He is a dragon," the *djinn* answered. "He has lived long before your gods birthed your tribe. The king is his grandson, and he is mighty with dragonblood coursing in his veins. Do you think he will be so easy to defeat?"

"Yes," the witch answered at once. "Because you will strike at him where he is most vulnerable."

"Ahh," the *djinn* breathed. "Wrath. Sweeter than a newborn's blood."

"I want you to strike them down."

"A dangerous task, and not without a price."

"I will pay it," the witch said.

"You do not wish to know what I will demand of you?"

She couldn't hear what else the Northerners said, but she did see the dark-haired one bring forth two small cups. When the king and his woman nodded, clutching each other's hand, the man gave one cup to each, and they, in turn, each fed a child from the cup.

"Now, creature—strike now!"

The *djinn* crushed the flame between his palms, and it exploded outward, knocking the witch down. From the ground, she looked up into the smoke left behind at what the *djinn* had wrought. The children screamed, one of them bursting into flames. Their parents and the dragon rushed to save them, but the witch knew it was too late.

Shaking, she touched a hand to her heart, then to her lips, and finally to her forehead. "For you, my sweet Mari. I do this for you."

"You did this for yourself." Hard hands curled around her arms, yanked her up off the ground. "And now, I take my reward."

The witch screamed, struggled in vain against the *djinn*'s hold. No, not a *djinn*; a true fire spirit would never have been able to leave its circle prison. In a rush of wind, the creature's face wavered, changed into something grotesque and terrible. Its eyes slanted crooked, its nose flattened into almost nothing, and its mouth stretched halfway around its head, opening on several rows of sharp teeth.

A *daeva*—a demon!

The witch screamed again, her own mouth forced open wide as the *daeva* forced noxious smoke down her throat. It became a living thing inside her, stretching her, pushing her aside to make room for itself. It hurt in unimaginable ways as the *daeva* cast her out.

Then the pain was gone, and she opened her eyes. She saw everything, the entire night, in every direction at once. She focused down on her body and saw it rise up from the sands. It looked back at her, its black eyes turned to red as the *daeva* smiled from her own face.

"Do not fear, no one," it said with her voice. "You may be nothing now, but a deal is a deal. I will give you the vengeance you so desired. The Imarah will pay for what they'd done, just as you wished. You simply won't be around to see it."

"What do we do?" a weeping woman whispered, turning the witch's attention back to the dissipating smoke of the *daeva*'s spell.

"I will take the girl," the dragon said.

"No!" the king cried.

"Be easy, Saeran. She cannot remain here. It is too dangerous. I will keep her safe, and you have only to think of her to be there with her. You must trust me. She is a Dragonblood, more powerful than any one of us, and until she can control it, she will need to be in a place where her fire will harm no one."

"And my son?"

A sigh. "He is a creature of water, not fire. I cannot help him."

"Then I will," the woman said fiercely.

Only when the witch heard the power in the woman's voice did she realize what she'd done. No human woman had a voice like that, one that could command the earth and heavens to move to her tune. *I have failed. I never stood a chance.* And she'd paid a terrible price for the attempt.

It was the last thought she had before the northern wind scattered her across the desert sky.

CHAPTER 1

"S*halla shanshber an Imarah!*" Clashing swords rang out over the screams of his dying tribesmen. "For the king and the tribe," they shouted, again and again. Seasoned warriors, workers, and even Magi, whose duty was to create, not to destroy. They fought as one to protect the women and children. Aesimar's warriors had attacked in the night, the cowards. On the one night in a moon's cycle when the *kharesh* trained away from tribe lands. They couldn't have known. Someone from his tribe must have told them. Imarah had a traitor.

"Tirasdunh!"

At Farraj's shout, Tir twisted sideways and backwards, barely avoiding an Aesimar blade. Rage simmered in his blood. He fell to the sands, rolled to his feet, but before the Aesimar dog had a chance to face him, Tir slashed across his back with his twin scimitars, the sharpest ever made. He was beset upon at once and blocked a sword and a spear in turn. Two against one were nothing for him; he was faster, stronger—he'd had to be to survive the ordeal of *kharashan*.

"To the east, Tir!"

Tir didn't question the order. He ran across the battlefield, fighting through when the path stood obstructed. At the eastern edge, he had a clear view of the entire fight. The Aesimar *shansher* sat his horse atop a dune with three of his assassin guards. He watched the fighting as one would a chess match and Tir knew that any moment now he'd turn and ride away, an unspoken order for his army to retreat.

It incensed Tir, knowing that the Aesimar leader didn't want to win this battle. He only wanted to show Imarah he could strike at any time, day or night. He sowed seeds of fear and let them destroy a tribe from within. Only if the people truly believed there was no more safe haven to be found on their lands would they abandon them. Imarah was very near that point again, and Tir would eat *daeva* shit before he allowed his people to be driven completely from their homelands.

Clutching his swords, Tir ran for the dune, weaving among enemy warriors without engaging, his whole being focused on the one target he needed to take out to end this.

The sand gave way beneath his feet, slowing him down, but he refused to relent. Gritting his teeth, he bore down, ran faster. Almost there. Almost at the crest. He could distinguish the markings painted in blood on the horses' bodies—symbols of Aesma Daeva, the god of violence and war, the one they worshipped and for whom their tribe was named. He knew those beasts would be sacrificed in an offering later that night in thanks for another successful raid. Their blood rites disgusted Tir.

One more reason to eradicate his enemy.

He was almost close enough to hurl one of his swords, when the company turned and rode away. Tir roared and pumped his legs, but by the time he'd crested the dune, they were long gone. "No..." He spun around. In the valley below, Aesimar's fighters were running. Several *kharesh* pursued and slayed a handful before Farraj barked the order to retreat, to tend to the dead and the wounded.

Tir sliced the air with his twin swords, the need to kill someone so strong he could hardly breathe. He'd failed his people.

Again.

Down in the valley, Farraj met his gaze and held it, until Tir ducked his head in shame and began to make his way back. The morning sun beat upon the sands, wavering the air in mirages to break one's spirit. Not far off, where a bountiful oasis once loomed, palm trees poked up like barren poles stuck in the sand. Rocks as dry as dust marked the remains of a deep well that once had enough water to not only soothe dry throats, but also irrigate a small field and a fig orchard. Those fig trees were gone now, years ago cut down for firewood when they stopped bearing fruit.

All of this had once been a verdant valley full of life around a burgeoning city, the tribe a thriving crowd of merchants and craftsmen, artists and singers. Now, the First Valley was dead, as his people would soon be, if he couldn't find a way to restore them.

"Anyone left alive to question?" Tir asked Farraj in passing.

"None I have seen yet."

Then there wouldn't be. Farraj missed nothing. Tir nodded and continued to the tents, where women stood outside, watching and weeping. He wanted to order them back inside, but it wouldn't do any good. They couldn't hide from this. Tir accepted a waterskin from an older worker who'd stayed to protect the women should any Aesimar dog make it through their front lines. "How is everyone?"

"The same, I'm afraid."

With a sigh, Tir nodded again and changed directions to go see to his family. His oldest sister, Halima, now a childless widow, tended to their father whenever Tir was away. She was the only one, besides himself and Farraj, allowed into his tent. None of them wanted the tribe to see their *shansher* this way.

The once-mighty Dhakir the Conqueror's spirit had deserted him after Aesimar scum had taken the life of his beloved first wife. Now, he was little more than a wasted shell, sitting listless in his chair, staring off into nothing. He never spoke, rarely moved. He'd eat when Halima fed him, drink when she held a waterskin to his mouth, but he wouldn't seek them out on his own.

"Father." Tir sank to one knee before his *shansher*. "Aesimar fighters have retreated."

He didn't answer, and Tir shuddered, feeling again as though he was speaking to the dead.

"You must do something, brother," Halima said, her dark, beautiful eyes pleading. "We can't go on like this. The wells we dig run dry within a day, there's nothing to hunt, and our crops dry out or rot as soon as we plant them. We are dying, Tir."

"I know."

"Then do something!"

"What?" As the *shansher*'s last living son, it fell to him to lead and provide for the tribe. Never did a prince want his station less. It never should have been his. Dhakir had had three other sons, all of whom had met their end in battle over the years. Tir was the youngest, and the last. "Tell me, Halima! If you know something I do not, please tell me."

Halima ducked her head. "Forgive me. I meant no offense."

Tir huffed, at his wits' end. They'd tried everything. The Magi had blessed the land, beseeched the gods, called to the spirits, and even tried to summon a *djinn*. Nothing had worked, as if everything had fled this land except for the foolish Imarah, the first Aegiran tribe to be birthed by the gods and gifted this valley as their homeland. And now, apparently, the first tribe to be abandoned by their makers.

What was he supposed to do? The Imarah had lived in this valley for so long, they knew no other way to live. If they left, they'd die. If they remained, they'd die.

Farraj announced himself and stepped into the tent. "Our dead are being prepared for funeral."

"How many?"

"Twelve in all. Seventeen wounded. The Magi are tending them now. We were fortunate to return when we did, otherwise we might have lost many more."

"What of the dead raiders?"

"We will leave their bodies in the desert far from here."

"I would praise your heartlessness, Farraj, but I think that might be their way."

Farraj bowed his head. He was the oldest fighter Imarah had, still unmatched to this day. He'd served the *shansher* all his life, loved him as a brother. He was as much a father to Tir as he was a commander and a mentor.

Halima shook her head in sorrow. "All this began when Mari died."

Farraj's gaze snapped up to her. "We do not know that."

That he'd bother to answer her at all put Tir on guard. "What do you mean, Halima?"

"Nothing, *sher'nah*," Farraj said. "It is only a woman's grief speaking. You must not give the words more meaning than that."

Tir focused on his sister. "Halima?"

She would not meet his gaze. "He is right, brother. I should not have said anything."

Tir swore. "Someone tell me what is going on—*now!*"

Halima met eyes with Farraj, who shook his head.

Tir shoved to his feet and, brandishing his sword, pointed the tip at Farraj's neck. "Either speak or leave this tent."

Slowly, Farraj raised a hand and eased the blade away with a finger. "As you command, *sher'nah*."

Tir lowered his sword but did not sheathe it. When Farraj motioned them closer, Tir and Halima sat on the ground by their father.

"Before you were born, your father led a raid on the North, hoping to win glory for our tribe with a great victory. Our warriors alone numbered in the tens of thousands then, and to the last, his men were ready to lay down their lives for their *shansher*."

Tens of thousands. Tir couldn't imagine it. Less than two thousand of the tribe remained, half-starved and dying.

"We thought ourselves gods, trained from birth for war. The Northerners would not stand a chance, and many of them did not. We razed their towns and cities, killed any who stood in our path. But the northern kingdoms are not like ours; they are great beasts with a heart city where their kings sit, and Dhakir wanted their golden crown for himself.

"When we came upon the crown seat of Lyria, we found a fortress made of stone, impenetrable. They had more horses, better weapons, and knowledge of the land to use against us, and their fighters wore armor made of metal that repelled our arrows. Fortune, too, favored them. The prince of Wilderheim was there, and to keep his son safe, his king father sent countless more warriors to protect him. We were not only defeated, we were destroyed."

"Dhakir retreated, and Mari was given to the Northern prince in *ramesh feh*." Tir knew this part, at least. A life for a life, *ramesh feh* used to be their custom for ending war through marriage. No longer. The attacking Aesimar tribe had no desire for peace, only war and death. All of the emissaries Tir had sent to offer a truce had been returned headless. The old days of honor were as gone as the water from their wells.

"Yes," Farraj said. "But she was only a babe still, and so we waited until she grew into a woman before we took her to become queen of Wilderheim."

Tir had only been a babe himself when Mari left. He couldn't even remember what she'd looked like. Still, she'd been his sister and he'd loved her. That much he knew. "So what happened?"

"We do not know," Halima said. "Not long after the wedding caravan returned, her guards and handmaidens came back as well, carrying her ashes. They said she became with child, and something went wrong. The midwife told me they did everything they could to save her, but she was too far gone. There were some who believed her Northern husband killed her to take another in her place."

Farraj swore. "Fools. They didn't know what they were saying. Their pride was thrice hurt—first with their defeat, then with Mari leaving, and the third time when King Saeran remarried. They would have fought ghosts to prove themselves, and they would have died trying."

"You think so little of your own men?" Tir challenged.

"No, *sher'nah*, but I have fought the Northerners, I've seen their magic men, and I have met their king. He is an honorable man. He would not have done harm to an innocent like Mari." He spoke with such conviction, Tir was tempted to believe him, but not convinced.

"Not long after that, our river dried up," Halima said. "With the water gone, the fig trees were the first to die, then the crops. Then the people began to sicken and then…"

"And then the *daeva* started flying through the night," Tir finished. In the absence of good and light, dark spirits had infested the valley. They came out at night, danced their wild dervishes, snatched any soul foolish enough to be wandering outside. Sometimes, they wouldn't appear for weeks; other times, they screamed and growled for nights on end.

The Magi were powerless against them, their spells and rituals all for naught. Two had died trying to banish the demons to whatever hell they'd flown out of. Only light seemed to keep them at bay, so the Imarah people had taken to sleeping by lamplight.

It would not be long before that comfort, too, disappeared. With nothing left to trade, their current oil supply was all they had left. What would happen when the last drop burned away?

"Simply because one followed the other, does not mean they were related," Farraj argued. "We have dry seasons and rain seasons."

"Yes, and the rain seasons grow ever scarcer," Tir said.

"Tir, think about this."

"I am. You spoke of magic men. If you fear them so, it means they are very powerful. Perhaps even powerful enough to cast a curse on our tribe."

"Why would they do such a thing?"

"To prevent us from riding against them a second time; to keep us too weak to seek retribution for the death of one of our own."

And they'd succeeded. The more he thought about it, the more sense it made. Imarah had struck out against the Northern kingdoms, and in retaliation, the Northerners had taken the life of their princess and made certain their tribe could never rise to retaliate.

Tir stood and picked up his swords.

"Tir, I know what you're thinking," Farraj said. "You cannot—"

"Oh, yes I can. You taught me that." He was *kharesh*, an assassin trained in the ways of battle and death. He couldn't raise an army against Wilderheim, but he could sneak into the kingdom to strike directly at its heart.

"No, I forbid it!"

"You forbid?" Tir snapped. "I am *sher'nah*, Farraj. You will do as you are told!"

Wide-eyed, his mentor stared a moment too long before lowering his gaze. "You would abandon your tribe, now, when they are most vulnerable?"

"I would do all in my power to rebuild what we have lost. If that means destroying the one who brought this misery upon us, then so be it. Kill the source, and the malady will lift."

"Tir—"

"Ready my horse. Halima, I will need whatever supplies we can spare. The *kharesh* are in charge until I return. You will see to the women and children."

Halima bowed.

"Tirasdunh!"

"I ride out at sunrise."

CHAPTER 2

Liadan took off her shoes to tiptoe into the tunnel. She schooled herself to breathe slowly, quietly as she picked her way, avoiding loose gravel and puddles of water that could betray her presence. She knew the tunnels by heart, so navigating them in the dark was no chore. To remain undetected was the hard part.

Sneaking past the treasure chamber, she peeked in to make sure the great dragon was still asleep before she turned to go deeper into the cave system.

You're in trouble now. Her brother's voice in her mind startled her, and she barely stifled a gasp.

Hush, you! Do you want me to get caught?

"And where do you think you're going, little miss?"

Liadan cringed, freezing in her tracks.

You see? Fal said. *You don't need me to get caught.*

She scowled at the wet cave wall. Fal's scrying powers were still a mystery to most, but Liadan was quite certain if there was even a sheen of moisture around, her twin brother could see through it at whatever it faced. That's why rain always exhausted him. When it rained, he could literally see everything, and he couldn't always stop it from overtaking his mind.

"Where have you been, Liadan?"

"Fal tattled, didn't he?"

The dragon stretched, bringing his snout an arm's length from her. When he sniffed, the puff of his breath almost knocked her over. "I am a dragon, child. I do not need your twin brother to tell me when you are up to something. Now, would you care to tell me which tavern keeper I'll be paying off this time?"

Liadan raised her head high. "None," she said. "I didn't go to any tavern." She only ever went to those when she craved contact. She could blend in among the rowdy tavern crowds far better than at the markets, where those who saw her asked far too many questions. Unfortunately, whenever she did visit, some drunk inevitably decided to make a conquest of her, often forcing to spark a brawl to extricate herself. It wasn't her fault! Why should she be made to answer for the actions of Wilderheim's inebriates?

"Well, are you going to tell me where you did go?"

Liadan crossed her arms. "You're a dragon. Shouldn't you already know?"

He growled a little, the ground rumbling beneath her feet, and Liadan knew she was in trouble. "Pick up your sword, girl."

She looked down at her new gown, the one she'd been saving for her friend's wedding to the village elder's son. "Now?"

With a swirl of fire and smoke, the dragon transformed into his almost-human body. In this shape he stood a head and a half taller than Liadan. He had the face of her father, but hair as dark as night and a pair of smooth, shimmery horns curling out of his temples, sweeping up and back along his head. His powerful build made him the perfect sparring partner. His tail made him a cheater.

"Sword. Now." He was already stalking out of the cave and into the clearing.

Liadan stomped.

"And don't stomp your foot at me, little miss," he said from the cave mouth.

Grumbling, Liadan retrieved her scabbard from the treasure room and strapped the plain-looking thing to her waist. The blade it held was without equal. Light as a feather, yet strong enough to shatter stone. The dragon had forged it for her alone, sharpened it on diamond rock and polished it with opal sand. The handle was wrapped in the softest of leathers; the pommel was a ruby encased in a cage of steel knotwork. Spells etched into the blade made it impervious to rust and fire, though provided no magical protection to the wielder. That would be cheating.

"Draw," the dragon said.

Liadan did, and almost fell on her backside when the dragon attacked, knocking his blade against hers with enough force to drive her back against the rock face.

"You were not ready."

"You were too fast."

He leaned his weight on the blades between them. "It does not matter how fast I am. The moment your blade is free of its scabbard, you must be on your guard."

Try as she might, she could not budge him. He was too strong. Magic was her only chance, and the mere thought of it summoned fire into her eyes and hands. She smelled smoke as the sword's leather handle began charring.

But before she could use it, the dragon huffed at her, and just like that, her magic was gone. He shoved at her as he disengaged. "What is the rule, Liadan?" he demanded.

Liadan blushed. "No magic when we spar."

She'd not taken two steps away from the rock, when he came at her again. This time, she blocked and twisted away from his sweeping cut. He could say what he would about her reflexes, but even he couldn't deny her footwork was flawless. Liadan didn't fight; she danced. Light on her toes, swift and precise, but when she bore down, she had strength enough to force her opponent back.

She hadn't been able to do it with the dragon, until now. As she charged forward to launch her attack, he retreated, swiped his tail at her, but she was ready, jumping and ducking the appendage with ease. Liadan kept an eye on her opponent and where she wanted him to go, and pushed him precisely there: to the edge of the clearing, where a single row of trees hid the sharp drop-off of a dead-fall gorge. She almost smiled at how easily she was winning. The dragon was fast, but she knew his tricks now, and even when a dagger appeared in his free hand, she wasn't worried. She had her own sheathed at her back. With two blades, she put on more speed, schooled her breathing, and kept aware of her surroundings. Several times over the years, she'd tripped on a protruding root or rock and had fallen face-first into whatever the dragon had chosen to place into her path. Horse dung was his favorite.

But not today. Today, she had him on the retreat.

Almost to the edge, Liadan twirled in a complicated block-and-thrust, then moved in for the kill, shoving with her shoulder to knock the dragon off balance.

But he was no longer there, and Liadan found herself tipping forward over the cliffside. Her scream cut short when the dragon grabbed her skirts, yanked her back onto solid ground.

Though she knew he'd never let her fall, the dragon kept her at the very edge while he stared her down through eyes slitted with displeasure. "What have you learned?"

"That you cheat!" she cried, heart racing, knees wobbly.

"Liadan," he warned.

"I wasn't paying attention. I got overconfident. I thought I had you."

"Yes. It's called strategy. Brute force and fancy footwork aren't always enough to gain you a victory. Sometimes you must outwit your opponent. If you can't maneuver them to retreat to your advantage, then you must feign retreat to achieve the same. But you must be careful not to reveal your path. Make your opponent think he has you in his grasp, let him toy with you, but never lose sight of the most important thing."

"His weapons?"

"His pride."

Liadan blushed.

"An overconfident opponent makes mistakes, and you can use that against him. But be careful not to let your own pride defeat you instead."

She nodded.

"So, what have you learned?"

"Pride is a weapon I must learn to use."

"And retreat is not only a coward's way out. You must remember that. Promise me."

"I promise, Grandfather."

"Good girl." He kissed the top of her head. "Now go pack your things. You ride before sunset."

"Where am I going?"

"Home, Liadan. You are going home."

She gaped at his retreating back. *Did you hear that, Fal?*

You're coming home, he said with a distinct lack of enthusiasm. She hadn't seen the brat in years. While she was stuck here with the dragon, Fal was sequestered in Frastmir, being tutored by their mother and the water sprites. She would have thought he'd be happy to have her home.

What's the matter?

Nothing. I'll leave you to it. You have a lot to do before you ride.

Fal—

He was gone.

Something was wrong. Liadan hastened to her chambers, where she began tossing things into a bundle on her bed. She stripped off her gown in favor of her leather breeches and tunic. Her deep blue linen shirt had been fashioned for a man, and bore the crest of her father on each sleeve, embroidered in golden thread.

When trying to pack and braid her hair at the same time proved to be too much of a challenge, Liadan abandoned both to pull on her riding boots. Then she finished braiding her hair and packing her bundle. Her weapons would be strapped to her saddle, and she'd bring food in the satchel she always carried. Once she had everything packed, Liadan looked around the chamber that had been her home for the last nineteen years, and sighed.

"Grandfather?"

"Yes?" He stood in the doorway, where she knew he'd be, hiding in illusion. Now, he showed himself, still mostly human and dressed in simple, serviceable clothes. For all the treasures the dragon hoarded, he rarely parted with the pieces.

"I will miss you," she said.

He shrugged. "I am not going anywhere."

Nevertheless, she ran into his arms and hugged him with all her might. "Why do I feel like something terrible is afoot?"

"Perhaps because it is," the dragon said. He didn't sound at all concerned.

She looked up into his face. "Why do I feel like I will never see you again?"

He cupped her cheeks in his large, scaled hands. "Listen well, Liadan. There will come a day when you will have to choose between your family and everything else. It'll be a terrible choice, and either outcome will bring pain. But that day is not today."

His words held the weight of portent, and cold fear slithered around her heart at the thought of losing her family. She loved the dragon dearly. Fal was her twin, her other half, and her parents were the only people in this world or any other on whom she could always rely no matter what. How could she ever consider giving them up? What else could be so important that the prospect of losing them would be an acceptable choice?

The dragon smiled. "There now. Don't fret. Here, something to remember me by." He produced a silver torc, an almost-full circle of twisted rods with thick rings at each end, etched with intertwining knots. As he settled the weight of it around her neck, its power thrummed against her skin.

Swallowing back her tears, Liadan took a deep breath. "I have something for you, as well." Fisting her hand, she summoned fire into her palm, stoked it white-hot, then hotter still until her skin glowed bright blue. When at last she was satisfied, she let the fire cool, then opened her hand. In her palm lay a ring forged of black gold that swirled with colors when held up to the light. On the inside, the language of the ancient race spelled out an incantation in symbols far older than any her learned mother knew.

No one could restore a broken heart. The dragon's had shattered the day his beloved had died, and not even his descendants could repair it. But they could remind him that there was still happiness in the world for him to grasp; they could show him his mate would not have wanted him to mourn her for all eternity and that giving up his pain was not a betrayal, but an honor of her memory. When he wore the ring she'd forged, he'd remember the happy times he'd shared with all of them, and he'd know he was not alone, never had to be, if he didn't wish it. The ring gave him the power to summon to him any and all of his blood kin.

When he took it, Liadan didn't know whether he'd put it on or destroy it.

He did neither. The great dragon closed his fist around the ring and brought it to his heart. Then he smiled, the first smile she'd ever seen crease his handsome face. "Thank you," he said, and truly, she needed to hear nothing else.

Picking up her satchel and weapons, the dragon walked her to the stables where her mount waited, already saddled and burdened with two large bags. He didn't look happy about the unwieldy weight on his back.

Liadan frowned. "What is all this?"

"I am sending something for your brother. Perhaps he will find it useful."

While she attached her weapons and her bundle, the dragon settled a heavy fur cloak over her shoulders. "Be safe, Liadan. Be happy."

"And you, Grandfather."

When she rode out into the woods, it was to the sight of the great dragon flying through the air, breathing great plumes of fire at the gathering clouds.

CHAPTER 3

With each village he passed, Tir hated the Northerners more. Such bounty, so much water he couldn't fathom it, and they wasted it in mindless play. He'd been welcomed into the inns as though he were an old friend; offered shelter, food, and a bath in a tub big enough to fit two of him. They'd filled it with water that would be tossed out the window when he was finished with it. The waste was inconceivable!

Everywhere he looked, people were well-fed, strong, and happy. They wanted for nothing, never knew a moment's worry. The sight of them only served to remind Tir his own people were dying in Aegiros. A single one of those lavish baths would have been enough water to quench the thirst of his entire tribe.

But as he neared the castle city of Frastmir, things began to change. From one village to another, Tir entered a different world. At first he thought his mind was playing tricks on him. He couldn't possibly be seeing this. Creatures he'd never seen before mingled with the villagers and townspeople, some with the ease of friendship, others with a cold distance, and still others with outright hostility.

When an old woman spoke to a little green girl with big eyes and vines for hair, Tir thought she had to be blind not to see it. But then, she took a vine into her gnarled hand, and laughed in delight when a bright pink flower bloomed in her palm.

A merchant selling earthen cups and plates looked on as a miniscule man with a giant nose and a crooked hat zipped from one item to the next, inspecting each. He licked the plates, and if he didn't like one, he made a face and shattered it on the ground. How could the merchant stand there and tolerate such abuse? Tir was about to intervene, when the little man-thing hopped onto a pedestal and shook a finger at the merchant. "You filthy cheat!" it shouted. "I gave you the best clay in all of Wilderheim to make my dishes, paid you a pouch of pure gold for your work, and this is what you give me!"

"I'm sorry, master," the man said, trembling. "I did not mean to offend."

"You did not think I would know the difference!" The little man-thing noticed Tir gaping, and growled at him.

Tir shook himself and continued on. He'd just about convinced himself not to panic, when a pure white mare with a horn growing out of her forehead trotted down the street, stopped by his mount, and nuzzled him. Tarabas tossed his head with a snort, then nuzzled her back. That was the last straw. "*Hyah!*" Tir shouted, kicking Tarabas into a gallop to get away.

At the river, he was forced to stop again. Across it lay the road to Frastmir; he could see the great, stone fortress from here. But the river was six wagons wide with a current so powerful it carried entire trees away. Along the banks were piles of broken logs that had washed downstream.

Fear gripped him. The bridge was sturdy; wagons, horses, and people crossed it with ease, not a worry on any of their faces. Still, he couldn't bring himself to nudge Tarabas forward. If it gave way, if he fell, he'd drown. No man could survive those waters, especially one who couldn't swim.

But the swell and dip of the waves unnerved him the most. For when they swelled, they rose to a person's height, and held the shape of one, too. Figures made of the purest water danced over the surface, leaping into the air, diving back. They had no faces he could discern, yet he sensed those creatures had teeth sharper than a scorpion's stinger.

Tir squeezed his eyes shut, squared his resolve, and nudged his mount forward. He kept his eyes closed, shuddering with every speck of water that hit his bare arms, imagining those creatures floating in the air next to him. They had no faces, he reminded himself. Still, he felt their eyes on him every step of the way.

Only when he heard Tarabas' hooves clop against packed dirt did he open his eyes. He didn't dare look back, only spurred the animal on faster.

If ever he had a lingering doubt that the Northerners were responsible for the slow destruction of his tribe, it was now completely eradicated. These people consorted with demons. Of course demons would be the method they'd choose to strike out against Imarah.

Frastmir was a thriving city with its fortress standing tall at the northeastern edge. The streets milled with so many people and… creatures, Tir didn't know where to look. Overwhelmed, he stabled his mount at the first inn he came across, then ducked inside. It was no less crowded in there, but at least it was quieter. Weary travelers sat together at large tables with plates of food and tankards of ale. They all spoke to one another in hushed tones and seemed a friendly enough bunch. Not a monster among them, as far as he could see.

Tir turned to the innkeeper, a beautiful, young girl with pale skin and red cheeks, and hair so light it was almost white. She smiled, and his heart lightened. "Aegiran," she said, and Tir was shocked to hear his language on her lips. "You've come a long way to us."

Dumbfounded, he nodded.

"A room, then?"

He nodded again.

The girl laughed, her voice a song to his ears. "Have you coin?"

Tir fumbled around for his pouch, pouring three copper coins onto the bar between them. It'd been enough in the other places he'd stayed.

The girl's eyes sparkled. "We barter in gold and silver here," she said, "but all manner of metal is precious to my kind." She met his gaze and swept her long tresses back behind her ear. Her long, pointed ear.

Tir almost ran, but he found courage enough to root his feet to the spot. His tribe depended on him to save them; he was meant to fight demons, not run from them.

"This will buy you supper for the night," the creature said. "But for a room, you will need to pay more."

Throat tight, Tir answered, "This is all I have."

Again that melodic laugh. "Coin is not what I want." She looked thoughtful for a moment, then said, "I will accept a kiss as my price."

"A kiss?"

She smiled. "Aye, a kiss can be a powerful thing. My kind feeds on passion. A kiss from one like you would sate me for many days to come."

At a loss for words, Tir looked around, seeking guidance, but no one paid him any heed. He was on his own.

"Do you accept the trade, son of Imarah?"

"How do you know my tribe?"

The creature pushed the copper coins around in a circle on the bar. "I know many things about you, Tirasdunh al-Dhakir."

"As a demon would," he growled.

She blinked her jewel-green eyes. "You must have never met a true demon to call me such. Know this, *sher'nah*, a demon would not barter for a kiss. He would take your soul. Demons are not welcome in Wilderheim, and especially not in Frastmir. Any known to consort with Dark creatures are executed by order of the queen."

"You expect me to believe a word you say?"

She shrugged a delicate shoulder. "Believe or not, but if you wish to stay the night, you must pay the price."

What would she do if he refused? Did he dare anger her?

No, until his mission was complete, he could not afford for someone to raise an alarm and alert his prey to his presence. Tir had one chance at this, and one alone. If he failed, all would be lost, and Imarah would be no more. He swallowed with difficulty. For his people, he had to concede.

Seeing the capitulation in his eyes, the beautiful creature leaned in with a smile. Tir met her halfway, pressing his lips to hers for the briefest of moments before pulling away again.

The creature gasped. Her cheeks flushed, her hair grew longer, her lips turned as red as blood, and when she opened her eyes again, they shone like bright green stars. Tir saw surprise in them. "You carry much pain in your heart, son of Imarah. And much darkness, as well. You must let go of the hate you feel if you wish to save your people. Your salvation lies in the bosom of the one you call enemy. Only a strong, pure heart can burn bright enough to banish your demons, and they'll not be defeated with hate, young prince. Only with love."

Tir snatched up the key she held out to him, then escaped up the stairs to where the rooms were. Unerringly, he chose the room the key unlocked and closed himself inside, away from the madness of Frastmir and its demons. With shaky hands, he removed his swords and placed them onto the bed. A pitcher of water sat on a small washstand, and he poured some into a cup, gulping it down to soothe his parched throat. With each drop he felt guilty. Had Farraj been right? Should he have stayed with his tribe, instead of running away to fight an enemy he didn't know?

He thought of his father sitting in his tent, of Halima feeding him what little water they still had. Then he looked outside at a gaggle of children splashing each other in puddles on the road and remembered why he'd come.

With renewed resolve, he sat on the bed and cleaned his swords of road dust and grime. Tonight, when the sun set, he'd make his way into the fortress to put an end to this, once and for all. He was *kharesh*, a trained assassin, the prince of his people. None would see him, unless he chose to show himself. None would hear his approach, until he had a blade to their necks. The demon summoner would die by his hand, and he'd know in his final moments that he was defeated at last.

When day turned to night, Tir shed his travel clothes and dressed in his assassin's attire: a sleeveless black tunic to allow for ease of movement, black pants to tie into soft-soled boots, and a black hood and mask to hide his face. He tied small sheaths to his wrists with black cloth and slid throwing knives into them. His poison pouches were neatly arranged in order on a special belt. They ranged from sleeping powders to incapacitate his opponent, to snake and scorpion venoms that could paralyze or kill a man in the blink of an eye.

A *kharesh* killed silently, and never let his presence be known.

The inn's guests didn't bed down at nightfall. Instead, candles were lit and musicians summoned to entertain them. Ale and honey wine would flow in rivers down in the main room; Tir had seen it before. He had no interest in their revelry, so long as it distracted them long enough to allow him to leave the inn, unseen. He crawled out through the window and left it open, silently jumping down into the street below. Torches lined the main road, and fires burned cheerfully in every house. Wispy, ghost-like creatures frolicked across the grass. He ignored them. Moving from shadow to shadow, Tir cut across the city to the stone fortress, where guards stood at the outer gate. The wall circled so far in either direction he'd lose precious time trying to find another way in. So Tir pulled out two of his knives and considered the stones for a moment, before he stabbed the blades into deep crevices, using them to climb up to the top.

At the edge he hung suspended, arms burning with strain as he waited for a pair of guards to pass by. Then he pulled himself up and onto the walkway. He was in luck. Not two paces from him stood a wooden staircase that led into the inner courtyard. Going down the stairs, Tir skirted the wall, keeping to the shadows as he made his way to the courtyard's gate. This one was guarded by a single armored man leaning on his spear. As he crept closer, Tir recognized the soft sounds emanating from the guard. He was fast asleep. Slipping in through the gate wasn't difficult. The hard part was finding where the king slept. Tir assessed the fortress' many levels, and the many windows in which light flickered. He could not hope to remain undetected while sneaking around inside. He had to find out which window belonged to the king's chamber and scale the wall up to it.

Then, as if by divine intervention, he noticed something odd: of all of the windows lit from within, only one was open. Though the day had been warm, the night's chill was in the air now. Tir was used to it; desert nights chilled the blood of even the hardiest men. But no one with any sense would let in the cold wind when he had a fire to warm himself. Only a king used to lavish comforts would be so wasteful.

Tir mapped out his route, shook out his arms, and started to climb. He scaled as high as the outer wall, then higher still. So far up, the cold wind snatched at him, seeking to tear him away. There were some footholds to make use of, but not enough to climb them with ease and his arms ached with strain. By the time he'd reached the window, he was out of breath, dizzy with the height, and even more determined to put an end to this.

Inside the chamber, the fire was dying down. By its fading light, he saw a massive bed with thick furs for covering. Tir circled around close to the walls, testing the floors first with his toes before putting down the weight of his entire foot. He sheathed his throwing knives and, reaching behind his back, drew out his long, curved dagger. The metal was tarnished to dull any flicker of reflected light, but the blade was sharper than anything else he owned; it could slice through flesh like butter, killing quickly and silently.

Close to the bed now, he distinguished two figures before the fire finally burned down to embers and the chamber became dark. The king and his queen slept like little lambs, tucked in each other's arms, with nary a care in the world. Tir pushed back his bilious anger and concentrated on steadying his breath and adjusting his sight to the darkness.

Imarah's salvation was his to claim. Tir would avenge his tribe, bring them back the fortune they deserved. He raised the dagger high above his head and, with all of his might, all of his grief and anger, sliced down.

The blade cut through fur, pillow, and mattress—the king and queen were gone.

"No." Impossible. He tossed aside the furs, dug beneath the coverings, and found nothing.

"You didn't think they'd make it that easy, did you?"

Tir spun, a knife already in hand. He threw it on instinct, expecting to hear this fiend die on the spot. Instead, metal clanged against stone. The dark figure moved with incredible speed, knocking his second knife from his grasp. He took a hit to his jaw, then three rapid ones to his midsection before he woke up from his stupor and struck back.

Tir caught his attacker around the throat and shoved, bending, kicking out with all his strength. The fiend grunted and fell back, coughing. Tir's satisfaction was short-lived. "You'll pay for that," the attacker whispered, and in a moment of utter lunacy, Tir thought he saw the figure glow. In the next, he was knocked backwards onto and over the bed to the hard stone floor. His training took over—he wrapped his legs around his opponent, rolled to bring himself on top, then curled his hand into a fist and punched down.

He struck the floor with enough force to crack a bone and a grunt of pain escaped him.

Hands curled into his tunic and a head butted against his nose, hard enough to make sparks of light flash before his eyes and Tir swayed, allowing his opponent to escape. No! He couldn't be allowed to live! Shoving to his feet, Tir followed.

As he lunged for the figure, fire burst into sudden life in the hearth, momentarily blinding him, but Tir saw enough of his opponent to drain all of the fight out of him. Soft, red-brown hair cascaded over graceful shoulders and framed a fierce, delicate face. A feminine mouth pulled into a vicious snarl, and beneath dark, arched brows, the woman's eyes blazed with fury, reflecting the fire's glow as though it shone out of her very soul.

Before his mind could comprehend what he was seeing, she knocked him to the ground with a well-aimed punch. His back met the hard stone surface of the floor, knocking the breath out of him and, head swimming, Tir watched the woman's blurry shape pick up his own dagger, knowing he was about to die.

Then the pommel slammed down onto his head, and darkness swallowed him whole.

CHAPTER 4

Liadan tossed the blade away and groaned, holding her side. The bastard had broken her rib. When Fal had called to her to ride hard, she'd not expected to find an assassin poised to kill her parents; Aegiran, by the looks of him. How in all the hells had he managed to even get inside the castle?

"Guards!" she barked.

They filed in before the echo of her voice had faded.

"Good of you to visit," she growled.

"Your Highness!" The one in charge bowed. "We didn't know you were back."

"And did you know my parents weren't here, either?"

The guards looked at one another. "Their Majesties were called away for important matters late in the afternoon," the captain said. "We were told not to expect them back until tomorrow at the earliest."

She frowned. "What important matters?"

"Other matters, your Highness."

Liadan rolled her eyes. Of course. Matters of Others took precedence over the return of their daughter.

When Queen Nialei had sworn to help repair the damaged Veil between the human realm and the Otherlands, she hadn't anticipated the intricacies of Other politics; everything required rituals and ceremonies, especially when the petitioner wanted a blood sacrifice. They only needed a drop of blood from each clan to reform the Veil anew, but with so many clans, and their blood so powerful, the Others had to be certain it wouldn't be misused. Those who requested it had to prove themselves worthy, true, and pure of heart, a test that involved lengthy tasks and ordeals, and time in Otherlands did not often move the same way as it did here. For twenty years now, Liadan's parents had worked to restore the order of the world, and they still had a ways to go.

Liadan limped over to the bed and gingerly sat down, jerking her chin to the fallen assassin. "Take him to a cell and fetch my brother at once." They'd be questioning the intruder as soon as she could mend herself.

The guards bowed. "Yes, Highness."

After they left, Liadan sighed, staring into the fire. She could command it, speak to it, and scry its flames; that was her gift, the only true magic she possessed. She couldn't speak to the animals or the earth like her mother could. Water was for drinking, not for divining the future, and wind was nothing but chill air as far as she was concerned. Liadan was a true Dragonblood, taking after her father and her grandfather, and while she couldn't change her shape into that of a dragon, she still possessed many of their strengths and skills. She could see in the dark, create fire from nothing, and manipulate it into different forms and shapes. She could even work metals with some competence.

Her mother dabbled in many arts, but Liadan was a master of a single one. It was her gift, and sometimes her curse. As powerful as fire could be, so was it wild and difficult to tame. The dragon had spent long years teaching her how to take control of it, and she'd succeeded with only one small exception. Yet that one weakness could prove fatal at the wrong time.

All of a sudden, water poured in through the doorway, and in its wake, moss covered the walls and miniscule, yellow flowers on long, sturdy stalks grew all around. Then a vision walked in, following the stream's path directly to her, and a strange, wavering face smiled from beneath a sopping wet hood.

"Fal." Liadan smiled, opened her arms to her brother. "Up to your tricks again, I see."

Her twin scooped her up off the bed to embrace her so tightly, her broken rib screamed in protest, until it melted whole again in the way water forged down its path when an obstruction was removed. Cool comfort covered her from head to toe, healing bruises in an instant. "Sister," Fal said, his voice echoing with at least three others. "Welcome home."

"It's good to be back. But I didn't expect this kind of welcome. What's going on?"

Fal released her with a sigh. "I saw him coming from a ways off. I don't know why he's here. As far as I know, we've been at peace with Aegiros for decades."

"He was here for a very specific purpose. Why didn't you warn the guards?"

"The dragon said not to. He said you, and you alone, were to handle this, and that no one was to interfere."

Liadan tilted her head. "Is there a reason why we're still in the glen creek? I'd like to see my brother when I'm speaking to him, Fal. Can you do away with the illusions, please?"

"I… can't."

"Come on, we all know you're an unmatched illusionist, you don't need to rub it in. Let it go already."

"Liadan, I can't."

She stared. "What do you mean, you can't?"

The creek dried out, its earthen bed cracking as the flowers died and the moss turned gray. "I mean, I cannot." His visage, too, wavered into a different face. "I can't stop the illusions. Believe me, I've tried. They happen whether I want them to or not, and the more I fight them, the more violent they become."

Liadan searched his face for any feature that might mark him as the Fal she knew. Before her eyes, his nose lengthened, then widened, his chin grew a beard, and in the next instant he was as clean-shaven as a boy. Only his eyes remained the same, steady and blue. There was her brother, her twin. She cupped his cheek, the tangible truth of him underneath the illusion.

"How long has this been going on?" she asked.

He shuddered beneath her touch. "Years."

"Oh, Fal." She embraced him, her heart breaking for him. "What do the sprites say?"

"That Halflings are always flawed. But not like this. Somehow, something went wrong when Da gave me the dragon's blood. I had no dragonfire within me until then, and it didn't fit inside me as it did you."

The dragon's blood hadn't taken well to Liadan, either; like tossing oil onto a flame, it'd made her volatile, dangerous. She had to be vigilant every moment of the day and night to keep the flames contained, but they were part of her, and she could command them. It would make sense that the fire that fed her strength kept Fal, a being of water, from mastering his own birth element. "And there's no way to undo this, is there?"

"If one exists at all, the sprites, the dragon, and our parents haven't found it yet. The rule of Wilderheim may fall to you by necessity, sister. No kingdom, even ours, will follow a king of false faces."

Liadan felt dizzy with dread. She loved Wilderheim, but she'd never wanted to be its queen. Her heart told her the path she was to walk led elsewhere.

But Fal might be right. Who would follow a king who wove lies with every step he took? The people's trust had been hard-won after everything that'd happened, and there was still unrest, uneasiness with the Others who'd made their home here. The kingdom believed in King Saeran and Queen Nialei and waited for the royal pair to make good on their promise of peace and equality, but they couldn't rule forever. When it came time for them to step down, with no one but Liadan or Fal to take over, Fal's condition might push their citizens into full rebellion if she didn't step in.

But I can't! She swallowed with difficulty. "So what do we do now?"

"I don't know about you, but I would love to find out what our Aegiran guest is thinking."

Yes, so would she. "I'll talk to him."

Fal laughed. "No, I will talk to him."

"But he'll like me better."

Fal grinned, and the chamber reverted back to its former state, the illusions condensing around him, settling over him like a cloak. "I am the prince of deceit, remember?"

Liadan shook her head at the perfect replica of herself. With leathers dusty from a long journey and boots muddied from the road, only her brother's blue eyes betrayed his true identity, flashing fire from behind skeins of tangled red-brown hair. "Don't be too proud of yourself. You still don't sound like me."

Fal winked, and in her voice, more delicate and refined than she'd ever sounded in her life, said, "If anyone can get the truth out of him, I can."

"And if you can't?"

"Then I'll get something to show us the truth of his heart."

Liadan winced. "It'll be messy. I hate messy."

Fal pulled a dagger, toyed with the tip, eyes sparking with menace. "One does what one must for the good of king and kingdom."

She could hardly argue with that. "Right you are, brother. Off you go, then."

CHAPTER 5

Fal left his sister to settle herself and returned to his own chambers. By the time he'd gotten there, the strain of holding such a small illusion had made him unsteady. The moment he closed the door, he shed the restraints, sighing when the chamber filled with water and fake sunlight glittered on the surface over his head.

You're making progress.

He went to the water stand to gaze into the bowl he always kept there. In its depths, Seol's face appeared, looking down at him like his own reflection. A water sprite, Seol rarely left his home in the deep underground well that fed the glen creek, but he could do what no other could: communicate through even the illusion of water. This made him a formidable ally and a master tutor, one to whom Fal owed his life.

"It was only a few moments."

A few moments longer than anything you haven't cast before. Seol didn't speak through voice, but through thoughts and images in Fal's mind. A sprite's voice was magic in and of itself, capable of killing a creature if they felt threatened, or of restoring life if they thought it necessary. They used it rarely and always with great caution.

Fal shook his head. "Why is it so difficult?"

It is your nature.

"It hasn't always been." Fal had been just fine, until he'd started making the transition from boy to man. Almost overnight, it seemed he'd cast one illusion too many, and they refused to go away. Mothers often warned their children not to make faces or they'd become stuck that way. Fal hadn't listened, playing with illusions the way a child made faces to delight his friends, and now he had his punishment: no other could look upon his true face, except through a veil of illusion.

Seol faded away, leaving the bowl empty. *See yourself,* he said. *You are still there, beneath it all.*

In the sprite's absence, the bowl reflected Fal's true face. His brows and nose were the same as Liadan's, his mouth was a more masculine version of hers, and his jaw was square with the grizzled beginnings of a beard.

Fal and his twin were alike in many ways, but their differences were marked. Both had inherited the dragon's dark hair, but Liadan's fire had painted hers in its hues, and while Fal's was straight like their mother's, Liadan's curled with a life of its own. Liadan had eyes the color of charcoal, which lit with fire whenever she was around it; Fal's were as blue as the clearest lake, the only constant in his ever-changing visage.

He was a creature of water more than anyone realized, his powers so vast, they leaked out of him in illusion, and more often than not, that illusion was water. Those few who knew him were used to it, but those who were not, believed it so real, they began to drown in the waters he cast. Fal's illusions were either all around him or all over him, and the farther they spread, the easier he breathed. If he pulled them in around his body, he became a different person. If he filled the chamber, as he did now, he could be himself for a while, but not many could tolerate the strangeness long enough to truly see him.

Lamia, his tutor before Seol, had thought it was Fal's nature trying to force him home, into the waters from where he'd hailed. Fal had followed her instructions, blindly leaping into the river, which had carried him for miles, and he'd nearly drowned trying to breathe under water.

Seol's theory was that Fal's illusions made up for his humanity, which denied him water, by creating a version of it his all-too human lungs could survive.

Fal hadn't inherited enough of his water sprite ancestry to live as they did, yet he wasn't human enough to fit in on land. He felt wrong, broken. Something had damaged him, but he still believed it could be repaired. Like the Veil between the realms, something inside Fal had come undone when the illusions had overwhelmed him. If he could divine what it was, perhaps he could repair it.

One day, perhaps you will, Seol said. *But tonight, you have more pressing matters to attend to, do you not?*

"Yes." The Aegiran assassin.

Fal took a deep breath and pulled back his illusions, forcing the magic into his own skin. As the chamber slowly emptied, his form changed. His hair grew longer, his face softened, and his figure rounded to mimic Liadan. He scowled down at himself. The dragon allowed his sister far too many liberties. No proper woman went around dressed in this fashion; it was indecent.

Then he shrugged. It'd worked in a fight. He picked up the assassin's dagger and turned it this way and that in the light. A plain-looking thing, but sharp enough that he wouldn't risk touching the blade. Fal slid it carefully through his belt, then squared his shoulders and headed down to the dungeons.

It was time he had a chat with their guest.

≪ »·◇·« ≫

Tir awoke slowly. He didn't want to. His head pounded and his right hand was a tight knot of agony, telling him he'd broken something. The instant he remembered what had happened, he shot to his feet and reached for his blade. It was gone. All of his weapons were, including his belt of poisons, his hood, and his mask.

He was in a stone cell with a thick, wooden door and a barred window hardly big enough to fit his hand through. He reached for it anyway and was pulled up short by the shackles locked around his wrists. The chains were anchored to the wall at his back, allowing him no farther than two steps away from it.

"Finally. I thought you'd sleep through the night." Fire sparked off a blade and onto a torch across the chamber, and in the meager light, he recognized the woman he'd fought.

"You," he snarled.

She arched an eyebrow. "You're angry with me? You're the one who snuck in here and tried to kill my parents. I should be the one angry with you."

"Then why aren't you?"

"Who says I am not?"

Tir yanked at his chains. "I have no time for games. If you are going to kill me, get it over with." He backed himself against the wall. The chain might be long enough to strangle her with, if he could lure her closer.

Instead of attacking, she pulled his own blade from behind her back and cleaned her nails with the tip. "Not yet. I have a few questions for you first."

"I'll tell you nothing!"

She smiled. "We will see."

"Kill me and be done with it. But know you are killing an entire tribe."

She stilled. "Do tell."

Tir bit his tongue and averted his gaze, cursing himself a fool. What had possessed him to say that? Desperation. He'd failed, and now had no way to remove Imarah's curse. He needed to go back and find another way; every moment he spent here, his tribe suffered.

"Come on, Aegiran, we both know you'll tell me eventually. Save yourself the pain."

Tir spat a curse at her in the language of the Magi.

The woman laughed at him. "Very good. If you had a drop of magic in you, I'd tremble in my boots." Then she scowled down at her boot. "Speaking of, I need a new pair."

He snorted in disgust. "A fool king to send a woman in his place. Weak. Let him come face me himself!"

"Sadly, my father is away on royal business. He's a very busy man, you know. He can't stop everything every time someone tries to murder him."

Taken aback, Tir struggled to find his voice, choking on his words. "Your father?" This was the demon offspring of his enemy? He regarded her where she sat like a man, across from him. A beauty, true; he'd never seen her equal, not even the demoness innkeeper.

Strong, too. To his shame, Tir had to admit she'd defeated him in single combat. Although, he amended, she'd had the element of surprise working in her favor. If they sparred again, he would not be so easily brought down.

She was undeniably a woman skilled in the art of combat. It showed in the set of her shoulders, in her thin but muscled arms. Her thighs encased in her leathers were powerful, well used to the saddle. She'd be a skilled rider, a fast runner, and he'd already sampled her kick to know its strength. Yet none of her mannish attributes marred her beauty; they seemed to enhance it.

If the fates had been kinder, if the coward king had been as honorable as Farraj had claimed, this woman would have been his niece.

No. No niece of his would behave in this way, dress in this way. This creature was completely shameless, and her fighting skills only proved what he'd believed all along—that the Northern king was some demon thing. He had to be, to have spawned this… this… "I will send you back to the hell you came from—"

"What is your name?" No rancor, no ire; she didn't even look at him, as if it didn't matter whether or not he answered.

Where he came from, names meant something. Tir stubbornly held his tongue.

She sighed. "What if I trade you answers? If I give you my name, will you tell me yours?"

"Demons lie," he bit out.

"And you think I am a demon?"

"It is known."

"Where? By whom?"

"In my tribe. By everyone."

She frowned. "Then your tribe has been misinformed."

Tir charged her, pulled up short by the chains. "You will not speak of them, demon!"

The woman rose. She was almost of a height with him, which unnerved him. Tir was tall among his people; few men matched his height, and he could fit most women under his arm. But this one faced him with her shoulders back and head held high, easily meeting his gaze like an equal. For a moment, Tir became mesmerized by her blue eyes. "I am Liadan," she said. "Daughter of King Saeran and Queen Nialei of Wilderheim. I am a princess of this realm and, under different circumstances, I would have welcomed you into our home as an honored guest."

"Lies."

"What reason would I have to harm you? Aside from the fact that you tried to kill my parents in their sleep. Were you too much of a coward to face them any other way?"

"Mock me at your peril, demon," he said, voice wavering with anger.

She gave him her back with a put-upon sigh. "Your name, Aegiran. I can force it from you if you make me. Don't make me."

He said nothing.

When she faced him again, her eyes were glowing. "Your name," she said, and her voice echoed.

Tir's throat locked tight; he couldn't breathe. His jaw stiffened even as his tongue moved behind his teeth, forming his name. The force of her magic stunned him. He'd never felt anything like it. His face heated, the need for air overcoming his desire to keep a secret. "Tirasdunh," he gritted out, and the force released him. Tir dropped to his knees, gasping for breath.

"Did you say Tristan? That is a Northern name. You wouldn't be lying to me, would you?"

He shook his head, opened his mouth to curse her blood, but when she held up a finger, his voice would not come.

"Truth, please."

Nothing but the honest answer to her question would come out, and the longer he remained silent, the more painful it became. He chose his words with care, revealing only what would do no harm. “Tirasdunh is my name. It is an old Aegiran name. Most call me Tir.”

“Tir is our god of war. It is not a name for mortals to carry.”

“Your god, not mine.”

She looked him up and down. “As you say. Why do you wish my parents dead?”

Again, her demon magic slithered around his throat, commanding more words. “They killed my sister,” he said, but stopped himself there.

The magic released him suddenly, and Tir hunched over, gulping in deep breaths of foul Northern air. If she wanted him dead, no better time to take his life than now, while she had him on his knees before her, head bowed, ready for a blade across the neck.

If Tir had had any pride left at all, he'd stand and face her. But he couldn't. Twice felled, he'd shamed himself and his tutors. His tribe would be well rid of him. They deserved better than a weakling who couldn't even stand up to a single demon. Perhaps he was the one cursed, and with his death, his people could be free.

But what if they weren't?

“Only one Aegiran woman passed into the arms of her ancestors in Wilderheim. Your sister was Queen Mari.”

Her name on the woman's lips sounded like an aberration.

She tangled her fingers into his hair, forced his head up to meet her gaze. “I know you're keeping something from me. And I know you will dance around it until all life has drained from your body before you let the honest truth pass your lips.”

“Then kill me,” he grated.

The woman shook her head. “Your death would serve no purpose. As your sister's served none. If you believe nothing else, then trust in this one thing: she did not die by my father's hand, or by my mother's. Her passing was a tragedy and many mourned her, my parents among them.”

Tir yanked on his restraints, the pain in his broken hand a paltry nuisance compared to the agony in his heart. She was lying; she had to be. Mari's death was the reason for everything. She had to be avenged for his tribe to live.

The woman sighed and released him. “If I can't get the truth from your tongue, I will get it from your blood.”

“No!”

But it was too late. With one smooth cut of his own blade, the woman opened his wrist and held it, bleeding, over a copper bowl. His struggles came to naught. “Damn you!” he screamed at her. “Damn all of you!” He called down curses upon her and her kin, invoked the dark gods whose names felt cold on his tongue and stabbed fear into his heart.

She didn't waver from her task. “Your gods,” she said. “Not mine.”

When she released him, Tir fought against his restraints, tried to kick the copper bowl out of her hands, but in three swift, long-legged strides, she was out of the cell and the door closed and locked behind her. He screamed himself hoarse, chafed his wrists raw, and all but wrenched his shoulders out of their sockets trying to escape.

Not until the torch had burned down to nothing and the light of day shone into his cell did Tir subside, sinking to the floor against the wall. Not until then did he realize the cut on his wrist had stopped bleeding and his broken hand felt whole.

CHAPTER 6

Liadan was bathed, dressed, and half asleep by the time moss once again announced her brother's presence. She sat up, searching another stranger's smiling face for Fal's familiar blue eyes. "Well?"

He produced a copper bowl filled with blood, and Liadan wrinkled her nose. "What did you do, slit his throat like a suckling pig?"

"I was almost tempted to," he said.

An odd way of putting it. "Almost?"

A rosy-cheeked woman's smile ebbed. "He's Mari's brother."

Liadan gaped. "Da's Aegiran wife, Mari?"

"The very same."

"He can't be much older than we are!"

"She was only a child herself when she came here."

Liadan couldn't imagine being bartered away like cattle to some stranger in a far-off land on the feeble promise of peace. The poor girl had paid a terrible price for her sacrifice. Saeran had done the proper thing—he'd honored his oath to Aegiros by wedding Mari, despite his love for Nialei. But back then, none of them had known the truth of his ancestry, and when Mari had become pregnant with her first child, her body had been too young, too weak to sustain them both.

Only dragonblood could carry dragonblood. Mari had paid with her life for her tribe's foolish customs.

"You are certain he spoke the truth?"

"Absolutely," Fal said, and for a moment, she glimpsed his true face beneath the mask of an old man.

"Then why the blood?"

"Because he held back something important. Shall I do the honors?"

"No, I will." Liadan took the bowl and stoked the hearth fire.

"Fire is unreliable," Fal argued.

"Not for me." Scrying from fire often showed two visions: the one the petitioner sought, and the one he most desired. It took a wiser man than most to distinguish the difference and set out on the right path. But Liadan was a creature of fire; it spoke to her clearer than to anyone else, and she trusted it without question. With something as elemental as blood, she needed only to cast it into the fire to see the pure truth inside. Motioning Fal to join her, she knelt before the hearth, dipped her finger into the Aegiran's blood, and flicked a drop of it into the flames.

At once, she was cast into a vision of vast sands and scorching sun. Everywhere she looked, the air wavered as if moments from catching fire and burning the world. Liadan frowned, flicking another drop onto the flames. "His blood keeps secrets as well as he does."

Now, she saw a pile of black rocks amid dead trees, some broken in half. Nothing else. "Damn it." Another drop.

"Give it here." Fal took the bowl from her and threw all of the remaining blood onto the flames, making them hiss and spark. Liadan gasped, plunging into a vision so powerful, she was right there in the middle of it.

She stood in the heart of a great, empty desert city, among silent earthen houses with rags billowing in the windows, not a soul in sight. They'd all been driven out by interlopers, who hadn't lasted long, themselves. Nothing lasted here; not without water, which had all but disappeared on this side of the valley.

Liadan followed the ghostly trail of an exodus across a long, narrow pass that snaked like a ribbon between sand dunes—a valley cut into the landscape by a once-mighty river that was now dry, just like the well in the oasis and every other underground well that lay dug up and abandoned. Everything had dried up, even the heavens. Liadan tasted the air, and all she sensed was sand and dust. This valley had not seen rainfall in a very long time.

Not far off, movement shivered in the air like one of Fal's illusions, and she flew closer to enter a small village of tents. They huddled together like children in the night; old, worn things anchored into the sand, just enough to serve as protection against the sun and sandstorms, but no true comfort for their inhabitants.

She saw people, too. Poor people, starving, sick. Dying. Terrified people who had nowhere else to go, hounded by the horrors they'd lived though—and there were many. As the sun raced to the west and the desert turned dark and cold, Liadan looked to the south where glowing shadows flew across the sky. Black, red, gray; colors of darkness, blood, and death. Demons. They swarmed the village, snatching up one person after another, feeding on their souls and leaving behind hollow shells of flesh and blood. Empty of spirit, those bodies still moved, hungry to fill the void inside. The dead walked the night, feeding on any meat they came upon.

Liadan cried out and fled the vision, slamming back into herself in her chamber. Shaking, she struggled to her feet, trying to get as far away from it as she could. Then Fal was there. Strong arms wrapped around her, and she squeezed her eyes shut to the lie of him and let her true brother hold her, rock her, until her heart had slowed and she could breathe again. "What happened?" he asked.

In halting sentences, Liadan told him what she'd seen. Saying it aloud made the vision real to her. This had happened, and was still happening, to the Aegiran's tribe.

"You're sure?"

Liadan nodded, extricating herself from his embrace. The fire had burned out, so she laid down more kindling, along with a fresh log, and sparked a new one the human way. Once it blazed strong and steady, she stuck her hand into the flames and let them snake up her arm. It warmed her, banished the chill of the vision and brought her comfort and peace instead. "He didn't come just to kill someone, Fal. He thought if he did, it would help his tribe. He believes we caused this."

Fal swore, and the illusory lake her chamber had become began to boil around her. It looked so real, the steam made her sweat. "What do we do?"

"What can we do?"

"We should wait for Father and Mother."

Liadan shook her head. "They could be gone for months. His people don't have that long."

"You want us to help them?" The lake started to swirl in a vortex.

"Don't sound so shocked. His actions may have been the wrong ones, but his intent was honorable. He sought to help his people the only way he knew how."

"By killing. He's an assassin, Liadan!"

"An assassin who sought help from us."

Fal, now a heavily bearded, balding man sitting on her bed, frowned. "If you think I'm going to fall for that—"

"By the charter drawn up by King Saeran and Queen Nialei, none who come to Castle Frastmir seeking aid for a people, our own or Other, may be turned away without being given some form of aid."

Fal shoved to his feet and began to pace, while the water vortex grew, following his step like a shadow. "I knew you would say that!"

"It is the law, brother."

"Our law, not his! He is neither Other nor a citizen of Wilderheim. He is the enemy come to slay the king in his bed! And you would choose to reward him for it?"

"I would choose not to punish his people for his actions."

"Then let him return to them! Mari was their princess, which means, as her brother, he is their prince. Perhaps even their king."

"And you would turn away a fellow royal so easily? What if it happened here? What if it was one of us desperate to save Wilderheim, the way Mother and Father are?"

"Liadan." His tone said he was done arguing. Good. So was she.

"Very well. I suppose in Father's absence, as his heir, you are in charge. I will obey your decision. The Aegiran will be released and escorted to our borders to return to his own lands."

"Thank you."

"And I will be the one to escort him."

CHAPTER 7

The argument that followed would go down in Frastmir's history as the worst thing to have happened since the Veil had been torn. Liadan didn't care. With her vision still occasionally making her shudder, she was in no mood to give in to her well-meaning but near-sighted and illusion-challenged brother. In the end, he could do nothing to stop her short of issuing a royal decree to keep her from riding out to Aegiros. But since her parents were nowhere to be found at the moment, a decree would not be forthcoming unless Fal forged their seal. And if he did, she'd know.

When Fal became so overcome with anger that the maids three floors below shouted about water leaking from the ceiling, Liadan put her foot down and walked out, effectively ending their sibling fight. For the moment, at least. She ran past the angry maids and the bewildered guards, straight down to the dungeons and the imprisoned assassin.

"Listen, you," she said, then stopped, temporarily robbed of speech at the sight of him. The guards had stripped the man of his weapons and his mask. Seeing his face for the first time, Liadan forgot what she'd been about to say. He was… unexpected. His hair was as dark as pitch and long enough to require a thong to restrain it, but shorter strands still escaped to frame his face.

And what a face it was. His dark skin made his pale brown eyes all but glow. He had sharp features with a proud, thin nose and a strong jaw. A true warrior, unadorned and unarmored, though his build and his scars warned her she'd be a fool to challenge him a second time. This one was used to war and pain, and there was a hardness to him, a mistrust and a stubbornness that spoke of many trials fought and won.

"Tir," she tried again, wondering if he even understood her language. "That is your name, yes? Tir?"

He said nothing, but if looks could kill, Liadan would drop dead where she stood.

She swallowed. If she couldn't make herself understood, this would turn out to be a lot more difficult. "Your petition has been heard and granted. We'll ride out tomorrow."

"What lies are you spewing now, demon?"

He had a deep voice as befitted a man of his size, and his accent gave his words a rough, mysterious quality. She could listen to him for days and never grow tired of the sound. Wait. Demon? "I am telling you that you will get the aid you came here to seek. Me."

The assassin glared for a moment, then laughed in her face. "You."

"Yes."

He laughed more, leaning forward where he sat, resting his elbows onto his updrawn knees. "You will ride to Aegiros with me?"

"Yes, that's what I said, isn't it?"

"And what can you possibly accomplish?"

Good question. Liadan had no idea what was happening to his tribe—she might never know—and going there might accomplish absolutely nothing besides getting herself killed. But instead of backing down, she produced the key to his restraints and took one of his wrists to free him. "We won't know until we get there, will we?"

He watched her face the entire time she fumbled with the shackle. Her hands shook. What was the matter with her? "Your eyes," he said. "They are different."

Liadan blushed as the first shackle fell to the floor. She took his other hand, unlocked that one, too.

The moment he was free, the assassin caught her wrist and wrapped his other hand around her throat. In the blink of an eye, he had her pressed against the wall, her feet dangling a fair distance off the floor. "You think you can play with me, demon?" he snarled.

Liadan grabbed his wrist, dug her nails into it, but he was too strong. Fire welled in her hands, glowed out of her eyes, a defense she usually pushed back in a fight like this, but these were special circumstances. Seeing her eyes change, the assassin's own grew wide, and he shouted something in his language.

Only a man, she thought. Not a dragon. A mortal. She didn't need her fire to best him. Pushing it back, she kicked the assassin right between his legs. He roared and released her, but he was in no way defeated. They moved apart to catch their breaths, and Liadan recovered just in time to duck his swing.

He was skilled in combat, but Liadan had been trained by the dragon, and fighting this man was no different. He was fast, but she matched him easily. He was strong, too—she still felt the reminder of how well he'd fought her last night. If she allowed even one of his hits to land true, she'd be done for.

Liadan fought defensively, against his erratic style, fueled by rage as much as by skill, and for a moment she was worried. If she lost, he'd kill her. He spun to put his weight behind a hit; Liadan spun the other way to dodge it. She caught his arm, wrenched it up behind his back, but instead of leaning into it, he somehow leaned forward and twisted around, bringing his arm before him while turning hers to such an awkward angle, she had to release him or risk breaking it. He grabbed her arm when she swung, and sidestepped when she would have stomped down on his feet. He now knew to avoid her knees, and when she tried to headbutt him, he flinched back, anticipating the move.

With speed to rival her dragon grandfather, he spun her around, wrapped his hands around her head and chin.

Liadan! Fal and the dragon shouted at the same time.

"Now you die," the assassin said.

Liadan had no ground to fight him unless she wanted to snap her own neck. Acknowledging her defeat with only a smidgen of regret, she closed her eyes, said good bye to her brother and her grandfather, and waited for the pain of death.

But it didn't come. She heard the assassin behind her rasp out big breaths so she knew time hadn't stopped. Yet she was still alive, and he wasn't moving.

All at once, he shoved her away, snarling a foul-sounding foreign curse. Daring a careful sigh of relief, Liadan turned to face him.

He stared at her as if she were a monster with thirteen heads. "Why did you let me win?"

"What?"

"You have magic and you held it back. I could have killed you!"

"Why didn't you?" she asked.

His shoulders slumped, and he shook his head. "What purpose would your death have served?"

"Liadan of Frastmir, what is the matter with you!"

Liadan winced as Tir whirled around to face the robed people rushing toward them. The speaker was Councilor Braith, second oldest member of the king's royal advisory council, surpassed in age only by the ancient Kvaran, who now shuffled his feet after the rest of the company. A more outspoken advisor had never shadowed the halls of Castle Frastmir.

"Councilors," Liadan greeted. "A fine welcome you give to your king's only daughter."

"If you want to be treated as a princess," Braith quipped, "then act like one. And you"—she turned on Tir, brandishing her walking staff—"settle your feathers or I'll make you see stars."

The threat was ridiculous, considering the source. But curiously, Tir's stance relaxed, and he dipped his head in a brief nod-bow.

Liadan gaped. "How did you make him do that?"

The Aegiran snarled at her, and Councilor Braith sniffed. "Follow."

The entirety of Frastmir's council turned to follow her out as if she'd charmed them into compliance. But Liadan knew better. Braith had earned her respect with long years of loyalty and wisdom, not to mention stubborn refusal to be subdued or overlooked simply for the handicap of her sex. Decades after King Saeran had taken the throne and placed a woman wizard at his side, Braith was still the only woman on his advisory council, and only because she held on to her post with tooth and nail.

When Tir looked at her with utter confusion in his honey-brown eyes, Liadan resolutely bit back a laugh. She shrugged, then did as Councilor Braith had ordered—she followed.

≪ »·◇·« ≫

Nialei couldn't move. The crystal encasing her was so thick, she could barely discern the shapes moving beyond it. It restrained not only her body, but also her magic; she was frozen, helpless to do anything but watch the skeletal wyvern swoop down on Saeran with a screech.

He dove to the ground to avoid its talons, then rolled as the wyvern sprayed acid from its mouth. Too close! Nialei desperately fought her prison to get to him, but she couldn't. This test was for him alone, and she was forbidden to interfere.

On the other side of the arena, the Northern Elf queen cheered the battle on with her horde of followers. Their lands were far removed from the human realm and any of its borders, sitting high in a frozen mountain range where no mortal would even think of encroaching. Thoroughly isolated, the Northern Elves saw no reason to do anything about the damaged Veil, and Nialei's petition had been met with powerful resistance in the form of apathy.

Worse, over the last few years, Others have spread the word of Saeran's agility in battle, and more often than not now, the chosen ordeal in exchange for their aid was to pit him against more and more imaginative opponents. The only way to secure the Northern Elves' aid was to give them something they rarely got to see: a spectacle—a true battle to the death between Wilderheim's greatest hero and one of this region's most vicious predators.

Wyverns were snake-like creatures with long necks and tails, covered in leathery skin. They had wings like a bat growing out of a short, barrel chest, and two clawed appendages that might have been feet. But between the length of their bodies and the awkward placement of those feet, they were physically useless. The wyvern's greatest asset was its glass-shattering screech and the acid it spewed the way dragons breathed fire.

As Nialei watched, the wyvern encircled Saeran in a wide, muscular coil of its body, then reared back to strike. Saeran had no way of retreat, and he'd lost his sword somewhere along the perimeter of the arena. Nialei tried again and again to cast her will through the crystal, to no avail. This, too, was part of the spectacle; the Elf queen wanted her to watch Saeran struggle.

She did not know Saeran.

As the wyvern paused, ready to spew a bellyful of acid, Saeran dropped to one knee and slammed his hands flat onto the hard rock surface of the arena floor. Nialei felt him reach deep inside the mountain to a lazy river of fire and draw it to the surface. The frozen rock cracked and broke at the force of the rising heat beneath his palms.

Confused, the wyvern released him and twisted in circles, watching the ground fracture. It beat its wings to escape, but the Elf queen's spell wouldn't let it; the creature battered itself against an invisible dome over the arena in a futile attempt to break free.

And all the while, Saeran drew strength from the fire, gathering it into his hands, his heart, his soul. With its added power, he rose, glowing from within like a lantern in the night, and when he held out his hand, his sword returned to him on its own, bursting into flames in his grasp.

Sensing the threat, the wyvern rounded on him and screeched. Saeran drew back, then hurled the sword, spearing the animal directly through its heart, pinning it to the dome overhead as it caught fire.

The Elven crowd fell silent.

Queen Taren rose from her seat, a warrior woman with silver hair arranged in multitudes of braids. She glared at Saeran and let the dome dissipate. The wyvern fell into a crevasse at Saeran's feet, and the queen's magic sealed it shut. With a jerk of her chin, she dissolved Nialei's crystal prison, releasing her to drop, gasping, to her hands and knees.

While Taren descended from her balcony perch, Saeran limped over to Nialei and helped her stand. "Won again," he said with a grin.

Nialei didn't share his enthusiasm; she was worried. An ordeal was meant to weigh the petitioner's heart and conscience, not the strength of his arm. And as the petitioner, Nialei ought to have been tested, not Saeran. In the past, both had been willing to submit to the will of Others for the good of all. But how long could they keep going this way?

"Are you hurt?" she asked him. Wyverns were venomous. A single scratch or bite could be fatal, even to Others.

"Nothing a hot bath and a kiss can't heal," he replied, rolling his shoulder with a wince. He looked somewhat the worse for wear, but she detected no bleeding wounds. A small blessing, but Nialei was grateful nonetheless.

The Elven crowds rumbled as they parted to allow Queen Taren passage. She was unlike any Other female they'd thus far encountered. Taren had no mate; she ruled alone with an iron fist, and it showed in her bearing. She dressed in breeches and leathers like a man, keeping her arms bare to show off the dark markings tattooed into her skin. Half of her face and the side of her neck were covered in them, making her look frighteningly fierce. She was scarred, muscled, and armed with two swords and a myriad of hidden knives.

She didn't need them. As a Northern Elf, Taren had natural control over snow and ice the same way Nialei controlled water, and as their queen, she could command every one of her kind to do her bidding with a mere thought. She lived for war, and when none could be had in her own realm, she sought it elsewhere, known to ally herself with any outnumbered, overwhelmed army, human or Other, to even the odds.

Saeran squeezed Nialei's hand. They'd long ago stopped trying to protect each other. Now, no matter what they faced, they stood side by side, working together. As Taren approached, Saeran's magic hummed against Nialei's palm, calling to her own. The queen didn't look happy; she'd bet a great deal on this battle's outcome.

"You owe me a small fortune, Halfling," she said to Nialei.

"And you owe me your blood, Majesty," Nialei replied.

Taren grunted, looking from her to Saeran, then back again. "Where is that beast of yours?"

Nialei smiled. "Behind you."

Head canted low, fur bristling, Varr stood at Taren's back, growling. He showed a mere hint of fang as a warning for the Elf queen to watch her step. No matter how many times Nialei ordered him to stay put, the wolf refused to leave her side. If she left him in the human realm, he somehow found his way through the Veil and tracked her wherever she went. If she tied him, he chewed through the binds, be they leather, cord, or metal.

Nialei wasn't quite sure what he was. He'd once died in her arms, and she'd worn his pelt about her shoulders, until the night the sorcerer, Jasper, had torn the Veil. Then, somehow, the pelt had come back to life, creating a creature who wasn't alive and so could not die, one who wasn't a true animal and so was not bound by the laws that governed them. Varr was a creature of in-between, a Halfling, just like Nialei and Saeran, both of whom he protected fiercely.

Taren snapped her fangs at Varr, and he snarled, which seemed to amuse the queen. Then she turned her back on the wolf, facing them with a terrifying smile. "I would forgive the debt in exchange for him. A fine battle hound he'd make. Fine, indeed."

"Varr is his own creature," Saeran said, not bothering to argue the debt. "He follows no one's orders, and fights no one's battles but his own."

Taren scowled. "I'd call you a liar if I didn't know better."

"The blood, your Majesty?" Nialei prodded.

"Are you in a hurry, Halfling?"

"Yes," she said, for the hundredth time. "Very much so."

Taren grinned, showing off her sharp fangs. "You ought to know better than anyone that time is irrelevant. It is a lie humans tell themselves to give structure to their lives where none exists. And by doing so, they make themselves finite." She leaned in as if to impart a secret. "That is why they die, Halfling. Not because they are human, but because they are so much *human*." With that, she sliced a sharp, crystal dagger across her palm.

Caught off guard, Nialei scrambled to produce the vial she'd brought, collecting into it several drops of Taren's blood. It was more than they needed—far more.

"I am the first," Taren said. "My blood is the purest of my kind. See that you do not waste it."

Before Nialei could utter her formal thanks, darkness engulfed her and Saeran, yanking them from the Otherland and back into Wilderheim. Nialei fought off the nausea this form of travel always induced, then looked around. They were in the east, at the edge of a long ravine that formed a natural border between Wilderheim and Ravetia, with a herd of goats grazing on lush green grass and bright yellow dandelions nearby.

"Thanks," Nialei muttered. It was past noon. Plenty of sunlight left to make their way across the fields. If they could reach the nearest village, they could procure horses and ride back to Castle Frastmir first thing tomorrow. "Was it necessary for you to show off?"

Saeran blinked. "What do you mean?"

"I mean, you could have summoned that fire at any time. You dragged that fight out deliberately."

He shrugged. "They wanted entertainment."

"And you wanted to play. Will there ever come a day when you stop risking your life in senseless displays?"

"Careful, love, you're beginning to sound like Loki."

She shoved at his shoulder. "You know what I mean!"

Saeran crossed his arms. "I seem to recall a time, not that long ago, when you were the one risking your life almost every day. Maybe it's time I put in my fair share."

She blushed, not appreciating the reminder of how much she'd changed over the years, from the young royal wizard, Nia, who'd once turned him into a toad, to Queen Nialei of Wilderheim, ambassador to the Otherlands. "It's not the same, and you know it."

It had taken years for Saeran to fully grow into his powers and learn how to control them. He'd learned from the dragon, and alongside their daughter, had slowly embraced all that his dragonblood had given him. He'd gained many of the dragon's gifts of Sight, Hearing, strength and speed, and even some mastery over fire. He could now hold his own in a physical battle as well as a magical one, but it hadn't always been so.

"You worry too much," he said. Along with his gifts, he'd also developed a sense of dragon arrogance. Nialei supposed all magic came with a price.

"I worry what this is turning us into."

"And what is that?"

Nialei rubbed her brow. "Puppets." Saeran didn't argue with that, and her shoulders slumped. He felt it, too. "This started out as a noble cause," she said, "but now it seems all we do is fight for entertainment and a few drops of blood."

Saeran pulled her close, pressed his lips to her temple. "It won't go on forever. We're almost finished. And once it's done and settled—"

"The Others will have made a laughingstock of us."

"What makes you think we were ever anything else to them? Was it not you who told me that Others live to play merry havoc with mortal lives and watch them implode?"

"It gives me such joy when my student recalls my lessons well enough to quote them back to me," she retorted, making him laugh. The sound of it rumbled from his chest, and she sighed, content to stand there for a while and simply be, without any duties or responsibilities pressing in from all sides. "We should get back home. I miss the children. And our bed."

"So do I. Especially our bed." Saeran gave an irreverent squeeze to her backside. "Well, love, we have two choices to get there: we can walk, or we can walk."

"I suppose we walk." Nialei reluctantly extricated herself from her husband's embrace and, closing her eyes, turned her face into the breeze.

Walk fast, the western wind said. *They need you.*

She looked at Saeran, who mirrored the face she made.

Saeran sheathed his sword, a muscle twitching in his jaw. "What are they up to now?" he muttered as he hopped onto a boulder and reached for her waist to help her up. He kissed her before he set her onto her feet, and Nialei sighed her aches and pains away. "Your children are a right menace, my queen."

"I wonder where they get it from, Majesty."

CHAPTER 8

And furthermore, a princess does not battle cloaked assassins on her own!"

Tir flinched, standing next to said princess being lectured by the old woman pacing before them.

"In point of fact," Princess Liadan said, "he was not wearing a cloak. Only a mask."

The old woman slammed the end of her staff on the ground. "Silence!" Then she turned on Tir. "What have you got to say for yourself?"

Tir drew back his shoulders, looking over her head at a point on the far wall. He refused to answer.

Liadan elbowed him.

He stood his ground.

She did it again, and when he glared at her, she gave him a pointed look, indicating the old woman.

Tir looked away.

"He's here to petition aid for his tribe in Aegiros," she said.

Damn her!

"Did he intend to petition it from the bleeding guts of your royal father?" the old woman retorted.

"What I intended—"

"Was to speak to my parents in private," Liadan cut in. "As you can imagine, this is a matter of pride. Naturally, the prince would not wish to discuss it in public court."

"Did he, or did he not attack you?"

"As you can see, I am unharmed."

The old woman narrowed her eyes. "Do not try to play me for a fool, Princess."

"You would do well to mind your place, Councilor Braith," the princess replied with steely authority. It was the first time Tir had heard her speak as one entitled to the obedience of her people. "I am still the crown princess of Wilderheim, and you will show me the proper respect."

"In the absence of your parents—"

"The rule of Wilderheim falls to the council of elders. But it does not give you the authority to overrule me or Fal. When I speak, it is with the full power of the crown of Wilderheim behind my words, and you will obey my wishes. Is that understood?"

Councilor Braith compressed her mouth into a thin line, anger written in the stiff set of her old shoulders and the white-knuckled hold on her staff. Her cheeks flushed, but she answered, "Yes, Highness. As you command."

"I would advise against this," the oldest man in the company said, voice weak and raspy as if he toed the brink of death already. "We do not know the Aegiran's true intent. His tribe has already lost a member of their royal lineage here, and I have cautioned his Majesty that retaliation might be imminent. There could be armies waiting at our borders as we speak. We should prepare for war."

"If there was an army, Fal would have seen it," Liadan replied before Tir could summon enough words to use the old man's suspicion to his advantage. "The Aegiran is here alone, and the truce King Saeran had procured by marrying Queen Mari obligates us to render him aid for his tribe. Failure to do so would be a direct breach of our laws as well as of the treaty with Aegiros, and then, Councilor Kvaran, then we would truly need to prepare for war."

The elders seemed unconvinced.

"Don't you see?" she pressed. "This is our chance to mend the rift caused by Queen Mari's death. Is that not worth the risk?"

"I say no."

Tir looked over his shoulder and on instinct reached for the weapons he no longer had. Walking through the giant doorway was a creature that defied definition. It had no steady shape of its own, its features constantly changing and shifting into different faces, speaking with many different voices. Its magic was so powerful, the world around it altered in its wake. Water flooded the chamber and grass grew from the stone at its feet as clouds gathered ominously overhead. "*Daeva*," he growled.

"Oi!" the princess cried. "No fighting in the great hall."

Tir roared and charged the creature, but as soon as his feet touched the water it had brought into the chamber, he fell through it as if a deep well had opened up beneath him. Except, it wasn't beneath him. Tir was engulfed in water, yet still in the chamber, looking at the creature. He fought to escape the prison, held his breath for as long as he could, to no avail. His lungs burned with the need for air, and he was getting nowhere.

"Not so frightening now, are you?" the creature taunted.

"Fal!"

At the princess' shout, the water dropped away from Tir, and he fell to his knees, gasping for breath, shaking, but he was completely dry. What magic was this?

Liadan went toe-to-toe with the *daeva*, arguing with it, shouting over it as Tir watched in stunned silence. The longer they bickered, the more the *daeva* began to resemble Liadan. Little things at first—the way its hands gestured, the way it stood, and then its clothing, its hair, and finally its face.

The same face he'd seen in his cell last night, with the same blue eyes that had watched him dispassionately as the creature had bled his wrist.

Liadan shoved at it, shouting, "Enough! This is *my* decision, Fal. You can go crying to Mother and Father later, but just you remember the dragon told you that *I* was to handle this and no one else was to interfere. Well, this is how I choose to handle it, so stop interfering!"

In the silence that followed, the creature's image wavered into a man very similar to Liadan. Its hands fisted at its sides and its jaw muscles twitched. While it glared at her and said not a word, Tir realized all of the water and grass had disappeared.

"You will be riding into the desert," the *daeva* said softly. "Without water, I will not be able to aid you should you encounter trouble and, make no mistake, sister, you will be riding into a kingdom full of trouble."

"I am aware," she said, subdued, staring at its face.

The creature's shoulders slumped, and water again flooded across the chamber floor, washing its face away like a mirage into something completely different. "Then so be it." The creature then turned to Tir, and crouched to put their gazes level. Tir felt dizzy watching its visage waver from old man, to young girl, to one of the elders, and even Liadan herself. "I place my sister's well-being into your care, Aegiran. Know that if any harm comes to her, I will destroy you and everything you hold dear."

When Tir found his voice again, there was only one thing he could say: "What are you?"

"I am the Halfling son of Halfling parents. The crown prince of Wilderheim, and great-grandson of a dragon older than you can imagine. His blood is in my veins, and Liadan's. And if I can do this with water"—water once again pooled around Tir, making him gasp—"only think of what my sister can do with fire." The water receded. "Be grateful she seeks to help you. Turn on her at your own peril."

"I came to end a reign of demons, and now I am to bring one back with me?"

"Bollocks this," Liadan muttered. She pushed aside the creature to kneel before Tir, pulling a blade from her boot. He caught her wrist, but before he could stop her, she closed her hand around the blade's edge and pulled, drawing blood. "A blood oath binds all things, mortal and Other. It is this way in Aegiros, as well, is it not?"

Tir nodded, and slowly released her.

She gave him the blade, and held out her hand. "Then let's dispense with all of the nonsense and finish this. Before the gods and mortals, I vow on my blood that I will not intentionally cause harm to you or your tribe, and that I will do all in my power to help you restore your tribe to what it once was. Now, vow you will not turn against me, and will grant me protection from your tribe so I can do all of that."

Tir searched her gaze for signs of deceit. She was not like her brother. Her eyes were a deep gray with flecks of white and black, like charcoal embers, and they looked into his without wavering, waiting for him to make his choice. She held steady as her blood dripped to the floor.

"My gods have abandoned us, and yours will not listen. I cannot fight demons with armies. If you fail, we all die. When you see them, you will run, too; abandon us despite your oath."

"I have seen, Tir," she replied softly, "and I vow I will stand by you and your tribe. If you agree to our deal."

"This is very ill-advised," the creature—her brother—said.

Tir looked down at the knife he clutched, the one she'd given him without qualm, placing her trust and her life into his hands. He drew the blade across his palm, then clasped hands with her. "I vow it."

Fal buried his face in his hands. "Bloody hell."

Liadan couldn't answer him past the shiver running up her arm and down her spine. She shook herself, then stood and pulled the Aegiran to his feet, as well. Aware of their audience, she dropped his hand and wiped the blood off on her breeches.

"Have you any idea what you have done?" Braith said, breathless.

"Have the servants show our guest to his chambers," Liadan replied. "Make sure he has everything he requires. We will ride out at sunrise. Is that soon enough for you?"

Tir dipped a wordless nod.

"Good. Now, if you will excuse me, I must go prepare."

She left the great hall, taking the stairs two at a time up to the royal wing. When the door was securely closed behind her, she leaned against it, willing her heart to slow. She couldn't breathe fast enough to keep up with its beat. Lightheaded, Liadan sank to the floor and rested her head between her knees.

Someone knocked on the door.

"Not now."

"It's me," Fal said from the other side with a surprising lack of censure.

Liadan stood and let him in. Within moments, Fal had transformed her room into the waterfall clearing where they'd used to play as children. Her bed became a massive, carved tree stump that served as an altar to the gods, and sunlight filtered in through the waterfall covering her window, like a treasure waiting to be discovered. Everywhere at her feet bloomed wildflowers in all colors of the rainbow. She was slowly learning to appreciate his illusions. "Is this a peace offering?" she asked.

"You'll go west through Lyria before turning south into Aegiros," he said. "I want you to ride into Dai, not around it, and pay the proper respects to Cousin Ulrich. He'll want to see you, even if it's only for one night."

"All right," she said. It'd be good to see her cousins. They hadn't seen each other since King Halden died some three years ago. His eldest, Ulrich, now sat on the throne of Lyria, with his two younger sisters as advisors.

"I have instructed the servants to pack supplies for you. You are not to eat them unless necessary. You have coin, and you can hunt. Use that while you can. Once you run out of inns and taverns, you will have a pack full of dried meats and fruits to tide you over. Water will be scarce, so ration it, but do not be foolhardy. You must drink, understood?"

Liadan nodded. "Yes."

"Good. Now, which mount do you want to—"

"Sleipnir. He's steady, doesn't spook, and can run for hours without cease if need be."

"He will serve you well. I would advise you to take guards with you but—"

"No one wants to ride that far south," she finished with a bitter smile. "I will be all right without them."

He reached out to embrace her, and she allowed it. "I wish to all the gods that you hadn't done this."

"I don't."

CHAPTER 9

Liadan had exhausted herself making arrangements for the journey ahead, but as the sun set, as tired as she was, she couldn't bring herself to sleep. Instead, she wandered through the castle, listening to every sound and every echo. Strange, this was her home and she knew each stone like the back of her hand, but it brought her no comfort to be here.

Unaccountably lonely and anxious about what sunrise would bring, Liadan sought her brother in his chambers. They were empty. Knowing Fal could only be in one other place at a time like this, Liadan turned on her heels and headed up to his private tower library—the farthest one could get from the servants' wing without leaving the castle itself. Padding silently on bare feet chilled by the cold, stone floor, Liadan passed through the great hall and hurried up the tower stairs.

At the top, she pushed open the door to step into an underwater kingdom. Surprised, Liadan gasped, feeling water fill her lungs. She choked and coughed herself out of the room, but as soon as she'd backed across the threshold, the sensation was gone. *It's an illusion,* she realized. Bracing herself, she took care going back inside. Instinct told her to hold her breath, but Liadan fought against it, closed her eyes, and breathed in.

Not seeing herself under water helped a little, though she could still feel the soft, cushioning sand bed beneath her bare feet. It took longer than she'd thought, but eventually she convinced her body of what her mind already knew, and she calmed. When she opened her eyes again, Liadan found this world Fal had created beautiful beyond anything she'd ever seen. Light flickered and danced all around her, while brilliant flowers bloomed and swayed in a warm current that caressed her skin. A dark, mysterious cave filled the hearth, and out of it swam a school of brightly colored fish. She herself looked different. Soft webbing stretched between her toes, keeping her feet from sinking into the sand, and when she held her hand up to the light, pearlescent scales shimmered across her skin.

"Amazing," she whispered.

Fal, of course, didn't notice. Seated at the central table with his back to the door, he hadn't even heard her enter.

The dragon had sent him a trove of knowledge: animal skins branded with markings, ancient tapestries, scrolls, even stone tablets, and all of them were now spread out before him.

Liadan sidled up behind her brother to look over his shoulder, marveling at the depth of his focus as he penned a translation onto a crisp piece of parchment. Fal handled the tools of a scribe with utter reverence, considering each word carefully before he committed it to writing. The markings he translated were in the ancient dragon tongues, as mutable as dragons themselves, with no two symbols alike. It took a keener mind than most to make any sense of them, let alone divine their true meaning. "So you were paying attention during Grandfather's lessons after all," she quipped.

Startled out of his half-trance, Fal jerked his hand sideways, scratching a jagged line of ink across the page. "Liadan!"

She laughed, but held up her hands and bowed her head in contrition, while he tried in vain to contain the damage. "So this is what you do on the eve of your one and only sibling being shipped off across hostile lands to aid a deadly enemy?" His sharp look spoke more than words ever could, and his grave eyes, miraculously glaring at her from his own face, sobered her, as well. "Couldn't sleep?"

He sighed, rubbed a weary hand over his brow. "I thought this would make time move slower. I was wrong."

The school of fish paraded before him, whipping their tails left and right to seduce him with their play of colors. Fal waved a hand to shoo them away, and they scattered.

Needing something other than tomorrow to think about, Liadan looked over the dragon's offerings. "What have you discovered?"

Fal blinked down at the piece of parchment as if seeing it for the first time, and his eyes widened as he read over the translation. "Did you know this?"

"I haven't a notion of what you're looking at, so no."

He frowned at the page, consulted the skin again, compared the two, scribbled a few more things, then blew on the parchment to dry the ink before he picked it up to read. Expecting him to have forgotten she was there now that he'd found something interesting, Liadan pushed her chair back, about to leave him to it, when he spoke again. "Ancient lore tells of the coming together of six elements."

Liadan, raised an eyebrow. "Six?"

"Yes. Earth, air, fire, water, light, and darkness." He quickly counted them off on his fingers, irritated by Liadan's lack of knowledge on the subject.

She merely shrugged.

"The elements were eternal and ever-present," he continued, "and so they remained in everything born of the clash: eternal and ever-present. Where one element overwhelmed the rest, a different breed of creature emerged, stronger with the dominant element's inherent…" Fal looked at the skin for confirmation. "Attributes, I suppose. Or powers, perhaps."

Liadan waved him on, before he got too distracted by the minutiae.

"Right, yes. Stronger with the dominant element's inherent qualities, but composed of all the rest, as well, in smaller quantities. At the point of absolute balance, where no single element held dominion over the other, the equilibrium birthed a breed foretold to master all six. Yet the struggle of each element to gain dominion over the others is what strengthened them and brought life to any being born of them. In its absence, at peace, the elements settled and faded, and with them, the body did as well."

"Humans," Liadan said, sitting up to attention. "That is why they age and die so quickly."

Fal nodded. "Struggle is the driving force of life. Without it, everything dies." Again he turned his attention to the skin, and this time, Liadan was certain he wouldn't look up for a good long while. She stood to leave.

"The elements are eternal and ever-present," he read to himself. "An aspect of one is but a small part of the whole, creating a tangible connection to the eternal, and thus making the passage from one to another possible."

Liadan stopped, hand on the door handle. "What does that mean?"

Fal didn't answer.

She shrugged and left him to it, carefully closing the door behind her. No doubt by morning, her brother would have discovered some ancient magic known only to dragons and he'd be too busy experimenting with it to notice her departure. His dedication made her proud. Fal wasn't someone who'd sit and wait for a miracle. He'd done his tutors and their parents proud by working just as hard to help himself as they had to help him.

She'd miss him in Aegiros.

Strange… now that the shock of what she'd done had passed, Liadan didn't regret her decision to accompany the Aegiran to his homeland. It felt right; more so than staying here. It felt as if this was the path she was meant to walk.

As she entered the great hall, a subtle groan of wood brought her head up. She found the Aegiran on the dais, peering hard at the queen's royal seat. What in the world was he looking for?

"It's called a throne."

Startled, Tir leaped away from the chair, lowering into a defensive crouch.

"I don't suppose you have those where you come from," she said. "That particular one is spelled for protection. You can neither destroy it, nor use it to destroy whoever sits upon it."

Tir straightened, embarrassed to have been caught. "I was merely curious about the markings."

"Ah," the princess breathed, drawing closer. "Those are called runes." As before, she was dressed in pants, but this time, her shirt hung loose to her knees, hiding her almost as well as a cape would. To Tir's shame, it frustrated him that he couldn't see what lay beneath. Only because he didn't trust her; she could be hiding weapons anywhere on her body and he wouldn't know it until she attacked. She mounted the stairs on bare feet, as silent as the night, watching him with a quizzical smile playing across her lips. "That one there, and the two next to it, mean protection against dark intents. And this one here is prosperity."

He studied the symbol she'd indicated. "These are words?"

"Not as such. They carry a broader meaning that can be interpreted differently, depending on their combinations. For example, these two together mean strength of arms, a victory in battle. But if I were to put this symbol next to that one and the one over there, it would mean strength of spirit, a blessing against corruption."

"I've seen symbols like these used before," he said, thinking of the blood marks painted onto Aesimar's horses. "They were not so benevolent."

The princess leaned against the throne's back, watching him. "Tell me about Aegiros."

"So you can destroy it more easily?" The harsh words had slipped over his tongue before he could stop them.

She had the temerity to laugh. "Yes, hateful foe, you have found me out. I dream of the day when the last Aegiran waters the sands with his blood. I have nothing else to concern myself with, except for the demise of your people."

"You mock me."

"You are astute."

"Do you not fear me at all?"

She grinned. "I do not see the purpose of it."

"You should." He stalked around the chair to her side. "In here, your warriors are but a call away. The cr… your brother has magic I would not dare incite. But when we leave, you will not have them to protect you."

She did not flee from his advance. Instead, she faced him and held her ground, her easy smile taking on a feral edge. "If I needed them to protect me, I would be worried." The princess held up her hand, then rubbed her thumb over the tips of her fingers. Her skin began to glow red, while tendrils of smoke curled up from the gentle friction. When a spark jumped, she curled her fingers into a tight fist, and when she opened her hand once more, fire nestled in the center of her palm. "Since I do not, I am not."

Tir steeled his spine against retreat. Though she'd performed the feat with frightening ease, he found himself curious about how she'd done it. He could feel the flame's heat, knew it to be real, yet her hand remained unharmed. Tir met her gaze and saw the fire's light glowing out of her eyes, as well.

The princess extinguished the flames, her eyes dimming as she did so. "Are we back to the beginning again?" she asked with the gravity of defeat behind her voice. "Is this what we will do every day until we reach Aegiros, as if a blood oath means nothing?"

Tir stepped back, then drew himself up, pride squaring his shoulders against her rebuke. "I honor my word."

"Good." She nodded. "Then I suggest you get some sleep. We leave at dawn." Giving him her back, the princess left the great hall, abandoning him in the cavernous chamber on his own.

There were no guards standing at the door, and the room they'd given him had no bars to lock him in. He could escape, leave and return to his people. But what would he bring back? Fear for them was a constant noose around his neck, choking him, pulling him back to Imarah. Tir wanted desperately to know how his tribe was faring, whether anyone was still left alive.

Prayer had never been anything but a last resort to him. Had he reached that point already, worlds removed from his homeland? Perhaps the time for it would never be more fitting than this very moment. Without an altar or any incense to guide him into meditation, he searched the wooden chair again for the symbol of strength. Placing his hand upon it felt like a betrayal, but if his own gods were too far away to listen, he had no choice but to petition the ones here.

Through a raw throat and a dry mouth, the words at last emerged. “I pray for my people. For those who cannot save themselves. I pray they be safe until I return to look after them. I pray for light to keep demons away, steel to fight off raids. I pray they know I bring back hope, and I pray it is true.”

There was no sense of relief nor hint of an answer to let him know his prayers had been heard. Though he was not a religious man, he'd felt the gods working through the Magi of his tribe and he knew in his heart there ought to have been something, some unknown feeling when one was in the presence of the divine. That he felt nothing only served to prove that the gods—all the gods—had well and truly abandoned him.

Weary beyond death, Tir allowed his shoulders to slump as he made his way back to his room.

CHAPTER 10

When morning dawned, Castle Frastmir became a beehive of frantic activity. Fal had given all of the orders himself, and it showed. Guards were posted at the gates and roaming the city to clear a path. Hostlers had readied four horses, two to ride and two drafts to carry additional supplies, bundles of which were either lashed to their backs or set aside to be added later. Cooks had prepared a hearty breakfast, none of which would be eaten, and packed heaps of dried meats and fruits, cheeses and breads for the journey.

Liadan greeted Sleipnir with an affectionate nuzzle, and an apple. "We're going on an adventure, you and I." The giant black horse bucked his head back and stomped, impatient to get going. Sleipnir was a spirited beast; he didn't like standing around unless there was a pretty mare to look at. Liadan couldn't blame him.

Across the courtyard, Tir watched the preparations, hisjaw clenching ever tighter. Liadan walked Sleipnir over to him. "This is Tir," she told the beast. "He will be coming with us." To the Aegiran she explained, "Sleipnir doesn't like strangers. He needs to get your scent, or he'll keep trying to bite you."

Tir's gaze warmed, and he held his hand up to the horse. When Sleipnir didn't nibble, Liadan nodded, satisfied with the successful introduction. "It won't be long now," she said and clucked her tongue to walk the mount around the courtyard for a bit.

Tir caught the reins, staying her as he looked into Sleipnir's eyes. "He is a fine animal," he said. High praise from someone who'd shown nothing but contempt to everything and everyone since he'd arrived.

Murmuring foreign words, he stroked an expert hand down Sleipnir's neck, made an appreciative hum as he patted the horse's deep chest. Following back across the mount's shoulder, he inspected the saddle, but it didn't hold his interest for more than a cursory glance. What he truly admired was the animal wearing it. Sleipnir was the pride of the dragon's herd. He'd been born wild, caught by the dragon, and tamed by Liadan. Standing tall, Liadan could barely see over Sleipnir's back, and he had hooves bigger and stronger than any other mount in Castle Frastmir's stables, so Liadan was shocked when the foreigner bravely bent down by Sleipnir's hindquarters to examine one of them. Even more so when the mount lifted his hind leg to show it off instead of crushing Tir like an insect.

By the time he'd finished his examination, Tir's mood had lifted a great deal. "You take good care of him," he noted.

"Sleipnir is very particular about his grooming." In fact, the mount was vain. He required frequent baths and brushing to keep his coat clean and shiny, and wouldn't let Liadan walk away after a ride until she'd brushed him down to his satisfaction.

"He is a proud animal, as well he should be."

Liadan smiled sweetly. "If it pleases you so much, I will let you groom him in my stead."

To her surprise, a smile lit up Tir's handsome face. "I accept."

Before she could quip a biting response, Fal appeared as a strapping warrior with muscled arms and scars crisscrossing his face. The courtyard overflowed with water, sending servants and hostlers scurrying for cover. Amazingly, the animals didn't even twitch. Could they see through the illusion?

As Fal approached, Tir tensed beside her, reaching for his dagger, but Liadan slapped his hand away, so he curled his fingers around Sleipnir's reins instead. Sensing his tension, the mount snorted, shifting his girth to shield Tir and bump Fal farther away.

Liadan glared at the horse. "I see where your loyalties lie."

"All is ready?" Fal asked as Sleipnir pushed against his side, making him trip sideways a step farther. Fal ignored it.

"As ready as it can be, I suppose," Liadan answered. "Thank you for all this. For everything."

"I only wish—" Another bump from Sleipnir. "I wish—" The mount chomped at his bit, glaring at her brother with one shiny, dark eye. "I wish I could—" Bump. "Stop it this instant," Fal snapped, changing into a wrinkled, old woman, "or I will put thistle in your mane."

Sleipnir tossed his head and shifted away from Fal, turning so he could slap him with his tail.

"Mane and tail," Fal growled, face rippling into a mask of menace.

Sleipnir whinnied and cowered against Tir.

Having settled that, Fal, now a lanky youth with gangly limbs, adjusted his robes and gave a nod of satisfaction.

Liadan bit back a grin.

"I brought this for you." He searched his pockets and pouches, finally withdrawing a plump, glass vial of crystal-clean water, small enough to be worn around her neck, holding no more than a swallow or two of liquid.

"What is this for?"

"I don't know yet," Fal said. "Last night I fell asleep in the library and dreamed of a great river sprouting from the desert sands. But all that water came out of a bottle no bigger than this." He shrugged, as if he couldn't understand it himself. Portents and visions divined from water were never clear in their instructions. "The dream doesn't matter. If nothing else, this will allow me to see you and speak with you if your drinking water runs out. Don't lose it."

"I won't."

Fal huffed and, pulling her into his arms, embraced her so tightly, her feet almost left the ground. He held her for a long while, not speaking, but Liadan didn't need any words.

“I will see you again soon,” she promised.

“Be careful.”

She nodded, then wriggled, asking to be released. Her brother stepped back, gave a farewell nod of his own, and retreated into the castle. Neither of them had had much practice with good byes.

“Mount up,” she said to Tir, pulling herself into Sleipnir’s saddle.

When the hostler, Micah, brought out Tir’s horse and handed him the reins, he was forced to release Liadan’s. After inspecting the new animal the same way he had Sleipnir, Tir looped the reins around his hand and walked the mare back to the stables.

“What are you doing?”

“I have a horse,” the Aegiran replied. “My Tarabas is stabled at the inn past the green.”

Liadan gaped at his back as he walked the mare all the way to her stall to remove every bit of man-made gear she wore. He then took more time to brush her down and speak what looked like a prayer against her forehead. And all the while, the hostlers stared at him as if he’d lost his mind. Liadan couldn’t be certain he hadn’t.

Sleipnir was getting restless, fidgeting and stomping left and right, shaking his head in irritation. His ear-splitting whinny finally summoned the Aegiran back out. He nodded to Liadan and her mount, then walked beside them when she nudged Sleipnir forward. The draft horses were tied to a lead, so well-trained, they didn’t need a human touch to tell them where to go. Nevertheless, as they made their way through Frastmir, Tir fell back to visit with them, as well.

It irritated Liadan beyond words, but she didn’t know why.

“Horses are precious to my tribe,” he told her. “We used to have herds of them. Others would come from the farthest reaches of Aegiros and beyond for the privilege of acquiring one from us. We never parted with a mount without looking into the eyes of the one who would ride him.”

“What happened?”

“What do you think?” He replied. “You should know; you said you have seen it.”

“I've seen only what your tribe is now, not what it used to be before.”

“You can only take the sights I possess. I have few memories of that time. They say our herds were scattered across the sands of Aegiros; our people chased them away to fend for themselves when we could no longer feed them. Some ran. Others stayed and starved with us.”

Liadan was tempted to inquire whether they’d killed the horses for food, but the way he leaned against the draft mare while she nuzzled him told her it wouldn’t be wise.

“Tarabas and another, a mare, are the last of their herd. Their sire died a good death in battle five moons ago. Tarabas and Zara will not leave, and my people do not have the heart to slay them.”

“How do you feed them if you have no food of your own?”

“However we can,” he replied grimly. Liadan didn’t ask more.

Past the weaver’s cottage, the road widened out into the market square, where merchants had opened their shops, preparing their wares for the day's crowds. In a little while, the square would be thick with people going about their daily tasks, but for now, it was still navigable on horseback.

To the left, the path forked down toward the rowan grove, and to the right, a vast expanse of the city green stretched on as far as the Hallowed Mountain. The meadow was tended by the clerics whose sanctuary sat atop that mountain peak. It was quite a distance away, across the green, through the woods, and up a long, treacherous staircase carved into the bedrock. Initiates entering the order's sanctuary for the first time walked the path on their knees to prove their humility and devotion.

"Over there." Tir pointed to the Wanderer's Tavern Inn.

A slow, wicked grin spread across Liadan's face. "This is where you bedded down?"

Tir glared, but Liadan ignored him and dismounted, headed for the tavern and for the innkeeper she'd known since childhood. *Won't she be happy to see me,* she thought with a wicked chuckle.

As the princess dashed into the inn, Tir gritted his teeth, taking hold of Sleipnir's reins to secure them to a post. Casting a wary glance all around, he saw many faces, none of which looked his way. Strange how the city's people treated the princess as if she were nothing more than another traveler. Did they even recognize who she was? What sort of ruler was unknown to her own people?

Loath though he was to leave the horses by themselves, Tir had no choice; gods only knew what manner of mischief the madwoman was up to now. He patted Sleipnir's neck. "Scream if there is trouble."

The dark horse nodded as if he'd understood.

Keeping an eye out for angry little man-things and creatures made of plants, Tir ducked into the inn after Liadan.

"Welcome back, *sher'nah,*" the fair-haired innkeeper greeted, though her coy smile was wary now that the princess stood before her. She was still as beautiful as the first time he'd seen her, yet she paled like a ghost next to the princess with her vibrant eyes and wild, red-brown hair, her skin as smooth as cream and cheeks flushed from the sun. "Have you found what you sought?"

Why had he not noticed before how lush the princess' lips were, or the way her jerkin molded to her body? "I do not know," he answered with a frown.

The fair-haired creature smirked. "Then all is as it should be."

"We are here for his belongings and his horse," Liadan said, a hint of warning in her tone.

"Are you now?" the female said sharply. "And whatever would he need the horse for? He has you, does he not?"

What did that mean? And why had the princess' face flushed, eyes heating with the fire that seemed to be her true nature? In her anger, she looked even more arresting, and Tir found himself drawing closer.

The innkeeper glared at her, a challenge no one in Imarah would have dared against the *shansher* or any of his kin. It incensed him on Liadan's behalf. He prepared to intervene, but as quickly as the princess' temper had flared, it subsided, and she smiled beatifically, leaving him stunned. "Where is my head today?" she said. "I apologize. It's been so long, I've forgotten all things are bought and sold in your fine establishment. Of course, you will want your due, yes?"

The innkeeper gasped a protest as the princess caught her by the back of the neck and kissed her on the mouth. The creature's cheeks flushed the same way they had when she'd bargained a kiss from Tir, but now her skin darkened, her hair curled, and her entire being glowed like a star. When Liadan released her, the innkeeper fell back and, clutching her chest, wheezing out, "Gods damn you, Liadan." A moan fought its way past her lips, and her fingers curled, sharp claws suddenly digging into her flesh.

"I would tell you to duck," Liadan said to Tir, "but I don't think it'll do any good now."

Tir couldn't tear his gaze away from the innkeeper. Her glow intensified, and then, as if she could no longer contain it, she screamed, and a burst of blinding light flooded the inn.

Tir reached for Liadan and pulled her down. Arms around each other, they held on while the world disappeared around them and the unearthly scream carried on.

In the next instant, the inn fell dark and silent. Liadan's head lifted, her nose bumped into his, and then Tir was kissing her, desperate for a taste of her lips. It was more pressing than the need to draw air into his lungs or to feel the ground beneath his feet. His fingers tangled into her hair while hers clutched at his belt, and Tir heard nothing but the slight catch of her breath, saw nothing but a flash of fiery eyes and red-brown hair. And he wouldn't have felt a blade pierce his heart past the delight of her body pressing against his.

Slowly, sounds began to intrude and the haze of blindness cleared. A man stumbled out the door. Another fell to his knees and retched. Somewhere near the back, yet another man wailed with such terrible grief, it wrenched Tir and Liadan apart. Her eyes were shocked and confused when they looked into his.

The innkeeper sagged against the bar with a heavy thud and spat venomous noises their way. Tir and Liadan ignored her, still staring at each other, holding their breaths, waiting.

When the man wailed again, Tir sucked in a sharp breath, recognizing the sound of a soul dying. It shuddered through him, making his fingers curl harder into Liadan's waist, fearing she'd be ripped away from him at any moment.

The princess squeezed her eyes shut, prying free of his viselike hold to push to unsteady feet. Nothing took her away from him; she left on her own, and the moment their connection broke, the desperate need to possess her ebbed in such a rush, it left Tir feeling drunk and confused, angry to have been played a fool.

Having summarily dismissed him, Liadan sought the weeping man's form in the shadows, then looked to the innkeeper once more. "Kala?"

The fair-haired creature begrudged a nod.

"No," Liadan whispered, rushing over to the grieving man. She caught his face in her hands, urging him to look at her, but he couldn't lift his gaze, sobbing his heart out on the tavern floor. Liadan spoke to him in words too strange and too quick for Tir to understand, but he heard the sentiment behind them. When nothing else worked, Liadan pulled the man into her arms and rocked him, wept with him.

Despite the sting of whatever trick she'd played on him, Tir sensed her heartfelt compassion, and his chest ached to see tears well up in her eyes. He couldn't stand the sight of it. With a hard look at the innkeeper still struggling to compose herself, he pushed to his feet, then ran upstairs to retrieve his belongings. On his way back, he bypassed the tavern altogether and headed for the stables instead. Tarabas was where Tir had left him, a docile mount with few cares in the world, aside from his next meal. Ever since they'd entered fertile lands, Tarabas had eaten his fill, and his ribs no longer showed through his brown coat. Tir greeted him, inspecting the animal from head to toe to make certain no harm had come to him since they'd parted.

Once he was satisfied his mount was hale and well-fed, Tir saddled him, then led him outside to join the other three, letting the horses sniff and nose each other until Liadan emerged, wiping her wet face on her sleeve.

Tir pretended to occupy himself with the supply packs, but he needn't have bothered. Liadan swung into Sleipnir's saddle and, without pause or a single word, steered him onward and away from the inn, the drafts obediently following.

Tir mounted Tarabas and nudged him to catch up, but even when he pulled alongside Liadan, she wouldn't look at him, staring straight ahead. With so many questions burning in his mind, he didn't notice they'd come up to the bridge until cold water sprayed his bare arm. Tir made the mistake of looking sideways and found a water creature hovering above the river's current, its head canted sideways as it watched them.

Tir nudged Tarabas on faster, but the mount refused to pull ahead of the larger Sleipnir. Crossing the bridge was the most terrifying experience of his life, but once they were all safely on the other side, Tir remembered his questions and he turned in his saddle to face Liadan.

"You needn't look at me that way," she said, avoiding his gaze. "It wasn't real. Galen is a succubus; they feed on passion and return it in kind. If they take in too much, their bodies can't hold on to it and it must be released. Those too close can't help becoming overwhelmed by the excess that gets absorbed into them. Succubi call it a purge."

Tir committed this to memory. "That man, who was he?"

Liadan's chin wobbled, and she pressed her lips together tightly. "His name is Geir. When the Veil thinned and Others began to walk among us in plain sight, he was a soldier in my father's army, charged with keeping order and peace. He was also the first human to be openly mated to an Other, a wood sprite who gave up everything to be with him. Kala's clan was against the union and shunned her. But wood sprites feed off the connection amongst each other, and without her clan, Kala began to change and weaken. Geir begged and pleaded with them to help her. He was willing to give his life to save her, but they refused. They told him she was beyond their help, too human already to receive nourishment the way she used to.

"Last I heard, Geir had petitioned my parents for help, but there was little they could do. Kala's body had become human, mortal, but her soul was still that of a wood sprite, and though she could ingest food the way we do, her soul starved."

"She died?"

"Yes. She held on for twenty years. Galen said she asked to be taken to the rowan grove two moons ago. She took her last breath in Geir's arms and turned into a sapling. When Galen purged, she brought his most powerful emotion to the surface, amplified it a hundredfold. Gods, I can still feel it. If I'd known, I never would have…"

"What did you tell him?"

"I told him…" Liadan sniffed and rubbed her eyes. "I told him to be strong for her, that an Other's mate-bond was as eternal as their souls. It bound them beyond strife, beyond death. I told him he would be with her again."

"Is that true?"

"I don't know," she said quietly.

Tir shuddered. "Gods save me from such a wretched fate."

"You don't need gods for that," she retorted. "Just keep to your own and don't fall in love with an Other."

CHAPTER 11

They rode almost without cease for the rest of the day, stopping only once in the town of Crossroads to take their midday meal. By the time the sun had dipped low, they were almost to the Western Ridge, a mountain range that formed the border between Wilderheim and Lyria. Though the pass was well-tended, it was treacherous to navigate at night, so they bedded down at the Royal Inn.

It was as good as its name suggested and was a convenient rest stop between the capital cities of Dai and Frastmir. Since the monarchs of the two kingdoms were related by blood, they visited often and were all well known to the old innkeeper, Jonah.

As soon as Liadan was recognized, Jonah summoned hostlers to care for the mounts. Liadan was too weary to object when one took Sleipnir's reins to lead him to the stables. She shuffled indoors, then collapsed into a plush seat by the hearth, already half asleep.

Magda, Jonah's wife, pressed a bowl of hot stew into her hands and set a bottle of mead beside her. Liadan managed a polite, "Thank you," but she couldn't eat more than a few spoonfuls. Setting it aside, she stared into the fire and let it soothe away her aches and sorrows. Next thing she knew, movement jarred her awake as someone scooped her up out of the seat and, startled, Liadan blinked to focus on Tir's dark face. "What are you doing?" she asked.

"Taking you to bed."

"You think highly of yourself."

"To *your* bed, Princess."

"Oh." He climbed the stairs slowly, carrying her as if she were a child. "I can walk."

"I know."

"Then put me down."

"I will." And he did. Once he'd reached the room they'd prepared for her, he laid her down onto the bed, then knelt at her feet to take off her boots. After setting them neatly to the side, he came back to cover her with a thick blanket. "Sleep well," he said.

"And you," she remembered to reply before he left, closing the door behind him.

With the light of the hallway shut out, Liadan couldn't fight her exhaustion any longer, and sleep claimed her as she was—fully dressed and dusty from the road.

In the morning, roosters announced the rising sun, crowing one over the other to impress the hens. Liadan hoped one of them would get cooked for lunch. She climbed out of bed and stretched, working the aches out of her sore muscles. By the hearth, her bath stood ready, gone cold from the night before. She stripped and stepped into the tub, calling up just enough fire to make it boiling hot. She washed quickly, redressed, and pulled her boots back on. No time to dry her wet hair. Tir would be anxious to move on, and she couldn't blame him. They'd tarried too long yesterday and had lost more time than they could afford.

Tying her wet tresses at her nape, Liadan hurried out the door and almost ran into Tir. For a moment, they stared at each other, at a loss for words. "Good morning," she finally said.

"And to you," he replied.

Silence.

Tir cleared his throat. "They have prepared the first meal down below."

"Oh, good."

He nodded. "Yes."

More silence.

"Are the horses ready to ride out?" she asked.

"Not yet. I will see to them." Happy to have something to talk about, he waved her to walk with him as he explained, "I took care of them last night and put our supplies away so I would know where to find them. It won't take long to get on our way again. Did you sleep well?"

"I don't remember," she said wryly. "I suppose that means yes. And you?"

"I slept." A mysterious answer from one who already said little. Unless horses were the topic of conversation, apparently.

"The innkeeper said there are merchants setting out for Lyria."

"Then we should hurry. We need to get ahead of them before they enter the pass, or their wagons will block the road and it'll take us twice as long to cross the range behind them. I'll settle our bill with Jonah, you start saddling up. I'll meet you in the stables in a moment."

He murmured in agreement and hurried ahead to see to his duties. Liadan, meanwhile, sought out Magda. "It's been a while since we've seen one of his kind this far north," the innkeeper's wife said, something brittle in her tone.

Liadan had no time to examine it. "I wish to thank you most kindly for your hospitality. We will need food to take with us, and then I can settle with you for the two rooms and your services."

"One room," Magda corrected.

"I beg your pardon?"

"One room, Highness. The Aegiran slept in the stables."

"Why?" Surely his love of horses didn't extend that far.

"I suggested he would be more comfortable there." Despite a flicker of unease in her eyes and a nervous folding of her wrinkled hands, the innkeeper's wife continued to speak her piece, nose in the air. "My husband fought alongside your father's men in the war. He knows what manner of people they are, and neither of us felt it appropriate for him to sleep under the same roof as one of the royal heirs. We thought your Highness would have requested it yourself, had you not been so worn out from your journey."

Fire burned through Liadan's veins, and she had to step away, take a deep breath to rein it back in. "You made him sleep in the stables?"

Realizing she'd misjudged, Magda sputtered. "W-we run an honest business here, and extend every courtesy to our royal guests. Why, we'd give the clothes off our back to one in need!"

"And you will," Liadan said thoughtfully. Reaching out to Fal in her mind, she made certain her brother was awake and listening. She wanted him to hear what she said next. "Listen well, Magda Westborn. You will pack your best food and wine for me and my Aegiran companion. We'll also require soaps and cloths, and spare clothing, if you have any."

"And you will, of course, pay for it all?"

"Oh, yes. A contingent of royal guards will be arriving from Frastmir before the day is done to give you what you deserve."

Magda paled. "Your Highness, please forgive us if we overstepped, but—"

"You've done far worse than that. You have insulted and mistreated the prince of Wilderheim's long-time ally. In your place, I would pray he is more forgiving than I."

What manner of punishment do you think will be fair? Fal asked.

The lofty bitch made him sleep in the stables. What would you do?

Leave it to me, he replied, and Liadan knew the next time she came riding into the Royal Inn, Magda and her husband would not be there. "Why are you still standing here?" she demanded of the woman. "I gave you an order. Move!"

Are you all right? Fal asked.

The nerve of them!

Yes, what nerve to be suspicious of a strange man travelling with the king's only daughter.

The stables, Fal!

I heard you the first time. Do you honestly think it'll be any different in Lyria?

She hadn't considered that. The war with Aegiros had been a terrible thing, but for decades, there had been nothing but peace between the northern kingdoms and the south.

Magda and two of her servants came rushing back in no time, carrying cloth bundles. They set everything before Liadan with bows so low, they almost touched the ground. Muttering pleas and apologies, Magda kissed Liadan's hand.

Liadan pulled away. "Leave me." *Why did you make us ride through Dai, if you knew this would happen?* she asked Fal.

I wanted you to see how he'd be treated—the mistrust, animosity, and hatred, perhaps even violence. He will have no friends there.

He will have me, she insisted.

As if she hadn't spoken at all, Fal added, *You need to see it and prepare yourself, because everything he'll encounter, you will feel twice over, once you step foot in Aegiros.*

And there was the crux of it. Lyria had won the war with Aegiros. Though it had sustained much damage, they'd had victory on their side, and a chance to reclaim their kingdom. Tir's tribe had been not only defeated, they'd been humiliated, and then hurt yet again when Mari had died in Wilderheim. They had more reason to stone Liadan to death than to trust she'd do anything to help them. A life for a life was meant to end a war. What if they demanded her life in exchange for Mari's to settle the debt?

Liadan snatched up the bundles and went in search of Tir. When she found him, he'd already burdened the drafts with their supplies and was saddling his own mount. "I would like you to change before we ride out," she said, handing him a bundle of clothes from Jonah. They wouldn't fit him well, but they'd make him look less threatening than his Aegiran attire.

"Why?"

"Please," she said.

Tir must have read something in her eyes. He accepted the bundle, but made no move to disrobe. "I do not care what they do or say. I do not fear Northmen."

"I know. But I do."

He stalled for a moment longer before he left to do as she'd asked. While he was gone, Liadan finished saddling Sleipnir, then checked to make sure nothing was overlooked. The innkeeper and his staff didn't come near either of them again, though several stuck their heads around corners to watch from a distance.

As the merchants started on the road headed west, Liadan led the horses outside. At last, Tir emerged. Jonah's pants were too short and too wide on him, but at least the shirt was serviceable. He'd tied back his long, black hair, but even though he was now dressed in the proper way, nothing could hide the dark shade of his skin or the proud set of his shoulders. His eyes dared anyone to cross him, and the swords strapped to his saddle made him look all the more menacing when he mounted Tarabas.

"Does this please you?" he asked, without looking at her.

"No," she said honestly. "Once we cross the pass, we will get you clothes that fit."

"I do not want more costumes!" Tir snarled. The clothes she'd made him wear felt ridiculous; nothing fit as he was used to, making him feel a fool for giving in to her request. When he sat on Tarabas, the pant legs pulled out of his boots, exposing the skin of his calves, and he was drowning in a huge shirt with sleeves so wide, he could have made two more shirts out of them. Everything hindered his movements, and it did nothing to disguise what he was.

"Then the next time a peasant tells you to sleep in the stables, you tell them who you are," the princess returned, matching his ire. "Tell them who you ride with." There was a challenge in her eyes as they locked onto his. Last night, when he'd taken over the care of their horses, he'd thought they assumed him to be a servant. He'd been given a pallet and a cold meal, but after he'd carried Liadan to her room, the proprietors had become outright hostile, all but chasing him back out to the stables.

Tir could have demanded better simply by telling them who he was. He hadn't, because he'd already known it would only make matters worse. He'd chosen instead to hide in the stables, where the animals showed him more courtesy than these Northmen.

Liadan wasn't trying to humiliate him; she was giving him a choice: Either try to fit in as best as he could and hide among these people for the time being, or show them who he truly was and hold his head up high when they threw their rocks.

Tir looked around at the merchants who'd stopped to stare at him. They took in his face and his clothes, then looked to his companion and sneered. Liadan noticed, too. But rather than abandon him and set herself apart, she stayed by his side, enduring their judgment while he made his choice.

"How hard can we push the drafts?" he asked. Tarabas might have looked half-starved, but he was strong and fast by necessity. Compared to what he'd been through to get there, the journey back would be a pleasure ride. Sleipnir had energy to spare, if the way he pranced restlessly was anything to go by. But the draft mares were so burdened, he didn't want to risk injuring them.

In answer, Liadan clucked her tongue, and Sleipnir took off, setting the pace at an easy trot. Tir hadn't come this way riding north, hadn't even looked toward Lyria, but had instead ridden straight to Wilderheim and its royal city. To see the mountains open up before them as if the rock had cracked under immense pressure was a marvel to him.

Inside the pass, the path wasn't straight, and it wasn't as easy as he'd hoped. The rocky walls stretched so high on either side, he couldn't see their tops, and the path's curves tricked the mind. If he held a hand just below his eyes to cover the dirt road, the walls looked like seamless rock, and when the path was too narrow for the burdened mares to walk side by side, Tir found it difficult to breathe. He kept his gaze skyward to remind himself he was not entombed, and to look for telltale signs that they were about to be buried beneath an avalanche of spine-crushing boulders.

It didn't help when Liadan said, "The path isn't usually this narrow. There must have been a rock slide recently."

"Are you frightened?" He was.

The princess grinned. "No. These mountains are the toughest rock anywhere in the world; there's little that will harm them. When the masons quarry it for stone to build up castle walls, they blunt their instruments a thousand times to remove a single block. The rock slide must have been triggered by lightning. And look up, prince. The skies are clear."

"Fortune favors us, then."

Liadan's whoop bounced off the stone in an endless echo.

Despite her confidence, Tir did not take a full breath until they'd emerged on the other side. From there, the road was clear across the countryside. Herds of cattle grazed here and there, and dark patches of forest dotted the landscape as if drawn on a map. More wagons and merchants came toward them, and Tir looked back into the chasm. How did they think to pass through, when those from the other side hadn't yet emerged?

"There's an order to the pass," Liadan explained. "Travelers must make their way from Wilderheim first, and all must be safely across before the sun is at its zenith. Those going the other way aren't allowed to enter until then, and if anyone is caught in the pass at the wrong time, those going opposite are entitled to force them to return."

Tir was only too happy to be through it.

The ride eased somewhat after that; the road was well-traveled and plenty wide. To spare the horses, they slowed down to a walk, and Liadan adjusted her seat in Sleipnir's saddle to lie back on top of him. A blade of grass held between her lips, she watched the clouds and hummed a tune, completely at ease and trusting her mount to know his way and take care of his rider.

"How can you do that?" he asked.

"It's easier than sitting on my arse for days at a time. Try it."

"I'd rather not."

Liadan laughed.

Tir's lips twitched in answer, but he schooled himself not to smile. "When we stop to rest, I am going to burn these clothes."

"Do you want to change now? I promise not to look."

He scowled. How easily her mood had improved from this morning. "Why are you so happy?"

She shrugged. "I am comfortable. The day is warm, the sun is high, birds are singing. My disgruntled companion has stopped growling at me, and I look forward to seeing my cousins. There is much to be happy about. Why are you so *un*happy?"

"My tribe is dying."

She squinted at him, shading her eyes from the sun. "Tell me about them. Do you have brothers and sisters?"

"Yes," he replied shortly, thinking again of Halima. Was his father still alive? What if another raid had happened in his absence?

There, at least, he did not worry. Farraj and his *kharesh* would fight to the death to defend them. What worried him more were the demons, and the thirst and hunger.

"Are you wed?"

"No."

"Is there a sweetheart waiting for you?"

"A what?"

"Someone you care for. Someone you might wish to court or wed one day."

Tir flushed when her teasing tone brought to mind the day before. He blamed the innkeeper's purge, as Liadan had called it, for making him lose his head, but regardless of what the magic had made him do, he couldn't deny a kernel of what it'd made him feel had remained afterwards.

Before, he'd viewed the princess as a strange and powerful creature, a skilled fighter with magic beyond imagining, whose beauty only made her that much more dangerous. Though he was still wary of her abilities, what he saw now was her spirit. Liadan embraced life, and everything it brought her, as a gift. Her joy made him forget his worries, and her smile, so easily given, coaxed one from him in turn, and although it made him feel like a traitor for wanting to embrace such happiness, Tir found the temptation of temporarily shucking off that immense burden almost too hard to resist.

Liadan made him want to be happy when he had no right to be, and that made her more dangerous than the fire she wielded with such ease.

When he failed to answer her, Liadan sat up in her saddle. "Anyone you fancy?" she prodded. He didn't say a word, and she frowned. "I am not sure what to make of that."

"Good."

She scowled, muttering something under her breath.

Satisfied to have won this small victory at least, Tir shifted in his saddle to ease some stiffness out of his legs. He'd almost forgotten the princess was there, when she said, "Teach me your language."

With a put-upon sigh, he said, "*Naras tograth fa toran di taprath.*"

She repeated the phrase smoothly, and Tir suspected that was all it took for her to memorize it. He'd have to be careful what he said in her presence. "What does it mean?" she asked.

"It is an old proverb. It means: a wise man knows to hold his tongue."

CHAPTER 12

Liadan continued to talk on her own, undeterred by Tir's lack of communication. If she'd prattled for hours on end, he would have been tempted to cut off his own ears. A wise man, however, would have learned by now that Liadan was unlike any female he'd ever met.

She talked, yes, but everything she said had some use to him.

She spoke of the northern weather patterns—how the sun sometimes mercilessly beat down for weeks on end, but when the heat wave broke, a massive storm cooled the air within hours. They were passing through just such a heat wave now, and knowing the signs of an approaching storm would help them seek shelter before it broke.

She talked of snow in the winters, when the air got so cold, water in the clouds froze and fell to the earth in white flakes, covering everything from valleys to mountaintops.

She spoke of Lyria as a kingdom of learning, open to all who sought knowledge of art, music, and philosophy, and eventually her story led into the war his father had waged.

Hearing about it from the lips of a Northerner grated on his conscience; he wanted to call her a liar every time she described the Aegiran armies as brutal savages who destroyed everything in their path, raped and killed everyone in sight, women and children, alike.

When she told him about the villages burned to the ground and wiped off the face of the world, he couldn't listen any longer. "Enough! Cease your lies. My father is an honorable warrior and leader of our tribe. He would never have ordered such atrocities."

Though momentarily silenced by his outburst, Liadan was in no way cowed. "It's easy to believe the best of our people and the worst of our enemies, when neither of us was alive to see them at war," she said, not unkindly. "You don't need to believe my word. The villages I speak of are south of Dai on the way to your tribe. We will follow the path your father took, and you will see for yourself."

Several villages lay along their path to Dai, but Liadan took them around whenever she could, or rode straight through when there was no avoiding it. The provisions procured from the inn would last them through their midday meal, but once night fell, they'd have to stop somewhere.

Late in the afternoon, they passed through yet another village, and this time Liadan stopped long enough to purchase roasted meats and fresh bread before they moved on. Even in that short pause, Tir got a good look at the disdainful faces all around them. No one dared show disrespect to Liadan, but plenty averted their faces from Tir, closed their shops, even herded their children away at the sight of him.

At the edge of the village, only fields and a road stretched as far as he could see. They wouldn't reach another settlement before night fell. "Dai is about a day's ride that way," Liadan said.

"Do you mean for us to ride through the night?"

"No, but we can't stay here."

Tir agreed.

"We will make camp over there by the willows." She pointed to a small group of trees with long branches of leaves like a woman's tresses. They had to leave the road to get to it and only then did Tir admit, if only to himself, that Liadan had a fine head for strategy.

Amid the trees, they were sheltered from the elements and hidden from easy view, but if he climbed one, he could see as far as the last village they'd passed before this one. Anyone searching for them in the night would be carrying torches, and he'd see them long before they saw him. The creek provided water, and the grass was softer than most beds. Tir much preferred it to the stables.

While he tended to the horses, Liadan gathered wood and prepared their evening meal. Nothing lavish, but even a scrap of meat was luxury to a man who went hungry most days.

With some sunlight still left after they'd finished eating, and with nothing better to do, Tir got up to stretch and put his body through its paces.

He'd never say so aloud, but the ride was taking its toll on him, too. His back and legs ached from long hours in the saddle. Exercise helped to loosen the sore knots in his muscles, and so he concentrated first on stretches, then on push-ups and sit-ups, and finally on his combat routines. Tir became so absorbed in the movements he knew by heart, he didn't notice when full night fell.

By the time he'd finished, his body was still sore, but more limber. He returned to the fire and spread his pallet beneath the willow tree.

"You do that well," the princess said.

"Make camp?"

"No, what you were doing before. Can everyone in your tribe do that?"

"Yes," he lied.

"Even the women?"

Tir glared, and Liadan smiled with a hint of gentle mockery, but no censure.

When she said no more on the subject, curiosity compelled him to ask, "Who taught you to fight the way you do?"

"My grandfather. He's really my great-grandfather."

Tir frowned. "How old is he?"

She laughed. "I don't think even he knows anymore. He was a king before humans knew such a word existed. Or so he says. I've never met another dragon to confirm his claim, and they are such solitary creatures to begin with, I doubt they would ever come together long enough to form a nation for a king to rule over."

"You're speaking nonsense."

She opened her mouth to reply, but then, seeming to think better of it, thrust her hand into the fire instead, rearranging the logs and making the flames dance to her tune. They contorted under the force of her magic, creating shapes like ethereal puppets. A great, winged lizard flew across the embers, and, by comparison, a miniscule woman looked up at it.

"Once, a very long time ago, there lived a great and mighty dragon. He was as ancient as the sky, wiser than the most learned mystics, and lonelier than an orphaned child. One day, a young maiden got lost in the woods and wandered into the dragon's lair. She was stunned by the riches she encountered. Her village was starving, their crops destroyed by famine. She looked through the treasures, and her heart swelled. A single piece of it would feed her village for a month or more. Surely no one would miss one shining jewel from a mountain of them."

The flames enacted her story, enchanting Tir with their display. His gaze followed the maiden through a dark tunnel, and as she reached out to pick up a piece of treasure, his heart beat faster, anticipating what was to come.

"The maiden picked up a heart-shaped ruby and slipped it into her pocket. But as she stepped from the cave, a terrible roar shook the ground beneath her feet and a great, lumbering beast chased her out into the clearing. She fell to her knees to beg forgiveness. She wept for her people, pleaded with the dragon to take her if he must, but to spare her village—save them."

In the fire, the dragon rose up onto his hind legs, beating his powerful wings in a show of dominance as the maiden cowered. But then the dragon stilled and settled, bringing his massive head down to look into the maiden's weeping face.

"The dragon took one look at the maiden and fell in love. He gave her a wagon of riches to make her village wealthy, then showed her the way home. Overcome with gratitude, the maiden took the treasure to her village elders, but although they rejoiced at her return, offered her anything she desired, the maiden's heart pulled her back to the dragon, in whose eyes she'd seen her very soul. She returned to his lair, and for her, the dragon made himself human and took the maiden as his mate."

Tir saw the beast transform and take the maiden's hands ever so gently into his. She fell into his arms, and the couple embraced, a passionate kiss sealing their joined fate.

"But their happiness was short-lived. As much as the maiden loved her dragon, she was still human. The child she conceived took her life as it came into this world, for only dragonblood can birth dragonblood. The child was a girl, and she became the dragon's whole world. She grew up learning from her father, sheltered from the sorrows and the treachery of human hearts. But when she grew into a woman, it was time for her to leave her father's lair and make her own way in the world. Not long after she left, she fell in love with a human king and wed him, never speaking a word of her heritage."

The scene split into two. In one, the maiden danced with her human husband while the whole kingdom rejoiced. In the other, the lone dragon paced his cave of treasures, roaring at the walls, breathing helpless plumes of fire, desperately worried for his child.

"When the queen conceived, she worried history would repeat itself, but she was half dragon and had faith in the power of her blood, and so she never shared her fears with her husband. Alas, faith alone was not enough. When the child was born—a boy to succeed his father on the throne—the woman died just as her mother had, for no one can live with only half of their being."

As the great dragon roared his grief, the human king fell to his knees at his wife's deathbed. He picked up his child, embraced him, but from the way his head turned toward his dead wife, Tir knew the king had loved her too much, and that no one would ever take her place.

And so it was.

"The king never remarried," Liadan said. "But the child his wife had given him grew hale and strong, beloved by his people. Strengthened by war, yet tempered by his goodness and the love he would find, he became a far greater man and a better king than his father could have ever hoped."

The old king faded, and his son took his place. Above his head swirled a circle with the shadow of a dragon in flight caught inside. The disc shrank and settled onto the king's chest like an amulet.

"That man is my father," Liadan finished. She released the fire, and Tir remembered to breathe again. Liadan's voice saddened as she told the rest of her tale. "He'd already fallen in love with my mother when Mari arrived in Frastmir to honor their pact. For the peace they had forged, my father wed her against his heart. My mother couldn't stand to see it, and so she left, traveling north, until she came upon the dragon the same way my great-grandmother had. That was when she learned of my father's bloodline. But by the time she returned, Mari was already with child, too weak to sustain herself and the babe. They both died."

"Yet you live," Tir said bitterly. "Your mother survived, while my sister died."

"Tir, my mother isn't human. I am a Halfling daughter of Halfling parents. There has never been a creature like me, or Fal, and not even the dragon knows the limits of what we can do. Our magics are too dangerous for us to test them."

"I do not wish to speak of this anymore," he said, lying down on the pallet and throwing an arm over his eyes.

Liadan sighed, but said nothing. Instead, she fed the fire to keep them warm through the night, then lay down to sleep.

Long after her breathing had slowed, Tir lay awake, hearing Liadan's tale again in her own voice. He couldn't rid himself of the words; they'd become seared into his mind. If her story was to be believed, then Mari's death was nothing more than the unfortunate result of a series of tragedies. An accident borne of ignorance.

If her story was to be believed, then the Northern king and his mate had nothing to do with the maladies plaguing his tribe.

The possibility offered him no comfort. Without the origin he'd been so certain to have found, Tir had no way of knowing what might lift their curse.

If there was anything at all.

CHAPTER 13

While quaint, picturesque little towns and villages abounded in Lyria, the castle city of Dai was very different by comparison—almost a kingdom in its own right. Even from a distance it dominated the landscape like a bright jewel sitting majestically among polished rocks. Purple and gold flags jutted out from each tower, indicating the royal family was in residence. Two massive banners hung down the walls on either side of the main gate: one for the royal house of Dai, the other for Frastmir. Fal must have sent word ahead. This was a not-so-subtle hint that Ulrich knew she was coming, and expected her to make an appearance in his home. Blast her brother's meddlesome ways. How much had he told Ulrich about her quest?

Liadan announced herself to the armored knight guarding the gate, then watched Tir's face transform as they followed a dispatched messenger into the city. Her father had told her much had changed in Dai since the war. Before, it'd been open, with no defenses to speak of aside from a poorly trained city guard. Now, a great wall surrounded the city, but its architects had created it in the same way they did everything else: as a work of art.

Past the gates, the city opened like a breath of air. Spires rose to the sky where temples and sanctuaries dotted the streets. Houses rose upward rather than out to the sides, creating wide, sunny passageways lined with trees and fountains. The castle road had been paved with colored bricks laid out in magnificent patterns, the houses painted in bright hues and hung with banners to identify the families or merchants who owned them.

In the city square, entertainers gathered to display their craft. Liadan and Tir passed jugglers and painters, but stopped to admire the dancers performing to match the singers and their musicians. They used instruments from all corners of the world, their unearthly music filling the square.

A small group of merchants had taken up a patch in the middle, facing every direction to display their wares: delicate glass beads, seashells from Synealee, ceramics from Ravetia, jewels made by Wilderheim's craftsmen, and cloths spun in Aegiros.

But while they all smiled at Liadan, eager to make a sale, the moment their gazes touched on Tir, their faces shuttered, eyes growing fearful. Tir had reclaimed his own clothing, dressed now in the way of his people; not the fearsome assassin draped in black, but certainly not like any Northerner. He held his head high and met each unfriendly gaze without flinching. Liadan admired his courage, but worried his pride might incite the citizens of Dai into a frenzy.

Tir dismounted to examine the tiles at his feet, and she noticed the inlaid metal plaque not two steps from him. She hopped down from Sleipnir and crouched next to Tir. "Amazing, isn't it?"

"This must have taken years to create."

"Yes," she said. "This square is a monument to honor those who've fallen in the war. Where you're standing is where they lit the first pyre to burn their dead. It blazed so high, citizens of the neighboring Synealee saw it and mourned with the city."

"I have seen the city wall. My father would not have been able to breach it if they closed the gates."

"The wall was not erected until after the war. When your tribe came riding in, they got as far as that pillar over there." She pointed to an old, half-destroyed pillar of gray stone, so damaged, so out of place in its modern surroundings, many believed it was a jest. "It used to be one of many encircling a bell tower that called the clerics to their meals."

A nearby soldier nodded his agreement. "It used to be connected to a sanctuary filled with scrolls and tomes," he said. "The pride of Dai's philosophers. It was the first thing the Aegirans burned to the ground. But not before they barred the doors to lock the clerics inside."

The fast-paced song ended, and in the quiet pause, Liadan watched consternation form on Tir's face. He didn't want to believe them; even with the truth staring him straight in the face, he didn't want to think his father had been such a monster. Liadan couldn't blame him.

A flute aired a haunting song; the first strains of a sorrowful melody. A female singer joined in, voicing the words of an ancient ballad, while the dancers tightened their circle, moving 'round and 'round, weaving together, hands joined, like a living knot. In seamless transition, they separated, scattering like a swarm of butterflies, moving through the square to every person present. They kissed the guards on their cheeks and touched hands with the merchants, who bowed to them in return. A pair drifted over to Liadan and Tir, and as one dancer with beautiful brown eyes lined with kohl caressed Liadan's cheek in welcome, the other, dressed in green-and-blue silks, took a flower from her hair and pressed it into Tir's hand.

At a loss, Tir stared at it for a moment, then caught the dancer's hand as she turned to leave him, and he touched his forehead to the back of her wrist in reverence.

"Our city welcomes all who enter it in peace," the soldier said. "Wherever they might have come from."

Face drawn, Tir rose and, without a word, took Tarabas' reins to walk him the rest of the way to the castle.

The grand structure was encircled by an open green to welcome everyone, its road leading directly to the courtyard, where the king and his family already waited to greet them. Ulrich's children, ten-year-old Esmee and eight-year-old Marco, squealed and ran to Liadan, throwing themselves at her. She laughed as she hugged them.

Ulrich, his queen, and his sisters were slower to approach, smiles cordial but restrained. "Cousin, welcome," Ulrich said.

Liadan embraced him. "It is good to see you. You look well." He'd inherited his father's kind eyes and warm disposition, but unlike the former king, Ulrich was shrewd when it came to the kingdom's defense.

"And you," he replied.

Stepping back, Liadan pulled Tir to her side. "Allow me to introduce Prince Tirasdunh of Imarah. I am escorting him to Aegiros to aid his tribe. Tir, this is my cousin, King Ulrich of Lyria, and his wife, Queen Aria; his sisters, Sidda and Penelope, and his children, Princess Esmee and Prince Marco."

Tir bowed to each in turn, showing a great deal more respect to even the little children than he had to her and Fal. Liadan didn't begrudge it.

"Any friend of Liadan's is a friend of ours," Aria said in welcome. While Sidda and Penelope shared a marked family resemblance with their brother, Aria stood out among them like a rare jewel, with her bright red hair and brilliant green eyes. She was a foreigner in Lyria. Her father had been a sailor whose ships supplied Lyria along their north-south coastal trade routes, and Aria had often accompanied him on his visits to Dai, and had played with Ulrich and his sisters while the king and the sailor negotiated prices.

She'd charmed them all from the first, eventually taking her father's place at the negotiating table, and it had surprised no one but Ulrich when he'd finally asked her to be his queen during a heated argument over the exorbitant price of sea urchins. All these years later, she still won every argument—and, from what Liadan had heard, her cousin was only too happy to let her. "Please, come in. You must be weary from your travels."

Esmee tugged on Liadan's sleeve. "Lia! Lia! Will you dance for us?"

"Yes! Please, Lia, dance for us!" Marco mirrored his sister, tugging her other sleeve.

"Children, let your cousin rest awhile," Ulrich said sternly.

"*Pleeeeaaaase*, Lia." Esmee pouted. "After dinner?"

Liadan laughed. "After dinner," she promised.

Squealing in delight, the children abandoned her and turned on Tir next. While Esmee stared at him, wide-eyed, Marco touched the curved blade sheathed at his side.

"Are you a demon?" Esmee whispered in awe.

"Can you kill a man with a finger?" Marco questioned suspiciously.

"Why is your skin so dark?"

"Why is your blade crooked?"

"Children!" Ulrich snapped.

They released Tir, running to hide behind their mother's skirts.

"My apologies, Prince," the king said, flushing. "They have never met one of your people in person."

Tir bowed a quiet nod in response.

To fill the awkward silence, Aria said, "My handmaiden will show you to your room, Liadan. We've prepared one for the Prince, also. Your Highness, if you would follow my steward, he will lead the way."

Tir was about to tell them he must see to the horses first, but they'd already been led away and he'd been too preoccupied watching Liadan with her family to notice where they'd been taken.

Liadan nodded in encouragement, which left him no choice. He followed the expressionless young man into a lavish chamber with a massive bed and a terrace overlooking a beautiful green garden. The satchel containing his few belongings had been set neatly on a chair by the bed.

"If it pleases you," the steward said, "the bathing room is just over here." The man showed him to an adjoining chamber with a square hole dug into the floor. He pulled a lever, and water pumped in. "If you require anything, the bell pull will summon a servant to see to your needs. The royal family shares dinner in the dining hall at sunset. I will see to it someone accompanies you to join them when you are ready."

Tir had no words. When the steward left, he didn't have the energy to wonder at the magic of pumping water from stone. Instead, he swirled his hand in the pool, shocked to find it warm. For a long time he sat there, mind and soul in turmoil, until the sky began to darken and the echo of children's voices brought him to his feet and out onto the terrace. A trio of servants lit lanterns and torches around the garden, while the royal children danced about, chasing fireflies.

He'd already been overwhelmed at the grandeur of Frastmir, with its massive castle and strange creatures. But Dai was far beyond even that. Tir had never seen anything like it, and he doubted he ever would again. All of the world's wonders seemed to have been gathered into this jewel box of a city, and he'd never seen a more beautiful sight.

To think his people had tried to destroy it made him want to howl in denial. The princess' word, he could have dismissed. Seeing it with his own eyes made all of his beliefs crumble around him. He'd thought the Northerners were savage brutes, hiding in their cavelike castles, massacring the scantily armored Imarah warriors.

But these people were more like children than fearsome fighters. They sang and danced, and opened their arms in welcome. There was no glory in destroying a place like this. That it seemed his father hadn't cared, so long as he'd gained his golden crown, troubled him immensely.

What was he to do? What would he say to his people when he returned and they asked him about the monstrous North?

The eve had darkened into night while he'd stood there and stared. Tir washed quickly and, dressed in his cleaner clothes, laced up his boots just as a servant knocked to escort him to dinner. He followed the woman, who kept her head down, perhaps to avoid the sight of him, meeting Liadan and her own escort in the entry hall. She wore a silken blouse that exposed her shoulders and billowing pants that narrowed at her ankles. He'd glimpsed similar attire once in front of a wealthy sheikh's harem, but those women hadn't worn embroidered jerkins to cinch their bodies.

Liadan blushed at his regard. "My cousin stands on ceremony. He insists his family wear their finest to dinner."

Tir looked down at himself. The clothes he wore were the finest he owned, but after weeks on the road, they were rumpled and dusty despite his best attempts to set them to rights. "Am I presentable?" he asked, not wanting to offend his hosts.

"You look fine," she told him with a smile, then threaded her arm through his with an ease of familiarity he didn't expect. "Come, they're waiting."

Expecting a grand feast and a hive of servants, Tir was surprised when they entered a rather small chamber with a single table for the diners and several more lined along the walls with food laid out on platters. King Ulrich rose to welcome them, and Tir bowed to him and his family.

"Family is important to Ulrich," Liadan said quietly. He had to lean his head closer to her to hear her whispers. "No servants are allowed in during dinner unless one is summoned. The king and his wife will fill their plates first. Then the guests, then the sisters, and finally the children last."

Tir nodded and took his seat by her side. The queen asked Liadan about her family, and they conversed easily while the king perused the food tables. When he took his seat, the queen followed his example, but Tir noted the king did not touch his food.

"We wait until everyone has had their turn before we eat," Liadan explained.

After the queen returned to her seat, Liadan nudged Tir to stand. He took his plate and followed her around the room as she pointed out what the different dishes contained. Tir wasn't particular about his meals; if it was edible, he'd eat it. But this bounty overwhelmed him. He stayed away from exotic dishes and instead served himself what he knew, taking only what he intended to eat.

Once the sisters and the children had had their turns, the king raised his chalice in a toast. "We welcome our honored guests. We share our food and wine, and offer shelter for as long as need be. Let us drink to their health."

Everyone echoed the blessing, and drank. At last, the king picked up a knife and the feast began. Among Tir's people, men and women took their meals separately, and children weren't allowed to sit with adults. Here, not only was the family all together, but they also conversed throughout the meal, speaking easily to each other, even the children. Esmee and Marco were much better behaved now than when he'd first met them; they sat quietly and ate the same as all of the adults, spoke up only when they had something to say, and caused no trouble at all.

"Prince, Liadan tells me your tribe has fallen on difficult times."

"Yes," he said. "Our valley has become barren and we are beset by maladies."

Ulrich frowned. "Forgive me, we don't often hear news of Aegiros. As I understand, there are many tribes, yes? Why not seek aid from one of them?"

"Our politics make such a petition unwise. The resources of Aegiros are scarce; most tribes struggle to keep their people alive. Imarah's valley may have lost its water, but it holds symbolic value as the First Valley, the origin of all Aegiran tribes, and many seek to overtake it. Another tribe would demand the land in exchange for any sort of aid, and if we gave it up, there would be nothing left for my people. We would die."

The king looked at Liadan, some silent message in his eyes, but she did not answer.

"Liadan," the queen said, "how is your brother faring?"

"As well as can be expected. I've brought him a small mountain of forgotten lore. I expect he will be too busy sorting through it all to notice my absence."

The queen nodded. "That is good. When we learned of his condition, we had our clerics search through the archives, but I'm afraid our knowledge of magics and Otherkind is very limited."

"He knows you would help if you were able," Liadan said. "The sweets you send are most comforting in his trying times."

The queen laughed. "I will be sure to send more."

At last, their plates were empty, and everyone sat back to relax.

Everyone, except for the little children, who quivered in their seats, staring at Liadan. She pretended to ignore them as they squeaked, trying and failing to be quiet, but their anticipation was palpable. Though the king glared at them, the women couldn't help the smiles they hid behind politely raised hands.

"*Liiiiaaaadaaaan*," little Marco whispered.

Liadan rolled her eyes. "Gods help me, all right."

Her capitulation was met with ear-piercing squeals of delight as the children jumped up and raced out the door.

Shaking her head, Liadan pushed to her feet. "Thank you for dinner," she said. "The food was wonderful."

"Yes," Tir added, standing to bow. "I am most thankful, as well."

"Now I beg forgiveness, as I am about to be set on fire."

Ulrich chuckled. "Don't keep them waiting too long, or they truly will take a torch to you."

Liadan gave him a crooked grin, then followed after the children.

Curiosity compelled Tir to go after her, but he wasn't familiar with the etiquette of leaving the room while the king remained seated.

Queen Aria saved him from making an awkward mistake. "Why don't we all go? It's been so long since I've seen Liadan dance."

King Ulrich indulged her and rose from the table. The women stood as well, but waited for the king to lead the way. "Come," he said to Tir, clapping him amicably on the shoulder. "I would wager a horse you have not seen her dance yet."

"You would not lose."

They went into the garden, where the servants had moved stone benches from the central area onto the grass. While the little heirs danced around Liadan, chanting in delight, she laughed and scolded them playfully, then chased them off. They ran to perch on the very edge of a bench, their bottoms touching it just enough to satisfy their cousin, but Tir could see by how tense they were that they might leap to their feet again at any moment.

The sisters seated themselves by the children to keep them in their place, while the king and queen took the opposite bench. Tir cast a questioning look at Liadan, but she only smiled a mysterious little smile, nodding for him to sit by the king. He did, waiting to see what she would do.

"Now, we all know the rules, yes?"

"Fire burns," the children chorused. "We do not touch it."

"That is right." Liadan nodded and, crouching down, rubbed her hands together as though chilled. When she breathed on them, a cloud of sparks blew out from between her palms.

The children cheered.

She did it again, this time pushing to her feet and spinning around, spreading that cloud of bright yellow sparks all around herself. Before it dissipated, she spun again, holding out one hand as if to throw something, and a plume of fire followed her movements.

And then she danced. Her toes traced fiery trails along the ground, her hands drew lines and circles of fire through the air; her entire body glowed from within, her hair transforming into flaming ribbons that whipped around her as she moved. The sight left Tir breathless. She was stunning, graceful, an accomplished dancer, to be sure, and the spectacles she created with her flames drew even the most timid servants and maids out to watch.

Her body swayed and rocked, twisted and spun to a rhythm only she seemed to hear. But Tir felt it; with every beat of his heart, he felt it. Liadan circled, seeking out each face to make certain her spectators were all paying attention, and when she returned to the center, her dance quickened, her movements so fast, Tir lost sight of her behind the streams of fire blurring together into an almost solid sphere around her.

Then the sphere exploded up and out, and the flames contorted into the shape of a giant dragon that rose high into the sky before it finally disappeared.

Applause and cheers drew Tir's attention back to the garden and to the winded dancer who grinned and bowed, laughing when the children mobbed her, demanding she show them again.

Next to him, the king laughed and slapped his back. "Breathe, my boy!"

Tir shook himself, then clapped in belated praise.

When Liadan managed to extricate herself from the young ones to come to him, Tir pushed to his feet, taking her hands in his to examine them.

"What are you looking for?" she asked.

"Fire burns," he quoted her, searching for any sign the flames she'd played with might have harmed her.

"Yes," she said coyly, "I do."

Startled by the jest, he met her gaze. She looked so happy; her spirit shone through her eyes, as if no moment in time was more beautiful and joyful to her than this.

King Ulrich cleared his throat, and Tir released Liadan's hands as if she'd scalded him. She might as well have. "It is late. You both must be wearied by your travels. Prince, are your chambers to your satisfaction?"

"Very much so," he replied, unable to tear his gaze from Liadan.

"Good, good. Then if there is nothing else you need, I think we should all retire for the night. Please excuse me, my royal decree will be required to corral the children back into their beds after all of this excitement."

Servants again escorted them back to their respective rooms. The same steward from before informed Tir the first meal would be served whenever he was ready, then left him alone with his thoughts. As exhausting as the day had been, as troubling as he found all he'd learned, Tir lay awake, staring at the ceiling, unable to think of anything other than Liadan and her flames.

When he closed his eyes, he saw her perform again, this time for him alone, and his heart raced at the artful mastery with which she controlled her element. He fell asleep imagining what it would be like if he could do the same, dance with her amid the flames.

In his dreams, the world around him burned, yet he was unharmed. He passed through the fires as if through gossamer veils, and in their center, found the princess Liadan. She danced, but not for pleasure. Her face drawn in concentration, her brow pinched in anger, she wielded her flames like a weapon that no creature could withstand. Shadows swooped down toward her, demons whose shapes he knew all too well. They clawed at her, screamed at her. Tir knew she felt the sting of their claws, but she never stopped. Her wrath burned them to cinders as they fled, and when at last the final demon fell, Liadan's hands dropped to her sides, her knees buckled, and she collapsed in a faint.

Crying out, Tir rushed to her side, but found no heartbeat in her chest, no breath on her still lips. The fires died around him, leaving the world as black as pitch, and in his arms, Liadan's body turned to ash.

CHAPTER 14

"She did what!" King Saeran boomed, and even the queen flinched.

Fal drew breath to repeat himself, but was instantly silenced.

"Don't speak a word. Gods damn it, boy, I thought at least one of my children would have the sense to think before they act!"

"Majesty—"

"And where in all the hells were you?" he demanded of the elders.

Braith hunched her shoulders. "We tried, your Majesty, but she was too fast. What was an old woman like me to do?"

Fal rolled his eyes, mirroring his father. Neither of them believed her to be helpless for even an instant. Old she might have been, but not *that* old.

"Your Majesty," Kvaran tried again. When no one interrupted, he seemed surprised, but regained his composure and continued. "Her Highness may have acted rashly, but her thinking was sound."

"How sound could it possibly have been if she swore a blood oath to an Aegiran?"

"She did worse than that," Fal murmured, bracing for an explosion of temper rarely seen from the royal pair.

"Woden have mercy," King Saeran prayed. Then, as if he could hardly speak the words, he asked, "How much worse?"

Fal looked to his mother for support, but she was too busy scrying the air for Liadan. "You won't find her," he said. "I already tried." The moment Tir and Liadan had entered the Western Pass, Fal had lost contact with his twin, unable to feel her in his mind. It was as if a Veil had descended between them, and he couldn't help suspecting it'd been deliberate. As closely as Liadan's disappearance coincided with his parents' return to Castle Frastmir.

Queen Nialei gave up with a frustrated sigh. "How much worse, Fal?"

"She swore a blood oath *with* him."

Silence fell upon the great hall, punctuated only by the clicking of Varr's claws on the stone floor as he paced nervously around the king and queen. The wolf pawed at Nialei's robes, whined softly to get her attention, but she didn't move, didn't even breathe, and neither did Saeran.

"I had no idea he would do it," Fal said. "I thought he would simply accept her oath and be done with it. But before I could blink, the bastard cut his hand and took Liadan's—"

"Everybody out," the king ordered on a harsh whisper, his face deathly pale.

The elders hurried through the door, and Fal wondered if any of them had the slightest notion about what he'd said.

"What words did she speak?" Nialei asked, her eyes gleaming with a fragile hope that the situation wasn't as dire as they thought.

Fal gathered water into a ball and summoned the past into its depths. The great hall appeared inside it, empty of all but the royal siblings and the elders. The Aegiran knelt on the floor, and Liadan pushed Fal out of the way to crouch face-to-face with him. She sliced her hand with the assassin's blade and said, "Before the gods and mortals, I vow on my blood that I will not intentionally cause harm to you or your tribe, and that I will do all in my power to help you restore your tribe to what it once was. Now, vow you will not turn against me, and will grant me protection from your tribe so I can do all of that."

The Aegiran hesitated. "My gods have abandoned us, and yours will not listen. I cannot fight demons with armies. If you fail, we all die. When you see them, you will run, too; abandon us despite your oath."

"I have seen, Tir," his sister replied, "and I vow I will stand by you and your tribe. If you agree to our deal."

Nialei pressed a hand over her mouth to contain a whimper. Her knees buckled, and she sank to the floor. Saeran wrapped her in his arms, but both king and queen were shaken.

In the watery vision, the other Fal said, "This is very ill-advised."

The Aegiran looked down at the knife he clutched, then drew the blade across his palm and clasped hands with Liadan. "I vow it."

Nialei sobbed, turning her face into her mate's shoulder.

"Have our horses saddled," Saeran ordered, voice quivering. "If they rode through Lyria, we can intercept them in the south before they reach Imarah."

"You can't," Fal said. "Mother's oath to restore the Veil prohibits her from leaving Wilderheim except to go to an Otherland."

"I swore no such oath," Saeran growled.

"But you are bound to Mother."

"He's right," Nialei said. "You can't go after her any more than I."

"I will not let my only daughter be tricked into this! Send the guards, round up a gods damned army, summon the dragon—just bring her back!"

As though he'd been waiting at the door, the dragon entered the great hall in his human form. Though he stood taller than Saeran and had darker hair, the two were mirror images of each other. And neither of them had aged a day since reaching adulthood. "You fret for nothing," he said. "Liadan is precisely where she needs to be."

His words shivered across Fal's mind with the same resonance he encountered whenever he tried to reach out to Liadan. "It was you," he realized. "It's your magic keeping us from Liadan."

Nialei gasped. "How could you?"

The dragon's distant gaze turned on the queen. "No one can undo a blood bond; not humans, nor Others, or gods. The girl chose her path and forged her own destiny. I would not keep her from it any more than I would have kept Saeran from taking you as his mate. Interfering now will only make matters more difficult for her."

"I trusted you with my daughter's safekeeping!" Saeran snarled.

"And she is safe, for the moment," the dragon replied.

Incensed, the king advanced on the dragon, but Nialei intervened. "Can you still bring her back?"

The dragon sighed. "I will not, and neither will you. There is a shroud of Darkness over the First Valley. I cannot see through it, but I sense its origins were the day the twins were born. Liadan might be the only one who can discover if there is a connection."

Nialei gaped. "What?"

"What are you saying?" Fal demanded.

Saeran rounded on the dragon. "You sent my daughter into Demon lands?" With each step he took, his ire rose until flames licked out of his palms and engulfed his arms like gloves. "You dare step foot into my home and tell me you sent my daughter to her death!"

"Saeran!"

Nialei's warning went unheeded. Saeran caught the dragon by his throat, eyes blazing with blue flames. Fal had never seen his father this way and prayed to all the gods he never did again.

"Saeran, stop!" Nialei broke his hold and stepped between them.

The dragon was unaffected by Saeran's attack, which incensed the king even more. "I did not send her anywhere. I merely afforded her the opportunity to choose on her own."

"She is my daughter!" Saeran fought Nialei's hold on him, but it was a halfhearted attempt. As powerful as she was, Saeran's love for his queen kept his own strength in check.

"Yes," the dragon said, "and the time has come to let her live her life, as I have done with my own."

The reminder of his mother, and of her death, ripped an anguished howl from Saeran.

"Da..." Fal tried, but words failed him.

"They have not yet left Lyria," Nialei said. "If you fly, you can stop them before they do. You can bring her back to us."

The dragon sighed.

"Please," the queen begged, another thing Fal hoped to never see again. Nialei, one of the most powerful wizards who'd ever lived, a Halfling daughter of a water sprite and some unknown woodland Other, had never had the need to beg anyone for anything.

"I cannot," the dragon said. "The path Liadan chose to walk cannot be altered except by her own choice. If she wanted to return, she could have done so a thousand times."

Fal couldn't breathe. He escaped from the great hall and the sight of his parents breaking down into helpless tears, slammed the doors to his chambers and rushed to the bowl of water. He slapped the surface to summon Seol.

His mentor appeared instantly. *Fal, is something the matter?*

"Can you bring her back?"

Seol blinked his overlarge eyes. *No,* he answered simply, without a hint of remorse. *Blood binds all things. The moment your sister joined hers with the Aegiran, her fate was sealed to his.* He cocked his head. *Did you not hear the dragon?*

"I heard every word."

Then you did not listen closely enough. If the Darkness plaguing the prince's tribe is tied to your births, then perhaps the answer to your control over the illusions you weave is hidden there. Liadan could mend you. If she survives.

The thought had briefly crossed his mind, but the feeble hope had quickly been extinguished by his fear for his sister's life. He would not sacrifice her to make his own existence easier. "If she dies—"

Then she dies, Seol retorted in a tone he always used when Fal tried his patience. *You will live. Damaged as you are now, but you will live. I will live. Your parents will live. The world will not mourn a Halfling's end, not even one as powerful as Liadan.*

With a roar, Fal hurled the bowl against the wall with enough force to break its copper shell in half. This was his fault; he'd listened to the dragon's instructions, when he should have listened to his own heart. If he had intervened as he'd wanted to, Liadan would never have handfasted the human; she would have fumed and blustered, and blamed him for all manner of petty grievances, yes, but she would have been home, she would have been safe.

What's done is done and cannot be undone. The chorus repeated in his mind until he thought he'd go mad with it. He had to do something.

Fal ran out of his chambers, headed for his tower. In all the gods damned lore, countless secrets forgotten by time, there had to be an answer. Fal would find a way to fix this, if it was the last thing he did.

CHAPTER 15

In the morning, the king's guard requested Liadan's presence. The captain, a longtime friend and companion to Ulrich, was familiar with the dragon's teaching methods and had offered to spar with her whenever she was in Dai. It was good exercise to keep her muscles loose, but it didn't offer much of a challenge. She half-hoped Tir would be there. Having fought him before, she itched to match her blade to his again.

Liadan was tempted to ask him but, although he'd stopped snarling at her and giving her dirty looks, he still kept his distance. She wondered at that, since he'd had no trouble carrying her to bed during their last night in Wilderheim, or taking her hands after her dance as if worried she might have hurt herself.

The Aegiran prince-turned-assassin confused her more every day. One moment, they were almost friends; the next, he retreated inward where she couldn't reach him. She wanted to understand him, if only to interpret his brooding silences as something other than contempt for her and everything she stood for. Liadan was used to all sorts of different reactions, but somehow, Tir's mattered more than anyone else's. That couldn't bode well.

She shook her head to rid herself of a frown, then picked up her sword and met the captain in the training ring. The dragon had taught her better than to let her mind wander during a fight.

Vale's preferred weapon was a spear longer than she was tall, with a metal point the size of her forearm and a weight that could tip Vale's page sideways if the youth wasn't careful. It gave him a farther reach than Liadan's sword; she'd need to be faster and more cunning to get at his weak spots.

With little more than a cursory bow, their bout began. Right away, Liadan felt the toll of having spent too much time in the saddle. She should have done as Tir had, practiced on her own when they'd stopped for the night. Now, the careless oversight was costing her.

"You've slackened in your training," Vale taunted as his men-at-arms gathered around.

Liadan grinned, refusing to show weakness. "I thought I would be kind this first time. You present a much larger target than I anticipated." She skirted his spear, then elbowed him in the gut.

Vale groaned, sweeping the spear to trip her. When her back hit the dirt, he leaned on his weapon like an old man on his walking stick, and jeered. "And you've slowed down."

Liadan pushed to her feet. "I'd like to see you after a week in the saddle." Their weapons clanged together, and the men-at-arms cheered.

"Delicate princess bruised her backside, did she?" Vale slapped said backside, to the wild hoots and shouts of his men.

"Oi!" she cried. "Did your mum not teach you it's rude to grope a highborn lady?"

Vale grinned. "She tried, but I liked my Da's lesson better." He spun his spear in the air, exposing his belly, a trick she wouldn't fall for again. Vale was wicked fast when he wanted to be; one cracked skull last time they'd sparred was all Liadan needed to learn that lesson. "He said there's no difference between highborn and lowborn when their skirts come up."

Liadan scowled, showing off her pants and lack of a skirt. Vale took the invitation, openly ogling her legs, which distracted him enough to lower his spear, and allowed Liadan to knock him back on his arse.

"Foul!" one of his men cried.

"What foul?" she demanded, singling him out.

The youth, a trainee by the looks of him, flushed and tugged at his messy hair. "Unlawful use of feminine charms?"

Liadan thrust an imperious finger at Vale. "He is swinging what amounts to an enormous wooden cock at my head, what is that?"

"Your lucky day," Vale answered, kicking her feet out from under her.

Liadan fell forward, but caught herself before her face hit the dirt. The guards whooped as Vale snatched her up by the ankle, and pulled her across his lap. Liadan gasped when his meaty hand delivered a stinging slap to her backside. Bracing herself, she curled her head down, then pushed off with her toes. The flying somersault hooked the crook of her knee around his neck and brought him down. Taking advantage of the new position, Liadan locked her ankles together to get a good choke hold on him. "What do you say?"

Vale grabbed for her thighs. "Thank you, gods?"

She smacked his head, and squeezed tighter. "Try again."

"Yield!" he choked.

"Better." Liadan released him and rolled to her feet.

As he sat on the ground, Vale rubbed at his neck, grinning while he caught his breath. "Must say, I've never had a sweeter defeat. Do you end all of your fights like that?"

"My father would skewer you if he heard you talk to me that way," she said, but she, too, was smiling.

"Then I say I must be lucky twice. First, to get my head between those lovely thighs; and second, to escape your father's wrath. The gods are generous today."

Liadan laughed, shaking her head at his banter, until she caught sight of Tir watching them from the shadow of a column. She saw little more than his outline but felt the weight of his stare, and a shiver of awareness ran up her spine.

"Liadan, a word?"

She'd only glanced away for a moment to acknowledge Ulrich's summons, but when she looked back, Tir was gone. Had she imagined him there? "On my way, cousin."

Vale pushed to his feet, then swept a cordial bow, though his eyes never left her face. His smile was wicked when he said, "Until next time, Highness."

Liadan winked at him before following Ulrich into his private study. He wasn't happy with her, she could tell, but he'd seen her spar with Vale before. The captain's mouth was perhaps bigger than was wise, but he was an honorable man. Ulrich wouldn't have appointed him to his post otherwise.

The king of Lyria seated himself in a smaller version of his lavish throne. "Do you know what you're doing?" he asked without preamble.

"I missed the first meal," she realized. "I apologize. It was bad of me to leave my companion unattended in your care."

"Gods damn it, I don't care about the meal, Liadan. I care about you prancing off to Aegiros on your own. Does your father know about this?"

Surprised by his outburst, Liadan answered carefully. "I imagine he will soon, if he doesn't already. I didn't wait to ask for his blessing."

"Because you knew full well that neither he, nor your mother, would have allowed this insanity if you had. And now you've put me in the position of having to make the decision in their stead."

"Nobody asked you to intervene, cousin. I don't need—"

"You do!" Ulrich insisted, then snapped his mouth shut and shoved to his feet to pace while he regained his composure. "I cannot pretend to know what all of this is about. I've not a drop of magic in me, thank all the gods, and I am well aware the rules are much different in Wilderheim than they are here, especially for one of your unique lineage."

"But…?"

"But you are so young—"

"I am a woman grown."

"Barely," he shot back. "Not a fortnight ago, you were living in seclusion in the dragon's cave, and the last time I spoke to your parents, they called you their 'little hatchling.' And now you expect me to let you go riding off alone with *him*? Do you have any idea what your people will say? What mine are saying already?"

"Do you think I care?" she challenged quietly. "You're right, Ulrich. You don't understand what's happening. If you did, you wouldn't be wasting my time on this discussion."

"I want you to take a contingent—"

"They'll slow us down. We can ride faster on our own. As it is, we've already lost time because of the drafts. We may have to leave them here and go on with Sleipnir and Tarabas alone."

"You've lost your bloody mind."

Liadan shrugged. "As my grandfather likes to say: you can't lose something you never had."

Ulrich shook his head. "No, I won't allow it. I can't let you leave."

She laughed. "What will you do? Lock me in the cellars?"

"If necessary."

"Ulrich, be reasonable. You can't keep me here any more than you can stop the tides from turning, you know this. I swore an oath to help Tir and his tribe."

"And you did so without a notion as to what would be required of you. Tell me something, cousin, when is your next cycle?"

Liadan felt the blood drain from her face.

Ulrich spat out a foul curse. "Foolish girl! What do you expect me to do now? Wish you well and pray?"

Liadan couldn't bring herself to say another word. Turning on the balls of her feet, she kept her pace just short of breaking into a run as she headed for the door.

"You'll kill him, Liadan," Ulrich called after her, "without ever meaning to."

She slammed the portal shut behind her.

"Princess—"

Startled, she spun around, swinging.

Tir caught her fist before it connected, but he showed no ire at being attacked without provocation. "Are you well?" he asked, voice too low, face too close to hers.

"Fine." She stepped back. He didn't release her hand. "I only need a moment to gather my gear, then we can be on our way."

Tir stared as though waiting for her to say more. When she didn't, he nodded and released her. "I will saddle Sleipnir and Tarabas with our most pressing supplies."

So he had listened to her fight with Ulrich.

Liadan hugged herself against the feeling that he'd somehow uncovered one of her secrets. When she returned to her chambers to pack, her hands were shaking. She tossed her sword onto the bed and paced awhile, rubbing the torc around her neck for comfort. She'd tried to reach out to Fal to let him know she'd arrived safely in Dai, but only silence had answered her call. She'd met with the same when she'd sought the dragon in her mind. His magic was fleeting in the torc's twisted rods, but even that soothed her. And it steadied her hands long enough to finish packing.

Ulrich didn't see her off. In his absence, Aria acted as ambassador wishing them both a safe journey, offering blessings for Tir and his tribe.

Liadan embraced her, grateful her cousin had found such a wonderful woman to rule by his side. "Be safe, cousin," Aria told her. "I will pray for you both."

"And you, Majesty. I will see you again soon."

They set off through the city, their mounts burdened with enough supplies to last them a week if they rationed properly, but they only had two waterskins between them. Refilling them in village wells along the way was no hardship, but Liadan worried what they'd do once there was nothing but dry dirt and sand beneath Sleipnir's hooves.

"I did not ride this way coming north," Tir said. "How long until we reach Aegiros?"

Liadan calculated the time from what she'd seen of Ulrich's maps. "Three days, if we rest the horses. Two, if we ride hard."

"Then let us ride." He spurred Tarabas on with a savage shout, taking off without a backwards glance.

Sleipnir reared and whinnied as if Tir had insulted him by starting a race without notice, and ran headlong after him, eager to prove himself better.

They didn't stop or speak again until late afternoon, when the skies darkened with a great thunderstorm that forced them to seek shelter.

They were in luck to find an abandoned stone cottage, half destroyed, but with three walls still standing and a roof that hardly leaked at all. Liadan built a fire where it was shielded from the worst of the rain. There was enough room for both of them and the horses, and once Sleipnir had herded Tarabas into one corner so he wouldn't stomp them to death in his panic, everyone settled.

They ate in amicable silence, Tir keeping a watchful eye on the storm, Liadan lost in her thoughts. She could tell the thunder made him nervous, but as a proud warrior, he didn't show fear beyond the occasional jaw twitch.

Liadan studied him across the flames while he was too preoccupied to notice. All her life her family had told stories about the Southerners, about how fierce they were, nigh unstoppable in battle. Fal used to say if an Aegiran ever met a true berserker, it'd be a battle people would sing about until the end of time. They'd admired them for it, seduced by the mystery of a people they'd never encountered.

Yet so many feared and despised them. In Lyria, even the mention of Aegiros was met with contempt, memories still too fresh, even decades after the war. Only now, having met Tir and spent time with him both on the roads and in Lyria, watching how the other Northerners looked at him, listening to what they said about him, could Liadan see the great pains her Da had taken to make sure neither of his children would ever know such hate.

Tir was his own man, strong and proud, but his pride didn't blind him to other possibilities. Liadan knew it was custom in Aegiros for women to be overlooked, but while among the Northerners, Tir had shown her and her family the same respect he would have afforded another man; he listened to her, even when he didn't want to hear what she had to say, and she wanted to believe he trusted her, as well. Not because he had to, but because he deemed her worthy of his trust.

That might change once they entered his homeland, where she'd likely be expected to adhere to his customs the way he'd honored hers, and Liadan wasn't certain what that would do to them. She'd never bowed to anyone in her life, nor had any reason to follow anyone's orders without question. In Aegiros, she might offend simply by meeting a man's gaze, and everyone would look to Tir for guidance where she was concerned.

One man's disdain she could handle, but she couldn't stand in opposition to an entire kingdom. Could she trust Tir not to betray her in favor of his pride? His blood oath bound him to keep her safe from those in his tribe who meant to do her harm, but there were many ways to do that, including locking her away in a cell somewhere until the end of time.

Tir met her gaze across the flames, and Liadan flushed to have been caught staring, but she didn't look away. Trust was such a fragile thing—so difficult to forge, so easy to shatter. Her heart told her this was right. The man sitting before her had already proven he'd do whatever it took to help those he loved, and Liadan admired him for that. She could only hope that, in time, he'd come to regard her as someone worthy of even a fraction of that devotion. Because without him, her life was forfeit in the desert.

Tir was the first to look away, turning his attention back to his meager meal. When he'd finished it, he gazed into the fire, his bright eyes heavy-lidded. *What does he see in the flames?* she wondered, when lightning struck outside, making him flinch. He tensed, staring at the rain as if it would come in and drown him in his sleep. Floods were common in this region, which was why they'd taken shelter on a hill, far from any danger. Tir was well aware of this, yet every time lightning struck, his body went so rigid, she could see his neck muscles go taut. Still, when the bright light had faded, he mastered his fear and relaxed a little.

"Thank you," she said to distract him.

His gaze swung back to her, and he frowned. "For what?"

Liadan blushed. "For not asking questions." If he'd heard her tell Ulrich they'd be leaving the drafts behind, he must have also heard Ulrich call his dire omen after her.

"Would you have answered if I did?"

She shrugged, ducking her head.

"I thought as much." She could tell he wasn't happy about it, but he didn't say anything more.

Liadan yawned. After another long day in the saddle, her back ached. She stretched up and to the sides, twisting left then right to work out the stiffness along her spine, wincing each time something popped. Then she set out her pallet and hunkered down for the night. Despite the storm's din, Liadan was so tired she fell asleep the moment she closed her eyes, without another care in the world.

Thunder woke her some time later as the worst of the storm passed overhead. What had started out as a downpour with an occasional distant lightning flash had quickly turned into a deluge mixed with ice as bolts struck the hill almost without cease. They lit up the night, shook the ground with deafening booms, terrifying Tarabas and making even Sleipnir nervous.

Liadan got up to soothe them, not even giving her riding companion a second thought, until she heard him roar outside. By the light of the storm, she found him in the middle of a clearing that used to be the village square. He was shirtless, soaked through, brandishing his daggers, and shouting at the heavens as though he dared them to strike him down.

He stomped amid the lightning storm, waved his blades, screamed at nothing, while fires sprouted left and right, extinguished almost immediately by the endless torrent.

Terrified he would get himself killed, Liadan shouted, "Are you mad? Get back here!"

But the storm was too loud for her voice to carry, and as the lightning intensified, the crazed Aegiran began to dance.

"Tir, get back here!" She waved her arms to get his attention to no avail. Her choices were reduced to throwing a fireball at him or going out there herself. He wouldn't have appreciated the first, and she wasn't mad enough to attempt the second. What in all the hells had set him off like this?

As he turned in a circle, she screamed at the top of her lungs, "*Tirasdunh!*"

Finally, *finally* he looked her way. His feet stilled, and his bare chest rose and fell with harsh breaths. Even from so far away, Liadan could see him shivering. She waved for him to come back inside, praying she wouldn't have to ride into Aegiros with his dead body slung over Tarabas' back.

Tir tilted his face up, catching the icy rain a moment longer to defy her. When he stalked back into the cottage, he flung his daggers to the floor and backed her against the wall.

Liadan felt the chill radiating off his skin. He had to be freezing. For his sake, she flicked her hand toward the fire to stoke it hotter. Without a log to keep it burning, it wouldn't last long, but at least the small burst of heat would help him recover faster.

Instead of gratitude, his face contorted into a snarl. "I do not fear cold," he spat. "I do not fear rain, or ice, or your thunderstorms."

"I never thought you did—"

"And I do not fear you." It was as much a challenge as a declaration.

Startled, Liadan looked into his honey-brown eyes. All she saw there was defiance and pride, and something else she had no name for, something that hadn't been there before tonight. She didn't know where it'd come from, but it burned as hot as her flames and dared her to provoke it.

Her hand reached up of its own accord to the side of his face, but she stopped herself just short of contact, and hovered there in indecision. Tir swayed closer, bracing his hands to either side of her against the wall. Though his skin was chilled, his breath blew hot on her face, while his heart beat loud enough for her to hear it over the din of the storm.

The memory of Galen's purge came back to her in a rush, making her own heart flutter in her chest. She could still feel the press of Tir's lips, the strength of his arms as he'd pulled her close, the passionate shudder that had racked his body, eliciting a pleasured moan from her in turn. Galen didn't create something out of nothing; her power could only seek out a seed of emotion and burst it to life. For her purge to have affected them both in such a way, a kernel of attraction must have already existed.

It was still there. Even knowing how ill-advised it was, Liadan wanted Tir to kiss her as he had then, she wanted to feel his arms around her, to lean on his strength, to share her fire in kind, and it frightened her.

Tir's gaze lowered to her lips, and he leaned in closer still. Liadan's breath hitched in anticipation, but prudence held her back and, cheeks flushing, she pressed her hand to the center of Tir's chest to stay him.

"Are *you* afraid?" he challenged quietly.

Liadan stuck out her chin. "I fear nothing."

"I think you do." He leaned into her, and her heart gave a hard thump from the sheer intensity emanating from him. "You stand firm against armed foes, look with contempt upon those who scorn you, true. But you do hold fear in your heart, and it is one that cannot be convinced away."

She scoffed.

Undeterred, Tir merely smiled. "You fear what happened in the succubus' inn was not her doing at all. You fear that if I kiss you again, you will respond the same way you did then." His tone dared her to prove him wrong, but his eyes weren't as certain; they gazed into hers and questioned, as if by guessing at her fear, he had revealed his own.

No, he was wrong. She felt nothing more than a remnant of Galen's purge, and she'd prove it to both of them.

They were of a height, and standing so close, their noses almost touched. Liadan had to only tilt her chin forward ever so slightly to press her lips to his. Tir sucked in a surprised breath and stiffened almost to the point of retreat, but then stopped himself and pressed into her instead. The chill of his rain-soaked flesh shouldn't have affected her, yet Liadan shivered. And just like in Galen's inn, she couldn't keep herself in check. Her arms wrapped around to lock at his back as his cold, trembling hand cupped her cheek, while the other slipped into her hair at her nape. And just like back there, Tir's lips moved restlessly over hers, harder, hungrier, until she opened to him, and he groaned, deepening their kiss.

For long moments, they strained together, as if nothing else mattered. The storm faded into silence, time ceased to exist, breath became secondary. Tir's arm came around her, squeezing hard. His hand fisted in her hair, snapping strands to bring her closer, to prevent her retreat. Fire lit her blood until her skin began to glow and heat, until the water trickling down Tir's chest evaporated with a hiss. Only then did he pull back enough to look at her.

And as she watched his lust-hazed mind comprehend what he was doing, Liadan recalled Ulrich's parting words. Her fire cooled in a hurry; her skin's golden glow faded, and her arms dropped away. She extricated herself from Tir's embrace, then looked away from his baffled expression. "You should come sit by the fire," she said softly. "You'll catch your death."

Face flushed, he stepped back and did as she bade. He'd stopped shivering, but water still ran from him in rivulets, a dangerous state to be in; a wet body succumbed to the cold much faster than a dry one. They'd been fortunate enough to have found shelter so quickly before, but with only their small fire for light and warmth now, it'd take too long for Tir to dry off on his own.

"Do you trust me?" she asked, lips still throbbing from the passion of his kiss.

"I do not fear you," he repeated sullenly.

"Yes, you said that, but do you trust me?"

Tir studied her while he made up his mind. His gaze held hers, then moved lower to her lips; he rubbed his mouth and chin with the flat of his palm in a move rife with frustration, then gave a curt nod.

Liadan stacked more wood on the fire, then knelt beside Tir. He turned to face her, wary but curious, and allowed her to take his hands into hers. "Don't move." She closed her eyes and called up her flames. They poured through her veins and into her hands, bursting out of her skin for just a blink before she tempered them with her iron will into a soft glow. Tir gasped, but she didn't let him pull away. Slowly, with careful manipulation, she sent the flames licking along his skin, close enough to warm, but not to burn. His breathing grew harsh as her fire covered his arms, his chest, and then the rest of his body, but he held as still as he could. Within moments, his hands had warmed, and when Liadan opened her eyes, she found his own squeezed shut. But his hair was dry, as were his pants, and his skin was flushed rather than chilled.

"Open your eyes," she invited.

He did, and through the shroud of fire, she saw his fear melt away into wonder as he looked down at himself. "How is this possible?"

Liadan smiled and called her flames back. "Fire doesn't have to burn."

CHAPTER 16

After a day and a half more, the border between Lyria and Aegiros loomed on the horizon. The change was sharp enough to make out from a distance. Forests gave way to grasslands, with little more than a lone tree or two to dot the landscape; shrubberies were dry and bare, the ground hard beneath their feet.

They'd dismounted to walk the horses across the divide. On their way through villages ravaged by war, all Liadan had managed to procure in the way of provisions was a small bundle of dried fruits and two additional waterskins, which might suffice her and Tir, but the horses would suffer. From here on out, she'd have to rely on Tir and his knowledge of Aegiros to keep them all alive until they reached the First Valley.

According to him, the valley lay at the heart of Aegiros, equidistant from the north and the south. While many oases of varying sizes lay scattered across the lands, the First Valley used to be the largest, carved out of the desert by a mighty river that had long since run dry. If his estimations were correct, they'd reach his tribe in three days. More, if they encountered trouble. With no roads to follow, they'd need to rely on the sun and the stars. Aegirans might have been master navigators and cartographers, but without a map or recognizable landmarks, Liadan felt utterly lost in their world.

Tir, on the other hand, seemed to gain confidence along the way. "We will ride through Sadirak," he said, pointing at nothing to the southeast. "You will need proper attire before we leave the grasslands."

She frowned. "Is this your idea of revenge for the innkeeper's clothes?"

His lips twitched. "You would think so."

The answer did nothing to placate her. "I have no need of different attire."

He shrugged. "As you wish. But I would advise otherwise. The desert sun can be merciless, even to one well-acquainted with fire, and the winds can strip tears from your eyes and make them as dry as dust in a blink." He looked her over from head to toe, reached out to brush a skein of hair away from her flushed face. A brief smile, almost wistful, disappeared all too soon as he pulled back and shifted in the saddle, nudging Tarabas a step farther away from her Sleipnir. "Your fair skin will suffer the worst, I think. Better to cover it, than have it blister and peel."

Since the storm, they'd both adopted a distant, formal air when conversing, as if that could somehow undo what had been done. It didn't work. The memory of their kiss, the burning quiescence it'd brought with it, and the sleepless night that had followed were all too insistent to be ignored. It all came back to her during unguarded moments, when conversation stalled yet again, and the landscape failed to provide sufficient distraction. Too often Liadan snuck glances at him, and too often she felt him watching her when he thought she wouldn't notice.

It'd been a mistake; she shouldn't have let it happen.

Determined not to endure another awkward silence, Liadan asked, "Is that why your people wear so many layers of robes? I thought it was to enforce modesty."

He nodded. "That, too."

The unapologetic way he'd said it made her laugh.

Her humor was short-lived. The farther south they ventured, the hotter the sun beat down. Liadan's legs chafed in her leather pants and her jerkin was cinched too tight, making breathing more difficult, until she began wishing for the comfort of skirts. Tir was right. She could not go on much longer dressed the way she was.

When tents and buildings came into view on the horizon, she spurred Sleipnir on faster, desperate for the relief of a little shade. Mercifully, Tir didn't mock her for it. He even haggled with a merchant on her behalf for some new attire. Liadan would have paid every last coin in her purse for something made of cloth instead of leather, but Tir knew better how to negotiate. Within moments the merchant handed him a bundle of clothes, gesturing to something farther away.

Tir bowed and paid the man a gold coin. "Here." He gave the bundle to her. "He said the market well is dry, but there is a fountain not far off. I will take the horses." The poor things were frothing at the mouth, they were so thirsty. "When you are ready, follow this path and turn right at the red tent. I will meet you there."

"Thank you."

He grunted. "Do not take too long. We should not tarry here."

His caution put Liadan on guard. She undressed in the privacy of the merchant's small tent, never so grateful to be out of her leathers. For a moment, she stood where a small breeze cooled her bare skin before she bound her chest and put on the clothes Tir had procured for her. She'd feared the long, cumbersome robes she'd seen the women wear. Much to her surprise, the bundle contained clothes meant for a man.

Liadan picked out dark blue pants to make riding astride easier, and a wide and roomy white shirt that was so thin it was almost sheer. It came with an embroidered tunic to match the pants, and some sort of headscarf she couldn't figure out how to knot. Liadan didn't care. When she finally stepped out of the tent, she took her first deep breath without choking on the hot air.

She could finally think, and the sights around her piqued her curiosity. Sadirak was more of a thriving marketplace than a city. Everywhere she looked, merchants displayed their wares as people and caravans milled about. There were tents that contained clothing, weapons, and earthenware, while in other places, meat cooked over an open fire and drink was sold in earthen jugs. Men and women alike were dressed from head to toe in robes and scarves with only their eyes and hands showing.

Liadan regarded the long piece of cloth in her hand. How had they managed to fold and twist it so neatly? She approached the merchant showing off his clothing to another passerby and bowed to him the way she'd seen Tir do. "Thank you," she said.

The merchant spat a few strange words at her, then turned his back.

Liadan frowned. Had she offended him somehow?

Since he refused to face her again, she decided to search for Tir.

As soon as she'd stepped away from the tent, however, the sea of travelers swept her along in its wake, and before she knew it, she was lost. Strangers glared, merchants shooed her away, men with scimitars shoved her aside as they passed, and it took all Liadan had to hold on to her temper.

She walked the passageways, trying to find her way back, but amid so much chaos of cloth and color, Liadan became hopelessly lost. Around one corner, a man paraded emaciated people in chains on a stage for an audience to see—slaves for purchase. Around another, cages lined a long wall made of sun-dried bricks. Inside them, wild beasts paced, snarled, lashed out when someone came too close, forcing their handler to crack a long whip to make them settle. He was missing an eye and his bare arms were riddled with claw marks, but his fingers were weighed down with thick, golden rings, and he walked like a king among beggars in gold-embroidered shoes.

In a covered alcove, a man dragged a woman to one corner and shoved her to her knees while she wept, her hands clasped together as she implored him. But the man showed her no mercy, striking her again and again. Liadan set out to stop him, but several other women rushed in, shoving her out of the way as they crowded into the alcove and hid the pair from sight.

Her hasty retreat brought her into a tent, where an old woman sat embroidering a length of silk. An oddly scented haze of smoke filled the space, turning everything as soft as a dream. A gossamer partition separated the front section from the back, and Liadan saw several other women sitting there together, drinking from golden chalices. They were draped in the most beautiful gowns, their hair fastened with golden chains and beads, their veils serving to accentuate their features rather than hide them.

Soft music drifted in from somewhere unseen; a dreamy melody she wanted to sway to. It was much calmer here than in the marketplace outside, a much needed respite that beckoned her deeper.

The old woman rose from her seat to bow to her, and Liadan smiled, returning the gesture. She beckoned Liadan closer and poured something into a chalice, offering it to Liadan on a polished silver platter. One sip of the syrupy-sweet wine made her waver on her feet, but did nothing to quench her thirst. Liadan wanted more.

When she stumbled, the old woman caught her by the elbow, steadying her, guiding her along. Already she was pulling Liadan toward the others, but something didn't feel right. Liadan frowned and shook her head, peering over her shoulder at the market street that suddenly seemed miles and miles away, bathed in a harsh light that wavered everything, split it in two.

The shadows were cool, the pillows looked so soft.

Liadan couldn't think. "No I must get back. My… Tir. He'll be waiting for me."

The old woman stroked her arm, kept pulling her along.

Perhaps she should stay awhile. Tir was probably looking for her even now. If she kept moving, they'd never find each other. Yes, better to stay here. Another step, and another pair of hands caught her elbow. She smiled at the younger woman to her right. A third approached, stroked her cheek, while a fourth at her back brushed her hair. Liadan's eyes closed, but she forced them open again. She was so very tired.

One by one, the women disappeared, and the world tilted, lurched. Instead of the sun-bathed chamber with the beautiful women, she was in the old woman's dark tent, with Tir staring into her eyes. "…leave you for one blink and you… *masiranah*…"

Liadan smiled, giggled. Tir cupped her face, and in the next moment, he was shouting at someone behind her. Then he was so close, prying her eyes open. She frowned and pushed at him, but her arms wouldn't work properly.

"Liadan… hear me?"

"'course I hear you," she groused.

More shouting and odd noises assaulted her. When he leaned her into him, her forehead fell against his shoulder, hiding away the world. Tir pushed her back, and her head lolled. How was she still standing? Again, he forced her eyes open, irritating her, but a dreamy sigh made her smile. "So pretty." She grabbed his shirt with her clumsy hands and swayed close, bumping her nose against his in an attempt to kiss him. But kiss him she did, and for a moment sweeter than the wine had been, Tir drew her close and kissed her back.

But then he pulled away and dragged her into the harsh light that forced her eyes to roll back in her head. Her knees buckled, and he slung her over his shoulder, bouncing her with every step. Blood rushed into her face until it throbbed, but the fresh air cleared away some of the cobwebs from her eyes.

When he set her down onto her feet again, she heard water nearby, and felt Sleipnir bump her with his nose. "What's… happening?" she asked, words slurring.

"Hush," Tir said, his voice strained even to his own ears. He steadied her by her shoulders until he'd ascertained her balance—precarious, but she was standing on her own. Rage simmered in his chest as he tied her hair back, then deftly knotted the scarf around her head, tucking in the veil to cover her face. "How do you feel?" he asked. The old hag had given her opium; he could still taste it from her lips.

Liadan nodded listlessly.

Tir curled her fingers around Sleipnir's saddle. "Do not let her fall," he ordered the horse. Tarabas stepped up on her other side, helping to keep Liadan upright between them, hiding her from sight, and Tir cursed himself again for the thoughtless mistake that could have cost the princess her life.

Only after he'd walked the horses to the fountain had Tir realized he never should have left her alone. *Masar*, drivers who specialized in acquiring pleasure slaves, were prowling the alleys in groups for new merchandise. Tir had spotted them right away; their distinctive scarves were unmistakable in the crowds. Their sheer numbers should have put him on guard, but he'd thought Liadan would be safe until she met him at the fountain. She should have been no more than a few steps behind.

When she'd failed to meet him, Tir had torn through the marketplace looking for her, leaving the horses to their own devices. It was a miracle no one had stolen them.

Taking their waterskins, Tir now returned to the fountain to refill them. His hands shook, and he kept looking over his shoulder for any sign the *masar* were trailing them. Once their harem keeper had a person in her clutches, *masar* didn't take kindly to someone relieving them of their prize. Liadan had been two steps and one golden lock on her collar away from becoming part of the *masiranah*. Her fair northern skin would have made her an exotic treat worth several fortunes, and the *masar* would come for her if Tir didn't get them out of Sadirak before the harem keeper told her men what she'd lost.

Tir hurried to retie the bulging skins to their saddles, then hoisted Liadan astride Sleipnir. Though she held on, she slumped, head lolling, and Tir didn't know whether she could keep her seat for the ride. Not willing to take the chance, he mounted behind her and tied Tarabas' reins to Sleipnir's.

Liadan leaned back into him, head against his shoulder. If she wasn't asleep yet, she would be soon. "Hold on, Princess," he murmured into her ear, kicking Sleipnir into a punishing sprint out of Sadirak.

He didn't slow until the marketplace was a dark smear behind them and the grasslands had begun to thin. They weren't being followed yet. A small blessing, but he'd take it gladly.

Liadan stirred with a tired moan. "Where are we?"

"Safe," he answered. For the moment, at least.

"What happened?"

"You walked into a slaver's den."

"Slaves. Saw them. Bad."

"Yes, very bad." Tir didn't want to think what might have happened had he not gotten to her in time. Imarah had had a run-in with the *masar* before. Years ago, an old woman who'd made for an innocent enough lure had passed through the First Valley with what she'd called her daughters. She'd managed to lure several of their maidens into her caravan before her *masar* had arrived and revealed her for what she was. Dhakir's *kharesh* had slaughtered the lot of them and retrieved the girls before they'd made it to the borders of Imarah. But other tribes, Tir knew, didn't always fare so well.

Liadan touched her hand to the arm he'd wrapped around her. She was steadier in her seat now. He ought to release her, but try as he might, he couldn't make himself move. "Saved me?" she asked.

Two little words, but so much fear and hesitation behind them. Tir flinched and clutched her tighter. "Yes."

She sighed, and her hand dropped away. She was asleep.

When night fell, the day's heat dissipated so quickly it left Tir chilled. In her sleep, Liadan had her ways of keeping warm—the fire that lit her blood gave her skin a gentle glow while it warmed her body to stave off the night's chill. The waxing moon gave plenty of light to ride by, but it was foolish to push the horses. Tir stopped at an outcropping and dismounted, then carefully lowered Liadan from the saddle to the ground. He rummaged through all of their supplies, pulling out every piece of clothing, every blanket, and every rag they had.

He rolled out the pallets, one next to the other, covering them with a blanket for more warmth. Without a fire, it would be a miserable night, but better than waking up to *masar* swords at their throats. The horses came next. Tir saw to each of them in turn, whispering words of reassurance and thanks. Had it not been for them, they might not have escaped Sadirak in time. A little water wasn't sufficient to show his gratitude, and neither was the care he took in brushing them down, but at least after two of their waterskins were emptied and the horses had settled, Tir himself was calm enough to face Liadan again without panic clawing at his chest.

She lay asleep on one side of the wider pallet. Tir knelt beside her, checking that her breathing was steady, that her heart was still beating strong. Opium was a dangerous drug; it could dull pain and induce sleep, but if used incorrectly, sometimes those who ingested it never woke up. But Liadan would recover. If nothing else, the heat of her skin assured him she was alive and well. In fact, she burned so hot, it warmed him, too. They might not need a fire after all.

Tir removed her headscarf to keep it from tangling around her neck while she slept, settled down next to her, closed his eyes, and willed himself not to dream, but the same vision that had plagued him since the night Liadan had danced pulled him into flames once again, unwilling to release him for even a single night. He knew where he was; despite the darkness, he knew the shape of each flame, found his way along the selfsame path to Liadan, the way he always did. He watched her battle dance yet again, watched her fight the demon swarm as he did every night, until the last one burned to cinders. And when it fell, when she looked at him and smiled, Tir's chest constricted until his own heartbeat caused him pain. He knew what was coming; dreaded it to the depths of his very soul. And he could do nothing to stop it. "We won," Liadan said, and before the last word had slipped from her lips, she collapsed in his arms and turned to ash.

Tir started awake as the first blush of morning lightened the eastern sky, to find himself entangled with the princess. She was pressed back against his chest, huddled as close as she could get. Tir didn't know when his arm had come around her, or when his face had found a cushion in the crook of her neck and shoulder, but he'd never before slept so well on the cold, hard ground.

Troubled, and far more comfortable than he had any right to be, Tir extricated himself, careful not to wake her. When he sat up and turned away to stand, Sleipnir was there, glaring one shiny, black eye at him. The stallion snorted, then adjusted his front hoof in an almost-stomp.

Tir held a finger to his lips to silence him. In answer, Sleipnir tossed his head, stepping back just enough to allow Tir to stand. Once they were eye to eye, Sleipnir shifted sideways, then bumped him away a step, and then another, and another, until he'd herded Tir away from Liadan. Having removed him from his mistress, Sleipnir took a stand at her back to guard her sleep.

Tir marveled at the mount's intelligence and loyalty. "Guard her well." Entrusting him with Liadan's safekeeping, he walked off a to perform his morning rituals.

CHAPTER 17

Frastmir was holding its breath. Word had reached the castle that Liadan and her companion had passed through Dai and crossed into Aegiros. Aided by the queen, King Saeran spoke to his cousin, Ulrich, and confirmed that both riders had been in good health, unharmed, and eager to continue their journey when he'd seen them last. Now that they'd left Ulrich's demesne, no one was left to aid the king and queen in bringing back their daughter, and the city waited tensely to see what they would do.

Fal had no time to dwell on any of it. The shroud hiding Liadan from his mind was thinning day by day, and he feared when it disappeared completely, she'd be beyond his help. He'd spent every waking moment in his tower library, poring over everything the dragon had sent him, praying there'd be something in all of those texts to fix this. He'd found the first bit of hope early on: the blood oath Liadan and the Aegiran had sworn was binding, but not permanent. As long as no feelings stirred between them, once Liadan had completed her task, she should be free to return home.

Queen Nialei had wept with relief when Fal had told her so. But the danger still remained. Liadan was clever, but rash. If she did something more to upset the balance, the bond would tie not only her fate, but also her soul to the Aegiran, and not even death would part them.

Fal had spent days since his discovery searching for ways to help Liadan fulfill her obligation; the sooner she was done, the better. But he hadn't unearthed anything on the subject of demons or curses. Instead, the dragon's lore was filled with tedious extrapolations of the elemental world, the laws of nature and Otherkind, politics and basic magics, but little on the interactions between all of them.

The more knowledge Fal uncovered, the less he felt he knew. There was so much humans had either forgotten or had never known about, things that could mean the difference between life and death. They walked a fine line every day, now that the Veil was disintegrating. Without its protection, stepping into the wrong Otherland could kill a human with a single breath. Some Others had magic so potent it shone out of them, and one look could turn a human into stone.

Fal's translations took time. Finding some sort of order to them took time. Figuring out whether it was immediately useful took time—time Liadan did not have.

Frustrated, Fal shoved to his feet to pace. His legs had gone numb from all the sitting, and his knees almost buckled beneath him. He braced himself on the table, and beneath his thumb he spotted the first translation he'd penned. The jagged line of ink across the page marked where Liadan had distracted him. Half smiling, he picked up the page and read what he'd written.

Frowning, he read it again. No. Impossible.

Eyes widening with every word seen anew, Fal read through the text a third time, and his heartbeat quickened when he realized what it could mean. He swiped clean an area of the table, then dug through the pile of materials for the branded skin the translation corresponded with. His eyes skimmed the markings, comparing the symbols to the words he'd written. No mistake, at least none that he could find. "Gods, this could be..."

He dropped everything and ran out of the library, tripping over his feet on the way down. In the great hall, he ran into his father, almost knocking them both to the ground. "Sorry," he said, pulling away. He didn't have time to hear what Saeran called after him, let alone to answer.

The waterfall he favored as his own secret hideaway was close enough to not require a horse. Even so, it took him a half-day to get there on foot when he wasn't rushing. At a full run, it was less time, but more frustration. The path wasn't clear through the woods; he had to fight his way through bushes and shrubberies, tearing his cloak along the way. He didn't care.

The woods opened onto a meadow, with the waterfall just on the other side. It wasn't very big, but it flowed into a basin large enough to form a small lake before it emptied into the creek. He'd used to bathe here in the summers, before his illusions had forced him into seclusion in the castle. It was the perfect size for what Fal needed to do now. After so much time at his studies, the run had wearied him; his legs wobbled as he stalked across the meadow to the lake, where he took off his shoes, shrugged out of his cloak, and waded into the waist-high water. Its chill embraced him, and he let the gentle waves revive him, clear his mind. He waited patiently for his strength to be restored, because what he was about to do would require a great deal of concentration and tenacity. As far as he knew, no one had ever attempted anything like this before.

Fal was about to make history, and he couldn't suppress an eager smile or the way his heart thundered and his limbs itched to move. And then he began, and all awareness of the outside world slipped away.

⫷ »·◇·« ⫸

Tir spent the day teaching Liadan his language. He also kept a careful eye on her, as though he expected her to fall asleep again at any moment. Liadan didn't remember much from the day before, but it must have been worse than Tir let on; all he'd tell her was that she'd stumbled into a slaver's den and he'd had to retrieve her. When she'd asked him why he still fretted, now that all was well again, he'd tensed and refused to answer.

As closely as he watched her, Tir also kept an eye on the endless stretch of cracked and barren earth behind them. Did he worry they were being followed? Liadan suspected her lessons were meant more to distract him than to teach her, but she didn't mind. With nothing else to do, it was as good a pastime as any.

It hadn't escaped her that Tir hadn't just saved her life; he'd saved her from a lifetime of pain. Liadan had seen slaves being sold, buyers fighting and bartering over them. Her own fate would have been much worse. Back in the marketplace, the old woman had drugged her to make her docile, but not unconscious, which could have only meant one thing: they'd wanted her pliant but awake for their use, and they would have continued drugging her to keep her that way. In time, her Other constitution would have helped her adapt—her body would have learned to resist the drug's effect. But if Tir hadn't found her, she might not have regained enough sense to defend herself from their abuse.

No meager thanks or gesture of gratitude would ever be enough. Liadan owed Tir her life. And instead of lording it over her, Tir seemed determined to forget it'd ever happened. It relieved her of the need to address his kindness, but made her wonder whether the real reason he didn't want to acknowledge it was that he'd rather have left her there.

When the sun approached its zenith, Tir pitched a makeshift shelter to shield them from the worst of its heat so they could eat a small meal and rest the horses. Now that they'd left the marketplace behind, he was keeping their pace slow, and for good reason. Everywhere Liadan looked she saw nothing but dry, cracked earth. Her eyes hurt from the sun's glare, and her feet ached from walking on the hard ground in the shoes Tir had bought with her gold. She was hot and tired, and missing her home and her family.

Even the horses were miserable. Sleipnir didn't do well with his black coat. In fact, he was so desperate to escape the sun's heat, he didn't even twitch when Tir dusted him with sand to dull and lighten his coloring. A small relief, but she could tell it made a big difference.

All too soon, Tir took the shelter apart, and they set out once more. Liadan's feet dragged, and she leaned on Sleipnir more than she wanted to as they walked the mounts to spare them the weight. They'd started the day with two of their waterskins already empty, and the other two wouldn't last much longer.

Time and again, Liadan imagined seeing a distant greenery, but it was all a trick of the unrelenting blast of sun. As a creature of fire, the heat shouldn't have bothered her as much as it did. It might have been a simple matter of getting used to it—a reasonable assumption, since she'd never had trouble acclimating to winter's snow and ice—but even during the worst, most miserable northern blizzard, she'd never lacked for water.

Amazing how easily one could take such a small thing for granted when it was in abundance.

"How do you say I would like some water?"

Tir spoke the words in his tongue.

Liadan repeated them, but she was starting to slur.

Tir laughed. "You asked me whether there is water in the goat."

"There probably is," she muttered.

Still chuckling, Tir handed her his waterskin.

She pushed it away.

"Drink," he insisted.

"I have my own."

"And you haven't touched it. Did I not tell you not to ignore thirst?"

"Yes, you did. You did, Fal did, almost everyone I've told about this journey, did. It doesn't change the fact that this water is all we have for gods only know how long. I am not about to drink it all the first day." Her next step dragged, and she tripped over her own feet, managing to right herself before she fell outright.

Tir caught her elbow, made her stop. "You would rather die of thirst?"

"Give me that." She grabbed the waterskin and took a swig. It was warm, but that didn't matter. As soon as it touched her tongue, Liadan wanted to drink all of it down as fast as possible. She was so parched, she wanted to weep, but she was still right—they had to ration what they had left. Unfortunately, the little mouthful did nothing to quench her thirst, only reminded her of what she was missing, and the longer she held the skin, the more it tempted her to drink her fill. Tired of fighting, Liadan took one more sip, then forced herself to give back the skin. "Happy now?"

"Yes, I am." He had to be as thirsty as she was, though she couldn't tell by looking at him. She hated him a little for the ease with which he moved, when her legs felt weighed down with lead.

What she wouldn't give for a tree. Just one. A great, big oak, with a heavy crown of leaves and a soft cushion of grass at its base.

When green on the horizon once again teased her tired eyes, Liadan couldn't help letting out a small squeak of misery.

Tir followed her gaze, then looked back with a dazzling smile. "Mount up," he said, following his own orders, and before she was even settled into her saddle, he took off toward that spot, leaving Liadan to catch up.

The green patch she'd thought to be an illusion grew before her eyes. "It's not going away," she said, breathless. An oasis in the middle of the desert, with several tall palm trees at the foot of a small pile of rocks that fairly passed for a mountain. Large-leafed plants grew there as high as her waist, and water glittered in the middle of it all. "It's real!" she cried, and spurred Sleipnir on faster.

Tir laughed when she pulled ahead. She didn't need to tell Sleipnir what to do; he was as thirsty as the rest of them. With a gleeful whinny, he charged right into the creek and all but threw her off to get a drink.

Liadan dismounted, slipped and fell onto her backside in the creek. Laughing, she lay back, never so happy to swim fully dressed.

But it wasn't enough. Tilting her head up and back, she saw water pouring out of rock to pool at the base of the mountain. She just knew it would be deep enough to submerge herself. Desperate to wash off all of the dust and the sand, Liadan got up and pulled the scarf from her head. Her tunic came next, and by the time she'd wrestled off her shoes, Tir was staring at her with what looked like tepidation.

"What are you doing?" he demanded.

She couldn't draw enough breath to answer him beyond one word: "Water."

Finally free of the shoes, she got to work on her shirt, which stuck to her back. She almost suffocated trying to pull it off over her head. When at last she did, she grinned triumphantly at Tir who flushed and turned his back. Modesty was the last thing on her mind. She shed her chest binds and pants, and waded naked into the water up to her chest. The chill of it took her breath away, but she ducked underneath and screamed in pure joy to be there.

Liadan would have stayed there forever, but the need for air forced her to resurface. She gasped, taking her first full breath since the day's heat had become almost unbearable. "Gods, I needed that." Treading water, she watched the trees sway above her, until it suddenly struck her she hadn't heard a word from Tir. Lifting her head, she found him exactly where he'd been a moment ago, still with his back to her, staring off into the distance.

"What are you doing?" she asked.

"Praying for patience," he retorted.

Liadan laughed. "Is the fearsome assassin shy?"

He muttered something she couldn't hear.

"Stop being stubborn. Who knows how long it'll be before we find anything like this again? You shouldn't waste it."

He didn't move.

"I promise I won't look."

His shoulders tensed, but beyond a backwards glare no doubt meant to shut her up, he did nothing.

He left her with no choice. Forced to resort to dirty tactics, she called, "Tir you smell. We both do. I am not going any farther until we bathe."

Tir shook his head and started unloading the horses. As soon as Sleipnir and Tarabas were free of their burdens, they waded into the water and soaked themselves, stubbornly turning their noses up at Tir's commands to come out. Letting them speak for her, she lay back and floated, ignoring Tir. She was beginning to doze off when Tir's curses brought her head back up to watch him wrestle his boots off his feet. Biting back a smile, she turned toward the waterfall to give him some privacy.

"You won't regret it."

"I already do."

It was truly beautiful here, reminding her of the glen her brother favored—the same waterfall, the same pool and creek, the only difference being the color of the rock and the foliage. That, and the fact that twenty or thirty paces in any direction lay a vast expanse of burning desert. If she looked past the waterfall, she could even see a little cavern, just like the one back home.

A soft splash and hiss heralded Tir's approach. Liadan was tempted to turn around, but the water was too clear to disguise their nudity. Tir didn't seem to mind; his gaze burned a hole between her shoulder blades. It would be only fair to see him in turn, would it not?

She swiveled, sinking lower, so the water rose up to her neck.

Tir must have had the same thought; she was left with a view of his back. A fine back he had, with lean muscle moving beneath his skin as he waved his hands back and forth in the water.

"It's deeper over here," she said.

"I know," he replied.

"No need to get testy. I only meant there's plenty of room. You needn't cower all the way over there." Oh, Da would have flayed her hide for this, but she couldn't help teasing a little. "I don't bite."

"But I might." He'd said it so softly she almost missed his words, but she shivered at the feeling behind them.

Liadan worried her lower lip between her teeth. From him, she might not mind the bite, but it wouldn't do for him to know that. "I should thank you," she said instead. "You rescued me from what might have been a very unpleasant situation in Sadirak."

"You would not have been in such a situation if not for me. You owe me nothing."

"Nevertheless, I am grateful." Without thinking, she reached out to touch him.

Tir flinched away. "Don't. I never thought you to be cruel; I don't want to start now."

"I only wanted to—"

He swore and moved away, wading to the edge of the basin. "This was a mistake."

"Wait! I offended you, and I'm sorry. I promise I won't touch you again. Look, I'll even turn my back." She did just that, facing the waterfall. "See? All is well. Please don't go."

Tir's movements stilled, and that sensation of his gaze caressing her returned. She heard him come back into the water and risked a sideways glance to see where he was.

"No looking!"

"Sorry!" Liadan faced forward, but she didn't need her eyes; the water displaced at her back as he came closer, and she sensed the heat of him on her skin the same way she felt the sun. Staring straight ahead, she started when her brother's image wavered in the mist. "Fal?" But it was gone as quickly as it came, and Liadan shook her head, wondering whether the heat had finally driven her mad.

"Liadan? Are you all right?" In an instant, Tir was so close, one step would bring him near enough to touch. Out of the corner of her eye, she saw his hand hover by her shoulder.

Before it could settle on her, someone reached out from behind the stream and grasped onto her, pulling her over to the other side. She sputtered, fought to free herself, but it was Fal's voice that cried her name, his arms that pulled her into a tight embrace. She wiped water from her eyes, heart thudding, to see where she was. "Wha… What is this?"

Trees towered all around under an overcast sky, and the water was a damn sight colder than it had been a moment ago.

"An aspect of one element is but a small part of the whole, creating a tangible connection to the eternal, and thus making the passage from one to another possible!" Fal cried. "I did it, Liadan! I figured it out."

Stunned beyond words, all she could do was stare. "What did you do?"

Fal pushed away from her with a gasp and slapped his hands over his eyes. "You're naked!"

"What did you do, Fal!"

"Why are you naked!"

Behind her, Tir's voice echoed, distorted by the water's flow. "Liadan? Liadan!" He was in the pool where she'd stood a moment ago, staring through the waterfall. Could he see her?

"Tir!"

He stepped away, searching the pool's surface. "Liadan!"

She slapped Fal's shoulder. "What did you do?"

"I'm sorry! I had to do something. Mother and Da are at their wit's end, we couldn't reach you, the dragon wouldn't help, and then you crossed into Aegiros and Da was this close to raising an army to go after you—"

"Stop!" Dear gods, how was she supposed to follow a word of that? "Will you put your hands down?"

"You're naked!"

"I was bathing, you dolt! The first bath I've had since leaving Dai."

"Then why is *he* in the water?" Fal demanded.

Her temper flared, warming the water around them. "Send me back. Now."

"I can't. Da will wring my neck if he finds out I had you and didn't keep you here."

"Fal!"

"You can't go back to him!"

"I have to! Or have you forgotten my oath? You were there when I swore it."

Fal dropped his hands to meet her gaze, eyes furious as he grated out, "I was there when you bloody handfasted yourself to the Aegiran assassin!"

Her jaw slackened. "What?"

Fal's features settled into his own face and, drawing in a deep breath for patience, he raised a hand to block her nudity, voice strained as he explained, "The words you spoke bound you to him, and his blood bound him to you in return. You are handfasted until your oath is fulfilled. The bond will fade, but only if you don't…" He gestured with his free hand. "You know."

"What?"

"You *know*."

Liadan shook her head. "What are you talking about?"

"Consummate!"

"Fal!" She slapped him on the head this time.

"Stop hitting me and listen. This is important. If you mate with him, it'll bind your soul to his. Not just until death, but forever. Do you understand? If he's slain in battle, you could die. If he grows old and passes on, he could take you with him."

Liadan struggled to understand. "I made myself mortal?"

Fal said nothing.

"But we exchanged blood. If his had this effect on me, what did mine do to him? He could just as easily have been made immortal." Or at the very least, longer-lived.

"It'll do you no good trying to understand it. None of us know what the exchange has wrought in both of you. All we know is that as long as you're with him, you're in danger. I can't let you go back."

Liadan shook her head. None of that mattered now. "You have to. The oath will compel me, no matter what you do, until I have finished my task, and Tir's tribe doesn't have time to waste."

Fal appeared to debate his choices.

"*Liadan!*" Tir called again, more frantic this time.

"Fal, please, you have to send me back."

His shoulders sagged in a sigh. "Remember what I told you, and don't lose that vial. Now, more than ever, water's my only window to you should you need help."

"Yes, yes. I understand."

"Gods keep you, sister." And he shoved her back through the waterfall, right into Tir's arms. The impact knocked him backwards, and they fumbled to untangle themselves. Liadan had no trouble finding the surface, but Tir struggled, and she had to reach down to help him. He couldn't swim, she realized.

"Are you all right?" Liadan asked, trying to look into his face.

He pushed her away, coughing up the water he'd inhaled. When he could breathe again, he turned on her with a fury she hadn't seen since that day in the dungeons of Castle Frastmir. "What tricks are you playing at?" he demanded.

Liadan backed off from his advance, cornering herself against the waterfall.

He grabbed her by the shoulders and, spinning her around, shoved her away from it. "I thought the *masar* had caught up to us! I saw someone pull you across the water, and then you were gone! Where did you go?"

"I didn't mean to, I—"

"Cease lying!"

Fire flared through her, and she struck without thinking, curling her fingers around his throat. She squeezed just enough to keep him still, but the heat of her fire sizzled against his skin, and Tir gasped, falling silent. "I've made allowances for you, Aegiran, time and again, and I am grateful for your help in Sadirak. But by the gods, if you call me a liar one more time, I will burn you to ash where you stand, blood oath or no. Do you understand?"

He gave a curt nod, as much as her hold would allow, and she released him with a shove. Tir wisely stepped out of reach and touched his throat, where the red mark of her palm print faded even as she watched. He'd feel no lasting effects.

She sighed. "I did not lie. Water is my brother's element, not mine. He found me and pulled me through, back to Frastmir to tell me—" She cut her sentence short.

"Tell you what?"

It would serve no purpose to tell him what Fal had imparted; neither of them could change what had been done, and telling him would only put more strain on their already difficult situation. "That my parents have returned and are angry with me for leaving. He tried to keep me home, but I made him send me back. To you and this godsforsaken dead land. Because I honor my word."

"Your brother can travel through water?"

"It would seem so. But he will not take me back a second time."

"You are right in that," he replied, his words a dire warning. "If I must leash you to me to keep you here, I will." Then his face flushed, and he quickly turned his back. She was still naked and, standing straight, the water wasn't deep enough to hide her. Before, the thought of being seen this way wouldn't have bothered her, but what Fal had told her changed everything.

There would be no more teasing the prince, no more breathless kisses, and no more bathing naked together. If mate-bonding with him wasn't the worst that could happen, then it came very, very close. She couldn't risk either of them living the same misery Geir felt every day, not even if the smallest chance existed they might be happy together for however long they had to live.

CHAPTER 18

The horses refused to hold still long enough for Tir to saddle them; every time he came near, they shook off his touch and crossed to the other side of the oasis. Nevertheless, he tried three times, and on the third, got pushed into the water, fully dressed, for his efforts.

"Leave them," Liadan called. "They deserve the rest. We can shelter here for the night."

Though the day was long from over, if the horses wouldn't leave, neither could they. Giving up, Tir waded out of the pool and squeezed as much water out of his clothes as he could without taking them off. Never again would he disrobe in front of the princess. Nor would he ask her to do whatever she'd done that night of the storm. He'd rather freeze to death.

Instead, he built a small fire and sat as far from Liadan as he could. If she noticed, she wouldn't meet his gaze long enough to mock him for it.

He shouldn't have looked. To see her suddenly disappear had scared years off his life—a depth of fear matched only by his anger at having her returned from her brother. Never would he have thought it'd be so easy for others to take her—right from under his nose!

Never would he have thought the idea of losing Liadan would bring him such—

Tir shook his head hard. No. He thought nothing. He felt nothing.

Gods, he shouldn't have looked.

But he had, and now the sight had been seared into his mind for all eternity. Liadan was exquisite. Her skin was as pale as milk, her body strong with muscle, yet graced with feminine curves. Tir rubbed at his eyes, wishing he could scrub away the image of her from the inside of his eyelids. If the princess noticed anything amiss, she said nothing. Risking a glance across the fire, he found her staring into its depths, lost in thought as she played with the glass vial from her brother.

Just as well.

After a silence long enough to make his tense shoulders relax, the princess opened her mouth. "Do people wed in Imarah the way we do in the North?"

Tir flinched, reaching a hand up to his throat. This was not a discussion he wanted to have today. Perhaps not ever. But to refuse to answer would mean admitting a weakness, and that was something a *kharesh* would never do. "Why do you ask?"

She shrugged. "Father told me Mari was chosen to wed him. But they wed in the Northern way, and he never spoke of Aegiran customs of courtship. Either he didn't know, or there aren't any."

"We wed," he said carefully. "Each tribe has its own customs, but the punishment for breaking them is the same everywhere."

She looked up, a question in her eyes.

Tir quickly focused on the flames. "Women who dishonor their husbands are stoned to death."

He could hear a disgruntled frown in her voice when she said, "I thought men were allowed to take many wives in Aegiros."

"They are. A man may have as many wives as he can feed and clothe."

"Then are women not allowed to have many husbands?"

"No."

"Why not?"

"It is the way it has always been."

Her silence carried a heavy weight of disapproval.

"This bothers you," he observed.

"Of course it bothers me!"

"Northerners allow only one wife for each man?"

"Yes. And we mate for life."

He'd already known this, but the way she'd said it gave him pause to consider the full implications of such an arrangement. "What happens when the woman dies?"

"Her husband mourns her," she retorted. "What happens to an Aegiran's wives when he dies?"

"If he has male kin, the wives go to them. If not, some tribes allow the women to be burned on his pyre."

Liadan looked horrified by the thought, and in truth, the practice had never sat well with Tir either. Imarah hadn't burned a wife in many centuries, but the mercy created complications of its own. Without a husband to care for them, women were forced to fend for themselves, to sell their crafts or their bodies to anyone willing to pay. Rare was the man who'd take into his household a widow not of his family, so the choice of starving on her own or dying with her husband was one each widow had to make. In some tribes, they fell willingly upon the pyre.

"You needn't worry. You are not human, remember?" He did, but the reminder changed nothing. What was seen, could not be unseen; did not want to be unseen. "You cannot be harmed by fire." Nothing good could come of this preoccupation he'd developed, but the more time he spent with Liadan, the easier he forgot that. She was becoming a flame he kept circling like a moth and he feared one day it would burn the flesh from his bones.

Her eyes sparked with fire as her face took on a faint glow. "Know this, *mortal*"—she spat the word as an insult, but through her bluster of anger, Tir saw a chink of hurt and instantly regretted his words. "When I choose to mate, it'll be with a male who is my equal in all things; who will love and cherish me as I do him. And I will no more abide him taking another than he would me cuckolding him for sport. When I breathe my last, it'll be with his arms around me, and I'll know I have loved with all my heart and soul, and have been loved the same."

When I breathe my last…

We won.

In his mind's eye, the vision of Liadan's naked form went up in flames, turning to ash as she died. "I begin to understand why Northmen only take one wife. If they are anything like you, one would be more than enough to keep a man busy for the rest of his life." He'd meant it as a good-hearted jest, but it only seemed to make matters worse.

"You mock me."

"No," he said in earnest, searching for the right words to explain. "To share such passion with another, to look into her eyes and see a helpmate rather than a helpless female in constant need of protection, I cannot imagine such a blessing."

Liadan's temper calmed, her eyes dimming to charcoal. "Your people depend on you a great deal."

"Yes."

"Your wives will as well."

Tir nodded. If his tribe survived long enough, he'd be expected to take a wife, perhaps more. With so many of their men dying of starvation or in battle, only a handful were left to care for the women. Of those, half were too young to wed and the other half already had two or three wives, and their children to look after.

"That must be a terrible burden to bear."

It was.

"But it is one of your own making. Aegiran men, I mean."

Ire heated his blood at her words, but he couldn't argue. She was right.

Liadan sighed and pushed to her feet. "I shouldn't have broached the subject." She put the vial into her saddlebag, retrieved her sword, and removed herself to the other side of the oasis to train on her own.

For a while, Tir watched her, absently noting the elegant mastery with which she wielded the blade. Aegiran steel was nothing like the Northern blades; their scimitars were thinner, sharper, and curved, meant to slice through flesh, not break apart metal armor. It afforded them more speed and less weight to carry in their scabbards.

He'd seen men in the North struggle just to walk in their armor, let alone draw their blades. Many had had massive swords strapped to their backs, the pommels sticking out over their shoulders and the tips all but dragging on the ground. Tir couldn't conceive of any use for such a thing.

He'd hefted Liadan's sword—a work of art if he'd ever seen one—and he'd found it wasn't as heavy as he'd have expected, but it was still more cumbersome than his scimitar. She must have grown used to it, however, because when she moved, the sword was not its own thing; it was an extension of her arm, and moved with her every which way, down to the smallest twitch of her wrist.

She practiced with her right hand, then switched the hold to her left. Finally, she drew a long dagger and repeated each routine with two blades instead of one. Each time she altered her weapons, she moved slowly at first, measuring each strike with precision borne of relentless training by a master. By the time she'd put on a burst of speed to repeat the whole thing, her movements were so ingrained in her limbs, he'd have been surprised if there was even a finger's width variation in them.

In practice, Liadan was a gifted swordswoman. But could she fight, too, or was this simply another form of dance to her? Tir pushed to his feet, intending to find out. If she was to fight with his *kharesh*, he needed to know she could hold her own. He couldn't have inexperience costing them lives.

But before he could make it across the oasis, Liadan suddenly dropped her blades and clutched at her stomach.

"Did you pull a muscle?" he teased.

Liadan cried out and dropped to her knees, hunching over.

"Liadan?" His steps quickened.

She looked up, face pinched with pain. With obvious difficulty, she struggled to her feet. "Sleipnir!"

The black mount answered her summons, reaching her a moment before Tir.

"What's the matter?" Tir asked.

"It's time again, my friend." She held her shaking hand up to Sleipnir, who sniffed at her fingers and tossed his head with an agitated snort, stomping his hooves.

Tir caught her hand to get her attention. "What are you doing?" Her skin was too hot; unnaturally so. "What's the matter with you?"

"Three days," she said, her voice unsteady. "I will meet you back here in three days."

"What?"

Sleipnir lipped her shoulder, and she pulled away from Tir to stroke the mount's forehead. "I'm sorry. It's not safe for me to stay here."

"You are not leaving!"

Her face contorted, knees buckling a second time, but when Tir reached out for her, Sleipnir shouldered him aside to support his mistress himself. He lowered to his knees so Liadan could mount. She barely kept astride, clutching Sleipnir's mane with a white-knuckled grip. "Please, Tir, I don't want to hurt you. This is something I cannot control. Stay here. I will be back in three days' time, I swear it."

"No," he growled and whistled for Tarabas.

Liadan moaned, leaning over Sleipnir's neck. All it took was one touch to spur the mount on, and he galloped off so fast, Tir was stunned. He couldn't waste time gathering their supplies. Refusing to let that female out of his sight again, he followed after her. But as fast as he knew Tarabas to be, Sleipnir was faster, and within moments, they'd left the oasis far behind.

She would not get away so easily. Tir kicked Tarabas into a hard sprint to catch up. When he did, Liadan was slumped over Sleipnir's back, moments away from slipping off, and the horse wasn't slowing down. Cursing himself a fool, he reached across to drag her onto Tarabas, but Sleipnir veered off, taking his mistress out of reach.

Tir tried again, but Sleipnir refused to let him take her. Risking his own life as well as hers, Tir squared his balance, pulled his feet up, and crouched on Tarabas' back, clutching his mane. The next time the mounts came close, he jumped, landing astride Sleipnir behind Liadan.

The instant he did, Sleipnir reared, throwing them both off. Tir took the brunt of the impact, landing on his back, Liadan on top of him, and she grunted, rolling off him, but she lacked the strength to stand. Breath knocked out of him, Tir sat up and reached for her, only to recoil when Sleipnir charged at him.

Sensing a threat, Tarabas intervened, and both horses reared, fighting each other. Sleipnir was bigger, stronger, and unrelenting, and he pushed Tarabas back as far as he deemed necessary, then turned on Tir with an angry snort.

Fearing for Liadan more than himself, Tir turned to shield her, but she was already crawling away from him, and what little distance she'd gained was enough for Sleipnir to get between them. Stomping his hooves ever closer, he herded Tir away. Tir pushed to his feet, trying to see around the mount, but he only caught a glimpse. "Liadan!"

His voice brought her head up, and Tir shuddered when she looked at him. Her eyes were pure fire, her face veined with bright red-gold cracks like the earth beneath his feet. Smoke curled up from her skin, and her hair billowed over it, turning to flame, one strand at a time. "Stay back!" she warned, and her shout turned into an agonized scream.

Tir shoved at Sleipnir to let him through, but with a sharp whinny, the mount half-reared again, kicking out with his front hooves to push him back even farther. Fear had widened his eyes, and his tail twitched with agitation. Tir realized the horse wouldn't let him through, because Sleipnir himself didn't want to be there.

A flare of heat struck him, pulling his skin tight and dry across his face. Sleipnir kicked out with his hind legs, tossing his head, desperate to escape. With no other choice, Tir relented, and went a distance farther until Sleipnir calmed somewhat and let him see Liadan.

Tir's heart stuttered. It had to be the distance making her seem so small. Yet even from such a distance, the waves of heat exuded by her huddled form overpowered the sun. He'd seen her engulfed in flames before, but this was different.

On her hands and knees, Liadan curled her fingers down to claw at the earth, and where they touched, fire erupted. But it wasn't the bright glow he'd become familiar with; these flames were darker, a sickening shade of blood, with little of the bright yellow. And they weren't just licking over her; they were burning her, bursting out of the cracks in her skin until her entire body was aflame, and then became the flame.

Liadan disappeared in that inferno, and Tir could scarcely make out the outline of her body. The flames flared out, then pulled in tightly, then burst out again—a cycle that repeated endlessly, growing bigger and hotter and so loud he heard nothing else.

Tir gasped for breath after he'd held it too long. He was rooted to the spot, unable to move or look away as Liadan burned. This was his nightmare brought to life. Worse, because he couldn't even go to her.

Beside him, Sleipnir stood and watched, waited for the gods knew what, his tail twitching every so often while his agitated snorts punctuated the ebb and flow of Liadan's fire. But he didn't move, standing loyal watch over his mistress, watching her die.

At the worst of it, the desert wind whipped a flare into a vortex that pulled the flames into the sky, and for a moment, Tir could almost make out Liadan's form. The next flare was smaller. The one after that, smaller still.

As the heat slowly died down, Tir and Sleipnir dared to approach, step by step. Tir followed the animal's instincts, trusting them more than his own, and didn't go closer unless Sleipnir matched him. The fire shrank, lightened, and then cooled, until it was once again the shade he'd come to associate with Liadan.

When it'd died down enough to reveal her, Tir stopped in his tracks. Her clothing had burned away in the maelstrom, the torc around her neck glowed bright, and her skin, still veined in blood red, flickered like a burning ember. She lay on the ground, unmoving, and he couldn't tell whether or not she was breathing; couldn't get close enough to see for himself.

Little by little, Tir inched his way forward, hoping and praying he didn't get to the princess only to have her turn to ash in his arms.

When at last he'd reached her, the red cracks had sealed into unbroken, luminescent skin, and the desert had become dark. Night had fallen while Liadan had burned, and now her faint glow was all the light they had. Tir reached out, tentatively touched her arm. She was hot, but no longer burning. He found her heartbeat, strong and steady in the side of her neck, then held his hand beneath her nose and felt her breath, soft, but sure.

Tir cupped her face, angling it up so he could check her eyes. The movement did nothing to rouse her. "Liadan, wake up. Can you hear me? Open your eyes."

She didn't stir.

Sleipnir nosed at her hair, then sneezed at the sharp scent of ash and soot, but didn't recoil. Instead he kneeled, jerking his head at Tir.

Tir shrugged off his shirt and threaded Liadan's arms through it to clothe her. He picked her up, but instead of slinging her over Sleipnir's back, he mounted with her in his lap. Sleipnir pushed to a stand, then began walking in what Tir hoped was the direction of the oasis. Eventually, Tarabas fell into step with them, eyes still big, wary of the larger mount and the glowing woman Tir held close to his chest.

When he saw the shadow of their oasis, Tir slumped with relief. They'd made it. The fire he'd built had gone out, but at least the plants provided some shelter from the freezing night. For the second time in as many days, Tir rolled out their pallets and settled Liadan on one side. He left her only long enough to gather more dried palm fronds for a small fire and several dry gourds he'd earlier seen scattered around, then sat nearby to begin his watch.

The flames swayed toward Liadan to mirror her breathing. It unnerved him enough to move her sleeping form farther away. Then he resumed his seat, pulled out his blade, and got to work on the gourds.

If he slept, all he'd dream about was fire. Better to stay awake and wait for Liadan to open her eyes. If she ever did.

CHAPTER 19

Liadan woke to shivers racking her body. It happened every time she literally burned herself out; her fire needed time to rebuild, and while it did, she was left chilled to her very soul. Opening one bleary eye, she found Tir's face a hair's breadth from her nose. She gasped, and he glowered.

"You're alive."

"You sound disappointed." Her voice was hoarse. She was parched and starving, and her arms quivered with strain when she pushed up onto her elbows. Oh, how she hated this.

Tir caught her arms and unceremoniously dragged her to lean back against one of their packs. Then he shoved a cup at her face, giving her no choice but to let him pour water down her throat. She would have fought him, but the water tasted so cold and crisp, she was too busy gulping it down. "More," she demanded when the cup was empty.

"Not yet. Eat." He curled her fingers around a piece of bread and dried meat as if she were an invalid.

"Your bedside manner is atrocious." Liadan took the nourishment and made herself chew before she swallowed each small bite.

"Are you ill?"

"No," she said around a mouthful.

"Are you hurt?"

She shook her head.

"Then you'll forgive me for being slightly irritated at having to watch you sleep for *three bloody days!*"

Liadan flinched. "I told you to stay here," she reminded him.

His face darkened with fury. Clearly, that had been the wrong thing to say.

"I'm sorry?" she ventured.

"You will explain." She could hear his teeth grinding. This was not good.

With a sigh, she stuffed the last bit of bread into her mouth, chewing slowly while she considered how much to tell him.

"You will explain in detail," he said, as if he'd read her thoughts. "And then you will explain this." Before she could react, he stuck his hand into the fire and pulled out a burning coal. Liadan's jaw slackened as she stared at his hand, black with soot but unharmed, proffering the ember as a silent accusation.

The last swallow of her dry meal stuck in her throat. "When…?"

"Sometime while you slept. A log cracked and rolled away from the fire. I reached for it and tossed it back on the fire without thinking."

"It doesn't hurt?"

He winced, more an expression of agitation than pain. "I feel the heat. It burns *into* me, but it doesn't hurt."

Liadan took the coal to inspect his hand. Just as when she'd branded him, the skin of his palm was red, but already fading. She looked at the coal in her free hand, turned it this way and that. The live ember, hot enough to sear any man, was no more than a warm, glowing gem in her hand, but *she* was fireproof. Tir should not have been. Unless… "It must be my blood. Somehow it's protecting you."

"It didn't when you burned."

"You didn't touch me then." She remembered that much; Sleipnir had kept him away.

"What happened to you?"

Liadan flushed, threw the coal back into the fire. Tir deserved an answer, no matter how much he might come to regret asking. "It's my moon cycle," she said.

He frowned.

Squirming beneath his relentless stare, she explained, "When mortal girls become women, their fertility is cyclical. A woman can't conceive a child until she's blooded, and when she is, once every month, her womb bleeds."

Tir paled, and two patches of bright red stained his cheeks. "I know this."

"Yes, well, Otherkind have cycles, too, except ours are different. Mine revolves around fire, my core element. Instead of bleeding, I burn. The pangs signal a firestorm, then the flames consume me. It exhausts me, and I sleep for three days afterward so my body can restore itself. My mother would call it a wizard's sleep. But I am Dragonblood, not a wizard."

She waited for him absorb that. For a long time, Tir didn't speak and had trouble meeting her gaze. To disguise his unease, he stoked the fire with his bare hand, then shook his head at the lack of damage and poured more water for her from a strange-looking bottle. "I should not have asked."

"You should not have followed. It's dangerous, for me and everyone else. I can't control the firestorm when it overtakes me. You could have died."

"I should have left you alone and naked in the desert for three days instead?"

Liadan grimaced. She hadn't thought of that when she'd mounted Sleipnir. Her only thought had been to get far enough away so she wouldn't hurt him. "I suppose not."

"This happens every month?"

She nodded.

"It looked… painful."

Liadan chuckled at the understatement. "Fantastically painful."

"How do you… How can you…?"

"Bear it? I've no other choice, do I? I can't change what I am. I wouldn't want to, if I could. All magic comes with a price. This is simply mine."

Sleipnir came to her, head low, and nuzzled her neck.

She smiled and patted his forehead. "You did well. Thank you."

The mount chuffed and lipped her shoulder.

"Why did you not tell me before?"

Liadan drank some more, then ate another bite of dried meat before she answered. "I don't usually make it a habit to reveal my greatest weakness to strangers. The firestorm may be deadly to others, but it doesn't last long; half a day, perhaps. And afterward, when I sleep, I am left completely defenseless. A tricky fellow might think to sever my head from my shoulders while I wasn't aware of it, and I couldn't do anything to stop him."

"You think I would do such a thing?"

"No, I suppose not."

Tir pushed to his feet, and Liadan suddenly realized he was shirtless. "You trusted your horse over me!"

"Not long ago you told me I should fear you, and now you want my trust?"

"That was before—" He cut himself off, frowning into the distance.

"Before what?"

He gestured with his hand.

"Oh, what is that supposed to mean?"

Tir scowled, and reached for her arm. "It means get up." He pulled her to her feet, then turned her north. "Do you see that?"

Liadan squinted into the distance. The day was hot, the air wavered, and she could hardly tell where the ground ended and the sky began, but as her sight adjusted, faint, dark smudges appeared on the horizon. "Are those riders?"

"We should go."

"Why?" she asked, but ran for her pack anyway to rummage through it for her spare set of clothes. No chest binds; she tore up her scarf to repurpose it, then retied her vial around her neck. It'd been a stroke of luck that she'd taken it off before riding out. The fragile glass wouldn't have survived the heat.

"We don't have time for this," Tir called while he saddled Tarabas.

In answer, she yanked off his shirt and tossed it at the back of his head. "Then stop dawdling and get dressed." It took her mere moments to bind herself and dress. She saddled Sleipnir while Tir secured their supplies, and only when she'd settled astride her mount did she remember she had no shoes. She'd left her riding boots behind in Sadirak, and the ones Tir had gotten for her had burned in the firestorm.

"Can you ride?"

How was she supposed to walk without shoes?

"Liadan!"

She met his gaze. "No shoes."

Cursing, he dismounted and ran for a low plant by the palms, cut off several leaves and shoved them into her arms before he mounted again.

"How are these helpful?" she demanded, balancing an armful of thick, green blades with hard, spiked edges.

"Ride!" he ordered, and took off.

Swearing as only a girl who'd grown up frequenting Wilderheim's taverns could, she stuffed the plants into her saddlebag, and spurred Sleipnir after him.

They put countless miles of sun-baked earth between them and the oasis, rode so hard and so long, Liadan lost all sense of time and direction. Nothing marred the barren landscape to tell her where she was, or which way they were going, and it terrified her. The sheer emptiness felt as if it would swallow her whole; she could disappear here, and no one would ever find her.

"Do you know where we're going?"

"South," Tir answered. How could he be so certain?

Liadan scanned for insects scurrying across the ground, but found none. No birds circled, and no fragments of bone showed any hint that a living creature of any kind had ever passed through here.

Tir had stopped talking altogether. His jaw was tense all the time and he kept looking over his shoulder. She hoped it was because he wanted to see whether or not they were being followed, and not because he was lost. They'd left no tracks, which meant they could have been riding in giant circles and never known it because they'd have never crossed their own trail.

Sleipnir was slick with sweat. The horses couldn't take much more. "Tir, stop!"

"A little farther, we're almost there!"

Tarabas jerked sideways with a scream, but Tir pulled him back in line.

"We're killing them!"

Tir leaned low over Tarabas' neck, spoke into his ear. Liadan couldn't hear what he said, but the animal seemed to gain some strength from the words and ran on, forcing her to keep up on Sleipnir if they didn't want to be left behind.

Ahead, the desert changed. At first, she thought the mounds were mountains, but the closer they got, the better she could see. Not mountains—massive sand dunes. Beneath them, hoofbeats softened, and Liadan stared out to the left and right, marveling at the change. Sand blew across the hard-packed ground in small flurries, lapping at the cracked earth like an eternally frozen sea and those dunes might as well have been waves.

Tir led them up the crest of one dune. Liadan worried they'd sink into the stuff, but although it was slower going for the mounts, they still managed, scaling the next one, and the next, until Tir finally deemed them far enough to stop. He dismounted and pressed his forehead to Tarabas', speaking soft words to calm him.

Sleipnir wasn't so easily soothed; he chewed at his bit, shaking his head as if the feel of his bridle irritated him. Liadan retrieved her waterskin and a hollowed-out bowl she'd found strapped to her supplies. She poured out as much water as the bowl could hold without spilling, then fed it to Sleipnir. When he'd drained it, she refilled the bowl again, and then one more time until the skin ran dry. Liadan stroked him a couple of times, as much in thanks as in apology, then she retied the skin and the bowl to his saddle before rounding on Tir.

"What is the matter with you? You could have killed us all!"

"I did not," he said shortly. Tarabas quivered beneath his hand. He'd given the stallion as much water as he dared, but despite the additional water he'd collected into the gourds, it wouldn't be enough to sustain them. They'd have to ration as much as possible until they reached Imarah.

"Who were those riders?" she demanded.

"I don't know."

"Then why did you run? They could have had supplies!"

"And you think they would have shared? Look around, Princess. This is not your world; it is mine. And in it, you eat and drink what you can steal. I counted at least seven in their company, maybe more. With luck, they would have taken the horses and every last bit of useful provisions we had and left us for dead. More likely, they would not have bothered fighting. They would have slit our throats and taken over the oasis." Worse yet, those riders could have been *masar*—the ones from Sadirak or elsewhere, it would have made no difference—they never traveled in groups fewer than a dozen.

"They wouldn't have dared. And if they did, they most certainly would not have won. I could have—"

"What, Princess? Killed them all?" He couldn't tell whether her cheeks were red from the sun or the heat of her blush. As powerful as Liadan was, he had no doubt she could have dealt with the riders handily, even weakened from her firestorm. But that had been the farthest thing from his mind when he'd rushed them away from the oasis. With Sadirak still too close for his liking, and the *masar* no doubt on their trail, he could only think of getting Liadan as far away as possible. How incredibly foolish of him; trying to protect the immortal fire warrior he was bringing back to save his tribe. He couldn't think it without feeling embarrassed. "That would make you no better than them," he told her. Better she believed he'd done it to spare her conscience, than to suspect him of being motivated by sentiment.

"Can one afford to be merciful in a fight to the death?" she challenged softly. "Tell me, *sher'nah*, I am certain you would know better than I." Before he could answer, she turned her back on him and mounted Sleipnir. "What now?"

Tir was only too happy to let the matter rest. "These dunes run north to south. If we follow them south, they will lead us to the First Valley." They were still too far west. They'd emerge in the First City, or just east of it. He hoped it was the latter.

He let Liadan set the pace. Now that she had at least some sense of direction, she didn't need him to lead, and she seemed to be calmer when she had control over where they were going.

Despite their mad race to reach the sands, Tir wasn't satisfied they hadn't been followed; the sensation of being watched prickled at the back of his neck, but no matter how many times he sought the source, he found none. The dunes hid their presence better than the open desert, but by the same token, they also hid whoever was on their trail. Not wanting to distress Liadan, he kept his suspicions to himself and his hand on the pommel of his sword.

They rode through the night in weary silence, which gave him too much time to think. He wanted to rail at Liadan again for keeping her firestorm a secret; she could have gotten them both killed!

But what worried him more was his newfound ability to touch fire without being burned by it. He'd never considered what mingling his blood with an Other might do, what it might turn him into. Was he still human? Was the relentless pull he felt toward Liadan, the maddening protectiveness and curiosity, a product of the blood oath, or of his own treacherous feelings? The closer they rode to Imarah, the more he questioned the wisdom of bringing her along, and each repeated nightmare strengthened the dread that he was taking her to her death.

Tir told himself his fear was unfounded; that she'd come along of her own volition—had forced him to take her along—and that her death, should it come to that, would mean little to him, even less to his tribe. But he didn't believe his own lie. Even knowing it was ill-advised, Tir cared whether Liadan lived or died. He cared whether she trusted him, whether she was tired, or hurting, or worried.

He feared examining those feelings too closely, lest he discover they ran deeper than was wise. They'd reach Imarah soon enough, and when they did, Tir would remember his duty, and Liadan would once again be nothing more than a tool he'd use to fulfill it. He would not do something as idiotic as fall in love with an Other.

But even with the waxing moon and millions of stars twinkling in the sky above him, he found no reassurance in the night's cool darkness; no comfort in its beauty, when all he saw was Liadan's gently glowing form swaying in Sleipnir's saddle. She turned to him, smiling wearily, and Tir was dismayed by his sudden hope that maybe none of his worries were as bad as they seemed. So what if Liadan's blood had changed him? Maybe its magic would make him strong enough to save his people, make him into the king they deserved. Maybe it had bound him to the princess in some elemental way, and she felt the same inexplicable pull toward him in return.

Maybe, just maybe, he wouldn't turn out like Geir at all.

By morning, the parallel sand dunes had shrunk into the hard, arid ground of the First Valley, and red clay houses appeared on the horizon. Tir's heart sank. The First City.

Liadan gave him a beatific smile. "We made it." With a triumphant whoop, she stood up on Sleipnir's back, spread her arms wide, and shouted strange words at the sky.

Tir swallowed, shifted uneasily in his saddle. He didn't share her enthusiasm.

How could he?

There was a reason Imarah had left the First City all those years ago.

CHAPTER 20

They entered the city as the last of the night's coolness evaporated and the sun reclaimed the earth. It was exactly as Liadan had seen it in her vision: empty, abandoned; a ghost town with invisible eyes, watching them from every dark window and open doorway. Eerie winds howled through the passageways, and small items blew across them, mimicking the sound of running feet.

At first, they stopped in every house, searching for any usable items. Shoes were Liadan's highest priority. But aside from broken shards of pottery and torn rags, they found nothing but dead air. Worse, it was death on the air. She wouldn't ask—didn't want her suspicions confirmed—but Liadan knew many had died here. Hundreds, perhaps thousands. There were no markers to be seen, but this whole city was a burial ground, and each step felt like she was dancing on her own grave.

The city sprawled along the sides of the wide river basin Tir had mentioned. Only dry clay remained of the once mighty river, darker than the surrounding earth and the obvious source of building material.

"How long ago did the river run dry?" She kept her voice barely above a whisper.

Tir's jaw muscle twitched. "Almost twenty years. They say it happened too quickly. One day, children played on its banks; the next morning, the basin was half empty, and dead fish were floating on the surface. The day after that, those fish were baking on the dry clay of the riverbed. The Magi said it was an omen, that the gods were testing our faith. They sacrificed three goats, three mules, and three horses to appease them. Instead of water, the gods sent us a swarm of locusts and a plague."

They turned onto a much wider street that led to a set of large buildings. Unlike the clay houses, these were made of stone and marble, with tall pillars supporting bright white roofs. One stood on each side of the street, and beyond them, straight ahead, loomed a massive palace with gilded ornaments and golden statues. "The First City must have been very rich."

"Yes. These used to be the stables. The troughs were filled by canals leading from the river, so the horses always had fresh water. And the palace was built by Khalil al-Raseph, the greatest of our kings. He built it to house his twenty wives and seventy-five children. Their orchards were so fertile, not even all of his kin could consume all of the figs. The fruits were left to rot on the ground to fertilize the next season's harvest."

"All this precious metal… Why is it still here? The city must have been raided countless times since then."

"What good is gold to a man dying of thirst, if there is no water to buy with it? The raiders took our wines, fruits, our animals, and sometimes our women. The gold and jewels would have been nothing but a burden."

Most of the palace windows had been broken out, but the remaining ones were filled with a mesh-like cage. The main doors must have been massive to fill the hole in the wall they'd left behind. Small pieces still hung off the hinges, and Liadan leaned close to examine one no bigger than her hand, but with a carving of a woman's face and hair easily recognizable. Such beautiful detail in so small a piece.

Tir joined her there. "The portals were covered with carvings like this. They said *shansher* Khalil wanted to immortalize the likeness of each of his wives and children. His first wife and his oldest son were carved into ebony statues for the palace orchard. When the raiders came nineteen years ago, my father set his eldest sons to guard the orchard and those statues." Tir shifted, and his voice became grave. "He should have had them guard the women and children instead. The first battle took three of his wives and seven of his smallest children. They threw the babes from the balconies. Those who survived were trampled by their war horses."

Tears choked Liadan. She didn't know what to say. He must have been old enough to remember it, and those children had been his brothers and sisters. She reached for his clenched hand to offer what little comfort she could, but he shoved to his feet away from her. "There used to be a well in the orchard, dug quite deep. With any luck, there will be a little water left in there. Do not stray too far. There is evil soaking every tile and every pillar here. We must stay together."

Horses in tow, they walked through the empty palace with its cavernous chambers, where the only thing supporting the floor above was a series of pillars. Beyond the main building, the orchard Tir had mentioned was a wasteland; what few trees remained were barren sticks in the ground, many of them no more than blackened stumps. Dried grass and weeds crunched beneath her bare feet, and Liadan winced each time she stepped on a thorn.

The well was housed in a wide circle of twelve pillars that used to support a roof. In the center, marble benches once provided a respite for tired feet. Now, all but one were shattered to pieces, their bright white shards littering the ground. The well itself was as wide as Liadan was tall, with a set of pulleys for lowering a water bucket into its depths. The mechanism was destroyed, but that didn't seem to matter to Tir.

He took the length of rope, tested its strength and, tying one end to a tree stump, tossed the other end into the well. "You can't mean to go down there!"

"How else do you think we will get the water?"

"If there even is any. Tir, that rope is twenty years old. What if it breaks?"

"Then I will use my blades to climb back out. Stop fussing, woman, and find me a bucket instead."

Growling, Liadan searched for anything that might be useful. She found three buckets, all broken. "I see nothing," she complained.

"Then look inside," he called back, already halfway down the well. "There might be more in the stables. But don't take too long."

Liadan ran, not keen on wandering alone if she could help it. The stables were as grand as the palace. She might have admired them, except their sheer size made her search more difficult. Liadan checked every stall, nook and cranny, but found nothing.

Until she looked up toward a loft not much larger than a shelf. There, stacked in a row and untouched by the violence that had destroyed this place, were at least two dozen wooden buckets. But there was no ladder. "Bollocks."

Her nape prickled, and she spun around, sword in hand. No one there. Nothing moved, no whisper of sound betrayed another's presence. But Liadan felt it. Wary, she kept her sword unsheathed as she looked through the stalls again. She found a frayed piece of rope and an old, warped horseshoe.

It would have to do. Tying the rope around the metal, she returned to the loft. Her first throw missed by a hair's breadth. Her second, however, caught in one of the bucket stacks, and the eerie feeling of being watched intensified. One sharp tug, and the buckets toppled from the loft. Two broke apart on impact, but the innermost one survived. She did it again with three more stacks until the rope snapped, but by then, she had four solid buckets in her grasp. Though it made her twitchy, Liadan sheathed her sword so she could carry them all at once, and raced back to the orchard.

The sight of Sleipnir and Tarabas grazing on dry grass eased her a little, but not enough. She needed Tir out of that well. "Are you still alive down there?" she called.

Tir cursed, and a large piece of marble flew out of the well. "Too much debris to see anything. I need to clear it out to get to the earth."

"Here." She pulled the rope up, tied a bucket to it, and lowered it down into the well.

Tir filled it with marble and rocks, and Liadan hauled it out. Empty bucket into the well, heavy bucket out of the well, over and over until her arms quivered with strain and her shirt was soaked with sweat. On her next pass, she sent him a waterskin, along with some bread and hard cheese.

"Thanks," he called up.

She sat with her back against the well while they ate and rested. "We should have taken Fal with us. He can find water anywhere."

"That might have been good to know before we left."

Liadan chuckled.

"Tell me about your dragon. Is he truly as fearsome as your fire story?"

Liadan smiled, missing her grandfather. "Oh, yes. He's as tall as a mountain, and when he stretches out his wings, they cover entire fields. One of his fangs is as large as I am tall." At least that's how she'd always thought of him.

"Does he have wings like a bat?"

"No. He… It's difficult to explain. He's scaled like a lizard, but the scales on his wings are softer, more flexible than the shield scales on his chest. They're almost soft enough to be cloth, but you'd break your sword if you tried to cut them from his wings."

"Sounds like magic."

She grinned. "It is. When he changes shape, he burns the old body and reforms the ashes into the new. But he can do it so fast, you'd miss it if you blinked."

"Can you do the same?"

"No. Perhaps if I'd been born in Otherlands, where magic saturates the air, I might have learned to harness the ability. Here, the taint of my human blood prevents it."

They fell into a companionable silence while they ate. Liadan imagined he mirrored her pose, sitting against the wall of the well, and if he weren't so far below, they'd have been back to back. It was pleasant outside, the kind of midday when the grass beckoned the weary to rest their heads upon it. The grass here was too dry for that, but if she strung up a blanket between those trees, it would do just as well. With the promise of shelter nearby, Liadan could even appreciate the sun shining down on her. How beautiful this place must have been before the drought—bright green grass all around, with pathways of marble stones here and there. She'd never seen a fig tree, but she could imagine them, weighed down with fruits. Children would play nearby, and beautifully attired wives would stroll through the orchard, arm in arm.

It's not so different from Dai.

Liadan didn't realize she'd spoken aloud until Tir answered. "No, it was not. Different people, perhaps, but the First City was as much a place of beauty as your Dai and Frastmir. The river was sacred to my people, blessed by the goddess Inaras. It could heal the sick, restore the weary. Travelers would come from all corners of Aegiros to fill even one bottle with it."

"And I am sure they paid well for the privilege."

"No. It is a great sin to sell what is given by the gods. Many left tokens of gratitude in our temples, but those offerings were for Inaras, not the Imarah." He sighed. "We should finish this."

They'd already cleared most of the debris. When he began to dig, he filled the bucket with earth and rubble, and Liadan lost count of how many times she'd hauled that bucket up. But as the day wore on, the dirt inside became darker and damper, and she redoubled her efforts, hope giving her strength when she didn't think she had any left.

Then Tir whooped in triumph, and she grinned. He'd struck water. "Bucket! Quick!"

Liadan lowered it down, and after a long moment, he tugged on the rope to signal it was full. She carefully pulled it up, then squealed in delight to see the murky liquid inside. She poured it into a waiting bucket and sent the old one back down. While Tir filled it, Liadan gave the first to Sleipnir and Tarabas, letting them drink.

She returned to the well, pulled up the second load, and poured it into a new bucket. "How much is there?" she asked. The horses could use at least two or three more turns each, but so could she and Tir.

"Keep pulling it up."

She did, and they kept at it until the horses were sated, wandering away to graze. Liadan filled every container she could find: the waterskins, the strange bottles and bowls, even some serviceable clay dishes she'd found inside the palace. With all of that and four full buckets, they ran out of containers, while water continued to trickle up through the dirt in the well. Giddy with excitement, she helped Tir up and out as the sun began to set. He was covered with mud, but his smile was as brilliant as hers felt, and as soon as he was safely out of the hole, she threw her arms around him.

He laughed as they embraced. "There is more down there if we can find something to get it out with."

"Isn't it enough to know it's there?"

"No. Tomorrow it might not be."

His waning good mood said he spoke from experience, and it sobered her, as well. They had plenty for a couple of days, at least, and it should be enough until they set out for his tribe, but who knew what they might find there, if anything?

They took the containers inside the palace and lined them up along one wall. Tir found an old oil lamp, Liadan lit the wick and, keeping close together, they searched through the building. In one chamber, furniture lay in broken piles, so they gathered the wood for a fire. In another, chests of silks and gowns lay scattered and forgotten, dirty with dust and soot. Liadan searched through them until she found a scarf to replace hers and spare clothes that would fit them both. Tir managed to dig out several pairs of shoes that would fit her.

The palace had no kitchens, only a cool, underground pantry, which was in somewhat better shape than the rest of the place. Tir found two more buckets and several bottles that looked sturdy enough to survive on horseback. They took them all, and returned to the great hall by the orchard.

Though Liadan didn't want him to, Tir crawled back inside the well to fill the new containers, still worried the water would disappear as quickly as he'd found it. It'd happened often enough to his tribe, and he refused to let it go to waste. When he came back out, he took one of the buckets to wash and changed out of his muddy clothes.

The garments he donned were familiar to him—they'd used to belong to his eldest brother, Zeke. At five years old, Tir had thought his brother a giant. Zeke had used to laugh, picking Tir up one-armed to show off how big and strong he was; had carried him on his shoulders and pretended to forget Tir was there. He'd died a year after their tribe had fled the city, his soul devoured by a demon. Now, Tir couldn't reconcile the memory of his brother with the clothes he'd put on. They were too small to have belonged to him, surely, but the ornate letter Z embroidered into the collar didn't lie.

By the time he'd returned to the palace hall, Liadan had started a fire, and set out their pallets and a small meal. She wasn't eating. Instead, she scanned the shadows for unseen threats.

"Keep the fire going and we will be safe," he said. "Demons fear light. They will not come near us while we're inside it."

Liadan scowled. "You could have said so." She got up and, sparking fire in both hands, went back into the orchard to call the horses. Once they'd clattered inside, she set fire to the ground along the entryway. "There, that'll keep them out."

"For a while." From that side, at least. The look she gave him made Tir laugh. "Eat. We are as safe here as anywhere." And while she ate, he retrieved the aloe leaves he'd gathered and cut a silk scarf into strips.

"What are those, anyway?"

He came to her side of the fire, pulled out his eating knife and, with a few careful slices of the blade, exposed the leaf's soft, juicy center, squeezing the excess juice into a small container he'd brought from the pantry. "Give me your feet."

"No, I need them."

Tir scowled.

Liadan rolled her eyes, proffered one foot, and he winced at the amount of damage it'd sustained in just one day. She'd not complained a single time, and he knew she'd been running over thorns and shards in the orchard, not to mention the hard, scorching city ground.

"There's no need for this, you know. They'll be healed by morning."

"Perhaps," he allowed. "But what if we need to run before then?"

Liadan made a face, but didn't protest when he dipped a cloth into the closest bowl of water to wash the wounds of dirt and dried blood. The skin was tender and cut up, redder than he would have liked.

"Urine helps," Liadan said, and when he looked at her, horrified, she shrugged. "That's what we use at home to stave off infection."

He shuddered. "Animals." Liadan laughed, coaxing a smile from him in return. "My people use honey." Since he didn't have any, though, he instead applied the aloe—it'd soothe the cuts and help them heal, but she'd have to be careful. Using clean silks, he tied strips of the leaf core to her soles and helped her put shoes on. "Try not to walk on them tonight, if you can help it."

"Don't worry, I won't run away into the night to battle demons on my own."

How easily she jested about things she didn't understand. "See that you don't."

The night was eerily quiet. Even without people, there ought to have been some noise—the hiss of insects, the squeak of bats, even the unearthly howl of wild dogs would have been preferable to this silence.

Tir hadn't slept a full night since before Sadirak, and his head dipped lower and lower until he dozed off where he sat, weary to his very soul.

Danna Tir...

Tir jerked awake.

Liadan blinked at him, bleary-eyed. "Sleep. I can tend the fire."

It must have been a dream; his mind was playing tricks on him. Settling a blanket about his shoulders, he lay down and closed his eyes.

Danna... danna Tir...

Half-asleep already, Tir tilted his head back toward the source of the childish voice.

In the middle of the gaping entryway stood a small girl dressed in dirty rags, long, matted hair covering half of her face. He sat up so quickly, his head spun, and Liadan started. "What is it?"

"Meagara bahran a mi, danna Tir." Please help me, uncle Tir.

"Tir? What's the matter?"

At Liadan's voice, the girl gasped and ran.

"No, wait!" Tir stumbled to his feet after her.

"Tir!"

He followed the girl out of the palace and into the streets, heedless of the dark night closing in on him. One of his kin needed help; Tir didn't stop to think how a child so small had found her way here alone. She was fast. He almost lost her as she weaved between buildings, but he kept going. "Wait! Please, I won't hurt you!"

Her sobbing cry broke his heart. He ran faster to catch up to her, and found her around the next corner, huddled with her back to him against a wall at the end of the pass. Her little shoulders rose and fell with harsh breaths. He stopped so as not to startle her. Then, moving ever so slowly, he approached the weeping child. "What is your name?" he asked in their tongue. "Where is your mother?"

"Dead," she wailed.

His step faltered.

Liadan slammed into him, almost knocking him over. "What—"

"*Shh!*" He righted her, never taking his eyes off the girl who'd now turned toward them. He still couldn't see her face. "What is your name, little one?"

"Tir…" Liadan warned.

He waved her away. "Go on, you can tell me."

"I have none," the girl said.

Liadan tugged at his shirt. "Tir, we should go back."

He brushed her off. "Don't tell me you're afraid of a child," he said, then turned back to the girl. "How can that be, dear one? Everyone has a name."

"Help me." She reached both bone-thin arms out to him. "Please help me, uncle Tir."

He opened his arms to her in return, but Liadan knocked them down and grabbed his wrist, her nails digging into his skin. "Children have feet!" she snarled.

Tir looked down to where he was certain he'd seen the child's toes curl into the dirt. There was nothing. She stood there, yet she didn't; the ragged bottom edge of her overlarge shirt hovered above the ground like a spectre.

"Please help me, uncle Tir. I am so hungry." The girl moved forward, her body swaying as if she'd taken a step, but as the wind billowed her shirt, it revealed no legs to carry her meager weight.

A fireball flew from Liadan's hand and struck the child, who stumbled back a step, head bowed to look down at her charred shirt.

"Run," Liadan said.

Tir backed up a step as the child tipped her head sideways, then snapped it up, her face contorting into a monstrous demon as her jaw unhinged, baring rows upon rows of needle-sharp fangs. And she screeched so loud, Tir almost fell to his knees.

"*Run!*" Liadan screamed, pulling him along when he tripped over his own feet.

They raced back toward the palace as more of those unearthly screams echoed throughout the city. Tir felt them gathering, closing in on them, like a swift frost creeping along the ground. Liadan started glowing, all but the hand she had on his arm turning bright hot to illuminate the passageways. She veered left and, with a blast of heat, set fire to an old barrel. Back right and an old sack of wood chips exploded in a burst of light.

One more turn, and they were on the main path to the palace. Shadows with gray, skeletal faces and glowing red eyes swarmed between them and the safety of those walls, their fury palpable, their claws and fangs glinting in the night. Tir had seen them before, knew well what they could do, and that knowledge made him falter.

Liadan squeezed his arm, nails digging harder into his flesh, forcing his gaze away from the ravenous swarm to focus on her. He twisted free and clasped hands with her instead, fingers entwined so tightly, they wouldn't be separated unless a blade sliced them apart. "We need fire!"

Flames burst from her in a bright flare. "Don't let go, and don't stop!"

The flames licked across her arm over to him, covering him like second skin, and Tir gasped to feel their heat—heat, but not pain. The protection of Liadan's blood held steady, keeping him safe within her fire, and she stoked it as bright as their mad dash would allow, building a shield in the front, with long tendrils trailing around to cover their backs.

Demons screeched and scattered as Tir and Liadan ran headlong through the swarm. All around, Dark shadows swooped down time and again, trying to sink their claws through the flames. Scraps of darkness caught aflame, forcing them back, incensing them further, but Liadan's protection held.

They ran up the palace stairs, and Liadan barred the entrance with a wall of fire so high, the flames licked at the ceiling. Before Tir had even caught his breath, she did the same with the orchard doorway, and then the hallways at either end. Only when she was certain they were safe did she extinguish their living shield and release him.

He was about to thank her, when her hand cracked across his cheek. Anger blazed in her eyes, hotter than her flames.

Demons howled outside, battering themselves against the fiery curtain, while Liadan stared him down without a word, daring him to break the silence. "Never—again," she grated after a while. "Do you hear me? We move together. We fight together. You do not run out on your own—"

"The way you did?" he shot back.

She struck out again, but this time, Tir caught her hand. Liadan broke his hold and shoved at his chest, hard enough to make him step back. "My risk was a calculated one and posed danger to no one but me! Yours could have killed us both, you thoughtless, arrogant—*argh!*" She left him to pace back and forth between one flaming doorway and the other. The demons' cries intensified whenever she neared one of them.

Liadan fisted her hands in her hair. "How long will they keep screaming like that?"

"Until the sun forces them back into hiding," he begrudged.

Her hands lowered uneasily, and she eyed the barrier she'd erected. "My fire didn't kill it," she said softly.

"No, it did not."

With those words, the fragile hope he'd nurtured to be bringing salvation back to his tribe, died.

CHAPTER 21

Neither of them slept a wink that night. Beyond Liadan's fear that the fires would go out if she closed her eyes, the demons were too loud to allow for rest. So many of them floated through the air; shadows and scraps blacker than the night, colder than ice, but at the same time, burning with a darkness Liadan had never encountered before.

And all she could think was: *My fire didn't kill them.* Hadn't even harmed the one masquerading as a child. Her entire strategy to defeat the demons had been to burn them. But if blades couldn't defeat them and fire couldn't harm them, what else could she do? And if fire couldn't kill them, why did it keep them out? Were the demons toying with them? She could believe it. Sometimes, when the fires parted just a little, she could see those soulless eyes staring at her, picking her out.

Though the demons were nigh indistinguishable through the fiery curtain, the longer they raged, the more familiar their voices became. She recognized the child by the way it wailed at the very edge of her flames, coming closer than any of the others; a steady, black shadow staring at her without cease, promising revenge.

She could pick out the ones who'd tried to score her back with their claws—they cawed in challenge with voices so powerful, they lured Tir to the fiery wall. He didn't cross, but when he retreated to her in the center of the room, he looked shaken, haunted. Worried he'd step through if she dozed off, Liadan coaxed him to sit beside her, linked her arm through his and sang bawdy drinking songs to drown out the demonic howls.

She knew the demons who'd eventually destroy her. They were the ones who, instead of ramming the fiery barricades, flew around the palace, searching for another way in. Several had already darkened the hallways, their screams echoing inside the palace. She felt the icy chill of those above them, heard them claw at the floor to dig their way through.

The worst of it came before dawn, when the demons' screeches began to sound human. Liadan flinched to hear three men scream in terror, then shivered with dread when, for a moment afterwards, the night fell deathly silent.

By the time the sun had chased them all back into hiding, Liadan was cramped from head to toe, and never so happy to see daylight. Tir stood first, wordlessly offering his hand to help her up, and she took it, wincing at the pins and needles in her legs. Tir steadied her, held her fast, when she would have pulled away. Startled, she met his gaze in silent question. Without a word, without looking away, he lifted her hand to his lips, then pressed it to his chest over his heart.

Humbled by the show of gratitude, she nodded a half-bow. "One life debt repaid. Only one left to go."

"There is no debt between us, *shai'iss*. But if there was, it would be mine. And I could never repay it, if I were to live a thousand years."

"*Shai'iss*? What does that mean?" Though Liadan was a quick study, she still had a way to go to fully comprehend the intricacies of the Aegiran language. One thing she'd come to understand, however: words beginning with that particular sound were usually associated with honor and respect. *Shansher*—king. *Sher'nah*—prince.

The brief smile Tir allowed never reached his eyes. "One day, perhaps I will tell you."

It was too dangerous for them to stay in the palace another night. After a quick, small meal, they gathered their supplies, studiously avoiding each other.

Tir checked the well and found it dry again. Deeper into the orchard, however, he found a two-wheeled cart in good shape. "From here on, we follow the riverbed. It is as good as a road, and will lead us to Imarah."

Liadan helped him load the cart with their supplies. All of their water was contained in three buckets, six earthen bottles, and whatever they'd brought with them to the First City. Five more canisters of oil were just enough to fill the cart's empty spaces, and a pile of clothes and blankets stuffed in between steadied the load.

Sleipnir and Tarabas had spooked badly the night before and now shivered, stepping out of the palace. Liadan spoke to her mount, touched him often for reassurance, but kept close watch on the shadows. She wanted to believe the demons were gone but couldn't convince herself of that when she kept seeing their eyes in every dark window and doorway.

Tir caught her hand when it began to smoke. "Save your strength. You will need it for the night."

"How much farther to Imarah?"

"Two days, perhaps two and a half with the cart." He eyed the rickety thing, which was serviceable enough, but jarred the load with each turn of the wheels. To preserve as much water as possible, Tir had covered the buckets with large platters and weighed them down with rocks, but it still seeped out through chips and chinks along the rim.

"Is it wise to be bringing it with us?" They could ride faster without it. Liadan didn't like the thought of getting caught out in the desert night again.

"It is never wise to leave water behind in the desert."

Liadan sighed. She knew that, of course, but last night's demon swarm had left her rattled and she couldn't help the urgency thrumming in her limbs, commanding her to move faster, to run away. Tir had warned her it would happen, and she flushed anew to remember how cavalierly she'd dismissed his words back in Wilderheim, thinking herself invincible.

Perhaps she was, but so, it seemed, were the demons.

Worry about them later, she told herself. *For now, focus on reaching Imarah.*

Tir wasn't the only one who'd ever had the idea of using the river as a road. At almost equidistant intervals, someone had built ramps down into the basin. Many were weathered and broken, but several still looked sturdy enough to be useful. With the cart between them, Tarabas and Sleipnir had to step carefully to avoid breaking a leg, but they managed, and Liadan breathed a sigh of relief when both horses and cart were firmly on the hard, clay bottom.

Dolls and wooden toys lay broken and trampled along the riverbed. Chests of treasures had been tossed aside as too useless to carry. Shattered cart wheels lay everywhere, but also weapons and saddles. “My people used the river to flee the city,” Tir explained.

Liadan imagined the tribe making their way east, children crying for their homes, women hunched under the burden of their earthly belongings; she could almost see dead horses on the north bank, men stumbling around, driven mad by thirst.

Eyes and ears sharp for threats, they walked quickly out of the First City. Solid buildings became sparse and the farther they went, the less debris they found, until all evidence of humans having come this way disappeared. What once used to be a fertile valley was now dried to dust; nothing smaller than a tree remained, and those had long ago fallen over, having lost all moisture until they littered the valley floor like bones.

Soon, they lost sight of the city, and Liadan’s apprehension of the setting sun redoubled. She wanted to move faster, to get as far as they could before night fell, but it would do no good. Darkness begot darkness. The demons they’d seen last night could just as easily come crawling out of the cart’s shadows, if they didn’t fear the light.

“You are quiet,” Tir said.

“What is there to say?”

“You need not worry. You are protected by the brave Tirasdunh al-Dhakir, remember? No harm will come to you here.”

His attempt to cheer her up didn’t have the intended effect. “One thing we never discussed, *sher’nah*, is what will happen if neither of us is able to fulfill our oath.”

“That will not happen.”

“But it might—”

“It will not,” he snapped, and stopped the horses to face her. “I swore I would keep you safe, and I do not intend to fail.”

“And what about me?”

Tir brushed back a stubborn lock of her hair, his thumb caressing her cheek. “You said you would do all in your power to aid us.”

“My power is fire, and we both saw how weak a weapon it turned out to be.”

“Did you not also tell me you have never tested its limits? You said it was too dangerous to try.” He gestured all around them. “Nobody here to harm. No homes to destroy.”

Had it been an order, Liadan would have fought him. But Tir had offered the possibility as an invitation and she was more than tempted to take him up on it. In Wilderheim, too many trees posed a hazard, and too many people and animals were in danger of being hurt. Here, as Tir had said, there was nothing.

Liadan looked to Sleipnir. “What do you think?”

Sleipnir snorted and nosed her sideways, all but shooing her away.

Tir took the reins from her. "Keep in sight of us, if you can. We will not stray from the riverbed. And if there is trouble, I expect you to scream."

"Likewise," she said.

With a bracing breath and watchful of anything out of the ordinary, Liadan crossed to the north bank and climbed out of the basin onto the hard desert ground. She kept step with Tir below, but let him take over the watch as she turned her sight inward.

Never before had Liadan questioned where her fire came from. Her soul felt like a tangible entity—a molten, fiery core swirling in endless eddies, flaring and condensing to mirror her moods. It fed her blood, and licked along the inside of her skin. She closed her eyes, imagining that core growing larger and hotter, and in her mind's eye, it slowly changed colors from red to gold, from gold to blue. The heat of it filled her chest, spread out into her limbs. The sun's rays were nothing compared to the inferno she stoked within her.

It frightened Liadan, made her stumble. There'd be no controlling such a fire if she let it loose. Worse than the firestorm of her moon cycle, which consumed only her, this blaze would explode outward as far as her soul could reach, and absolutely nothing living would escape it. If she lost control, Liadan could burn this world to ash.

Hands shaking, she pulled the fire back. It fought her control, refusing to be banked and imprisoned, now that it'd tasted the freedom of fresh air, the power it could hold, and the battle with herself left her breathless. Too much too quickly, and she tripped over her own feet, falling to her knees, gasping. But her fire was contained.

Down in the riverbed, Tir sent her an encouraging nod.

To stop would mean disappointing him.

Liadan pushed to her feet, closed her eyes again. When she reached for her soul's flames a second time, she drew out only a little, and in her hand, it swelled into a ball as large as her head. Bit by bit, she grew and shrank it, testing the ease with which the flame could be manipulated.

Red fire was the easiest; it was the coolest, and warmed rather than burned. Yellow fire was more willful; like the sun in the sky, it warmed from a distance, but too much or too close, and it began to burn. This was the fire she'd hurled at the demon last night and it'd done little more than tickle the thing.

Liadan shrank the orb. The smaller it was, the hotter it burned, until a bright blue marble circled around in her palm, jumped up and down, and then, of its own accord, levitated out of her grasp and shot into the sky. She'd lost it. "Bollocks!"

"What do you need?" Tir called.

"Something to hold the flame," she returned.

In answer, Tir tossed her sword up to the bank.

Liadan stared at the blade by her feet, while Tir moved on with the horses and the cart. Between one breath and another, she lit on an idea. The dragon had spelled the blade to be fireproof. She picked it up, called a small flame into her free hand, and polished the blade with it as she would with oil. As the steel heated, it caught the flame and held.

Liadan raised the sword aloft, swung it left to right, concentrating on the fire, and grinned from ear to ear when it didn't extinguish. She tried a combination or two; slowly at first, then at her fastest. The blade and the fire held.

With a few running steps, she caught up to Tir and kept pace with him as she gradually fed the blade more heat. Red flames turned yellow, then to blue, and still they held. She dragged the tip along the ground, charring a thin, black line alongside her path.

With the blade upside down, the flames licked up to her hand, coating it, and she eased them up to her elbow, but no farther. When her sleeve began to smolder, she was forced to extinguish her experiment. Liadan was fireproof, but her clothing was not, and she couldn't afford to lose another pair of shoes.

After wiping soot from her blade, she returned to the basin and accepted the waterskin Tir handed her. "Well?"

"I suppose we'll find out when the sun goes down."

CHAPTER 22

When the shadows turned long, it became too dangerous to continue. Their pace had brought them to a fork in the riverbed, a natural rest stop, where remnants of old fires still marked the red clay with black soot. Tir remembered this place only too well; it was one of his earliest memories from childhood.

The night his tribe had stopped here, there'd been no music, only the sound of a people mourning—women had wailed, children had screamed, men had argued. Fights had broken out over which way the tribe should go come morning. Many had believed there'd be water and hope where the river branched out into creeks, and they'd hoped to find another flood plain like the one that had sprouted the river at the foot of the Silver Mountain to the west.

But Dhakir al-Bashir, Dhakir the Conqueror, hadn't wanted to stray from their eastward path, convinced their salvation lay where the sun was born each morning. Surely the source of light and life would succor them and restore their strength. He'd described visions sent to him by the gods each night, of black caves deep underground, caverns where crystalline lakes glistened and diamonds glittered in the walls.

Those who'd heard him had been scandalized—they were desert people, not cave dwellers!—and fights had become brawls, which had grown into a small revolt. In their fear and desperation, the once-proud people had turned on each other like savage beasts, tearing into one another worse than any demon could. By dawn, the tribe had split into two, each half going its own separate way.

To this day, Tir didn't know what had become of those who'd gone south, following the lead of Khiron, Dhakir's last remaining brother.

"Do you think they'll follow us?" Liadan asked as they dragged a dead tree down into the basin for firewood.

"I do not know."

When they dropped the wood onto a charred patch of red clay, Liadan worriedly wiped her hands on her pants. "There won't be enough."

The firewood would last through the night, but Tir knew she wasn't talking about that. Fire only burned with something to hold the flame. In the absence of wood or oil, Liadan could sustain a blaze, but for how long? Already she'd tired herself out practicing throughout the day, and neither of them had slept the night before. Tir was exhausted, and could only imagine the weariness Liadan must have felt.

She wiped the sweat from her brow with one shaky hand. With the other, she clutched the vial her brother had given her, and Tir didn't need to hear her thoughts to know what they were. "You are afraid."

"I'm tired," she lied. "That's not the same thing."

Tarabas fidgeted, tossing his head, prancing left and right. Tir went to soothe him, and glimpsed a familiar sight to the north. "Liadan!" He raced back and began to unload the cart.

"What are you doing?"

He grinned at her. "Help me turn the cart over."

"What?" She tossed pouches and bundles to the ground, and carefully arranged bottles to one side.

"No, over here. We need to cover them with the cart."

"Have you lost your mind?"

Tir only laughed.

For all its age, the cart was damned heavy, and when they tipped it over, they had to carefully manipulate it to keep it from buckling under its own weight. With their belongings safely stowed, Tir unsaddled the horses. "Find my tent and put your veil on."

"Why do I have a very bad feeling about this?"

"Because you are a smart woman. There's a dust storm coming."

"And you want to outrun it?"

Taking the tent from her, Tir herded Liadan toward the north bank. "That would be a waste of a perfectly good storm," he said. "Keep close to me."

"What about the horses?"

"We have to leave them behind." Horses had better instincts when it came to natural phenomena. They'd be better off on their own than where Tir planned to take Liadan: straight into the heart of the storm.

She saw the billowing wall of sand rushing to meet them, and gasped, stopping in her tracks. They needed to reach the dunes before the storm washed over them. Tir grabbed her hand and dragged her along, running as fast as his feet could carry him. They reached soft sand with mere moments to spare, and Tir quickly pitched the small tent. Not enough to cover more than their upper bodies if they stretched out, but that's all they needed. The storm was almost upon them with a roar so loud he couldn't make himself heard, and winds so powerful they snatched at his clothes and hair.

Liadan fought him, refusing to go into the tent, but Tir wrestled her down into the shelter just as its sides bowed inward with the force of the storm. Her eyes widened, and she gasped for breath. She snatched off her veil, clawed at the tent wall. "W-we're getting buried!"

"Shh," he soothed, catching her flailing hands against his chest so she could feel his steady heartbeat. "We're getting hidden."

Liadan shook her head, struggling to free herself. "No! We'll die!"

"Liadan—"

"And Sleipnir—the demons—"

"Liadan, stop!"

"—they'll kill him!"

Tir silenced her frantic tirade with a kiss, and Liadan stilled against him so completely, she stopped breathing. Her heart raced, pulse throbbing in her lips against his. Tir had only needed her to calm down before she fainted, but once he'd had a taste of her, he wanted more. Shifting closer, he tangled his hand in her wild hair, pulling her tight against his body, relishing the way her hands curled into his shirt.

Little by little, she softened, and he rubbed soothing circles over her back until the fear had ebbed out of her. Until she kissed him back.

But all too soon she pushed away. Tir allowed her enough room to break their kiss, but not enough to pull out of his embrace. "Have you changed your mind about taking an Other as your mate?" she asked.

Tir's mind was slow to catch up to her words.

She took his silence for an answer and shifted farther away, as far as the small tent would allow. "Then you shouldn't do that again."

⯬ »·◇·« ⯮

At its strongest, the sandstorm tore at their meager shelter, winds howling worse than the demons had the night before. Still, the worst of it came when all sounds dulled to almost nothing. Liadan's legs had become buried in the sand, its weight pinning her in place. In the tomb-like darkness, she desperately pushed against the tent wall, marking the depth of the sand by the amount of resistance she met. Tir had set the tent with one corner against the coming storm to carve a wedge into its force. Had he built it with the flat side facing north, the cloth would have torn apart in moments.

As it was, Liadan schooled herself not to panic. From the floor of the tent, she traced the cloth up to the height of her shoulder. Nothing but a solid wall on the other side. A few hand widths farther up, still more sand. Liadan paused, glancing to where the tent's ceiling marked her final hope in two meager hand widths. With a shuddering breath, she licked her dry lips, then eased her hand higher. At the very top, barely two finger widths of cloth depressed into a softer layer. Still not emptiness, but enough to tell her the surface was within reach.

The bastard Aegiran had buried them! A small sound escaped her, and she held her breath to contain more of them. But her fire betrayed her weakness. As her fear rose, Liadan began to glow, illuminating the cramped space. Had it somehow gotten smaller?

She pushed at that small patch of tent, testing its give to reassure herself that there was still a way out.

Tir curled his fingers around hers to stop the frantic movement. "Be at ease," he said. "Sleep."

"Will that make dying easier?" She couldn't take a deep enough breath to satisfy her lungs; they screamed for air, but with each gasp, there was less of it, and the tent walls were pressing closer with the weight of the entire desert.

"We will not die," he insisted, pulling her hand down and to her front. With his chest against her back, he embraced her, speaking quietly into her ear. "Every storm passes eventually. Every fear can be overcome. Close your eyes, and see yourself standing on the surface."

Struggling for breath, Liadan closed her eyes, firming her chin against a quiver.

"Can you see it?"

She imagined the hard, cracked ground they'd crossed to get to the sand dunes, and pretended her feet now pushed against its sturdy surface.

"Feel the sun on your face. Breathe in the hot air." Tir's voice was so steady, its timbre reassuring enough to calm her mind.

Liadan inhaled, and by some miracle, her throat opened, allowing for a full breath. She let it out slowly, then tried again, picturing herself soaring on the dragon's back. She grasped on to the vision, with the whole of the sky open to her, every which way she looked, and Tir at her back, flying with her. For a moment, lost in thought, her body felt lighter, cushioned by feathery clouds; her quick heartbeat echoed her exhilaration, not her fear, and Tir's arms were a welcome embrace. She reformed her courage from his strength, found comfort in his voice, and slowly released her fear, placing her trust wholly in him. And for just a moment, Liadan felt at peace. Despite the near-suffocation inside the tent, Tir's words lulled her, and she began drifting off to sleep.

And then the first demonic scream reverberated through the night sky.

Liadan gasped, tensing against Tir.

"Be still," he said, pulling her closer. "They will not find us here. Not before the morning sun forces them back into hiding."

"B-but they're out there," she replied.

"Yes."

"That means the storm has passed." Which meant they could get out! How the bloody hell did he intend to get them out? And why wasn't he doing it?

His stubbled cheek rasped against hers in a smile. "Yes. Now we need only wait for morning light."

What? No! "I can protect us," she said quickly, clawing at the tent to get free. "If we dig our way out, I can make another shroud like before. The demons won't touch us—"

"You would choke us on smoke before we managed to dig ourselves clear. You must be patient." He pulled her hands down a second time, and a third when she fought free of him.

"I can't breathe!"

He caught her hands one more time, pressing them to her chest with his arms around her, binding them in place so she couldn't move. "Then how can you speak?"

Liadan shut her mouth. Her struggles eased, but her mind still raced with the possibility of getting out, breathing real air.

"Try to sleep," Tir said. "In the morning, this will all have been a dream."

"How can you be so calm?"

He smiled. "What should I be instead? Sometimes in battle, all you can do is wait. During the ordeal of *kharashan*—"

"The ordeal of what?"

"Our tribe used to train some of the fiercest warriors in Aegiros. They were legion, back in the day. When we were driven out of the First City, most of the *kharesh* took the path south with my uncle and his family. He was the one who'd trained them all. He thought my father was mad for continuing east, downstream of a dead river. Only Farraj and a few others chose to stay with the *shansher*. They had sworn their lives to him, and refused to break their oath. My father knew strife would follow us, and so he ordered Farraj to continue training the men in the same way they had always been trained. He does so to this day."

Liadan absorbed all of this in silence.

Tir waited for her to offer an opinion, and when she didn't, he continued. Speaking of his people was a balm to his restless soul. While they were still in his mind, they were still alive. "When men train with the *kharesh*, they are not called as such. They are still only men. To become true *kharesh*, they must pass the ordeal of *kharashan*. We hold these rites sacred, and each man must face the ordeal on his own. Some succeed and become *kharesh*. Some fail, and return to their family homes in shame. A few, too foolish or proud to admit defeat, fight to the death in hopes of making it through."

"You are one of them now, yes?"

He grunted in answer.

"You must have found it easy, being the prince of your tribe."

Tir tempered his laugh into a chuckle. "Hardly. The *kharesh* make no exceptions for anyone, regardless of station. When I faced my ordeal, I still had two older brothers who would have led the tribe after my father's death. I was no better than any other in training, and I was treated no differently."

"I see."

"Do you?" he replied, greatly amused. "Would it surprise you to hear I almost died during the ordeal?" In truth, he should have died. He'd been too young, forced into the *kharashan* too soon, because Imarah had needed every man they could spare. But that was no excuse. A true *kharesh* was always prepared, no matter what the circumstances. His ordeal had lasted three days, and by the end of it, he'd been reduced to crawling back to his tent, too weak and too sick to walk upright. But he'd made it back. Five of the others had not, their bodies forever lost to the desert sands.

Liadan replied with a thoughtful hum.

In the ensuing silence, demons swooped down toward the sands, screaming their rage. Liadan gasped, tensing in his arms.

"What does that mean, *hmm*?" he asked to distract her.

Her breathing ragged, she said, "I-I was only thinking of my grandfather, and what he would have made of the *kharesh*."

"Was the dragon's training any easier for you, being his granddaughter?"

"Ha! I think not. And if he ever says otherwise, he is a gods damned liar."

The demons quieted for a moment.

"He thinks I'm cursed, you know," she continued, and from the way she said it, Tir couldn't be certain of her meaning. There was a definite note of mockery in her voice, but also unease, as if she herself couldn't decide whether or not to give it credence. "Halflings are always complicated. When Fal and I were born, the dragon thought to spare us a lifetime of anguish. He fed us a drop of his blood to settle our magic and make it easier to control. It had the opposite effect. More so in Fal than me, but you've already seen proof of that. To this day, the dragon swears on the soul of his mate that some outside force must have interfered, else it never would have turned out the way it had."

"Why is your brother so different?"

She sighed. "Perhaps because of our elements. Fire is volatile, but also short-lived. It needs to be nurtured into a blaze, and when its fuel is removed, it burns out. Water is eternal. It flows infinite and holds no shape of its own. It is life itself."

"Water can extinguish fire," Tir said.

"Yes," Liadan replied. "If there's enough of it, even the fiercest blaze will die in its path."

"This does not worry you?"

"Why should it?"

"Your brother's power is unpredictable; he could kill yours without meaning to."

"Never. We are Dragonblood at heart. We are not only twins in body, but in soul, as well. To kill me, he would kill part of himself." Liadan rolled her shoulders, shrugging off his hold. "I'm all right now. You can let go."

"What if I do not want to?"

"You should," she said gravely.

"I would not have expected a woman as brave as you to be shy of a man's touch."

"Perhaps I simply don't like yours."

Her sharp retort hit its mark only too well, and Tir released her, shifting to the other side of the tent to put as much space between them as their shelter would allow. "So fire does burn after all."

Liadan said nothing. She curled in on herself, away from him, and as she did, her glow dimmed, leaving them in darkness once again.

CHAPTER 23

They judged the time of night by the demons above the sands. Whenever their dervish died down, it heartened Liadan that they could start digging their way out, but then the noise picked up once more and with such force, she felt as though they were right on top of the tent.

They screamed for so long, she feared the sun would never rise again. But eventually it did, forcing the demons back into hiding. After a sufficient amount of time had passed, Tir declared it safe to reemerge. "Move over," he said, and Liadan shifted as close as she could to the tent wall.

Tir grunted, moved around, elbowing her a few times as he carefully extricated his legs from the sand. Crouching free, he tore into the tent's top on his side, and light flooded in. Liadan cried out, looking over her shoulder. The sands were nowhere near as high there as they were on her side, and Tir crawled out easily, then reached back in for her. Grasping her forearms, he pulled her out, a task much more difficult than it had been for himself, but once she stood in the sun, Liadan wanted to weep with joy. She turned in circles, clutching the vial of water in one fist, thanking the gods for allowing her to see the sky again.

"We made it!" She whooped and laughed.

When Tir didn't reply, Liadan turned around. He was already walking away from her, the torn remnants of their tent tucked under his arm. He gave a shrill whistle to summon Tarabas, but kept heading toward the riverbed, leaving Liadan to her own devices.

"Are you angry with me?" she called after him, rushing to catch up.

"No." He whistled again.

"You are! Why are you angry?"

"I am not angry with you," he said.

Liadan shook her head. "You might as well tell me. I won't stop asking until you do."

Tir rounded on her. "I am angry with myself!" he snapped. "For allowing myself to be distracted from my goal. For wasting my thoughts on you, when I should be thinking about how to save my people." His face darkened with the force of his words. "What do you want from me, Princess?"

"Nothing!"

"So you say. Yet you've done nothing but try to seduce me ever since we have ridden out of Frastmir. You lure me closer, then you push me away and turn your back. I'm sick of it!"

Taken aback, Liadan gaped. "*I* try to seduce *you*?"

"Bah!" Tir threw his hands up in the air and walked away from her.

"Wait!" Running to catch up a second time, she grabbed his arm, but he shook her off.

"Tarabas!" There was no sign of either horse.

"Tir, stop!" Liadan pulled ahead of him to bar his way, to force him to meet her gaze, but he slipped sideways around her. "What do *you* want?" she called out, tired of chasing him through the desert.

Tir halted in his tracks.

"I know my sole purpose here is supposed to be to save your people, but is that all you really want from me—you, not your tribe? Is that why you kiss me for every time I kiss you? Why you looked at me just now as if I broke your heart?"

His hands fisted at his sides, shoulders rising and falling with deep breaths. He wouldn't face her, staring off into the distance while he composed himself.

"Play the innocent victim of my heathen wiles if you want, *sher'nah*, but let's have it all out now and settle things between us before we move on." This time, when she stepped closer, he didn't move away. "Tell me I offended you with my forwardness. Tell me being so close to me is unacceptable. Tell me a prince of Aegiros would never stoop to desiring a Northerner who so readily accepts a man's touch. And then tell me why you so readily give it anyway."

A few more steps brought her up to his right, and his gaze flickered sideways before it skittered away again. His jaw was set, his arms taut at his sides.

"I don't say this to challenge or offend you," she said, voice lowered. "I say it, because when we reach Imarah, none of it will matter anymore."

Tir turned to her, his mouth, not long ago so soft and warm, now set in a thin, angry line. And still she saw how hard he fought himself to hold on to that anger, even as his gaze warmed, if only a little. It saddened her, and softened her voice further still, almost down to a whisper. "Out here, only the sky and sand can see us, and one man and one woman mean little enough to them. Among your tribe, you will no longer be just a man; you will be their prince. I will be a stranger at best, an enemy at worst, and you will need to convince them otherwise. Can you look them in the eye and make them believe I can be trusted, when in your heart, you resent me?"

The tension in his shoulders dissolved. "Resentment, Princess, is the farthest thing from my mind."

Hers, as well. But Liadan couldn't tell him so, lest she kindle a hope that would destroy them both. "Remember Geir?" she said instead.

"Remember the ember?" he returned.

With an ear-piercing whinny, Sleipnir bounded toward them from the south with Tarabas on his heels. Liadan was immensely relieved both horses had weathered the storm. Sleipnir almost knocked her off her feet with his nuzzle, and Liadan embraced him around the neck, then ran her hands down his back and sides, checking for injuries. Aside from being covered in a thick layer of dust, the mount was perfectly all right. "Hello, handsome," she crooned. "I've missed you."

Sleipnir snorted and tossed his head, throwing off a cloud of dust.

They walked the horses back to the river basin and to their cart of supplies which, to Liadan's surprise, was still there, exactly as they'd left it. When they turned the cart onto its wheels once more, the buckets and canisters underneath were still whole. Parched, Liadan snatched up one of the waterskins and drank her fill, throwing caution to the wind as Tir and the horses did the same.

"We lost about half of our water to the desert," Tir said after a while. They'd likely lose even more along the way.

"Do we have enough left to reach Imarah?"

"Difficult to say," he hedged. "We have another day's ride to find them; plenty of water left for that."

"But no telling what we'll find when we get there," she finished for him, "if anything."

Or anyone, Tir thought, rubbing his chest to soothe away the pain of it. Anything could have happened to his tribe while he'd been away, and the dust storm would have been the least of it.

"But that's not all that worries you, is it?" Liadan said gravely.

Tell her, his mind urged. *Tell her everything.* Yet his heart refused. How could he tell her what he feared? That the dreams that troubled him nightly were a portent of the future. That he might be bringing her to his tribe, only to watch her die. That she truly might save them all from the demon plague, but at the cost of her life.

Every night before sleep, Tir prayed for guidance from the gods, and every night they sent him visions of fire. He'd sworn an oath to keep the princess safe. He'd also sworn one to bring salvation to his tribe. Tir was coming to understand he would have to break one of these oaths before long, something he'd never done in all of his life.

Instead of answering her, he said, "From here on, we will be riding through battleground. The Aesimar tribe has been riding on Imarah every chance they get. They have claimed territory between the First City and the eastern edge of the valley where my tribe now sits, and they patrol it tirelessly."

"I thought you said Imarah still claimed the First Valley as their home."

"Yes," he replied, "by virtue of our birthright. But we do not have the men to protect it. Most tribes have already heard of our curse, and fear of demons keeps them from the valley and our abandoned city. But Aesimar worships the dark god, Aesma Daeva, for whom demons are kindred spirits. They fear neither darkness, nor pain, nor death. They live for war and murder, and each of their kills is an offering to their god. And so, to honor Aesma, they keep attacking to crush our spirits, rather than to kill us all outright. They will continue to do so, until the last *kharesh* falls, and we become chattel. Until that time, we are still an enemy, worthy of sacrifice."

"Demons bent on devouring my soul, tribesmen out for my blood, is there anything else I should be wary of, that you have not yet mentioned?"

Tir scowled at her irreverence, but her unconcerned smile put him at ease. "Scorpions," he replied.

"Well, come on, then. It seems we have our work cut out for us." Liadan set about repositioning what was left of their supplies on the cart. Tir watched her try to wrestle an unwilling Sleipnir to pull the cart, but the stubborn horse rooted his hooves. She pulled his head close and spoke to him softly until he finally huffed and relented. And all the while, she showed not a morsel of unease; she hummed, for all the gods' sake! The same way she had on the ride into Dai, lying across Sleipnir's back as if everything was right with the world.

"Why are you so at ease?"

Liadan shrugged. "The wait is the worst. We're close enough now that I need not anticipate; I can plan. I like that much better."

Tir shook his head in disbelief. "Only a fool feels no fear when confronted with death."

Liadan grinned. "Death is easy," she replied, securing the cart's harness to Sleipnir. "It only concerns those who are left behind. Try living for endless ages after everyone you've ever cared about has passed on. My mother used to say she'd rather die a thousand deaths with my father, than live a thousand years without him." Her hands stilled on the pack she'd been about to tie to Sleipnir's saddle. Her shoulders tensed and she turned her face away.

"What is it?"

Liadan shook her head, but couldn't meet his gaze. "Nothing. We should head out. The farther we can get before noon, the better."

"As you wish," he replied. Checking to make certain they'd left nothing behind, he set an easy pace east along the riverbed. Liadan had strapped her sword and her dagger to her waist and draped a veil over her head, loosely looping it around her neck to keep it in place. She bore the heat as well as a Northerner could, and Tir had to admit he was glad to have brought her back with him.

But long after they'd left the last remnants of human settlements behind, Liadan was still tense and quiet, and wouldn't tell him what was bothering her. With one hand holding on to Sleipnir's reins and the other loose by her side, it wasn't battle readiness that affected her so. Her mind was far away, her gaze lost in some distance Tir couldn't breach; she might as well have been back in Frastmir.

At noon, when the heat had become unbearable, Tir pitched the remains of their tent and handed her a waterskin. But when she would have taken it from him, he held on. "Tell me your greatest fear," he said.

Liadan raised her chin a notch higher in challenge. "Tell me yours."

"I fear that, in the end, nothing I do will make a difference. I fear the gods have forsaken my tribe and will turn on anyone who tries to save it. And I fear that one day soon, I will stand alone on the crest of a dune, the last of my tribe, and watch the valley burn at the hands of Aesimar."

Liadan acknowledged this with a nod. "I fear losing the ones I love." With a wry smile, she added, "And I'm not very fond of being buried alive in sandstorms, either. Have I earned my drink now?"

Tir inclined his head, relinquishing the waterskin. When she handed it back, it was still heavy with water, and Tir drank as much as he dared, hoping his tribe had found another water source in his absence, though the odds were against it. "I should mention," he told Liadan, "Aegirans are very superstitious people."

"Superstitious? No!"

He grinned, welcoming the return of her good humor. "Yes, indeed. I know, it comes as a great surprise."

"You want me to hide my fire," she guessed.

"Yes. For your safety, as well as theirs. Save your flames for the demons. Please."

Liadan tilted her head. "What would they do to me if they knew what I can do?"

It didn't bear thinking. "The Imarah would kill you."

"They might *try*."

"Aesimar would seek to possess you. Their magic men are very powerful; they can summon *djinn*, even *daeva*, and keep them prisoner in chains that are inscribed with dark spells. Only the one who spelled them locked can unlock them again."

"And, being immortal, if I were to be taken, I might be enslaved for all time."

"Yes." He coughed to clear the coarseness from his throat.

She nodded and pushed to her feet. "Thank you. Forewarned is forearmed. We should get going."

"Even this does not frighten you?" he asked, baffled.

Liadan slowly turned to face him. "A few days before I left the dragon's cave, I had a strange dream. It frightened me at first, but the more I think about it, the more accepting I am of what I saw in it."

Tir's breath locked in his chest; his hands on the burning sands were suddenly cold with dread. "What did you see?" he made himself ask. It couldn't have been the same dream he'd been having each night.

"I think… I think I saw my true form, the way I would have looked had I been born in Otherlands, rather than in the human realm. This body is mine, but it's only one incarnation of my being. The other is a reflection of my true soul—the Halfling daughter of Halfling parents, a Dragonblood with human blood in her veins." She smiled, but her eyes were sad. "Believe me when I say, demons or raiders, dark gods or magic men, I am not the one who should be afraid."

CHAPTER 24

Where the river had cut its path through the valley, once-lush grounds were now as hard as rock, sun-baked by the incessant heat. To a certain distance on either side, the world was a flat and empty wasteland of otherworldly wrath. Beyond that, golden sands rose in great dunes, lapping ever closer as the desert reclaimed the river's former demesne.

And all was deathly quiet.

They passed the dead oasis where Imarah had camped. Not a scrap of their presence remained, save for mounds of fire ash. Tir hadn't expected to find them there; their water would have run out, as it always did, and forced them farther. He'd discussed it with Farraj before leaving for Wilderheim, and both had agreed the only choice was to keep heading eastward toward Temple Mountain. If any water remained in the valley's underground streams, with Inaras' blessing, they'd find it there. The mountain range was another day's ride away as the cart rattled, and as anxious as he was, Tir had to force himself to keep a steady pace.

The farther they went, the shallower the dry riverbed became, widening until he could no longer tell where it ended and desert began, and then the hard earth once again disappeared beneath a sand dune. It didn't burn their feet any less. Nor did the breeze offer any comfort from the day's heat.

"Say something," Liadan said. "I can't stand this silence."

"What should I say?" he returned.

"Anything. Sing, for all I care."

Tir chuckled and checked the sun's progress in the sky. Night would come quickly. He hoped they reached his tribe before then. His nape prickled with the unease of one being watched from a distance, and Tir swept his gaze across the dunes to the north and south, searching for any hint of people. He found none, but his mind's disquiet didn't ease.

"Well?" Liadan prodded, clutching Sleipnir's reins so hard, the mount tossed his head in agitation. Could she sense the same?

"Perhaps you should talk," he said. "You are much better at it than I."

Silence.

He frowned. "Princess?"

On the other side of the cart, Liadan squinted into the distance ahead. "Do you see that?"

Tir blinked hard, then looked where she pointed. On the horizon, with heat mirages obscuring the view, shimmered a dark spot—there one moment, gone the next, and then back again. "I do," he replied, but he wouldn't trust his eyes until they'd gotten much closer. He clucked his tongue, urging Tarabas on a little faster, and Sleipnir matched him.

"Is it your tribe?"

The shape solidified for a long enough moment for Tir to recognize the western mountain range. "It should be."

"That's good, isn't it? We made it."

Tir shook his head. "Something is wrong." The tumult of shadows writhed halfway in between, too far from Temple Mountain's oasis. He mounted Tarabas. "Keep going with the cart. I will ride ahead."

"Oh, no. You are not rushing out on your own again." Faster than he would have thought possible, Liadan unhitched Sleipnir from the cart and mounted. "We can come back for all of this later."

Rather than argue, he urged Tarabas into a gallop. With each mile they passed, the feeling of dread grew until they'd gotten close enough for Tir to see figures milling about. He sucked in a sharp breath. "Ride!" he shouted, digging his heels into Tarabas' sides. With a sharp whinny, the mount reared, giving Tir just enough time to draw his blade, and then he took off straight toward the embattled *kharesh*.

Behind him, Liadan whooped, a signal that propelled Sleipnir forward so fast he overtook Tarabas in moments.

Tir swore. "Wait!" He raced to catch up, but the princess wouldn't be stopped. She plunged into the fight with no care for consequences and without knowing which side to fight for. But as Sleipnir reared, his massive hooves striking out with enough force to instantly kill a man, Tir saw he needn't have worried. The Aesimar raiders had decked themselves out in full armor, all the better to intimidate, and wielded two blades each, both polished to a shine. In comparison, the starving Imarah wore nothing but their linens, their swords dirty and worn from long years of constant fighting. They were also vastly outnumbered. This was no raid. Had the Aesimar *shansher* finally lost his patience? If so, then this could be the end of Imarah.

Tir roared his battle cry and dove straight into the fight, keeping his seat on Tarabas' back for a better view and cutting through the enemy with cold efficiency. He evaded attackers unless he had a clear opening to kill, methodically working his way deeper into the throng, while Liadan cut outward and split the forces into two. Tir had no choice but to leave her to it. Aesimar wouldn't have attacked like this unless they'd sensed a mortal weakness, which could only mean one thing.

Dhakir the Conqueror was dead.

No, he wouldn't believe that until he saw it for himself. Tir shut his ears to the sounds of his people dying, refused to look at the half-pitched tents, torn and bloodied, with bodies lying dead inside. Aesimar must have caught them unawares as they were setting up camp for the night. Bloody cowards! Giving his back to an enemy he'd fought against his entire life, Tir rode straight for the camp's center, to the one tent that stood taller, larger than the rest. Dismounting at full gallop, he cut through five

Aesimar dogs to rush inside.

The walls billowed in the breeze. The carpets were covered in sand, and pillows were scattered around everywhere; large water jugs lay overturned and empty, and Dhakir's ebony seat was fallen over onto its side.

The tent was empty.

None of his father's possessions were there. Halima was gone, her veils and loom removed, probably to the women's tent, where she'd huddle in fear with the children and unwed women of the tribe.

Tir staggered back, but no matter how far he retreated, he couldn't escape the sight.

"To the south, Tir!" Farraj's voice broke through his shock, and Tir whirled around, expecting a blade to descend.

It didn't.

Instead, he watched the battle shift away from the camp and back in the direction of the Aesimar leader, who once again observed the fray from his high perch atop the crest of a sand dune. He was draped in pure white, his armor fashioned of polished gold, and from such a distance, he shone like the sun in stark contrast to the black mount beneath him. He looked like the Dark god himself, come to reap Tir's tribe from the face of Aegiros.

Then Sleipnir screamed, and Tir's gaze shifted lower, picking him out in the fight. He was riderless, striking out at those closest to him as if he'd been bred for battle, hooves crushing bones and bodies, massive girth shoving people aside, forcing them to retreat or die.

Where was Liadan?

"Stop gawking, boy, and move!" Farraj snapped, running forward to contain the damage. He limped, his clothes were stained with blood, and his left arm was bandaged. How many raids had the tribe endured in Tir's absence? How many of his tribesmen were still alive?

Tir clutched his sword tighter, drew his second and followed.

↞ »·◇·« ↠

Liadan rolled to her feet and charged the bastard who'd pulled her off her horse, running him through and turning on the next. These were trained fighters—fearless, methodical, and without mercy. Their blades were sharp, their strikes swift, and they moved so easily across the sand that always pulled Liadan into its depths. Nevertheless, the dragon hadn't wasted years training her for her to fall in her first skirmish. Drawing her dagger, Liadan faced the enemy, with her back to Sleipnir, trusting him to protect it. Forward press, clear some room; pull back and draw them in. Right into her blades. Aegiran scimitars were curved, shorter than her own, which gave her a longer-reach advantage. But theirs were lighter and sharper, which meant they moved faster, sliced easier. Her strategy became to strike fast and kill, rather than wound. The longer the fighting continued, the more she'd tire.

An armored fighter rushed her with a shout, and she twisted out of the way, then followed through to slice his back open from shoulder to hip. The next landed on her dagger, straight to the hilt. Two more came at her at the same time. Liadan whistled, then clashed with one, listening for the bone-crushing thud of Sleipnir having taken out the other. Through the fray, Liadan looked for Tir but saw no sign of him. His people, however, were everywhere.

She could tell at a glance which ones were Tir's *kharesh* and which were not. Though all looked thin and haggard, slowly dying of thirst and hunger, the *kharesh* stood out by the force of their relentless attack. They fought like madmen, throwing themselves at the enemy, driving them back in sheer recklessness. They opened themselves up to being wounded in order to deliver a killing blow, and while Liadan admired their devotion to their tribe, their fighting technique frightened her. They didn't fight to win; they fought to take down as many as they could, then die a heroic death. Tir's arrival had gone unnoticed, and until they saw him, they'd think their cause was hopeless.

Liadan kicked out, shoving an Aesimar fighter back. "Sleipnir," she barked, and the mount pivoted toward her, striking down more of them with his hind legs. After sheathing her dagger, she caught the edge of Sleipnir's saddle and swung up. "Steady does it," she told him before she stood on his back to make herself as tall as possible. She only had moments, so she raised her sword high and shouted as loudly as she could, "*Imarah! Sher'nah bahrai sephri! Kharesh gavoran!*"

Sleipnir screamed and reared, throwing her off. Liadan landed hard, breath knocked from her lungs and her sword from her hand. As she stared at the bright sky, her vision darkened, the surrounding warriors nothing but shadows blending together. She shook her head hard, wiped sand from her face, then gasped, rolling aside just as a curved blade sliced down. Her attacker followed, separating her from Sleipnir and the sword lying behind him. Liadan scrambled backwards, hands and feet burying in the sands. *Too slow!*

When he roared and cut down again, she fell back and, kicking her legs up and over her head, rolled smoothly until she had her feet under her again. The curved blade slid deep into the sands, and Liadan pushed forward, drawing her dagger. But her feet slipped, and instead of stabbing him through the heart, the blade buried into the flesh just above his hip. Liadan lost her balance, the weight of her descent sliced him open, and when he shouted and reeled back, arching away from her, his innards spilled out before him.

A hoarse cry rose up from one of the Imarah, followed by another, and then the whole tribe seemed to be screaming into the dying light. "*Shalla shansher an Imarah!*" they shouted, rallying for one final push against Aesimar. The raiders hesitated, eyes flashing with uncertainty for just a moment before they, too, rallied, and the fighting intensified.

Liadan grabbed the dead man's blade and shoved to her feet, heart racing with the heat of battle, blood boiling in her veins, the fire of her soul licking across the underside of her skin. It wanted to burst out, to roar in answer to Imarah. But she ruthlessly pushed it deep down and fought her way back to her own sword. With its comforting weight in her grasp, she shouted into the sky, echoing Tir's tribe. "*Shalla shansher an Imarah!*"

From some distance off, Sleipnir whinnied and galloped full tilt toward her, swinging his head back and forth to clear the path. As he ran by, she caught onto the saddle, swung easily into her seat, and renewed her press south, toward the group of Aesimar generals overseeing the battle from the crest of a dune.

One of them blew a horn, its deep sound reverberating across the valley, and down to the last, the Aesimar raiders fled after their departing leaders. Liadan followed, cutting down as many as she could, but eventually, Sleipnir stopped in his tracks, refusing to go any farther, letting the survivors escape. Only then did she notice him shuddering with each massive breath he took. Liadan dismounted and came around to his front. "Oh, no…"

Sleipnir's chest was cut open from shoulder to shoulder, dripping blood onto the burning sands. His great head drooped and he rested his forehead against her shoulder.

"Easy, handsome," she crooned, even as her heart fluttered with fear for him. "It's only a scratch, nothing more. You'll be stalking pretty mares again in no time."

The *kharesh* headed toward them. Now that the enemy had retreated, they were in no hurry to reach as far as Sleipnir had taken her. Liadan couldn't see Tir among them. Where was he?

Sleipnir huffed. He was losing too much blood, and if she didn't do something, he'd die before they could get him back to the camp. Licking her dry lips, Liadan made a decision. With the tribesmen still a ways off, she turned Sleipnir around so his hind quarters faced them, then called up her fire. "I am sorry, my friend, this will hurt terribly, but please, please trust me." Pulling together the edges of the wound with one hand, she dragged a glowing finger across the seam as quickly as she could, searing it shut.

Sleipnir screamed, lifting his head, eyes wide with fright, but he held still for the gruesome procedure, trusting her with his well-being.

The *kharesh* ran forward, spurred by Sleipnir's obvious distress.

"Easy," she soothed, and she tugged off her scarf, draped it around his front like a necklace to hide the raw wound before the warriors descended on her in a flurry of angry shouts and pointing fingers. Liadan understood not a word, but she did comprehend what they wanted when someone tried to tear Sleipnir's reins from her hands. She knocked the man sideways and drew her dagger.

In an instant, she was surrounded by a group of very angry men all armed with swords pilfered from corpses. Liadan's fire flared inside her, this time refusing to settle so easily. They wouldn't harm Sleipnir, that much she knew. But none of them would hesitate to slit her throat from ear to ear, if it came to that.

Liadan steadied her gaze on the man she'd shoved. He looked furious, his eye twitching, no doubt unaccustomed to a woman staring him down. She refused to look away. The moment she did, these men would lose all respect for her, and she couldn't have that. For their sakes, they had to acknowledge her as a person, not as a woman; not one of them, not a member of their caste to be pushed aside and ignored. As her mother had done before her, Liadan needed to establish herself as separate from the hierarchy, neither superior nor subject to anyone.

"*Revroha thran,*" the man said. She recognized *thran* to mean north, or northern. *Revroha*, whatever it was, didn't sound very respectful.

Where in all the hells was Tir?

"*Haromi preh thum rekar, revroha thran.*" Long journey and dying. If Liadan guessed correctly, he'd just told her she'd come a long way to die.

"*Rheo, kharesh,*" she replied in greeting, introducing herself the way she'd seen people do in Sadirak. "*Baikal Liadan al-Saeran, shansher thranai fasgaoi ben.*"

They fell silent at hearing a Northerner speak their language.

Then, as one, they all burst into laughter.

It wasn't quite the reaction she'd expected. Flushing furiously, she clutched the dagger tighter, eager to beat them down a peg, when she noticed riders approaching from the camp. Tir on Tarabas led the charge, with another behind him on what had to be the last remaining horse of the Imarah tribe. Bloody finally! Though they were too far away to hear properly, their shouts turned the men's attention away from Liadan.

She shifted around Sleipnir to get to the sword still strapped to her saddle, but another *kharesh* barred her way, placing a blade to her neck. Liadan stilled, inclining her head just a little to let him know she understood, and wouldn't move again.

Tir shouted in his native tongue, and the *kharesh* exchanged looks amongst them. He rode full tilt toward the man who held Liadan at swordpoint, forcing him to back away or be trampled. Free of him, Liadan unsheathed her sword, preparing for another battle, if necessary.

As the second rider approached, Tir wheeled Tarabas around and dismounted, shoving Liadan behind him and her sword down to her side. More angry, foreign words followed, too fast for her to catch their meaning; he was arguing with the *kharesh*, while the second rider, still mounted, gazed steadily at Liadan.

He was older than the *kharesh* on the ground, hair streaked with white and weighed down with golden adornments. She drew herself up and met his gaze, waiting for another outburst.

To her surprise, he touched a hand to his heart, then his mouth, then to his forehead, and he bowed as deeply as the saddle would allow. "I offer greetings to the daughter of the North," he said with more respect than she'd encountered in a long time. "I am Farraj al-Talib, faithful servant of the *shansher* and *shensari*."

At his words, the *kharesh* quieted. They stared at Farraj first, then at Liadan, while Tir openly gaped.

"Well met, Farraj al-Talib. I am Liadan of Frastmir, daughter of King Saeran and Queen Nialei of Frastmir, crown princess of the realm of Wilderheim."

He bowed again. "Well met, and welcome." He dismounted and handed the reins to a *kharesh*. "We are in your debt, Princess. Without your timely arrival, our tribe would be no more. Please accept my humble thanks."

She bowed respectfully. "How many dead?" she asked.

Farraj glanced at Tir, then replied, "Too many. Eight *kharesh* have met an honorable death in battle. At least fifty brave men died defending our weak and wounded. The rest were women."

"And how did they die?"

"By the grace of the gods, swiftly. They died fighting for their children."

"A death as honorable as any warrior would receive in battle."

Farraj inclined his head. "As you say."

"The sun is setting," Tir said. "We should get back before darkness falls."

Farraj barked an order, and the *kharesh* moved out, back to camp, leaving Liadan in the company of Tir and Farraj.

CHAPTER 25

"What do you think you are doing?" Tir demanded the moment the others were out of earshot.

Farraj dismounted and, ignoring the outburst, approached Liadan and her mount. "My lady, will you permit?" he asked, indicating Sleipnir.

"Farraj!"

"The Aegiran fascination with horses is well known to me by now," she replied, glancing warily between Tir and Farraj. "But might it wait until after we return to camp? Sleipnir needs seeing to."

Farraj inclined his head. "Of course." Rather than ride, he walked his own horse to keep pace with Liadan, giving Tir his back, an insult he'd never have dared with Dhakir.

Tir grabbed for Farraj's arm. "I asked you a question," he snapped.

With a swift move belying his obvious injuries, the *kharesh* leader sent Tir sprawling into the sand in front of Liadan's feet. "While you catch your breath down there," Farraj said in their native tongue, "consider carefully your actions today. And *think* before you speak. It is not my place to mentor the *shansher*, nor, by the gods, do I wish it to be. But mark me, boy, too many have laid their lives on the sands today, believing you had abandoned them. Too many more survived, thinking they'd be better off if you had never returned. You have lost more here than you can imagine in your absence, and you will lose more still if you act the hothead you were before you left."

Stunned, Tir said nothing.

Farraj offered his hand to help him to his feet and, speaking in Liadan's language, he added, "We have much to discuss, I am sure. But this is not the place, or the time."

The sun always set quickly; already it'd lost its warmth. It would be dark soon, and they were quite a distance from the safety of the tribe. Flushing, Tir allowed Farraj to help him to his feet, but not before noticing the glistening trail of blood that matted Sleipnir's coat. Before Liadan could protest, he pulled away the scarf she'd tied around the horse's neck, then sucked in a sharp breath.

The princess drew herself up, raised her chin. "As I said, my horse needs seeing to."

Farraj pushed Tir aside to take a closer look and, with a gentle hand, caressed Sleipnir's quivering chest above then below the wound. The animal was visibly shaken and in pain, something no one of Tir's tribe would ever ignore. Farraj scrutinized Liadan, no doubt searching for whatever she'd used to cauterize the wound. Finding nothing, he said, "Your father is King Saeran of Frastmir. I knew him when he was a boy. I was there when he offered himself in *ramesh feh* in the war, and later, when he wed our Mari. Is he well?"

"As well as can be expected, I suppose," Liadan replied uneasily.

"And your honored mother? I have not stood in her presence, but I heard she is an extraordinary woman."

"Yes, many do say so."

"We should hurry back," Tir said before Farraj could ask more. For Liadan's sake, he tempered himself, biting his tongue against more angry words. If he was to gain the tribe's favor for her, and regain it for himself, he'd require the older man's aid.

"As my *shansher* commands," Farraj replied, not taking his eyes off Liadan.

They walked the horses back swiftly, racing against the setting sun. "You fought well today," Tir offered, earning a confused look from Liadan.

"Are you truly so surprised?"

Her voice betrayed neither remorse nor grief—that did surprise him. "You do not weep for the lives you have taken?"

Farraj turned his head to better hear her answer without seeming too curious.

Liadan held Tir's stare, seeming to give the question serious thought before she replied, "No. I respect and honor life, and I will fight to protect it. But I will also show no mercy to those who try to destroy it. Those men I killed today would have killed many others, had I not stopped them. No, I do not regret taking their lives."

"Women are meant to give life, not take it," Tir said.

"Then perhaps you should not think of me as a woman, but as a weapon," she returned immediately, then clicked her tongue to urge Sleipnir on faster. Had he offended her? Tir looked to Farraj for guidance, but found no help in the general's responding shrug.

Numerous fires began to flare ahead, lighting the way home. As they neared, Tir saw Imarah had become much more resourceful in his absence. The tribesmen had gathered up the dead Aesimar, stripped them of their weapons and armor, then arranged the corpses around the camp. Although they gave off a noxious reek, they burned steadily, and would do so for a long time.

The tribe had already gathered, desperate faces eager to see if the news spoke true about Tir's return. Many had tears in their eyes; more still glared angrily as the three of them passed, with the young *shansher* in the lead. No one stopped the company and no one offered any greeting. Instead, the tribe waited for Tir to explain himself or to offer hope.

Tir's throat felt tight, his jaw stuck, unable to form words. Shamed by his actions and Farraj's reprimand, he could only look straight ahead as they passed through the tribe's midst.

At the *shansher*'s tent, Farraj called to one of the men who'd followed them. "This is Matek," he told Liadan. "He will take good care of Sleipnir for you, and he can be trusted."

Liadan nuzzled the mount, while Matek led away Tarabas and Farraj's Zara. They all waited with the princess until he'd returned for Sleipnir. When Liadan relinquished his reins, the mount snorted and rooted his hooves, refusing to be budged. But Matek spoke to him, lavishing praise in a soothing tone until Sleipnir relented and allowed himself to be led away.

Tir entered the tent first, followed by Liadan, and Farraj last. He righted Dhakir's seat, but couldn't bring himself to sit in it. Instead, he carried the heavy chair to the edge of the tent, then sat on the pillows and motioned for the others to do the same.

A short, veiled woman hurried inside, carrying a silver tray of libations. The repast consisted of three small flatbreads, a little cheese, and a bottle of wine. Tir glanced at Liadan to measure her reaction.

The princess nodded her thanks to the woman, and said, "There is a cart of supplies to the west. We left it behind when we saw the fighting. Someone ought to retrieve it."

"At first light," Farraj said, as the woman hurried out of the tent. "It is not safe to venture outside the camp during the night."

Though clearly displeased by that answer, Liadan nodded in acceptance. Had Sleipnir not been injured, Tir would wager she'd have ridden out on her own for that cart, consequences be damned. And Farraj had called *him* a hothead.

"Where is Halima?" Tir asked, breaking a flatbread into halves and handing one to Liadan. When she shook her head to decline, he firmed his mouth and forced the bread into her hand. He had no stomach for food, either, but to refuse an offering when the tribe already had so little would have been an insult.

Rather than reply, Farraj leaned back and regarded Tir. "You rode out of Imarah, determined to slay the bringer of this demon curse. Without a word to anyone, you left your tribe to seek the blood of the Northern king and his wife. And now, you come riding back with a woman at your side. A warrior, no less, who not only slayed three score Aesimar fighters, but also seems to have an unknown ability to cauterize wounds without fire, and introduces herself as a crown princess of Wilderheim, daughter of the very man you wanted to kill. You will explain."

Tir drew himself up. "You forget your place, Farraj."

"I forget nothing! Do not sneer at me and call yourself my better, whelp. Dhakir earned my loyalty by caring for his tribe to his last. He heard the raiders coming, when he had not heard a single word in many years. He saw them drag Halima from the tent, and he roused himself to defend her. He may have languished as one brokenhearted for too long, but he died a warrior, defending his daughter, when his only remaining son had fled and abandoned them!"

Tir blanched, hands growing cold. *I never thought… Never imagined…*

Into the silence, Liadan quietly asked what he couldn't. "Did Halima survive?"

Farraj didn't answer right away. When he did, he lowered his head. "Forgive me. It is not my place to speak of these things in front of outsiders. These are private matters of family; I should not have said what I did."

Tir was bursting to know the answer and, by Farraj's covert glare, the old man knew it. He was deliberately withholding it to prolong Tir's torment. "For a faithful servant of the *shansher* and *shensari*," Tir grated, repeating his earlier words, "you show neither faith nor servitude."

"What was your plan, Tirasdunh?" Farraj returned, then indicated Liadan with a polite wave of his hand. "You have brought whom most of the tribe consider a blood enemy into our midst, not in chains, but armed with blades. How would you have explained to us?"

"I most certainly would not have introduced her as my wife!"

Liadan's back shot ramrod straight. "What?"

"You are a fool, boy. A damned, naïve fool. They would have stoned her before you could think up a proper excuse."

"What is this about a wife?" Liadan demanded.

For the first time since they'd sat down, Farraj hesitated, seeming at a loss for words.

Tir couldn't resist an opportunity to put him in his place. "When he introduced himself to you before the *kharesh*, he called himself a servant of the *shansher* and *shensari*—the king and queen. As he said, Dhakir the Conqueror is dead, which makes me the *shansher* of Imarah."

"It was safer for them to think Tirasdunh has returned with a queen by his side," Farraj told Liadan, glaring at Tir. "As *shensari*, you are under his protection, and no one may lay hand on you. I did it to spare you their wrath."

Liadan shot to her feet. "Well, undo it!"

A queen! Had they been anywhere but in Aegiros, Liadan would have admired Farraj's quick thinking. Even a fake queen had immense power to dictate her will unto her people. She could have ordered the entire tribe to break camp and trek across the desert back to the First City, and farther west in search of more fertile ground, and they would have obeyed instantly. They might have quietly questioned her actions, but they would not have dared to oppose her. She'd have had no reason to fear displaying her fire; indeed, it would only have solidified her authority over them.

But where, except in Aegiros, did the title of queen hold so little meaning? Among the desert tribesmen, women were regarded as little better than chattel—they were bartered with, bought and sold, kept under lock and key, disallowed to keep company among the men or even to speak their minds. A queen's station in Aegiros meant nothing other than she belonged to the king.

Farraj pushed to his feet to face her. "You are too young to understand the ways of our world. We have not the time for me to explain, but you must believe me when I say, you would not have survived the night had I not said what I did."

He spoke the truth Liadan already knew. That didn't make hearing it any easier. Earlier, she'd taken a calculated risk in joining the fight. What better way to earn the tribe's trust in her fighting skills than by showing them she could hold her own? Liadan and Sleipnir had saved lives today, of that she had no doubt. She'd been well on her way to establishing a unique position among the Imarah, and before she could have solidified it, Farraj had undone it all.

"You wanted to be accepted," Tir retorted.

Liadan shook her head. "This cannot be the only solution." If for no other reason than her blood oath, the closer she and Tir got, the more dangerous it would become for both of them.

"It is," Farraj said.

"No, you don't understand," she insisted. "What I came here to do, I cannot do while shackled to Tir's side like a shadow."

"Would it truly be so bad, pretending to be my wife?"

A handful of words, and Liadan was pulled back to the riverbed that morning. The same sadness now darkened his golden gaze, the same pride drew back his shoulders, and the same subtle challenge lowered his head.

Once again, he put himself on the line, and once again left it to Liadan to be the rational one.

Gods, but she was weary of fighting this same battle for both of them. "Think, Tir. You know what I am, and you know I won't be able to hide it. What will happen when your tribe discovers you not only brought a creature like me among them, but also bound yourself to her in marriage?"

Tir knew the answer, and if Farraj's flush was any indication, he did, as well. The Imarah wouldn't abide another betrayal from their king, especially not one so grave. They'd rise against him, banish them both at best, murder them at worst.

She'd come here expecting to change the world, not realizing the world was much too big to be changed by one woman, even a Halfling.

Without another word, she shook her head and stalked out of the tent. Tir called after her, rising to follow, but she quickened her step, and Farraj's voice stopped him in his tracks, giving her time to get away. She didn't slow until she was certain neither of them would come looking for her.

Full night had fallen while they'd talked, and while the sand beneath her feet was still warm, the air had grown cold. But it was the scene before her, not the night air, that chilled her to the bone. Hugging herself about the middle, Liadan strode through an unfinished camp devoid of people. Many tents had been erected, creating pathways and alleys, but at least half of them were dark, empty, gaping tombs and markers for those who should have lived there, and the closer she got to the edge, the more such tents she passed.

Not a soul stirred out in the open. Those still alive huddled around small fires, safely hidden by billowing cloth, and their whispered prayers hissed on the wind. Liadan didn't need to understand the meaning; she felt the fear behind those words.

At its very edge, the camp's boundary was stark enough to give her pause. Behind her stood a multitude of tents. Before her lay a line of burning corpses, and beyond that was nothing but sand. She gazed up at the stars, recognizing few. They twinkled, so far away, they seemed unreachable, yet at the same time so heavy, Liadan felt as though they'd crush her.

What am I to do?

She looked around. Not a human in sight, no signs of any demons. After two nights of their howling screams, Liadan had expected them to swoop down the moment the sun set safely behind the horizon. But now, alone in the night, she sat on the sand with her back to a tent and, drawing the water vial from around her neck, held it up to the firelight. "Fal," she said softly. "Can you hear me?"

No answer.

Liadan sighed. "I suppose it was too much to hope for at least that little comfort of your voice. Well, I found them. I traversed the desert and found the Imarah tribe, and brother, it's even worse than we thought." She rubbed her brow, hating the lack of response. "I wish you could see it. There are endless stretches of sand everywhere you look. The sky is so blue, there's no word to describe it, and the sun's so bright, at its zenith, it feels as though fire's eating you alive. But at twilight and gloaming… Oh Fal, it's so beautiful, it takes your breath away." She imagined what the First City must have looked like back in its day—streets filled with people, groves of fig trees, marble fountains spraying glistening drops of water toward the sky. She could almost smell the spices perfuming the air.

All gone now. Nothing but an exotic dream, faded into ruin.

"*Beela thran.*"

Liadan jumped to her feet, tucking the vial into her belt at her back.

An old woman melted out of the darkness between tents. She was short, stooped, her step uneven with a heavy limp. Her clothes were rags, a tattered scarf slipping off her grizzled white hair, her bare feet sinking into the sand as she walked. "*Rah, beela, beela thran. Tosma beela, rah. Abu rekar semerekara a tibokar.*"

"I'm sorry, I don't understand what you're saying."

The woman smiled, further creasing her wrinkled face to expose a mouth with only two stumpy teeth. She nodded, reaching out to Liadan. "*Rah, beela thran, nomarehraba dath. Mea idrah shensari preh thum aiii.*" She shook her head, on the verge of tears. "*Bahran a mi. Meagara, bahran!*"

"*Ves!*" Farraj suddenly shouted, rushing to intercept the woman, pushing Liadan behind him.

"What are you doing?"

He ignored her, pointing furiously in the direction the woman had come from. He crowded Liadan away, but never took his eyes off his target. "*Aseti, ves begos!*"

The old woman hissed, eyes sparking angrily. "*En emeil baseeri, kharesh*!" She spat on the sand. "*Hamme daeva deogobor feh. Kalikarai a ti an ebeo Dhakir!*"

Breathing hard, Farraj drew his shoulders back, and his blade sang out of its scabbard. He gripped the hilt so tightly, his knuckles stood out stark white.

"Stop!" Liadan cried, grabbing for his arm. "What is the matter with you? She's just an old woman!"

Farraj shook her off. "Do not interfere," he ordered.

The woman laughed, pointing at Farraj. "*Daeva emeil baseeri. Baseeri an el tiath Imarah.*" She spat again, then turned her back on Farraj, shuffling away into the shadows whence she'd come.

After she'd disappeared from sight, Farraj turned on Liadan. Sword still in hand, he grabbed her arm and dragged her off in the other direction, closer to where the flames were at their highest. "You will not go near that woman again," he said.

"I will do as I bloody well please! Release me, Farraj, this instant."

After turning her to face him, he did. "Do you have eyes, Princess? Yes, I see that you do. Do you know how to use them? Then look around. Do you see anyone walking the night here? Not a one! Everyone who values their soul is too afraid of the darkness to leave the safety of their lights. Yet there, a feeble old woman, brave enough to wander the very edges of our camp, all on her own. Did you not wonder why that is?"

"Perhaps she has more courage than you," Liadan retorted. "And she was not the only one walking around in the night. I was there, as well."

"You were there, because you do not know any better. *She* had other reasons."

"And what were they?"

"She is *aseti*. An outcast—a witch. Damned by the gods to wield evil powers."

"I have powers," Liadan told him, head high. "Will you cast me out, as well? Your *shensari*, as you called me? Do it! I'd rather keep company with that old woman than with any man who regards my very nature as a scourge!"

Farraj seethed, sword arm quivering with tension. "She is different," he insisted. "*En emeil baseeri, kharesh*. Do you know what that means? My curse upon you, *kharesh*. *Hamme daeva deogobor feh*. May the demons drag you into hell. *Kalikarai a ti, an ebeo Dhakir*. You will suffer my eternal wrath—"

"Along with Dhakir," Liadan finished, her anger cooling slightly. She'd understood that part, at least. No wonder the *kharesh* had reacted so badly. Superstitious, Tir had called his tribe. The word was too trite to describe the true depth of their fear of magic. "She cursed you."

"Me, and all of Imarah."

"And still you let her live."

"It is said a witch cannot be killed by an ordinary weapon. If a man slays a witch by human means, her soul will be reborn from his wife, devour his children, and drive him to madness."

"If it eases your mind, Farraj, she may have spoken the words, but there was no power behind them. I would have felt it. You are safe from the old woman's curse."

"Perhaps," he allowed. "Perhaps her words were nothing more than that. But make no mistake, *shensari*, we are all already cursed. The *shansher* is even now pacing in his tent, mourning his family, thinking grave thoughts of his tribe, no doubt. And he has cause."

Yes, that much, Liadan believed. No natural thing could so quickly bring a thriving civilization to this. Mighty rivers didn't just dry out overnight, and demons didn't leave their hellish worlds unless someone broke through the Veil and summoned them. But something else worried her. Liadan hesitated before asking, "Did Halima survive?"

Farraj heaved a great sigh. "She did," he replied. "Gravely injured, dishonored, she lived to see the next sunrise, to watch her father's pyre be built. In her delirium, she called for her brother, and when he did not appear, she joined her father in the flames."

Liadan's stomach clenched, eyes stinging with tears. "Why would she do that?"

"She believed, as we all did, that Tirasdunh would never return. You can plainly see the state of our people. There isn't one among us who can afford to take on another hungry mouth, when the ones he already has are starving. Halima would have been *aseti*, an outcast left to fend for herself. She would not have lasted long. She knew this and chose to die to spare herself long days of suffering."

The thought was incomprehensible to Liadan. She'd been born blessed with so many gifts she used to take for granted: a loving family; a kingdom rich in magic, food, and water aplenty—all gifts she'd known not many shared. But never in her life could she have imagined this much suffering. How much pain and grief must Halima have endured; how defeated and helpless must she have felt to have done what she had?

"I am deeply sorry. For everything you and your tribe have endured."

"As am I."

Silence stretched between them, heavy with meaning, and broken up by the roar of fire all around them.

Back home in Wilderheim, a night like this would be filled with music and song. In towns and villages, the kingdom's people took great joy in coming together at the end of each day to share a meal and to entertain each other. On the outskirts, in the wilds, Others roamed relentlessly, their ethereal voices lilting on the breeze; they could be heard in the hiss of wind through the trees, and in the gentle gurgle of creeks and rivers.

Liadan hadn't realized until now how much she missed those sounds.

After a while, Farraj sheathed his sword. "I have given you some thought, *shensari*."

She winced. "You call me queen, but I'm not one of you. I'm not Tir's wife, and I never will be. A union between us would be disastrous."

He regarded her with unabashed curiosity, and Liadan felt as if he could see through her, as if she'd somehow revealed far more than she'd intended. "I think you do him a disservice. Yourself, as well. But that is not my place to ponder. Of course, you both have your reasons for it, and I am not one to pry. I am but a humble warrior who can only see what I see in your eyes." He smiled, kindly, mysteriously, then just as quickly, turned and indicated she should walk with him. "My point was that perhaps there may be a solution to the dilemma of your presence more suitable to your character. A title better suited to a weapon than a woman."

With no solutions of her own forthcoming, Liadan inclined her head and joined him. "Speak it then, my good man. I am all ears."

CHAPTER 26

"You may speak."

Itamar al-Jiri, right hand to the Aesimar *shansher*, and the High Magus of the tribe, licked his dry lips with a sticky tongue. The *shansher* had removed his armor, and now sat behind his writing desk, glancing over reports neatly written on papyrus sheets. He didn't raise his head to acknowledge Itamar, and nothing in his tone of voice or demeanor betrayed any hint of his displeasure at the disappointing outcome of their earlier push against Imarah.

And that was precisely what worried Itamar so gravely. The *shansher* was at his most dangerous when he seemed the calmest. *He is only a man,* Itamar reminded himself. But a man was never only a man when he used demons to do his bidding.

"We have suffered losses," he reported, his own voice so tremulous, it brought the *shansher*'s head up. Tensing his hands by his sides to hide their quiver, Itamar pulled his shoulders back and continued in a stronger voice, "Six score dead; one hundred wounded."

The roving remnants of the once-powerful Imarah tribe had been slowly dying for a long time. Itamar didn't understand why the *shansher* had allowed them to continue. But last night, on word that their prince still hadn't returned, he'd ordered an end to it. Their warriors had gathered in the hundreds, armed in full regalia, and set out at daybreak to claim a glorious victory for Aesimar—and they'd nearly had it in their grasp; so close, Itamar had almost tasted it.

They hadn't lost the battle; they'd ceded it. "We had not expected Imarah to rally as they did," Itamar added with a note of apology, though he had nothing to regret. His preparations had been flawless; his plans executed to perfection. It was the *shansher* himself who'd ordered the retreat.

"No, indeed." The *shansher* set aside his reports, and for a long moment, he quietly stared into the shadows behind Itamar with such intensity, it made the High Magus want to look over his shoulder. But one didn't turn his back on the *shansher*, unless he wished it marked with a whip. "Tell me, Itamar, what did you see through your longlooker, down in that valley today?"

Itamar blanched. "I… I—"

"When the rallying cry went up, and Imarah caught its second wind, you saw something through that tube that made you doubt your eyes. I saw it in your face. What did you see?"

Itamar couldn't find the words. How was he to describe to the *shansher* what he could scarcely believe himself?

"It must have been that young warrior," the *shansher* pushed. "The one who rode in on the black hellbeast. Magnificent animal, was it not? At least a score of my men fell beneath its hooves, and it protected its rider as I've never seen a horse do before." He smiled as though imagining such an animal in his possession, and Itamar breathed a small sigh of relief at the change in subject.

The *shansher* adored horses, and in years past, one such mount would have proven invaluable. The newly formed Aesimar tribe had warred and conquered constantly, absorbing smaller, weaker tribes and training them to act and think in accordance with their laws. Back then, the *shansher* had always been the first to ride into battle, and the last to leave it.

But those days were gone. Having acquired enough men that even today's losses didn't weaken their forces, the *shansher* no longer partook in the battles, instead watching them from a high perch like a performance put on for his enjoyment.

Why did you sound retreat? Itamar thought, struggling to understand. *They were ours! The last dregs of Imarah, kneeling at our mercy! Why did you not finish it?*

Coming back from his internal musings, the *shansher* once again looked Itamar in the eye, silently demanding an answer. "Did you recognize him? It was not Tirasdunh; the prince kept to the edges of the tribe to protect his people. The stranger pushed outward into our line of offense. Who was he?"

"Your Highness," Itamar said, using the lofty Northern title he knew the *shansher* preferred. "He was… He was a *she*."

Never before had the High Magus thought he would feel such fear from so small an action. For no more than two blinks of an eye, the Aesimar *shansher* stilled so completely, the entire tent seemed to grow cold. "A woman?" he asked quietly.

Itamar shuddered, and coughed into his fist, embarrassed by his weakness. "Yes, your Highness. A Northerner, by the looks of her. As pale as the sands."

The *shansher* leaned back and stroked his long beard. "I will know everything there is to know about her."

Itamar bowed low. "I will consult our seer—"

"No. I will have it from Kaliban."

"Your Highness…"

"A woman roused the dying *kharesh* to rally and fight like devils against my army. Six score of my men are dead, and all of them her fault. This is no ordinary woman, Itamar. I will know her. Make me ask again, and I will send you to her to ask in person."

Itamar schooled himself not to whimper. "As my *shansher* commands."

Bowing out of the tent, he hurried across the camp to the western edge, where the Magi had settled. There, he summoned Rafi, Pirro, and Dar, the three who, along with him, were the keepers of Kaliban. The four of them together hefted the heavy, metal chest, carrying it back across the camp to the *shansher*'s tent. Despite the heat of the day, whether placed in the sun or in the shade, the chest's metal was always cold. Itamar's hands had cramped by the time they'd set the chest down before the *shansher*.

Chanting their spells, the Magi circled it four times, then each knelt on one side to unlock the clasps that held the lid. After removing it, they reached inside to pull out another box, this one smaller, made of ebony, and carved with intricate protection spells. Placing this chest onto the carpet next to the metal one, they once again chanted prayers before repeating the procedure of removing the lid. Inside the ebony chest lay an even smaller one made of ivory and white crystal; a chest small enough that one man should have been able to lift it out himself, yet it took all four of them to remove it.

One last ritual of spells, and Itamar unlocked the tiny white chest with a shaking hand. From it, he removed a golden oil lamp, shined to a polish, its surface dulled by patterns of black frost. The lamp chilled Itamar's hands so much, he couldn't hold it for longer than a moment and, turning quickly, he placed the lamp down onto the *shansher*'s desk, then stepped far back to kneel by the others, and joined them in droning a quiet prayer.

The *shansher* pulled his sleeve down to cover his hand, then rubbed the oil lamp, disrupting the frost pattern. At once, a plume of noxious black smoke streamed out. Unlike smoke from a fire, which rose into the sky, this one was so thick and so heavy, it poured like water across the surface of the desk, congealing until it formed the figure of a man-shaped creature, solid yet as insubstantial as mist. Itamar wrinkled his nose at the stench of rot and death that always accompanied Kaliban's appearance, and lingered for days afterwards.

"My master summons me," Kaliban said, his voice a hissing rattle reminiscent of a venomous snake. It struck fear into the soul of any unlucky enough to hear it, and the *daeva* relished that fear, savored it like a treat. "What is your wish?"

"A woman of the North thwarted my victory over Imarah today," the *shansher* lied, holding his hand over his nose and mouth. "My wish is to know who she is."

Kaliban raised his hands high above his head, the chains that bound him rattling loudly. Power, ancient and cold, gathered along the tent's ceiling, swirling to create a vortex to another world. In it, terrifying and incomprehensible shapes began to form, Only Kaliban could decipher them and convey their meaning to the *shansher*. Itamar had warned the *shansher* many times that creatures of Darkness, even imprisoned ones, often mixed truth with lies; he wouldn't have believed the *daeva* had he told them the sky was blue and the sun set in the west. But the High Magus was merely a tool of the *shansher*'s ambition, just like everyone else.

An ugly, scornful laugh rattled around the *daeva*, and his form shivered as if he would dissolve into mist. "Your first wish gave you a tribe," he jeered, "and your second brings its demise!"

Itamar shuddered, faltering in his prayers as the *daeva* spun his evil spell. The vortex above the *shansher*'s head stretched down, spinning with visions and demons reaching out to claw the unwary. "You wish to know the woman of the North? She is Vengeance. She Who Walks Through Fire will not be stopped by magic, or by sword. She will cut darkness with a blade of fire, and tear hearts out of the bodies of her enemies. She will claim yours, Khiron al-Bashir, deserter of Imarah, and you will see it burning in her hand before your soul has left your body." The *daeva* laughed cruelly, jangling his chains with such vigor, Itamar feared he would break out and destroy them all. For the first time since they'd bound Kaliban, Itamar feared those chains were nothing but a cruel trick, worn willingly to give them all a false sense of security while the *daeva* bided his time and schemed.

"*Enough!*" Khiron slammed his fist down onto the desk, overturning the oil lamp. "Begone, fiend! Back into your prison!"

Still laughing, Kaliban's form dissolved into smoke, taking his vortex with him. Little by little, he streamed back inside the lamp, his final words rattling softer, as if for Khiron alone: "You will call again, *shansher*, and your third wish will cost you dearly. You will call. You will. And I shall answer… for the price of your soul."

The *daeva* was gone.

Dar rushed to return the lamp to its resting place. His flesh sizzled when he touched it, rousing the others from their stupor to come to his aid. The lamp steamed when they placed it into the white chest; the ebony sealed in its warmth; and by the time they'd locked the metal, the entire chest was cold once again.

They rushed the whole thing back to its resting place in the Magis' tent, but when Itamar returned to the *shansher*, Khiron was as pale as a sheet, wide-eyed gaze fixed on the table where the lamp had scorched it.

"What does my *shansher* command?" Itamar asked timidly.

"Bury the chest," Khiron rasped, breathing hard, "deep in the desert, where no one will ever find it."

"And what of the woman?"

Khiron al-Bashir, deserter of Imarah and *shansher* of Aesimar, stroked his beard with a shaky hand. "She is merely a woman," he mused, "and as you like to remind me, *daeva* lie. I will not give its words credence."

"Indeed." Itamar bowed low. It wouldn't do to point out the sweat on Khiron's brow, or the quiver in his voice. Only a fool would throw his *shansher*'s weakness back in his face, and a fool Itamar was not.

For all that he claimed to have the Dark god's favor, the leader of Aesimar feared him as much as any man, and for all that he pretended to use Aesma's creatures as his minions, as any other mortal man, Khiron was nothing but their puppet.

The *shansher* had bought three wishes from a *daeva* for the price of his soul. It wouldn't matter where Itamar buried the chest, Kaliban would not be cheated of his prize; he'd come from the ends of the world to collect on his debt, with interest, and Itamar intended to be far away when that happened. Better to be executed as a traitor; better to slowly waste away of thirst in the desert and pass into the arms of his ancestors, than to relinquish his soul to a *daeva*'s eternal hunger.

Win or lose, Khiron would never see the First City again.

Perhaps that was for the best.

CHAPTER 27

Sleep eluded Tir all through the night. He paced the tent like a tiger denied his prey, reeling from the news Farraj had so callously delivered. Dhakir the Conqueror was dead, his only remaining daughter burned on his pyre, and Tir was the last of his family left alive, a prince who'd never wanted to be king.

He'd failed to break the curse, his tribe was doomed to slowly die on the scorching desert sands, and Tir was helpless to stop it.

Passing by the ebony seat again, he felt a chill run up his spine, as if his father's ghost still sat there, watching him and demanding his due. Imarah was now Tir's responsibility, and with all of their lives resting on his shoulders, Tir couldn't breathe.

He wanted to scream, to curse the Northern king again, to lay the blame at Liadan's feet. Her fire storm had cost them three days; if they'd ridden straight to the First City, straight through to Imarah, he might have saved them, and his sister might still be alive.

But his anger found no easy victim. Liadan didn't return to the tent the entire night. He waited for her with angry words lodged in his chest, ready to let loose—and he desperately needed to let them loose, the ache too great to keep contained. But she didn't appear.

When light caressed the tent wall, Tir held his breath, waiting for Liadan to enter; she'd shone that brightly many times before. To his disappointment, it wasn't Liadan, but the morning sun illuminating the world outside that thin sheet of cloth. Day had quietly dawned while he'd walked countless miles in circles throughout the night.

Weary, he rubbed the sleep from his eyes and stepped out into the open, preparing to face the impossible task of bringing his people solace.

"*Imarah, awaken!*" Farraj bellowed somewhere nearby, and dozens of little bells rattled in unison. "*Imarah! I summon thee!*" The bell staff thumped in rhythm to his words. Like the rest of his tribe, Tir followed the noise, curious.

In the small gathering space among the blood-stained tents, Farraj stood tall, slamming the bell staff down and shouting, "*I challenge the brave and the strong! I challenge Imarah! Who will answer? Who will submit to the ordeal of kharashan?*"

"Farraj! Have you gone mad?"

The man ignored him. "*Who will answer?*" he repeated, casting his gaze over the gathering of men and women who looked at each other, frightened, confused. They hadn't seen a *kharashan* for many years, not since Dhakir had lost his will to live and their people had begun to die off like flies. Courage had deserted them long ago, their strength sapped more and more every day.

Imarah didn't need a trial of strength now; they needed help. "Leave off, Farraj," Tir said, tired of pretending to be strong. "Do not make a mockery of us."

"*I challenge the brave and the strong!*" Farraj shouted again, voice booming as very few could. "*Who will submit to the ordeal of kharashan?*"

A hum of confusion swept through the crowd as a man stepped forth, joined by another, and then a third. As they each came forward, the tribe hailed them with cries of honor, quietly at first, afraid of making too much noise, but by the fifth, they cheered as loudly as they could, and Tir was left speechless.

"*I challenge the brave and the strong! Who will answer?*"

Two more stepped up, and Tir's people raised their fists in the air, chanting for their braves. From the other side of the gathering, a boy of no more than thirteen crawled out and ran to join the petitioners. People laughed when his mother dragged him back by his ear. Even Tir allowed himself a chuckle, his dark mood lifting as he beheld his tribe's spirit and realized the wisdom of what Farraj had done. Even in their darkest time, he gave them cause to feel strong, to act brave, to face a challenge they could overcome.

He felt Liadan approach before he saw her; the familiar heat of her fire, the scent of smoke and woman ever present around her. He turned to her with a smile, but she paid him no attention, her determined gaze focused on Farraj.

Someone had given her a change of clothes. Billowing pants tucked at her ankles into soft leather shoes, the same kind the *kharesh* wore into battle. Instead of a shirt, she wore a laced vest to cover her torso, leaving her arms bare, painted like a heathen warrior with swirls and symbols that also marked her uncovered face. Her hair, plaited tightly back, shone with red streaks in the sun, and the twisted torc at her neck gleamed. She looked like the Othercreature she was, and Tir realized at once what was about to happen.

"Do not—"

"Will you do something for me?" Her charcoal eyes flickered red-gold with her fire as she pressed something into his hand, curling his fingers around it. "Keep this safe," she said.

Tir gazed down at the small glass vial of water from her brother. What was this? By the time he looked back up, she'd stepped out to join the petitioners. "Liadan!"

She ignored him, standing tall next to the ninth man to make an even ten, and the crowd fell silent. With all eyes trained on her, Liadan didn't flinch; she kept her chin up, her back straight, her gaze forward.

Farraj stopped shouting for the brave, and as people hummed with displeasure, *kharesh* entered the circle, no doubt to remove Liadan, to beat her for showing such brazen disrespect to their men. Tir stepped forward to intervene, but Farraj once again thumped the bell staff onto the flat stone, hard enough to crack the shaft. He did it again, and again, in a slow, steady rhythm that demanded their silence and attention. He looked at each of them in turn until the *kharesh* retreated one by one beneath the authority of his stare and everyone else quieted in deference to it. Farraj lingered longest on Tir, sending a silent message: *Do not interfere. Do not let her be undermined again.*

Tir curled his fingers into fists at his sides, mindful of the fragile vial Liadan had entrusted into his keeping. His feet cramped, aching to move, to drag Liadan away from the center and into safety behind tent walls. The ordeal of *kharashan* was no laughing matter; men had died during its challenges, some had disappeared, never to be seen again, claimed by the desert forever. He knew what she was thinking—to prove herself a warrior among them, strong enough to lead and defend them. A fool's errand, and one that would get her killed.

And Tir knew Farraj had helped her orchestrate it. The man wouldn't have called a *kharashan* for any other reason now, of all times, when they grieved their *shansher* and so many others who'd fallen. The two of them had schemed behind his back to do this. He'd wring both of their necks when all this was over. Starting with Liadan's.

If she made it through.

Gods, please let her make it through.

CHAPTER 28

They wanted to stone her. Every last one of them, beginning with the *kharesh*, who'd see her participation as the ultimate insult, wanted to see her broken and humbled on the ground at their feet. Well aware of the turmoil she'd caused just by stepping into the circle, Liadan steeled herself to stand tall. This was only the beginning.

She felt the tribe's animosity like countless sharp needles pricking her skin, but didn't dare show her unease. She was strong; she could and would complete the ordeal. To think any less meant allowing weakness into her heart, and Liadan couldn't allow that when so much was at stake.

Tir bristled twenty paces away. He was furious with her, of that she had no doubt, but he was allowing her to do this without interference, and that humbled her. He'd told her how difficult the ordeal of *kharashan* was, as had Farraj, and now both of them showed incredible trust by letting her prove what she could do.

Liadan didn't intend to fail them. A polished scimitar waited for her at the end of the ordeal and, by the gods, she'd make it far enough to claim it.

The man standing next to her huffed his anger; the tribesmen sneered, shaking their heads. And through it all, Farraj continued to beat a steady rhythm, demanding respect and obedience to the ordeal. He did so for a long time, until the tribe joined in, clapping to the rhythm he set. The beats came faster, and faster, until the tribe shouted and cheered once more, and then Farraj roared to the heavens and shouted a summons.

One by one, the petitioners followed him through the crowd to the first challenge. Each was touched by the people he passed, receiving a blessing for success from the men and women of Imarah. They showed no such deference to Liadan, who brought up the rear; instead, they withdrew, some turning their backs. One man spat at her feet, but was quickly yanked back and admonished. Liadan didn't catch the angry words, but she heard "*shensari*" among them.

When she felt a hand on her shoulder, she braced for a blow, but it was Tir who'd suddenly appeared beside her, walking tall and daring anyone to question whom the *shansher* chose to favor. "Thank you," she said softly, knowing what it cost him to do this.

"By the gods, do not thank me for walking you to the gallows," he grated in response.

"Would you miss me if I were to perish?" she asked, fighting back a smile.

"As a horse would miss a swarm of gnats. All the same, I will keep your trinket safe, if you do something for me in return."

"What is it?"

The line stopped in front of a black tent strewn with animal skins, and Farraj placed himself at the entrance to stand guard. After a ritual of hopping and huffing to give himself courage, the first petitioner stepped inside.

Tir grasped Liadan's chin, gently turning her face to meet his gaze. "Come back alive, *shai'iss*." His golden eyes burned with so many words he couldn't say before he pressed a chaste kiss to her forehead. Then he stepped back into the crowd.

Stunned by the gesture, Liadan searched for him, wanting to reassure him somehow, but she couldn't see him anywhere. *I'll make it through,* she vowed. *You'll see. I'll prove you haven't made a mistake in bringing me here. I will fulfill my oath.*

The petitioners entered the black tent one at a time, summoned by a strike of Farraj's staff. Liadan watched them each prepare in their own way before they stepped inside, and while she waited her turn, she recalled everything Farraj had told her last night.

The ordeal of *kharashan* consisted of three trials through which the petitioners proved both their worth and their strength. First, a trial of the spirit. Inside the black tent sat the last remaining Magus of the Imarah tribe. He was ancient, his face covered by a black veil so he couldn't be recognized. Upon stepping inside, the petitioner drank a potion known only to the Magi, one forbidden to anyone else, as it induced visions and hallucinations, lowered one's guard and forced them to speak only the truth.

Once the potion took effect, the petitioner was asked three questions, each with only one acceptable answer, and the petitioner had to speak it truthfully.

Who are you?

I am a blade of Imarah.

What do you want?

To serve the shansher and my tribe.

What will you sacrifice?

My all, and all of myself.

If the wrong answer was spoken, or spoken dishonestly, the petitioner was expelled from the ordeal and shamed by the tribe, never to attempt it again.

I am a blade of Imarah, Liadan repeated to herself as the seventh, and then the eighth man entered the tent. None had yet emerged; they'd all continued on to the next trial. *I wish to serve the shansher and my tribe. I will sacrifice my all, and all of myself for the good of the tribe.*

The ninth man entered, leaving Liadan alone in the circle of people who'd grown as quiet as death. She schooled herself not to fidget. *I am a blade of Imarah.* A blade did not waver.

The sun rose higher. Liadan's mouth felt dry; already she'd been standing there for a long time. But no one offered a drink of water, and she wouldn't ask for it. Every pain and discomfort, Farraj had warned, was part of the ordeal. And so she waited, keeping her eye on the tent's entrance and on the staff in Farraj's hand. Any moment now it'd strike to announce her turn, and she'd step into the tent to face the Magi.

Suddenly, the tent flap billowed, and the ninth petitioner crawled out. A collective gasp sent the tribe a step backwards from the weeping man whose limbs shook as he dragged them forward. Though he had no injuries that Liadan could see, his eyes were haunted, terrified, and he wailed, cried out words she didn't understand as he crawled toward those closest to him. They stepped away, spat on the sand. Abandoned, the man collapsed onto his side, curled in on himself like a child, and wept. No one came to help him.

Farraj struck his bell staff against stone, summoning the last petitioner.

Tearing her gaze away from the crying man, Liadan licked her dry lips and stepped forth, faltering only the slightest bit as she stepped from the searing light of the desert sun into the tent's total darkness.

The scent of smoke and incense hung thick in the air. Carpets had been laid one over the other to cushion her feet from the sand. The Magus struck a wooden stick against a brass bowl, in a soft gong to direct her toward him.

With her dragonsight, Liadan had no trouble seeing in the dark; yet even so, she saw little more than shadowy shapes. Everything inside the tent was black: black walls, black carpets, black veils draping over the Magi, black bowls and chalices. Only the polished brass gong gleamed bright. She approached and knelt before the Magi, bowing so low her forehead touched the carpet before she sat back on her heels and waited.

Who are you? What do you want? What will you sacrifice?

I am a blade of Imarah. I wish to serve the shansher and my tribe. I will sacrifice my all, and all of myself for the good of both.

Without a word, the Magus pressed a black cup into her hand.

Liadan brought it to her mouth, and the sharp, herbal scent stung her nose. Whatever was in that cup would be more potent than any spirits she'd sampled in the past. After taking a deep breath, she drank down the bitter brew underlaid with an unfamiliar sweetness that lingered on her tongue.

At once, the ground swayed, and the cup tumbled from her numb fingers as she tried to hand it back. Her heart raced; sweat broke out on her brow and upper lip. She braced herself forward on her hands as her stomach clenched, trying to cast out what she'd drunk. But Liadan gritted her teeth and swallowed it back.

Head swimming, she tried to focus her gaze on the brass bowl, waiting for the questions to be asked.

Who are you? What do you want? What will you sacrifice?

The bowl began to glow so brightly, she had to squint against its glare, and she felt herself falling forward, felt immense power pierce the darkness and reach out for her.

It didn't ask her identity.

It called her by name.

Liadan shuddered at the whispery voice that screamed inside her mind with such strength, her skull threatened to explode. She bit back a cry of pain and squeezed her eyes shut, pressing the heels of her hands into them to keep them from popping out. Without support, Liadan slumped forward, her forehead falling to the carpet once more.

Who are you? What do you want? What will you sacrifice?

The questions didn't come. Instead, in the thick darkness of her own drugged mind, pale shadows formed into blurry shapes. White smoke thickened to form the ghostly face of a beautiful woman with eyes shining like stars. In an instant, it dissolved, replaced by a pair of graceful hands dancing through the air in intricate patterns, shaping a wordless spell. Once again, the darkness broke the vision apart, thickening, fighting to keep the apparition away.

It was a Veil. Although she'd never seen one, Liadan nevertheless recognized that the darkness was some sort of barrier holding the apparition back. It seemed to have a mind of its own, moving, swirling, repairing itself every time the pale woman of light managed to break through even a little.

She called to Liadan, summoned her by name, and Liadan was helpless to disobey, pulled into the suffocating black sea that blanketed the entire valley.

"You risk much, young Dragonblood, by undertaking the ordeal," the woman whispered, and Liadan fell to her knees, covering her ears. The woman spoke in Aegiran, but somehow, Liadan understood her perfectly. "Do you seek Imarah's approval? They will not give it. Not for this."

"I… I am a blade of Imarah," Liadan said, choking on the darkness that poured down her throat every time she opened her mouth to speak. If only she could get the words out, speak the answers, the first trial would be over. "My wish is to… serve the *shansher* and my tribe."

The apparition formed long enough to laugh in Liadan's face before the darkness banished it back again. "You are not of Imarah, young Dragonblood, and you serve no one but yourself."

A terrible wind knocked Liadan sideways, swirling the darkness so thin, she could almost see through it. Lights flashed in the immeasurable distance, a different face inside of each; they called out to her—some in anger, some with hope in their eyes—and their voices touched her mind, imparted knowledge she'd never had before. Their language became hers; their names as familiar as her own family's; their history became etched in her mind like a memory of her own.

They were gods. Once worshipped by Imarah, they'd been banished beyond this black Veil that none but the mighty wind god, Vayu, could penetrate.

"Do you know what you have done?" demanded Inaras, the great Mother of Life, as the black Veil once again reformed to hide the others.

Liadan could no longer tell which direction she'd come from. She couldn't breathe, until that great wind once again swirled around her, diluting the black sea enough for her to take a breath and find her voice, and desperate to escape this in-between, she quickly said, "I will sacrifice my all, and all of myself for the good of my tribe." As soon as she'd finished, the Veil once again reformed. It leaked into her eyes until she feared she'd go blind, and in her fear, magic pooled beneath her skin, glowing out of her like a living flame.

The darkness squealed, but instead of retreating, it forced its way deeper into her.

"Yes, that is true enough, at least," Inaras replied, her terrible voice thoughtful.

Liadan felt the goddess' gaze on her.

"Am I… finished?" Liadan gagged. All around her, the Veil screamed soundlessly, imposing its terrible will on her soul, and the more Liadan fought it, raising her fire to glow brighter, the harder the darkness struck her. If it couldn't expel Liadan, it would rend her apart from the inside. She wouldn't last much longer here, but Inaras held her fast by the force of her will alone.

"No, young one, your trial has only just begun."

The wind returned on its third pass, fanning her flame and providing a small respite. *She weakens, Inaras,* hissed the great god, Vayu.

Taking heed, the goddess spoke quickly. "Listen, and listen well, Dragonblood, for many lives depend on you. Lives of *my* people. Are you worthy of them?"

The darkness had filled her limbs, turning them as cold as ice, and Liadan shivered. "N-no," she answered, humbling herself before the great Mother of Life. "Your people are great, and incredibly strong. I am… not worthy of them. I have… not proven myself to be as strong. I… don't know if… I am."

Ghostly hands caressed her face, forcing her to look up into a pair of shining eyes. "You must be," Inaras said. "It was one of my own who summoned the demon for her revenge. No outsider could have banished me from my own people; only one of the Imarah could have done so, and the curse will keep me from them until the Veil's maker is dead, or I am.

"I weaken in exile, young Dragonblood. Without my people's prayers, soon, even I will not have enough power to restore the First Tribe. You *must* triumph! You must draw out the demon and slay him; destroy the shroud of Darkness over the First Valley. You will never be a blade of Imarah, young Dragonblood; you will be my Vessel, the flame with which I'll burn my way back to my people. And you will burn so bright, it'll reduce you to ashes. That is the oath you swore to my prince, and that is the price your oath will exact. Do you understand now what you have done? Are you willing to sacrifice yourself so they might live?"

The goddess' face dissolved and her hands faded away. Liadan was forcefully shoved out of the Veil, slamming back into herself, her physical body convulsing to expel the residual darkness. Sporadic bursts of light flared from her, reflecting off the brass bowl into dozens of sharp beams.

The Magus' voice trembled with fear as he asked, "Who are you?"

At last, the question she'd been waiting for. But Liadan could no longer answer as she'd been instructed. Shaking, disoriented, she rose to her hands and knees and answered the only way she could: "I am the flame of Inaras." She spoke the words in Aegiran, the sounds effortlessly flowing over her tongue as if she'd spoken them all her life. Her skin's glow settled, burning away the chill of the Dark Veil and feeding her strength.

The torc at her neck, the dragon's gift to her, vibrated against her skin, reminding Liadan of her heritage. *I am a Dragonblood, the Halfling daughter of Halfling parents, a crown princess of my people, and an Other with powers none have yet seen, not even*

I. And now, with the goddess' hand on her shoulder, those powers would be greater still. They'd consume her in the end.

Perhaps that had always been her fate.

The moment she thought it, her inner light intensified enough to illuminate the Magus' face behind his veil.

Eyes wide, mouth slack, he gasped softly, leaning back. But despite his fear, he asked, as ritual dictated, "What do you want?"

Dizziness assailed Liadan as she pushed herself up to sit back on her heels. Although the Veil's darkness had burned away, the potion's effects still ravaged her body and her mind, and Liadan couldn't focus on any of the six shadowy Magi now floating before her. When she reached up to wipe her brow, her hand passed over her hair instead, and she dared not shake her head, lest she topple over and never get up again. "I wish to fulfill my oath, to break the curse and restore Imarah to what it once was."

"W-what will you sacrifice?"

Silence followed. Liadan stared at the brass bowl, and in its depths saw the reflection of her own eyes, glowing as brightly as the goddess' had done. The final answer would seal her fate. In Wilderheim, she hadn't known what she was doing when she'd foolishly spoken her oath. Now it was too late to undo it. She had no choice but to keep going forward. Her life, her very soul was bound to the Imarah tribe by that oath, and the only way to free herself was to free them.

Her light dimmed, plunging the tent into darkness once more.

"My all, and all of myself," she finally answered the Magi.

The first trial was over.

CHAPTER 29

Farraj stepped away from the tent to indicate the final petitioner had passed the first trial, and Tir's shoulders slumped in relief. She'd made it through.

Then he saw his shadow, barely peeking out past the tips of his toes. Midday. The ordeal of *kharashan* had no time limit; whether a petitioner took a day or seven to return to the tribe, it only mattered that they return at all. But there was a reason why they'd stopped calling for it. When the threat of demons loomed over everyone the moment night fell, the risk was too great for any one man to venture out into the desert on his own.

Today's first petitioner would already be well on his way to the final trial. Liadan, the last, had lost a half-day waiting; she'd have even less time to finish the ordeal and return to the relative safety of the camp before nightfall.

She will make it through, Tir told himself. Her oath would compel her to return, would give her the strength to meet each challenge quickly and without delay.

And if the demons came…

Fear for her and for his tribe suddenly lodged in his throat. He looked at the glass vial he still clutched, raised the looped thong to hang it from his neck, then reconsidered and took the vial to his tent instead. He wrapped the delicate bottle in cloth, then in leather, and finally in sheepskin, then placed it into the ebony chest where Dhakir had kept all of his most treasured possessions. It was empty now, those treasures burned with him on his pyre. Swallowing back his grief, Tir forced himself to his feet. There was work to be done.

Emerging from the tent once more, he caught Farraj just passing by.

The older man sighed. "Leave her to it, Tirasdunh. She must complete the ordeal if she is to be one of our tribe on her terms. It is the only way."

"I know," he replied, causing Farraj to raise his eyebrows in surprise. "That is not what I want to say to you." Liadan had been right; she couldn't have remained *shensari* for even a day. If she had, the tribe might have come to accept her, but only as an extension of him. For Liadan, that would have been a slow, withering death.

"Then what is it?"

How to explain? "I know you don't believe I am worthy of leading Imarah. No, do not interrupt. You are right to doubt me, but I ask you to trust me now. Something bad is heading toward us; I feel evil coming on the wind, and I need your help."

"Anything," Farraj answered at once.

Tir nodded. "Gather the *kharesh*. Liadan and I left a cart of supplies in the east. Water, oil, clothes, shoes; anything we could take with us from the First City."

Farraj blanched. "You rode through the First City?"

He ignored the question. "I will need two riders to come with me to fetch the cart. I fear we will need every last scrap of those supplies before the night is through."

"Yes." Farraj nodded. "It will be done at once."

≪ »·◇·« ≫

Liadan stumbled out of the tent, falling to her hands and knees a few paces from it. The sand burned her palms, the sun seared her back, but the air was clean, and she breathed in deeply, hoping it would ease the potion's effects.

When she felt strong enough to look up, she saw no one around except one veiled woman sitting before her. The black tent was far behind her. She'd walked farther into the desert than she'd thought.

Sitting back on her heels, she wiped the sweat from her brow and faced the veiled woman—the second trial. Seven bottles sat in the sand in front of her, all identical, all neatly aligned. This was the trial of the mind. Last night, Farraj had told her that each *kharesh* was not only a warrior, but also a trained assassin; they learned to kill by any means, with weapons, trickery, or poison, and to that end, each wore a belt lined with these same venoms and poisons in varying degrees of potency. The weakest would make Liadan fall asleep for days and, by the rules of *kharashan*, she'd be left to her own devices until she awakened—*if* she awakened. The strongest would kill her instantly.

The poisons would be unmarked, but always arranged the same way on a belt. Not by potency, but using a code each *kharesh* learned before taking the ordeal. They learned it early on, and repeated the lesson often, so that, should the need arise, a *kharesh* wouldn't need to think about which bottle to reach for; he'd know it instinctively, wasting no time when it mattered most.

The veiled woman waved her hand over the row of bottles, then brought it to her mouth, tipping her head back. Liadan was to choose one bottle and take a drink. What was the order Farraj had taught her? Her memory was excellent on most occasions, but with the potion still muddling her mind, Liadan couldn't recall his words. There had been a rhyme to it… Venom, poison sleeping draft. *Wasting time! Gods, what was the order?*

The veiled woman pointed at the sky, then eastward to the mountain range. Liadan was far from finished; she had to make haste.

She reached for a bottle, then hesitated. Thirst made her tongue stick to the roof of her mouth; she'd give her sword arm for a sip of water. Liadan glanced to the east, where the mountain range loomed dark red above the sands, marking the location of her third trial. She couldn't head toward it until she'd passed the second.

No more time to waste; the longer she stayed there, the worse the heat would become. And what would it matter, anyway? Liadan was Other; she didn't react to poisons the same way humans did. Whatever was in those bottles wouldn't kill her—it couldn't. At worst, she'd fall asleep for a few days, but she'd recover eventually.

Liadan snatched up the third bottle on the right, downed its contents in one swallow. Warm liquid slid down her throat, and hope surged that she'd made the right choice. Liadan's questioning look to the woman was met with a bow of her head and a motion of her hand to indicate she should continue.

She stood, ready to move on—

—and her knees gave out under her. She dropped to the sand, stomach twisting painfully. Her entire torso clenched in a merciless cramp as the poison she'd just imbibed contorted her insides. She embarrassed herself by vomiting in front of the veiled woman, but she was still alive.

Struggling to her feet again, Liadan took a shaky step and, by the grace of the goddess, she didn't fall. One more step, and the cramps subsided a little, but ten steps farther, they returned with a vengeance, sending her sprawling once more. Liadan writhed on the hot sands, tears of pain stinging her eyes. This was worse than the pain heralding her firestorm. The poison exacted its price for her foolishness by making her crawl when she ought to have been running.

But Liadan refused to give up. She crawled ever eastward, gaze locked on that mountainside as her guiding beacon. When she could, she got up and walked; when the pain knocked her to her knees, she crawled. Step by step, Liadan approached the mountain, and when she got there, the pain had become too much and she blacked out.

By the time she woke, the sun was already kissing the edge of the horizon. *I'm alive,* she thought. Potions, poisons, trekking through the desert—none of that had stopped her, and Liadan was so close to her goal, she could almost see it. There, halfway up the mountain, something glittered in the saddle. Her prize beckoned—a shining scimitar to mark her a *kharesh*, worthy of looking the tribe in the eye instead of staring at their feet in submission. *I am a blade of Imarah.*

You will be the flame with which I'll burn my way back to my people.

Liadan smiled recklessly, reaching up for a small outcropping above her. "Wait until Mother hears about this."

CHAPTER 30

The sun was halfway behind the horizon when the eighth petitioner, now a *kharesh*, returned to camp with a gleaming scimitar in hand. Farraj stood on the ceremony of clasping forearms with him to welcome him back, but Tir refused to waste any more precious time. They'd already distributed the clothes and shoes to those most in need of them, and what little water had remained, they'd given to the returning *kharesh*, but Tir had kept two bottles back for Liadan.

No one had glimpsed any sign of her yet.

"It's taking too long," he muttered, hands clenching at his sides.

"She is strong," Farraj replied. "She will come back."

"Before the sun sets?"

Farraj said nothing. If she wasn't already on her way back—and someone would have seen her if she were—the only way Liadan would return from that mountain before nightfall was if she truly sprouted dragon wings and flew.

"What does the woman say of her second trial?"

"She says nothing," Farraj answered, "as it should be. The trials are Liadan's to overcome, not ours. If any of the stories about her parents are true, if anything you told me about Liadan is true, then you need not worry about her. Worry instead for your people."

Tir forced his gaze away from the setting sun to look around. The *kharesh*, old and new alike, stood ready with their scimitars at their sides. Their celebration cut short, each had been given a bowl of oil and a cloth with which to varnish the blade, and each had been instructed to light those blades on fire at the first sight of a demon. The rest of his tribe knew nothing of it, but they must have sensed the same thing Tir had: as bright and as hot as the day felt, a chill seeped up from the sand and the air felt heavy with dark magic. Not a single breeze swept by to lighten the oppressive weight of portent. Tir had felt this way before, while riding through Lyria with Liadan, just before the storm had broken right over their heads.

Not knowing what else to do, Imarah had gathered in the center of the camp, forming a circle with the women and children in the middle, and the men standing guard around them. Everyone watched the eastern mountain, though whether they watched for Liadan or for a demon swarm, Tir didn't know.

The sun dipped lower; his shadow grew a little longer. To the north, the horses whinnied, and Tir ran to them at once. He passed the Magus' tent with a cursory glance at the old man drawing giant concentric circles in the sand.

When he'd left Imarah, only two horses had remained: Tarabas and Zara. Now, the shelter held six horses in all, some still wearing the symbolic markings of Aesma Daeva that couldn't be washed off except with water.

At the very back of the shelter, Sleipnir tossed his head, kicking at the post his reins had been tied to. Sensing his fear, Tarabas, too, tried to rear away from his tether, and their distress riled the others into a panic.

"Easy," Tir soothed, approaching with his hands raised. "Calm yourselves. Calm…"

Sleipnir reared, tearing the post from the sands. It swung wildly, still attached to his reins, and Tir ducked to avoid a blow. He took two running steps, vaulted astride the black stallion, and hung on for dear life with his legs as he struggled to free Sleipnir from the straps. The horse reared again, then dropped forward and kicked out, jumped and twisted, doing his worst to shake Tir off his back.

Tarabas and the other horses squealed, drawing others of the tribe to try to calm them. They were dividing the group. Tir almost had the strap undone, when Sleipnir reared again, this time so far back, he lost his balance and toppled over. Tir couldn't move away fast enough; his foot caught beneath the horse's girth, and something popped painfully in his ankle. The stallion scrambled back to his hooves, leaving Tir in the sands, but with the straps now loosened, Sleipnir shook out of them and galloped off toward the mountains in the east.

Tir was glad. "Run quickly," he said, wincing as he probed his ankle. Nothing broken; the pain would ease in moments. "Run to her, and keep her safe." He got up, keeping his weight on his good foot, and shouted, "Everyone fall back! Free the horses; they can take care of themselves! Set them loose and fall back!"

⋘ »·◇·« ⋙

The final challenge, a trial of the body, was the longest, and the most grueling. Farraj had warned Liadan it wouldn't be what it appeared; the trial didn't begin until the petitioner had reached the point of total exhaustion. The trek through the desert to the mountain range had been a pleasurable respite compared to the wretched climb to the saddle. Liadan steadied her foot on a hold, then reached up with her opposite hand. The red rock was searing hot, something that wouldn't normally have bothered Liadan, but it was also sharp and brittle, with blade-like edges that cut into her palms and broke off in her skin. Every time she let go, she had to wipe her palm to remove the debris, wasting precious time and energy.

Her mouth was parched; her lips were cracked and peeling. She squinted against every breeze, but dared not completely close her eyes, even with sand constantly blowing into them. She had no tears left to wash it out. What was worse, every so often, her stomach clenched with painful cramps, remnants of that accursed poison she'd drunk. Weak and shaky, she had to test the security of each hand- and foothold twice before trusting her whole weight to it. Wasting even more precious time.

At an outcropping large enough to hold both of her feet, Liadan stopped to catch her breath, squinting against the sunset. In the distance, she saw the Imarah camp huddling small on the vast expanse of glistening sands, its people like miniscule dots moving rapidly among the tents. The other petitioners had no doubt made it back to camp already. There would be celebration and much honor bestowed on all of them. Would anyone notice she hadn't yet returned? Would they care? Like as not, they'd be happier for her to disappear altogether.

Not about to give them that satisfaction, Liadan gritted her teeth and looked up. The saddle wasn't far; already she'd made it two-thirds of the way. *One final push,* she told herself. *I can make it there. I will stand with the kharesh as one of them.*

So determined, Liadan launched up and caught a protruding lump of round rock. It gave, detaching with a soft crack, and she cried out, swinging from her one secure handhold. Blood on her fingers made her weakened grip slick and as she dangled hundreds of feet in the air, her hand began to slip.

In a desperate bid to save herself, she swung for another hold, and the tips of her fingers brushed it without gaining purchase. She swung again, stretching farther… *There!*

A sharp point speared into her palm, but at least the natural hook anchored her, even if it did hurt like hell. She braced her feet and pushed up.

The sun dipped lower, two-thirds down behind the horizon by the time she'd reached the saddle. By then, Liadan couldn't keep her feet under her. She sat down hard, head lolling back, and allowed herself a moment's rest to catch her breath. When the sun set, she'd have to summon her fire to climb back down, and wasn't sure of the wisdom of that.

Her eyes began to close.

Can't fall asleep… Liadan forced herself back to her feet to look for her blade.

Breath left her at the sight before her. Fifty paces ahead rose four majestic columns with intricate symbols and patterns carved directly into the rock face where the saddle met the higher mountain. Behind them, a small flame flickered deep inside a black tunnel. Its light drew her forward, and she cautiously entered the abyss, tracing the ground with her toes before shifting her weight forward. Her feet dragged, her knees were weak, her hands throbbed with a bone-deep ache that overpowered even the sharp pain of her many bleeding cuts. The flame danced somewhere just out of reach, singing to her of a beautiful, gleaming sword set on an ornate pedestal. She kept going, steadying herself against the tunnel wall, unconcerned about the bloody streaks she left across the faded paintings.

Not far ahead, Liadan rounded a bend in the tunnel, and all at once, there it was—on a small stone altar in the center of a cavernous chamber, a shallow bowl of oil had been set aflame to illuminate the polished scimitar set on a carved ebony frame. The blade shone, its metallic melody sharper than any sword she'd ever wielded, aside from her own. The guard was darker, an intricate construction of brass and gold that sang to Liadan in the purest of tones. The handle was wrapped in leather dyed a deep red, ending in a pommel shaped like an onion with a bright red tassel dangling from its tip. Beneath the stand lay a leather scabbard, a whetstone, a cloth, and a small vial of oil. A more magnificent prize, Liadan had never seen.

Mesmerized by the beauty of such an offering, she approached the altar.

The fire suddenly flared a warning.

Liadan gasped, pulling back a blink before a scimitar sparked against the altar's edge.

"You did not think it would be that easy, did you?"

Liadan leaped aside as the warrior launched his attack. She spun a clumsy pirouette to the left and ducked another swing of his blade, retreated from his merciless forward press until she found herself with her heel past the edge of the chamber. He'd almost expelled her back into the dark tunnel and, having done so, he backed up to the altar to guard her prize.

"Save yourself the pain of death, Northern scum," he said in scornful Aegiran, every word of which Liadan now understood. "Go back to your demon homelands and leave us in peace!"

Undeterred, Liadan started forward again. The warrior brought up his blade, slashed in an arc, driving her back a step farther into the tunnel. The gleam in his eyes told her that was precisely what he'd wanted. The tunnel was dark and narrow, a much more difficult place to maneuver around a swinging blade. If she let him, he'd force her all the way out and off the cliff.

Liadan needed to stay in the chamber; it was her only chance of getting that sword. She tried again to get past him, and again he drove her backwards. Feigning left, she dove beneath the swing of his blade to the right and rolled along the floor, back inside the chamber. He roared as he came after her, his sword sparking off the stone walls. Liadan kept low, kept moving, but her strength sapped quickly, thighs burning with strain as she rolled and crawled around the chamber in a pathetic display. The dragon would have been ashamed.

The fire called to her, singing enticingly; it was just there, a tool to be used, and a weapon much easier to wield than a sword. Fire was light; it moved on its own, an extension of her. But to use her power over it against the *kharesh* would forever deny her the respect she needed. No, to win this trial, she had to do it on his terms—as a warrior, not a Magi.

Of course, that didn't mean she couldn't make use of it the mortal way. Shoving to her feet, she stepped into the warrior's next swing, drove her fist into his stomach, kicked his feet out from under him. He recovered in an instant, now enraged and out for blood, and when he came at her next, he held the scimitar in one hand and a dagger in the other. Liadan turned and ran at the wall, launched off of it, twisted in a graceful somersault over his head to land behind him. Her balance was off; she stumbled and fell onto her backside, striking her elbows on the hard stone floor as the warrior crashed into the wall and howled with rage.

An opponent quick to anger is one easily defeated, the dragon had always said. As the *kharesh* spun around, hurling his dagger at her, Liadan ducked it, using her momentum to get back to her feet and grab for the bowl of fire. Its metal was searing hot, the oil inside it sloshing as she swiped it off the altar and flung it at the *kharesh*. A speck landed on her arm, and fire flared eagerly along the back of it up to her shoulder, igniting her hair.

The warrior didn't escape it, either; he screamed as burning oil coated his left side, boiling his skin off, and the smell of charred flesh filled the chamber instantly.

Liadan shook out her hair, extinguishing her own flames with a thought, before she rushed to put him out. The ground was on fire where the oil had spilled; she kept them safely away from it despite its seductive call.

Tears of pain ran down his face, but he made not a sound. The warrior would be in a great deal of pain for a long time; his left arm would be scarred, disfigured for the rest of his life, but he'd survive and would retain the use of his limb.

Liadan stepped away to let him catch his breath. His eyes were bloodshot, his breaths rattled, lungs filled with smoke. He coughed, swayed on his feet, then leaned back against the chamber wall, shaking the entire time. From there, he stared at Liadan for a long time, fighting a silent internal battle, then finally allowed himself a small nod of thanks.

Liadan inclined her head in reply. "Do you need help down the mountain?" she asked in fluent Aegiran.

In answer, the *kharesh* pushed away from the wall with a groan and raised his sword. He could barely keep his feet under him, but the blade, even quivering in the space between them, didn't lower, the tip pointed squarely at her chest.

"I just saved your life!"

"A *kharesh* fights to the death!"

"Eight others must have come through here before me. Did you kill them all? You must have, since you're still alive."

"A *kharesh* fights!" he repeated. "A *kharesh* is not *kharesh* until he crosses blades with the enemy." His gaze flickered to the scimitar still resting on the altar.

Understanding dawned. Liadan slowly reached for the sword, keeping a wary eye on her opponent.

Her hand met the warm softness of leather; her fingers curled around the handle. The warrior didn't move, save to shift his feet farther apart for balance. He wouldn't last much longer. She eased the weapon off the stand, then brought it forward, touching the flat of her blade against his.

The warrior nodded. "Hail *kharesh*," he said. "Liadan of the North, *shensari* of Imarah. I am Muhammad al-Hassan, and I claim you as a sister, in battle and in… blood—"

Liadan caught him before he hit the ground.

All at once, the fire went out, plunging the chamber into darkness, and a great wind swept past Liadan. "*Riiiide…*" commanded the whispering voice of Inaras. Then again, louder, "*Riiiide!*"

Liadan lay the fallen *kharesh* on the ground, then ran out of the cave. The last rays of sunlight had winked out, its dying glow still painting the western sky in hues of purple and pink, but in the distant south along the foot of the mountain range, a pitch-black cloud obscured the stars. That blackness raced across the desert toward the Imarah camp, and even from so far away, Liadan heard the demon screams piercing through the night.

She froze. Not a single flame burned in the camp. "They'll be massacred…"

A sharp whinny echoed far below her. Sleipnir stomped at the base of the mountain, tossing his head, kicking out at the rock with enough force to make it crumble. He could feel them coming.

Liadan glanced back at the tunnel behind her. This was a temple to Inaras; it had stood for countless centuries, and though the chiseled inscriptions had faded, the goddess' power was palpable in the very stone it'd been carved into. She had to believe Muhammad would be safe inside.

"*Riiiide!*" the wind commanded again.

Liadan moaned, drawing on the dragonfire in her soul. Her skin began to glow, flickering like a living flame caught inside her. Its heat banished the growing chill, made stone hiss when she touched it with her bare hands. With her scimitar sheathed at her waist, Liadan scrabbled down the mountain toward Sleipnir. His whinnies became louder—more screams of fear than cries of alarm—and he pranced back and forth. As soon as she'd mounted his bare back, clutching his mane, he bolted off so fast, it stole her breath away. They flew like the wind over the desert sands, and still couldn't hope to outpace the demon swarm. *We'll never make it,* she thought, watching darkness descend upon the camp.

CHAPTER 31

Faster than a sandstorm, more powerful than a northern gale, the demon swarm swept through the camp, razing everything to the ground. Tents blew away beneath its force; stands and stalls splintered. Knocked off their feet, the people of Imarah screamed in terror. They saw nothing, felt nothing but the icy wind that stole breath from their lungs and drew tears from their eyes.

"Hold!" Tir shouted, though he could barely hear his own voice.

The *kharesh* scrambled to their feet, sparking flints to light oil, but the wind was too strong for it to catch.

"Hold!" Tir repeated. "It's only wind!"

No one heard him, and with sand kicking up and no light, they couldn't see him waving for their attention.

Tir grasped the arm of the closest *kharesh* and shouted by his ear, "Get everyone close together and hold steady!" If they could shield the center from the wind, fire would catch more easily.

The *kharesh* nodded, passing the message on to the next, and little by little, the tribe drew together, with the warriors surrounding the women and children.

Someone screamed, a sound Tir knew all too well. He couldn't see who'd fallen to demons, but when the scream cut short, he knew a warrior had dealt him a mercy blow.

Then, all at once, the wind stopped. Shouts faded into silence, and the tribe raised their heads, casting frightened gazes all around.

Tir let out a cautious sigh, and his breath misted. "Is everyone all right?" He shivered, chilled to the bone, and looked down to see white frost creeping across his skin.

"Hiru is dead," came the answer.

"Nai'mah needs a bandage!"

Farraj joined Tir, gaze roaming for the threat that seemed to have disappeared. "What happened?" he asked. With the tents gone, they could see for miles to the west and to the south. All was empty, the night perfectly still and quiet, but neither of them believed the demons had truly gone.

"I don't know," Tir answered, uneasy in the dead silence. Demons didn't leave when they had their prey surrounded and helpless. Why would they take only one and then give up? "*Kharesh*," he called softly, "light the oils."

Flints sparked and oil ignited, illuminating the night. Someone set the fallen Hiru on fire as a precaution. He'd be given the proper honors another time—if anyone survived to speak the words. For now, they needed light and assurance that he wouldn't rise as Forsaken.

"Too quiet," Farraj murmured.

Tir hummed in agreement.

"Where did they go?" asked someone else.

Tir circled the group, looking out in every direction, his gaze lingering on the eastern mountain range. No movement, no light, no telltale flash of fire among the dunes. He didn't allow himself to contemplate what that might mean.

She's not dead. Their blood bond would have told him if she were. As long as his tribe was in danger, Liadan's oath would compel her to aid them. "Where are you?" he whispered.

"Uncle Tir," a small voice suddenly said, freezing him in his tracks. He turned his head to the west and again beheld the bedraggled little girl-child from the First City, standing alone and a fair distance off, with her dark, matted hair falling over her eyes and her small, dirty hands loose and defeated by her sides.

Tir wasn't the only one who saw her.

"Zia?" one of the women cried. "Zia! It's you!" Three *kharesh* held her back as she desperately tried to run to the child, screaming for her daughter.

"Where is she, Uncle Tir?" the demon-child asked in a soft, quivering voice, ignoring the woman and the commotion she'd caused.

"Tir," Farraj warned quietly, "she has no feet."

"Where did she go?" the demon asked again, more urgently this time. "I can't find her."

"Everyone stay together," Tir ordered, not daring to look away from the demon. "Keep to the lights." They needed more fire. It had taken a wall of it to keep the Dark creatures out of the palace when they'd attacked in the First City. But what else could they burn here? The demon storm had swept everything away.

"Where did you hide the daughter of fire?" the Dark child demanded, body quivering, hands fisting. Her voice changed as it grew louder, and Tir shuddered at the terrible sound.

Farraj grabbed Tir's arm. "They want Liadan?"

"They want her *first*." He pushed Farraj off to draw the sword he'd strapped to his side, and the heavy Northern blade sang out of its scabbard, briefly reflecting firelight. The demon hissed furiously.

"We want the daughter of fire!" The child grew bigger, rising higher off the sand. A gust of icy wind swept past Tir. "She belongs to us!" Inside a whirlwind of its own making, its dark hair turned into misty shadows, revealing a horribly deformed face. "*Where did you hide the Northern bitch!*" It rushed Tir with a scream, knocking him to the ground, giving him no chance to shout a warning as the floodgates opened and demons descended from above. Someone shouted for fire; someone else screamed.

On his back, with claws of ice digging into his chest, squeezing his heart, Tir couldn't breathe. The demon's eye sockets glowed red with bloodlust, and a hideous grin mocked him as it sank its incorporeal fingers into his core. A pained groan escaped Tir as the demon latched onto his soul and slowly, so very slowly, began to pull it out.

Viscous saliva dripped onto his exposed flesh, burning like acid, and all the while the demon watched, enjoying Tir's torment. Tir's hands and feet went numb; his lips turned cold. *This is the end,* he thought. The last of his tribe would not only die, their souls would be devoured, never to rejoin their ancestors in the afterlife. In one fell swoop, Imarah would cease to exist.

The demon gave a hard tug, and Tir's back arched, head tilting backwards. Blurred flashes of fire danced across his vision—Imarah's vain attempt to fight back, to survive just one more night. Their desperate voices blended with the unearthly demon screams; bodies flew up, never to fall back down. Tir fought the demon's pull, dug his fingers into the sand, commanded his heart to keep beating. But no matter what he did, he couldn't break free. The demon shrieked louder—a dark cackle of delight.

Desperate for his last sight to be something other than the thing's filthy visage, Tir squeezed his eyes shut and thought of Liadan. Her fire dance lit up his memories, filled his mind and his heart with searing heat and wonder.

The demon screamed, released him, rearing away as though burned.

Tir sucked in a harsh breath, his body a twisted mass of agony. Before he could recover, the demon snatched him up again, so high, Tir's feet left the ground. It roared, the bones of its face contorting into a furious snarl before it unhinged its jaw to bite off his head.

Something slammed into its back, and a fiery, golden aura flared around it, bright enough to make Tir squint.

The demon swiveled around to seek its attacker and, with a shrill call, dropped Tir to streak off in pursuit.

Tir groped for his sword as volleys of fireballs assaulted the demon swarm. All around him, his people dropped from the sky like flies, some alive; some broken and contorted, their bodies crushed beyond recognition. Those still alive huddled around the flames, took up swords and raised them high to catch a fireball.

Tir struggled to stand, shaken, unsteady, and weak, and braced to fight against the demons murdering his tribe.

But none of them faced him; the mass of swirling darkness thinned as its venomous shadows streaked across the sky toward the greater source of fire. The sky brightened with countless stars, and its sudden vastness sent Tir back down to his knees. He dared not look behind him, couldn't bring himself to face what he knew he'd see.

Farraj helped him to his feet, held him steady, spoke urgent words Tir couldn't hear past the ringing in his ears. Heart thrashing, head pounding, Tir stared at the older *kharesh* and waited for him to say the only thing he could: that Liadan was dead, and they were doomed.

"…working! The fire…"

Tir frowned, shook his head, and focused on Farraj's mouth to read his words.

"…fire alone did not harm them, blades passed right through. But when the blade burns, the fire gets *inside*! It kills them from within!"

Tir looked down at the Northern sword imbued with magic that thrummed into his hand, and forced his grip to tighten.

“She is winning, Tir,” Farraj said. “Your *shensari* is winning, and she is magnificent!”

Tir whirled around to see for himself, and nearly fell to his knees once more.

On the other side of what used to be their camp, the night was bright with Liadan’s fire dance. Demons flared, one after the other, exploding in spectacular showers of sparks as she cut through them with her flaming scimitar, and with each one dead, the oppressive darkness lessened, the chill eased, and the survivors cheered louder. Even at such a distance, Tir felt the heat of that dance, knew it was brighter, hotter, and bigger than she’d ever conjured before.

She cut them down in a glorious display of beauty and grace, her face pinched in concentration. Just as she always did in his dreams.

And just as it always did in his nightmares, it would kill her.

CHAPTER 32

Tir saw it happening. Her flames ebbed as her strength waned. The demons saw it, too, attacked harder, scored her with their claws and retreated before the fire could hurt them. Liadan's body glowed, her hair escaped from the confines of its braid to halo her head in a mane of living flames.

He'd seen her like this in Dai, but there'd been no smoke then, only fire and light. He'd seen her smoke, too—in the desert, when her flames had consumed her like dry wood.

"Magnificent," Farraj repeated in awe. He didn't know any better.

Tir did. "Fall back..."

"What?"

"Get everyone away. Fall back, as far as you can—"

Another flare, and the following ebb extinguished her almost completely. "Liadan!" Tir took off running, even as the demons swooped down on her, so many, so thick, that her light disappeared in the center of their dark mass. He ran straight at the demons, turning a deaf ear to the cries of alarm sounding his reckless advance. Blade cold, with no light to protect him from their wrath, Tir roared, desperate to draw their attention away from Liadan, to give her just a moment more to recover her strength.

He was close enough to swing his blade at the outer circle, when a swirl of fire blazed out, cutting through the swarm in an arc so wide, Tir had no hope of avoiding it. He felt the fire pass through him. Its searing heat sank into his skin, flared across his heart, and came out the other side. But where demons squealed, and burst, and scattered before him, Tir remained unharmed. Shock stopped him in his tracks. Liadan was not fifteen paces away, slumped, gasping for air, but she was still alive. For just a moment, their gazes met, and her eyes widened in surprise to mirror his.

A moment too long. The demons regrouped and attacked once more. Though their ranks had been thinned, their fervor had grown. Liadan threw a fireball Tir's way, then she was engulfed again, fighting for her life. The sand burst into waist-high flames at his feet. Tir felt their warmth, but nothing more; just like in his dreams, he passed through the burning veil as if it were made of the softest gossamer. Ah, but now he had light.

In the middle of the swarm, Liadan cried out in pain, and rage lit his blood. Clutching his sword tighter, its blade holding fire as if made for that purpose, Tir smiled and picked out his first target.

⋘ ››·◇·‹‹ ⋙

Liadan's fire was running out; she didn't have the strength to keep up a steady attack. A burn like that required both concentration and fuel, both of which she had in short supply after the ordeal. Sooner or later, she'd weaken enough for the demons to take her. She couldn't let that happen.

Her retreat tactic had worked. Feigning weakness had brought the Dark bastards to her in droves, and she'd culled a good number of them in one shot, but it wouldn't work a second time. They were too smart; they sent in decoys to draw her fire, while others snuck up on her blind side. While Liadan was shrouded in flames, they couldn't kill her, but they could and did reach through her fire's weakest points to strike at her. Liadan's back stung where they'd clawed her. Blood seeped from her wounds, adding the wrong kind of fuel to her flames. When it burned, it smoked, hazing her vision, and with each drop she lost, Liadan's strength waned even more.

Slash, twist, duck, turn, slash. Decoys to the right. Throw a flame, pirouette to cut off the main attack at its knees—or where knees ought to have been. Didn't matter where she cut them; their human-like shape seemed to be only an illusion. As long as the burning blade slashed through the outer layer, the fire burned them alive from the inside out.

But two or three had burst from the heat alone earlier. At least she thought they had. Liadan could almost hear the dragon's voice in her mind: *Hunches and guesses will kill you faster than an arrow through the heart.*

Two demons swooped down from opposite directions, and Liadan rolled out of the way, using her escape to gather a fireball in her free hand, feed it heat until it turned blue. When she pushed to her feet, she let it fly, striking one of the pair in the face.

Others charged her shroud of fire to keep her off balance and disoriented, but even as she fought them off, Liadan kept an eye on the one she'd struck. It screamed, flying backwards into its brethren, but it was too late for them to help. Its face disintegrated, and the rest of its body followed, raining down onto the sand in a shower of sparks.

It worked!

You got lucky, a memory of the dragon retorted, and it was right. She'd hit the demon by accident, not by design. Blue fire required more energy to build, and it was erratic, shooting off without warning in any way it pleased. She might hit a demon, she might not, but she would waste precious energy in the process. She might also hit one of the tribe by accident.

Duck, swing, slash, flare. Three more demons down. Too many left, and she was tiring. No, individual shots wouldn't work, but if Liadan could build enough strength for one massive burst, as hot as she could handle, she might be able to take them out all at once.

Demonic shades parted, and for just a moment Liadan saw Tir not fifteen paces away. Her fire didn't burn him; he stood in a pool of it, the flames licking at his waist and higher, and instead of running, he used it to fight. He kicked up burning sand, infuriating demons into attack, and any who flew too close died beneath his flaming sword. But it wasn't the weapon Tir was used to; it was longer, heavier, and he wielded it too slowly. He wouldn't last much longer than Liadan.

That's that, then.

She spun, scoring the sand with her swordpoint, and a circle of fire shot up, high enough to camouflage her for a few moments. Drawing her fiery shroud back into her core, she banked the flame until it barely shone, then she fed it every last bit of power she possessed, drawing on her soul, her life essence. The fire turned blue, threatening to escape. She held it steady, fed it more, more, until the pressure almost shattered her. Her skin stretched to its limits, her bones ached with the strain of holding on to far too much. With all of her focus on her last weapon, the circle of fire began to die down. Liadan didn't need it anymore.

When she opened her eyes, everything looked blue, and the night had turned to day, the air wavering with Liadan's heat. Demons drew back, confused. She glowed, flickering like a star; not as bright as before, but much, much hotter. Liadan held out her hand, watched veins pulse with heat beneath her skin. Her every breath fanned the flames inside her, and each time it flared the slightest bit, her hand turned transparent, as if her body itself was becoming fire.

It frightened her. Too much power, too much fire could destroy the wielder as easily as his opponents. A true dragon might have withstood the heat longer, but Liadan's blood was diluted, too human, and already her core was burning as it never had before.

Twelve paces away, Tir cut through a demon and braced for more, but none attacked him, all of them intent on Liadan. He met her gaze, shook his head in a wordless message. He feared for her. He should.

A demon screamed, and the rest echoed it, launching another attack.

"Burn," Liadan ordered venomously, not recognizing her own voice. She threw her arms out to the sides, let the fire out. Its full force ripped out of her, exploding so fast, Liadan had no hope of containing it, and she prayed the tribe was far enough to escape the inferno. It lasted no longer than three frenetic heartbeats, during which Liadan was unaware of anything but the blue fire tearing through her.

When it ended, darkness reclaimed the night, and Liadan sagged, dizzy, naked, shaking from head to toe. She had nothing left in her, not even a spark to call up to defend herself. Her scimitar dropped from her numb hand, and she was relieved to be rid of the extra weight. Blinking hard against the gloom, she searched for any hint of movement, human or otherwise. As her eyes adjusted to the darkness, she saw the sand had turned black as far as she could see. Hard lumps marked charred remnants of whatever hadn't blown away in the demon storm, but she saw no sign of people, save Tir, lying still in the sand a fair distance away, tendrils of smoke rising from the last shreds of his clothing.

"Tir?" she called, anxious and hoarse. Her legs were too weak to carry her to him; she was barely keeping upright. "Tir, answer me!"

He moved, then stilled again.

Were her eyes playing tricks on her? She took a step, stumbled, and cursed. "Tir!"

He groaned, sitting up with a wince. "Calm yourself, woman, you haven't killed me yet!"

Liadan would have laughed if she'd had the strength. Instead, she looked up, basking in the glory of millions upon millions of stars and the bright, waxing moon. Cold seeped into her tired, aching bones, and she shivered in her nakedness, wincing at the twinges of pain in her back. In all of her young life, Liadan had never felt cold like this; always, her soul's fire had warmed her, even in the deepest winter, when tears froze on the cheek before they could fall. Now that it was depleted, Liadan felt hollow, yet heavy at the same time. She was tired.

"Are you all right?" Tir asked, getting to his feet with all the grace of an old man. He scowled down at himself, shaking his head.

Far behind him, shadows moved as the tribe began to emerge from hiding. Off to the side, a lone, hunched figure shuffled closer, rattling a string of bones. The Magi. He droned a chant of some sort, moving rhythmically around Liadan, tracing a large circle in the sand. She didn't know what he was trying to do, had no strength left to wonder, save to think it'd have been more helpful for the man to bring them some clothes instead.

Oh, who bloody cares, anyway? Breathing deeply of the chill night air, Liadan tasted nothing but ash and cold on the back of her tongue. The demons were gone, their taint burned away for all time. *We've done it. Inaras, you are free… And I am still standing.* "It's over," she said, allowing herself a smile.

CHAPTER 33

She smiled. Shivering, moments away from collapse, Liadan smiled at him, and a terrible dread gripped Tir's heart. "It's over," she said, as she always did in his nightmares just before she turned to ash.

"No…" He made his feet move, rushing forward to stop what he knew was coming.

"We've won—"

The tip of a scimitar suddenly punched out of her chest.

"*No!*"

Liadan looked down, blood gurgling past her lips as her murderer yanked the weapon back out, let her crumple to the ground.

"Liadan!" Tir fell to his knees and gathered her limp form into his arms. Her eyes were closed, her heart silent, and she was cold as ice. Tir shook her. "Liadan! Open your eyes!"

Her head lolled.

"By the oath you swore to me, I command you—wake!"

Her murderer cackled. Not a demon, not a warrior of Aesimar, but an old woman *aseti*, one of their own, had done this.

"You?"

The old woman tossed the bloodied scimitar to the ground. "A deal is a deal," she said.

"Tir!" Farraj shouted. "Get out! Get away from the witch!"

Tir snatched up Liadan's scimitar, still hot from the flames, and launched at the old woman. With a single cut, her head toppled. Her body swayed, held upright by some invisible force.

Fire flared in a perfect circle around them, and Tir stared down at Liadan's face, searching for signs of life. But it hadn't been her spark. The Magus had set the fire, and even now chanted loudly, moving out to light the second of the three concentric circles Tir had seen him trace earlier that day. They were in the center, he and Liadan, and the old hag.

"Tir, get out!"

The tribe had followed Farraj, *kharesh* circling the flaming perimeter, but none dared to breach it while the Magus worked his spells.

"Hurry! Before—"

The outermost ring burst into flame, pushing Farraj and the *kharesh* farther back.

The tribe fell silent, while the Magus chanted louder, his fire circles flaring so high, Tir lost sight of them all for a moment. But against that bright backdrop, the black mist was easier to see as it seeped out of the witch's neck and poured to the ground like blood. It congealed there, taking on its true shape—that of the demon who'd possessed her. As it escaped its mortal prison, the witch's body withered like a prune, clothes disintegrating into dust until nothing was left but rattling bones raining to the sands.

Before Tir now stood—*floated*—a sight more evil than even the child had been. The *daeva* was incredibly tall, but as thin as a waif, with long hair elegantly pulled back into a queue that coiled on the sand where his feet ought to have been. His face was pale, but more human than any of the others Tir had encountered thus far. Red eyes slanted beneath dark, winged eyebrows; a narrow, regal nose slashed down between sharp cheekbones; and a thin, cruel mouth smirked at him with an arrogance borne of immortality.

The demon emanated evil so deep, Tir felt it down to his soul. It made him feel weak, frightened. His grip on the scimitar slackened until he felt it begin to slip from his hand as the demon circled around the very edge of their fiery enclosure, growling, "Clever little Magi. Fire will not save you. It'll die down eventually, and I will be free once more."

Tir drew back.

Attracted by movement, the demon turned, tipped his head. "Is something the matter, *shansher* Tirasdunh? Have you lost your fighting spirit?"

Tir forced his hand to curl tighter. He raised the blade sideways into the flames, then brought it burning before him.

The demon laughed. "You think to defeat me with that? A burning blade might have sufficed for my court, but I am their prince; I draw on the strength of Darkness itself. Go ahead. Swing your sword." He spread his arms wide.

Tir dug his heel deeper into the sand, refusing to fall for the trick.

The demon rolled his red eyes, hissed a sigh. "I suppose you require incentive. Very well." He streaked forward, claws outstretched for Liadan.

Tir slashed through the black mist of the demon's incorporeal form, severing it mid-stream. The two halves veered off in different directions, circling the prison's perimeter before colliding together across from Tir to mend whole again.

The demon prince smiled. "Do you believe me now? You cannot win against one as powerful as me. Nothing so trite as a little fire can destroy me."

Again the demon circled, regarding Tir with what might have been amusement. "I must admit, I am intrigued. You guard that dead body as if it means more to you than your own life." He tipped his head the other way. "Tell me, *shansher* Tirasdunh, Tir the Demonslayer, did you love your Northern wench?" He sucked in a sharp breath, and his smile stretched wider in delight, revealing rows of pointed teeth. "You did. I can smell it in you. Poor little Dragonblood. She tried so hard to keep the oath from consuming you both. How selfless of her. How brave, and utterly futile." Circling left, the Dark prince hissed at the Magus beyond reach. "For your bravery, *shansher*, I will give you a gift."

"I want nothing from you!"

The demon speared him with a venomous glare. "This, you will want very much. Do you not want to know why your tribe has suffered so? What had brought so many torments down upon your people? Yes, I think you do. Listen well, Tirasdunh the Demonslayer. Listen and suffer! Do you see that pile of bones? It was she who summoned me into your midst, she who traded her soul in exchange for revenge.

"Your father sent the innocent Mari to her death in the North, and when her ashes were brought back, the proud Imarah did *nothing*. Like beaten dogs, Dhakir's defeat had broken all of you. Fabled warriors—*ha!* Even the *kharesh* tucked tail and retreated into mourning. No one thought to raise arms to avenge her. So the witch did it herself. And for their cowardice, she doomed Imarah to a long, miserable, painful death so they would all be swallowed by the desert sands, forever forgotten by man and god alike. One of your own tribe destroyed you, little king, and in your blind hatred, you brought an innocent from the North here to die for it. The young Dragonblood was not your executioner, *shansher* Tirasdunh; you were hers."

"No!" Tir slashed the laughing demon from shoulder to hip, severed the head from its body, speared his blade through the demon's black heart. He raged and cut, and all the while the demon remained unaffected, screeching with laughter at Tir's feeble efforts.

With one solid strike to Tir's chest, the demon sent him flying backwards against the fiery barrier. Tir struck it and bounced off as if it were solid. He fell to his hands and knees in front of Liadan's body. Her lips were pale, her sun-kissed skin turning gray. No heat to her, no telltale sign of even a spark of life.

His fault. "Liadan…" *Forgive me… Come back.*

"What happens to a Northman when his woman dies?" the demon mocked by his ear.

A cold breeze wavered the wall of flames, ruffling Tir's hair with a silent command: *Fight*! He didn't recognize the voice, but somehow it ignited a memory inside him. Demons feared light; they only came out in the dark of night, retreating into their lairs at the first hint of dawn.

The demon prince's long, forked tongue snaked out to lick across Tir's cheek. "Mmm… But you are not a Northman, are you? Your soul smells of the desert, not of snow. Your heart burns for battle, not for the heat of a woman's love."

Another cold breeze. *Stand and fight!*

Tir glanced to the east. He'd lost track of time through the night, but it had to be nearing sunrise.

"You've lost, Demonslayer. And oh, how I savor the taste of defeat." The demon inhaled deeply, his form wavering like a mirage as if he felt true pleasure at Tir's anguish. His smile was drunken, his eyes deepening to almost black as he asked, "What happens to an Aegiran when he loses his reason for living?"

"He prays to the gods for the strength to fight on," Tir replied, and stuck his arm into the flames. As fire licked along his skin, he clenched his jaw against the pain.

Only there was none. Even in death, the bond of Liadan's dragonblood protected him from its heat.

The demon drew back warily as Tir pushed to his feet and raised his hand to the sky. Instead of burning upwards, the flames licked down to his chest and across his body, enshrouding him in protective heat. Another gust of wind turned it blue, and his skin pulled taut. He stooped to pick up the scimitar, then faced his enemy, head-on. "You want my soul, demon? Then come and take it!"

The demon screamed, streaked at him, but veered off at the last moment, circling around from the other side. He tried to get around Tir, to attack from his blind side, but with a bracing cold breeze, Tir's flaming shroud flared brighter, and he caught his second wind. Striking faster than he ever had, Tir followed the flames—moving where they swayed, spinning where they swirled, slashing where sparks jumped. Drunken on his premature victory celebration, the demon was too slow to react. Tir's dance was not as intricate as Liadan's, but it was fueled by a rage that set his blood boiling.

He couldn't defeat the demon prince.

He didn't need to.

All Tir had to do was stay alive, distract him long enough for the sun to do the rest. The Magus had forged a prison strong enough to contain the Dark prince, and his own minions had razed the camp so not a single tent remained to cast a shadow. When dawn came, the sun's rays would destroy the demon, and with him, the curse he'd wrought upon Imarah. Tir only needed to stay alive long enough to see it through, and that meant keeping the demon at arm's length.

The Magus' voice chanted louder, echoed by many from the tribe. The fiery circles flared with different colors as they tossed magic dust into them, agitating the demon into a frenzied, reckless attack. He knocked Tir down, clawed through the flaming shroud to score Tir's chest. A green flare made the demon flinch and rear back. Abandoning the sword, Tir rolled away. Sand stuck to his open wounds, the fiery shroud banked to nothing, and he was left exposed, disarmed, bleeding, crouching once again between the enraged demon and Liadan's lifeless body.

The circles flared blue and red, green and white; faster, brighter, until the demon suddenly raised his head to the sky. His shape wavered, dissolving almost completely before it reformed. Instead of attacking Tir again, the Dark prince threw himself against the fiery prison walls, seeking to escape. They repelled him as they had Tir, and each time he tried to rise higher to escape over the top, they flared up to keep him in place.

The demon screamed, and through his madness, Tir heard something he'd never thought demons could feel much less convey: fear. Again and again, the demon streaked upward to fly over the barrier, but with each attempt, the height of his jump decreased, as if his strength was fading. He squealed, shrank to pathetic proportions as the sky lightened, and with the demon the size of a child, Tir dared to take his eyes off him to look to the east. The sun peeked out from behind Temple Mountain, still weak, but already Tir had to squint against its brightness.

"You'll never be rid of me!" the demon growled, shrunken to all fours like a dog.

His red eyes blazed at Tir, then shifted behind him to Liadan with dark intent. Desperate to escape his own doom, the demon hissed, streaking across the sand toward her, faster than a snake.

Tir leapt to intercept, forcing the demon up and over him. As the Dark prince rose waist-high, the first rays of sunlight speared through his shadowy, raven-sized form like dozens of flaming arrows. The demon screamed, fire bursting from him in sickening explosions of black slime and burning sludge. Tir fell over Liadan's body to shield her, to take the searing pain against his own back, when a flash brighter than day lit up the sky, accompanied by an intense burst of power that nearly extinguished the fire around them. Tir never felt a single drop of burning demon touch his skin.

When the glare had finally eased, he looked up. From a single point of light, a myriad of white flashes streaked to every corner of the desert lands, and with each one, the oppressive weight of misery he'd lived with for two decades lifted a little more.

In years to come, Imarah would recount the event to their children and their grandchildren, and consider themselves blessed to have been gifted with such a vision. For by the time the last streak of light had dispersed, the central glow had dimmed and reformed into a shape they all recognized: the welcoming, benevolent form of their patron goddess, Inaras. She reached down over the tribe, and Tir felt the warmth of her restorative touch deep in his soul.

Her divine power shivered through him, returning the strength he'd lost. His injuries mended, his heart beat stronger, breaths became easier to draw, and he knew all of his tribe would feel the same.

At once, his gaze shot down to Liadan again. Inaras had healed his tribe; surely, she could bring their savior back to life.

But the pale, Other female lying in his arms didn't stir; her eyes remained closed, her face serene in death, her heart still and silent in her chest. And Tir felt as if he'd lost her all over again.

Outside of the circles, the surviving Imarah cheered their victory. The demons were defeated, the curse was lifted, and at last, they felt hope again for their salvation. Many raised their hands to the sky, thanking the gods, while others bowed to the rising sun and kissed the sand at their feet.

Only the Magi, Farraj, and his *kharesh* looked deep enough into the circle to see the cost of their victory. Only they saw their *shansher* mourning over the lifeless body of his brave, fallen queen.

⋘ »·◇·« ⋙

In the middle of the night, the sleepless, cavernous great hall of Castle Frastmir echoed with an unearthly scream of agony. The dragon raced out of the chamber, the royal couple following close behind. Terrified, led by that awful sound through the bowels of the castle and up the tower stairs, they burst into the library to find it engulfed in flames.

Queen Nialei cried out, fell to her knees, as the dragon boldly stepped into the illusion to kneel by the writhing body of Prince Fal. The boy screamed as if his soul were being torn in two. His skin smoked, his eyes burned bright gold, a living flame caged within his watery soul.

"Fal!" the dragon shouted.

In answer, the crown prince of Wilderheim fell silent and arched up off the floor, tensing so hard, bones cracked beneath the strain. When he collapsed, the illusion broke, and his parents rushed to his side. For the first time in too many years, they beheld the young man in his true form as if all of his illusions had been burned out of him. His mother caressed his cheek, and yelped in pain. Fal was a living ember, burning to the touch with far more heat than a water creature could hold.

Laying a hand against the center of the prince's chest, the dragon called to those flames, pulled them out of the boy to ease his fever. Fal gasped, roused a little to mumble incoherently. He tried to open his eyes, but they kept rolling back, and his heart thrashed too hard, too fast. He was in terrible pain, too weak to heal himself.

Queen Nialei did it for him, channeling her own magic into her son, mending bones, healing tears, soothing aches. But even when the prince was whole again, he would not wake.

King Saeran laid a hand on his son's forehead, adding his own strength to the two already fighting for his son's life. He soothed the fire burning in the boy's mind, searching for the cause of this firestorm, already knowing, and fearing, what he would find.

Tears streamed down the prince's cheeks, and his body jerked in quiet sobs. "She's dead," he said. "Liadan's dead."

CHAPTER 34

For the third time in as many days, Dar knelt before his *shansher* with tidings both good and bad. For the third time, his hands grew cold, his mouth dry, and his spine weak. Acting as the *shansher*'s eyes and ears, a task in which he'd foolishly taken great pleasure, had now become a dangerous gamble the new High Magus dreaded most with each new sunrise. Ever since Itamar had disappeared into the desert with Kaliban's chest, Khiron had been plagued by terrible dreams that deprived him of sleep at night and haunted him during the day. Many times during their conference, the *shansher* stared off into the distance as though lost in memory. Sweat broke out on his brow, his hands quivered, and for long moments he neither saw nor heard anyone inside his tent. When the spell finally passed, the *shansher* was always shaken and unsteady. Dar suspected it was Kaliban himself tormenting Khiron from his desert grave, but Khiron would hear none of it, and so the Magi could do nothing to help.

Now, Khiron stroked his beard, deep in thought. "You are certain she is dead?"

"Our scouts have said it is so, your Highness. They have watched the survivors for two days. The camp has been moved to the northern oasis at the base of Temple Mountain, and the woman's body is laid out in the open. It has not moved a single time."

"Why have they not burned it? There is plenty of dry wood there."

Indeed, the oasis had plenty of wood. The grove of palm trees so old, their trunks were thicker than two men put together, had once provided shelter and solace there for journeymen visiting the temple of Inaras. It had all dried up, along with the underground river that used to feed it, many seasons ago, and was now as dead as the rest of the First Valley. "The young *shansher* will not permit it, your Highness. He keeps vigil by her body day and night, and will not allow it to be touched."

Khiron al-Bashir grunted his disgust. "The boy must be possessed."

"Perhaps not, your Highness," Dar ventured, uncertain how the tidings should be conveyed; whether he should speak them at all. Had Itamar been there, he would doubtless have conjured up the appropriate words. But for all of his dedication and study, Dar was still young—an apprentice, rather than a Magus in his own right—and with his master tutor gone, he floundered, wholly unprepared for such grave duties. Rafi and Pirro were younger still, untried in the ways of magic and politics, and though only three seasons older, Dar had, by necessity, become their master. *May the gods lead us true,* he prayed, for if ever the tribe needed divine intervention, it was now.

"Well? Go on. Do not keep me waiting."

Dar licked his dry lips, risked a glance at his *shansher*. The thunderous expression he'd expected to see wasn't there. Khiron al-Bashir looked haunted. "The scouts say the body does not change. For two days, she has lain in the heat of the sun, and has neither dried, nor burned, nor withered. They say she looks as if she only sleeps."

"Hmm..." Khiron fell silent, staring at the tapestry of his once proud Imarah lineage. "How did she die?"

Dar shivered. Though the query seemed a casual curiosity, this was the part he'd most dreaded relaying. The moment the scouts had returned with news of the woman's demise, the Magi had conjured a vision of that night. Horrified, they'd watched as the massive swarm of demons descended upon Imarah, a black stain on the desert. They'd borne witness to the tribe's bravery when facing their death head-on, and they'd stared in awe at the woman's majesty and courage in battle with the swarm. She'd reduced them all to ash, burning so hot, the sand at her feet had melted into glass.

And having defeated them so masterfully, for her end to have come in such a cowardly fashion had outraged all of them, even knowing she was the enemy.

"She was stabbed through, your Highness."

But that did not concern Dar. Death was death, whether dealt instantly at the point of a blade or transpiring after long years of disease and torment. What concerned him was that even in death, her body didn't yield to the natural process of decay. He'd not forgotten Kaliban's malicious jeer when he'd last been summoned; those words had tormented him every night since. *She is Vengeance. She Who Walks Through Fire will not be stopped by magic, or by sword. She will cut darkness with a blade of fire, and tear hearts out of the bodies of her enemies.*

Will not be stopped by magic, or by sword.

Did the *shansher* remember?

"Do you believe she is truly dead?" Khiron asked.

Dar hesitated. "No, your Highness, I do not."

"Neither do I. *Vengeance* does not perish so easily. Hmm... Yes. Perhaps Kaliban was right. She Who Walks Through Fire. Yes... You will bring her to me. In chains."

Dar blanched. "Your Highness?"

The *shansher*'s ire boiled up, flooding color into his sunken cheeks. "Was I not clear? Bring me the Northwoman! Dead or alive. Bound in chains."

Dar touched his forehead to the ground in supplication. "As your Highness commands. But we will need time to spell the chains. A creature like that is different from a demon. We will need to pray for guidance and power, to ensure she does not escape."

"The moon peaks full tomorrow night. I want the chains ready by then. We will attack after sunset and put an end to this, once and for all."

"Tomorrow night... but your Highness—"

"I weary of living like a gods-damned pauper, Magi! I want my birthright back, and she is the one who will win it for me! If the last dregs of Imarah aren't dead by the time the sun rises in two days, I will cut out your heart myself and burn it before your eyes as an offering to Aesma. Now leave!"

Dar scurried from the tent, cursing the traitor Itamar for abandoning their tribe to a madman.

CHAPTER 35

The northern oasis at the base of Temple Mountain, once an inviolable place of worship, had become Imarah's refuge. Perhaps the final one. The tribe was defeated, and though no one had seen a single shadow of a demon threat since the battle, people were still terrified of closing their eyes at night unless fires burned high all around. Luckily, the oasis, once so lush and green, had plenty of fallen, dry wood to burn. Needlessly, perhaps, but it was worth their peace of mind.

Since they'd made camp, Tir had spent every waking moment sitting vigil over Liadan's lifeless body.

The tribe had built a great funeral platform for her, an honor befitting the bravest of warriors, but Tir wouldn't allow them to lay her upon it.

For three days, she'd lain in the desert as one dead, only to awaken again as if from a long sleep. Tir knew in his mind this time was different, but his heart refused to believe it. With each day Liadan persevered, untouched by the ravages of death, his hope grew that she'd eventually awaken. In a day. In a week. In a month, perhaps. One day, her heart would beat again; her chest would rise and fall, and her eyes would open.

And because the alternative was unthinkable, Tir kept his vigil, turned a blind eye to the pile of wood awaiting the *shensari*, and a deaf ear to Farraj telling him it was unseemly, that Tir dishonored her by keeping her on display and that his people were beginning to think him mad.

Perhaps he was. It hadn't escaped him that he was behaving in exactly the same way Dhakir had years ago, after losing his beloved first wife. The demon prince had mocked Tir for his Aegiran love of battle, but the men of his line seemed to carry in their hearts a passion just as powerful for their women.

She is not yours, an insidious whisper in his mind insisted. *Liadan was never* shensari. *It was a ruse. Your blood oath only bound you until your tribe was saved, and now she is free of you, and your ignorance, and your scorn.*

A hand on his shoulder broke him out of his dark musings. It was time for Farraj's daily visit. "Any change?" he queried softly. Since they'd made camp, he was the only one brave enough to speak to his *shansher*.

Tir shook his head.

Farraj sighed. "How long can this last?"

Tir pried his lips apart to answer, "As long as it takes."

"We must send word to her father."

Tir ignored this. If Liadan and her twin brother were truly as close as she'd said, then he already knew.

"The tribe is restless; they fear another raid. I had the *kharesh* gather weapons and prepare a path of retreat, but the only safety left to us here is up the mountain, and even Inaras' temple will not save us if Aesimar does attack again. They will not honor her sanctuary. We lined the cliff with scimitars, bows, and as many arrows as we could make, and instructed the men to do what needs to be done. Our women will not become slaves to that horde of savages." He paused, then huffed, adding in a softer tone, "Tir, we cannot stay here. We *must* move on."

"Sleipnir."

"What?"

"Her horse. Sleipnir. Where is he?"

"Run away, probably. No one has seen him since he broke free that night. Zara and Tarabas are gone, too. Just as well. We have nothing to feed them anymore."

Never had Tir seen that mount abandon his mistress. Even through the fury of her firestorm, he'd stood a distant watch over her until it had passed. Why would he leave her now?

"It's been three days, Tir. Even if this was the same sleep she'd slept before, you said yourself she would have awakened by now. You must allow us to burn her body. If we do not, her soul might become trapped here and haunt us forever, as surely as the demons did."

Better a vengeful Liadan, than no Liadan at all.

As if he'd heard Tir's thoughts, Farraj crouched down beside him. "Would you truly keep her from her ancestors? She has saved us, Tir. Even the Magus confirmed the darkness of our curse is lifted. She has done what no other could. She rescued us from the brink of death! And this is to be her reward?"

"What would you have me do?"

"Let us honor her. We have waited as long as you asked: three days, to allow her time to rise again, and still she lies lifeless. She is gone, Tir. Let us send her off the way she deserves."

Tir shook his head. "Our ways. Not hers."

"Perhaps," Farraj allowed. "But more than a Northerner, she is a creature of fire. What better way to pay our respects than to acknowledge her nature, return her to the element of her soul?"

He spoke wisely, and the longer Tir listened, the less he had to say in argument. Farraj suggested they give her the honors and respects of a *shansher*, something a mere woman would never have garnered before in Imarah, or any other tribe. The entire tribe would be summoned, dressed in their finest clothes, which now amounted to the golden armor and white robes pilfered from Aesimar corpses. To honor her Northern ways, men and women alike would strap scimitars to their sides, and draw them in salute. The *kharesh* would stand her guard as they would one of their own, armed against any who'd interfere with the rites. The Magus would speak his spells, bless Liadan's soul on its journey into the afterlife, and Tir himself would light the pyre.

With her death, the Northern princess, once scorned and hated by the entire tribe, had won more respect and adoration than she ever could have in life. Imarah no longer cared about her origin; they worshipped her bravery as if she'd always been one of the tribe—the best of them. The flame of their goddess, Inaras, shining their way to victory.

"Allow us to do this for her," Farraj pleaded. "It is the only way we have to thank her for her sacrifice."

"One more day."

Farraj paused. "What difference makes a day?"

For the first time in three days, Tir looked him in the eye. "I ask you the same. Tomorrow night the moon peaks full. We will light her pyre at sunset so all the stars will see it and welcome her among them."

Farraj's throat moved with a swallow, and he bowed his head in assent. "So shall it be," he said with difficulty, then left to relay Tir's instructions to the waiting tribe.

In no time, the preparations were under way. Gold gleamed in the corner of Tir's eye as his tribe scurried about, dressed in Aesimar colors, to do his bidding. He ignored them, his attention fully focused on Liadan as he watched her closed eyes for any hint of movement that might betray her awakening; held her cold, limp hand in his to feel her skin begin to warm with signs of life. But there was nothing.

Yet even when his mind insisted that Farraj was right, that she was gone, he still couldn't leave her side. Her skin, though pale, was as soft as it always had been. Her lips, though bloodless, just as plump. Hope, even as false as he knew it to be, was a fierce, stubborn beast inside him, insisting Liadan was still alive, somehow.

The next morning, the sun rose bright white over the desert. At Farraj's urging, Tir relinquished his vigil to prepare himself for the ceremony, and allow the women to do the same for Liadan. She'd be washed and dressed in clothes as befitted a queen; her hands and face would be painted with henna, her hair adorned with gold, her feet covered with silk slippers—the same way she'd have been attired for a wedding.

Tir, for his part, was ushered into the Magus' tent, where he submitted to a modest bath, then bowed his head for the cleansing ceremony that set his teeth on edge. The words were not ones of honor, but of protection—a plea to the gods to sever any remaining connection between him and the deceased, to guide the spirit into the afterlife, to banish it from the world of the living and to protect the tribe from its vengeance and wrath.

Tir refused to speak his part of the ritual.

Rather than insist on it, the Magus continued, concluding with a prayer to Inaras for Liadan's loved ones. When all was said and done, the Magus left Tir to his meditation and went to oversee the pyre preparations.

The imposed solitude did nothing to soothe Tir's mind, or his heart. Again and again, he remembered the heartbroken man in Frastmir, the terrible agony with which he'd wailed his grief over his mate. Not for the first time since Liadan's death, Tir wondered whether Geir had embraced the pain as readily as he. Liadan was gone; his grief was the only remaining proof that she'd ever touched his life. He'd rather remember her and ache, than dishonor her by forgetting.

At sunset, Farraj summoned him out of the tent. The *kharesh* lined a path directly to the pyre, each holding a scimitar in one hand and a burning torch in the other, creating a lighted passage, at the end of which a small bowl of oil had been set aflame—Tir's tool for lighting Liadan's pyre. They'd piled it up with even more wood, raising the platform so high, he couldn't see Liadan on top of it. What he did see were three horses standing solemnly in front of it, facing Tir in anticipation. Tarabas, Sleipnir, and Zara.

Tir frowned at Farraj.

"I was as surprised as you are," the older *kharesh* said. "They walked into camp to that very spot, side by side as you see them now, and refused to be led away. I think… I think they are waiting for you."

Tir nodded. What could he say? Tarabas was trained to return to Imarah whenever he wandered into the desert. So was Zara. But to see Sleipnir between them, head held high like a king in his own right, staring at him steadily… Tir didn't know what to make of that. He walked down the path, gaze focused just above the top of Sleipnir's head, but below Liadan's platform.

His people had gathered around at a safe distance in a silent congregation, faces solemn and hands clasped together. No one uttered a word as Tir took up the small torch and dipped it into the oil. Once it caught the flame, he moved forward again, meeting the final obstacle: the horses. Tears had tracked dark lines down Sleipnir's dust-covered face. The mount rested his forehead on Tir's shoulder with a bone-weary sigh, holding still as Tir stroked his neck and clenched his jaw against tears of his own. Sleipnir wouldn't act this way unless he knew his mistress was well and truly gone.

Once he'd realized this, the last of Tir's hope died silently inside him, and he whispered his condolences into Sleipnir's ear. The proud stallion huffed, stomped a hoof, then shifted sideways to allow Tir to approach the pyre.

The wood was so dry, it flared up instantly, and within moments, the blaze roared to the sky so hot, it forced the tribe to retreat a few steps farther. Tir watched the dancing flames, imagined shapes taking form inside of them.

For a moment, he thought he glimpsed Liadan's shadow twirling about. The next instant, he almost made out the shape of a dragon; a rearing horse; a warrior brandishing his sword—all fanciful illusions conjured by his grieving mind.

When the fire blazed at its hottest, Zara became restless, and finally allowed someone to lead her away to be brushed down. Tarabas and Sleipnir remained, standing guard to either side of Tir, and the three of them watched the massive pyre burn.

A log collapsed, sending an explosion of sparks flying outward. The women on that side cried out, pulled their children away, but the men remained steady.

Tir drew his dagger, and the rest of the *kharesh* followed suit. As one, they held up their arms and cut a long, shallow line across the backs of them—a sign of respect and affection. No less than they would have done for Dhakir, or Tir himself.

Farraj shouted a farewell, and his *kharesh* echoed him.

Then someone on the outskirts of the tribe screamed a warning.

CHAPTER 36

From the south, a sea of torches spilled across the desert toward Imarah, with a roar worthy of a sandstorm. Aesimar in full strength: legions of foot soldiers, as well as mounted cavalry, polished blades flashing in the torchlight.

Farraj raised his sword high. "*Kharesh*, to arms!"

The tribe scattered in a burst of activity, men racing south to confront the legions, women herding children toward the mountain and the treacherous climb up to the temple, the only refuge left to them. Tarabas stomped. Sleipnir reared angrily.

"Tir!" Farraj called, mounted on Zara and ready for battle. "We need you!"

With Liadan's sword strapped to his back and his own at his side, Tir grasped Sleipnir's mane and mounted the warhorse, bareback. Tarabas was a faithful mount, but Tir had seen what Sleipnir could do in battle. He would need that fighting spirit today. "*Hyah!*"

Sleipnir took off at a breakneck pace that forced Tir to lean low over his neck as they raced straight into the fray, trampling foot soldiers, bowling over warhorses several hands smaller than the Northern stallion. Between Tir's knees, Sleipnir's girth all but vibrated with a furious energy that mirrored his own. Tir drew his scimitar and attacked, moving with the mount as a single being. He felt when Sleipnir tensed to rear, secured his seat, and leaned back to cut down the men attacking Sleipnir's flanks. When the mount kicked out with his rear hooves, Tir cut down the warriors to his right, then switched hands when Sleipnir twisted, and cut down those on the left.

He didn't echo his *kharesh* in their battle cries; instead, he left Farraj to bellow orders to keep Aesimar from cutting off their path of retreat. Tir was silent in his wrath, slicing through the Aesimar ranks like death itself. Under the cover of night, the farther he got from Liadan's pyre, the darker the battlefield became. Torches fell, banked as their bearers died, and men shouted for more light, but each time a new torch was lit, someone extinguished it. Lighted targets were easier to take out. Soon, the entire battlefield was shrouded in darkness with only the full moon left to illuminate the chaos reigning over the sands.

Tir looked to the southwest, where the Aesimar *shansher* presided over the carnage from a high sand dune, illuminated by the blaze of a brazier and two torches as tall as he was, protected by mounted riders to either side. Tir nudged Sleipnir to turn in their direction, then spurred him forward.

They didn't get far. Mounted Aesimar cut in front of him, pushed him back toward the main throng of Imarah, to crush them all at the same time. A lucky strike knocked his scimitar from his hand; a blade sliced across his arm. Sleipnir reared, throwing Tir as he attacked one of the other horses.

Lying in the dust, Tir saw nothing but massive, swirling shadows and hooves striking the sand too close to him. He was surrounded, vulnerable, and for a moment, he lay still, expecting a hoof to smash his skull to pulp. For a moment, he even prayed for it—a quick end, an honorable death, and peace at last; freedom to join Liadan in the afterlife. It would have been so easy to simply give in, to let go and fade away. Even with the curse lifted, Imarah still had nothing left and no strength to make it back to the First City. Less than fifteen hundred Imarah men, women, and children remained, and all of them would die.

He'd failed.

Sleipnir reared, screamed, and kicked out, intimidating the other horses into retreat. They collided, threw off their riders, toppled over in their haste to get away from the black stallion, and as the air cleared around Tir, the battle on the ground thickened.

A screaming Aesimar appeared above him, blade raised to strike him dead.

Tir rolled, instinct proving more powerful than his defeat. He pushed to his feet, then fell back again to avoid a flaming arrow. From Temple Mountain, arrow after fiery arrow launched into the warriors below. Such weapons were considered a coward's last resort; a true warrior faced his foe head-on, not from a distance. Aesimar, for all their cowardice in attacking them during the night, had never stooped to them in all the time they'd been raiding Imarah, but Tir's tribe no longer had anything left to lose. In the hands of their survivors—women, young boys, and old men who'd climbed up to Inaras' temple to escape the battle—the long-range bows proved to be an effective, deadly weapon.

Aesimar scum sprouted burning, wooden shafts from their chests and limbs, hungry flames quickly engulfing their oiled flesh. The fire spread from one to the next, culling the Aesimar ranks with swift efficiency. The archers aimed high and far, taking out the rearguard rather than the front advance. With so many pouring toward them, they had no need for practice or precision; their arrows found marks with ease.

Rather than cower and pray, the daughters and sons of Imarah stood their ground and fought. They wouldn't yield their own to the enemy. How could their king do any less? With renewed strength, Tir shoved to his feet and drew Liadan's Northern blade. It was longer than his scimitar, allowing a wider reach and more power behind each strike, and in the moonlight, the blade glowed an unearthly blue. The Aesimar were fast, but they were not *kharesh*. Sloppy technique, no discipline. He felled them one after the other, moving from memory rather than strategy. His feet knew where to step, his arm knew how to swing without Tir having to consciously command them.

And still, he uttered not a sound. In the face of enraged, shouting Aesimar, he cut his opponents down with silent precision, wasting no time on defense. He took injuries in stride, ignored the blood trickling from his many cuts, and never cowered, never retreated. Soon, his stoic attack unnerved the Aesimar fighters into wary retreat, and they began to part before him when he advanced. With Sleipnir at his back, Tir stalked across the battlefield toward his true enemy: the Aesimar *shansher*.

He no longer stood atop the dune, yet his warriors weren't retreating.

Scanning the fray for any sign of him, Tir held out his glowing sword sideways, a silent summons for Sleipnir. As if he understood what Tir needed, Sleipnir pranced closer so Tir could mount, and from his high perch, Tir once again surveyed the battlefield. From the south, the mob parted to allow through a mounted contingent bearing torches, with the *shansher* himself wading into the battle, straight for Tir.

A battle horn sounded his approach, and the Aesimar rallied, swarming Tir once more. He fought back, losing sight of their *shansher* as Sleipnir turned in furious circles, battling as hard as any warrior Tir had ever fought. But against so many, they stood little chance. For the second time, Tir lost his seat astride the stallion, and gazed up from the sand as Aesimar fighters bore down on him. He cut them down at the ankles, then rose again to launch into a frenzied offensive, heedless of who fell beneath the arc of his sword. The handle warmed in his grip as if Liadan's fiery spirit still lived within the blade, and he clutched it tighter, embracing its heat, drawing strength from it when he began to wane.

An Aesimar fell. Then another. A third slashed his cheek open, and Tir ducked under his second swing, slicing him open just below the edge of his armor, then thrust upward, spearing him through the bottom of the chin. Kicking the dead weight off his blade, Tir swung around and connected with a scimitar.

Old, familiar eyes stared him down from a face he hadn't seen in too many seasons to count. Taken aback, Tir broke off, stepped away in retreat as the Aesimar *shansher* advanced.

For so long after the tribe had separated, Dhakir had consulted nightly with the Magi, always asking the same questions: *Where is my brother? Is he still alive? Has he found refuge?* For so long, he'd held on to the hope that some of his people at least might have found salvation, that one day his brother would find them again and lead them to fertile ground where the tribe could reunite and rebuild.

And here he was. Khiron al-Bashir, returned at last—to destroy them all. "You look as if you've seen a ghost, boy."

Khiron was the leader of Aesimar. Uncle Khiron, who'd taught Tir how to throw a dagger and saddle a horse, who'd regaled all of the children with wild tales of *djinn*, and beautiful princesses, and treasures hidden in secret caves that opened on command.

The tip of Tir's sword lowered to the sand. "Why?"

Khiron's mouth arched into an ugly snarl. "Dhakir was a spineless fool. Imarah should have been *mine*!"

"You destroyed our tribe out of greed?"

Khiron threw his head back and laughed. "Dhakir knew better than anyone: *might* is king in Aegiros. Look around you, boy. You have no more tribe to speak of. I have created a new Imarah, born from the blood of its enemies. With the Dark god's blessing, we've grown more powerful than Dhakir could ever have dreamed. The First Valley belongs to us now, and you will bend a knee to me, Tirasdunh, here and now, or I will give the order to slaughter the rest of your pathetic flock and mount your head on a spike!"

"*Never!*" Tir brought up the sword, guiding its heavy, blue blade with surprising ease. Khiron blocked, twisted aside and, using Tir's momentum against him, sent him sprawling into the sand with a kick to his back. Tir rolled, threw sand into the traitor's face, then launched up and forward, aiming for his heart. They locked blades, shoved apart, clashed together again. Khiron might have been old, but he was a trained *kharesh*, and his agility had not abandoned him. Assured of his victory, he toyed with Tir in a game of cat and mouse.

"Still the impassioned hothead." Khiron shook his head in disappointment, parried another blow and twisted, ramming his elbow into Tir's side. "What have I always taught you, boy? I, and Farraj, and your father, alike." Their blades sparked against each other, and with a palm to Tir's chest, Khiron shoved him back a few steps. "The fastest way to defeat your enemy is to make him angry."

One of Khiron's men attacked from the side, and Tir twisted to intercept, foolishly turning his back on Khiron. With a wide swing, he cut the warrior underneath his sword arm, but to his surprise, Khiron followed through and severed the man's head from his body. Then he roared at the others locked in battle around them—he wanted Tir for himself.

Khiron met his gaze in silent challenge. "Where is your Northern whore? Surely, it is not her burning so brightly in your camp. Northerners bury their dead like dogs." Khiron feigned an attack, sneered when Tir twitched in readiness. They circled slowly. "Was she as good in bed as I've seen her on the battlefield? Tell me, what was it like bedding a woman who may as well have been a man? How many did she have before you?"

Tir bit his tongue, refusing to rise to the bait. When their blades clanged together again, he reined in his temper, took measure of his opponent, adjusted his strategy. Everyone had a weakness; Khiron would be no different. He'd already proven himself a formidable opponent, but the longer they circled, waiting each other out and seeking the best angle of attack, Tir noticed something odd.

"Shame I did not have a chance to try her out for myself. She might have proved entertaining. For a night or two." Khiron struck, pushed Tir back, herded him around the circle until their positions were reversed with Khiron facing the pyre and Tir's back to it. Every time they circled, Khiron forced them into this position. He wanted to keep the pyre in sight. "Well, perhaps I might get another chance."

Tir shuddered at the implications. He'd once warned Liadan that Aesimar had the means to imprison a demon, and probably even an Other, like her. If they could do that, what was to stop them from raising a soul back from the dead? Once Khiron had Liadan in chains, she'd be enslaved to him forever.

Tir snarled and struck out at Khiron's left. The Aesimar *shansher* deflected, shifting right, quickly launching a counterattack to reverse their positions once more, to keep his eye on the pyre. Tir wouldn't let him. He kept Khiron off balance, distracted enough to give up watching the flames, at least for the moment.

Khiron's temper rose to the fore and his strikes became sharper, more unfocused, his blocks and parries sloppy as time and again he tried to maneuver Tir around. They clashed and broke apart three more times before Khiron lost his patience and shouted for his guard.

Four came at Tir, faster than he could defend. He dropped one and knocked another back, but the remaining two overtook him, while the first recovered enough to slam his dagger's hilt into Tir's wrist. Pain pierced up his arm as bone shattered, and the sword fell from his grip. He braced against their hold, jumped up and, kicking out with both feet, sent the Aesimar scum stumbling backwards into Khiron.

The traitor of Imarah righted himself, ran his own guard through, then shoved him aside, coming for Tir with his blade raised to kill.

All at once, Sleipnir barreled through the press of bodies with a shrill whinny, heading back north, past Tir, toward the camp, where light flared brighter than midday. Khiron froze in his advance, eyes wide, mouth agape at the sight, and his guards loosened their hold enough for Tir to twist around.

In the sky above, a bright flash of light faded, then flared anew, as if the night was breathing. The pyre below mirrored it, throwing its flames high, then banking low to blue in an eerie cycle. With each burst of light, more heat drove back those closest to it, and the sounds of fighting and death stilled as, one after the other, the embattled warriors broke off to direct their gazes north.

Released from distracted holds, Tir faced the spectacle, breath locked in his chest as he witnessed the burgeoning flames dance and bend—higher, brighter, hotter. Sleipnir's shadow reared against the glare, hooves kicking out as if to add his strength, until a massive burst of fire exploded and spewed forth a cloud of thick, black smoke. The plumes swirled together and quickly condensed into a shape the likes of which none had ever seen.

Awestruck, the two tribes of Aegiros watched a creature unfurl its great, black wings, beat them in powerful thrusts to gain more altitude. Like an ember fanned to life, its body glowed and flickered, building from the smoke until a fully formed beast screamed to the sky, and the unnatural heavenly light faded.

"The chains..." Khiron muttered behind Tir, then found his voice and his resolve to shout, "Magi! The chains!"

The creature aloft turned its head south and speared the Aesimar *shansher* with a fiery glare. Its wings pulled tight to its body as it dove back through the flames, crashing into the pyre. Its wings unfurled once more with a snap, and scattered burning logs to catch the wind as it glided over the warriors toward Tir and Khiron.

"The chains! *The chains!*" Khiron screamed as his men dodged the fiery beast. He swirled his scimitar in the air, calling on his guard, his Magi—anyone! But in the face of such a monster, Aesimar held no allegiance to its *shansher*. The men scrambled for their lives, trampling over each other in their haste to escape.

Drawn by the commotion of fleeing prey, the creature flew right for them.

For a moment, as it passed overhead, Tir caught a glimpse of human arms and legs, the hint of curve around the breast and hip.

No, his eyes must be playing tricks on him in the darkness.

And yet…

Fire burst from the creature's hands in streams, instantly incinerating the fleeing Aesimar. It banked left, gained air once more, then swooped down for a second pass, and a hundred more Aesimar were reduced to ash in an instant. Those along the periphery screamed in agony, their bodies engulfed in flames they couldn't put out. A few brave souls launched an attack, scimitars raised high to slash at the creature. One must have struck true, because the creature twisted in midair with a scream, rose higher, and looked down at the culprit.

Close enough for Tir to see.

He couldn't believe his eyes.

Demons or raiders, Liadan had told him, *dark gods or magic men, I am not the one who should be afraid.*

She'd been right.

In the dark of night, Tir beheld what could only be Liadan's true form—a Halfling daughter of Halfling parents, a creature born of dragonblood, yet too tainted with humanity to completely take on one's true form. Her body, covered in shimmering black scales, was held aloft by massive black wings shaped almost like a bat's. Her hands were clawed, feet more dragon than human, a long, powerful tail snaking left and right behind her with a life of its own. Her eyes glowed red-gold; her hair was a mane of living flames that whipped around her. She had one pair of sleek, black horns that curled from her temples, over her head, and another, smaller pair that spiked up and back from her forehead, creating a bestial crown.

Her fangs gleamed pale white as she snarled at the men below, singling out the one who'd struck her. She snatched him up from the throng, flew him high overhead as he screamed. Holding him by the throat at arm's length, the Dragonblood princess brought her mouth to his and exhaled. The Aesimar warrior stopped struggling. His body lit up, briefly, then turned black like a piece of charcoal, disintegrating into ash that rained gently down onto his comrades below.

With a powerful beat of her wings, Liadan rose higher, twisted around, and let loose a spiral of flames in a grand display, then dove through them at the warriors.

"Now!" Khiron shouted, and from amidst the warriors, chains whipped upward as Liadan flew past.

"Liadan!" Tir shouted, but his warning came too late. One of the shackles clasped around her ankle, pulled her up short, and she tumbled to the ground. The troops descended on her like a pack of starving hyenas, falling onto her prone form to kill the beast before it could strike at them again.

Tir raced toward her, the pain in his wrist forgotten. With his good hand, he snatched up a scimitar and slashed through the thickening crowd, while Aesimar Magis chanted somewhere nearby. He had to slay them to break the power of those chains, but he spared them not a glance. The warriors would kill her faster than anything Khiron might conjure. He needed to free her first.

All at once, the mob exploded outward, bodies flying left and right as Liadan burst free and launched into the sky. But the chain again pulled her up short, and three men were dragged into the air in her wake before more took hold of the tether and yanked her back down. She screamed, extended her hand to throw her flames, but nothing came from her palm. The chains would weaken her ever more, until she was forced to bend to Khiron's will.

"Hold her!" Khiron ordered. "Get more chains! To me, men! Take hold! The beast will be ours!"

The mob had grown again, too thick for Tir to get through, all of them so intent on Liadan, they no longer fought him, hungry instead for her blood on their swords. Tir cut through them without mercy as they dragged Liadan down, little by little. Her tail whipped out, slammed a warrior into another, and she rose a little higher.

Then another chain was tossed, the shackle locking around her wrist. Liadan struggled to break free, but even with her added strength, she couldn't overpower an army of this size.

"Liadan!" The mob's roar swallowed Tir's voice. He cut down a warrior, then twisted and cut down two more, working his way toward the ones who held the chains.

Liadan's light and the mob's sway and rhythm were Tir's only indications he was moving in the right direction. When bodies did shift, what little they could, they pushed Tir forward and deeper into the center. He was close enough to hear blades scrape against a hard surface, men shouting taunts and dares, and Magi chanting their spells to keep the prisoner confined.

As he neared the center of the throng, the warriors parted enough for Tir to glimpse Liadan struggling on the ground. They'd dragged her flat, face-down, where she beat her wings against the sand like a trapped bird, limbs chained in place by the strongest of Aesimar's men. The weaker ones kicked her, stomped on her wings, and chopped down with their blades to break her skin, but her scales were impervious. Several blades lay broken on the sand, mocking Aesimar's bravest to test their might against her.

And Tir knew this stalemate wouldn't last. Already, Liadan's flaming hair was dimming; her eyes, when he glimpsed them in her struggles, darkening to the charcoal-gray he knew. As the chains weakened her, she seemed to be reverting back to her human form, and if it was really so, without the protection of her scales, the first blade cut might well kill her.

Tir fought harder, pushing and slicing through men disinclined to give up their view. So intent were they on the battle in the middle, they fought with each other to get closer, and Tir's advance went unnoticed.

Khiron shouted an order from the other side, but no one paid heed. He dragged one of his own men away from Liadan, shouted again, and this time, his loyal guard obeyed, corralling the impassioned warriors away from Liadan to make room for a Magus carrying a black, metal collar.

Liadan screamed when they dragged her up from the sand to kneel, and she fought against their hold, swiped out with her tail, flared her wings to beat them back. Several fell, broken by the powerful blows, but for each Aesimar who died, three more rushed in to replace him.

The Magus raised the collar high, chanting louder, and a chill seeped down from the dark sky, centering on the circle of black metal in his hands. Tir shuddered with dread, ran his blade through the warrior in his way, then burst into the center, sword drawn back to slash. The Magus' arm dropped to the sand, the collar still clutched in its hand, and Tir spun, putting his entire weight behind one more strike. The Magus' head dropped, followed by his body.

Khiron, drunk on his own power, had turned his back on the Magus to rile his warriors for more bloodshed, and didn't notice right away. Not until the groan and snap of a chain link freed one of Liadan's arms. The loose end whipped out, struck Khiron in the shoulder, and he twisted around in time to see Liadan regard her claws with a slight tilt to her head. When she looked up at him, her eyes flared brighter than ever, and Tir shuddered at what he knew would come next.

CHAPTER 37

Sand. Blood. The reek of men.

Liadan smelled the desert on the air, felt the vast open sky above her, and yearned to soar up toward it. But they held her down. Cold metal locked around her ankles and wrists. It refused to obey her command, screamed in her mind with a voice dark enough to overshadow her glow and bank her fire. That darkness leeched strength from her core until she felt too weak to defend against the human onslaught. Their blades couldn't touch her; their soft human feet couldn't hope to cause her pain, even when they put all their strength behind the attack.

But that metal would kill her.

Dark chants echoed inside her head, throbbing down her spine and crawling into her wings until she couldn't raise them to protect herself. Her fiery blood cooled, her head swam. They raised her up, yanking on the chains, thrusting a blade against her back to arch her. She struck out with her tail, and felt the satisfying crack of bone; flared her wings and knocked a half-dozen warriors off their feet. Still not enough.

That gods-awful chant grew louder, reverberating through the metal of her chains like the gongs of a massive bell, rising to the sky, but leeching her strength down into the sand. Ice crawled across her forelegs, up into her thighs, and her eyes rolled back in her head, body quivering with a forced command: *Shift!*

And it began to obey…

Until that chanting voice suddenly fell silent.

Liadan breathed in, fresh air stoking her fire into a full blaze once more. She flexed her arm, strained against the pull of countless mortals. No need to overpower them; she only needed to snap one link.

And then she did. The deadened chain whipped across to the other side, and Liadan looked down at her free hand. Her fingers were tipped with thick, black claws, sharper than a well-tended blade, and she couldn't wait to make use of them. Another deep breath, and the weight of her hair lifted as it flared to life. Night illuminated into day in her dragonsight, and she looked up at the source of her misery, the one who commanded the magickers with their evil chains. Already the ones left alive were renewing their chants.

Liadan yanked her other hand free, then launched into the air, spinning to snap the chains that bound her ankles. The remains trailed from her like jewelry and she tore them off, hurled them down to the sand, and unleashed her flames.

The vermin below began to scatter.

Oh, but she had other plans for them. Liadan flew high, then swooped down in a wide arc, searing the outliers as they ran, cutting off all paths of retreat. Her fire was a living thing; it sang under her command, danced to the tune she set, leapt from man to man, raced across their skin and clothes to spread like a thick blanket over the lot of them. No mercy. No prisoners. The ground below lit up quickly with the blaze of hungry flames, but one man in the middle remained untouched.

She'd saved him for last.

With a thought, Liadan extinguished the fire in her hair and eyes, becoming a dark shadow against the sky. Then, with a shrill cry, she dropped straight for him, flaring her wings at the last moment to scoop him up from the inferno, high into the air. No quick death for this man; she wanted to feel his soul escape his mortal shell.

The Aesimar scum stared at her, wide-eyed, too terrified to scream his fear, too stunned to weep. Liadan allowed herself a feral grin, and his eyes widened even more, his mouth opening to shout for aid. She ran a single claw down the center of his chest, hard enough to scratch a thin, bloody line into his skin.

He did scream, then. "Kaliban! I summon you! Free me!"

Darkness pulsed in his core, a thin, cold link stretching deep into the desert night. At his cry, it throbbed, strengthened, drawing the chill around them both, and Liadan knew true evil lurked at the other end.

She snarled into his face. No one would rob her of this prey! As the black frost raced toward them, Liadan speared her hand into his chest, curled her claws around his heart, and ripped it out. His gaping chest rose and fell as blood bubbled out from his lips. He saw his heart beat in her palm, saw it compress and burst into flame as Liadan crushed it.

Then a black shadow swooped down between them and, tearing the human from her grasp, spun away with him. Liadan screamed, surged forward to reclaim her prize, but the demon didn't go far. With a skeletal hand to the human's chest, the Dark creature bared rows upon rows of sharp teeth, grinning at its dying captive. "I told you it would come to this," it hissed, its voice pulling Liadan up short to hover before it. "You wish to be freed, Khiron al-Bashir? Then I can do no other than oblige."

Liadan watched as Khiron's body convulsed under the demon's evil spell. A thin, pale mist of a soul seeped out from the hole in his chest, barely aglow. It carried too much darkness to rise to the sky as Liadan knew it should. Instead, it stretched like slime the demon swirled and looped around his finger until the last of it was in his grasp. "Your third wish is granted, *master*, and in return, I claim your soul as payment." Green saliva dribbled down his chin as he brought the wisp to his mouth and gobbled it down with a groan of pleasure.

He let the empty shell drop to the desert floor and with a curious sniff, turned his gaze on Liadan. "I smell dragon in you. You and your humans killed my brother." Liadan braced for an attack, but the demon merely grinned. "I thank you for it. With his death, his power passed to me." He inclined his head slightly. "We have no quarrel between us, Dragonblood. I certainly have no wish to follow my brother's path against the flame of Inaras. The valley is yours." Then he streaked away to the west, and disappeared.

Liadan scanned the ground for more enemies to tear apart, but found none. Above her, the sky glittered with countless stars, and a heavy moon crawled ever lower toward the horizon. Soon, the sun would rise to put an end to this wretched night.

Below her, the desert was ablaze with burning corpses. No one left alive, at least not to the south. To the north, where the remnants of a pyre still burned, the Imarah survivors huddled around their wounded, quietly weeping. Their fear was like an invisible mist hanging low in the air. Liadan could taste it at the back of her throat. Sweeping down over the enemy troops, she recalled her fire to restore herself, then caught a high wind to soar toward her tribe, basking in the freedom and beauty of flight.

For too long, her essence had languished, confined in her human shell. She'd never realized how small a prison it'd been, until the fire had set her free. Caught in the darkness of eternal sleep, she'd felt it calling to her, but she couldn't answer its summons until a bright light had shown her how. Spinning high toward the stars now, Liadan sent her quiet thanks to Inaras. Without the goddess' help, she never would have known this feeling of pure happiness.

As the patron goddess of Imarah had foretold, Liadan had, indeed, burned to ash in her service. But her dragon's blood had brought her back, reformed her in the way a dragon could, into something much more powerful. *I am free at last! A true Dragonblood!*

At the base of the mountain, she descended gracefully, stretching out her wings as she touched down on one knee, before she folded them against her back. The talons hooked together at her neck like the clasp of a cloak, the feathery soft membrane billowing around her. With a light step, she approached her tribe, taking stock of how many had survived, how many were injured, and how many wouldn't make it through the night. Imarah had been culled to almost nothing. She counted less than a thousand, their eyes haunted, terrified, but she didn't realize the true source of that fear until she drew close and people backed away from her, muttered prayers, and herded their children behind them.

Liadan stopped, tilted her head, and truly looked at them. Each soot-smudged, blood-stained face was turned toward her, eyes wide with fright and mouths set with the last of their courage. A lone child wailed pitifully nearby. Liadan started for it, to offer comfort, to help find its parents, if they were still alive.

Before she could reach the babe, a woman gave a shrill cry and raced over, snatching up the child and backing away from Liadan as if from a demon hungry for her soul.

Liadan frowned.

Where the woman retreated, several *kharesh* limped up to shield her, taking a stand between Liadan and the rest of the tribe. They could barely keep their feet under them, many bleeding from wounds that had yet to be dressed, yet each and every one had his scimitar drawn. Against Liadan—one of their own! She'd earned her rank, her sword, and her place among them!

But that had been when they'd still thought her human.

Liadan looked once more at her hands. Sharp, black claws; skin as soft as silk, yet as impenetrable as marble. Her body was covered in scales, and her hair was still a mane of long strings of fire. Her tail swished out and around her feet, which were more like a dragon's hind claws, balanced on the toes with sharp talons buried in the sand, the back spur on what should have been her heel, gleaming sharp.

No wonder they fear me. I am a monster.

"Stand down!" Tir called from a distance, racing across the sands on Sleipnir's back. "Liadan!"

Finally! He'd talk some sense into the tribe. They didn't know her; Tir did. He'd explain, and all would be well. Liadan had destroyed the demons, and Aesimar. Imarah was safe at last, the curse lifted. They could return to the First City, rebuild what they'd lost. And she could help. Flying ahead, she could chart the easiest route, spy out water to quench their thirst, hunt game to feed them on the journey.

She acknowledged Tir's approach with a glance, inwardly wincing at all the wounds he'd sustained, but when she noticed how quickly they were healing already, her attention returned to the *kharesh*. Why hadn't they dropped their guard? Their *shansher* had commanded them to do so.

King or no king, however, it seemed she'd been right after all. Their fear of her was stronger than their loyalty to him. They'd no longer obey Tir where she was concerned, and there would be no making them understand she was not a threat. Their king had brought her among them; bound himself to a monster, made her his queen—or so they thought. His judgment was impaired, and he couldn't be trusted. That they'd stayed their weapons this long was a sign of their respect for him. But it would only last so long. They needed someone they trusted to vouch for her.

Where was Farraj? Even with Tir's authority in question, surely they'd obey their commander.

But the old man was nowhere to be seen.

"*Kharesh*, stand down! Do not harm her!" Tir dismounted at full gallop, running up to the group locked in a standoff, but stopped ten paces away from Liadan, kicking up sand.

Liadan flinched. They stared at each other, and the longer the silence stretched, the heavier it became. He wouldn't approach. His gaze swept over her, from her flaming hair down to her clawed toes, pale eyes wide to take in all of her. And he wouldn't approach. "I thought you feared nothing," she said, not recognizing her own voice.

She wanted to shift back to her human body, but dared not make herself that vulnerable. Without her scales, she'd be defenseless against an attack, which seemed more and more imminent the longer Tir just stood there, staring. He schooled his features admirably to hide his true feelings, but Liadan could guess what they were, and for the first time in her life, she felt something utterly alien to her: shame. And hurt. And sorrow.

The torc at her neck felt cool against her hot skin, reminding her of home—water, snow, her brother's healing touch, and the dragon's ancient understanding. When the first rays of sunshine peeked out from the east, it threw Imarah's fear and mistrust into sharp relief. They didn't want her among them; they'd drive her off, or kill her, to restore their mortal balance.

"I do not," Tir replied to her question, yet he didn't move any closer. "I thought you were dead." How horrifying she must have looked in the growing light, for him keep so far. He was tense all over, stuck between a tribe who depended on him for their survival and the creature who could destroy them all with the ease of an afterthought.

Her fire banked. "That which is immortal cannot die." If only she *had* died. Then she'd never have known what true scorn felt like, from someone she'd come to regard so highly.

"I am… glad," he said, looking over his shoulder at his people.

Liadan's mouth twitched in a wry smile. "Yes, of course." She bowed formally at the waist, so he wouldn't see her blinking back tears. "Fear not, brave king of Imarah, our bargain is finally finished. Your people are safe. And by the oath we swore, this monster is free to return to her demonlands in the North."

"What? No, wait—"

"Farewell, Tirasdunh al-Dhakir. May your tribe flourish once more."

"Liadan—"

She crouched low, then launched herself into the sky, spreading her wings to soar. The warm air currents pushed her higher, and she rode them westward, away from the little tribe, and the little king who'd managed to destroy her so easily without ever drawing his sword.

CHAPTER 38

"Wait! Liadan!" Tir ran after her, whistled to Sleipnir, and heard a sharp whinny in answer, but the stallion wouldn't come. He ran as far as his weary feet would go, strained to keep Liadan in sight, but she was too fast and disappeared over the horizon without the smallest trail for Tir to follow.

When he couldn't run anymore, he stumbled in defeat and fell to his knees, breathing hard. "I don't want you to leave," he said. Too late; she was gone, and he had no hope of tracking her.

Another whinny brought his attention back around to the east, where the rescued tribe of Imarah stared at their king in fear and disgust. Three *kharesh* held Sleipnir's reins, preventing him from going after his mistress. If they hadn't stopped him, could Tir have caught up to Liadan on horseback?

His tribe stared, waiting.

The war was won; Imarah was safe. Would their king abandon them for the fiery creature with dragon wings?

Might is king in Aegiros. In that, Khiron hadn't been mistaken. Imarah might be safe now, but they were still weak, vulnerable. They needed someone to lead them, to restore their strength.

They needed *shansher* Tirasdunh the Demonslayer, and though it broke his spirit, turned his heart cold and hard with resentment, Tir still had a duty to protect his tribe. He got up, turned his back on the west, and returned to his people.

His hands curled into fists at his sides before he remembered his shattered wrist. But the pain did little to distract him as he walked back among his tribe, trying to guess where Liadan might have gone. Home, no doubt. The crown princess of Wilderheim had had more than her fair share of the desert. She'd go home, back to her family, and a people who didn't fear her.

And Tir couldn't find it in his heart to begrudge her. As she'd said, their bargain was finished; she'd delivered his people from the jaws of death and, having done so, had moved on.

Liadan was gone.

How foolish he'd been to think, even for a moment, that she might have chosen to stay a while longer. How foolish to think Imarah might have let her.

Curling his injured hand tighter, he focused on the pain to keep from turning on his own *kharesh*. They'd not only dared to raise arms against Liadan, they'd disobeyed his direct order to stand down. He'd been too soft on them, too preoccupied with keeping them all alive to insist on obedience, when he himself had been ignorant.

No more.

"Tir."

He pulled himself out of his dark thoughts to focus on Farraj's second-in-command. "Report," he said hoarsely.

Sami bowed. "We have many wounded. Two score dead. The Magus has not yet returned from the temple." After a hesitant pause, he grudgingly asked, "What are your orders?"

Tir glared, but chose not to address the insult. "How many *kharesh* are still battle-ready?"

Sami looked around, counted nods, then replied, "Twelve."

"I want them to ride out south at once." Before Liadan had scorched the battlefield, a handful of Aesimar horses had managed to break free of the fight; he'd seen them wandering around as he'd ridden back on Sleipnir. They'd be there, still. "Find the Aesimar camp. If any are left alive, kill them. Whatever supplies they have, bring them to us, as much as the horses can carry."

"It will be done at once."

"Send someone up to the temple; make sure the Magus is safe. And find Farraj."

"*Shansher*," Sami said, "Farraj has been gravely injured. The women are tending to him, but he has not awakened since he was struck down."

Swelling fingers curled tighter still. "I will see him. Go do as I ordered."

"*Shansher*… The creature…"

Tir barely stopped himself from driving his fist into Sami's face. "The *creature* is the only reason any of us are still alive," he snarled. "The creature has a name, and if you value your life, you will speak it with reverence from this moment on." He raised his voice to address them all. "And if I see *anyone* draw a weapon against *that creature* again, they will taste the edge of my blade!"

"It's a monster!" someone objected.

Tir drew Sami's dagger out of its sheath and advanced on the old man whose head had been bound in bandages. Two *kharesh* intercepted him, moving slowly, worn out after the war. Tir struck one in the throat, ducked the other's swing, and drove his elbow into his side. Incensed beyond reason, Tir felt no pain as he grabbed the old man's shirt collar with his injured hand and pressed the dagger tip beneath his chin.

"Tir!" Farraj's hoarse voice cut through his haze of anger, just enough to stay Tir's hand. "We cannot afford for more of us to die," the *kharesh* commander said. His head dipped wearily as two men supported him between them.

The old man in Tir's grasp whimpered, wide-eyed, terrified. Tir shoved him down in disgust, then stood to his full height. Might was king in Aegiros. If Tir had any hope of keeping his tribe under control, there could be no doubt in their minds that he *was* in control. He looked closely at the faces surrounding him, met each challenging gaze and stared them down until each man bowed his head in submission. He turned on Sami last. "I gave you orders. *Move!*"

The man scrambled to obey.

Farraj sighed. "Sit me down." His handlers gently lowered him to the ground. He hadn't weathered the attack well—his arm was in a sling, his torso bandaged; he was covered in soot, and blood had dried on his face from a wound Tir couldn't see. The strongest, most fearless, most unwavering man Tir had ever known now looked exhausted, much older than his years.

Tir tossed Sami's dagger to the ground and sat down next to his mentor to watch his people go about the tasks he'd set them. One of the women, her veil torn from her face, approached timidly, keeping her head down. She carried splints and bandages and, after looking over his wounds with a cursory glance, gestured to Tir's hand, which he proffered without argument, though he kept his attention on Farraj to spare her modesty. "You look as if you just faced down an army of demons."

Farraj grunted a chuckle. "I am not so sure I didn't. Oh, stop fretting like an old woman. They have not killed me yet."

"And none have lived to attempt it again," Tir assured him.

Farraj groaned. "*Daeva* take them all. What am I supposed to die of now, old age?"

Tir allowed himself a smile. "If I'm lucky."

Farraj studied him for a moment in silence. "So, *shansher* of Imarah," he mused, wincing as he shifted to face Tir, "what do we do now?"

Tir rubbed his face, suddenly exhausted. "As soon as the *kharesh* return with supplies, we'll set out back west."

"After your dragon *shensari*?"

The woman binding his wrist paused, listening intently, while trying hard to pretend she wasn't.

"No," Tir replied after a heavy silence. "Liadan is gone. We will go back to the First City, reclaim what is ours, by right."

"You loved her," the woman said, surprising both men. Blushing fiercely, she ducked her head lower and tied off the bandage.

Tir caught her wrist before she could run off. "What is your name?"

She bowed low. "Nai'mah, *shansher*."

"Nai'mah, I would like you to do something for me. Gather the bows and any arrows we have left, and distribute them among the women."

Her gaze flicked up to his, before dropping away just as quickly. "*S-shansher*?"

"We don't have enough able-bodied men left to defend the tribe along the way, and we have no way of knowing what dangers lie between us and the First City. We'll need everyone who can carry a weapon to arm themselves and be prepared to fight for those who cannot. Do you think it can be done, or am I asking too much of our women?"

Farraj raised an eyebrow, but didn't say a word.

Nai'mah seemed to give the matter some serious thought before she answered, "It can be done."

Tir nodded. "I am grateful. And, to answer your curiosity, yes, I did love Liadan. I would have had her sit by my side as queen, had she accepted me. And, though it makes no rational sense to you—it most certainly does not to me—I will never stop wishing it could have been so."

The *kharesh* returned with news that the Aesimar camp had been dismantled, with not a soul left to fight, but in their haste to escape the burning scourge, they'd left everything behind: tents, livestock, barrels of water and oil. On the first trip, the *kharesh* brought back enough to feed all of Imarah, and for each to drink their fill, with still enough left over to properly clean and dress wounds.

Once they'd unloaded everything, the twelve took seven more men on a second trip. At sunset, they came back with horses, wagons, clothes, shoes, goats, weapons, skins filled with water for travel, and even musical instruments. As the tribe warily settled in for the night, someone struck up a mournful tune, and several women lent their voices to the melody, singing their soft lullaby.

Tir walked among his people, sat with each of them for a while, spoke with them, assuring them all would be well. His people were frightened, tired, hurt, and as many times as he repeated they were now safe, as many times as they nodded obediently, he knew they weren't convinced. They'd carry that fear and insecurity in their hearts for many seasons to come.

He also visited Sleipnir, who'd settled as soon as Liadan had disappeared. He'd allowed himself to be led away and brushed down, and now he stood silent among the herd, spurning even Tarabas' presence as he brooded alone in the roped enclosure. He turned away from Tir's approach, refused to suffer his touch, snorted and tossed his head to hear him speak.

Tir couldn't tell whether Sleipnir blamed Liadan for abandoning him, or Imarah for keeping him from following. Either way, the result was the same: Sleipnir's heart was as broken as Tir's. He merely lacked the words to say so.

"I can't bring her back," he told the mount with a sigh. "I can't even follow, no matter how much I want to." And gods, how he wanted to. Tir gritted his teeth and untied the rope from the closest post, opening the enclosure right in front of the great stallion. "But you can."

For a moment, Sleipnir stood there, staring at Tir with one big, shiny eye, as if he couldn't comprehend what Tir had done. As if he waited for something.

"Go on," Tir urged. "Safe journey to you both."

Sleipnir turned his head to look at his own back, then stared at Tir again.

"Not this time. You must go alone."

The horse snorted with obvious disdain, then took off toward the west. Plumes of dust billowed in his wake, and Tir wished again he could have gone along. But when the dust settled, Sleipnir stood there, facing west, tail twitching. He raised a hoof, took two more slow steps, then looked behind him at Tir. Head bowed, he walked back into the enclosure, lipped Tir's shoulder, then dipped his head lower to nose the rope in Tir's hand.

Tir caressed his neck, touched his forehead to Sleipnir's. "No more binds. One of us, at least, should be free."

By morning, the Magus still hadn't returned, so Tir himself scaled the mountain to find him deep in a trance inside the temple, guarded by two *kharesh* who knew better than to interfere with religious rites. Tir nodded his thanks to them, and waved them out, back to the tribe to rest.

This was the first time he'd entered the temple of Inaras as a grown man. At her altar, Tir bowed his head in supplication, then gazed up at her statue, twice as tall as a man, pale marble arms outstretched in welcome. Her divine power seeped into every corner of the temple, from the largest boulder above to the smallest speck of dust at his feet, humming along his skin, soothing his mind, and Tir found himself relaxing enough for his eyelids to droop.

Soon, the ground melted away and warmth cushioned him on an invisible current that carried him outside to hover far above his tribe. He didn't linger there; the vision carried him west, across the desert to the First City, through its empty streets and abandoned houses, and on into the dry river basin, following the deep trench ever westward, faster, lower, until a bright light flashed and Tir found himself in a dark cave.

Narrow shafts of light speared down from a hole in the ceiling, illuminating rock as black as pitch, shaped by countless millennia into crevices and protrusions like a giant, tooth-filled maw. To the east, the cave narrowed into a black tunnel large enough for four men to pass through, side by side. To the west, the bubbling wall had been carved deep with symbols he didn't recognize. They looked ancient, but uniform, like magic spells embedded into the stone. And from the center of the floor, a small water well bulged up, spilling across the maze of rock formations toward the tunnel.

The Source.

Though he'd never seen it himself, Tir recognized the place from his father's impassioned ravings. Now, this strange vision showed Tir the truth of them. Before his eyes, time shifted, racing back through the ages. The cave changed, its rocky teeth receding into a smooth surface, the carved symbols fading from the western wall. Within moments, it was empty of everything, even sunlight.

But within its dark recesses, Tir heard the soft drip of water. It welled beneath him on a glow of divine magic, and out of the puddle emerged men and women made of clay. Light flared, searing their shape solid, giving them each a heartbeat. The First Tribe opened their new eyes, sucked in their first breath, and fell to their knees before the well of light, touching their foreheads to the ground in supplication. A spark floated up to caress the western wall, and a man traced its movements, carving spells into the rock. When he'd finished, the cave shuddered, the ceiling crumbled, and sunlight streamed inside to guide the First Tribe to the surface. As they emerged, the waters rose behind them, filling the cave, overflowing, forming the flood plains at the base of Silver Mountain.

Where the sun sets, life begins, a soft voice whispered across the vision.

Water continued to well, pooling, then pouring east, carving out a basin for its path. Tir followed the small creek as, over time, it grew into a river; as the First Tribe grew in numbers; as the First City sprouted and grew in the now-lush valley. He saw the tribe flourish, spread, war, and fragment, and then the river itself carried him farther east on a mighty current. But even as it did, Tir sensed the selfsame current deep underground. Two sister rivers: one in the light, and one carving its way through darkness underground, both emerging from the same place in the west, both flowing to the same endpoint in the east.

Eventually, the rivers slowed. The surface one, having split a dozen times, trickled along the eastern edge of the valley, then quietly disappeared underground once more, dragging Tir with it back into darkness. This time, he saw light reflecting off diamonds as water pooled in a multitude of pits and caves, and dripped down the walls. This was the place Dhakir had sought for Imarah.

Where the sun rises, life begins anew, that soft voice whispered, and the vision wavered to show him the fleeing tribe of Imarah in the surface of a dark pool. Led by Inaras' visions, Dhakir took his people east instead of west, searching for this very place, for even had they found water at the Source, as long as the curse remained, Imarah would still have perished. Only here, in her temple where she still held some power, could the goddess of life have aided them. In her oasis, her light might have overpowered the *daeva*'s dark spell and freed Imarah. If only they'd reached her in time.

But war, famine, demons, and disease slowed their journey, and with every passing day, Inaras grew weaker, her call softer until she was banished behind the dark Veil and could no longer aid the First Tribe. And so they lost their way. Khiron fragmented the tribe, taking off to the south. Dhakir's beloved *shensari* died in his arms, and with her passing he lost his will to live and rule. Without his guiding voice, Imarah withered, while far to the south, Aesimar grew stronger, and as time once again moved forward, the diamond cave dried out, its countless pools shrinking down to puddles, then to nothing at all.

"Why show me this?" Tir demanded. "What meaning am I to take from it? That there's no hope left? That no matter where we go, Imarah is doomed to die?"

As if in answer, a nearby diamond glittered brightly, drawing his gaze. The spark detached, floated like a firefly around Tir, only to dash off down a dark tunnel, dragging him along. He saw nothing but what little the tiny spark illuminated. Miles passed him by in the dark, unchanged, until Tir noticed a second light beneath the first. A reflection. *Water!* The farther east he flew, the larger the puddles became, until they turned into a small but steady trickle, which spat him back out again into the first cave, with its maw of teeth, and spells carved into the western wall, now faded with time.

Where life once began, it can be restored, the voice whispered. *Seek salvation in the First Temple...*

With a gasp, Tir found himself back in the temple of Inaras, breathing hard, staring at her altar without seeing it at all. The Magus rose to his feet, touched Tir's shoulder, and nodded a bow when Tir finally focused on his face. "Inaras is weakened," the wise old man said. "She can guide us to salvation, but cannot restore us."

"Then what are we to do?"

"Find another way." The Magus bowed again and shuffled his ancient feet out of the temple, grumbling, "I am too old for magics like these. If only Imarah had someone younger to take over, someone who understood the ways of gods and men…"

Tir remained in front of Inaras' altar until the torches burned down to nothing, but no answer came to him. By the time he'd returned to camp, the sun was low and the tribe had settled in for the night. Tir sat with Farraj, needing someone to help him make sense of what he'd seen, but before he could utter a word, Sami approached to report the day's progress.

The Aesimar camp had been emptied of all supplies. They now had enough to last them a good week or two, if they rationed, but after that, they'd need to find another source of water. Having been informed of the plans to head out west, Sami assured them the day hadn't been wasted. Everything had been packed and prepared for travel, and at first light, they could break camp. Too many dead around this place; the tribe was eager to move on.

Tir thanked him, then ordered the preparations to be made.

"I have something for you," Farraj said, after Sami took his leave. "The women found it among the debris." He pulled cloth off a charred lump of a chest sitting beside him, motioning Tir closer. The chest had been burned beyond recognition on the outside, but had somehow retained enough of its shape to hold together. The iron clasp on the front caught Tir's eye and sparked a memory.

He pried it up, careful not to damage the seal of Imarah's *shansher*, then opened the chest he'd last seen on the morning of Liadan's *kharashan* and carefully withdrew the bundle within. He unwrapped its many layers, uncovering the treasure at its center, perfectly preserved and untouched.

"I'm no Magi," Farraj said, "but I don't think one would carry such a thing without reason, do you?"

"No, I don't," Tir replied, tying off the thong to hang the glass vial from his neck.

"Perhaps its owner will return for it."

Tir almost smiled. "Thank you, old friend."

He didn't speak to Farraj about his vision.

That night, he dreamed of the Source. He stood before the western wall, facing Liadan, their hands clasped together. A chalice appeared before him, a choice to be made, and as he reached for it, a deep, male voice warned, "There will be no going back after this, for either of you."

CHAPTER 39

Liadan had learned a thing or two in her time alone in the desert lands of Aegiros. Her ordeal of *kharashan* had been nothing compared to the daunting task of surviving on her own in a land where only the heartiest did. While flying over the endless sands was faster than walking, her black dragon scales absorbed more sunlight, which intensified her thirst and her need for shelter during its strongest hours.

Out of necessity, Liadan returned to the only place she recognized: the First City. There, at least, the palace had tall ceilings to provide shelter from the sun and clothes to replace the ones that had burned away on her pyre. But it still had no water, forcing her to fly out daily, training her keen eyesight to distinguish real oases from mirages. Few and far between were places where water pooled on the surface enough for her to drink it. More often than not, only greenery marked where underground wells and streams existed. Her claws were ill-suited to the task of digging, so each time Liadan found a source, she had to revert to her human form to dig it out. With each try, the process became easier, but it still wearied her.

She ought to return to Frastmir. Her family had to be worried sick with no word from her for so long. But each time she peered into a pool of water, with Fal's name on the tip of her tongue, she drew back. Each time she caught a current north, she veered off, back to the First City. As much as Liadan missed her family, she wasn't ready to return to them. She knew what awaited her in Wilderheim: a lifetime of imprisonment behind Other politics, duties to people on both sides of the Veil, and one day, if Fal's condition didn't improve, the weight of the crown. If she returned, she might never again leave the confines of Castle Frastmir. After two decades of living sequestered in a cave, she'd spend the rest of her life in one—better appointed, but still a cave.

No, Liadan wasn't ready for that.

Here, all of Aegiros was spread out for her to explore. From above, its landscape readily revealed its secrets, and lured her in with more mysteries yet to be solved. Despite appearances, life did thrive across the desert sands—small creatures scurried about, day and night; people roamed on horses and camels, built settlements, towns and cities, traded goods, sang, danced, loved, and warred. She could spend several lifetimes exploring these lands and never grow bored.

The life of a wanderer had its merits.

Until she remembered the looks of horror Imarah had gifted her for saving their lives.

At night, when the desert cooled and Liadan had time to think, the truth of who and what she was became inescapable. Perched on the palace roof, she gazed eastward, waited for sunrise, and remembered. They feared her, as anyone else would if they'd seen her true form. No matter how far and wide Liadan wandered, sooner or later, she'd be seen this way, with her wings spread wide, and her hair aflame, dark horns adorning her head like a demonic crown. She was well aware of how she'd look to the superstitious people of Aegiros. They'd hunt her, chase her off, or worse, try to imprison her again, as Aesimar had done.

For now, she was safe. But even now, Tir's tribe would be making its way back to reclaim the First City, and if they found her here…

I left Sleipnir behind.

It pained her to admit it. In her haste to escape Tir and his scorn, she'd left behind her every possession, as well as her companion and old friend. For days, she'd waited for Sleipnir to follow her, as he always did, but after so long, Liadan was forced to accept that this time, she was on her own.

I can go back for him.

But what good would that do? Even if she could sneak back into camp without being seen, she couldn't fly the stallion all the way back to Wilderheim. She'd have to ride the entire trek, however long it took, and how would Liadan feed him when she could barely feed herself? As much as she hated the thought of leaving Sleipnir with the Imarah, at least she knew he'd be safe and cared for among them. He'd be king of his herd, lavished with affection and the best of what little the tribe had to offer. He might hate Liadan for abandoning him, but at least he'd be safe, which was more than she could say for herself.

Forgive me, my friend. I'll see you again one day.

"Inaras, I call to you," she whispered. "I summon you. Appear to me."

A cold wind fanned her flames, but no godly light appeared.

"Vayu, god of Veils and in-betweens, ruler of the void between light and darkness, you spoke to me once, I beseech you to hear my call. Come to me again."

Silence answered her.

Liadan raked her claws across the roof. She should have known better than to expect gods to care about her problems; she, better than anyone, ought to understand their fickle nature. What use did deities have for humans and Others? None, save to alleviate an eternity of boredom.

Inaras had used her. She'd needed a powerful champion to free her and the other gods, and she'd found one. Now that the task was finished and she had her people and their prayers back, she would become powerful again and reclaim her world, and Liadan no longer had a place in it.

"I didn't ask for this," she grated. "I've fulfilled my oath; the tie is broken. Why does it keep calling me back?"

Back to Imarah. To Tir.

Gods, she hated this sick feeling in the pit of her stomach, twisting inside her, yanking her back eastward and at the same time shredding her like a knife in the gut with the knowledge that Tir wanted nothing to do with her anymore. He'd looked at her that night and had seen nothing but a monster. She'd known it would happen—in some part of her mind, she'd even expected it—but nothing could have prepared her for that look in his eyes, as if honor alone kept him from thrusting her own sword through her demon heart.

She could have left a thousand times, flown back to Wilderheim, or even Lyria—anywhere else, as long as it was far from here. She hadn't. Because some part of Liadan still hoped she'd see him again, look into his eyes and see something other than disgust. When she slept, Liadan dreamed of him holding her. She remembered the pressure of his kiss, the warmth in his eyes after their first night in the palace.

We are no longer bound, she reminded herself. Whatever he'd felt for her before had died the moment he saw the truth and realized she'd been right all along, that Others and humans did not mix.

Whatever she still felt would fade, too; in time, she'd close her eyes at night and no longer see him in her dreams. She'd remember her time in Aegiros as a battle she'd won, and she'd be proud of it. But none of that could happen here. If Liadan wanted to forget, she'd have to go where everything she saw and touched didn't remind her of the man who'd broken her heart.

It was time to leave Aegiros for good.

Standing tall, Liadan folded her wings, and burned herself back into her human shape. By some trick of magic she had yet to understand, the clothes she wore now became part of her when she shifted; they disappeared somehow in her half-dragon form, then reappeared when she was human. A useful thing, that.

As the sun peeked out and stretched long rays of light across the city, Liadan closed her eyes to bask in its caress. Her skin had darkened with her transformation, not into the brown shade of Aegirans, but no longer the pale cream of a Northerner, either. The sun's bright majesty, once a burning nuisance, was now a warm comfort.

Soon, night's chill had burned away, and the paved streets of the First City were awash in daylight. Liadan once again called to the dragonfire in her soul and dropped forward, shifting as she fell to catch the air before she hit the ground. She rose above the city, veering north. In no time, she crossed the parallel dunes and flew over the waterfall oasis. Not far off, she spotted a patch of charred ground where the firestorm had claimed her. Liadan kept going.

The market city of Sadirak appeared ahead, and she banked low, out of sight. Too many people there; too much danger of being seen. She circled in place a few times, debating what to do. Sooner or later, she'd have to touch down and continue on foot. Even in Wilderheim, winged creatures weren't a commonplace sight among the Others, and it wouldn't do to attract too much attention. She might have to rest by day and travel in the dark of night. A tricky proposition, but better than being mistaken for a malevolent beast and shot out of the sky.

The oasis would be a good place to rest. From there, she could fly straight north into Wilderheim; a much shorter path than the one she'd taken with Tir.

Yes, it was a good plan.

Liadan rose higher to catch a breeze back east, when a flash of color caught her eye. To the west, south of Sadirak, a caravan crawled across the desert—ten camels in the lead, four tent-carriages drawn by horses, and eight more camels to bring up the rear. All of the men were dressed in the same way, with the same striped scarves tied around their heads and faces and the same scimitars strapped to their sides.

Liadan remembered those colors only too well—they'd adorned the old woman's tent in Sadirak. She remembered, too, the taste of her sweet potion, the scent of smoke, and the hazy glitter of a golden collar.

With a furious beat of her wings, Liadan shot upward into the sky. Wilderheim could wait. First, she had a score to settle.

CHAPTER 40

There were shadows, and within them a prison so dark, so powerful, even the Halfling god of trickery and deceit couldn't escape it. The walls of smoke have long ago stopped reverberating from his outbursts of maddened rage, the black corridors silent, allowing neither sight nor sound to intrude.

A once magnificent, fearsome creature, the Trickster was much altered by his imposed solitude. His bottomless eyes no longer carried their usual mischievous spark. Now, only madness and wrath swirled in their depths. His voice, once as melodious as the sharp twang of a breaking lute string, now growled ominously—if he chose to speak at all.

For two decades, the fabled Loki, lover of whimsy and practical jests, had wandered blindly through world after world, at first to flee the All Father's punishment, and later to seek a creature—any creature—powerful enough to restore him. But, to his utter frustration, this Shadowland was of his own making, flawlessly constructed to hide his presence from all beings—human, divine, or Other. Woden could not have devised a punishment more cruel than this, and with each passing day, Loki's hatred for him grew.

But the world of Northern magic was changing. The Veil, still weakened from Lady Nialei's fabled battle with the dark sorcerer, continued to grow thinner, leaking power—Woden's, and all the gods' with it. Loki sensed it first on a stray breeze flowing through the cavernous darkness of his prison, and as he inhaled the scent of sand and spices, he smiled, baring teeth too sharp to look human any longer.

Aegiros. He swirled the dark shadows with a wave of his hand and gazed out into more darkness. Unfolding his lanky body, Loki stretched and stepped forward. The Shadow moved with him, hazing his view once more, but he swept it aside again, forming the first window he'd managed in far too long, and he found himself strolling through the desert night.

The First City sprawled abandoned before him with its deep river basin bone-dry, and wind howling through empty clay houses. This was the result of a mortal's wish and, not unlike the one he'd fulfilled himself, it was beautiful. The night air was perfumed by decades of death, famine, and disease; destruction flowed in a clear path from the tall palace, through the heart of the city, down into the river, and eastward across the valley. An entire tribe brought to its knees, its legacy slowly devoured by the desert sands. And had the creature who'd wrought it been punished in any way? No! The divine laws were different in Aegiros. Humans bore responsibility for their own folly.

Snarling at nothing, Loki whirled around and streaked across the city to the palace. He sensed a trail of smoke, a familiar scent of homeland, and followed it up to the roof, where an odd creature perched. Lying low to avoid being seen, Loki watched the creature spread its wings as far as they would go to reveal a shapely, though odd, female body. Fiery hair, a horned crown, clawed hands and feet, and a restless tail…

Who was this? *What* was it?

She cocked her head toward him, and Loki shrank back, curious to see, but not to be seen. Scenting the air, the creature rose to her full height and faced east as the sky began to lighten. Her wings pulled in around her body and smoke rose from her skin, her form lighting from within like a live ember. The smoke crackled and hissed, billowing out briefly, before it settled back into her skin. Her pale, human skin.

Loki slithered closer across the roof, flattened the Shadow to blend in with its surface and, from a thumb's width in front of her toes, gazed far up at the Halfling's human face. Rage suffused him as recognition took hold. He knew that face! Its makers tormented his memory and stoked his fury every time he recalled them. This was the warped spawn of Nialei and her Dragonblood king—how dare she exist!

The sun emerged at last, its hot rays sliding across the Shadow, into it, and Loki shrank from its sharp glare. He clawed at the window he'd created, but though his hand passed through, on the outside, it became invisible, incorporeal. The Northern Veil had thinned, true, but it had yet to completely disappear. Its power was still potent enough to keep him prisoner, allowing only a glimpse outside its walls. As much as he ached to twist the Halfling's head from her body, he could not.

But he could bide his time, keep close, and wait for his opportunity.

Yes, he could, indeed, wait. And scheme. And plot.

The Halfling closed her eyes, spread her arms wide, and smoke once again swirled as she leaned forward and dove off the roof. Loki leapt after her as her half-dragon body took shape mid-fall, wings flaring out to catch the air. She glided gracefully down the empty street, then beat those great wings to rise above it.

Following her path, Loki felt a sudden rush of freedom from the illusion of flight. So simple a thing, the smallest of pleasures, but one he hadn't felt in far too long. He was almost tempted to thank her for it.

Almost.

She banked left ahead, turning north, carried along on a strong air current that held her aloft over the vast expanse of golden sand. When she'd had enough of floating, she beat her wings, flying north so fast Loki's Shadow fell behind, hindered by too much light. Nevertheless, he kept her within sight, following her flight path over a lush oasis and toward a market city. She kept her distance, flew low to remain out of sight, circled in place several times as if unsure of where to go next.

Then something changed. She rose higher, and her fiery gaze locked on to something to the southwest. For long moments, she stared into the distance, clawed fingers curling and stretching at her sides, throwing off bright, golden sparks. Something had angered the Dragonblood.

I know the feeling.

With a sparking hiss, the female shot upward and, trailing her into the sky, Loki was momentarily blinded by light. Snarling, he swirled the Shadow thicker around himself and looked out again—

—at the furious visage of a bright, white goddess before him. Her eyes shone like stars; her face ageless, timelessly beautiful. "You do not belong here," she whispered, and Loki's Shadow squealed beneath the sheer magnitude of her power.

He shrank away, lowered into a respectful bow. This was Aegiros, wholly unaffected by the turmoil Wilderheim and its gods—Loki himself—currently faced. "I beg forgiveness of the great Mother." He shaped the foreign words with a voice he no longer recognized as his own. It was too dark, too deep and growling; more like the crack of thunder than the lilt of a sinister song. "I seek no trouble in her demesne, only what is mine."

A great, cold wind swirled his Shadow prison with an unseen presence that made Loki's insides quiver with unease. *And what is yours?* that presence hissed in question by his ear. It was inside the Shadow with him. How…?

Loki shuddered, feeling like a mouse in a lion's den. He greatly disliked it. "Revenge," he answered.

Seek it elsewhere, Trickster. There is nothing here for you. The wind god retreated, streaking out of the Shadow as if its walls were insubstantial.

Loki rushed after him, hoping to escape through whatever gateway the other god had created, and collided with the wall of his prison. "Oh, but there is!"

Inaras blazed, forcing him back into darkness. "You dare oppose our will!"

"The creature—"

"*She is not yours!*"

Her scream shoved the whole of his Shadow into a vortex of blinding light, threw him end over end to the edges of Aegiros and beyond, across realms and worlds so distant he'd only heard of them in stories.

By the time it had settled and darkened once more, Loki peered out at nothing. The glowing bitch had banished him to the very edge of the universe. It would take him months to get back. With a bellow of impotent rage, he struck out at the walls of his prison.

And felt them crack.

CHAPTER 41

A journey that had taken Tir and Liadan two days would last twice as long in reverse for the whole of Imarah. Even with horses and carriages to ease the way, moving so many people at once was no easy task. With Tir in the lead, they walked for two days just to reach the river basin. Once there, the path was clear and Tir could fall back, check on the wounded, feel the pulse of his tribe. Everything seemed different now. A sense of hope had taken hold, keeping them on the move, even when they were too weak to continue.

During the day, conversation often turned to reminiscing, with the old ones telling the children about their once-beautiful city. They described its wonders, the carefree happiness and comfort they'd enjoyed before the curse.

In the evening, the tribe gathered around fires, told fables of brave heroes and beautiful maidens. Tir often found himself listening as raptly as the little ones, smiling and wishing Liadan was there to share in the wonder of it all.

He missed her.

Every time he glanced down at the vial of water hanging from his neck, every time he strapped on her sword in the morning or brushed down Sleipnir at night, she was there. She'd left them all behind when she'd flown off, and although Tir kept hoping she'd return for them, with each day that passed without any sight of her, his hope diminished. Even Sleipnir sensed it—he was surly, obstinate, and refused to let anyone but Tir come near him. He always pressed forward, ahead of the tribe, quivering with tension to run hard, but whether he wanted to chase down his mistress or simply get away from everyone else was impossible to tell.

The worst of it, however, came at night, when Tir finally succumbed to sleep. He no longer dreamed of fire, but water: the First Temple's underground well swelling, and the flood plains darkening with water that would eventually spill back into the eastern river basin. He dreamed of Liadan, too, sitting next to him on golden pillows, a diaphanous red veil covering her face and a spiked, golden crown adorning her head. Fanciful things. Impossible things. Things for which he'd have traded his sword arm.

As they neared the First City, talk among his tribe changed—men whispered to each other; women flocked together, clutching the weapons they'd been given for the journey. Tir doubted anyone would ever pry those bows out of their hands again.

"...the *shensari*?" one of the *kharesh* said, as Tir passed by on his way to the rear of the procession. His name was Matek, the man who'd taken Sleipnir into his care upon their arrival and, if memory served, one of the first to draw a blade against Liadan.

Unaware the *shansher* had heard, his friend, Ali answered, "Yes! With the hand of

Inaras on her shoulder. I swear by my sword it was her."

"I dreamed the Magus was with her," Muhammad offered. His charred arm was covered in ointment and had to be tormenting him, but he betrayed not a hint of pain, guiding his new mount with one hand on the reins. "He was chanting as the goddess placed a crown on her head."

"Do you think…?"

Matek spotted Tir, and coughed, cutting off whatever Ali had been about to say.

Checking a scowl, Tir nodded to them and kept going.

"What happened then?" a woman asked breathlessly, a little farther back. Something in her voice gave him pause. He turned Sleipnir around, kept behind the group of women to listen in.

"She danced," came the answer, "in a way I've never seen before. I cannot describe it. You wouldn't believe me if I did—"

"I would!" another woman chimed in. "I saw it, too!"

"What did you see?"

"Fire! But it… it was alive. It obeyed her…"

"Tirasdunh."

Tir flinched, turning to Sami beside him. "What is it?"

"Farraj is asking for you. Something's happened."

Tir followed the *kharesh* toward the front, where the wounded warriors rode on horseback and on carts. Farraj, for all his insistence that he was fit enough to ride, still couldn't keep his seat on Zara. Having him sit next to the cart driver was as much to preserve his pride as to free up space for those more gravely wounded. Allowing him to keep his scimitar across his lap was purely for the sake of appearance; he couldn't lift it if he tried.

Having delivered Tir to the general, Sami bowed in his saddle, then veered off to give them what little privacy he could.

"Have you slept well, my king?" Farraj asked without preamble.

"As well as can be expected."

"No strange dreams to disturb your rest?"

Tir frowned. "No stranger than usual. What's this about, Farraj? Since when is my sleep any of your concern?"

"It is not your sleep that concerns me, *shansher*. There's been talk among the tribe about the mother goddess walking through our dreams—"

"So I've heard," Tir muttered.

"—showing favor to your *shensari*."

"What?"

Farraj bowed his head in a deep nod. "Ever since the princess Liadan rose from her ashes, it seems. At first, no one thought anything of it. But then a boy asked his mother whether the fiery one would be waiting for us in the First City, and word began to spread. We've all dreamed the same dream every night since Aesimar was defeated."

"And you think it's by the will of Inaras?"

Farraj rolled his bound shoulder and winced. "I am a warrior, not a mystic; I merely know what I see and hear."

"And what is it you see and hear?"

"I hear Imarah whispering about the *shensari*—their queen, not a beast. I see children dancing with veils and scarves and pretending they're flames. I hear men recall seeing her in battle, wielding a sword that sang when it slashed through the air, boasting about her intercepting a blow that would have killed them. I hear little girls talk of wearing armor one day and standing with the other *kharesh*."

"Easy enough to honor a hero without having to look at her true face. How quickly they've forgotten about that. But they'd remember just as quickly if they ever saw her again, of that I have no doubt."

"Perhaps," Farraj allowed. "But what if…?"

"What if, what?" Tir snorted. "What if Liadan came back and became my queen in truth? The only way she would, is if she sat beside me on a throne of her own. Do you truly believe Imarah's men would tolerate a woman giving them orders?"

"Not at first. Perhaps not for long years. She might go to her death many years from now, never having earned the respect she deserves. But what she has begun here, Tir, will outlive us all. Look around. Our tribe might be returning to the beginning, but it is a much different tribe than it used to be."

Tir scoffed. "I never knew you to be so sentimental. You grow soft in your old age, my friend."

"I've witnessed the misery love can wreak when denied," the commander replied gravely. "I would not wish it on anyone, least of all my *shansher*. There must be a reason why Inaras has chosen to appear nightly in our dreams, with her hand on Liadan's shoulder. Perhaps she wishes the same. We've all seen her above Liadan's pyre that night. She brought the princess back from the dead, and now she shows her to us, seated by your side, with a golden crown on her head and fire in her hand. One of us. Our queen."

"Indeed. It must be a sign, then."

Farraj ignored the retort. "If ever the chance lived for that dream to become real, it is now. *Now*, before we remember all the reasons why it shouldn't. When we reach the First City, we can go back to the way things used to be, or begin anew, find a different way."

"Rewrite the laws we've lived by for centuries to accommodate a Northern queen in our midst," Tir replied dryly. "Even if the goddess herself could appear in the palace and spell every man, woman, and child of Imarah to adore their new Northern queen, you forget one thing, Farraj."

"What?"

Sleipnir fidgeted, picking up on his rider's restlessness. "Liadan is gone. And she's never coming back." He kicked the horse into a gallop, pulling ahead of the front riders, then gave him free rein. The great stallion whinnied, raced like a shot to put as much distance as possible between himself and the rest of Imarah.

They reached the First City just as the sun set behind the horizon. Standing on the outskirts, Tir stared down the alley before him. Not a flicker of light to be seen anywhere, but the faint scent of smoke lingered in the air, teasing his senses to take a different path than the one leading directly to the palace.

Liadan is gone, he told himself again. The scent was nothing but his mind playing tricks on him. Nevertheless, his hand tightened on the reins, just enough to turn Sleipnir into the breeze and follow that scent to its source—if there was one.

The waning moon wasn't bright enough to illuminate the path, and if he lit a torch, he'd lose the scent trail, so Tir kept going in the dark. The shadow of the palace loomed to his left, but the smoke trail led farther west, more proof it couldn't have been Liadan. If it had been her, she'd have bedded down in the palace itself.

The farther he went, the stronger the scent became, and the more uneasy Tir felt. He pulled Sleipnir to a halt by the old marketplace, earning himself a grumbling snort. He held a finger to his mouth for silence when he dismounted. Drawing Liadan's sword from its scabbard, he waved Sleipnir back and continued on foot alone. Not far ahead, faint light flickered through a bare window. Tir approached silently, watchful for any movement in the shadows. Voices hummed inside that house, too deep to be women.

"What do we tell the sheikh?"

"A pox on the sheikh! A pox on all of them—*argh!* Watch it!"

"If I don't burn it, you'll bleed to death!"

Tir flattened himself against the wall, then leaned over to peer through the small window. Two men sat in front of a small fire inside, their clothes torn and covered with dust. One had removed his shirt, exposing four long, deep furrows across his chest, with the deepest still bleeding.

"Do it, then. But for all the gods' sake, be quick about it!"

His friend pulled a small dagger from the fire, then pressed the red-hot blade to the wound.

The injured man screamed, shoved his friend away, and curled in on himself, reaching out a shaking hand to rummage through a pile of cloth for a bottle. He spilled more out than into his mouth when he tipped it.

"Careful," the friend snapped, yanking the bottle away. "That's the last of the opium wine."

The injured man spat at him, belched, and leaned back against the wall.

With a sigh, his friend set the bottle aside, out of reach. "What do you think it was?" he asked after a while.

"Who bloody cares what it was?"

"You should. It killed..." The man shuddered. "*Everyone.*"

The opium drinker gave him a drowsy, lopsided grin. "Not everyone. It let the women go. Stupid. Kinder to kill 'em like the rest."

"Did you see what it did to the matron?"

"*Hmph!* A pox on the old hag. A pox on all of 'em. Soon as I heal up, you wait an' see. I'll hunt down the demon bitch myself. I'll—"

Tir's dagger struck him in the throat, cutting off the rest of his threat. Before the other *masar* had a chance to scream, Tir leapt in through the window, caught him by the throat, and slammed his back against the stone wall.

"W-wha—"

"Tell me what I want to know, and your death will be swift. Lie to me, and I'll make it last a week."

His eyes bulged in terror as he nodded, shaking from head to toe.

"Your *masiranah* was attacked?"

Another nod.

"When?"

"T-this morning. North of here—"

"By what?"

"I d-don't know. Never saw anything like it. Please—"

"What did it look like?"

His eyes darted to his dead companion, then back to Tir, and whatever he saw in Tir's eyes made him wail in fright. "Big, black demon thing! Wings… tail. It b-breathed fire—"

"Did you see where it went? What happened to the women?"

"No, please! I saw nothing, I swear!"

Tir squeezed his throat a little tighter, pulled a throwing knife out of his boot and pressed the tip to the man's cheek, just below his eye. "Think very hard."

"I don't know! On my soul, I don't. We ran away, fast as we could. It killed all the men—tore the matron limb from limb! Burned our caravan. Gods, please, I don't want to die!"

His fear was genuine. A kinder man would have taken pity on him, shown him mercy and let him go. But kindness wasn't a virtue Tir had in ready supply where the *masar* were concerned, especially the ones who'd have sold Liadan into slavery as an exotic treat. A man of his word, Tir gave the *masar* the quick death he'd promised in exchange for his cooperation. In truth, Tir ought to have thanked him. Without him, he never would have known Liadan was still in Aegiros.

Now, all he had to do was find her.

CHAPTER 42

Wholly focused on her revenge, watching her flames consume the remains of the slavers' caravan, Liadan never saw the sandstorm coming. The powerful winds slammed into her back, knocking her to the ground and blowing her across the desert like a small sailing boat over a raging sea. She choked on sand, lost all sense of direction; no more fire, no sky, only sand—everywhere. She tried to shield her face with her wings, but the winds pushed even harder against the solid wall of their span. She could neither stand in place nor rise above. Against this desert force, Liadan had no protection, no path of escape; it carried her along, and all she could do was keep moving, keep the sand from burying her alive.

By the time it had finally ended, night had fallen, and Liadan was alone in the desert, far from familiar territory. Flying up for a better view helped little; as far as her dragonsight reached, the sands were dark, with not a single flickering light to betray any hint of a human settlement, and only a shadow in the distance to provide a focal point. With nowhere else to turn, Liadan flew toward it. She'd rest by that mountain range and find her way back north by daylight.

But the distance stretched longer than she'd expected and, exhausted by the flight, Liadan burned her wings the moment she landed at the base of the mountain. Her breath misted in the cold, and her skin began to glow to ward off the night's chill.

"Where am I?" This wasn't the red mountain she'd scaled for her scimitar. This rock face was a pale gray, almost shimmering in the moonlight. She took a step closer and gasped as the ground gave way beneath her, dropping her into an underground cave on a cloud of dust. Liadan landed hard. Her foot caught in a crevice, and she lost her balance, slamming into a rock protrusion.

"Ow!" Temper flaring, her skin glowed brighter, and fire sparked off her fingertips. She smacked the wall to level herself off the ground and nearly broke her own ankle to free her foot, stumbled again and fell onto her hands and knees in a puddle.

"Water..." Clean, cool water bubbled up from the ground and trickled between the rocks to disappear down a vast, black tunnel. She didn't wait for divine invitation, just stuck her face into the puddle and gulped down as much as her stomach could hold.

Her thirst finally quenched, Liadan sat back on her heels and looked around properly. The cave felt smaller than it ought to have been. Massive stalactites drooped from the ceiling, melting into stalagmites rising from the floor. It felt like being inside a giant maw filled with fangs, complete with a pitch-black tunnel of a throat stretching far to one side.

"Hellooooo!"

The echo of her voice bounced deep into the tunnel. No stranger to caves, Liadan was fairly certain this particular one stretched for endless miles far beneath the sands of Aegiros. It was definitely large enough for any number of creatures to live there, and with a steady supply of water, it'd make an excellent lair. With a small bed, a few tapestries and candlesticks, it might as well be home.

Liadan shook away the fanciful idea. What on earth was she thinking? She already had a home, and it was far away from here, where grass and trees painted the landscape green instead of gold, and water froze in the sky in winter, falling down in flakes of snow to cover the land like a fluffy, white blanket until spring.

Liadan gazed down at the bubbling surface of the ground well. "Fal. Brother, can you hear me?"

Nothing.

"Fal!"

The puddle glittered with firelight. "Liadan?"

Tears burned her eyes, even as she smiled at the image of her brother's baffled face.

"Liadan, is that you?"

She nodded, not trusting herself to speak. Her throat was too tight to form words anyway.

"I thought… Sweet gods, we all thought… Say something! Where are you? What's happened?"

Liadan wiped her nose, her wet eyes, and sucked in a deep breath. "I'm still in Aegiros. Alive and well, and free of my oath."

Fal gaped. He was pale, gaunt, and very much himself.

"What's the matter with you?" she demanded. "You look like death itself. Are you ill? Has someone died?"

Her brother rubbed his jaw. "You did."

"Oh… I suppose I did, at that."

Fal still hadn't blinked. "Is… are you real?"

Liadan looked down at herself. The blouse and pants she'd pilfered from the palace were covered with dust, the vest drenched from her earlier dive into the puddle. "I think so."

He reached out, mouth moving with a silent incantation. His hand broke the surface, and Liadan pressed her palm to his, felt him shudder. "All the gods above, you're alive!" Tangling his fingers with hers, he pulled her hand across the divide. "Bollocks. The surface is too small to bring you across. You have to find a bigger pool."

"I'd love to. Only I've no idea where I am. Have you got any food?"

Fal released her, and moments later a plate piled high with meats and cheeses appeared in the puddle's surface, pushing up and across. Liadan snatched it to her, dug in with her bare, dirty hands. The first proper meal she'd eaten in who knew how long and, gods, it tasted like heaven. Fal let her eat her fill before he began firing questions at her: Where had she gone? What happened to her? What was Tir's tribe like? How did she defeat the demons?

Belly full and heart content in her twin's distant company, Liadan recounted the whole of her journey, from the moment they'd crossed into Aegiros to the moment the last Aesimar had fallen. She skimmed over nothing, took heart in her brother's exclamations of outrage over the slavers and the Dark chains Aesimar's Magi had almost locked onto her.

She told him about Tir and his tribe, the *kharesh* and her ordeal to become one of them, then she listened to everything that had happened in Wilderheim since she'd left. The curse had kept all of them from Seeing into the First Valley; they'd had no news of Liadan, until the moment Fal had felt her die. He told her how the fire had seared across his mind, burning away the bond between them, and how he'd been bedridden for days after, refusing to speak a word to anyone.

"Mother and Da are inconsolable. They blame the dragon for…" His eyes suddenly went impossibly wide. "I have to tell them!"

"Wait, don't go yet!" If she let him, Fal would disappear and leave her alone again in this cave. "They've been mourning for days. One more night won't make any difference now. Stay with me a little longer. I've missed you so much."

He sighed. "What will you do?"

"Wait until sunrise, then climb out of this cave and look for north."

"Are you sure that's what you want?"

Liadan was proud of the way she was able to smile through the stabbing pain in her chest. "Of course I am. I want to go home."

"And you can, any time. I can teach you the incantations for passing through elements, and you can step through a pool of water, or even a tall flame, and be back in Frastmir in an instant. But…"

"But what?"

Fal huffed. "Will it make you happy?"

Home, family, a lifetime spent between stone walls; stuck in a land of green and white, far away from Imarah and its king. The stabbing pain turned into searing agony. "What should I do instead? Fly back to Imarah and hope they don't kill me before I can finish saying I mean them no harm?"

"You could speak to Tir."

Liadan shook her head. "It's better that I don't. Nothing good would come of it. Any of it."

"You can't know that. Look at Mother and Da. The entire kingdom was against their marriage in the beginning, and now… well, a good part of it is still angry, but we manage just fine. There hasn't been a rebellion in years."

"The dragon told me there would come a day when I'd have to choose."

"But this is not that day," Fal insisted. "Who says you can't have both? As long as we inhabit the same realm and the elements remain eternal, the passage between their aspects is only a spell away. You can fly across the whole of Aegiros during the day, and return to your own bed in Frastmir for the night."

How easy he made it all seem—simple, magical, and completely attainable. But it wasn't.

"What do you want, Liadan? What does your heart yearn for?"

"The impossible," she replied, tracing the grooves of her torc.

Fal kept her company until long after sunrise, until exhaustion dragged Liadan into deep sleep and strange dreams. She saw a powerful river pour out of a small bottle and a golden crown shaped into horns and flames, glittering in the hands of Imarah's Magi. She saw Tir holding a wooden chalice, heard the dragon's voice speaking words she didn't understand.

She awoke to a fresh plate of food, a bottle of mead, and a travel bundle on the ground by the bubbling pool, with Fal nowhere to be found. Likely he'd told the royal pair the good news, and they were even now scrying for her whereabouts.

Liadan yawned and stretched, working out the soreness from her muscles and joints. While she ate, she untied the bundle to see what her brother had gathered for her. A thick cloak, proper boots, a pair of knives, a pouch of coin, and two large waterskins—everything a Dragonblood princess could ever need on a long journey. Fal's thoughtfulness included the bundle itself, as well. It was small, with long straps that would easily tie around her shoulders and waist, with the bundle resting between her wings in flight.

"Thank you, brother."

Now all she had to do was find the waterfall oasis again. Fal had brought her back through it once. He could do it again.

Is that really what you want?

Yes. *It's all I can have.*

After packing up the treasures, Liadan sat on the ground to remove her silk slippers in favor of the sturdy leather boots. The oasis couldn't be far, but if she couldn't find it, she'd explore farther, look for another. She might even fly over the mountain range, try her luck on the other side. Aegiros didn't go on forever. Somewhere on its western edge lay the border with Synealee. Not a friendly place for Others, but it had water aplenty—

Sounds above. Hoofbeats galloping toward her, echoing along the tunnel in a familiar rhythm. Liadan moved everything into shadow, then crouched down by the rock wall, clutching her new blades.

Rubble rained down as the horse halted and stomped the ground a few paces from her. Liadan winced, pressing herself tighter against the solid wall. That ground was unstable. A little more weight and it would crumble, as it had where she'd fallen through last night.

A thump. Footsteps. A lone rider? No, that couldn't be. No one rode alone in Aegiros; the desert was too harsh and treacherous. Liadan hadn't seen groups of less than three anywhere, and they always had at least one extra beast of burden to carry supplies. A loner could only mean one thing: he was strong, and familiar enough with the desert to survive for long periods on his own, by any means necessary. He could be trouble.

Sand dusted down along the edge of the hole she'd made, and a shadow fell across the ray of sunshine spearing into the cave before a figure dropped silently inside with a much softer landing than hers had been. The man's back was to her, his head and neck covered with a scarf, a long, curved dagger sheathed at his waist. Definitely trouble.

But he only had one blade against her two, and one of his hands was bandaged. Liadan liked those odds. She shifted her weight to get a better look. He stared at the far wall, where something had captured his interest for the moment, but he'd move on soon enough. The trickle of water would distract him, and then he'd find her and try to rob her, or kill her and take over the watering hole before she could tell him he was welcome to it. Liadan was cornered where she crouched; no room to maneuver, and on the wrong side of the cave, with him standing between her and the way out. If he came at her, she'd be at a disadvantage. Better to take her chances in the open.

While his back was still turned, Liadan pushed away from the wall and rushed forward. He heard her, twisted around, blocked her thrust, knocked her blade away, then rammed his shoulder into her middle. Liadan fell back into the stream and took advantage of their momentum to keep rolling, throwing him over her head, deeper into the dark cave. They leapt to their feet at the same time, Liadan with one knife left and the man brandishing his own.

Their positions had reversed; Liadan now had a clear path to the surface, but the man didn't seem inclined to let her escape. He charged her head-on, so fast, she barely spun out of the way of his blade. She kicked out at the back of his knee hard enough to buckle it, but he caught himself against a stalagmite and stayed upright, pulling his injured hand away before she could grab it. Again, they clashed, and Liadan's back slammed against rock, knocking the breath out of her. She refused to go down. The man yanked her forward, bodily threw her back into the light and followed her down. But she was ready for him, clawed the scarf around his neck for a choke hold and pushed up, rolling them both until she ended up on top with her blade to his exposed neck.

"Liadan?"

She froze. "Tir?"

Metal clattered to the ground, and then his bandaged hand fisted in her hair so hard it hurt, yanking her down, and he cut off her cry with a hard, punishing kiss. She forgot to breathe beneath the pressure of his arms around her, lost all coherent thought in the taste of him, the desperate clutch of his hand in her hair, the curl of his leg around hers as if he feared she'd be ripped from him.

He rolled to trap her beneath him, but by then, her hands were entangled in his shirt, and she was kissing him back for all she was worth.

"Gods, I missed you, *shai'iss*," he said against her lips, and Liadan thrilled. She knew what it meant now. Her body warmed to his touch, her skin began to glow, and steam rose from her wet clothes.

All at once, she remembered herself, broke out of their kiss, pushed at him, and where her hands touched, his clothing charred.

But Tir wouldn't release her. "Calm, Liadan." He cupped her face, made her meet his gaze, and smiled. "You can't hurt me." To prove it, he kissed her again, slowly, then traced her jaw with his lips, caressed the side of her neck. His every touch stoked her fire hotter, yet he didn't withdraw. Where his clothing smoked, he pressed her hand directly to the center of his chest, looked into her eyes and made her see. "Your fire burns in my heart. It will never hurt me."

Uncertainty flickered in her eyes; Tir saw the memory of hurt in them and knew instinctively how much this frightened her. Imarah had turned on her once already, how could she trust one of them again?

But this wasn't a cowering mortal in his arms; this was the Dragonblood princess Liadan, and she feared nothing. "Kiss me," she whispered, and Tir could do no other than oblige. Her lips were life itself; her touch, the answer to questions he'd never thought to ask. Nothing would ever compare to the feel of her in his arms, and he had no intention of ever letting her go again.

Tir soothed her frantic breath by giving her his own, calmed her nervous quiver by letting her feel his steady heartbeat. They shed their clothes in a hurry, eager to touch, desperate to feel. Water hissed beneath them and filled the cave with a sensuous steam, a dreamy haze to soften every sight and sound.

Liadan's skin took on its familiar glow, bathing him in light and warmth, and he savored every inch of it, thrilled in the scrape of her nails against his back, the nip of her teeth at his shoulder as he sank into her welcoming embrace. Theirs was not a gentle joining—after everything they'd endured, neither of them had any patience left for feathery kisses and soft sighs. Too much death had shown them how short and how precious life was. Every moment apart was a moment wasted.

Liadan's impassioned cries echoed in the cave with each of Tir's thrusts; his pleasured groan rumbled from deep within him whenever she squeezed him closer, deeper. Alone in the desert, only the sky and sand could see them, and one man and one woman meant little enough to them. But for Tir and Liadan, even all of the desert and the sky, the entire world and the whole of creation became inconsequential for a few moments of the deepest happiness either of them had ever known.

They didn't move for a long time afterwards, content to simply lie together, to touch, to kiss, to pretend nothing existed outside of their little hideaway. Long after night had fallen, Tir finally made himself climb back out to check on Sleipnir. He removed the mount's saddle, gave him oats and water, then endured a lot of sniffing and stomping before Sleipnir allowed him to return to the cave and to Liadan.

She'd dressed and brought out a few small items from deeper inside the cave. With his hands full of blankets for the night, Tir stopped in his tracks, staring at the packed bundle by her feet. "What's going on?"

"Nothing," she said, though her smile faded much too quickly. "I just wanted to make sure I wouldn't leave anything important behind."

"Even if you did, the palace has everything aplenty. You can have your pick of whatever you need."

"Tir—"

"No, don't say it."

"I'm not going back to the First City."

Sharp pain shot up his arm from his injured wrist, and he forced himself to relax his hand. The blankets dropped quietly to the cavern floor. "Why?"

"Because nothing has changed."

He blanched. "What?"

"I'm still the same monster you couldn't come near of back there. Your people still fear me like a swarm of demons, and I still have no place here. Not among them, not anywhere in Aegiros. My family is waiting for me in Wilderheim; it's time I returned to them."

A thousand different arguments stuck in his throat. None of them would sway her. What could a mere man, even a king, offer an Other? What possible reason could he give to make her stay with him? "What if you're with child?"

She swallowed hard, touched a hand to her abdomen. "I'm not. I'd feel it if I was. But even if… More than likely, it'd… b-burn away with my next firestorm." Her voice quivered too much for him to believe the callousness behind her words. "Halflings are volatile and rarely breed. That my mother was able to birth me and Fal was nothing short of a miracle. I don't expect it to happen again."

"So you'll run back to your fortress of stone and ice, to live out your eternal life alone."

"What other choice do I have?"

"Stay here!"

"And do what? Hide in caves so humans won't try to kill me? Wait for you to sneak away from your kingly duties for a clandestine tryst every now and then?" Smoke curled around her, billowing out to hide her completely. When it retreated once more into her skin, Liadan stood before him in her true form. Black, shimmering scales covered her body, her wings pulled tight against her back, and her eyes shone red-gold from a familiar face turned alien with sharp cheekbones and pointed fangs. "Have you forgotten already? *This* is what I am. Look at me now and tell me I can walk into your palace and have my pick of whatever I might need."

In this form, she stood a hand's width taller than Tir, and with one flick of her tail, she could flatten him against the cave wall. But she was still his Liadan. Her eyes burned fiercely, but not with anger; her clawed hands clenched tightly, but not to attack. Tir had never seen a creature more magnificent. "*Shai'iss*, I did not offer you a single thing from the palace. I offered you the palace itself. And the First City, along with the entire valley. I do not want you to hide in caves. I need you to sit by my side, sleep in my bed, eat from my plate, and drink of my wine."

"And wait for your *kharesh* to cut off my head in the night?"

"The *kharesh* are even now singing of your bravery. They have their hands full with young men pestering them to be trained, insisting another *kharashan* be held so they can test themselves, now that you made it look so easy. The women have started plaiting their hair the same way you do, and little girls run around waving sticks in the air and pretending they're swords. How could nothing have changed? You saved us all, Liadan—*you* changed *everything*."

Her flaming hair banked down to red-brown tresses. "Centuries of laws and customs won't change overnight for one woman, even an Other."

He'd said the same thing to Farraj only two days before. The general's answer, before so naïve and shortsighted, suddenly seemed like the most sensible wisdom. "No, not overnight. But with time—"

"Do you remember what I told you before my firestorm? I'll only take a mate who is my equal in all things, and I will no more abide him taking another than he would me cuckolding him for sport. Do you expect me to sit in shadow of your reign, stand idly by while you take ten more wives to give you heirs when I can't?"

"Never." His simple answer seemed to startle her. "I remember what you told me, Liadan, and I remember what I said, as well. To share such passion with another, to look into her eyes and see a helpmate, would be a blessing beyond imagining. You are right, Imarah will not bow to a Northern queen right away—perhaps not ever—but they will show respect to the one who saved them, accept you among them. And when we breathe our last, *shai'iss*, you'll be in my arms, and you will know that I have loved you with all of my heart and soul, all the days since first we met."

She said nothing for so long, Tir began to lose hope. Then smoke and fire crackled around her and she emerged from them human again, her beautiful gray eyes flickering gold. "I'd never be a proper Aegiran wife. I never stop myself saying what needs to be said. I'd be brash, and do the wrong thing, and offend the wrong people. I wouldn't stop training or sparring, and I'd dance whenever the fire's song moved me, probably terrify your court with the flames. I'd disappear often, sometimes for days or weeks, to see my family, and if ever anyone threatened me or mine, Imarah would see my true form again."

Tir caught a lock of her hair, smoothed its silk between his fingers. "I've had a tribe's worth of proper Aegiran women to choose from and never once thought of taking a wife, until you. Say whatever needs saying. Do whatever needs doing. If the wrong people take offense, only remember you are *shensari*, and you'll always have me by your side, in court or in battle. I want you to train, and I'll happily spar with you day and night, if that's what you wish. Dance, fly, make a fortress of your flames, go to your family whenever you need them. I would never deny you any of these things, as long as you come back to me when all is said and done."

"You'd make enemies."

"You've already defeated more in one week than I could accumulate in another lifetime."

"You'd be scorned for taking an outsider to wife instead of one of your own."

"They already think we are wed, remember? And even if they didn't, how could I take another when your blood runs in my veins now? Fire cannot touch me. Who knows what other changes it had wrought?"

Liadan flushed. "About that…"

"What is it?"

"Our oath was fulfilled before…" She gestured to the ground, where rock had charred from their lovemaking. "The bond was already broken. Whatever changes it caused will eventually fade."

"Good."

She gaped. "*Good?*"

Tir smiled in the face of her outrage. "I do not want a wife bound to me by an unintended trick of magic; I want her to cleave to me of her own choice. If she so chooses."

Again, she fell silent, and Tir held his breath, waiting for her to make up her mind. Then her shoulders drooped, and she huffed. "You make it all sound so simple, and it isn't."

"Nothing worthwhile ever is."

Liadan rubbed the torc around her neck. "We should get you back to your tribe. They'll think you abandoned them again." She brushed past him, shouldered her pack, and climbed up to the surface.

Tir followed quickly, afraid she'd disappear again if he let her out of his sight. But when he finally clambered up to the desert sands, he found her standing frozen where she'd emerged. "Liadan?"

"You've been missed, child."

Tir turned on the stranger, dagger in hand, but couldn't move a single step. Not ten paces away stood a tall, pale man, dressed in nothing but billowing pants, with his hands clasped lightly behind his back, but his body so incongruously rigid, he may as well have been carved out of marble. His mouth smiled, but his ageless eyes were cold. Were it not for the horns adorning his head—the same ones Liadan wore in her dragon form—and the three floating fireballs illuminating the desert night, Tir would have gutted him on the spot.

Instead, he stared, baffled, as Liadan ran straight into the man's arms, with a happy cry of, "Grandfather!"

CHAPTER 43

The dragon chuckled caught her up in an embrace so tight it hurt. Liadan didn't care. Her heart sang and her eyes stung with tears to be with him again.

"Hello, little miss." He squeezed her a little harder, then set her back on her feet. "I am glad to find you alive and well."

"When did you get here? How?"

"Midday. I… didn't want to interrupt."

Liadan flushed. He must have heard… Gods, this would be bad. "Grandfather, this is Tirasdunh al-Dhakir."

"*Shansher* of the First Tribe," the dragon finished and inclined his head formally. "I've heard a great deal about you."

Liadan nudged the gaping Tir, who glanced at her, then touched a hand to his mouth, his forehead, and bowed deeply. "I humbly welcome the great dragon. I've heard much about you, as well."

"Well met, young man. You do your people proud. Most would flee at the sight of me."

"Are Mother and Father with you?" she asked to fill the silence. "And Fal? Did he bring you through water? How is everyone?"

"Easy, girl. All in good time. First, let's have a look at you."

Liadan grinned and stepped back to change. When her shape settled, she proudly flared her wings wide, swished her tail left and right.

The dragon smiled again, one those impossibly rare smiles that warmed his eyes for the briefest moment. "Well done," he said thickly. "Will your wings carry you?"

"Yes, but flying tires me."

"The muscles are the same as your human ones. They need practice. In time, flying will be as easy as riding a horse. I am proud of you, Liadan. We all are."

Tir, oddly subdued and silent during the exchange, sheathed his dagger. "You've come to take her home."

The dragon looked at him again. Liadan knew that piercing stare; the dragon could cow the bravest of the brave just by looking directly into their eyes. Most fell to their knees and swore to do anything the dragon commanded if he spared their lives. She quickly burned back into her human form and prepared to face off with the dragon, if need be. Tir had done nothing wrong, and she would not let the dragon shame him.

But Tir stood his ground, met that ancient gaze head-on. "I know I can't beat you. I know you could whisk Liadan away to the end of the world and keep her from me forever—"

"And I know you would never stop searching for her if I did," the dragon replied calmly. "I know your heart, young king; it burns as brightly for Liadan as hers does for you. I am not here to take her away; she's not mine to take. But neither is she yours to keep. Do you understand what that means?"

Tir drew himself up. "I do."

"Then, my girl, the choice is yours."

"I…" She looked to Tir, but he wouldn't meet her gaze. He'd already said all he needed to say down in the cave, offered his heart and his kingdom at her feet. The dragon, too, kept silent; he didn't need to tell her what she already knew: if she stayed, she'd forever give up her claim to Wilderheim's crown. Demons take it; she didn't care. But she needn't give up her family. If Fal could open a doorway through water, she could find a way to do the same with fire, and if not, she could always fly.

One thought, however, still kept her from speaking the words she so longed to voice: Tir was mortal; eventually, he'd die, and she'd have to go on, unchanged, for decades, perhaps even centuries, after his ashes had blown away across the desert sands. Everyone here would live out their lives before her eyes, and no matter how many friends she made, if she stayed here, among mortals, her existence would be a long procession of funeral pyres as, one after the other, everyone she cared about passed from this world. The same shadows that always swirled in the dragon's eyes would grow in hers, as well—ghosts of her loved ones, of Tir, until the pain of loving became too much and she retreated into solitude the same way he had.

Is it worth it?

Yes. She didn't need to read the answer in the dragon's eyes; it was already there, deep in her heart. If all she would ever have with Tir was a human lifetime, then she'd fill that lifetime to the brim with enough love and memories to sustain her for eternity.

Liadan touched a hand to Tir's shoulder, then drew his dagger from its sheath and pulled the sharp blade across her palm. "My choice is you."

"There'll be no going back from this," the dragon warned, "for either of you."

Before he'd finished speaking, Tir snatched the dagger from her, tore the bandages from his hand, and cut open his own palm, pressing the wound to hers as they clasped hands. His hand was swollen, bruised black, but he didn't feel any pain at all. He pulled her into him and kissed her right there in front of her grandfather.

The dragon cleared his throat and, with great reluctance, Tir pulled away enough to take a breath. "Blood binds all things, human and Other," the dragon said. "It'll forever join you, in this life and the next."

"We know," Tir replied.

"Then it is done."

"Thank the gods."

Liadan laughed, and the dragon's eyes twinkled. "Allow me to offer a gift."

Tir frowned at the wooden chalice the dragon held out to them. He accepted it, held it steady as the dragon produced a bottle of wine and filled the chalice, then raked a claw across his own palm and added three drops of his blood. The wine hissed, smoked, bubbled, swirling so hot, the cup itself warmed in Tir's hand.

"But he's human," Liadan protested.

"That's precisely why he must drink."

She took hold of the chalice. "It could kill him!"

The dragon remained unmoved. "You proved yourself willing to give up everything for the mortal you love, Liadan. You've passed your test. Now it's Tir's turn. Will you drink for her, human? Even if it kills you?"

Tir looked into Liadan's worried face. "My choice is you—always." And before she could stop him, he raised the chalice and downed the searing wine in three gulps. The heat blinded him. The world tilted, fell away as fire scorched him from within until he couldn't even draw breath enough to scream. His muscles clenched, his bones groaned. Tir gritted his teeth, stubbornly rode out the pain, felt it brand his very soul. But at the moment he was sure it would burn him to cinders, the fire banked into a soft glow at his core, and he breathed in, his lungs easily filling with air once again.

His head in Liadan's lap, he stared up into her eyes, brushed away her tears with a hand suddenly whole, as if it had never been broken. A thin, pale line cut across his palm, the wound mended with the dragon's magic blood. Liadan was now forever part of him.

"My blood will not protect you from injury or disease," the dragon said, "but it will help you heal much faster. Likewise, it will not make you immortal, but it'll prolong your natural life a great deal. And while it won't give you magical powers, it'll protect you from them for as long as you live."

Tir grinned and stood up, snatched Liadan around the waist and twirled her in circles until she squealed, clinging to him as hard as he held on to her. Then he set her back down to face the dragon once more with a deep bow. "Words will never be enough to express my gratitude."

The dragon nodded.

"We should get back," Liadan said. "Imarah is waiting for you."

"For *us*," he corrected.

"Aren't you forgetting something?" the dragon asked. "Your tribe is safe, but it still has no water."

Tir's heart sank. "He's right. If we can't bring the river back to life, we'll never revive the First City."

Liadan sighed. "Water is Fal's power, not mine."

"Your brother gave you the means before you left," the dragon said. "Don't tell me you lost it."

Tir caught her hand in his. "The vial. I left it in Sleipnir's saddle bag."

The dragon whistled a loud, shrill call, and within moments, the thunder of Sleipnir's hooves galloped toward them through the dark of night. He ran straight for Liadan, nearly bowled her over in his excitement, and she laughed while he lipped her hair, bumped his forehead against her. Tir couldn't help smiling at the sight as he crossed over to the pile of gear and supplies he'd removed from Sleipnir earlier. In the first light of morning, he withdrew the glass vial, held it up for the dragon's inspection. "I don't understand. How can a handful of water produce a river?"

"The vessel is only a conduit. All water is connected, eternal and unchanging. But it has no shape of its own. For a connection to the Eternal source to endure, it must be anchored, in shape and position."

Liadan grinned. "I think I can do that." She took the vial, and jumped back into the cave.

"Liadan, wait!" Tir dropped down after her, followed by her dragon grandfather.

"You saw this before I did," she told him, tracing the carvings in the western wall of the cave.

At first, the symbols seemed random, but from far enough away, their pattern became obvious: concentric circles, like endless ripples on the surface of a lake, and in the very middle, a small crevice. Yes, he'd seen it before. Inaras had been guiding him to this place from the moment she'd returned from her exile. *Where life once began, it can be restored.* This was the Source, the forgotten First Temple of Inaras.

"Fire burns," Liadan murmured, pressing her palm flat against the center point. Her hand began to glow, brighter, hotter, searing the rock beneath it.

"Slowly," the dragon said. "Too much too fast, and the rock will crack."

Steam rose from the stone, air wavering from the heat, and when Liadan pulled her hand away, her handprint remained, the rock bright yellow and *malleable*.

The dragon cocked his head. "You'll need to cool the rock quickly, or the glass will shatter."

Liadan stared at the vial in her hand. It had survived weeks of travel and elements, so it had to be stronger than it looked, but Tir still couldn't imagine it standing up to rock so hot it melted. Liadan seemed to have her doubts, as well. "I may need your help with this, Grandfather."

The dragon nodded, placed his hand on the stone beside her handprint. "Set the vial, and I'll cool the rock."

She touched the center crevice, manipulated it to open wider, and quickly placed the glass vial inside of it. In an instant, the heat's glow began to dim, and as the rock set around the glass, it darkened once more to natural gray. It happened silently, in the span of a few heartbeats, and everything seemed to be fine, until the faintest *chink* froze them all. The glass had cracked.

The dragon pulled his hand away, while Liadan leaned in close to check the damage. "I can't see anything."

Tir joined her to look for himself. "The glass might have cracked, but it looks like the rock sealed around it. I think it'll hold."

Liadan rubbed her brow with a shaky hand. "Now what?"

"Fal," the dragon called.

From somewhere behind and below Tir, Liadan's twin spoke up. "Remove the stopper, then I suggest you get back up top."

A hand pushed up from the surface of the bubbling pool, bathed in a pale blue glow.

When Tir would have reached out to it, Liadan caught his arm and pulled him away, up and out of the cave after the dragon. The three of them stood well back from the opening, waiting for something to happen. When the ground rumbled beneath them, Sleipnir reared, removing himself even farther and, familiar with his superior senses by now, Tir pulled Liadan to follow him. But the sound of rushing water brought them all back to the edge of the precipice.

Tir gaped at the impossibly powerful geyser bursting out of the western cave wall. The current was so strong, water filled the cave within moments, spilling down the underground tunnels to the east. Soon, it bubbled up from the hole, flooded out into the surrounding area, turning the ground dark with more moisture than the Flood Plains had seen in decades.

So much misery, pain, and suffering, so many years of wandering, dying… all of it undone with one small glass bottle and a handful of water.

"We did it…"

Liadan whooped and jumped, splashing about in the pool growing around her stoic grandfather and speechless husband. She caught Tir's hands, pulled him into a dance, infecting him with her boundless enthusiasm. "We did it! We saved everyone!"

Someone laughed. "Liadan, the savior of Imarah. Is this any way for a queen to behave?"

Once again, Liadan pulled away from Tir and raced into the arms of another man—her brother this time, cloaked as before in layers of illusion. But this time, when Liadan stepped back, Tir caught the man up himself, heedless of custom and propriety. He'd have kissed Fal for this miracle, but he still had a smidgen of manly pride left, so he twirled Liadan around and kissed her instead.

When the pool began to spread into a small lake, the group set out back toward the First City. The water, Fal assured them, would flow and follow, filling the riverbed as it had long ago.

"Will you stay awhile?" Tir asked. "I'd be honored to have you both as my guests in the palace, as neglected as it is."

"I can't. Mother and Da will be looking for me. They still aren't allowed to leave Wilderheim." He turned a stern look at Liadan. "So they'll expect you to visit—*soon*."

Liadan leaned against Tir, hugged herself to his side. "We will. As soon as Imarah is taken care of." If possible, her words made him love her more.

They spoke a little longer, shared a midday meal beneath a small tent, and then Liadan's kin took their leave, with promises to see each other in a few days. When they were gone, Liadan sighed and set about packing away their tent.

"Are you sorry to see them go?"

"Always," she replied. "But not as sorry as I would have been had I gone with them."

Tir took the bundled tent out of her hands and kissed her knuckles.

She smiled. "It's strange, I always knew in my heart my path would lead me far away from them. I just never imagined how happy I'd be to arrive at my journey's end."

"Ah, *shai'iss*, my love, but this is not the end. We have only just begun."

EPILOGUE

In the realm of the Divine, the wind god gathered everyone around a massive copper bowl. Swirling the sand therein, he summoned a vision of Aegiros. The First City took shape in the center, a mighty river flowing lazily from west to east. Inaras shone with pride at the sight of children playing on the banks, horses filling the stables, farmers tending the first harvest. After years of lying fallow, the earth once again bore fruit, more abundant than ever before, and the First Tribe flourished.

The great palace at the heart of the city bustled with activity, droves of merchants and traders arriving and leaving under the watchful eye of the *kharesh*. The king himself presided over court, alone, listening patiently while angry men told him how his queen had defied tradition yet again. He cared not a whit—smiled in the face of their rage, laughed at their threats, then sent them off without punishment. Old men considered it their duty to complain, but unless one took action against the order the *shansher* and his *shensari* had established, Tirasdunh the Demonslayer had far more important matters to think about.

Far in the back of the fig grove, the new queen's guard-in-training encircled a clearing where Liadan faced off with two *kharesh*. All women with muscled bodies and uncovered faces, they shared many of their *shensari*'s traits: defiance, strength, courage. She hadn't called them; they'd come to her, seeking purpose, a way to carry on after losing their husbands, brothers, and sons. They came from all across Aegiros, and they'd each taken a knee to swear their fealty to Liadan, as any knight would to a Northern lord. As any *kharesh* did to his general. They cheered their queen as she sparred, listened intently when she explained to the *kharesh* how and why they wound up on their backs. Rare was the battle Liadan lost. Whenever she did, she smiled brightly, praised her opponent, and offered him reward.

"What is to come of this alliance of north and south?" Inaras asked. Although she rejoiced to have reclaimed her demesne, like the others, she fretted over the many changes her people had undergone since her exile. The minutiae of everyday life blinded her to the inevitability of their fate.

Vayu swept among the gods, seeking confirmation of what he already knew. It was there, in each of them, though they didn't know it yet. *A great storm is coming. It will sweep across the North and reshape it in the image of a lone god.*

The news was met with but a faint gasp. "Shall we help them?"

No, Vayu replied. *We are none of us yet strong enough to stand against such a force. We must gather our strength and look to our own, for once the storm is done with Wilderheim, it will come for us, as well.*

Inaras hugged herself, her beautiful glow dimming. "What of Aesma?" She would not look at the dark god standing next to her. Like a sheath to her blade, his darkness absorbed her light, his cold robbed her of warmth. Part god and part shadow, Aesma was everything men feared: war, death, pain, suffering. Merely looking at him could reduce a brave man to tears.

Vayu remained unaffected, impartial. *He is not responsible for our exile, only for using it to his own advantage.* Indeed, Aesma Daeva had had no hand in shaping the barrier Veil, but neither had he been imprisoned by it, and his influence over Aesimar, the violence it had caused, was simply a manifestation of what he was. No one could be held at fault for carrying out their purpose. Balance had to be maintained. Life could not thrive without death.

Still, Aesma's influence had unduly disturbed the delicate balance, endangering not only the First Valley, but all of its gods as well. Reparations would need to be made. *Inaras, you suffered the most among us. His judgment is yours to carry out.*

The goddess of life turned her gaze upon death, shuddered delicately when he smiled, revealing black, rotted teeth. His shape was as much blood as it was shadow, and it dripped from him in congealed chunks, only to reabsorb into his dark form in a sickening cycle. "If it is as you say," she answered at length, "then we may need him for the battle yet to come. But can he be trusted?"

Aesma bowed his head, poured rivulets of crimson tears over the sand bowl. "I would not dare oppose the will of Vayu," he grated in a voice as sharp as a thousand swords scraping together.

Vayu looked to Inaras and saw acceptance in her shining eyes. Fealty to Vayu, once given, was eternal. She calmed, her face once more settling into a mask of serenity, certain in Aesma Daeva's obedience.

She could not see what he saw. None of them could. The force rising to sweep over them would not come gently. It would flood the world with blood, and none of them would survive it any better than myths told to children around campfires. Aesma himself would become a facet of the new faith. The lone god would feed on his strength, use him to conquer the world, and then banish him into the darkness to reign over demons and corrupted souls.

All things must come to an end, Vayu thought.

Perhaps it was for the best.

PRINCE OF DECEIT

And from the icy mist rose, like a great beast of Shadows deep, a new world, wrought of the blood and bones of the old. Fragmented, deformed, its first cry was one for war; its first thought one of hatred and fear. And so the Bringer of Light shaped his world—with a fury of steel and flame that consumed all that was into all that was left.

PROLOGUE

"The Son is rising. I can see the light."

"The sun has risen long ago, My Queen," replied one of her holy knights.

He will expect to find a powerful kingdom to rule.

"Yes, and He shall have a kingdom worthy of His glory." She let the heavy curtain fall back into place and turned away from the window. As beautiful as the light was to behold, it hurt her eyes.

"Your Majesty?" the knight questioned. Jonah was his name. One of the First, the five knights who'd journeyed to the land of heathens and brought her the Cup of Eternal Life.

Such tales they'd told upon their triumphant return. They'd awed and entertained the court with fables about a land filled with magic, and a powerful witch seated at the right hand of its king—a woman who had his ear in all things. A woman who'd led the knights to the hermit's cave for the Cup they'd sworn would restore Queen Genevieve's youth.

It hadn't worked, of course. These things never did—unless one was worthy of them. The knights had all fallen under the heathen witch's thrall, and with their fall from Grace tainted the Cup before it'd reached Queen Genevieve's hands.

For many years thereafter, she had prayed to her God for guidance, seeking to become worthy. She'd purged the disbelievers and heathen heretics from her lands. She'd established order with laws to purify the soul and safeguarded her kingdom against the evil of pride and the temptation of sin in all its forms.

Still, the glory of God, His guiding voice, had been denied to her for all these years until one day, in her despair, she'd sought to purify her withered body with boiling water. No pain had been too great for the majesty of her God. No sacrifice too much for the promise of eternal life in His all-encompassing embrace.

And as the scalding waves had lapped at her knees, His voice had spoken to her from the shadows. In His mercy, He'd declared her devotion divine. He'd named her His prophet and shared with her a glimpse of His power. At once, the water had cooled to soothe her burns. Her pain had disappeared. And when she'd managed to tear her gaze away from the miracle, He'd shown her another—the briefest glimpse into her just reward. For a few moments, her youth had been restored, and she'd looked and felt as she had in her prime.

A glimpse, but a promise, as well. "Serve me well, and I shall give you youth eternal, and you will dwell in my kingdom for all time."

Awed by His power, Queen Genevieve had prostrated herself at once and sworn fealty to Him and no other.

His counsel had never left her side since.

Her court might think her mad, but Genevieve now knew the Holy Truth. She was its bearer, her God's chosen messenger in this world until He came to speak for Himself. Until He deigned them all worthy of His presence.

Your knights grow suspicious. Send them away.

Genevieve nodded and allowed the knights to help her to her seat by the hearth. Her weary bones creaked as she lowered herself into it. She held her gnarled, twisted fingers up to the fire's warmth.

After so many wars, so many villains slain, so many glorious victories won, age had turned out to be the one enemy she couldn't defeat. Once, she'd walked with her head held high, her thick, black hair draping over her shoulders like a veil. Now, her hunched, dried out husk of a figure curled in on itself so much she had to tilt her head up to look straight ahead. Men who would have been of a height with her in her youth towered over her and made her feel weaker still. And her once beautiful hair had been reduced to a few wiry white strands she hid beneath a silken veil held in place by a golden circlet.

The crown she hadn't worn in years sat on a pedestal against the far wall, a symbol of her political power and her physical weakness. Were she to don it now, her neck would break beneath its weight.

Her frail form failed her more and more every day. She no longer possessed the strength to hold court in her grand throne room as was expected. She could only walk the distance from her bedchamber to this sitting room, with its plain wooden floors and sparse tapestries. Her servants had draped it in gold and filled it with plush seats and dozens of candles, but it was still a paltry substitute, and a hateful inconvenience she tolerated because she had no other choice. "Leave me now," she ordered. "Find me Sir Arnaud. He is summoned before the queen."

The knights complied at once, closing the heavy wooden door behind them, but not before it admitted a chill breeze to sneak underneath her thick robe and make her shiver.

Yes, well done.

"Why him? There are hundreds of them now, and more flock to the Holy Order every day. Any of them could carry out Your commands better than the traitor."

It is not service I require. It is knowledge. He alone has spoken to the heathen queen.

Not so. There were others—Frederick and Lucca. Oh, but yes, yes. Her weary mind remembered. Frederick was dead, long years ago now. And Lucca, the heretic, had been made an example to the rest of them. He'd screamed his dead wife's name as he'd been pulled apart, a final affront against their God.

Bearing witness, Sir Arnaud had sworn himself into silence and solitude. His ominous words that day had sent a chill down Genevieve's spine. "The next time you hear me speak will be my last. But my words will live on long after my death!"

Of the five knights who'd braved the heathen lands to bring her the Cup, only Arnaud and Jonah remained. And Arnaud alone refused to obey her royal orders, yet suffered no consequence.

As an elder of the Holy Order, he ranked highest among them, save for Genevieve herself. Sequestered in his cell, shrouded in silence, he placed himself at the mercy of others. Younger knights cared for him, provided food, water, and clean robes. Genevieve questioned them often about Sir Arnaud's condition. They always replied the same, "He prays in silence and never speaks a word."

For twenty years, he had done this. For the strength of his conviction alone, she ought to have him executed—his piety surpassed her own.

She stayed her hand for one reason. With all his devotion, piety, and silence, God still hadn't chosen him. He'd chosen the queen of Synealee instead. As long as Arnaud remained silent and didn't publicly oppose her will, Genevieve was content to leave him to his barren cell to rot.

When the knights returned with Sir Arnaud, she stood once more to face him. Age had left its mark on the former knight, as it had on Genevieve herself. What a pair they made, the queen hunched at the shoulders, and the knight whose legs no longer straightened all the way. But at least Genevieve still took pains to ensure her looks befitted her station. Sir Arnaud did not. His hair was white, grown past his shoulders in shameful disarray. His beard, too, reached past his chest. The plain linen robes he wore were as clean as she'd ever seen them, save for the two dark spots that would forever stain it where his knees pressed into the ground during endless prayer. This was one of his nicer robes. She'd seen him before in ones with holes worn through.

But none of that mattered when she stepped close and looked into his eyes. Such unusual eyes he had, so steady and serene, filled with utter peace. It was said he never faltered in his routine, never displayed a hint of fear or doubt. It was said he was the silent prophet, and any who sought him with questions found answers in those eyes.

It was said…

Genevieve despised him for every scandalous whisper bearing his name. The queen had defied death. She was by far the oldest regent ever to sit the throne of Synealee. She was God's chosen, His instrument and herald.

Yet her people—her knights—spoke of only *him*. In their whispers, he was no longer Sir Arnaud. He was Saint Arnaud the Silent.

No audience, God decreed.

"Leave us," she ordered.

Arnaud showed no reaction to her command.

"I am told you speak to the heathen queen of the north."

The witch who'd sat by her king had staked her claim most thoroughly by stealing his heart along with his reason. Rumors traveled far and wide about Wilderheim and its king and queen. It was a land of faeries, elves, trolls, and all manner of inhuman creatures never meant to be seen by human eyes. The people of Wilderheim called them Other. Genevieve called them what they were—demon spawn crawled up from the deepest pits of Hell to corrupt the righteous.

Their king had broken royal protocol and defied the laws of his ancestors by taking the witch to wife. Genevieve had prayed for dissent among his nobles to finally bring Wilderheim to its knees, but she'd been denied. Wielding untold power of their own, the heathen monarchs had calmed the unrest and bewitched their people to love them.

"What is said between you?"

Not a word or a twitch in answer. Arnaud didn't blink an eye.

"What would your acolytes think if they knew their Silent One wasn't so silent after all?"

The knight stared at her.

"You've drunk from the Cup, haven't you? All of you must have. The pride of men hath no limits. Nor does their irreverence. But it did not work. Here you are, as old and decrepit as time itself, no better than you would have been without it. Worse, for knowing your prayers went unanswered. And do you know why? None of you were worthy."

A slow blink.

"You will tell me what was said between you and Nialei the Whore."

He remained silent.

"Your queen orders you to speak."

He will not part with his secrets so easily. Perhaps he needs a little incentive.

Arnaud's gaze darted to the side and back to Genevieve. As if he'd heard.

She rushed him. Her hand raised of its own accord and struck him across the face. She felt tainted by that brief contact, her palm stinging with the coolness of his flesh. "I can make you speak. The dungeons have no shortage of clever devices and implements to unravel even the most tangled of tongues."

No, God said from his shadow. *Do not give your knights cause to doubt your judgment. They must not witness him suffering unduly on your order.*

Sir Arnaud tilted his head in the direction of the voice, his mouth twisting in displeasure, and oh, how she wanted to defy God's will and make the knight suffer for his insolence.

God, too, seemed to notice. When He spoke again, His question was directed to the silent knight. *Has she found the song?*

The knight dismissed the voice of God as if it meant nothing to him, turning back to Genevieve.

"Answer Him," she wheezed, feeling heat rise up her neck as her heart thrummed in her chest. She knew nothing of this song, but if it was important to God, it had to be a powerful thing, indeed. She would get the answer out of Arnaud one way or another.

Sir Arnaud leaned down to match her stoop and dared to meet her gaze with a stare so direct Genevieve felt herself falling forward.

Shadows closed in around Arnaud, then swallowed all but those cursed, knowing eyes of his. She lost herself in them. Her aged heart thrashed, and her lungs labored to keep up as visions took shape before her. A woman with golden hair and magic in her eyes. An endless winter. A dark cave, and inside, a hermit older than time itself, yet possessing youth eternal. And the Cup. She sensed no pride in what she saw. Only humility, awe, and love.

Genevieve whimpered, broke away, and turned her back on him, suddenly cold and weary. So weary…

Enough. You tire yourself needlessly. I have all the answers I need.

Then His will was done, and Genevieve was free to deal with the heretic as she must. Sir Arnaud had the power to induce visions with nothing but his stare. He was tainted with heathen sorcery, and still, his acolytes worshipped him. He was a threat to everything Synealee stood for. She couldn't allow such a man to live. "Guards!"

Seven knights rushed in, swords drawn in readiness.

"Take him to the stake."

They hesitated.

"I said take him! He is accused of practicing witchcraft and consorting with demons. In the name of God, burn the heretic!"

Two of the knights seized Arnaud with obvious reluctance. God's guiding voice said nothing, yet she still felt His presence. Surely He wasn't displeased with her.

Arnaud stayed his guards with a simple look. "You dare invoke the name of God," he rasped, "and accuse me of witchcraft when the Devil himself whispers in your ear."

The knights gasped, drew away in shock.

"I know what you seek. You think to earn God's favor by tearing down those who oppose Him, but you are wrong. Queen Nialei's world is not yours to conquer. She has her own gods to obey and has little care for ours. I have glimpsed the future, False Prophet—yours and hers."

"Silence!"

No, let him speak.

Genevieve flushed.

"You will fail," Arnaud prophesied. "Your armies will march into Wilderheim, waving your banner with pride, and they will find nothing but snow and death. Thousands will fall and none by the Queen's order. Her progeny will be the ones to raze your armies to the ground. Her son will be your undoing, and his cause will be just. And you, *My Queen*, will not live to see this come to pass."

His ominous words fell like physical blows on Genevieve's shoulders, driving her to hunch lower. She couldn't catch her breath to speak.

But her guards did. Into the shocked silence following Arnaud's prophecy, one of them found voice enough to say the only word that mattered. "Treason."

"Burn him," she ordered, clenching her shaking hands to her belly. "Take him from my sight and burn him at once!"

The knights took him away quickly but without force. None was necessary, as Arnaud walked out with his head held high. Genevieve hurried to her window overlooking the courtyard and, beyond it, her beautiful seaside city of Palos. Dozens of church spires proudly pierced the sky in those streets. They marked places of sanctuary and worship, tracing the shape of a cross laid over the city. Whenever Genevieve felt at her weakest, she sought the sight of those spires to lift her spirits and strengthen her resolve.

They failed to do so now. Feverish with doubt so deep it made her shiver, she raised her hand to shield Palos from her view and squinted against the sun's blinding glare, eager to see Arnaud swallowed up in flames. The centerpiece platform was as high as she was tall, made of steel and stone, and the sight of it made her shivers ease.

God's soothing voice whispered in her ear, *Fear not, My Queen, while I walk by your side. Your armies will know the taste of victory. I will allow no other outcome.*

Genevieve watched Arnaud walk up the steps to the post and stand with his back to it. He didn't resist when the executioner tied him in place, showed no fear as the wood was placed around him. No quick death for Saint Arnaud the Silent. He would not have the luxury of flames lapping up his robes. The fires would burn high around Arnaud but never touch him. He'd die in slow agony, suffocating on the heat and smoke. She would hear his voice once more as he screamed.

The pyre was lit. Flames spread to encircle him, then rose high over the top of the post. Smoke obscured her view, but Genevieve thought she glimpsed Arnaud's face turned toward the sky, his eyes closed, and his lips moving in silent prayer. She stood there, waiting for his screams, but she was denied.

A shudder of apprehension rocked her ancient frame. Could he have spoken true? "Show me again," she pleaded, desperate for reassurance of God's power. "Show me as you did that day. My faith weakens. Doubt grows in my heart."

Look away, He crooned. *All the heathens in Wilderheim could never hope to equal my power. Look at yourself and believe.*

Genevieve turned away from the sight of Arnaud the Silent slumping against the post. She shuffled her feet to the hearth, feeling the weight of all her fourscore and eight years pressing on her shoulders. Retrieving a mirror, she gazed at her reflection.

A beautiful young maiden stared back at her, with pale skin and hair as black as night, and lips as red as cherries. She smiled, her strength once again restored, and her faith renewed. With a reverent young hand, she reached up to touch her cheek and twirled on the polished wooden floors, her slippered feet as sure as they'd been decades ago.

A fleeting glimpse, nothing more. But she treasured it for the promise it held. God had not and would not abandon her. She served Him well, and He would reward her for it in the end.

And so she danced, and laughed, and thanked God for giving her this moment of strength to fortify her against the struggle still to come. For, when the battle was won—and it would be—this strength would be hers for all time. She looked at herself in the mirror and smiled with such joy in her heart.

And she never once looked away to see the creature in Shadow disappear.

CHAPTER 1

Why so sad, my love?

The dragon sighed, watching water drip steadily from the stalactite overhead. Each droplet grew the protrusion by an infinitesimal amount before it fell into the puddle below, sounding the only music he had in this place. Distracted from his reverie, he puffed out an annoyed cloud of black smoke and brought his horned head around to rest over a forepaw.

Will you not speak to me?

He did not, though his heart ached to reply, to have the apparition hear his words and respond in truth. Instead, the dragon closed his eyes against the ghostly vision, reminding himself yet again that it was not real, no matter how much he might wish otherwise. The voice existed only in his mind, where her memory lived unchanged, preserved against time itself.

Dragons were the keepers of memory. Their gift and burden were to remember the things time had eroded to dust and scattered into obscurity. Within his mind, infinite worlds collided, and swirls of magic mixed together. The Beginning of All was born again and again, each time as brilliant and wondrous as the first. Lands rippled alive, creatures big and small formed into being and just as quickly disintegrated.

He remembered everything since the moment of his awakening, but only one memory out of an infinity of them could make him doubt what was real and what was not. Only she could escape from the past to invade his present and make him lose track of both.

It was becoming more and more difficult to sort her back into her rightful place. Perhaps his mind was slipping. Or perhaps he simply did not want to keep her in the past. Her rightful place was by his side, and she would have been there with him now, if only…

If only.

A sigh, like the promise of a kiss, blew across his snout. His scales bristled at the imagined touch. His tail lashed around to curl toward his head to catch the sensation, hold onto it before it disappeared again.

The ground thrummed with nervous energy, sending waves of soundless drums reverberating throughout the cave. An early warning the dragon had long anticipated, now an annoyance he couldn't escape. What good was knowing the end was nigh when he could do naught to change it?

Yet through that deafening din of silence, he heard an incongruous sound: the patter of soft feet. His nostrils flared, catching an impossible hint of a familiar scent.

The dragon tensed, listened, but then shook himself off and made himself turn his bulk around within the chamber's confines and settle again. Nothing but a dream. Beautiful, but fleeting.

It's coming. Can you feel it? The cold breath of endless winter. Fenrir's binds are weakening. He is breaking free.

The worry in her voice cut him to the quick. How could he leave her to suffer alone? He could not, and so he relented, aware that acknowledging her presence would make it that much more difficult to push back later. "It is as it was always going to be," the dragon said, his deep, low voice rumbling with the force of an earthquake. Sometimes it eased his heartache to talk to her. Even if she wasn't truly there.

Are you ready?

Ready for the end? With all of his soul. He craved it, eager for the promise of seeing his beloved once again. And if not, eager to embrace the endless abyss of nothing. There, perhaps, he might finally find peace at last. A respite from this wretched hollow that breathed and yawed inside him, growing bigger, erasing more of him with each year that passed.

"I miss you," he said fiercely, willing the vision to linger.

Another sigh, another almost-touch he could feel beneath his scales. A memory snuggled in the crook of his shoulder, leaning its soft, nonexistent weight against his neck.

Had he the ability to smile, the dragon might have attempted to do so. "Remember that first Mabon? You asked for a bonfire bright enough to banish the night. I watched you dance around it, and the flames sang for you." She'd always loved the flames he'd built for her. As human as she'd been, her heart had been pure fire, bright and hot as the sun, searing him with so much love he'd thought it could fill even a lifetime as long as his.

And when she'd died, she'd taken that fire with her, leaving him cold.

"I should have held on tighter."

How does one keep the wind from blowing away?

"By closing the door."

An ancient argument the dragon relived in his mind a dozen times a day. It had made no difference then, or ever since. In the end, she'd known only one could survive, and she'd chosen to sacrifice her life to save their child.

Why worry about the inevitable? she asked as she had then, smiling through the sorrow in her eyes, for his sake. *Why waste away our happiness? Dance with me. Dance with me…* "Dance with me."

The dragon opened his eyes, gaped at the sight before him. There she stood, her flaxen hair wild, flowing down her back, a skein of it veiling her eye. She wore a peasant dress, as plain as she was beautiful, her feet bare, stepping left and right in a familiar dance. "Solveig…"

"Dance with me," she said, laughing. Her delicate hands curled around one of his claws and tugged. Her touch had once moved mountains inside him. It was no different now. The dragon's beastly form burned away, swathed him in thick smoke as he compressed his essence into the shape of a man. Claws became fingers and toes. Scales smoothed into soft, vulnerable skin. Everything he was and ever would be squeezed into the shape of a man, leaving only a pair of horns and a tail to mark him as Other.

Solveig had always loved his dragon form. But in his human shape, he could love her back as she deserved to be loved.

A delighted smile lit up Solveig's face as she threw herself into his arms, burying her nose in the crook of his neck to breathe him in. He felt her. He scented her. An impossibility to his ancient mind but one he could not bring himself to give up. His human arms came around her, hesitant for fear they'd sink through nothing as they'd done so many times before.

This time, they touched upon firm, solid flesh.

The dragon dared not breathe. He clutched her to his human chest as tightly as he could without hurting her, painfully aware of her mortal frailty. So many opportunities wasted, so little time left. He was desperate to hold on, to somehow keep her from slipping through his claws a second time.

Not real…

But how could it not be? Her warmth seeped into him. Her laughter awoke his heart to life. Her hands clutched his hair with so much strength and vitality—how could she not be real?

Solveig pulled back, her brilliant green gaze tracing his face. She cupped his cheek, wiped away an errant tear. "My love," she crooned.

The dragon hardly trusted himself to speak. "You're here."

"Yes," she whispered.

"But how?"

Solveig pressed her smiling mouth to his, whispered her answer between his lips. The dragon heard not, and cared not. She was there. He'd dreamed her back into being, and this time he wasn't letting her go. Fenrir would escape anon; the End of All was nigh. What little time any of them had left, the dragon wanted to spend with her.

"Dance with me," she said.

He danced. Slowly, at first, savoring the feel of her in his arms, the smile on her face. Then faster, twirling her around, tossing her up, and catching her again to make her squeal and laugh. The dragon danced her through the tunnels that ran past his treasures and Liadan's old bedchamber, all the way to the underground lake. Sparks jumped from his fingertips, flying through the air around them like swarms of fireflies. Some of them landed on torches he'd had no use for in many years, and they flared up, filling the caves with light.

Solveig laughed and laughed, the music of her voice echoing back to him from every direction, and the dragon forgot. The decades he'd spent mourning her melted away in an instant. He felt younger than he ever had, brimming with joy to have her with him. He'd waited so long to find her, and the time he'd had with her had been but a wink. A gasp of delight followed by pain and sorrow.

But she was there now, healthy and hale and in his arms. Afraid to let her go, when she pulled free of him to dance away, the dragon caught her hand and held on, following her lead with unabashed eagerness.

"Your legs have grown as stiff as trees," she teased.

The dragon laughed. "Aye, so have other parts of me." But for her, he lightened his step, smoothed out his stride, and when he caught her against his side for a turn, the movement felt as lithe as a breeze.

How does one keep the wind from blowing away?

Blowing away...

Away...

He faltered, stopping by the scorchmark where a small fire had used to warm her after she'd bathed. The memory of its heat still remained, as did the one of Solveig wringing water out of her long tresses all over him.

"You came back." Even to his own ears, the words sounded strange, disbelieving and hopeful at once.

Solveig's smile softened. "I came back. For you." She kissed him, and her lips tasted so sweet... "Come with me," she said. "I know where we can be together. Safe. Forever."

The world spun, making him sway, but he had her to hold onto. The dragon clutched her hand, looped his tail around her ankle, just tight enough so he knew she was there beside him.

Her free hand raked through his hair, scratched lightly over his horn, making him shudder. "Come with me," she repeated. "Be with me."

Gods, how he wanted to. With a thought, he summoned Liadan's ring onto his finger. A gift he'd all but forgotten. Forged in dragon's fire, it had the ability to summon any of his blood kin to him. He had but to think it, and his descendants would be there, all of them together again. And Solveig would make them all safe. "Yes," he answered, eager to get out of Fenrir's path; to go anywhere, as long as Solveig was with him.

She smiled, tugged on his hand to lead him down a tunnel he didn't recognize. "I have missed you so much, my love."

"Woman, you took half of me with you when you left."

Died...

"I am back now."

Dead...

"Yes." The thought of his family faded before it could summon them. The ring settled on his finger, ready to work its magic, but dormant for now. Time enough still. Time he could spend with his mate alone. He needed that—needed *her*.

"And we can take back the time Fate stole from us. I want to be with you."

The dragon nodded, not trusting himself to speak. His body quivered, and his legs weakened as he followed her down the dark tunnel, staring into those beautiful green eyes, afraid to blink, lest she disappear and prove herself a dream.

If she was, he never wanted to wake again.

The tunnel became a passage, the stone around him shimmering into slabs laid with mortar. The ground beneath his bare feet evened out, and the sound of dripping water became the rush of a stream. He raised a hand to summon fire, but Solveig pressed her palm against his, keeping his flame at bay. No matter. Solveig knew where she was going, and the dragon trusted her implicitly. Even when the shadows deepened and black emptiness swallowed them whole. As long as he felt her with him, the dragon kept going.

At long last, she slowed, stopped, and in the darkness, pressed her body into his. Her hands caressed his face, swept down his shoulders and arms, and squeezed his wrists. She brought each of his hands to her lips, pressed a kiss to each knuckle.

"Solveig..." The dragon reached for her face, needing to kiss her again. The bite of rope around his wrist pulled him up short. "What—" He tried with his other arm, reaching for her waist, and a length of rope snapped taut, yanking him back by the wrist.

The instinct to protect his mate flared into a snarl, and he tugged with his tail to pull her closer into the shelter of his arms, but as he did, she disappeared. His tail curled around nothing—the press of her body against his melted away like mist. Between one moment and the next, Solveig was gone, leaving not a hint of her scent behind.

The dragon groped around the darkness, searching for her, fearing for her, and each time he let the ropes grow slack, they drew tighter, reeling him backward. He shouted her name, raged against his binds, but with all his might, he couldn't budge them, and only endless echoes answered him.

Until she spoke. "Solveig is dead," she said in his beloved's voice, but it wasn't her. It changed on each sound, lost its melody and warmth, and became something foreign, unfeeling.

Torches flared to light left and right, illuminating a stone cell. He was standing in ankle-deep water, beside a wrought-iron cage through which it ebbed and flowed. He sensed his surroundings, rather than saw them, his gaze rapt on Solveig's beautiful visage as it faded into a different shape.

The woman standing before him was tall and thin, her lips deathly pale, and her dark hair braided into dozens of ropes that swayed around her on an unseen gale. She stared at him with eyes as black as pitch, and the dragon saw nothing in them. She was empty.

"Whoever you are, I will kill you for this."

"I am Hel, and you are welcome to try." No emotion in her voice. No smirk of victory on her face. He would have welcomed even boredom, but there was nothing. Nothing for him to respond to. Nothing to sharpen his claws on. The goddess who ruled the realm of the dead regarded him with all the passion of a stone.

He yanked on his binds with all his might, but they held him fast. He summoned fire to burn them away, but they didn't weaken in the slightest. He tried to shed his human form and transform into his dragon self. His feet stretched into hindpaws; his hands grew scales and claws; his teeth sharpened into fangs, but the magic imbued in those ropes froze him there. His fire spread to engulf him but brought him neither heat nor strength. He was stuck.

And all the while, Hel watched him without reaction. As dead inside as hear entire realm. As mad and ruthless as her entire family was said to be. What else could he expect from the spawn of Loki?

The dragon shuddered. "Why?"

"Because my father asked it of me."

Then she was gone.

Sanja's face felt cold. Her lips were numb, her cheeks ached, and her eyes stung for lack of blinking. She hid her clenched hands beneath her skirts, but as hard as she tried, her aching fingers wouldn't straighten. She was frozen. *Gods, it can't end this way...*

"Well, child? What do you say?"

Sanja blinked to focus on her father's aged face. Gerhart was a good man, a carpenter who'd made an honest name for himself in his day. He'd worked himself raw to become the most sought after craftsman in the entire city, and even received a commission or two from the royal family. He'd wanted his legacy to carry on through his sons and had been dismayed when, after two miscarriages, his wife Olga birthed a daughter.

Their elderly neighbors told Sanja her mother had wept for days over it. When another miscarriage had nearly taken her life, and the Other midwife declared Olga would never bear another child, she'd wept for weeks longer.

Gerhart could not love his daughter more, but the lack of a son left him with a heavy burden to carry through his advancing years. Sanja had watched his eyes turn bleak each time a neighbor shared happy news of a wedding or birth. She knew he longed for his only daughter to marry, but this...

"Daughter," Olga whispered with a nervous smile. In her grief, her once beautiful face had aged a great deal more than it should have. But her love for Sanja shone out of her as bright as the sun.

Sanja turned her frozen smile to their guest of honor.

Jarl Steen was a man who revered hunting, brawling, and all other manner of manly pursuits, and it showed. He towered over Sanja when standing and made the worn chairs creak and groan when he sat. Perhaps his bulky frame and thick neck wouldn't have been as intimidating if the man deigned to smile once in a while, but his brows appeared to be forever set in a foreboding frown over his cold gray eyes.

He wore his light brown hair shaved along the sides to display the decorative scars he'd had cut into his scalp. The rest of his hair was braided down the center of his head to his nape and matched the braids in his beard. Both were adorned with golden beads, each one, the rumors said, signifying a victory or achievement of some sort.

His fearsome presence alone overwhelmed the old cottage so much Sanja felt it holding its breath. One hard stomp from him, and it would come crumbling down around them.

And his temper was reputed to be just as mighty.

Gods, he'll crush me with a thought.

As the border lord to the east, Jarl Steen had vast holdings. He was titled, rich, and celebrated far and wide for his strength. By all accounts, he ought to have been married long ago.

Alas, despite all this, no one would have him.

Gerhart cleared his throat, reminding Sanja she still hadn't said a word. But what could she say? "I, umm..." She looked to Olga for support, but her mother could only offer a wan smile. If she wouldn't come to Sanja's defense, then the situation had to be worse than either of her parents let on. Gerhart's hands were no longer steady enough to carve his masterpieces. He'd been reduced to pounding together rough stools and tables for the poorer denizens of Frastmir, but it still caused him pain. To make up for the lack, Olga had become a washerwoman, laundering merchants' clothes and linens in the freezing river day after day, but despite both of them earning coin, their home had fallen into disrepair, and visits from friends had turned into uncomfortable silences and subtle reminders of unpaid debts.

Sanja, too, tried her best to help. She'd apprenticed with the weaver, the seamstress, the miller, even the fisherman. Each had sent her back to her parents as a bothersome nuisance. No two ways about it, Sanja was clumsy. Her hands never seemed to be steady enough for delicate tasks, or strong enough for harder ones. She dropped instruments constantly, had no eye for art or design, and worst of all, she had the unpardonable habit of talking too much.

Except, it appeared, now.

"Sanja," Gerhart whispered, giving Jarl Steen an apologetic smile.

Her mind was her best feature by far. She had an excellent memory, a good head for numbers, and an insatiable curiosity about everything Divine and Other. Alas, such qualities were only sought after by the upper classes of human society. Unlike Other communities, humans valued practical skills over abstract thinking.

Under the pretext of pouring himself more water from the jug that ought to have held ale to show their guest proper hospitality, Gerhart bumped into the table, startling Sanja back to the matter at hand.

Shivering, she answered the only way she could. "N-no."

The room plunged into silence. Gerhart paled, his hands shaking so hard he almost dropped his cup.

"I am sorry, Da. And I apologize to you as well, Jarl Steen. You honor us with your proposal of marriage. Honestly, I am well and truly flattered that a man of your stature would approach a young girl of my humble means, and any woman in her right mind would consider herself lucky to receive such a generous offer, and please don't think I refuse you out of stubbornness or because I would prefer someone else..." She prattled on for so long she stopped paying attention to her words while her mind raced with desperate ideas on how to put him off without bringing his wrath down upon herself and her parents. "You exhibit the finest qualities a man could possess…" Gerhart leaned back, gaping at her with an increasingly alarmed expression on his face. *Think of something quick.* "And you have means to rival the king, all this is true and makes you a fine man, indeed, and if I were free to marry, no doubt I would say yes. Yes! A thousand times, yes!"

Jarl Steen raised his giant hand to stop the tirade. Closing his gaping mouth, he frowned. "Are you saying you are not free to marry?" As softly as he spoke the words, his voice still boomed so loud Sanja flinched. He looked to Gerhart for confirmation. This was a courtesy meeting to introduce Sanja to her husband to be. The agreement had already been struck, and all the particulars negotiated at length between Jarl Steen and Gerhart earlier that morning. To now be told otherwise was as unexpected as it was insulting.

"I assure you, Jarl Steen," Gerhart rushed to say. "My daughter might be a strange one, but she is of marriageable age, and she *will* marry."

"She will not," Sanja dared, suddenly striking on the perfect solution to all of this. "She—I mean *I*—have chosen another path."

"Another path?" Jarl Steen repeated, uncomprehending.

Olga worried the edges of her apron. "Sanja?"

Sanja nodded and, pulling her shoulders back, declared, "The path of the cleric." Why had she never considered it before? Clerics were reclusive, studious people who had given up the pleasures of city life in favor of becoming lifelong students and teachers. Their lives were dedicated not to the worship of any particular god but to knowledge. Most spent their time in their temple high up in the mountains, transcribing and preserving ancient books and scrolls. But some did travel to teach what they knew to those willing to learn. Some, like those in charge of Frastmir's massive library, were honored with a lifelong position as the keepers of books for kings and queens. Such a life would be perfect for Sanja.

Gerhart paled. "Daughter, no."

Sanja frowned. Why was he looking at her like that? This wasn't a jest; she was in earnest. She certainly didn't care that clerics couldn't—or rather *didn't*—marry. While there were no restrictions on marriage for clerics, their lives were not easy to share. No wife would want to raise children on her own while her husband traveled the world. No husband would want a wife who spent months at a time in the clerics' temple. Better, as recompense for losing one of their line, the clerics paid homage to the initiate's family, oftentimes equivalent to a dowry or bride price. Her family's debts would be erased with that sum, and Sanja would be forever safe from another of Jarl Steen's ilk sniffing at her skirts. For the chance to expand her mind, she would gladly give up marriage, a life of servitude to her husband, and the perpetual cycle of pregnancy and child rearing. None of those things had ever appealed to her, anyway. Sanja longed to see the Otherlands, to walk different worlds, and learn their secrets—

Jarl Steen laughed, his thick shoulders twitching up and down. "A cleric? You?"

"Just so," she confirmed, puzzled. He was certainly taking the news well.

The jarl laughed harder. "A cleric!" Wiping his tears, he made an effort to contain his mirth as he turned to Gerhart. "Master Carver, be easy. I know what this is and how to handle it. The girl suffers from maidenly shyness, she said so herself. My offer is so generous she cannot contain herself."

Gerhart attempted a smile, knowing full well that wasn't the issue. Sanja was, indeed, of marriageable age, fast approaching its end without a single offer so far. While young men weren't shy to talk to her, none of them had asked for her hand. She was a strange one, and they seemed to know it right away. Jarl Steen's offer of marriage might well be the only one she'd ever receive.

Her intended looked at each of them in turn, then waved some internal thought aside. "No matter. I know what needs to be done. The girl wants to be wooed. All these Others prancing around with their poetry and songs of love have turned every head from here to Lyria. Not a-one sensible female left in the kingdom. But mark me, Master Carver." He leered at Sanja as he made his pledge. "I am decided on this matter. I will have your daughter or none at all, and I will be relentless in my pursuit." His gaze briefly turned unfocused as he added, almost to himself, "Any wild beast can be brought to heel. Even the stubborn ones. All it takes is a firm hand."

Sanja shuddered as she watched his hands curl into fists.

Seeming to come back to himself, he turned back to Gerhart with a determined nod. "The girl wants time? She will have it—I will give her a full month. She wants courtship? I will show her what true romance is. Our nobles can surpass any Other in Wilderheim." He spoke of courtship like an unsavory task that had been laid before him.

Although Wilderheim's marriages now modeled after the devoted, loving relationship of its ruling couple, there were still too many who believed women inferior to men, those who considered a woman nothing more than a piece of property whose only purpose was to birth children. The jarl was very much one of that ignorant lot.

"In a month's time, she will be only too happy to don her wedding gown."

The gods only knew what her fate would be afterward. Sanja was determined not to find out. "In a month's time, I will be making my way up to the clerics' temple."

The jarl's indulgent smile set her teeth on edge. "In a hair shirt, as all the rest of them? Autumn is already upon us, girl, it'll be a cold day when you start on that path, and snows come early high in the mountains." He shook his head, dismissing the idea. "You will never make it to the top. Certainly not on your knees, as they demand."

True, that part of her plan was somewhat troublesome, but Sanja was nothing if not determined. "I will make it to the top. On my knees, and in a hair shirt. I promise you." The physical ordeal of the Journey seemed paltry compared to the alternative—a lifetime of nights with this mountain of meat climbing on top of her. Her stomach churned to think of it.

"Then perhaps a wager is in order," Jarl Steen suggested. Sanja didn't like the sudden interest in his eyes. "If you make it to the top, I will readily admit defeat and offer my apologies. I will also keep *my* word"—he glared at Gerhart—"and pay your bride price, though I will have no wife for it."

At this, Gerhart set down his cup and clasped his hands together. Sanja could see in his face he wished to say something, but he kept silent.

Olga looked wary. Her large, brown eyes spoke volumes, but Sanja understood none of it.

"If you fail," the jarl continued, "I will have your hand for one third the bride price your father negotiated. And you will give me complete obedience in all things."

Sanja swallowed past the lump in her throat. *Complete obedience.* To a man not known for his restraint.

Olga whimpered. "Sanja, don't." Her hands were clenched so hard around her apron, its threads snapped.

"I don't intend to fail," she assured her mother despite her own doubts. Men far stronger than Sanja had failed the Journey under the best of conditions. Sanja would have none of their advantages, but she would happily take the risk for a chance to choose her own path in life, unfettered by the demands of a husband and children.

"Neither do I," Jarl Steen replied, his gray eyes sparkling at the prospect of a new challenge. "Do we have a deal?"

Gerhart stood, about to intervene.

"We have a deal," Sanja said before her father could speak a word.

"Shall we seal it in blood?"

"No!" Gerhart cried, taking a stand in front of Sanja. "You will not spill a single drop in this house."

"It's all right," Sanja told him. "I will swear on my blood if that is what Jarl Steen demands." When Gerhart opened his mouth to argue, Sanja took hold of his hands and leaned close to whisper. "Please, trust me." Win or lose, at least the oath would guarantee her parents would be provided for. The rest, Sanja would sort out later.

"You do not know what you are doing."

Sanja met Gerhart's worried gaze with her own, determined one. "Yes, I do." She knew her father meant well by inviting Jarl Steen into their lives, but Sanja was not meant to be a wife to anyone, much less a man like that.

"I insist on a written contract," Olga announced. "Sanja is a clever girl. She can read and write, and she can most certainly sign her own name. Gerhart and I will witness. Not even the king will have cause to negate it."

"A pox on the king," Steen spat, and Sanja gasped. He dared—in the castle city, no less! Seeming to realize his mistake, he made an effort to calm himself. "Very well. But we will sign in blood." His gleeful sneer sent chills down Sanja's spine. "Let's have it done, then. Parchment and quill!"

Gerhart moved to comply, but Olga gently pushed him back down and retrieved the items herself. Seating herself at the table, she dipped the quill in what little ink they still had. In neat, even script, she penned the terms of their wager. She took her time to write everything just so, with all three of them standing at her back, looking over her shoulder. At the bottom of the page, she added one more sentence:

Should Miss Sanja receive another suit and marry within the month, this contract and all its terms shall be null and void, releasing Miss Sanja from any obligation.

No sooner had her quill left the parchment than the jarl tore it out of her hand. "What is this?"

"My own terms to this foolish endeavor. You men have had your say. Now I will have mine. Sanja is my daughter, too."

"Meaning no offense, My Lord," Gerhart rushed to reassure his noble guest. "A mother's worry, you understand. Women and their silly notions. They do not understand the world as we do."

"Da!"

Jarl Steen dropped the contract back on the table. "Let the women have their say. I will agree to her terms." He smirked at Sanja. "If the girl hasn't managed to snare a husband yet, she certainly will not find one in a month." He produced a knife from his belt sheath and cut across the tip of his finger to draw blood. Taking the quill out of Olga's hand, he dipped it into the welling crimson drop and clumsily scratched his name on the parchment.

When he thrust both knife and quill at Sanja, she pushed them both away. Instead, she went to the cupboard and pulled out a large sewing needle to perform the dreaded deed. She winced as she stabbed herself in the thumb, and then a second time when the first failed to bleed sufficiently. Her hand shook as she coated the tip of a different quill with her blood, forestalling any possibility of it mingling with Jarl Steen's in any way. Hesitating only a little while everyone stared, Sanja signed her name, sealing her fate. Her father then added his mark, followed by her mother, to witness the contract.

It was done.

One month. Four weeks to prove herself worthy of a cleric's robes.

Steen inclined his head in a mock bow. "You will be seeing plenty of me anon."

Sanja didn't take another full breath until the door closed behind him, and air returned to the cottage. "Riddance," she muttered, allowing herself a triumphant little smile.

Rather than enjoy her daughter's victory, Olga brought her fist to her mouth. "I think I will have a rest now." She retreated to the bedroom, closing the door with undue care.

As soon as she was gone, Gerhart sank back into his chair, his head in his gnarled hands. "Daughter, what have you done?"

Sanja sank to her knees next to him. "It will be all right, Da, everything will work out, you will see."

With a heavy sigh, he straightened in the chair and took both of her hands in his. Those hands had once carved intricate symbols into the queen's own throne. Twisted by age, they could now barely hold an eating knife. Whenever it rained, his fingers knotted with pain he couldn't conceal. "All I wanted was to see you wed," he said.

"To a man like *him*? I would rather die."

"Hush!"

Sanja flushed, biting her tongue against more harsh words. But she wouldn't take back what she'd said. Had Gerhart consulted her before speaking to the jarl, Sanja might have had a chance to tell him what sort of man her intended was said to be. Why would he have gone behind her back?

"Listen to me, child. Life is not like they write it in those books of yours. When all is said and done, beauty fades. Strength wanes. In the end, even your clever mind will fail you. People like us don't get dashing warriors riding to our rescue. We make do with what we have. Jarl Steen might not be a gentle man—"

Sanja scoffed.

"—but he is here," Gerhart insisted. "Oh, I know how much you love your books. But those books will be a cold comfort once your mother and I are gone."

She begged to differ. Give her a library full of knowledge still to be explored, and Sanja would happily devote her life to it.

"One day, you will want someone to share them with. Someone to keep you company, give you a family of your own."

"Not Jarl Steen."

Gerhart smiled with regret. "Daughter, there is no one else around."

CHAPTER 2

A massive crack of thunder shook the stone walls of Castle Frastmir, rousing the royal family from a deep sleep. The crown prince of Wilderheim sat up in his bed, sweat beading on his brow, heart thrashing in his chest. Disoriented, he braced himself for the flood of visions rainstorms always brought, but his thoughts remained clear.

He threw back his covers to go look out his window. From there, he had a clear view across the courtyard, past the castle gates, all the way to the river on the other side of the city. There was no rain anywhere near Frastmir.

Yet no sooner had the echoes faded than another bolt of lightning struck the tower, exploding stone and shingles into the courtyard below. Another set the stables on fire, and one more roused a blood-curdling scream from the kitchens below. A storm of bright blue streaks turned the night brighter than day. The sky above Frastmir looked like a massive, cracked eggshell. Not a cloud in sight, no waft of a breeze to indicate a summer storm. Only the lightning flared in an endless web above, obscuring the moon and the stars. Fal's ears hurt from the sharp assault on his senses.

He squinted against the bright lights in search of some coherence in the world. The stables and kitchen were burning. He made out the shapes of people looking on from doorways around the courtyard, but no one dared step a single foot outside.

Needing to do something, Fal raced out of his chambers to the castle's front entry. He called to the creek in the gardens, altered its flow, and urged it on faster to pour where it was needed most. As far as his magic reached, he sought water, used it to put out flames and herd people into safe corners where the fury of lightning couldn't reach them.

He didn't realize his parents had joined him until Queen Nialei touched his shoulder and pointed to the sky.

A sizzling sparkle now accompanied each branch of lightning, as if it was burning the sky itself. Nialei's fingers dug into Fal's flesh, turning his attention back to her, but as hard as he tried, he couldn't make out the words she shouted. Shaking her head, the queen released him to take hold of King Saeran's arm and raised up her free hand. Her skin began to glow as she bent the laws of Nature to her will, and within moments, the great din outside dulled to a low rumble as a bubble of silence enveloped them, leaving Fal breathless.

Nialei made a fist to hold on to her spell. "The Veil," she said. "It's falling apart."

Fal reeled. The Veil not only formed borders around the human realm, the Otherlands, and the realm of gods, it was also a repository for divine power. If it broke, the gods themselves would be rendered powerless. This was what Nialei and Saeran had spent two decades trying to prevent.

And now it was too late.

Never one to run from a fight, Saeran squared his stance as though presented with an enemy he could battle and best. "What do we do?"

A sharp cackle echoed from the shadows. "You pray." Before the words faded, darkness exploded toward them. Tendrils of black smoke and shadows swirled around the royal family, then congealed before Fal and his parents, shrinking until, like a glamour peeling away, it revealed the figure of a man. He was tall and ghostly pale, with dark runes and symbols twisting beneath the surface of his skin as if they had a life of their own. His coppery red hair, adorned with warrior braids, reached down to his waist, and with each of his movements gave off a soft screech like twisting metal.

Nialei tugged at Fal's sleeve while addressing the creature. "Loki."

The Trickster god grinned, baring sharp, white teeth in a feral snarl that creased his ageless face and made his pitch-black eyes all but glow with evil intent. "Halfling." His growling voice hurt Fal's ears.

"The Veil is breaking apart," Nialei said with an edge of desperation. "Please, you must help us restore it!"

"Help you?" Loki's laughter echoed with the unearthly sound of a thousand blades scraping together. "Oh no, my dear. I am merely here to settle a debt."

Casting a quick, worried glance at Fal, Nialei retreated a step away from him, taking Saeran with her. *Do not speak,* she commanded in Fal's mind. *Do not interfere.* Focusing on Loki once more, she asked, "What debt? I owe you nothing."

"Oh, but I owe you," Loki replied, stalking her retreat.

She was distracting him, guiding him away from her son, drawing the Trickster's wrath so Fal might be spared.

Fal refused to let her. They would fight as one, or not at all. Shoring up his strength, he moved to follow his parents, to stand with them and battle a Halfling god if need be. But, raising one clawed finger, Loki froze him in place. "Not your time, princeling," he said. "Not your battle." Then he flicked that finger and sent Fal shooting across the great hall to slam against the wall behind King Saeran's throne.

His bones shattered on impact. Screaming agony stole the breath from his lungs, but urged on by his pain, Fal's magic rose within him at once, forging a mighty path across his body and mending whole each break and tear it came across. In two blinks, cool comfort blanketed over him even as lethargy stole across his mind.

The sound of his mother's scream forced him to climb back to his feet. Weakened to exhaustion, he tripped like a newborn foal and tumbled down the dais steps, sprawling face down at the bottom.

Loki's terrible voice punctuated his fall, "When we last met, I made you a promise, Halfling."

Fal struggled up to his hands and knees. He felt coarse fur brush past him as his mother's wolf charged across the great hall toward the trio backlit by an endless blaze of lightning outside. Varr was a creature unique to all the realms. Pulled back from death by powerful magics, he was neither alive nor dead. He had no magic, yet seemed to be immune to it. Binds could not restrain him, and wards could not keep him in or out. He wasn't fooled by Fal's illusions and could somehow pass through the Veil to any Otherland he chose. And he was ever faithful and protective of his mistress.

Fal watched the creature of in-between race to aid the royal pair, and he knew Varr wouldn't make it in time. Terrible portent squeezing like a fist around his heart, he watched shadows and darkness once again swirl up Loki's body. "Time to meet your sire." Shadowy tendrils shot forward as he launched at Nialei. Her scream was cut short as the Trickster's darkness swallowed up all three of them.

Varr leaped at it but passed through and landed just outside the door.

With a shout, Fal pushed to his feet and charged forward—to nowhere. The Trickster and whatever magic he'd wrought had already disappeared, along with Fal's parents.

Nialei's spell broke, and the deafening boom of thunder once again assailed him, shaking the floor beneath his feet and the stone walls around him. Varr took no notice as he sniffed the place where Nialei had disappeared. Fal prayed to the gods that the wolf would find a scent to track, as he had so many times before.

When Varr raised his head to look outside, ears pricking forward and back, Fal thought his prayer had been answered, but the wolf went no farther than the threshold where, tail tucked between his legs, he gazed up at the blinding lights in the sky.

Terrified of what he might see, Fal caught hold of the heavy portal for balance and looked for himself.

Against the lightning storm's constant, crackling blaze, behind a multi-hued gossamer veil of sparkling lights, the shadow of a massive lupine form raised its head, and individual beats of thunder joined together into a single, prolonged howl of noise.

Fal shuddered, watching as the lightning ceased all at once, leaving only a faint, colorful haze against the dark backdrop of the sky. When the booming howl faded, the night plunged into stifling silence, sealing their fate for all time.

The Veil was gone.

The great wolf Fenrir was free.

Ragnarok had begun.

CHAPTER 3

Two days later, the rising dawn found Fal standing in front of the stairway to his damaged tower library. Dust and rubble were spilled all the way down into the hallway. A pungent scent lingered in the air—smoke, hot metal, and burned magic, all underlaid with what he imagined to be the scent of despair. It was so heavy it oozed down the stairway and across the hallway floor, soaking into his cloak.

A small, charred piece of parchment with the remnants of an ancient spell still glowing softly on its surface wafted through the air. Fal held out his hand to catch it, only to have it disintegrate in the palm of his hand.

Despair. Yes, that seemed an apt description for the current state of affairs in Frastmir and, from what the messengers reported, all of Wilderheim. Dread had settled over the kingdom so thick nothing seemed to lift it, and it was only made heavier by the strange lights ever streaking across the sky.

Fal unstuck his feet from the hallway floor and, with infinite caution, stepped into the stairway. Around the first bend, light spilled in through a hole in the wall. A little higher, the wall was gone entirely, the steps crumbling away at the outer edges. The higher he climbed, the more debris littered what remained of them until he was forced to cast magic just to keep his footing steady.

With each half-burned, buried tome he passed, the ache of loss clenched a little tighter around his chest. Years of research and translations, stacks of scrolls, texts, and ancient skins with knowledge all but lost to time. And somewhere within them, perhaps even his undiscovered cure. Had any of his work survived the fire?

Did it matter anymore? With his parents gone, his research destroyed, and Fenrir racing toward Wilderheim, Fal's malady seemed like a minor inconvenience by comparison.

Fal's parents were both Halflings born of the union of two different species. Such beings were always powerful, dangerous, and most importantly, unable to produce offspring. Nature's way of preserving balance, he supposed.

Yet somehow, Nature's rules broke when Nialei not only conceived but managed to survive the pregnancy and give birth to twins. As far as Fal knew, he and Liadan were the first and only ones of their kind, blessed and cursed with powerful magics they themselves couldn't always control. And it seemed Fate was determined to make them pay for it.

Liadan's gifts were rooted in fire and metals, making her an unrivaled warrior. A true Dragonblood, she could burn her human shape into something not quite human, but not dragon, either. But her magic was so volatile her moon cycle burned her from within each month, and she slept for three days thereafter as one dead while her body recovered. Nature taking desperate measures to ensure she never bore a child. If Liadan suspected this to be the case, she never spoke of it, and Fal never dared to broach the subject.

His own gifts were rooted in water and all manner of visions. He could scry farther than anyone he knew, travel through water, control its flow, and cast visions for others to see. But, like Liadan, his magic was volatile, growing stronger with each passing year. What had started out as little more than a trick of the light when he'd been a child had evolved into visions so convincing and far-reaching he could no longer contain them as a grown man. Swathed in a cloak embroidered with dampening spells and armed with golden cuffs etched with channeling runes, Fal still couldn't pull them back completely.

Those who looked upon him saw an endless parade of faces masking his true self. He'd learned to hide beneath the hood of his cloak. Those who dared to step into his watery illusions found themselves drowning on dry land. For the safety of his people, he'd learned to keep his distance.

Everywhere he went, the world changed, right along with him. Fal had never spoken an untruth in his life. But when his own people looked upon him, all they saw was a lie. And so they'd dubbed him the Prince of Deceit.

Sequestered in Castle Frastmir, he'd spent years searching for answers in obscure texts and magics lost to time. He'd found nothing. And his illusions continued to grow stronger and bigger. One day, they would overwhelm him, and he would disappear.

If Fenrir didn't put an end to all of them first.

At the top of the stairway, two-thirds of the chamber were gone, leaving a yawning hole and an unobstructed view of the castle gardens below, the fields beyond the wall, and the shadowy line of a forest in the distance. Only one bookcase remained along the inner wall. The rest was either burned to ash or buried beneath a mountain of rubble below.

He collected a handful of journals, stacked the remaining books onto one pile, and sent the lot of it to his chambers for safekeeping. If nothing else, at least the condensed summary of his studies had survived. Fal would take what he could get.

With the first task complete, he turned his attention to another. He righted a copper scrying bowl and filled it with water, speaking softly into its depths to bring up a vision of his parents. He'd scryed for them five times already since they'd disappeared, but each time he'd cast his will into the water, only darkness had answered his call.

Fal refused to believe the Trickster killed them. Loki was many things, but never thoughtless. He thrived on chaos, often giving gifts disguised as curses and curses seeded within powerful gifts. As all the gods did, Loki toyed with the lives of mortals and Others alike, but, unlike the others, he took perverse pleasure in sowing seeds of discord and fed on the resulting carnage. Killing was easy and, in the end, useless to Loki. He would not have ended lives he could torment. Wherever he'd taken Nialei and Saeran, they would live long enough to entertain the Trickster to his dark heart's delight first.

Loki had said something about Nialei's sire. Perhaps he'd transported them to his realm. But where was that? None of them, not even Nialei herself, knew what manner of creature her sire was, or which Otherland he'd hailed from. Without any guidance at all, Fal was left literally fumbling in the dark, looking for them. He was beginning to lose hope of ever finding them.

But he had one more thing yet to try. It was dangerous. He'd have to risk losing himself by forcing enough magic into the water to punch through its connection to the Eternal. Fal had been holding back from it, sensing any contact with the source of all water worsened his condition. But he couldn't wait any longer. Wilderheim needed the crown now more than ever, and Fal was a poor substitute for his honored parents. Praying it was the right thing to do, he pushed harder, driving his will through the bowl's bottom into the realm of Eternal water, and straight to its source.

He almost panicked as a chaos of infinite windows opened to him, not just in this world, but every Otherland, as well. The copper bowl grew hot in his grasp, its rim taking on a dangerous glow as the water in it boiled with magic. Fal kept it up, focused his intention on finding Nialei and Saeran. He pushed until his palms began to sear, and he'd almost lost hope, and then the surface suddenly settled on a burst of light and a vision.

He was looking out of a puddle straight up at a beautiful clear blue sky and his parents plummeting to the ground. It happened so quickly he didn't have time to gasp before they landed with an impact that rippled across the puddle, blurring the vision.

They can't die, he told himself. Any moment, the surface would settle, and he'd see his parents on their feet, alive and well, taking measure of the place so they could find a way back.

Fal waited and waited, but the surface didn't settle. Instead, as it continued to ripple, he saw blurred shapes flashing by in droves.

A giant hoof came down on the puddle, making him flinch. The vision shattered into dozens as droplets sprayed out around the puddle, showing him flashes of half-human, half-beast creatures with cloven hooves and antlers growing out of their heads. These were no savages, but well-trained warriors, armored and armed with swords and bows.

Fal didn't recognize the creatures, but they bore the mark of Cernunnos, the god of wild things. He was a secretive but benevolent deity, said to have the power to bring natural enemies together in peace. Little was known about him, but ancient songs hinted at his ability to create different kinds of demigods, all of them bearing his mark—golden eyes, deer-like antlers, or a circle around the neck like a symbolic torc. Could this be one of his realms?

A droplet or two briefly held on to hooves that took him almost to the place where his parents had landed. Fal dared not move. His clenched jaw ached, his eyes burned from lack of blinking. The vision shifted, bringing him high up, where a warrior near the front of the herd had poured water over her face. He could see everything she saw.

Saeran wasn't moving. Nialei herself looked little better, struggling to raise herself up on one elbow while keeping the herd in check with a glow of magic in her free hand.

Nialei reached for Saeran, and her magic redirected to him.

“Please,” Fal whispered, terrified he might be watching his father die. But Nialei wouldn't let him. “Please, don't let him…”

The warrior who held Fal's vision looked down, stomped her hooves in agitation. Fal couldn't sense what she did, but he could guess. Nialei's connection with the earth was powerful. She would call on its strength to restore herself and save Saeran, as she'd done many times before in Wilderheim.

“Wait!” he cried, knowing she wouldn't hear. The Otherlands were different than Wilderheim. Magic in them was raw, wild, and far more powerful. She wouldn't be able to control it the way she did at home; it would burn them both to ash if she couldn't hold on, which Nialei knew very well. She had to be desperate to do it.

As the wild torrent surged up, shuddering through the ground, the water in Fal's bowl rippled in response. Fal forced it to settle just in time to see Saeran's body bow off the ground beneath a force he was helpless to resist. He saw sparks jumping off the surface of Saeran's skin, and then a bright blue glow as he burst into flame. His scream chilled Fal to his soul.

And then Nialei screamed, too. The Other's face began to dry, but she moved closer for a better look, and through her, Fal saw his parents change. Black smoke billowed out from beneath Saeran, solidifying into wings. His face contorted, hardened, and then reformed with a pair of smooth, black horns growing out of his temples and sharp fangs filling his mouth. Though Saeran's eyes were closed, Fal could see them glowing blue with the same flame that burned golden in Liadan. *Dragonblood.* As direct descendants of their dragon ancestor, both Saeran and his daughter had inherited his fiery magic and the ability to transform their shape into something far more than human. Liadan had had to die to awaken that ability. Saeran, to Fal's knowledge, had never been able to do it. Until now.

And while Saeran transformed, Nialei did, too. But she was a creature of water, like Fal. Instead of burning, her skin rippled, taking on a pearlescent sheen as small antlers erupted from her forehead and temples into something like a beastly crown—the mark of Cernunnos, or at least one of his creations. Loki had, indeed, kept his word and taken Nialei to her sire's realm. She would finally know who and what she was. And she was beautiful, inside and out.

Welcome home, Nialei Waterborn, whispered the Otherland's waters. They welled up around her, cushioning her fall as she collapsed next to her mate, giving Fal a brief window straight to his parents. It was a courtesy for which he was grateful because it gifted him not only with the sight of his parents' new, transformed faces, but also the feel of their hearts beating strong within their chests, and their magics glowing within them, out of them, leaving no doubt that they were alive and well.

Fal took a chance, altered the spell, and dipped his hand into the water. The bowl was too small to accommodate travel, but at least he could reach through and touch his parents, somehow let them know he was looking for a way to—

His hand struck the bottom of the bowl, dispersing the vision.

Frowning, he pulled it back and thought of his parents again, needing to reopen the window to wherever they were. It wavered briefly over the bowl's surface as the puddle he looked through dried out. One more time, he focused his intent, pouring everything he had into the thought of pushing through to them.

Once again, his hand pressed against the bottom of the bowl, and when that window closed, he could tell it wouldn't reopen a third time.

"No, that can't be." He'd never been denied this way, not by water. "Seol, I need you," he said into the surface, sending the message through its depths into the realm of water sprites. If a being existed who could help him now, it was his mentor. "Seol!"

The water rippled, but though he sensed his message had made it through, no response came from the other side.

"Seol, please answer me. Where are you?" He cast for a vision, but the water remained still. "Are you even still alive?"

Alive, Seol's voice whispered back so softly Fal had to put his ear almost to the water to hear him. *For now.*

"Where are you? I can't see you. The Veil is gone and—"

The water sprites are aware.

"—I need to reach my parents… Wait. You know?"

Yes. We all felt the Veil give way.

"Are you doing anything about it?" How could they not? Of all the Others, water sprites had the most vested interest in helping Nialei restore the Veil. They were her mother's people, after all. Seol himself had been the first to offer his support when the Veil became damaged, and he'd stood by the family ever since.

We are saying farewell.

Cold dread settled into the marrow of his bones, so deep he thought he'd never be warm again. "You've given up?"

We have accepted the inevitable, Seol replied. *We feel the frost coming. It will take us soon.*

"Get out, then! Run while you can!"

We cannot, came the succinct response.

"What do you mean you can't?" Water sprites were incredibly powerful creatures with voices that were said to have the ability to kill as easily as restore life. Their watery realm connected to every lake and river in the human world and in every Otherland. Seol should have been able to snatch Nialei and Saeran right back from her sire's realm; his people should have been able to scatter to the streams to escape Fenrir.

No one can; the waterways between worlds are already frozen. We are trapped.

No waterways? "Tell me how to help you."

He felt the water ripple with Seol's sorrow. *Help your own kin. Find King Saeran and Queen Nialei. Find the dragon.*

"I saw my parents, but I cannot reach them. Please, Seol, what do I do?"

Farewell, son of water.

"Wait—" He felt a wrenching rift sever his connection with Seol. The water froze into a moment of shocked stillness, then resumed its natural form, softly rippling in the bowl. Seol was gone.

Wearied from the effort of his casting, Fal sat with his back to the bookcase and stared into the distance. He sat there until his magic restored itself, throwing illusions of deepwater across what remained of the floor, spilling in an endless, silent fall over the edge. He sat until the sun dipped behind the horizon, and only the colorful lights in the sky remained to illuminate the lands. Numb with cold and loss, Fal didn't notice anyone approaching until a too-warm hand settled on his shoulder, sending heat like a blanket of golden flames across his body from the neck down.

He turned his head to meet his sister's glowing gaze. "Liadan."

She must have sought him out immediately on arrival. Still in her Other form, Liadan was terrifying and beautiful at the same time. A full head and shoulders taller than him, her body was covered in impenetrable black scales. Her massive wings could hold her aloft for days if need be, and her claws were sharp enough to tear through metal armor. Her hair transformed into living flames in this shape, and her eyes burned with the fire of her Dragonblood soul, but she could extinguish both and become invisible in the night sky to rain down fire on unwary enemies.

Gods, it was good to see her.

Liadan smiled at him in greeting, already burning away her wings, tail, and horns to reclaim her much less intimidating human shape. "I should have known I'd find you here." As she shrank down to her human size, her features became a much more feminine version of his own. She had grown more beautiful since the last time Fal had seen her. Like a flower blooming in the sun, she'd taken to the desert lands of Aegiros far better than anyone could have predicted, and he could feel her happiness and vitality shining out of her. Dressed in a simple blouse, breeches, and bodice, with her red-black hair in dozens of braids held back by a golden crownlet, and her skin burnished golden brown, no one would ever suspect her northern roots. Unless, of course, one was familiar enough with Aegiran customs to know that every single thing Liadan wore went against them. "Your library is gone, have you noticed?"

Fal threw his arms about her and squeezed as hard as he could. He was bigger, but Liadan was still stronger, and when she squeezed back, she made his ribs groan. He didn't care a whit. "So are Mother and Father."

Liadan released him and pulled back, her eyes dimmed to their usual gray. Rather than drag him into the castle, she sat with him shoulder to shoulder. "Tell me what happened."

And so he did. He told her everything in as much detail as he could recall. Liadan remained silent while he talked, watching the light of her flames flicker across his water illusion. Like its caster, the illusion stubbornly refused to acknowledge the chaos in the sky, reflecting only Liadan's fire and a clear sky of brilliant stars.

But it couldn't change the truth.

When he finished his tale, Liadan looked up, flinching the same way Fal always did to behold the chaos above them. "What do you suppose it is?"

Fal followed her gaze, and a bitter smile twitched across his lips. "You are looking at a map of our closest Otherland neighbors. Without the Veil, what once was hidden now reveals itself to human eyes. "

"It makes me ill."

"Me too." The constant swirl and sway of those lights made the ground feel like it was about to fall out from under him. Some lights streaked across the sky, racing back and forth with restless vigor, others spun and churned in vortices, and still others swayed in place, pulsing with some unnamable energy. It was breathtaking for a moment or two. But the longer Fal stared, the more it unnerved him until he could bear it no more.

Liadan pointed to a bright green cloud to the right of the moon. "That one looks like it is fading."

And so it was. They watched all color leech out of the cloud, and then it dimmed by slow degrees until nothing was left but a dark gap where something ought to be.

"Does that mean…"

"It's gone." Fal rubbed his chest. He'd seen it happen several times over the last two days. Some lights went out quick as a wink, while others disappeared little by little. Each time one of those lights went out, someone thanked the gods that the sky was clearing. Fal didn't know how to tell them an entire world had just died, along with everything and everyone in it.

"And it will be our turn soon," Liadan guessed.

"Is it like this in Aegiros?" He'd already spoken to their cousin Ulrich, but the king of Lyria hadn't heard a whisper of what had transpired in Wilderheim, nor could anyone in the kingdom see anything like Wilderheim's sky. It hadn't breached their western border, then.

Likely not the eastern border, either. If it had, King Gavriil of Ravetia would already have done something about it. He was a superstitious sort who abhorred magic in all its forms, and he wouldn't tolerate such a blatant breach of their peace treaty.

And that left their southern border with the desert lands of Aegiros. Aegiros wasn't a kingdom, but a nation of independent tribes. Its resources were scarce, forcing the tribes to fight one another for control of them. Although Liadan was now the queen—or *shensari*—of its oldest tribe, there were still many others over whom she held no sway. Fal didn't consider them a threat as a whole, but smaller raiding parties weren't unlikely if something spooked them.

Liadan slowly shook her head. "As far as I could see in my flames, only Wilderheim has a sky like this. At our borders, the lights fade away."

That confirmed everything Fal had read thus far. Wilderheim didn't merely lie on the border between the human realm and Otherlands—it *was* the border. At least as far as Woden's reach stretched. By Liadan's account, Aegiros had its own gods and realms, as sovereign as the kingdom itself, and as isolated. Crossovers were not tolerated.

"The moon will be full in three days' time," Liadan said. "I can stay until then."

"And do what?"

"Whatever needs to be done. I'm hardly going to leave you here to face this on your own."

"You are needed in Aegiros." Full moon meant time for their warriors to train. After decades of suffering at the hands of demons, Liadan's tribe was finally restored to their ancestral home in the First City. But, though they worked hard to rebuild their way of life, their numbers were low, making them vulnerable to attack from rival tribes. While their warriors went off into the desert to train, it was Liadan's duty to patrol the city and ward off any potential threats. "Mother and Father will be back soon and—"

"You don't know that. There is no telling how time passes where they are. They could be gone for centuries, for all we know."

"They will be back before Fenrir comes for Wilderheim." Of that, he was certain.

Liadan nodded in agreement. "And in the meantime, our people will have their two heirs to look after them. Two heads are always better than one."

Fal looked off to the side where water trickled down the wall. While his illusions had free reign in so much open space, the sheen reflected his true self, but as soon as he returned down the broken staircase and pulled them back, his face would disappear beneath multitudes of others. Nothing had changed. The Prince of Deceit still couldn't show his true face to the world, unless he wanted it to drown. "Yes," he agreed with Liadan. "Especially when one of them cannot be seen."

In the brief moment of silence that followed, Liadan must have realized the implications of what she'd said. "You know that is not what I meant."

"But it is what they will understand. Your presence here will speak to my inability to rule. You may as well usurp me now and get it over with."

"I refuse to waste time on a pointless argument. We are not talking about the rule of Wilderheim. We are talking about the end of everything we have ever known. There will be panic, and possibly war, both of which you have only ever read about. You will need all the help you can get to keep the peace, and someone still needs to continue Mother's work."

"I can do all that!"

"No, you cannot," she snapped, her eyes briefly flickering to gold as her skin brightened with the glow of angry fire. Taking a deep breath, she banked both and continued more evenly. "No one could. It is too much, Fal. Even with a council of advisors and an army at your back, you cannot be in all places at once. Wilderheim needs you to focus on what you do best." She took his hand in both of hers and held on despite Fal's attempts to free himself. "I need you strong and focused on restoring the Veil."

Fal grunted unhappily.

"The fate of everything rests on you now, do you realize that? I wouldn't even know where to begin, but you have spent your life learning about it. You know what needs to be done."

"But not how." Therein lay the bitter defeat of all their efforts. Having the ingredients to restore the Veil meant nothing if they couldn't figure out how to use them.

"Then keep studying and figure it out. Give Wilderheim a way to survive what is to come, and let me deal with the little things."

"By which you mean panic, rebellion, war, and widespread destruction?"

Liadan waved a careless hand. "Child's play."

Fal chuckled, despite himself. "What about Imarah?"

"I am sure my king can handle it in my absence," she said with an impish twinkle in her eye.

Since it was his tribe, her king most assuredly would do just that. Even so… "Go back to him, Liadan." Seeing she was about to argue, he swiftly cut in. "I promise to keep my fire burning so you can come back at a moment's notice if things go awry." As Fal could travel through water, Liadan had mastered the art of traveling through fire, as long as it burned large enough for her to fit through. Their parents always kept a strong blaze burning in the great hall for her, and their dragon great-grandfather kept one in Liadan's old chamber in his cave. She rarely used either, preferring to flex her wings and fly. "But I need to do this on my own. I need to try."

Liadan made a face. "Very well. But I will be keeping my eye on you. And I am still staying until the full moon."

Fal let her pull him to his feet. She kept hold of his hand as she turned for the staircase, but Fal pulled her up short. "Speaking of keeping an eye on me, have you had any word from the dragon?"

"I tried calling to him a time or two," she said. "No response. But you know how Grandfather is. If he doesn't want to be bothered, he won't be. He is probably in one of his darker moods and wants to be left alone."

"Perhaps," Fal allowed.

Even by dragon standards, their great-grandfather was extremely solitary. He'd existed in complete isolation in a cave far to the north of Wilderheim ever since his mate died giving birth to their only child. Were it not for a group of foreign knights and a ridiculous quest for a cup that had led Nialei straight to his cave, no one would ever have known of his existence.

Since his discovery, so to speak, the dragon had become a constant, yet distant part of the family's lives. He'd fostered Liadan in his cave since birth to teach her how to control her volatile flames. But while Fal believed the dragon cared for all of them, he still chose to remain in his solitary cave rather than join them in Frastmir. Some habits, he supposed, were hard to break—especially if they'd been formed over millennia.

"But I should think he would care at least a little that Loki abducted his grandson."

Liadan shrugged.

"It doesn't bother you that he has abandoned us?"

"He has not abandoned us, Fal. He is a dragon. He has dragon things to do. For all you know, he is working out the spell to restore the Veil as we speak."

Fal shook his head and helped Liadan down a broken step. "I don't like it. He has always been there when we needed him."

"He hasn't always helped," Liadan reminded, shaking off his helping hand on another step to hop down on her own. "Remember when he let me go off on a quest to Aegiros and then hid me from you so you couldn't interfere? I died there if I recall correctly."

"Is that what we are saying happened?"

Liadan gave him her most innocent look. "What else would we be saying?"

"That you chose to run off to Aegiros with a known assassin, against all common sense—and despite all of my objections, I might add—to go battle a horde of soul-stealing demons by yourself because you thought it would be an adventure. And yes, you did die there. But if I recall correctly, you rose from your own ashes stronger than ever before. Which turned out to be a good thing, since you then decided to stay among a people who fear you enough to want to kill you, and marry the assassin who started you on this little adventure in the first place."

At the bottom of the stairs, his sister opened her mouth to say something, then closed it and crossed her arms over her chest. "Well, it doesn't sound nearly as heroic when you say it like that."

CHAPTER 4

The Order of Clerics was the only one of its kind, unique to the whole of the human realm. It was an order that worshipped knowledge above all else, including the gods. They had but two tasks to which they devoted their entire lives—preserve and share knowledge.

Their temple was built high up on Hallowed Mountain to create distance from the petty problems and politics of everyday life. There, master scribes carefully copied ancient texts, and master bookmakers painstakingly cut, sewed, and bound the volumes to be disseminated by traveler clerics wherever their paths might take them.

It was said the temple burned beeswax candles for light and always smelled like honey. Each cleric had a small bedchamber with only a bed, a writing table, and a bookcase.

Sanja smiled at the mere thought of it.

In theory, anyone could join the Order of Clerics if they proved their devotion to knowledge and reason by completing the Journey of body and mind.

In truth, very few earned the distinction of donning one of their hooded white robes.

The Journey began with a torturous trek from Frastmir's grand library to the top of Hallowed Mountain. The fifteen-mile path led through the city, across the river, past the fields, into the forest, and up a steep stairway carved directly into the rock face. And Journeymen had to traverse the entire length of it on their knees.

Companions carrying food, water, and other essentials were allowed, but only as far as the stone stairway, and they could not interfere with the Journeyman's progress in any way. Breaks, sleep, and healing salves were allowed as well, as long as the Journeyman picked up in the exact spot where they'd stopped. Some took days to complete the trek; others took months, and some never finished at all. And that was only the beginning.

Once the Journeyman made it to the top, on the brink of death with exhaustion, hunger, and thirst, he or she was led directly into the inquisition chamber where the clerics launched into a merciless interrogation of the mind. They said no two Journeymen were asked the same questions. Each inquisition was unique to the Journeyman, removing any possibility of preparation or cheating. If even one question was answered incorrectly or dishonestly, the Journeyman would be turned away for good.

Standing at the top of the library steps, Sanja could see the thin line of a stairway snaking up Hallowed Mountain. Where it ended, sunlight glittered off the glass steeple where clerics lived and worked. It all seemed so impossibly far.

No, do not think like that. She had three weeks, plenty of time to prepare and complete her Journey. No other choice. If she failed to reach the temple, she might as well throw herself off the mountain because she would *never* let Jarl Steen lay a finger on her.

True to his word, he'd been coming by the cottage every day, forcing her to sit with him even when he had nothing to say. He had nothing to say about anything! Even the lightning storm hadn't elicited more than a grunt from him, and though he kept glancing out the window at the lights dancing across their sky, he waved away any attempt on her part to discuss them. All he wanted to talk about was himself and his fighting skills.

Sanja had no patience for it. She would happily discuss any number of subjects of a cerebral nature and had made many attempts to do just that, but each time she had, Jarl Steen's face had turned an angry red, and he'd emitted a displeased growl that sounded to Sanja as if he was choking.

To make matters worse, Sanja suspected he had her watched. Four times now she'd gone to the market and noticed the same man lurking around whatever stall she happened to be perusing. Once, she'd gone so far as to smile at him and said hello, but he'd ducked his head and hurried away without saying a word. But why would Jarl Steen want to have her watched? Why would anyone care how many fish she bought, or which of the colorful ribbons she admired, dreaming of one day being able to afford it? It couldn't be for fear of her finding another suitor. As Jarl Steen and her own father had been so quick to point out, if she hadn't found one by now, he wouldn't magically appear in her time of need.

"A fine day to begin a Journey, no?" Sanja looked up at the bookish young man standing next to her in a plain hair shirt and trousers. He was looking up, smiling. "Aye, the gods show us favor. It is a fine day, indeed."

Sanja followed his gaze up toward the shimmering greens and reds swirling together like ghostly snakes across the bright blue sky. They've been fading away one by one over the last week, but day and night, the hundreds of remaining lights continued to distress humans and Others alike. The city was poised on the tense edge of some kind of disaster. Everyone felt it, but no one spoke of it aloud. People looked at the Others among them with suspicion, and in return, the Others have begun to retreat from human society. Formerly amicable interactions have turned into cold, silent stares. Merchants turned Others away, and Others turned their backs on those who sought them out for help.

And then there were those, like this young man, whose unbridled optimism blinded them to all but the beautiful lights.

"Why would that be a sign of the gods' favor?" Sanja replied to what she suspected had been a rhetorical question. "Could it not as easily be a sign of their displeasure?"

The Journeyman looked at her with a quizzical expression. "Have you never heard of Valkyries, girl? Lights like those always accompany them across battlefields, and their favor is the gods' favor."

She frowned, shifting a step away to make room for the young man's companion carrying heavy sacks of supplies. "Yes, I have heard of them. But Valkyries don't ride willy-nilly. They are drawn to battlefields and the fallen warriors lying upon them. We have not had a war in Wilderheim in generations."

The young man's smile turned somewhat sour.

"Furthermore," she continued, "lights in the sky have preceded the great battle of Crossroads, and the Age of Maladies. Both of which were considered terrible tragedies at the time."

Had he paled a little?

"There was also a falling star the night before King Halder's mother died, two months after giving birth to his stillborn sister, and a solar eclipse on the day of King Bjarke's coronation—and as you will recall, King Bjarke was killed by a bear that same year, which was an ironic end for him, given his name. So, if anything, reason would say lights in the sky are, more often than not, a bad omen, rather than a good one."

"Gunne, let's go," the young man said, glaring at Sanja. "It is time for us to set out."

"Oh, but I didn't mean it had to be a bad omen for you," she called after them. "I am sure you will don your white robe in no time!" Having clattered his way down before his master, Gunne adjusted the sacks across his back as the young Journeyman got on his knees and hurried down the stairs as fast as he could manage. Sanja winced, watching them disappear among the market crowds. He'd wear his knees bloody before he reached the fields, the poor thing. "May your Journey be short and painless," she added belatedly.

Fiddlesticks, I shouldn't have said anything.

As she watched them hurry away, Sanja became aware of someone else standing behind her. She turned and looked far up into the kindly face of an old cleric.

"Can I help you, child?"

"Oh yes, please, Brother Erik! I am looking for books on a very specific subject." She had no intention of giving up on her quest, but it never hurt to be prepared for the worst.

Brother Erik chuckled, waving her ahead of him into the library. "Well, you have come to the right place. Our volumes encompass almost every subject known to man and quite a few known to Others. What is it you are looking for?"

"Anything there is to learn about courtship, beauty, and love."

He opened the door for her, ushering her into the library, and Sanja breathed in the heavenly aroma permeating the air. Centuries of knowledge rested within these hallowed walls, and it almost brought tears to her eyes. "Ah, you seek to attract a suitor," the cleric said. "I believe we can find something to—"

"Oh, no, quite the contrary," she said, catching sight of a beautiful old leather tome.

"Pardon?"

"I do not want to attract a suitor," she clarified, tracing the tome's decorative grooves. "I want to repel one."

"I am not sure I understand."

Every detail of the book's cover was meticulously wrought, and each individual page was cut and stitched precisely. This book was a work of pure love of the written word. She could feel it permeating through her skin where it touched the cover.

No! Remember why you're here! Curling her hand into a fist to stop touching the beautiful tome, Sanja focused back on what she needed to do. If her charms weren't enough to attract another suitor, then she had to find a way to get rid of the one she had. "I need to learn what attracts a man so that I can do everything opposite and make myself as unattractive as possible." She had no way out of a blood oath, but there were any number of ways in which Jarl Steen could make her quest to escape him difficult, even impossible, to force her to fail. Perhaps if she made herself undesirable enough, she could make him only too happy to let her succeed just to be rid of her. It might cost her the chance of attracting another suitor, but Sanja was desperate enough to try anything.

"Err…"

"Well, perhaps unattractive is the wrong word. Repugnant! Yes, that is much better. How do I make myself utterly repugnant to a relentless—Brother Erik, where are you going?"

≪ »·◇·« ≫

"Any word of the dragon?" Fal barely recognized his own voice. He was exhausted after only a week. Though he'd sooner die than admit it to his sister, Liadan had been right. Fal had not slept a night through since he'd taken over the rule of Wilderheim. He'd know it would be difficult, but he could never have anticipated the hundreds of little details that would require his attention.

"No, Your Highness," the runner answered. He was the sixteenth messenger in the last week who'd returned with nothing of use. Fal had sent them north, east, and west in search of any sign of his absent grandfather, desperate for his counsel. He needed the dragon's ancient wisdom now more than ever.

The careful balance of justice and magic which King Saeran and Queen Nialei had fostered and preserved for decades was disintegrating before Fal's eyes, and nothing he did seemed to help. Soldiers now patrolled the streets of Frastmir to keep the peace, and instead of being reassured, humans and Others reacted with scorn and resentment, accusing the crown of monitoring its citizens like criminals. If Fal ruled a dispute in favor of an Other, he was said to be taking *their side*. If he ruled in favor of the human, Others accused him of shirking his duty to the balance.

The smallest ripples of unrest in the streets caused tidal waves among the nobles. Their positions of power and influence had already been undermined with the arrival of Others as welcome members of society during King Saeran's reign. While the balance had held everything in check, they'd remained silent, fearful of reprisal. But the shattered sky made politics and money all but irrelevant. People didn't look to their lords' coin for protection, they sought Other magic.

Every day, Fal's noble court issued demands for the Others to be banished once and for all. And every day Fal refused, their malcontent grew deeper and louder. Most had already declared they would not pay taxes again until their demands were met. Some had threatened to revolt. Though he couldn't prove it, and therefore couldn't mete out punishment for such a heinous offense, Fal was certain some of the nobles had posted bounties on the Others dwelling on their lands.

Fal was at a loss for an agreeable solution. With the noble houses watching his every move, he feared a single misstep would send the kingdom spiraling into civil war. If it did, he would be on his own, with no support from the Others, who had already decided fleeing to kinder realms was preferable to weathering the coming storm in Wilderheim.

The Sidhe had disappeared on the night of the lightning storm, leaving a short, cold note of warning for Fal to finish what his mother had started or else. With them gone, the dwarves were becoming worse than usual, lashing out in fits of temper, breaking things, and insulting innocent passersby.

A triad of succubi had been attacked five times in as many days, forcing them to defend themselves the only way they could—by draining their attackers of all passion and feeling, leaving them to waste away without the ability to sleep and dream.

The higher order of Others at least had the ability to communicate freely and hold their own against the frightened humans who'd decided Other magic was at fault for Wilderheim's current predicament.

The more exotic Others weren't so fortunate. Fearing for their lives, tree nymphs have retreated to their trees, which wouldn't protect them from saws and axes. Someone had started a rumor that grinding a unicorn's horn to powder and sprinkling it over the threshold would protect a home from magic. One had already been butchered, forcing the rest of the herd to flee.

As Other creatures slowly retreated from Wilderheim, the humans took their voluntary disappearance as proof that magic and Otherkind were at fault for their troubles, adding fuel to the noble court's ire.

To make matters worse, word of unrest and cursed skies was spreading far and wide. Trade with Aegiros, Synealee, and Ravetia had stopped completely. Lyria held fast to familial ties, but its king could no more order his people to trade with Wilderheim than Fal could restore the sky to its former state.

Staring at the stack of reports on the chair beside him, Fal was beyond the point of absorbing anything he saw or heard any longer. It was simply too much. Too many troubles and complications. Too many rules and laws to observe. Too many mistakes he'd already made and would continue to make, because none of his advisors knew any better, either. Simply put, Fal was ill-equipped to rule a kingdom in turmoil.

While his parents had spent all their energies over the last twenty-two years on getting the Others' cooperation to rebuild the Veil, Fal had focused his studies on dealing with the results. All of their clerics, Other advisors, and councilors, had been working all this time to aid in those two endeavors. They couldn't afford to contemplate the alternative.

Now, they had no choice.

"What are your orders, Your Highness?"

A map of Wilderheim and its neighbors had been laid out in the center of the table. Colorful wooden tokens were lined up on either side of it like the troops they were meant to represent. This meeting had been called to discuss the kingdom's military defense strategy. Councilor Tarben, a former general, anticipated an invasion if or when certain monarchs realized Wilderheim's protections were compromised.

Fal couldn't concentrate on any of it. He sat in the seat King Saeran usually occupied during these meetings, his embroidered cloak controlling the erratic outpour of his illusions until it merely looked soaked through, dripping water on the floor, and he saw nothing of the map or the people speaking around him.

"We should address the people," Councilor Braith said, filling the silence when Fal didn't answer. "Keeping silent is only making them create their own explanations and blame one another. If there is any hope of restoring peace among the people, they must be told the truth. They must be given the choice to stay or leave."

"Yes," Fal replied slowly. "We should inform our people the Veil we have sworn to repair is destroyed. But the common folk likely won't know what that means. So we should tell them the whole truth. The gods have lost their power over us, could well be dying as we speak, and a great, immortal wolf is coming to devour our world. Mind you, it might not cause an exodus large enough for our less friendly neighbors to notice, so we should also say that the king and queen on whom Wilderheim has depended for protection are gone, replaced by the heir, whom Frastmir's denizens have so charmingly dubbed the Prince of Deceit. Excellent idea. You do it."

Braith twisted her mouth and glared, but remained silent.

"What other option do we have?" asked their newest member, Eira, only the second woman to ever sit on the advisory council.

"We say nothing." That from Councilor Kvaran, who, at an age so advanced he himself had lost count, needed to be transported from place to place on a long-handled seat carried by four servants. His voice was barely a wheeze, and they expected him at any moment to close his eyes and never open them again, but every word he said was worth his weight in gold. "Wilderheim and all its citizens are one. All of us are bound together by eons of magic. It is steeped in the ground we walk upon, the water we drink, the food we eat. It dies with our elders and is reborn in our children, and it will call to Fenrir no matter where our people choose to run. This is not something anyone can hide from. I am afraid with their Majesties gone, there is little the rest of us can do to prevent it. Our world as we have always known it *will end*. But that does not mean we should let panic consume us. Our people deserve to live their lives without fear for as long as they can, and it is our duty to ensure they do."

His words were met with grave looks and bowed heads. It was no easy thing for any of them to accept defeat, but Kvaran was right. Wilderheim was structured like an Otherland nestled within the human realm. Anyone who'd lived within its borders for longer than a year, who'd seen its every season pass, became bonded to the land. They might not feel the magic within them, but it was there, nonetheless. It gave their people longer, healthier lives, made their minds more open and resilient to the presence of Others. Now, it put them all in the path of the end.

The Veil could only be reformed from the blood of each Other clan. Nialei and Saeran had collected much of it over the years, despite immense opposition from Others for whom the passage of time meant nothing, but no one knew where it was. Because of the immense power even a drop of Other blood held, Queen Nialei had kept it hidden where no one could find it or use it for Dark purposes. But with her and Saeran gone, the rest of them were left powerless to continue their work. Even if all of the remaining Others magically decided to appear in the great hall this very moment to volunteer their blood, it would never be enough without the rest.

They all stood guilty of the greatest folly in the world: thinking time would be plentiful and infinite.

"We will hold our tongues and pretend their Majesties are simply on another mission in the Otherlands. They have gone on extended trips before. The people are used to it by now."

"And what of the lights?" Eira asked.

Kvaran stroked his long, white beard. "The anniversary of Wilderheim's inception is coming up. We will say the lights are in celebration of it."

Braith shook her head. "But the storm—"

Tarben waved that aside. "Prince Fal's studies have resulted in many sights like it in the past. It can be explained away."

"And if someone chooses to speak otherwise?" Braith asked, and all eyes turned on her. "Oh, not me," she defended. "My loyalty is to the crown. But we have Others in our population, and clerics who of a certainty know better, and people with enough magic to feel the end coming. What of them?"

"They must be made aware that there is nowhere they can go to avoid what is coming."

Eira's words caused Tarben to chuckle. "Knowing and feeling are two different things, my dear. Knowing the end is coming will not stop thousands of frightened people from trampling each other to death trying to flee from it." He was not wrong, and they all knew it.

"Councilor Kvaran will speak to the clerics," Fal decreed. "Make them understand that, in the name of peace, they must not share their knowledge of Ragnarok too freely. They are to call back all their members immediately and begin studying the forgotten lore. If there is anything that has been overlooked, anything at all that might help us, they are our only chance of finding it. They will understand and obey. I will speak to the Others. If they wish to leave and take their human friends and families along, no one will stop them, but there will be consequences if they try to incite a panic."

"And what of our own people?"

Fal thought about it for a moment. "Let them say what they will. The best way to squelch a rumor is to ignore it. To react in any way would only give it credence." He stood, forcing all others to their feet as well. Taking a stack of silver tokens, he placed them on the map. "But just in case word reaches Ravetia or Synealee, we will reinforce our border keeps here, here, and here, and warn Ulrich to do the same here and here.

"Councilor Tarben, you are now in charge of monitoring our neighbors. I will see to it that you have all the resources you require. Keep our troops well fed, well trained, and ready to move out, but do not sound a call to arms without my say-so. We do this quietly and slowly. Have an excuse at the ready in case someone does notice and asks questions."

"I suppose it is the best we can do," Braith said, shaking her head. "But I still don't like it."

"Our world is about to end," Tarben retorted. "What is there to like?"

CHAPTER 5

As soon as the council meeting concluded, Fal sent a simulacrum of himself to his chambers, cloaked himself in invisibility, and snuck out of the castle. The courtyard was eerily silent as wary faces looked to each other for explanations or reassurances. They knew something odd was afoot, but no one dared speak of it aloud, and with each day that passed without an official acknowledgment of what was happening, the anxiety grew deeper and colder. It was a palpable chill carried on the northern wind, seeping into the marrow of Fal's bones.

He hastened through the gateway, breathing a sigh of relief once the oppressive castle walls were behind him and the city of Frastmir opened up before him. Out here, the chill gave way to bright sunshine and cautiously smiling faces. This close to the castle, people still kept up at least the pretense of goodwill. But Fal knew the farther out he went, the less peaceful his city would be.

The market roiled like a giant anthill with merchants in the center and customers flitting from one to the other. The library doors glittered as sunlight reflected off their golden inlays each time they were opened. A line of carts and wagons stretched over the bridge. Music carried from the inns, magic glowed around the Others in the crowd, and autumn spiced the air so sweetly, Fal stopped for a moment to simply take it all in.

This was true freedom: the ability to go anywhere without hindrance. In that moment, standing at the edge of the road, Fal envied everyone around him, as far as the eye could see, for having been born to the immense privilege of a simple life. What Fal wouldn't give to trade places with any one of them.

Bypassing the crowded market, he took a long way around to the city green. From there, he had an unobstructed view of the mountains, the fields, and the river crossing, without the risk of anyone running into him—always a concern when invisible. Fal lay down on the soft, green grass and closed his eyes, pretending there were no strange lights in the sky, only the sun. He pretended the shrill chirps he heard were of a migrating flock, instead of one confused and unable to find its way as it had done for generations past.

He pressed the palms of his hands into the dirt, feeling for the familiar connection with the earth that was now altered in some inexplicable way and told himself it was only natural to feel out of sorts in his current state.

But, of course, none of that was true and, try as he might, Fal could not make himself believe it. As the inevitability of his fate and the fate of his kingdom returned, he began to feel the chill once more, seeping up from the ground like an early frost. Far too early for this time of year, when the sun still beat down with vigor.

"*...fair maiden, look once more down that secret forest trail.*"

Fal frowned, listening to the intrusive voice drift closer. What was this? No one except children and their nurses ever came to the green, and only after noon. It was early morning still.

"*Come sit with me when the moon peaks full, and the night is at its deepest.*"

Soft footsteps neared, the earth humming at their approach and, without looking, Fal sighed and picked himself up to move out of the way. Better that than to be trampled by some featherbrained girl with her nose stuck in a book of bad love poetry.

"*For a loving glance I offer, without duty or a price, nothing less than the gift of my heart.*"

He scoffed.

To his surprise, so did the girl. "Right. An Other whose glamour can only be broken by the light of the full moon. There is a dream of a lover."

Fal turned around just as she snapped the book shut and picked up her step, nearly bowling him over. He managed to step out of her path in time, but couldn't move his foot fast enough to avoid her heel as she abruptly turned and stomped back the other way. Luckily, she wore soft shoes and didn't amount to much.

"Like as not some slimy, pustulent monster, or a man cursed for eternity to look like one," she said to herself, pacing around at random. Fal scrambled to clear her haphazard path, mesmerized by the girl darting back and forth like a temperamental squirrel. "What woman in her right mind would want that? Haven't we got enough problems of our own without trying to save someone else from theirs?"

It was surprisingly shrewd and level-headed reasoning from a girl who looked anything but. Her hair was a cloud of black curls that refused to be restrained by the thick red ribbon tying it at her nape; her pale cheeks were smudged with soot; and her sharp, green eyes stared ahead as if there was someone there to speak to. She wore a simple brown and gray dress, well made, but worn and faded, with threads hanging loose from her sleeves. The frayed hem of her skirts flared up each time she did a sharp about-face to stomp a few steps before turning again like an agitated squirrel twitching its tail.

Then, as if breaking out of some unfathomable spell, she sat on the ground and opened the book once more to read aloud, "*For such a joy and such a burden is love, that one may never look upon it directly, but will forever feel its tethers binding heart and soul to its true intended. Beyond time, beyond distance, beyond even death itself.* Bah!" She let herself fall back, the book still in her lap, and glared at the sky. "Useless, maudlin tripe. How is any of that supposed to help me?"

Fal couldn't help himself. He laughed. "What exactly did you expect a book of poetry to help you with?"

The girl screamed, sat up, and threw the book so hard it flew over his head to land in the grass a distance behind him. No sooner had it thumped down than she gasped and crawled over to it. "Look what you made me do!" She made a valiant effort to brush off the dirt, but only managed to rub it in deeper. "Where are you, you fiend?

Show yourself!"

Charmed despite himself, Fal leaned down to say at her ear, "Only by moon—*oof!*" The book thwacked him across the face and, had the girl had any physical strength to speak of, she would have laid him out. "Gods damn it, girl."

"Care for another?" she challenged, her eyes wild and her cheeks flushed as she looked around for the unseen enemy.

"Do you always strike friendly, invisible strangers for no reason?"

"Friendly? You're invisible—you could be a demon or an assassin!"

"Do you have many of those following you?" He wouldn't be surprised. "What say you put the book down before you hurt yourself?"

"Not until you leave."

"All right." He'd be more than happy to oblige. "Fare thee well, madwoman."

Yet despite knowing full well it was beyond foolish to meddle with any human, especially one of his royal subjects, Fal couldn't walk more than three steps before he turned right back again, curious about the girl who met a magical anomaly with the same indignation she would have shown the basket weaver. She might have startled easily, but she didn't seem to be afraid at all. Clutching her book as a makeshift weapon, the girl looked ready to dispense more bashings to anyone who would dare come too close, be they human or Other, visible or not.

She had courage. And excellent aim, he added, rubbing his temple with a reluctant smile. Fal couldn't remember the last time he'd met someone new who hadn't run away or cowered at the sight of him. Invisibility did have its benefits. Perhaps he ought to take advantage of it.

Fal quietly circled around the girl as she scanned the green for hidden threats. She kept up her guard for so long Fal thought she might be onto him, but eventually, she settled her ruffled fur and breathed a little sigh, shaking her head as she gazed down at the book. "So much for scholarly wisdom." Not one for conversing with strangers, apparently, but quite the chatty little squirrel when talking to herself. "Probably would have gotten better advice from the Other." She frowned, then smacked a hand against her forehead. "Why did I not ask the Other? Stupid, stupid, stupid, Sanja! You never think before you speak."

Fal sat beside her—well out of striking distance—to observe her a little while longer. She was quite pretty, this Sanja. Not a great beauty like the Other females in Frastmir, not even like the human maidens in the city. Still, something about her made him want to keep looking. Her boundless energy hummed along his skin. She was an unrestrained spirit—freedom embodied in this slip of a girl who quite possibly had lost her mind a long time ago.

After a morosely quiet moment, she once again opened the useless book and read another verse. "*Seek not love in a flower's bloom, nor in the face of the rising sun. For love is a sigh, a glance, a touch that lingers eternally and renders time a fleeting afterthought.*" She had a lovely voice, soft, yet full of emotion. She seemed to hold nothing back as if she couldn't. "Yes, but how do I stop it!"

"Stop what?" The words were out before he could bite his tongue against them.

With a shriek, she swung again and missed. "Gods damn you, leave me alone!"

"A moment ago, you were lamenting not asking me for help," he pointed out in his most rational voice. "Therefore, I shall, just this once, overlook your alarmingly violent impulses when startled and give you one more chance to—"

THWACK!

"Will you stop hitting me!"

"Ha!"

THWACK!

"That does it." Fal snatched the book out of her hands, rendering it as invisible as he was, and moved out of her reach.

"Give it back!"

He led her in a merry chase around the green, following the sound of his laughter and nothing else. "Not on your life, savage."

"I need it! I need to learn how to get rid of a suitor."

"I'd say running circles around the city green while shouting at nothing might be a good way to do it," he retorted.

Sanja stopped in her tracks, looking around as if she expected this suitor of hers to be there, watching her.

"There's no one there. And you look relieved." And why should that disappoint him?

"Of course I am," she hissed in his general direction. "I may want to rid myself of *him*, but that does not mean I want to shame my parents even more." Her words were impassioned, but the way her gaze skittered sideways convinced Fal they were not the whole truth.

Still, he decided to pretend her answer sufficed. "*More?* You cannot be more than eighteen years old. How could you have managed to shame them already?" Was there a sordid affair in her past? Did this suitor get a babe on her before the wedding night? So many questions. Fal didn't intend to let her go until she'd answered all of them to his satisfaction.

"I am a score and one years of age, sir." The proud announcement was followed by a defeated slump. "And if you must know, I have committed the most unpardonable offense of all: being useless."

He would have laughed at the absurdity of her claim, were it not for the embarrassed flush in her cheeks and her inability to tear her gaze away from the toes of her shoes. "You are not serious."

Sanja shrugged as if there was nothing else to say on the matter, and Fal's levity drained out of him in a rush. Someone must have gone to great lengths to make her believe it. Fal knew of a thousand ways to destroy a person with spells, but it never ceased to amaze him how quickly humans could do it to each other with a mere handful of words and not a spark of magic behind them.

"You have a clever mind and a strong instinct for self-preservation," he said. "I would hardly call that useless." If anyone could attest to the true strength of the mind, it was

Fal. Knowledge was, indeed, power, if one was willing to seek it out. But it required a keener mind than most to adapt theoretical texts for practical applications. Fal had spent his life doing it, and he recognized the same curiosity and tenacity in the girl.

Sanja worried the loose threads of her sleeve. “Yes, well, neither is a quality prized in a woman. We are not supposed to be clever. We are supposed to be pretty, and quiet, and know how to cook and sew, and always defer to our husband’s higher intellect. Even when he hasn’t got one. May I have my book back, please?” She held out her hand in his general direction, looking at her own palm as if expecting the book to appear there.

It was unfair to hold it hostage, but Fal couldn’t think of another way to keep her still a while longer. Strange little Sanja, whose head barely reached his shoulder, was the first human he’d spoken to outside of the royal court since he’d been a child. Fal was loath to let the moment end. “Am I to surmise from your little speech that you do not know how to cook or sew?” he asked to incite a flare of temper to banish her gloom.

He was denied. “Surmise what you will. Just give me back my book.”

Never one to admit defeat, Fal tried again. “It seems to me that if you are such a useless burden on your parents, marriage would be the simplest solution. Why chase away the one man who would have you?”

He may as well have struck her, the way she flinched, and Fal immediately regretted his harsh words.

Without giving him a chance to apologize, she turned and headed back toward the market.

“Wait, stop!” Fal followed after her as she picked up her step to escape him. “I apologize. I did not mean that the way it came out. Truly, I am not usually so crass. I just wanted to stop you feeling sad.”

“Well done, you,” she shot back, darting left and breaking into a run.

Fal should have let her go—he told himself so, even as he ran to catch up and overtake her. “I still have your book,” he reminded her just before she slammed into him.

“Keep it,” she cried, changing direction. “Perhaps it will teach *you* a thing or two.”

She definitely wasn’t sad anymore. *Well done, Prince of Deceit.* And still, he couldn’t let her get away. In a last-ditch effort to stop her mad flight, he threw the book in the air, then guided its path to land a distance in front of her so she would see it and stop before it tripped her.

She did stop in time and stared down long enough for Fal to catch up and see what had so thoroughly caught her interest.

The book had fallen open on a page depicting two trees twined together on one side, and a short poem on the other:

Thus marked the world a true love’s end:
It did not end at all.

Her ire seemingly forgotten, Sanja gazed at that poem for a long time. “Do you ever wonder if it's real?" Her abrupt change of pace startled Fal so much he thought she might have suffered some sort of injury. He was about to ask if she was all right, but then she slowly leaned over and picked up the book, tracing the words with a reverent touch.

"If what is real?"

"True love."

Taken aback, Fal didn't know how to respond.

Sanja, however, didn't seem to need a response. "It always seems so magical. Two souls meeting at the right moment in the right circumstances, and they are somehow able to forge a bond that cannot be weakened or broken. Not by treachery, evil, or even death. We write about it, sing about it, and dream about it. But can it truly exist? Or do we simply wish for it so hard we make ourselves believe it does, even if we never find it ourselves?"

Fal had asked himself those same questions often enough. The tragedy of his curse was to be surrounded by love and know he'd never find it himself without risking someone else's life along with his own. His parents, his sister and her husband—Fal envied them all bitterly.

Oblivious to the feelings she had stirred up in the invisible Other, Sanja traced the drawing with the lightest touch. The elusive emotion soaked into the page like a perfume she could sense with her heart. It made her wistful and loosened her tongue to speak things she probably ought not say aloud. "Sometimes it seems so real I see it everywhere I look. Other times it feels as if true love is meant for everyone but me. I do wonder if it is worth believing at all. It hardly seems practical on the face of it. With all the people in the world, that there should be one alone born just for me…" She looked up at the spot where she imagined her invisible companion to be standing and grinned. "Then again, I have never been a practical sort."

There was a moment of silence in which she thought he'd disappeared, but then the air shimmered, and right in front of Sanja, a figure took shape. She gaped at the sight of a white-haired, bearded man—but then he was a red-haired young woman. And in the next instant, the woman's skin darkened to almost black, and she became a young boy. "What are you?" Sanja whispered in awe as a blink later, a different man stood in front of her, this one portly with a red nose. But before she'd taken in his features, he became a beautiful woman about Sanja's mother's age, and then a young girl, and another man, and a woman once again.

"In truth, I do not know," the Other answered, and even his voice changed between one word and the next as the woman became a bald man with slanted blue eyes.

"How is it done? Are you doing it on purpose? What kind of magic is this? Where did it come from?" So many questions. She did not intend to let the Other disappear before she got answers to all of them. "Does it hurt? It is almost as if you don't have a physical shape at all—oh!" She was touching him. Definitely a *him*. Despite appearing to be fondling a young girl's generous breast, the flesh beneath her hand felt harder, flatter—the chest of a man, not a woman. "It's an illusion." It looked so real, if she wasn't touching him, she'd believe this creature to be the beer-bellied man with a long mustache he appeared to be in that moment, but her hand felt the soft fabric of a well-made, embroidered shirt, not the sweaty chest hair of a shirtless man-at-arms. "How amazing."

And Sanja somehow became part of the illusion. Her hand appeared to change distance from her body, her arm extending or pulling back so that her palm always appeared to be on the chest of whatever shape he took, even though neither of them moved.

As her fascination with that particular phenomenon eased, she glanced down and gasped. The lush green was now a brown, murky marsh, and she was standing ankle-deep in it. Though her feet were cold, the ground beneath them still felt hard and steady. When she raised one foot, steadying herself against this strange Other, it came out looking covered in mud and muck. With her free hand, she reached down to touch it. Nothing but warm, dry slippers on her feet.

"Oh, you must tell me how it's done!"

"It does not frighten you?"

"Frighten me?" Sanja laughed. "I could spend days watching it. You always take a human shape, but they never repeat, do they? How can that be? How can so many people exist?" Caught up in her excitement, she ran her hands over the parts of him she could feel. "Yet your own shape never changes." She felt a large clasp of a cloak of some kind at his neck and slipped her hands underneath the heavy fabric to his shoulders, down his arms, to the thick metal cuffs that encircled his wrists. "I have read about illusion magic before, but nothing like this." The metal was warm from his flesh, precise grooves indicating it was engraved. How she wanted to see it. Were there illusion spells etched into each cuffs? Was that how the magic worked?

"You probably never will, either."

Sanja blinked up into eyes bluer than the clearest sky. "Why is that? Is it a secret of your kind?" And if so, why had he revealed himself to her?

"Because by the time I find the answers for myself, even your great-grandchildren will probably be long dead and buried."

"Oh." Spirits deflated, Sanja stilled her hands at the edges of his metal cuffs. "I suppose there is a reason why they say humans and Others ought not mix."

What a shame that was.

Sanja let her hands fall away, lamenting yet again the limitations of her own nature. Still, curiosity was a dangerous, relentless thing. It compelled her to know this creature, somehow. Was his flesh scaled? Did he have horns? Were there eyes in the back of his head? Fully aware she might and probably was breaking some ancient Other rule, Sanja reached up one more time, tracing the hood of his cloak to the top of his head, then down over his face.

He sucked in a sharp breath when she touched his bare skin, and then, like the waves of a lake settling into a glassy surface, he changed once more, became as steady and solid in her eyes as he was beneath her palms. The hood of a dark gray cloak cast shadows over a surprisingly human face. His hair was dark brown, pleated with a braid on each side, with stray wisps falling across his blue eyes. He had a strong nose and a close-cropped beard, and lips that seemed to droop at the corners into a perpetually unhappy frown. He was taller than her, and quite handsome, and somehow familiar.

Sanja squeaked and jumped away, clutching her skirts. “You're the Prince of Deceit!” Though no one outside the royal court had laid eyes on the crown prince of Wilderheim since he'd been a boy, his likeness was struck into every silver coin of the realm. Oh gods, she'd touched the crown prince of Wilderheim. She'd bashed him over the head with her book!

He scowled. “My name is Fal.” Even as he spoke, his visage began to change once more, disguising his true face beneath an endless parade of strangers. A silvery haired young woman blinked at Sanja in surprise. “Wait, you can see me?”

Sanja dropped to her knees, bowing her head. “Forgive me, Your Highness. I did not mean to, I—”

“Bollocks that, girl, get up!” Big hands, appearing to be encased in thick leather gloves, grasped her arms to pull her up to her feet. “Can you see me?”

Sanja felt the warmth of his skin through her sleeve, yet now he looked like a half-frozen waif with deathly pale skin and blue lips. She shivered at the sight of him; couldn't find the right words to say in reply.

“Answer me!”

Sanja shook her head. “N-not anymore.” Her eyes stung from staring, yet she could not make them blink.

Disappointment hooded the eyes of a weary old man whose long beard touched the ground when he hung his head. His hands slid away from her, and he stepped back.

Sanja looked down, spotted the book she'd dropped from excitement earlier. It was sunk almost completely in a puddle that glittered with white frost around the edges. She scooped it up through tendrils of cold mist that swirled around her wrist as if to pull her down. As with her slippers, the book was unharmed, but the chill had somehow seeped into its cover, and it would not warm to her touch.

“It's no use,” the prince said, shaking his head. He looked like a young soldier just returned from battle, covered in mud and blood. As he sat on the ground, his features softened into a pretty woman with hands chapped and red from the cold. “It's no use.”

He was distracted; Sanja ought to flee while she had the chance. Instead, her feet brought her closer, and her legs bent to make her sit. Clutching the book to her chest, she watched strangers ripple across the prince's features as he stared at the ground in front of him.

“You cannot see me, no matter how hard you stare.”

Sanja snapped her gaze forward; stubbornly stopped herself from turning back toward him, despite the ache taking root in the back of her neck from the effort.

“Prince of Deceit, they call me, though I have never uttered a lie in my entire life. I *am* the lie, it seems. Everything I touch becomes a lie. Every place I go turns into an illusion.”

"Are you doing it on purpose?" Sanja asked, her eyes open wide to catch a sideways glimpse of him without looking.

"No," he replied.

"Then you are not a lie. You are an Other truth that mortals cannot comprehend."

He scoffed, and his voice turned deep and gravelly as another mask settled into place over him. "How can something be true if it changes constantly?"

"Well… That is…"

"You see? Even you don't believe it yourself."

Sanja clutched her book harder to keep from bashing his shoulder with it. "Kindly don't put words in my mouth, sir. I know my own mind quite well, thank you. It's only that I sometimes cannot find the right way to articulate it quickly enough."

"Please, take all the time you need," he retorted.

The crown prince of Wilderheim was mocking her. Sanja ought to be insulted, yet the corner of her mouth twitched to smile. Sitting on the city green with him, arguing over impossible things, felt easier and more pleasant than any other conversation she'd ever had. Settling herself more comfortably, she considered the ideas flitting around her head and tried to put them into some semblance of order. It wasn't easy; each time she opened her mouth to speak, the sentence she'd thought up changed in her mind before she could utter it, and she lost the meaning she'd grasped onto a moment ago.

It didn't help that Sanja felt the prince watching her so intently her scalp prickled as if her hair would stand on end like bristled fur, were it not restrained by the ribbon that tied it back. Her cheeks heated, and her mouth became dry. *Say something!* Sanja looked up, squinting at the sun right above them. "Change is the only truth," she murmured.

"Pardon?"

Did that make sense? Yes. Yes, it did. The more she thought about it, the more Sanja realized the brilliance of it. With a bright smile, she turned to him and looked straight into the blue eyes of what might have been a plumper version of herself. "Change is the only truth. Day becomes night, blue skies grow thunder clouds, summer becomes winter, life becomes death—everything changes all the time. Nothing is eternal in its original form. The surface of a lake ripples endlessly, and no two waves are ever alike. Does that make it a lie? Rocks weather and crumble. Does that mean they are not real or true? And what of fire? Have you ever seen it burn the same way twice?"

"Enough," he said with a laugh. "Please, you have made your point. Quite brilliantly, I might add."

Sanja's chin twitched a little higher, a little prouder.

"However, it still doesn't change *this.*" Passing a hand in front of his face, he changed it from a mud-splattered young boy to a cleric with his hair cropped close to his skull and a scar across one cheek. He did it again, and the cleric became a haggard old woman with missing teeth. One more time and the old woman turned into a swarthy young man.

"Enough," Sanja said, repeating his earlier capitulation, "you have made your point."

She took his waving hand to stop it, and once again, his features settled into the face of Prince Fal.

She tried not to react, but he must have glimpsed something in her face, and his gaze dropped to their joined hands. When she would have pulled away, he held her fast. "Tell me what I look like now." All previous good humor gone, he didn't look at her when he issued the order.

"You are the… You are Prince Fal of Frastmir."

He looked her in the eye once more, his gaze brimming with so many things, Sanja had no names for them. She dug her heel into the ground to keep a shiver at bay as he finally let her slip free.

As the last contact between them broke, his face changed into an older woman with one eye grown shut. "And now?"

Sanja shook her head, her gaze skittering away. She still felt his touch lingering in her palm and frowned down at her hand to see if he'd changed it in some fundamental way. It appeared to be the same, but, like his illusions, there was something more underneath. Sanja felt as if she held the warmth of sunlight in her palm. Tendrils of it snaked up her arm with the comfort of a stout fire on a cold winter's day and settled across her shoulders like a warm blanket.

Prince Fal grasped her chin, adding a new spark to the flame, and gently coaxed her to look at him. "And now?"

Cheeks heating, she said, "You are the crown prince of Wilderheim, Your Highness."

His thumb skimmed lightly across her jaw, then his head tilted, and he released her. She saw one of his eyebrows go up in question before he became a young girl with blond curls falling over her eyes.

"Gone," she said.

The blond girl reached out, tugged on one of Sanja's curls, but released it too quickly and became a dark-skinned foreigner. When his fingers tunneled into Sanja's hair, molding to her scalp, Prince Fal appeared once more. "And now?" he asked, much too close.

Sanja forgot to breathe. He was so close she felt his breath on her chin and saw specks of silver in his bright blue eyes. She held still, poised at the edge of something monumental, and it thrilled her, as it terrified her. The prince's palm seared her ear. His hooded gaze mesmerized Sanja until her own eyelids began to droop. Her limbs were rigid, yet her spine melted, pushing her forward, closer…

A bright spark of sunlight glinted off his golden cuff, breaking her out of the strange reverie. Gold. A wide band of it circling the wrist of Wilderheim's future king. Sanja gasped and reared back. What was she doing?

"I must go now," she said, tearing away from his hold and pushing to her feet before he could stop her.

"Sanja, wait!"

"I'm sorry," she said, all but gasping for breath as her heart thrashed. She took off running and didn't dare look back to see if he'd followed her.

CHAPTER 6

"Wait, stop!" By the time Fal regained his mental faculties and pushed to his feet, the quick little squirrel had already made it to the edge of the green. He ran after her, cloaking himself in invisibility before he dived into the market crowd, but as small as she was, Sanja disappeared from sight almost instantly. Fal stopped before a weaver's stall, turning circles and craning his neck to see over the crowds, but saw no sign of her. She'd well and truly disappeared.

His fingers dug into the thick cloth of his cloak. *Fool!* He'd had the first glimmer of hope in his grasp and let it slip right through his fingers. Fal had no notion of what'd happened on the green, but he didn't need ancient scrolls in dead languages to tell him it had been *something*. Something significant and quite inexplicable. He needed to learn what made her the only human in Frastmir who could see his real face. What magic did she hold that could make him so thoroughly lose his own, along with his higher reason?

And why in the bloody world had he let her get away?

A black, winged stallion strolling through the crowds tossed his head in agitation as he passed Fal and abruptly spread his massive wings, sending everyone in the vicinity scurrying for cover. Winged horses were notorious for their tempers—when threatened or angered, they breathed fire.

Having cleared almost half of the market square, the stallion stomped his front hoof, snorting smoke. His wings beat as if he was preparing to take flight, swaying wicker baskets where they hung from lines behind Fal. Large black feathers broke loose and floated to the ground, instantly turning to ash where they landed—a natural precaution that prevented anyone from using them to bend the winged horse to their will.

With one red eye trained in Fal's direction, the stallion snorted again and tossed his head. Then, as if he'd lost interest, his wings settled back against his sides, and he continued on, the frightened crowds parting before him to give him a wide berth.

In the open space the stallion left in his wake, Fal caught a flash of movement and, without thought, he ran after it, away from the market, into the maze of small alleyways of Frastmir's underbelly.

Here, the castle's walls cast long shadows over weathered little shacks and tents where the criminal gamblers, brawlers, and pickpockets fleeced unwary travelers. Armed soldiers patrolled the area day and night but, unless they caught a criminal in the act, they were forbidden from interfering, which made said criminals very clever about hiding their activities out of plain sight.

Fal slowed his step. Out of direct sunlight, rainwater pooled in constant puddles, rendering all wooden slats soggy and soft and creating a gloomy, ominous sight. Fal did not frighten easily, but so much water altered his senses by force. He could see the alley from every angle as if looking out through those puddles, all at the same time. What ought to have been an invaluable advantage became a lethal weakness as his mind struggled to make sense of it all, to sort it into some kind of order and give it context.

A multitude of his own reflections moved around him in flickers of a billowing cloak, making him flinch each time. Water was not fooled by a magic trick as paltry as invisibility. Natural elements could never lie, and thus always reflected only the truth.

Fal pulled his cloak tightly around him, made his steps as slow and fluid as possible, while fragments of reflections flashed across his mind's eye, blinding him to his surroundings. The farther he went, the worse it became until he was forced to stop and lean against the wall of a shack to regain his bearings. His heart beat too hard. His breath came too quickly, and his head swam, making him sway on his feet.

And then the reflections began to move again.

Impossible to tell where from, or how many. Fal, already off balance and half out of his mind, panicked. Rugged, dirty faces flashed in grotesque swirls all around him, gruff voices echoed, incomprehensible but threatening all the same. The glint of a weapon caught his eye, reflecting a dozen times from different angles. Was he surrounded, or facing a single opponent? Had his invisibility spell failed? Fal had no way of knowing. Shaking from head to toe, he did the only thing he could think of. He pushed away from the wall, leaped for the largest puddle on the ground, and bent the element to his desperate will, falling through the surface into its primordial core.

Water enveloped him instantly in a cocoon of glittering light. His soul responded to its embrace, opening eagerly to join with the element, even as he perceived ice crystals beginning to form. Even as his human body struggled not to breathe—not to drown. He sent his will into the element one more time, creating a current to carry him back to his own world. In his own chambers, a shallow copper basin spat him out with a splash, and Fal collapsed onto his side, gasping for air.

With shaking hands, he undid the clasp of his sodden cloak and fought his way free of its weight. With a thought, he dried the rest of his clothes, returning scattered water droplets back into the basin.

Hands roughened by swordplay grasped his arm, pulling him up to his feet. "I leave for a few days and come back to find the crown prince of Wilderheim on his hands and knees. Is this your idea of having everything under control? I am not impressed, brother."

He blindly pulled Liadan into his arms, as much for comfort as for balance.

"You're shaking."

Fal chuckled. "I noticed."

"What's the matter?" Her entire being heated just short of bursting into flame. The warmth melted the chill in his bones until, by the time she released him to spark a fire in the hearth, Fal was almost back to himself.

"Something's happened, sister."

"Tell me," she said, pushing him into a chair and taking the other for herself. "I cannot bear to lose you, too."

So he told her about the girl with wild black hair and a restless mind, and her quest to make her suitor break his troth. He must have sounded like a raving lunatic when he described their conversation and the girl's inexplicable ability to see his true face because that was where Liadan held up her hand to stop the flood of words pouring out of his mouth.

"She could see you? The real you?"

Fal nodded. "But only when she touched me. Skin to skin. She was not at all shy about putting her hands all over me, but nothing happened until she reached a part of me not covered by clothing." At her raised eyebrow, he clarified, "My *hand*."

"And as long as she held it, she could see you?"

"Yes. And when I pulled away, the illusions swallowed me up again."

"Naturally, she must have been terrified. No wonder she ran from you."

Fal flushed. "She wasn't terrified." At least not at first. Not until he'd tried to kiss her. *Why did I do that?*

The infinitely perceptive Liadan tilted her head at that. "She saw your illusions and *wasn't* terrified? Was she stunned into silence?"

A sudden burst of laughter startled Fal. "Hardly. She would have asked a thousand questions had I not stopped her. She talks incessantly, even when no one is around to listen."

Liadan studied him for a moment before a wicked smile made her eyes spark gold with firelight. "You like her."

"What? No!"

"You do, I can see it in your eyes. I must meet this girl. What did you say her name was?"

Fal scowled at his sister as she added more wood to the fire in preparation of seeking out answers from its flames. Fire was an element of the heart, and as such, it always offered multiple visions: those a Seer sought, and those he most strongly desired. Liadan had a singular ability to see the real truth in them—a feat even those with the gift of magical Sight found impossible. But then, his sister didn't merely play with fire; she *was* fire, as much as Fal was water.

Noticing he hadn't answered yet, Liadan sent him a questioning glance, to which Fal responded by shaking his head. She scowled at him and sat back on her booted heels, turning to face him. "You must know this could be the only chance you will ever get to learn more about your affliction and how to heal it. Why do you hesitate?"

"Because I rather think the prospect of the end of all we have ever known takes precedence over my personal problems," he retorted. "Did you yourself not tell me I should focus on that?"

"Yes, I did," she snapped. "Days ago, when I didn't know there might be a chance to accomplish both."

"There isn't."

"But—"

"Liadan, there is no time."

She flushed. "What if she could help?"

"She is human. The only thing she could do is die." He knew the words were a mistake the moment he uttered them.

"That is beneath you," Liadan hissed on a crackle of carefully controlled fire. Fal's apology never made it past his lips as her ire poured out on a torrent of rapid words. "She must have some kind of magic to see through your illusions, and you said she has a sharp mind and can read. Did it never occur to you to wonder if perhaps a fresh pair of eyes might see something we have all missed—precisely because they belong to a human?"

Fal winced, thoroughly chastised and ashamed of himself. It should have occurred to him, and well before now. All these years, the royal family had been so anxious to keep the full truth of his condition secret for fear of the repercussions, none of them had ever thought to consult anyone outside of their own.

How paltry and insignificant it all seemed when there was so much worse to fear now.

Once more, he opened his mouth to respond, and once more, Liadan spoke over him. "And what good do you think you will do against Fenrir if your condition worsens?"

Fal flinched. She was right. He hated to the core of his soul that she was right, but she was still right. He could not answer her.

Still staring at him, Liadan inclined her head the slightest bit, throwing her eyes aflicker. When she spoke again, her voice was softer, kinder. "You know all this, brother. You are far too clever for none of this to have crossed your mind already, and you have never been one to cower away from what must be done. What's holding you back this time?"

What wasn't? Sanja was a human commoner with no magic or formal education. If his people saw him summon her to court on royal business, it would appear as a final act of desperation, or worse, madness. If he approached her informally, he would be seen as wasting time chasing skirts while his kingdom was in turmoil. Either path would risk what little political power he still held, and put her in danger from those who would see him deposed.

But instead of any of that, Fal said, "She is betrothed." It had no significance whatsoever to their current dilemma, yet he couldn't seem to separate the two, and clever Liadan noticed. Her eyebrows raised in quiet speculation, but she stayed silent, letting him talk himself deeper into the muck. "The match was arranged, I assume, to benefit her family. She does not want it, but it seems she cannot refuse the suit." A wry smile turned up one corner of his mouth. "What sort of human girl spends her time looking for ways to get rid of a suitor?"

"One desperate to forge her own fate, I would imagine. The desire for freedom is not restricted to Other creatures."

That was certainly true enough. "What do you suggest I do?"

"Seek her out," Liadan said, sounding annoyed at having to state the obvious.

"Liadan—"

"We agreed. You said I could come back any time and step in if I thought you needed help. Well, like it or not, brother, that time has come. I told you you couldn't do it all on your own. Even Da had Mother by his side to help him rule," she added reasonably, forestalling any argument he might have voiced to the contrary.

She was resolute. Any attempt to drive her out would only result in her throwing a fireball at his head. Fal was grateful. But when it came to the topic of Sanja, "There is another reason for not involving myself with her."

Liadan rolled her eyes in exasperation. "And what is that? What else could there possibly be to keep you from her?"

"That I'm the bloody Prince of Deceit!" Fal exploded from his seat, and as he did, water appeared to flood out of him in every direction until the entire chamber was submerged, and the wooden floor turned soft with shifting sands. Above their heads, the surface churned and foamed, casting long shadows as clouds of sand kicked up around his feet, making the waters murky.

Aside from a wince, Liadan appeared unperturbed by the display. She was still the only one Fal had ever know to withstand the deepest depths of his illusions without drowning in them, including both of his powerful parents.

"I can't simply walk through Frastmir, knock on her door, and ask her parents for an audience with their daughter."

"And so," Liadan said in a thoughtful tone as he paused for breath, "rather than take a chance and hope for the best, you choose to give up. Rather than ask this girl her thoughts on the matter, you choose to take the decision out of her hands completely."

He did not dignify such nonsense with an answer.

His scowl didn't deter Liadan in the least. She seemed determined to make her opinion known. "Fal, you are the most objective person I know. Think it through. Take yourself out of the picture, and think the way that young girl would. You are being forced to marry a man you do not want. What would you do?"

"Seek another solution."

"And what would that be?"

Fal shrugged helplessly.

"Come now, don't tell me you have spent all these years watching your people and learned nothing. That is not like you at all. You *know* the answer. It is only that you don't want to say it."

"You're suggesting I court her myself," he accused.

Liadan shrugged. "I merely asked a question. *You* suggested a courtship."

"The prince of Wilderheim cannot court a girl already betrothed to another man." It would be seen as a gross abuse of power and was forbidden by the laws of Wilderheim's Charter.

The smile she gave him was as sharp as it was wicked. "Who is to say it has to be the prince of Wilderheim who comes knocking at her door?"

The waters around them stilled. Fal met Liadan's glowing gaze, a dangerous idea blooming in his mind.

The fire in the hearth banked low and bright blue, casting heat enough to sting and drawing Fal's gaze into its depths. As the flames flickered, they took on shapes he recognized: himself and the girl. In one moment, the figures stood facing each other, stray flames leaping between them to mimic them holding hands, at first separate, then melding into one. In the next, another figure replaced the one representing Fal, and the flame joining the two figures flared out sideways, *through* the girl, who then disappeared. The fire flared high once more, dozens of individual flames reaching up like a violent clash of spears and swords before it abruptly died down to embers.

Fal blinked his vision clear as Liadan intoned, "They all call you the Prince of Deceit. Perhaps it is time to prove them right."

CHAPTER 7

The preparations are progressing well.

Genevieve smiled, a dark burden lifting from her heart at the voice of her God. His shadow hovered by the heavy drapes the servants had pulled aside so she might see the green.

There, her army generals have assembled to present themselves for inspection. Five hundred generals, each in command of two thousand soldiers, all ready to march on Wilderheim at a moment's notice. The symbol of their faith, a red cross on a field of white, billowed proudly in the hands of the bannermen at each corner and adorned every tabard and shield in a smattering of red and white on the bright green meadow. The sun glinted off their armor, nigh blinding, but a glorious sight to behold.

"Look at them." She preened with pride. "Are they not beautiful? Their armies will reshape the world in Your image. They will bring honor to the rebirth of the Son."

And you shall rule by his side.

Genevieve shivered as a wicked northern breeze swept around her. Summer was at its end and, though these lands never saw a single snowflake, her old bones have become greedy for each waft of chill, soaking it in so well not even her ermine cloak could keep it out. "Is it time?"

Not yet, God replied, his voice contemplative. *But soon. The stars must align just so when the march begins. Else we risk great losses along the way.*

Yes, she knew this all too well. Messengers from Lyria have already delivered no fewer than fifteen missives with King Ulrich's seal, all containing warnings that Synealee's armies would not be tolerated on their lands. Genevieve had expected this, of course. Ulrich was Saeran's cousin, and a close one, at that. Wilderheim had aided Lyria in a time of war once already, and now Lyria was eager to return the kindness—one Genevieve was eager to repay as well.

It was because of King Manfred's familial ties to his brother, Halden, that he had sent Wilderheim's troops to protect Lyria from the Aegiran threat. He'd rushed to their aid, though Lyria hadn't asked for it, and ignored Genevieve's desperate pleas for help as the Aegiran scum had razed village after outlying village, creeping ever closer, forcing her to cede control of a vast tract of land on the other side of Silver Mountains, which now marked the new border between Synealee and Aegiros.

A third of her kingdom—gone.

And all because a man loved his brother more than a lady in distress.

Both were long dead now, but their progeny yet lived, heir to the sins of their fathers. She would show them. Before they died, they would know that Hell had no fury worse than a wounded queen.

I see great turmoil within you. What troubles your mind?

Genevieve hid her quivering hands in the folds of her cloak. She closed her eyes and lifted her face up to the sun, breathing deeply. "I want them to suffer," she confessed. "I want their kingdoms to bleed and turn the ground into rivers of red!"

A cold silence closed around her, making her cheeks heat with shame. The longer it continued, the deeper her shame burrowed, causing her knees to weaken. *Take heed,* God warned on a sharp whisper, *that you do not forget yourself. My mercy is infinite, but so is my wrath. Your duty is to* me.

Genevieve turned at once toward the source of His voice and lowered to her knees, touching her forehead to the woven carpet before her. "I beg forgiveness, Divine One. I have not forgotten Your kindness or the duty You have bestowed upon me. I will not fail You. I swear it on my life."

Your life is not long for this world if you fail. Swear it on your soul instead.

"I do! I swear on my soul I will not fail in the task You have set before me." She would destroy Wilderheim, as her God had commanded her to do. She would kill the crown prince and lure out his whore of a sister, who'd taken up with an Aegiran of all things. Both would water the ground with their blood, and the royal line of Wilderheim would be stamped out for all time.

But it would never be enough. Once her holy charge was finished, she would turn her armies on Lyria, and then Aegiros itself.

God sighed, his shadows billowing out like black smoke. *Rise. It is no good for an old woman to kneel.*

Genevieve obeyed, struggling to raise herself upright. Standing tall once more, winded and flushed, she faced her God with her gaze humbly downcast. "God, I trust Your will and judgment in all things. You have helped me build a vast army to defeat Wilderheim, but how am I to get it there?" He had forbidden her to step foot into Lyria, and that left only a long, arduous, and dangerous march over Silver Mountains and through Aegiros, where bloodthirsty tribes would attack them on sight without the slightest provocation. Even if their losses were minimal, the march alone would weary her soldiers and weaken them before they reached Wilderheim's borders.

When the time comes, have faith, and all will be well, God intoned, filling her with strength and confidence once more. *Do you think I would allow you to fail before you have begun?*

Had she any strength left, she would have fallen to her knees once more, this time in gratitude.

Now, worry no more about what may come to pass. Turn your thoughts to what is.

"Have I overlooked something?" She couldn't have. Her plans have all been guided by His wisdom.

This, I have been saving for the final step. It is a gift I offer. The shadow billowed out once more, and Genevieve held her breath, yearning for a glimpse of her God. She almost thought she saw Him. The shape of a tall figure moved within those shadows, lean and beautiful, youth personified in flawless pale skin and red hair, and ageless wisdom written across His face. Glorious, breathtaking, and terrifying, even cloaked by darkness. Genevieve clutched at her chest, her heart thrashing painfully, perceiving the awful power contained within the confines of His form.

Overwhelmed by it, she was grateful when darkness once more hid Him from sight, leaving behind God's offering: a gleaming sword, standing upright on the tip of its blade, with a sturdy crossguard separating the blade from its handle. It was a magnificent thing, hewn by the Divine. Genevieve could feel it pulsing; could almost hear the sharp blade singing in a shaft of sunlight.

Your army is, indeed, vast, God said, *but your soldiers will need a reason to give their lives for you, one they will be able to see every day, that their faith may be reaffirmed. This sword is imbued with my power. If its wielder be worthy, it will slay any foe with a single blow and protect him from harm. But take heed. If it spills but one drop of innocent blood, its purpose will be lost, and its wielder cursed for all time.*

The warning sent a shiver down her spine. "Who would be worthy of such a weapon?" And such a burden! Genevieve had seen enough of war to know that anything could happen in the heat of battle. When one's life was in peril, a soldier didn't stop to think, only reacted. And when the fight was finished, he took his reward in any form available to him. That brutish, animal part of man was ever controlled by the Devil and could never be stamped out completely, only suppressed and controlled with prayer and thoughts of duty.

Any man who wielded the weapon of God could meet with eternal glory or eternal punishment. Genevieve herself would not have dared such a risk.

This is the final task I set before you, God said, and the sword moved toward her, scratching across the carpet. *Find me someone worthy of this gift. Someone who will be my voice on the field of battle and your successor on the throne of the largest kingdom ever to exist.*

Genevieve reached out to grasp the handle like a cane, and it leaned toward her as she leaned on it in return. Its power thrummed into her palms, made her blood heat with the thrill of upcoming battle. The promise of victory was so close at hand, she could taste it on the wind. Were she a young man, she would march out this instant to join the soldiers on the green.

Such heady power. It terrified her how difficult the sword was to set aside. When she spoke, her words, though meant for her God, were directed to the gift with which He had burdened her. "Your will is my command. I will not fail."

⪻ »·◇·« ⪼

The task of finding one person in a city as crowded as Frastmir turned out to be easier than Fal had imagined. One small scrying spell had revealed Miss Sanja to be the daughter of Gerhart the Carver, currently dwelling in the Wood district on the far side of the city. Now all he had to do was come up with an innocent enough pretext for crossing paths with her. And what could be more innocent than a day at the market?

Cloaked in invisibility, Fal kept to the center of the gathering crowds. Usually, he would avoid making contact with anyone, but with so many people milling about, they hardly noticed a stray bump here and there. And if they noticed, they blamed someone they could see.

Fal enjoyed walking among his people, becoming part of their lives without them knowing. He listened to their stories, watched them go about their days. He knew the merchants closest to the castle so well he could call them friends. Their lives were filled with everyday struggles, little victories, love, and heartbreak. They lived each moment to the fullest.

Or they used to before the sky shattered above their heads.

Here in the western market, the people were strangers to him, and Fal itched with curiosity about them. The market itself was much smaller and sparser than the one he usually frequented. It served the needs of the poorer districts and the occasional traveler with necessities and practical wares, rather than exotic luxuries. But the people were no less fascinating.

He indulged in a slow stroll, stopping by each stall and table to listen in on town gossip.

The beekeeper had suffered a great loss overnight. His bees had dropped dead, and the honey in their hive had turned dark and bitter.

The seamstress smiled, however, for having sold three woolen dresses to fancy travelers the day before. She spoke about buying some expensive cloth at the central market to sew a new dress for her daughter, who was to marry the butcher's son.

But as Fal made his way over to the butcher's stall, he found the family in a somber mood, talking in whispers and forcing smiles when a customer stopped by. The mother kept glancing at the sky before turning her gaze to the cart piled with cloth-covered bundles. The father relented whenever a customer haggled down a price, and the son wouldn't acknowledge either of them, sitting off to the side with his head in his hands.

They would be gone as soon as the last of their meats were sold.

A crystal merchant nearby spun a piece of glass on its thong, reflecting sunlight into Fal's eyes. He squinted, turning away, and his gaze snared on a familiar figure.

With a basket hanging from one elbow, the girl who dreamed of true love strolled from stall to stall, examining the wares. Her curious fingers touched various items of interest, as though she couldn't help herself. The merchants scowled when they saw her approach. When she stopped by their stalls, they turned away, shouting their wares louder to the crowds, but kept a wary eye on their merchandise.

Undeterred, Sanja asked a question or two, and her smile never dimmed when she received a terse, dismissive answer. Fal didn't understand the merchants' reaction. They behaved as if disaster walked among them, yet Sanja didn't seem to mind, taking each scowl and every brush-off in stride.

The customers, at least, treated her with more kindness. Older women smiled and asked about her family. Young men greeted her with winks but, though they spoke to her briefly, they moved on again in haste.

Sanja continued on her path. Curious to know more about her, Fal decided to follow at a discrete distance. Her next stop was the cheese stall, where the merchant came around to stand in front of a low shelf laden with milk jugs when he saw her coming.

Sanja greeted the man with a cheery smile, either oblivious to the nervous twitch in the man's eye or ignoring it. He flinched whenever she raised her hand to point at something. Finally, he accepted a coin for a round of hard cheese and shooed her on her way. Sanja gave him a nod of thanks and a wave farewell as she whirled away with a burst of energy that snapped her skirt out sideways, tipping the outermost jug on the ground. It teetered on the edge of its base and would have settled, had the merchant not rushed forward and accidentally nudged it over himself. The jug broke, spilling milk all over the ground.

"Pox rotted nuisance! Who'll pay for this now, eh?"

Fal shook his head as he passed the cursing merchant. Normally, he would take no pleasure in seeing a man lose even so small a portion of his livelihood. But for the way he'd treated Sanja, Fal was tempted to knock over a few more of his jugs.

Instead, he hurried to catch up with Sanja as she collected root vegetables from a farmer on her way to the baker. There, she stopped and perused the delicacies. He could see by the way her hands clenched in her skirts that she would dearly love to sample several. But when the baker offered her a meat bun, Sanja shook her head and, with a wistful look, walked away.

Could her family be so low on coin she couldn't afford a single bun?

The idea sat ill with Fal. Passing by the baker's table, he quickly snatched up several buns, leaving behind a silver coin for payment.

At the far end of the market, the crowds thinned out. Merchant stalls gave way to shops and taverns, and a little farther down the road, the river marked Frastmir's borders. A wide stone bridge allowed carriages to safely cross its churning white waters. For a moment, Fal's gaze caught on the leaping waves and stuck, watching the foamy figures twirl in the air before splashing down.

The spectacle was breathtaking to him but unnerved those crossing the bridge as the figures leaped in giant arcs over the bridge, raining water down on wary travelers.

So caught up was he in their display, he fell a ways behind Sanja. Luckily, she'd stopped in front of the clothier's shop to admire a cloak hanging on display beside the door. It was a fine thing, to be sure. Thickly woven and embroidered around the edges with an intricate knotwork of vines. A garment his sister might well have worn—and one Sanja might never be able to afford.

But as he studied her face, he saw no sadness or envy, only a sense of wonder as her admiring gaze traced the lines of embroidery from top to bottom. She savored its beauty for its own sake, no doubt wondering how it'd been done.

The same way she'd looked at him on the green.

The longer he watched, the more Fal realized Sanja didn't merely see. She studied everything and everyone.

She tore her gaze away from the fancy cloak to examine her own clothes. They were far inferior and worn through, yet she didn't seem perturbed. Instead, she gamely plucked a carrot from her basket, tore off the limp stems, and wove them in and out of the frayed neckline of her dress. Satisfied with her new adornment, she smiled to herself and raised her chin proudly.

Fal was entranced. He drew closer, careful to keep out of the way of passers-by. With her dark hair and pale skin, and her cheeks pinkened from the sun, she looked like an enchanting earth elemental snuck away to play in the human realm. When she turned away, he followed and, just to see her reaction, let out a stream of illusions to frame her path with wildflowers.

She didn't notice, staring into the distance before her as if she could see over the horizon if she looked hard enough.

He closed the distance between them until his toes nearly brushed her heels as they walked. She was humming to herself.

Distracted by her voice, Fal didn't notice they were on the bridge until water rained down on them. Sanja squealed in surprise, then laughed and twirled back and forth, dancing with the figures. Travelers glared when she got in their way, but Sanja remained oblivious. And the undines delighted in her reaction, performing ever more daring leaps and drenching anyone who complained.

They sent Fal a few looks, too, invisibility notwithstanding. He sensed some kind of playful challenge in the gesture, but they chose not to make themselves understood. They often did that, just to make him feel stupid.

Fal made a rude gesture at them, causing them to whistle back an equally rude response.

Sanja danced back toward him, and he hastily stepped out of her way, nearly knocking himself off the bridge. The undines burst in the air—their form of laughter—and from the river below mocked him for behaving like an untried schoolboy. Another challenge came to him, a dare of some sort, once again incomprehensible, but somehow connected to Sanja.

"Who needs human lads, anyway?" Sanja called to them with a fond smile. "I'd much rather dance with you!" Her words caught him off guard.

Making sure she would see it this time, he wove an illusion across the bridge's stone rail. A swirling line of moss and little white flowers raced from a stone in front of her toward the landing back in Frastmir.

Sanja frowned at it, reached out to a flower, but pulled back quickly without touching it. With a wary look around, she muttered something to herself, then waited.

Fal sent a ripple down the mossy carpet and conjured a bright red flower at the end to draw her eyes.

The invitation was too enticing to refuse. Sanja followed the trail he'd created for her, running her hand over the top of it without touching until she reached the red bloom. That one was real. Fal had anchored it in a crevice between two stones, rooted it all the way down into the ground. Unless someone tore it out, it would bloom again and again with each new season.

But he didn't want Sanja distracted by a flower. Before she could touch it, he bent the flower, drawing her gaze to a trail of bluebells that led away from the bridge, along the river toward the green.

"H-hello? Is anybody there?"

A passing traveler tipped his hat at her.

Sanja blushed and smiled in answer, then quickly turned away, gnashing her teeth. "Show yourself," she hissed under her breath.

Fal kept quiet.

After a moment, Sanja's temper cooled, and she leaned close to smell the red flower, smearing yellow pollen on the tip of her nose. Her fingers closed on the stem, about to pluck it, but she seemed to change her mind. Releasing the bloom with a lingering caress, she turned her back on the bridge.

She was going to head back toward the market, he realized with no small amount of disappointment. But two steps along the path, Sanja stopped. She was muttering to herself again, earning more strange looks from passersby.

To entice her further, he made the bluebells deepen in color.

With a glance at the basket full of purchases that her parents were no doubt waiting for, Sanja sighed, bit her lip in indecision, then resolutely took off, following the bluebells so quickly Fal had to jog to keep pace with her. He grinned to himself, enjoying her unbridled curiosity more than was wise.

When they were out of sight, the trail came to an end at a large round boulder.

"Well, that was disappointing."

Was it now? Fal placed one of the buns atop the boulder and made it visible.

Sanja dropped her basket and stomped her foot. "I knew it! I knew it was you! Where are you, you fiend?"

Fal bit the inside of his cheek to keep his laughter in check. She didn't have a book on her, but there were plenty of other things she could bash him with. Better not risk it. Instead, he placed a second bun next to the first and quickly stepped out of reach as she whirled in angry circles with her arms outstretched, looking for him. The buns went unseen and, worse, uneaten.

"Show yourself! Why are you following me?"

Fal took a bite out of the third bun and held it visible in the air where she would notice. "So, you have never been asked to dance?"

Sanja gasped. "You heard that?" Her cheeks turned red, and she growled. "Oh, I wish I had never met you!" She launched herself at the bun, her only point of reference, and Fal shifted to stay out of her reach.

"Is that any way to speak to your prince?"

"Is that who I'm speaking to?" she countered. Abandoning her assault, she searched the ground for something. Probably a convenient rock or large stick. "How would I know? I cannot see anyone around. I could be talking to myself. I do that often enough."

"And you answer yourself, as well. An admirable gift. Whenever I question myself, I never seem to get an answer."

"Perhaps you are asking the wrong questions."

Fal conceded the point. "Why have you never been asked to dance? You are pretty enough." Enough to snare his attention most thoroughly. Were the young men of Frastmir blind that they didn't see her?

"I am not speaking to you anymore. Aha!" Good gods, she'd found a stick.

"Now, let's be reasonable about this," Fal said, raising his hands in a gesture of peace, though she wouldn't be able to see it. "I am not here for a fight. On the contrary, see the buns? I bought those for you. As a peace offering. And an apology." Of sorts. Though, if she asked him for what—

"An apology for what?"

Bollocks. "Er…"

"You're apologizing, and you don't know what for?"

Fal's shoulders raised in a helpless shrug. "Is that not what a man is supposed to do when a woman is angry?"

The contrary wench swung the stick.

"Yield, yield! I'm sorry!"

"Go away!" She swung again, harder. "I do not have time for this."

"Gods curse it, then let me help."

Sanja froze, stick still raised, but she frowned. "What do you mean?"

"If you put down the stick, I will show you."

After a moment's hesitation, she complied, propping the stick against the boulder within easy reach. "Well?" Curiosity. That was her weakness. She couldn't resist a mystery; he could use that to his advantage.

"I would like it noted that I am willingly putting myself in physical danger to meet you halfway."

Sanja rolled her eyes. "I thought princes were supposed to be fearless in the face of death."

"Death, perhaps, but I don't know a-one who would risk his neck facing you and that stick."

She ducked her head but not before he caught the twitch of a smile. He found himself grinning in return. She was quite charming—when she wasn't trying to kill him for no good reason.

Fal reached into the pouch tied at his waist and brought forth a small, leather-bound book. The cover was unevenly cut and tearing, the spine stitched with a careless hand. The pages within were crumpled and stained, but what they contained could prove quite useful for Sanja. He'd thought it'd been lost years ago and had found it last night purely by chance in Liadan's old chambers. His sister had a wicked sense of humor, and it would pay off for Fal.

"A gift for you. Perhaps it will help you with your suitor dilemma." Making the book visible, he extended it to Sanja, coming only close enough so she could take it from him, but far enough to flee the stick, should she decide to use it again.

There'd be no danger of that, he realized, as long as a book was nearby. The stick forgotten, her eyes widened, and her fingers twitched. "For me?"

"As I said."

"To keep?"

He grinned. "Indeed."

She took the book from him ever so gently and held it before her with both hands, admiring the haggard cover front and back. "What's in it?" she whispered with such reverence, as if he'd handed her a box of untold treasures.

"Unsavory tales no young woman should ever come across," he replied. "Tales of bad men getting their just comeuppance, vengeful women doling it out, all manner of lurid acts, and all of it delivered with a great deal of inappropriate humor by a writer I strongly suspect wasn't all together literate. You will want to read them straight away."

"And I can keep it?"

With her fingers curling tightly around its edges, Fal wouldn't be able to pry it from her if he tried. "Yes, it is yours forever."

Sanja opened the book, traced the words written in a clumsy, untrained hand. "I don't know what to say." She considered it even more beautiful for its humble origins. It was a precious morsel of someone's life forever immortalized on a few worn pieces of parchment and stitched together in a rough leather cover that might have once been a boot or an old garment.

Such a book would never have a place in Frastmir's grand library, yet it had been read by the crown prince of Wilderheim. And now it was hers.

"Your love of books is a thing to behold," the prince said, disturbing her out of her reverie. "I have met clerics bowed over with the weight of their years of study who have never looked at a tome the way you are looking at that thing."

"You don't understand. Someone like me wrote this. This person scraped together whatever was available to create a book so he could document as many stories as could be fitted onto its few pages. And he did not do it for any reason, other than sharing a piece of himself in a way that might endure after his passing. This is…" She fumbled for the right words to describe it. "It is a letter written to me by someone I never knew I wanted to know. It is magic."

"I never thought of it that way," he said after a pause.

"No, of course you would not."

"What do you mean by that?"

Still enraptured by her gift, Sanja shrugged. "Only that books for you mean something different. I imagine you have been surrounded by them since early childhood. You have been taught to read for the purpose of ruling a kingdom. Therefore, books for you are a responsibility, whereas, for me, they are a privilege. Do you ever read for pleasure, Your Highness?"

Another pause. This one lasted so long Sanja feared he'd left. She was about to say more when he chuckled a little without humor. "Do you know, I don't think I ever have." His voice sounded strange. Without seeing his face, Sanja couldn't identify the emotion behind his words, and she wanted to.

"Will you not show yourself, Your Highness? I would very much like to thank you properly."

"It is better that I don't."

"Yes, of course," she demurred, hugging her treasure close. It wouldn't do for the prince to be seen in the company of a poor peasant girl.

"I wanted to apologize for the way I behaved on the green. It was not my intention to insult you or frighten you. I acted selfishly, and, as my sister pointed out, that is not at all like me."

"Then I should apologize for striking you with a book."

"To me, or the book?"

Sanja smiled, flushing with relief. "Both, I suppose. It seems neither of us was quite ourselves." She bit back a wince as she subtly toed away the stick she'd meant to use on him. Violence was not at all in character for her. Except, it seemed, when Prince Fal was nearby.

Happily, he didn't say anything about it. "Peace?" he offered.

"Yes."

She heard him sigh, then felt something brush past her and turned to see one of the buns disappear. "Good," he said around a mouthful. "Now, have a seat, and let's see that book."

Obediently, Sanja sat, and the remaining bun transferred from the boulder to her lap. It was still warm from the baker's oven, and Sanja's belly growled hungrily for a taste. She took a bite and nearly swooned. The bun was so soft it melted in her mouth, the filling just warm enough to make her shiver in delight. She savored that first bite, then devoured the rest of the bun in two more.

After licking her fingers, she wiped her hands clean before picking up the book. "How did you come by this?"

"I strongly suspect my sister either won it in a gamble or stole it from a tavern drunk during the early years she spent in the north."

Sanja gaped at the empty space where his voice was coming from. "The crown princess of Wilderheim spent her youth gambling and stealing?"

"And drinking and brawling. Never to excess, mind. And, according to her, never as the instigator. Liadan has always insisted that any unprincesslike behavior was always provoked. She conveniently leaves out her liking to visit places where such provocation is wont to occur."

"I don't know what to say to that."

"Neither did my parents. But since she has never caused undue harm, they decided to make allowances for her behavior."

Sanja scoffed. "The privileges of royalty." Had she ever attempted anything like that, her parents would have boxed her ears—deservedly so.

She heard him shift about in his seat. "You must understand, both Liadan and I are very much at the mercy of our elements. Liadan's is fire, mine is water, and they rule every aspect of our beings, whether we want them to or not. Liadan requires activity to burn off the excess energy. She is a born warrior who thrives in battle but, without a war, that energy burns too bright to contain."

Sanja absorbed this in silence. "If what you say is true, then the princess must be thriving with her new husband in Aegiros." The region was constantly at war with itself, different tribes fighting for control of its limited resources. "But what about you?"

"I have been asking myself that question for the last six years and—"

"Wait, don't tell me. Your magic is like a lake, isn't it? Fire burns out unless you feed it, but water continues to accumulate. Without at outlet, the lake grows and grows, until it spills out and swallows up everything. Am I right?"

Once again, it seemed she'd rendered him speechless.

"A-are you still there?"

"Our grandfather used to tell us we were cursed at birth," he said, his tone hesitant, as if he was debating how much to reveal. "He performed a ritual on us, a blessing of sorts, but something went wrong, and he swears it was some outside force interfering, swears he felt it twist the magic inside us somehow. When Liadan broke free of her curse in Aegiros, I expected it would heal me as well, but it did not. I never stopped looking for my own cure but, inside, I keep hoping it is only a matter of time, and the curse will eventually cure itself. I keep thinking if I am patient enough, wait long enough, something will eventually change. And then it does, and it is always for the worse."

He stopped there, his pause heavy with the need for some sort of response. Sanja wished she had some advice or words of comfort to offer, but in matters of magic, she was at a woeful disadvantage. "How did Princess Liadan free herself?"

"She died. And then she rose from her own ashes reborn. As you said, fire burns out eventually, until you spark it anew."

"I hope you never attempted to test that theory on yourself."

"Once or twice," he admitted. "As you can see, it didn't quite take."

"Well, of course not. Fire and water aren't in any way similar." And how dare he try to take his own life—the royal heir!

"What do you suggest I do instead?"

"Find a suitable outlet naturally. If the problem is too much magic then, Your Highness, you have an entire kingdom to loose it on. You could cure yourself and help your people at the same time."

"If only it were that simple. But Wilderheim is already steeped in so much magic it cannot absorb any more."

"Then go elsewhere."

"I can't, Sanja. The magic I hold is so great, it could only wreak destruction if I let it loose. Why do you think I have been sequestered in Castle Frastmir all this time? My own parents are worried about the consequences—as are all the Others. They have now banned me from their lands altogether."

"But there must be some way to overcome this, surely."

"Indeed, there must," he replied with a heavy sigh, then seemed to rally. "But it will not be discovered today, so we might as well occupy ourselves with pleasanter things." An invisible finger tapped on the book in her lap, and another bun appeared before her. "You have a lovely reading voice. Will you not read me a story?"

Sanja accepted the bun and opened the book to the first page. Between small nibbles, she obliged the prince and read such stories as would never be told aloud within an innocent girl's hearing. Sometimes, the words were almost indecipherable. Sometimes they made her stutter and blush crimson. And sometimes they made her laugh so much she could hardly breathe.

But all the while she read, Sanja couldn't help thinking of the prince's illusion curse.

She was still thinking about it when she reached the end of the last story but, when she turned to Prince Fal to ask more questions, only silence answered her.

Sometime during the last story, he'd left her without a word farewell.

CHAPTER 8

If the prince's magic could be siphoned off, how would it affect his use of magic? And if he wasn't allowed into Otherlands, might there be a way for him to purge the excess in Lyria, where his royal cousin might give him leave to do so? Or Aegiros, perhaps? No doubt the desert region could do with more water. And why hadn't he tried either before?

These thoughts occupied Sanja's mind most thoroughly during Jarl Steen's next unwelcome visit. She'd learned from previous occasions not to voice any opinions or questions pertaining to magic or Otherlands, as he seemed to be resentful of both. Sanja couldn't determine whether it was because of his lack of magic or his lack of understanding, but evidence continued to mount on the side of the latter.

Given the restrictions imposed on possible topics of conversation, Sanja and the jarl sat together in a room where the only sounds were those of the hens frolicking outside.

He'd put in the effort to make an impression today. His embroidered shirt was fit for royalty, stretching across his shoulders and arms. With his wide belt cinched too tight, he was forced to sit perfectly straight, and whenever he twitched a foot, his polished leather boots groaned.

She'd never seen anyone look so uncomfortable in his own skin before.

The man's face was flushed and sheened with sweat, but a wooden smile remained plastered across his face. Every once in a while, he would take a deeper breath as if to say something but, at a loss for words, he would release the breath on a sigh and hold his silence.

At last, he spoke. "Do you like your gift?"

Sanja mustered what she hoped was more of a smile than a wince. She'd made no attempt to take the offering from him and refused to touch it now as it lay spread out on the table before her. "It is very generous," she said, eyeing the array of iron and leather adornments meant to hold her hair in intricate braided patterns.

Jarl Steen drew himself up and smiled wider, taking her deliberately vague words as praise. "I can't wait to see them on you. Such lovely hair you have. It should be worn in a crown."

A crown of iron. Sanja's head ached just thinking about it.

Leaning toward her, the Jarl said softly, "If you please me well, my dove, I'll buy you a set made of gold." He made some sort of winking grimace she assumed was meant to be seductive. But then his gaze touched on a curl of her hair, and his mouth twisted in subtle distaste.

Come to think of it, his last gift to her had been a set of ribbons. It appeared the jarl had a strong preference when it came to hair. To test that theory, Sanja pretended to sneeze and shook her head to dislodge the thong loosely tying her curls at her nape, letting them slide free and bounce over her shoulder and across her forehead. "Apologies," she said with a smile. "It's a bit dusty today."

He looked from her to the adornments on the table, then back at her with an expectant raise of his eyebrow.

Sanja smiled blandly and folded her hands in her lap, her thoughts drifting.

Were the changing faces an aspect of Prince Fal's overflow of magic? If so, it was imperative he find some way to siphon it off. Illusions were one thing, but what if they were only the first stage of the process? What if, with enough magic behind the changes, they became real and permanent? He might never hold his own shape again. A man whose identity had been instilled in him since birth—how would he bear it if he lost that identity for all time?

"Red," Jarl Steen said at random.

Sanja frowned at him, trying to recall what else he'd been saying.

He grinned. "Red would look striking on you." His gaze slid down her body, and Sanja felt it like slime oozing down her skin.

"Do you intend to choose my dresses for me? If so, I favor more earthbound colors. Greens and browns. Blue is my favorite." It was also the most expensive pigment available.

Jarl Steen chuckled. "My dear, if I had my way, you would have no use for clothes at all. They only get in the way, in any case."

"Then what…?"

He didn't seem to hear her. "Skin like yours should never be concealed. So lovely…" His breathing became more labored as he spoke, and Sanja shrank back in her seat, eyeing the kitchen as her most efficient path of escape.

"You know," he continued, staring at her chest. "Some clans still mark their skin with permanent patterns."

Yes, many Others still practiced the same, and the markings always looked to her like beautiful jewelry they could never lose. Some could even move beneath the skin, which fascinated Sanja.

"They brand their women so the world will know at a glance whom they belong to."

"That is a lie," she blurted out and bit her tongue. She ought not have said that aloud. But how could he make something so beautiful into something so base and offensive? Most such markings, like his own, were a sign of strength and bravery, often awarded to warriors and other accomplished clan members as a great honor.

His fervid gaze met hers, his face darkening redder. "I should like to see them put my clan's mark on you," he said, the threat all the more disturbing for the amount of pleasure he seemed to derive from making it. "It hurts a great deal. But you will bear it for me, will you not?"

"Do you take pleasure in seeing people in pain?"

His palms rubbed along his legs, and a vein began to throb in the side of his shaved head. Eyes growing unfocused, the Jarl's voice became distracted, monotone. "Pain, pleasure. You would be surprised how often they are the same thing." He licked his lips. "I always seek the Moment. I hear it in their voice, a sort of…keening whimper. And I look into their eyes, and I see it there, so beautiful, begging me. Begging…"

The Jarl's mind was somewhere else, a terrible place she instinctively feared as much as he apparently loved. His hands were balled into fists, his shoulders tight, almost up by his ears. Breathing hard, he leaned forward, staring through her, somehow dragging her with him into whatever torment he imagined playing out until she almost heard herself keening, begging him—to stop.

She surged out of her seat and escaped to the window. Hugging herself, Sanja stared out at the sky, counting the lights to distract herself away from the waking nightmare sitting across the table from her. The empty spaces between the lights widened every day as the sky slowly cleared. It ought to be a good sign—the jarl certainly thought it was—but deep down, Sanja worried it was a sign of worse things to come.

As if rousing from a deep sleep, she heard the jarl's husky voice behind her. "I should take my leave."

Sanja shuddered. "Yes, it is time you did." Propriety be damned, she refused to face him as he struggled to lever his bulk out of the chair. She didn't return his farewell when he gave it, nor did she walk him to the door. Instead, she remained hunched over at the edge of the window, hiding from sight, watching him depart. He showed little consideration to his sturdy riding mount, yanking him close so he could swing up to his back. The poor beast looked broken, dragging his hooves slowly down the road, quivering and snorting until the jarl delivered a vicious kick that sent him into a mad, screaming sprint.

She waited only long enough for him to disappear around the nearest corner before she scooped up the offensive hair adornments with the corner of her apron and tossed the lot of them onto the hearth fire. The iron would survive, but at least she could watch the leather burn to ash.

As she did, a full-body shiver overtook her. Sanja shook herself out, wiping off the front of her dress, desperate to remove any lingering sense of Jarl Steen's regard. A shame she'd never be able to wipe his words from her mind.

And I am supposed to be his mistress and share his bed. Subject to his perverse proclivities.

The thought sent her running out the door. She ran into the wind, breathing deeply of the fresh scents of grass and mist it brought her as it swept through her hair and clothes. Sanja held her arms out to embrace it, gave herself up to its cleansing chill, and welcomed it against her skin.

She ran without thinking and found herself at the boulder where she'd read to the prince the day before. Today, the bluebells were gone, but a sea of dandelions spread out from the boulder, atop which sat a tray of sweet buns. "Your Highness?"

"I did not know which flowers you liked best," he said from somewhere nearby. Before her eyes, the yellow dandelions shrank down into the ground and, in their place, sprouted bright red poppies.

Red. Sanja shuddered. "Definitely not those."

They disappeared at once, and tall, thick stalks of sunflowers took their place. They were so tall, their blooms so large, the boulder and its sweet offering disappeared from sight completely. "Too big," the prince decided, reducing the sunflowers to nothing. A carpet of clovers sprouted in their stead, interspersed with bluebells and dandelions in glorious disarray.

The riot of colors soothed her mind and the tension began to ebb from her at last. "Yes, I like those the best," Sanja said, feeling lightheaded with relief. "Are they real?"

The blooms wavered, then settled, filling the air with their sweet scent. "They are now."

Sanja knelt in their midst, unexpected tears stinging her eyes. So much beauty right there at his fingertips. Such a wonderful gift he'd given her. "Thank you," she said. "If you only knew… They are beautiful."

"The buns are real, too. And quite tasty." The tray levitated off the boulder to the ground beside her, and the flowers shifted to make room as the unseen prince seated himself on the other side of it. "I did not know if you would come back."

"I did not know you wanted me to. You disappeared yesterday without a word."

"I fell asleep. And when I woke, you were gone."

"You fell asleep while I was reading? Those stories were anything but boring." Except for the last one. The writer had finished his volume on a sweet, wistful note with a letter to his beloved. Sanja had found it touching and heartfelt.

The prince had fallen asleep. *Men…*

"I think it was your voice."

Sanja gaped. "My voice is boring?"

"No! Not boring. Soft and soothing. Have you ever been on the lake when the winds are calm? The water is never still, and at times like that, it rocks the boat ever so gently. And when the sun shines down to warm you, it makes you feel like a child, with the world itself rocking you to sleep. There is no better lullaby in the world. That is what your voice felt like."

Sanja tugged on a clover's petals, at a loss for words. The casual praise, delivered so earnestly, humbled her and brought her a secret thrill of unexpected pleasure. With a few words, the prince transformed her from a silly, chattering girl too clumsy to learn a trade and too strange to attract a husband, to someone special. Someone worthy of a few stolen moments reading a book. It awakened something inside her that she'd thought she'd extinguished for all time. An impossible hope in happy endings, in the kind of love that filled pages with poems and emotion. An effortless bond the likes of which she'd given up the moment she'd signed her name in blood.

"Why have you come back?" she asked.

"I come with a nefarious plan and ulterior motives, of course."

Sanja gasped. "Dear me, surely not. How fiendish of you!"

Before she'd had a chance to regret her impetuousness, he chuckled. "Indeed, the

Prince of Deceit lives up to his name. I have lured you here with sweet buns to take advantage of you in a most unscrupulous way."

"Oh?" Sanja prudently shifted her seat farther away from him.

"There is no need for alarm," he assured her. "I brought you a puzzle." A small stack of parchment sheets appeared beside the platter of buns. Nothing at all like the book she now kept underneath her pillow, these sheets were perfectly trimmed and starched, the writing on them neat and orderly. "I would like to see what you make of it."

"Is this a test?" Even if it was, Sanja didn't care, already reaching for the puzzle, the sweet buns forgotten.

"Would it bother you if it was?"

She shrugged, but already her attention was focused on the writing in her hands. "You wrote this," she guessed. "But it is not your work."

"How do you know that?"

"The writing feels old. It was transcribed from somewhere else."

"Correct," he confirmed, "on both counts."

Sanja read to the end of the first page, then carefully set it aside to move on to the next. The text had a rhythm to it like a silent melody, and Sanja began to hum to herself, trying to fit the words into a song. At times, she almost felt like she knew it, but it never lasted more than a word or two before she lost it again.

It was the story of the great wolf Fenrir, and the enchanted ribbon forged to bind him. The great wolf, a ravaging beast sired by the Trickster god, Loki, was said to be so terrible not even the gods could best him. He destroyed and devoured everything in his path and was foretold to devour the gods themselves in the final days of Ragnarok, the End of All.

Desperate to escape their fate, the gods tasked a clan of dwarves to forge a chain strong enough to contain Fenrir. If they couldn't kill him, they could at least imprison him for all time. What the dwarves gave them was a delicate ribbon hewn from the blood of Otherkind and the power of all the gods combined.

But the great wolf was a formidable opponent, impossible to overpower, and so the gods devised a trick. They presented the ribbon to Fenrir as a challenge. After all, he was so mighty, and the ribbon was so fine, surely he wouldn't balk at testing its meager strength.

As proud as Fenrir was, he was no fool. He agreed to try the ribbon, but only if Tir, the god of war and their best warrior, agreed to put his hand in Fenrir's mouth as insurance. Tir agreed, the ribbon was placed around Fenrir, and the wolf tried to break it. He tried and tried, but the ribbon held him fast.

Incensed, the great wolf slammed shut his maw, biting off Tir's hand, but it was too little too late. The seemingly delicate ribbon was unbreakable and inescapable, and it bound Fenrir in stasis forevermore.

An odd way to put it. Stasis. A state in which nothing changed—it went against the laws of Nature. The ribbon itself was described in such a way that Sanja imagined not a physical bond, but something that more closely resembled a precise melodic chant winding around the beast in an endless current.

"How interesting." She turned another page.

Once the wolf was bound, the gods took a piece of the ribbon and extended and expanded it to fashion it into the Veil to separate Otherlands from one another and from the world of humans. "I have never read this version of the tale."

"What do you make of it?"

"It's the song of worlds," she replied, lacking a better way to describe it. It did feel rather like a song drifting between realms. And it made an ironic sort of sense. To keep two things separate, there had to be something between them to form a barrier. And that something meant a connection between the two, however unintended. "By forging a tangible barrier between the realms, the gods bound them all together."

The prince made some sort of reply, but Sanja didn't hear. Lost in thought, she studied the text, awed at the secrets it revealed.

If someone could perceive the song, they could find the borders between realms. And if they could feel the breaks and pauses, they could drift in and out of them, pass through the Veil between verses as if through doorways or portals. The wall the gods had intended to forge thus became a series of pathways between Otherlands for anyone who knew what to look for.

When one verse came to an end, the pause before another began weakened the barrier. The Veil thinned at such times, allowing for more beings to pass through with ease. That was why human rituals centered on solstices and equinoxes. The rhythm of the world was part of the song itself. Humans with no magic in them would never be able to pass through the Veil on their own. But when the Veil was at its thinnest and powerful beings were more likely to hear their prayers, humans could beseech Others and the gods, and offer gifts in exchange for their magic.

It explained so much.

"And here, is this it?" The last pages had no words at all, only drawings of different shapes scattered in incomprehensible patterns across their surfaces. Tilting her head this way and that, she studied the edges of one page. "It is almost as if..." Setting the rest of the stack aside, she laid out six of the pages before her with their edges touching. "No, that's not right." Sanja rearranged them another way. "Not that way, either." The symbols didn't match up exactly, and somehow she knew it wasn't because of transcription mistakes. The pattern was precise and meticulously copied.

She felt the prince shifting closer as the platter of buns disappeared to give her more room. As she moved the pages about and muttered to herself in frustration, Prince Fal nudged the sheets into different positions but, no matter how they arranged them, the patterns never fit quite right.

Sanja sat back in defeat. "It's no use. There must be pages missing."

"There aren't. These are all of them." Fal moved two of the pages to different positions, continuing to work the puzzle. Three years of staring at those pages and it had never occurred to him that they might be parts of a larger pattern. Sanja had taken one look at them and seen more than he had after staring at the original tome for days on end. Now that he had the promise of progress, he couldn't stop himself trying to solve it.

A song of worlds…

Why did that sound so right?

He put two pages together, fitting the edges in such a way that the partial shapes on one page completed those on the other. All of them seemed to fit that way, one page completing the other in different configurations but never all at the same time.

A strong breeze blew across the green, snatching several pages up into the air. "No!" Fal gave chase, with Sanja right behind him. He managed to catch two of the pages, but two more slipped through his fingers. Sanja caught one of them while the last flipped over and over in the air out of her reach. Fal secured his own pages, then went to her aid but, as he reached for the page, the wind snatched it sideways. Fal spun around to follow and collided with Sanja, knocking them both to the ground.

With his hand over Sanja's on the page, Fal collapsed next to her, glaring up at the swirling sky above them while Sanja laughed. "It's not funny," he groused. "I almost had it figured out."

"You did not," countered the irreverent imp, still laughing. "Oh, don't frown like that. I am sure you will put it all together again."

Startled, he realized she could see him. He was still holding her hand over the page. Did whatever magic she possessed to see through his illusions also allow her to see through his invisibility spell? Did her touch make him visible to the world, or did it merely pull her into his invisibility spell with him?

Fal ought to be more concerned about that. But, looking into her dancing eyes, he felt himself being pulled into her happiness, an answering smile tickling his insides.

Sanja looked away, up to the sky, her cheeks pinkening with a pretty flush. "So I take it you cannot control the wind." One of her curls had tangled around a clover bloom. With a thought, Fal severed the stalk and wove it through her hair to secure it there. She didn't notice, so he added a few others, adorning the wild black mane with flowers.

"All wizards have some control over the elements. Some more, some less. We tend to focus on our strengths and neglect our weaknesses. My greatest strength is water, and I have dabbled some with earth during my lessons with my mother. I have never had cause or opportunity to work with air, and so it remains a mystery."

Her curious gaze once more settled on his true face with ease, without any comprehension of how impossible a feat it ought to be. "And fire?"

"Definitely a weakness," he answered, burning to know what she thought of him. Did she find his features pleasing? "Fire and water do not mix." Before he'd changed, he'd been considered quite handsome, even by Other standards. Lasses had been forever smiling and winking at him, amusing his father and annoying his mother, who'd pushed him that much harder into his studies to prevent him from becoming vain about his looks.

And then his nature had destroyed any possibility of that all on its own.

"They say the two elements ought to be mutually destructive. Yet somehow, they converged in just the right way inside my sister and me to make us into something unique."

"I heard rumors about a dragon," she said, her voice timid.

"Have you, then?"

"When Others speak of your family, they call you Dragonblood."

"It is true," he said, choosing his words with care. "My father's mother gave us the gift of dragon's blood."

Rumors of King Saeran's growing magic had been raising questions long before he'd defied tradition and taken his royal wizard to wife. The two of them had decided early on that, for the sake of everyone involved, it was better to give their people a small part of the truth than let their curiosity lead them where they ought not go.

Better for everyone to believe a long-ago ancestor had inherited blood from an extinct Otherkind than reveal that a true dragon still lived not far to their north. He might well be the last of his kind, and he'd survived this long by hiding from those who would make a trophy of his head. No one wanted to see him hunted for sport. Human and Other alike, the few who were aware of his existence paid him homage by protecting his secret.

Sanja's expression turned dreamy. "I wish I could have met a dragon. Can you imagine how powerful they must have been for their blood to still affect you this way countless generations later?"

"They must have been a sight to behold." Not a lie. Fal had seen the dragon's true form soaring across the sky. He could only imagine how magnificent an entire horde of them must have been, with their scales glittering in the sun and their massive wings casting shadows across the land.

The dragon rarely spoke about his kind. Fal didn't even know how they came to be, or if they'd once had a world of their own. Alas, on this one subject, his great-grandfather didn't indulge unfettered curiosity. Fal had learned not to ask anymore.

"And here you are, wielding water magic with dragon's fire."

"A poetic way to put it," he retorted. "The truth is, many would consider me and my sister to be abominations."

Sanja turned to her side, quirking an eyebrow for him to keep talking.

Fal shifted to match her, intertwining their fingers to a more comfortable position. In the tall grass, no one would see them unless they came looking. The world at large felt far away, as if the two of them had created a secret little Otherland of their own where no one could trespass on their conversation.

Despite that, or perhaps because of it, Fal kept his voice soft enough that not even the wind could carry his words elsewhere. "We defy everything anyone has ever known of magic, Others, and Halflings. We ought not exist."

"Why?"

A bumblebee droned around Sanja's adorned hair, passing clumsily from bloom to bloom. Any of the noble ladies he'd known would have squealed and flailed to get it off, but Sanja didn't seem to notice at all. Fal weaved more flowers through the seams of her frayed dress, shaping them into patterns of knotwork similar to the ones on the cloak she had so admired the day before. The colorful adornments suited her better than gold and gemstones.

She noticed the subtle movement, but Fal didn't want her attention to stray. He enjoyed having her gaze at him so openly, without fear or disgust. He enjoyed being himself for once without any effort at all. "Different Otherkind can mate," he said to keep her focused on him. "They can sire children, but the bloodlines usually end there. Halflings are always complicated. Their magics are strange, unpredictable, and often destructive. Many die before reaching adulthood. Of those who survive, none have been recorded to have children of their own—until my parents. In fact..."

"In fact, what?"

In fact, it had taken dragon's blood to allow Queen Nialei to conceive and give birth to the twins. To this day, Fal didn't understand the magic behind it—the dragon refused to tell him. All he knew was that it had been powerful enough to change Nialei's soul. It had spared her the fate of King Saeran's first wife, a young, human girl whose life had been drained by a child she'd been too weak to carry.

But Sanja didn't need to know that part. The royal couple's story wasn't Fal's to tell. "In fact," he said instead, "my parents defied all the odds by having twins. Liadan and I are, in many ways, more complicated than ordinary Halflings."

"I heard a wise man once say that the greatest struggles are allotted to those meant for the greatest achievements. The gods put obstacles in our path to make us stronger for what is to come. By overcoming them, we prepare ourselves for our ultimate destiny."

Struggle is the driving force of life, he'd once told Liadan. *Without it, everything dies.* "If that is true, then the gods mean for me to save the world," he retorted, but his poor attempt at humor didn't negate the truth of his words. He had, indeed, been tasked with saving the world. And he felt wholly unequal to it.

Sanja smiled. "Songs will be written about it, I am sure." For a moment, her gaze grew distant, and her smile turned sad.

He didn't like the change and couldn't stop himself asking, "What is it?"

She shrugged and shook her head. "I was thinking about destiny. How strange that my path would cross with yours here and now. In the present, something wonderful can occupy the same stretch of time as something terrible. But years from now, which one will be remembered better?"

"You don't think it can be both?"

She reached out to touch the edge of his hood with a delicate fingertip. "I think memories are a strange thing. We choose which events hold importance to us, but our choices change with subsequent events." As she had done with the cloak the day before, Sanja traced the embroidered patterns along the edge of his hood.

His eyelids grew heavy, but he refused to let her out of his sight for a blink. Fal wanted her touch on him so much he held his breath, held perfectly still for fear any move would disrupt her reverie, and spook her into flight. But he couldn't stop his thumb stroking lazy circles over her hand in his. Whatever spell she cast, whatever magic she employed to snare him so thoroughly, Fal was more than willing to succumb.

"A year from now, you might remember me as the girl who read you a book on the green. Or, when you get back to the castle, you might see, or hear, or do something so momentous, it will define this time in your mind, and you will forget all about me."

Never. For as long as Fal lived, he would remember the strangely brilliant girl with flowers in her raven locks, whispering secrets into his soul. "And what will you remember?"

She met his gaze, her eyes at once determined and vulnerable in a way that roused a strange feeling inside him. "I want to remember this moment." A deliberate way to say it. Fal sensed something else hidden behind her words. He wanted to question her about it, to make her tell him what had put such a look in her eyes. Yet, at the same time, all he wanted to do was make that look go away, to chase off whatever fears she harbored and make her laugh again with the joyous abandon she'd shown mere moments ago.

He reached out and caught one of her shining black curls between his fingers. Holding it up to the light, he watched the tumultuous colors of the sky play across its glossy surface. In Wilderheim, it was tradition for a young lass to gift the lad she fancied with a lock of her hair as a keepsake and an unspoken invitation to courtship. To give of oneself showed trust, for it left one vulnerable to magics.

Fal had never expected or wanted such a token from anyone before. Until now.

Above them, a flash of white briefly lit up the sky, drawing his gaze up. When it had faded, Fal watched in dismay as the last sparks of a blue-green swirl faded from the tumult, leaving behind a tangible void. He didn't know which of the Otherlands had just fallen, but he felt its loss like a burning piece of charcoal lodged in his chest.

"People in the market talk about the sky clearing and pray for the day the last light disappears," Sanja said. "But it's not that simple, is it?"

"No," he replied. "Magic never is." Letting go of Sanja's hair, he sat up and reluctantly released her hand, disappearing back into his invisibility spell. "I must go now. They will be looking for me."

Sanja frowned but didn't argue sitting up in preparation to stand. "Yes, of course. Good day, Your Highness."

He hated the look of disappointment that came over her, the way she shrank in on herself, and looked down. But in doing so, she finally noticed the flowers he'd woven through her dress and hair, and Fal allowed himself to linger a moment longer to watch her stand up and crane her neck this way and that, trying to see it all at once.

He savored her laugh of delight and let it carry him from the green all the way to the castle. Beyond all the troubles of his world, and any other, Fal knew no other sight would be more momentous or memorable as the girl dressed in flowers, dancing in sunlight on the green. And for that, he was grateful.

CHAPTER 9

The new day dawned on a soundless flash of red lightning so bright that, for a moment, all the world turned red, and somewhere in the distance rose an unearthly chorus of wailing howls. It sounded as if dogs all over Frastmir were being torn asunder.

"Gods preserve us!" Olga prayed in the kitchen below.

Sanja, still dressed only in her nightshirt, clutched her windowsill and held her breath as the howling went on and on, piercing straight to her soul with such wrenching fear it set her shaking like a leaf.

And then, as abruptly as it had begun, the howling stopped, and the world outside her window became deathly silent. She watched for movement, but no one dared step foot out of doors after that. Even the animals were quiet, huddling out of sight.

At long last, the red haze cleared, but the silence stretched on.

"All right, then?" Gerhart asked softly.

"Yes," Olga replied.

"All right, Sanja?" he called up the staircase.

"I-I'm all right!"

"Then you best get yourself ready. Jarl Steen will be calling anon."

"Do you think he will?" Olga asked. "Now, after this?"

Sanja didn't hear her father answer.

Prying her hands off the windowsill, she clutched her nightshirt and shored up her courage. It was nothing. Soon, the citizens of Frastmir would flood the streets for the morning market, and by sunset, the entire episode would have been forgotten. What was one more oddity among so many?

But she didn't believe her own lie. Gods, she had not needed a bad omen to weaken her resolve today, of all days.

Taking a deep breath, she sat in front of her table and reached for the shears.

The first cut was the hardest, marking the point of no return. Sanja winced as a curl of glossy black hair severed from her mane. She had to take a breath or two to restore her equilibrium, but after that, the task became easier—a snip here, a snip there, and a few more all around. By the time she'd finished, a fluffy nest of hair lay on the floor at her feet, and her head felt light and chilled.

Sanja assessed her reflection on the surface of a polished brass disc. She'd shorn her hair to just below her ears, and now the curls stood out at all angles around her head in a chaotic display that pleased her immensely. She could have cut it shorter still, all the way to her scalp, as some of the male Journeymen did, but that would have been too neat for her purposes. Satisfied with her achievement, she gathered the shorn locks and tossed them out the window.

Next came her clothes. From the wooden chest beside her bed, Sanja withdrew the bundle she'd hidden at the bottom. Inside was her hair shirt and trousers, procured from the weaver in exchange for Sanja's ivory comb. An exorbitant price, but well worth it in the end.

The garment itched her all over when she put it on. The shirt was too big, causing the V of the neck to gape too wide over her chest and the sleeves to dangle past her fingertips. The hem reached the middle of her thighs and was split down both sides up to her waist. Underneath, the trousers bunched at her waist, where the too-wide opening was cinched with a length of string. It wasn't comfortable or attractive.

It was perfect.

And just in time, too. Someone was knocking on the front door.

Sanja heard her mother's footsteps rush over from the kitchen, and the door groan open on Olga's ready greeting of, "Jarl Steen, welcome!" She raised her voice deliberately so Sanja would hear and come down without needing to be summoned.

Sanja hated when either of her parents did that. Out of spite, she remained where she was, listening in as their guest entered and made himself at home, no doubt by occupying Gerhart's favorite chair. She pressed her ear to her door, but their conversation had hushed to murmurs. She wouldn't be able to hear anything unless she came out.

Well, it would have come to this sooner or later. Sanja raised her chin and reached for the door, but at the last moment, pulled back. Her gaze strayed to the jug filled with wildflowers. What a change a day could make. How different she was today from the girl covered in flowers only yesterday. It all seemed like a beautiful, faraway dream now, but those flowers were real. They were her proof that at least for one afternoon, Sanja, the daughter of a humble carver, had lain in the grass hand in hand with a prince. Whatever awaited her downstairs and forever after, at least she would always have that.

Holding the memory before her like a shield, Sanja squared her shoulders, raised her chin high, and stepped out of her room. Her insides quivered as she padded down the creaky stairs toward her destiny. She traced the wall with one clammy hand to keep herself steady while her mouth and throat dried out more with every step. *Don't falter. He must never suspect the slightest hesitation.*

Gerhart heard her first and came to meet her, already anxious at having kept their guest waiting this long. When he saw what she'd done to herself, his face turned ashen. Sanja gulped to see his hands tremble, but all he said was, "You have a visitor." He did not wait for her response, turning his back as if the sight of her was too much to bear.

Like a lamb to the slaughter, Sanja followed him toward the rest of their meager company until she had no choice but to step out from behind him and face Jarl Steen on her own. *This is it. Fare thee well, Jarl Steen, and good riddance, too!* She was ready to see this done.

Only there was no jarl waiting for her with a quaff of wilted flowers clutched in his meaty fist. Instead, a young man stood there, facing away with his hands at his back as he conversed softly with Olga. Had the jarl sent a messenger in his stead? He didn't wear Steen colors. His clothes gave no indication of rank, station, or trade, though, by his lean form and clean attire, Sanja would guess him to be a merchant or scholar of some sort. Clean trousers and tunic, a long blue jerkin, belted at the waist, and knee-high boots neither old nor new. He had no weapons or purses, nothing she would have expected a messenger or errand boy to carry. Odd, that.

At their entrance, Olga gasped, causing the young man to turn around. He was handsome, by all accounts, but in so common a way he could have been anyone. If Sanja had ever met him before, she had no recollection of it. His ready smile waned a bit in surprise before it spread wider, his blue eyes crinkling at the corners with suppressed mirth. "Miss Sanja," he said in greeting, "it is good to see you again."

"Again? But I—"

"I was just telling Mistress Carver of the book you asked about on your last visit to the library. A truly fascinating volume and a rare one. The brothers were quite impressed with your request."

Sanja's face felt hot with embarrassment. "Forgive me, but I—"

"I must apologize on their behalf. Sadly, they were unable to locate Master Valco's Third Treatise on Elemental Governance in the archives." At this, he turned to Olga to say, "It would have been a wondrous find if they had, you understand. In his day, Valco was renowned throughout Wilderheim as the authority on elemental magics, and his work has formed the foundation of magical study ever since. The brothers were very excited at the possibility that one of his original works might be housed under their roof." Facing Sanja once more, he continued, "But it appears Brother Otto, who had originally brought the volume and recorded it in the registry, took it with him again when he resumed his travels some years ago."

By the time he shook his head with dramatic regret, both Olga and Gerhard wore identical expressions of utter perplexity. Sanja would have laughed, if only she weren't equally as confused. But she repeated the book's title in her mind so she would know to look for it later. It sounded fascinating!

Elemental magic was considered to be the purest of all, and extremely difficult for humans to master. Each element was said to possess its own temperament. To manipulate it, a witch or wizard first had to woo or cajole the element's cooperation, and even then, success was never guaranteed. Those who possessed elemental magic were few and far between. Those who survived its awesome power into adulthood were rarer still. They carried a high rank among wizards and were the only magic workers allowed to hold the title of Mage, though Sanja suspected that most of the clever ones declined the honor. Elemental Mages tended to die young and always in the service of someone whose ambitions far surpassed the limits of the natural order.

"...readily volunteered to deliver their offering," their guest was saying. "I hope Miss Sanja forgives my saying so, but I have never met such an intelligent young lady before."

Gerhart wrung his hands. "All well and good, but books are no substitute for a husband and children."

Looking at Sanja as if her father hadn't spoken a word, the young man added, "I could not resist an opportunity to see her again."

Sanja flushed, grasping for something to say in response. He must have mistaken her for someone else. She'd never seen the man before in her life. Had she?

He broke their shared stare first to face Olga again. "Forgive me. I'm rambling."

Yes, he was. And she *wasn't*—he didn't give her a chance.

"Master Falwyck, I do not wish to be rude, but we are expecting company at any moment. Noble company. Sanja's suitor. You must be familiar with Jarl Steen? And, well—"

"He must not find another keeping company with his betrothed," Gerhart said, glancing out the window as if the jarl was already waiting there.

"Da!"

Gerhart flushed as his wife and daughter both glared at him. But he found his voice to remind them, "You have a contract, daughter."

"Aye," Olga returned, raising her chin, "and what does it say?"

Gerhart began to answer, then stopped himself.

Olga winked at Sanja. "You were saying, Master Falwyck?"

The young man inclined his head. "I have come at a bad time. And I cannot help but impose upon you further. You see, I did not come only to deliver the Brothers' books to Miss Sanja. I came to ask your permission, Master Carver, Mistress Carver, to court your daughter."

Was Sanja dreaming? Was this some fevered hallucination? He could not have said what she thought he'd said.

"We give it gladly," Olga answered at once. "You are most welcome here at any time, young man. And, husband, now we ought to feed the livestock. Let the lovebirds talk awhile." Ignoring his protests, Olga took hold of Gerhart's arm and dragged him out the kitchen door.

Sanja could hear them launch into an argument as soon as the door slammed shut, their voices fading as they went a ways off, well beyond their little chicken coop. How could they leave their only daughter alone with a stranger? He could be a vagabond or a murderer!

"That was unexpected," Master Falwyck said. "Well done, you. The hair, the costume—I am impressed. But I trust you do not expect it all to chase *me* out the door."

Sanja whirled on him. "Who are you?"

The man grinned, his blue eye aglitter. A trickster of some sort, no doubt. And of all the houses he could have chosen to pester, he'd walked into hers. "You don't recognize me? Good. Then no one else will, either."

There was something familiar about him now that he'd shed his polite manners. The wry tone, the subtle note of insult somehow mixed with respect in the same breath, the eyes…

Sanja gaped. "*You!*"

He grinned, and his face rippled in a shift so subtle she would have missed it if she weren't looking for it. "Did you know Castle Frastmir has its own royal library? It houses all official records and census documents. Three of my most thorough people have pored over all of them, going back a score of years, and do you know what they discovered?"

The crown prince of Wilderheim was standing in her father's decrepit old cottage, wearing a stranger's face, talking about records and census documents. How had her life come to this level of absurdity?

"It appears there is only one Sanja currently living within the city of Frastmir. An incredible stroke of luck, wouldn't you say?"

Sanja was speechless. Meeting him on the green had been one thing, more like a spell-induced vision than anything resembling reality. Out there, it'd been easy to pretend they were on equal footing, two strangers crossing paths at random on their ways elsewhere. But this…

There was no escaping the harsh contrast of the prince filled with so much magic it created an entirely different shape for him in Sanja's groaning, dark little abode. His presence was no less overwhelming than Jarl Steen's. But instead of making her feel like a helpless doe about to be shot down, Prince Fal left Sanja in a state of utter confusion, feeling out of place, throwing into stark focus how unworthy she was to stand in his presence.

His wicked grin waned. "You are not saying anything. Are you all right?"

"All I wanted was to escape Jarl Steen."

Prince Fal looked around pointedly. "And by his absence, I would say you must have succeeded. My compliments. Was it the hair or the hairshirt that did it, do you think?"

"What?"

He gestured at her, and Sanja remembered what she'd done to herself before coming downstairs. Embarrassed, she ducked her head and fingered the quaff of curling hair at her temple. Though Sanja had fully expected and prepared for her eventual Journey knowing all of Frastmir would see her this way, she hadn't cared about what they might think of her. The opinions of strangers had never mattered to her before. Why should they now?

But she'd never considered that she might find herself in Prince Fal's presence again before then, or that she would feel like an utter fool with him bearing witness to the depth of her desperation. Sanja was battling for her life and freedom the only way she could, but to him, this would be nothing but a jest, a momentary amusement at her expense.

"I think it was the hair," Prince Fal guessed. "Most noblemen like their women pretty and biddable, and *biddable* is not a word I would ever ascribe to you." Sanja wanted to take offense, but he said it with so much appreciation in his voice. Was it part of his illusion? "Take away the beauty of your hair, and… Well, suffice to say your strategy was good." He huffed. "Please say something."

"It wasn't me," Sanja said. She chanced a look at him long enough to see his questioning frown before she dropped her gaze to the floor. "We heard the dogs howl this morning. No one will come out through the city after that."

His mirthful voice gentled when he said, "I did. And others will, too, eventually."

"Why did you lie to my parents about wanting to court me? They will take you at your word, you know."

"Good."

Sanja frowned. "You truly intend to court me?"

"I..." He winced, rolling his shoulder as if it pained him. "Forgive me, I don't want to frighten you, but wearing a single face for so long is extremely uncomfortable. I have to release it." He hunched over, and his borrowed form shivered, falling away from him with a splash. From the resulting puddle, a geyser welled up, flooding the room up to Sanja's knees. She gasped, but aside from a slight chill around her feet that could just as easily have been caused by a draft, she felt nothing.

It's another illusion, she told herself and kept repeating it in her mind as the water rose above her waist to her chest, then above her head, all the way to the ceiling. Breathing was an awkward exercise when each inhale felt as if she was about to drown, but Sanja persisted until her mind adjusted to the strangeness of it.

"I fear I come to you on grave business today," Prince Fal said in his own voice.

Tearing her gaze away from a massive eel twining around her legs, she found the crown prince standing a mere handful of paces away, the hood of his cloak pulled back to reveal his true face. With Master Falwyck's good humor stripped away, he looked a little sad. Tired, too. He was a mere two years older than Sanja, but as the future king, the weight of Wilderheim sat heavy upon his shoulders, causing him to hunch a little.

His dark hair was neatly trimmed just below his shoulders, with warrior braids framing his face on either side. His true clothes, unlike Master Falwyck's, befitted his royal lineage, sewn from rich fabrics and embroidered by a hand far more talented than hers. He wore a silver chain about his neck, and one more at his waist, partly obscured by his cloak. Sanja suspected the adornments served a magical purpose of some sort. He didn't seem the type to wear his wealth on his sleeve—he wasn't even wearing his crown.

"Don't be afraid." His mouth twisted into a bitter smile. "This is merely the truth of what I am—illusions upon illusions, and no way out. I can contain them for a little while, but they always pull me back under in the end, along with everyone around me. This is the only way I can be myself—by flooding everything and everyone around me in illusion. And if I give it free rein, it will only keep growing larger and more convincing."

Fal could feel the water begin to push past the boundaries of this little room already. The walls would appear to be leaking from the outside, water pouring down to pool around the cottage. It would draw notice before long; he didn't have much time. "Take my hand."

Sanja clasped her hands behind her back, shifted farther away. She looked frightened yet unharmed.

"Look around you, Sanja. Do you see the water? The fish? The mud beneath your feet?"

"It's only an illusion," she replied. "It's not real."

"Yet others would already have drowned in your place." He chanced a step closer, relieved when she stood her ground. "Please, take my hand. Let me show you what you do to me."

"Am I meant to swoon at such pretty turns of phrase?"

"What? No. Gods, girl, you must stop wasting your mind on those bloody maudlin poems. Nobody speaks that way."

"You just did."

Fal bit back a frustrated growl. "You have my word as the crown prince of Wilderheim—"

"The Prince of Deceit!"

Fal glared at her until she flushed and drew back. "As charming as I find that name, I would have expected better from you by now."

Head bowed in meek submission, she worried the frayed edges of her hair shirt. "What do you want from me?" Any more of her tugging and the cheap garment would unravel altogether.

This had been a terrible idea. He should never have come here.

But even as he thought it, he took a seat, hoping it would put her at ease and restore her temper. He didn't like seeing her so subdued. "Will you sit with me a moment?" Otherlands were falling ever faster. Time was running out; he needed Sanja's help, and he could not wait any longer.

With the gravity of obeying a distasteful order, she took a chair, then furtively moved it farther away from his.

Fal was at a loss as to how to begin. He'd rehearsed the speech several times in his chambers, and again on the way here, and now that the moment had come for him to speak, he couldn't think of a single word.

Sanja's foot tapped out a nervous rhythm, waiting for him to say something. "What, already?"

"Do not rush me, woman, this is important."

She scowled.

Her lack of concern was unsurprising, given she didn't know what was happening, but even so, "Have you not seen the lights in the sky? Did you sleep through the storm that caused them?"

Sanja stilled. "I noticed. People said it was world's end. Many have left already, and more are whispering about fleeing to Ravetia, of all places. They say if ever there was a place safe from magic…" She frowned, shaking her head. "It's all nonsense, of course." It wasn't a question, but the way she looked at him, with hope and expectation that he, the crown prince, would surely allay her fears, made it one.

Fal struggled to speak, the words heavy and creeping their way out barely above a whisper. "It is not."

"What do you mean?"

"The people are right to fear. Our kingdom is ending," he said.

"Our kingdom is…"

"Ending," Fal supplied. "The storm, the sky, the howling… The Veil is gone, Sanja. Ragnarok is coming for us fast. The lights fading from our sky? Each one is an Otherland falling to Fenrir's advance. He will destroy anything with the smallest trace of magic inside it."

Her face grew pale, and her eyes rounded even as her eyebrows drew together in a frown. "Respectfully, Your Highness, such jests are in very poor taste." Despite her dry tone, her voice was unsteady.

"I think there may be a way to keep Wilderheim safe. But I need your help to find it."

"You are serious."

"The end of everything is not something anyone would jest about. You already knew there is more to the lights than meets the eye. You said so yourself. Now you know what it is."

"If the Veil is gone, then…" Her eyes grew wide. "Then that means the gods themselves will lose their power anon. There will be no one left to pray to. Nothing left to stand against our destruction."

"There will be me," he insisted. "And, I hope, you."

"*Me?*" She shoved to her feet, toppling over her chair. He reached out to catch her as she tripped over it, but Sanja pulled away from his reach, keeping him at a distance. "Have you lost your royal mind?" she demanded, flapping her arm to shoo away a bright red fish swimming too close past her face. "This is a matter for Mages and Others, not a useless, common human. The only thing I could do is die." Color rose in her cheeks while words continued to pour out. "A horrible, bloody death at the hands of some monster, or my own people, desperate to escape. And even if you wanted to sacrifice me for virgin blood—" Suddenly, she became completely still, the annoying fish forgotten. Her terrified gaze met his. "Is that what you want from me?"

"No!" How had she come up with that?

"I don't believe you!"

"Will you let me explain?"

"I think I have heard quite enough, thank you."

If she wouldn't hear reason, he'd have to show her.

Fal reached out and swiftly caught her hand in his, holding on tight when she would have pulled away. "Look," he ordered, stopping her struggles with the power of a royal command. "Look around you, Sanja, and look hard." When she cast a baleful glance about the dry room, he released her and winced as water once again welled up around them. "Do you see now? This is why I came to you."

When he reached for her hand again, Sanja's fingers curled around his, and for a moment, both of them stood in silence, taking in the miracle of a perfectly ordinary room.

His voice, subdued into soft, grave tones, disturbed its intrinsic serenity. "My parents were interrupted in the middle of a long, involved working of Other magic that would have prevented this very thing. When the Veil disintegrated, they became trapped in an Otherland. I cannot reach them, and I cannot wait for them to find their way back on their own. The magic they began must be brought to completion if we are to survive Ragnarok. But how can I finish it like this?"

Gently disentangling himself from her hold, he stepped away, allowing the illusions to return. They didn't flood back, merely faded into being like a trick of the light, or a desert mirage. Underwater, the old, worn chamber took on an eerie air of ageless antiquity. The longer the illusion remained, the more it began to change their surroundings, turning faded drapes bright and new, and worn wood smooth and polished. The old little cottage revived within the water's reach, restored to what it must have looked like when the family still had the means to keep it up.

"You are far from a common human, Sanja. You took one look at the puzzle I gave you and saw something I had never noticed before. You affect me as no one, and nothing ever has. Magic or not, whatever is inside you is strong enough to do what no one else, wizard or Other has ever managed to do before. Including me. And that makes you something I had not dared to pray for in many years: hope."

At this, she brought her gaze to his, speaking volumes while her lips remained sealed by a terrible, wondrous silence.

"If I am to stand against the end of everything, I will need powerful allies to stand beside me. I will need you."

"But I—"

"I cannot promise it will be easy. If half the tales about Fenrir are true, what we're about to face will terrify the bravest of men, and I hate to the bottom of my soul that I must ask you to face it with me. But ask I must. Because if all you do is hold my hand, it will be a gesture far more powerful than any spell I could ever speak."

"Your Highness, I…" She reached over her shoulder as though to tug on a curl of hair that was no longer there. When she encountered nothing, an odd look passed quickly over her face before she bowed her head and clasped her hands before her. "Duty alone would compel my obedience."

He frowned. "No, that is not… I am not giving you an order, Sanja, I am—"

"And, given a choice, it would be my honor to stand by your side and do whatever I could, even if it cost me my life," she said louder, more forcefully, before quieting once more. "But I am not free to make such a choice."

Fal noted the nervous clutch of her hands, the high points of color in her cheeks. She was tense, but not with fear. The boundless energy making her all but quiver in place was nothing as simple as that. It was something else. "There is a contract," he recalled her father mentioning something of one. "With your intended, I presume. Jarl Steen?" Her mother's admission, and a most unwelcome one.

She gave an infinitesimal nod.

"Your father wants this match." But while the man seemed intent on handing his daughter to a titled noble, his wife, at least, had given the impression she might want better for Sanja.

Living in the heart of Wilderheim's castle city, the family must have been either too busy or too disinterested in royal gossip to have escaped the rumors about Jarl Steen. All of them were true. Steen was a savage, refused by every honorable woman he'd ever courted. The only reason King Saeran tolerated his presence at court was that he had no choice. Steen's clan occupied a long swath of land on the Ravetian border. His keeps and his men-at-arms formed the first line of defense against their attacks.

Steen's forefathers had earned and amassed more wealth with their service to the crown than any one man could spend in a lifetime—a fact which had not stopped Steen from trying. He poured as much gold into his lavish keeps as ale down his gullet, and his coins flew as quickly as his massive fists.

Sanja would not last a fortnight as his wife.

And if it came to light that Fal had interfered with his betrothed in any way, Steen would declare war on the crown immediately, and he'd find ample support from the other nobles. Fal would lose the kingdom and any chance of stopping Ragnarok.

"My father was trying to protect me by securing me a husband who could provide for me and settle my family's debts with a bride price. Neither was a prospect he could refuse." Another wretched twist of her hands as she admitted, "I was sold for a pouch of gold coins. My mother insisted on a contract to be drawn to that effect, and Jarl Steen demanded it be signed in blood."

Cold fingers of dread ran up his spine. "By whom?"

"By me."

Blood bound all things with powerful magic not even the gods could undo. A promise sealed in blood could not be escaped, save through death. "What are the terms?"

"A wager, of sorts. One month's reprieve, during which time I must either marry another or complete the cleric's Journey and take my robes. If I succeed in either, my father will receive the full bride price from Jarl Steen, and I will be free of any obligation. If I fail to do either, I must marry Jarl Steen for one third the bride price." Her mouth twisted unhappily. "I have a fortnight and five days left."

Fal gaped, feeling his illusions swirl out like mud around his feet. "What in Frigga's name would possess you to sign such a contract—in blood no less!"

Sanja raised her gaze, her eyes burning defiant. "I—had—no—choice. The agreement was struck without my knowledge. All I could do was mitigate."

The mud spread out, sinking Sanja's feet, and she didn't notice while Fal choked on an irrepressible urge to shake her; to personally drag her father to the stocks and rip Steen's innards out through his throat. "But you said you wanted to rid yourself of a suitor. You must realize the oath will still compel you to wed him, whether he wants you or not."

"Of course I realize that—I am not a simpleton."

"Then why bother?"

"Because I presented Jarl Steen with a challenge, and I am afraid he will do whatever it takes to win. Part of the reason he keeps coming back to sit here with me and endure the painful silence is to take away my time to prepare for the Journey. I fear…"

"What?"

Sanja wrung her hands together, staring out the window to escape his gaze.

"Tell me."

"I fear he will put as many obstacles in my path as possible to make me lose the wager. But if he no longer wants me, he will step back and at least allow me to make the Journey unhindered."

Her insight into the man's character was accurate. Steen hated losing. If he could cheat his way to victory, he would. Knowing he could not interfere with Sanja's Journey once she began, he was doing his best to delay it until she ran out of time.

A blood oath, for all the gods' sake.

Despite facing a most formidable opponent, Sanja's strategy was admirable. To have refused Steen outright would have sent the man into a rage; he would have destroyed Sanja and her parents to save face. Instead, she'd bought herself time to escape his clutches—and Fal suspected she'd made him think the whole thing had been his idea. She'd thought of everything, considered each angle, and addressed every threat to the best of her abilities. It proved to Fal that Sanja's mind was, indeed, a force to be reckoned with.

But wits alone would not be enough to bring her safely through a challenge of this magnitude. Sanja would need all the help she could get to win. "You truly intend to undertake a Journey?"

She shrugged. "No one besides the jarl will have me, Your Highness. What else is a girl to do? The only way out of a blood oath is death."

The way she said it made him tense. All around them, mud churned up into clouds of murk that shaped themselves into a vision. There, just behind Sanja's left shoulder, a bulky figure fell back onto the flat surface of a bed while another, smaller one turned away. The bottom of its cloud flared out into skirts, the top swirling tighter into the shape of a woman's curves as one tendril split off, forming an arm. A second tendril kicked up from the ground, straightening into a long dagger that floated into the female figure's grasp before she stabbed it straight into her own heart.

Fal sucked in a sharp breath, knowing the vision was true—he could read it in Sanja's fervid gaze. If she failed to escape the binds of her contract, Sanja was prepared and resolved to take her own life.

Fal could not permit either to happen. "What if Master Falwyck did?"

She frowned.

"Have you, I mean. Court you." He'd already committed to that much, at least. As long as he kept his mask firmly in place, no one should suspect he was someone else.

"It would not be enough. The contract is specific. I must *marry.* And I cannot marry someone who does not exist."

Then marry me.

The words were there in his mind, not to be spoken aloud. Even if Fal were free to marry by choice, he was still Other, and Sanja was not. Without the dragon there to spare her the ravages of illness, old age, and the magic of his bloodline, the way he'd done with Liadan's mate, Fal dared not bind himself to her. He could not become the reason this inexplicable, vibrant girl's finite life shortened further still.

Nor could he bring himself to walk away. He could feel the boundary beyond which disaster loomed. It was a line so close that one wrong step would bring him across; so thin, a strong puff of air would blow it away. And on the other side, Sanja with her shorn hair and large, sad eyes. The boundless energy within her called to something inside him, keeping him still when he ought to be running the other way, pulling him toward her—toward her doom.

We are all doomed, anyway.

"Then I will simply have to help you through the Journey."

If anything, the proclamation seemed to deepen her confusion. "Why would you do that?"

"Because I need you." With a wry smile, he added, "And because I don't believe it occurred to you that the death to release you from the blood oath need not be yours."

"It occurred to me," she admitted.

His esteem for her rose another notch. "Then, by now, it must already have occurred to you that I need you enough to have your unwanted suitor permanently removed if you asked."

Her guilty flush was answer enough.

"Yet, you have not asked."

"And I will not," she declared stubbornly. "I am not a murderer, your Highness, and I would no more ask someone to kill for me than I would carry out the deed myself. No matter the circumstances, my path was set the moment I signed the contract. The consequences are on my head and mine alone." Fal wanted to argue, but she shook her head and changed the subject. "In any case, you cannot help with the Journey. It isn't allowed."

"No one is allowed to interfere in a Journey, true. But there are ways to ease its torments without breaking the rules. For all I am asking of you, it is the least I could do." Fal knew healing spells that could mend her wounds. He could make certain Sanja had food and drink each night and shelter from the cold so she might rest and recover her strength for the next day. He could mentor her through aspects of the second part of Journey, as well. There were scrolls in the royal library dedicated solely to the Journey procedures and rituals. Fal would have to be careful not to reveal too much, but it could be done. "And once you have passed, you will be free to help me."

"And if I fail regardless?" she asked quietly.

If she failed, that dagger would take her from Fal before he got the chance to learn why Sanja alone in all of Frastmir could disarm his wayward illusions. If she died, Fal would slowly disappear, and Ragnarok would tear Wilderheim apart.

Marry another, or complete the cleric's Journey. "You will not," he declared with a confidence borne of desperation. A fortnight and five days. With Fal's help, Sanja could enter the clerics' sanctuary in as little as a week. "I give you my word. Steen will never have you." Fal would dispatch the wretch if it came to that, whether Sanja wanted him to or not. She was too important to Wilderheim to die so senselessly. Keeping that part to himself, he offered his hand to seal the pledge. "Are we agreed?"

Sanja hesitated for so long he thought she would refuse, but then she put her hand in his. "Agreed."

The moment she touched him, the mud around them drained down through the wooden floor. Bright morning light spilled in through the open window, warming Fal through his cloak. He took a deep breath and drew his shoulders back, the weight of his illusions suddenly gone. He felt stronger, lighter, entirely in control of himself. He could see better and hear the softest sounds as if the fog he'd been wading through for years had suddenly lifted, and all for a simple handshake.

Loath to give it up, Fal held on longer than he ought, enjoying the feel of Sanja's hand in his, the play of light in her eyes, and the charming disarray of her shorn hair.

Sanja's tongue darted out to wet her lips. "Gods all bless, I hope you keep your word."

"I always do."

She closed her eyes and whispered, "Because if you can't…"

He didn't need to look into her mind to know she was thinking of the only other alternative she was prepared to accept.

"It will never come to that," he said, squeezing her hand a little tighter to press the promise into her skin. She swayed forward, her feet shifting her a half-step closer, and when she looked up at him, he saw all of her in the depths of her moss green eyes. All her passion, her fear, her determination, and a sense that, no matter how hard she fought, she would still lose. But she would fight, nonetheless, ready to lay down her life, if need be, rather than give in to despair. As stalwart as any warrior Fal had ever met.

Long ago, during one of his many lectures on warfare, the dragon had told the twins, "Never lose sight of what you are fighting for. The moment you lose your purpose, you have lost the war."

"We fight for Wilderheim," little Liadan had declared proudly.

"Which part?" the dragon had countered. "Wilderheim is a big place, little one. A kingdom is too vast a dream to protect. Your purpose must be small enough to hold onto, and treasured enough to fear losing. For your parents, you are that purpose. And when you are old enough, you will find yours, and that will become your Wilderheim."

Sanja was fighting for her freedom.

And I will fight for her.

As if she'd heard his thoughts, her eyes widened a little, her lips parting in breathless surprise, and once again, Fal felt an intense urge to catch those lips with his own, to steal a taste he had no right to crave. He touched a soft curl at her temple, brushed it back, tracing the delicate curve of her ear. Sanja tilted her chin up a little higher…

Behind the kitchen door, Olga and Gerhart's voices floated closer. *Out of time.*

Fal reluctantly released Sanja and stepped back, painstakingly resuming his shape as the forgettable Master Falwyck. "Your parents are returning," he said when she blinked at him askance. "I will call on you again tomorrow. In the meantime, I have brought you a gift." He indicated a stack of books beside the door, neatly tied together with a length of string.

"But… That is…"

"A fortune bound in leather. Yes, I know. But you cannot very well help me if you don't know what is happening, can you? This is but a fraction of everything I have studied over the years, along with a journal that condenses my findings up to this point. Within those pages are secrets of magics so ancient they have been forgotten by all but time and one very old dragon. I told your parents they have been loaned to you by the library so they would not be tempted to sell them."

"Master Falwyck," Olga called from the kitchen, "will you share a meal with us?"

"To my regret, I cannot, Mistress Carver. Perhaps another time. I must take my leave now." Fal bowed to Sanja's parents, then to her. Holding her gaze, he promised, "Tomorrow."

Sanja nodded, but she was already turning away from him to explore the books. He grinned, charmed by the delicate reverence with which she caressed the topmost book.

Tomorrow they would have more time to talk.

If Sanja could tear herself away from the treasures he'd brought her.

And if he could keep his thoughts on anything other than her lips.

CHAPTER 10

He dreamed of battle. Two great armies clashed all around him, swords clanging and arrows flying. Fire scorched a nearby field, filling the air with thick smoke and obscuring his sight with shadows. The sky was as black as night, throwing into stark relief the soundless flashes of colorful lights winking out into darkness—Otherlands disappearing in rapid succession

Fenrir was coming for them all.

Fal blocked a speartip with his shield, his feet slipping on a fallen banner as the enemy forced him back. He twisted the shield, snapping the tip off the spear, and ran the soldier through. The grip of his sword was drenched with blood, and more of it dripped down his face. He adjusted the chipped shield on his arm and wiped his wet cheek on his shoulder.

Time seemed to slow as he looked at the carnage all around him. The battlefield was littered with hundreds of dead soldiers already, their bodies trampled into the mud by hundreds upon hundreds still locked in battle. He sought Liadan's fire amid the chaos, but far too much of it already blazed left and right, and the din of screams disguised her battle cry.

At his feet, the ground had turned to dark mud, pools of blood reflecting the sky back at Fal. It hurt like a long needle stabbing into him to witness each light going dark. He had no time to mourn them when his own world was dying. Thunder rumbled above, threatening a storm and fear knotted his insides. He looked up once more, hoping it had only been a fluke, but a fat raindrop splashing down onto his cheek confirmed his worst fear.

Fal had to retreat. Already, the air felt thick, and flashes of the battlefield miles away obscured his sight. Shadows flickered all around him amid flashes of a brightly polished blade cutting down his soldiers. He sensed magic in it, as he had each time he'd seen that sword in his visions, yet each time he sought its wielder's identity, he met with darkness.

A soldier came at him, the red cross on his tabard no longer distinguishable beneath the muck of battle. His mind weary and his body weak, Fal blocked the soldier's battle ax with his sword, rather than duck out of the way. The impact forced him to his knees. He gritted his teeth, pushing back with all the strength he had left, to no avail. He could not hold out much longer. That ax would cleave him in two.

Suddenly the solder spit up blood as the tip of a curved blade forced its way out through his chest. Wide-eyed, he tipped sideways, taking his ax with him.

Liadan grasped Fal's arm and pulled him to his feet. Her eyes blazed with fire behind a braid that had fallen over her black horn-crown. Her being glowed with fierce strength like a berserker drunk on the rage of battle. With entire fields burning bright, his sister would not lack for power. "Wilderheim will not die on its knees," she snarled at him through the sharp fangs filling her mouth, reminding him so much of their dragon grandfather. Her grip fed strength into his exhausted body, but nothing would shield him from the madness the rain was about to bring.

As Fal recovered, still connected with his sister, he felt something within her that made him grow cold with dread. "Take to the sky," he ordered. "Now!" Away from the armies, beyond the reach of their weapons.

"And leave you to die?"

"Liadan—"

She shoved him aside to meet another enemy soldier head-on, her curved blade making quick work of him and his three comrades. The two coming for her from the back met with Fal's sword and fell in short succession.

Liadan retrieved her other sword and put her back to Fal's. They were surrounded.

"You must go!" Fal tried again. "For the child's sake, if not mine." Against all odds, his sister had managed to conceive. If there was any chance for the child to survive, Fal had to get her somewhere safe.

He felt Liadan tense at his back. "Won't be the first time I have lost a child. Or the last." She tried to make it sound careless, but Fal wasn't fooled. Her grief was a living thing, coiling inside her, biting at her heart—and now at his.

A vision of women running through a nearby raided village blinded him just as the soldiers attacked. He gave a shout, bringing up his shield to block a thrust and slashed sideways. Between rapid blinks, he saw his enemy again, then Liadan's, then another place entirely.

"Oh, no," Liadan whispered as a few random drops turned into a downpour. She looked back at him, her eyes dimming anxiously. Then a furious snarl turned her face into something beastly, and she faced her enemy once more and screamed, bursting into flame, scorching their foes to dust where they stood as she transformed.

Within moments, the thick mud at their feet turned into pools and creeks, the earth already soaked with too much blood to drain the rainwater away. Fal became blind and deaf to the world around him as everything the water touched flooded into his mind. He saw everything, heard everything for miles around. He felt a thousand deaths, smelled smoke mixed with blood and bile, and tasted hopeless prayers on his tongue, knowing there was no one left to answer them.

His sister's voice echoed through the madness: "Wake up! *Wake up!*"

Fal started awake to the sound of someone banging on his bedchamber door.

"Wake up, brother, you're flooding the castle!"

Drenched with sweat, shaken to his core by the vision already fading from his waking mind, Fal got out of bed and unlocked the door, making an effort to pull back his illusions.

Liadan glared at him from across the threshold. "We have been summoned to a council meeting."

"I can't," he replied, rubbing his face to wake himself up. He felt exhausted. "I have somewhere I need to be."

"Yes, you do. At the council meeting. It was not a request." She frowned at him. "Are you all right?"

There was something he ought to ask her, wasn't there? Something important. Something… The fleeting thought faded away, leaving him with the unnerving sense that a vital detail had slipped his mind. "Make excuses for me, will you? I need to set myself to rights before I can present myself to that hornet's nest."

Liadan nodded. "You look like you fought through a war last night."

The distant sound of clashing swords chased a chill up his spine. "I must not have slept well. It's nothing. Go, you know how they hate to be kept waiting."

His sister snorted. "Our parents have allowed those old dotards far too much freedom if you ask me."

"Spoken like a true queen," he teased, closing the door in her face.

It didn't take him long to put himself to rights and make his way to the council chambers. He walked in intending to tell them the meeting would either be postponed or carry on without him. Sanja was waiting for him, no doubt with plenty to say about the books he'd left with her yesterday.

But there'd be no shirking this meeting. Not when maps were laid out on the long table with bright tokens stacked on either side. Liadan looked up from the map before her, her gaze worried. Something was wrong.

"Your Highness, at last. Now we can begin."

Liadan came around the table. "A moment, Councilors."

"What's happening?" he asked her in a whisper.

"Our ally in Synealee sent word of armies gathering for battle," she said. "The council is of the opinion that we should prepare for war."

"Why? Has there been any indication that they mean to attack us? They could be arming up against Aegiros."

"The thought has occurred to me, and I already spoke to my mate to make sure he will be ready. Not that I needed to." Of course not. The Imarah tribe had only recently reclaimed their valley. Their numbers might be small, but they were all fierce fighters, always at the ready to defend their home by any means necessary. Whoever came to the First Valley seeking trouble would find a swift death on the burning sands.

"Does he want you back?"

Liadan smiled. "Always. But he knows my duty lies with Wilderheim as much as with Imarah." She made her eyes briefly spark with golden fire as she sent him a glare, silently daring him to argue that point. When all he did was nod, her eyes dimmed back to gray, and she added, "Also, he thinks if Synealee does attack Aegiros, I will be safer here."

Fal would wager every book he'd rescued from his tower that Liadan hadn't told her mate Synealee could just as easily turn on Lyria and Wilderheim. If she had, Tir would have demanded she return to his side forthwith.

"But you and I both know Wilderheim is no longer untouchable." She glanced out the window at the colorful tumult in the sky. "Our neighbors know the kingdom is in distress and ripe for picking."

"Where did this warning come from?"

Liadan hesitated. "Sir Jonah. Remember him?"

How could he forget? Some of his favorite childhood bedtime stories had revolved around the group of knights who'd come to Wilderheim in search of a magical cup. It was the stuff of legend, a story of lovers cursed by fate. The royal wizard Nialei, sworn to stand as the neutral right hand of the king she secretly loved. The young King Saeran, pining for his wizard, but sworn to marry an Aegiran for the sake of peace. Nialei couldn't bear to watch it happen, and so she volunteered to act as a guide for the knights.

Their quest led them to the dragon's cave far in the north. And when they returned, everything had changed, including Nialei and the knights.

Over the years, Nialei had remained in contact with them, mourning each one's passing as a brother's until only two remained. Sir Arnaud was a deeply religious man who'd vowed himself into silence in the service of his faith. Sir Jonah was a stalwart soldier in service to Synealee who didn't share the queen's beliefs. Having witnessed magic in Wilderheim, he kept Nialei informed of anything that might pose a threat to her people. He did so at great risk to himself, for in Queen Genevieve's court, treason was met with swift, cruel punishment.

"He sent two messenger birds," Liadan told Fal. "One with news of the armies and the other to inform Mother that Queen Genevieve had Sir Arnaud burned at the stake."

Fal shuddered. "Gods, she's gone mad."

Liadan hugged herself. "Remember what Mother used to say? 'Beware those who blindly bow to one lone god.'"

Yes, he remembered. "Faith is a powerful thing, my dear," Nialei would tell him any time he giggled at the silliness of it as a child. "Even moreso when it is all a people have."

Queen Genevieve was known far and wide as a ruthless zealot. She had outlawed anything she'd deemed offensive to her god, and punishments for such offenses were said to be brutal. Yet her people suffered willingly for the promise of great reward in the afterlife. They prayed no less fervently than anyone in Wilderheim. The difference was, they all prayed to the same god.

Their faith bound them together. It made them dangerous.

"Is Sir Jonah safe?"

Liadan shrugged. "We know nothing of his whereabouts. It used to be safer that way. The less contact between him and Mother, the better. Now? I hope so, but…" She pulled him out into the hallway and whispered, "When I tried to seek him in the fire, my flames went out."

Fal gaped at her. For a tool of Sight to go blind was one matter. For it to disappear completely...

"This is bad, Fal. Very, very bad."

Again, that distant echo of battle teased his mind with hints of something he'd forgotten. "So, we prepare for war." The words felt ominous, final. He clenched his fists at his sides, wishing to all the gods that Nialei and Saeran would come walking in the front gate to take over for their ill-equipped son.

Liadan laid a hand on his shoulder and squeezed. "I am with you, brother. No matter what. Say the word, and my *kharesh* will ride to defend us."

Fal reciprocated the gesture and touched his forehead to Liadan's. "I am grateful. But you were right from the first. We must speak nothing of this to Tir."

Liadan drew back.

"No, I will not have him weakening his defenses to aid us. Your *kharesh* are spread thin enough as it is. I will not have the Fist Valley fall again because of us."

Liadan dropped her gaze and nodded her acceptance. "Very well."

"Liadan, if we go to war—"

"You will have me at your side, guarding your flank." Her eyes sparked with flames as she said it. Sometimes, this side of her frightened Fal a little. "I have my purpose, brother. I will fight for you, and I will not fail." Liadan was a brilliant warrior and a formidable creature in her own right when she shed her human skin and took to the skies as a true Dragonblood. Still, she was his twin sister, as reckless as she was powerful, and that recklessness had already led her to her death once before.

"You will obey my command and retreat on my order," he told her sternly.

She grinned. "I live to obey."

Councilor Olgier cleared his throat in the doorway. "Shall we begin?"

Fal nodded and unstuck his feet from the floor, shoring up his courage for his first war council meeting. But as he crossed the threshold following Olgier, he stopped once more. "I have a task for you, sister, if you are up to it."

≪ »·◇·« ≫

The elements are eternal and ever-present. An aspect of one is but a small part of the whole, creating a tangible connection to the eternal, and thus making the passage from one to another possible.

Sanja read the passage again to make certain her eyes had not deceived her. They had not. If she understood correctly, then Prince Fal had discovered a means of travel through the elements themselves. How fascinating.

She could read his excitement in descriptions of the travel he'd already attempted and was so engrossed in the accounts, the dark stain obscuring the last section of text brought her to an abrupt halt. Underneath it, at the bottom of the page, a hastily scribbled note read, *Waterways between Otherlands frozen. Travel from one to another no longer possible.*

"Oh." How disappointing. But could he still travel without leaving the boundaries of a particular world? Wilderheim, for example?

The journal didn't say. The note must have been made recently.

The next page began with accounts of Ragnarok, citing several different sources.

Prince Fal, it turned out, was meticulous with his record-keeping. His journal was detailed, but concise, written in a neat, steady hand. Sanja was certain he must have volumes of random notations and scribbles somewhere within Castle Frastmir, but what he'd given her showed no sign of them. This was a transcribed summary of what must have been years of intense study. And he wanted her help.

Carefully closing the journal, she glanced at the stack of books she had yet to pick up. If she lived a hundred years, Sanja would never hope to attain as complete an understanding of magic as was contained in only one of Prince Fal's journals.

Yesterday, she'd been worried about failing her Journey. Today, failing *him* worried her even more. What ailed the crown prince of Wilderheim was nothing as simple as a broken bone that could be set and healed with time. It appeared to be more akin to a wasting disease that was slowly robbing him of his ability to exist in reality, and it could not have begun at a worse time. If Prince Fal was Wilderheim's last hope of survival, then he'd just placed the fate of the entire kingdom into her clumsy hands, along with his own life.

What was her Journey compared to that?

And still, he'd agreed to give her all the time she needed to complete it—time he didn't have.

From his accounts, Sanja now knew his condition began to manifest when he came of age. Little things, at first, water appearing to pool where it ought not be, strange leaks where no source could be found. Then the illusions had turned on him, changing his appearance and voice. As more magic had poured out of him and into them, the illusions had grown bigger, more elaborate, and so convincing they'd fooled others into drowning on dry land. Now, the man who always spoke the truth was a living, breathing lie.

His journal described in detail how the illusions spilled out of his control and how the larger they became, the more difficult they were to rein in. Yet containing them required so much effort it exhausted him. His soul was not strong enough to keep so much magic contained for much longer. At this stage, Prince Fal might well be right. If he were to let it all loose, he could destroy all of Wilderheim.

Where was he, anyway? They hadn't agreed on a time, but Sanja would have thought he'd be knocking at her door after first light. They had so much work to do and no time to waste.

He'd almost kissed her. Right there by the open window, with the sun shining down on them, and Sanja's hand in the prince's, he'd looked at her with those brilliant blue eyes and touched her so gently…

And, foolish goose that she was, Sanja had wanted that kiss. Even knowing naught would ever come of it, she'd wanted her first kiss to be magical. Decades from now, when she was old and wrinkled, and reading to little children in the library, how wicked it would be to tell them she'd once been kissed by the king?

And if Ragnarok came for them all, Sanja could face the end of her ordinary life with a smile on her lips for having stolen the smallest taste of magic.

The most dangerous words in the world were *what if.*

What if Gerhart had been right? Only the day before, the idea of living her life surrounded by books had filled her with defiant joy. Today, Sanja wondered…

What if life could be better? What if she could escape Jarl Steen, and have her books, and find happiness with someone all at the same time?

What if the prince himself would have her?

At last, there came a knock at the front door.

Sanja raced down the stairs, waving Gerhart aside so she could admit their guest herself. "There you are—oh."

Across the threshold, Jarl Steen paled. "What have you done?" He shoved his way inside, tossed the flowers he'd brought to the floor, advancing on her with angry steps. "What is this?"

Sanja barely heard Olga speaking to Jarl Steen past the thrum of her heart. She put Gerhart's chair between herself and the jarl's advance, grateful to have speed on her side, but she'd underestimated his fury.

The cottage shuddered with each of his heavy footfalls. He took hold of the chair and threw it at the wall to get at her. "I have made allowances for you, girl. But by the gods, this is too much!" One of his massive hands fisted in her shorn hair dragging her closer as he roared in her face, "Am I to have a hairless bride? I will tear out what you have left, you little bitch! I will teach you what happens when you cross me!"

Sanja screamed, tears of pain stinging her eyes. She clawed at his hands, but against his brute strength, her meager struggles were for naught.

Olga ran for the front door, shouting, "Help! Guards! Guards!"

Sanja was about to die, she was sure of it. Because for all of her qualms of conscience about murder, Jarl Steen did not share them. Prince Fal had been right. She should have asked…

A new voice rang out clear as a bell over the fray: "Halt! Unhand the girl, Jarl Steen!"

"Mind your own," he barked back, shaking Sanja hard enough to make her teeth rattle.

There was movement, then Jarl Steen cried out in pain and dropped to his knees. Sanja broke free, falling to her backside. She scrambled all the way to the wall, with the window right above her and huddled there, watching an Aegiran tilt Jarl Steen's face up with the tip of a curved sword. "You will obey when a soldier of the crown gives you an order," the stranger informed him coldly. The accent was crisp Northern, the voice clearly female, but Sanja would never have guessed her sex, dressed as she was in desert men's garb, with a headscarf covering her hair and face. The crest of Wilderheim embroidered in bright blue on the sleeves of her white shirt loudly proclaimed her an emissary of the crown. It gave her the king's authority to dispense any justice in his name, including executions, if necessary, regardless of the culprit's station.

Sanja had seen many a guardsman wear the crest with pride, but never one dressed like that.

"Poxy desert strays running the streets of Frastmir," the jarl spat. "Mark me, one day you will all get yours." He reached slowly for the sword. If he managed to take hold, he would overpower the guard in a wink. Sanja wanted to shout a warning, but her voice wouldn't work.

She needn't have worried. The Aegiran knew how to handle herself. She pressed the tip of her sword harder into his flesh, drawing blood and forcing Steen back into his place. "Assault and talk of treason. A busy day for you, isn't it?" Without looking away from him, the woman turned her head a little to address Sanja. "My sword could end him here and now if you wish it. You have but to say the word."

Jarl Steen's eyes flashed raw hatred as his gaze darted from the foreigner to Sanja. He dared not utter another word, but his hands quivered. It ought to gladden her to see him in such a state after what he'd almost done. She ought to be leaping at the chance to rid herself of him and his cursed contract.

Instead, Sanja felt sickened by the sight of him, as much as by the knowledge that she was now the source of his fear.

"Sanja," Olga pleaded, though she herself didn't seem to know for what.

As much as Sanja wanted to be free of the jarl, she couldn't stomach the thought of living the rest of her life knowing she'd ended his. "No," she whispered, regretting the word as soon as it left her mouth, but unable to take it back. "Let him go, please."

The Aegiran glanced at her with what might have been surprise. She stood there for so long, Sanja feared her sword would cut the jarl down regardless.

He did, too. Breathing hard, Jarl Steen flushed almost purple as a single fearful moan escaped unchecked past his lips. It was as close as a man like him could allow himself to come to begging for his life.

Sanja almost hoped the Aegiran would kill him. To return to his clan after such a humiliating defeat at the hands of a woman would be a crushing blow to his pride and standing.

After a long, miserable pause, the woman pulled her blade from his flesh. "Hear me now, and listen well. Your life was spared today because of that girl. But make no mistake, the crown will know of your conduct here, Jarl Steen, and it will watch your every move. One wrong word, and it will come down upon you without mercy. Do you understand?"

Jarl Steen nodded as much as the threat of the sword allowed, and the stranger stepped back to let him stand. On his feet once more, he seemed to regain enough of his courage to spit on the floor as he speared Sanja with a nasty glare. Then he turned on Gerhart and Olga, both standing behind the foreigner. "We will have this out another time."

The Aegiran soldier didn't sheathe her sword until the door slammed shut behind him. She came to Sanja and helped her to her feet. "All right?" she asked.

Sanja nodded, dashing away her tears. "Thank you."

Eyes like cold embers studied her. "What was Jarl Steen's business here?" The question was routine enough, but her tone implied she already knew the answer.

Sanja glanced at her parents to explain, but Olga was beside herself, and Gerhart could hardly meet her gaze. "He is my betrothed," Sanja admitted.

The woman shook her head. "No wonder."

"Pardon?"

Her eyes smiled. "Nothing. Pay me no mind. I am only glad I happened by just now. I heard your mother's call for help."

"We are grateful," Olga said at last. "But I am afraid it only delayed the inevitable. I worried this might happen. My girl, you made yourself a lifelong enemy in him now."

"Then why did you make me do this?"

Gerhart sighed. "I wish I had never let him into this house. Forgive me, daughter."

His remorse was genuine, his pain and shame too deep to conceal.

If only it had come before Sanja wrote her name upon that cursed contract.

"Will you walk me out?" the Aegiran asked, already tugging Sanja along. They went out onto the street and circled around to the back, the stranger keeping a sharp eye out for any threats. Jarl Steen was long gone, but he would be back, and next time Sanja might not have a guard to save her from his wrath.

"You have my thanks," Sanja said.

"I should have killed him."

"No, I do not want that." Not for her sake.

The woman looked duly unconvinced, but she let the matter drop. "Has he done this before?"

Sanja shook her head. "No."

"My brother will want to know about this."

"Your brother?"

When they were sufficiently out of sight of any neighbors who might happen by, the woman held her finger to her veiled lips for silence, staring at Sanja until she nodded in understanding. Then she pulled her veil aside to reveal her face.

Sanja wilted against the wall. "Y-you're—"

"*Shh!* No one must know I am here, understand?"

"Yes. Yes, of course, Your Highness."

Princess Liadan of Frastmir, *shensari* of the Imarah tribe of Aegiros, had just saved her from Jarl Steen.

Sanja tried to bow, but the princess pulled her upright again. "What did I just say?"

"Forgive me, Your Highness."

"Call me Lia. Listen, I came on my brother's behalf. He wanted me to give you these." She brought forth a bundle of three small books tied together with string and pressed it into Sanja's arms. "And to tell you that urgent crown business requires his immediate attention. He will not be free to call on you for a few days. He sends his apologies and asks you not to fret. Fal will honor your agreement; he has no intention of abandoning you." Her eyes momentarily warmed to a golden glow as she added, "Neither do I. If we can keep you from that monster Steen, you have my word we will. I will inform the castle guard. They will watch him and make sure he does not come near you again until your contract is fulfilled." *One way or another.* She didn't say the words, but Sanja felt them regardless. "For now, study the books. Fal will send more in a day or two."

Having spoken her piece, Princess Liadan hid her face once more and nodded her farewell.

Their entire world was about to come to an end, his life hung in the balance, and Prince Fal was wasting what little time they all had on petty politics? "What crown business?" Sanja whisper-called after her.

"War," the princess replied over her shoulder, then disappeared down the street.

CHAPTER 11

Sanja heard no word from Prince Fal or Jarl Steen the next day. The house was so quiet the slightest creak of old wood made her flinch. Olga and Gerhart weren't talking and, having no wish to witness their awkward silences, Sanja spent the time in her bedroom, reviewing the tomes on a cleric's Journey Prince Fal had sent by way of his sister.

With everything she'd read already, her mind was as prepared as it could be. It was the physical trek she feared the most. With servants, tents, supplies, and favorable weather, a great number of Journeymen still failed before ever reaching Hallowed Mountain. Sanja would have none of those things, and now that the prince was occupied with matters of war, she could not expect him to help her, either.

To make matters worse, the gentle cooling of autumn felt more like an untimely freeze of winter, casting each morning into a thick, white fog while frost hardened the earth. Patches of snow already adorned the mountain peaks. When the winds were high up there, Sanja could see it blow off in tendrils of translucent white clouds.

If the conditions turned bad, she might be forced to give up to save her own life.

The growing chill could only be a sign of Fenrir's approach. The books had described him as a being of endless winter, heralded by ice and snow that froze not only things but spirits as well.

With the way people had been acting since the lightning storm, Sanja could well believe it to be true. Jarl Steen wasn't the only one whose temper flared more readily these days. Prejudices long-buried and hidden had begun to rise all over Frastmir, and the anger fed on itself, spreading from person to person, turning cool heads hot, and hot heads volatile.

Steen's animosity would only grow worse. A clever man, he was not, but the jarl was powerful in his own right and devious. He would blame Sanja for his humiliation and retaliate. He would have his way sooner or later, despite Princess Liadan's warnings. *I would rather freeze.* Better that, than face Jarl Steen again.

Her scalp had ached through the night, and her stomach had been in knots ever since his assault. Several times she'd woken up in a cold sweat, searching for Steen's hateful face leering at her from the shadows. She'd felt a taste of his violence now, and the threat of more had made her fearful of leaving the house. How much more of this could she take?

None, she decided. With the weather growing worse by the day, Sanja felt her chances of success dwindling. If she waited any longer, she might not make it to the forests, much less up the Hallowed Mountain staircase.

When the sun's light suddenly dimmed, and she saw rain clouds passing in the sky outside, Sanja's path became clear. She closed her book and sought her parents in the kitchen. "I cannot wait anymore," she told them. "I must begin my Journey tomorrow."

Olga clutched her apron. "It's too soon. You are not prepared!"

"I will never be as prepared as I need to be. But my chances are best while the days are still warm." And more time to complete the trek wouldn't hurt, either. She'd already wasted almost a fortnight as it was, and the more she thought about that lost time, the more desperate she became to be on her way.

"But what about that young man, Master Falwyck?" Gerhart tried. "He asked to court you. You could encourage him some."

Sanja blushed. "No, Da." As wondrous as it would have been to have the prince or even Master Falwyck on her side, neither could get her out of the contract. *People like us don't get dashing warriors riding to our rescue. We make do with what we have.* Sanja had her wits, and she had a plan. It would have to be enough.

"But—"

"All the encouragement in the world would not bring Master Falwyck to wed me. I will take the Journey as planned. It is the only chance I have."

Olga whirled away and began rummaging through the cupboards. From one, she withdrew a small clay pot, from another, a worn leather pouch. With shaking hands, she upended both on the table, revealing a handful of coins. She counted them unhappily while Gerhart stared.

"Where did you get that?" he asked.

"Anywhere I could," Olga said, glaring at him. "Don't just sit there, fetch your own. Or do you truly want your daughter to die out there in the cold?"

Gerhart flushed and ducked his head but, though his shoulders were hunched the whole way, he went out to the shed and returned with two more coins to add to the meager pile, and something round wrapped in old sackcloth.

"What is that?"

His face red and his gaze unable to meet hers, he carefully folded back the cloth to reveal an engraved copper plate. The light caught on intricate symbols and patterns around the rim as he placed it on the table next to the coins, and Sanja gaped, feeling its magic crawl like an army of ants across her skin.

"I have seen that plate before," Olga said, staring at it with dawning horror. "At the fisherman's cottage. This… This is Hans'!"

Gerhart dipped a guilty nod.

"You stole it?"

"I did not!" For all the conviction in his voice, he still couldn't meet his wife's gaze for longer than a blink. Looking anywhere but at Olga or Sanja, he confessed, "But I did take it. I went to Hans to beg for a scrap of netting for Sanja this morn. But his cottage was empty. Tools gone, wagon gone, candles burned down."

"Gods, so they did leave after all," Olga whispered, sinking onto the stool. "I bought fish from Astrid just last week. She said Hans cast his nets into the lake three times, and three times they pulled up as many fish as dead things. *Other* things," she clarified.

Sanja shook her head. "So they fled in the night, but left this behind? It looks valuable."

"It would not go with them," Gerhart said. "I saw it where it hung in the kitchen. The wall around it was gouged all over where he tried to pry it off, but it would not go."

"Then how did you get it down?"

"Hang me if I know," he replied. "I touched the rim all gentle-like, and the curst-odd thing dropped from its hook. Right into my hands."

Olga, still staring at the plate, brought her fist to her mouth. "Astrid used to say it was dwarven magic. To bring them luck and keep the house safe. She would never say where she got it, only that it was a blessing in their house. What could be causing this, Gerhart?"

Suddenly cold, Sanja hugged herself. It had to be Ragnarok at work. Whatever magic had bound the plate to Hans and Astrid's house, it was now faded enough to be removed. And that could only mean the Others who'd created it were dying if they weren't dead already.

But she couldn't tell her parents. How could she? They were terrified already, brought low by their bargain with Jarl Steen, and in no position to flee the way Hans and Astrid apparently had.

Sanja bit the inside of her cheek and stubbornly lowered her arms to her sides, clenching her fists. No, she would not lay more troubles at their feet.

With startling swiftness, Olga roused from her stupor and pushed to her feet. She quickly gathered the coins into her leather pouch and pressed it into Sanja's hands. "Take this and go to market. Buy what you can for the Journey. You will need warm blankets and wine to warm you, and dried meats."

"A fire spark, too," Gerhart added, bundling the plate back into its cloth. "The wood is bound to be wet in the forest. You will need something that will help you get it burning in the night." Handing her the bundle, he said, "Take this, as well. Get what you can for it, and don't you let them swindle you! It's worth a silver piece, at least."

Sanja was loath to touch the thing while her skin still crawled with its magic, but Gerhart pressed it into her hold, giving her no choice in the matter. Her father may have started her on this path, but, in his own way, he was trying to make amends and help her succeed.

For his sake, she mustered a smile. "It will be all right," she told him, praying it wasn't a lie.

"Go before the crowds pick apart the wares."

Sanja went.

The market was quieter than usual. The crowds Gerhart had feared were thin, and the merchants wary. Sanja haggled down the price of a thick, woolen blanket until the old weaver woman—a foreigner by the looks of her—shoved it into her arms for a fraction of its true worth. "Take it, curse you. Not worth the trouble, it is." With Sanja looking on in shock, the woman threw her remaining wares into a basket and hurried away.

Several stalls and tables throughout the market fare stood empty, and many a door were closed up tight. Sanja slowed her progress, listening to idle talk and frightened whispers.

"Wilderheim will fall," one voice said. "Mark me, the sky will rain down upon it!"

"The Others have all gone," whispered another. "To the last—disappeared overnight. If you had any sense in that silly head of yourn, you'd run for the hills, same as them."

Sanja paused, frowning at the people around her. She couldn't see a single Other anywhere. Indeed, among those closed stalls and cottages were plenty owned by an Other, including the Wanderer's Tavern Inn.

Those humans who'd come to buy wandered from merchant to merchant, their eyes hollow, and their smiles wan. They conversed little, tarried even less as they gathered what they needed from what was still left. Horses clattered by, some of them pulling wagons piled with possessions, and all of them headed across the river out of Frastmir.

The sense of being watched once more spurred Sanja to keep going. With the merchants wanting for business, she managed to get more for her coin than she'd expected. Not halfway across the market, her basket was filled with small necessities: a fire spark, salve for wounds, charms for warmth, a sturdy satchel, the wool blanket, and a simple pallet for sleeping.

The butcher and the goatherd refused to budge on their prices. It was to be expected. Even in times like these, people still needed to eat and, like it or not, they would pay any price to do so while they could still afford it. Sanja bought a good round of hard, aged cheese from one, and some dried meats from the other. It would have to do. The more supplies she acquired, the more she would have to carry all the way.

The sky lightened with a flash of bright green, then darkened as the clouds above grew heavy. A cold breeze made Sanja shiver. She hugged herself for warmth, ducked her head, and hurried away toward the jeweler's shop. She had but two coppers left and the plate. Succeed or fail, without a means to earn their keep, her parents would starve in her absence. Sanja had to sell Hans' ornate plate to make certain they were provided for. Perhaps the plate would fetch enough to buy a good mule and a small wagon. If Sanja never made it back, at least Gerhart and Olga could escape to safety.

The old man Varrik was just closing the shutters on his shop.

"Wait, please!"

He squinted at her, pulling the collar of his shirt tighter around his neck. "Shop's closed, miss. Come back tomorrow."

"But it's not even midday! Please, I am desperate. I will only be a moment."

Varrik looked around, clearly eager to be away, and she noticed through the shutter he hadn't yet closed all the way that the wares he usually displayed on the shelves behind his counter were gone. Was he leaving, too? Would he be there to see her tomorrow?

"Please," she said again.

He waved her inside, then closed up and lit a branch of candles, illuminating nothing but empty shelves and bare tables all around the shop. "Be quick about it," he told her gruffly. "What do you want? As you can see, I have precious little to sell."

Sanja found her voice as she pulled the copper plate from her bundle. "I am here to sell, not buy." She placed it before him so the light might catch its polished surface. The carvings were deep and meticulous, an intricate design of runes and knots. Though the crawling sensation hadn't left Sanja completely, it had waned a great deal. Its magic was fading.

Old Varrik scoffed at it at first, but then he appeared to notice something worth a second look. Placing his flat palms on either side of the rounded edge, he picked up the plate and turned it toward the light, studying the designs on its face with a thoughtful frown. After a moment, still holding the plate, he glared at her. "What do you want for this?"

At least a silver piece, her father had said, but from Varrik's reaction, Sanja guessed the plate was far more valuable than that. She took a chance. "Twenty silver pieces."

Varrik laughed. "Not on your life, miss. I will give you eight, no more."

"It is worth at least eigh*teen*," she insisted.

Scowling, he set the plate down. "Fifteen. And that is all I have to give. If you don't want it, take your blessing elsewhere."

"I want it!"

Grumbling to himself, Varrik retreated behind a thick curtain. He came back with a pouch of coins and counted them out on the table, scoring each with a sharp implement to prove to her they were silver through and through. Only when Sanja nodded and collected the coins did he pick up the plate and wrap it in a soft length of cloth. "Bad time to give up any bit of magic, let alone one like this. Heed me, lass, take yourself to Lyria or Ravetia. Even Aegiros will treat you kinder than what's about to happen here." Then he amended, "For a while, at least."

He ushered her out the door and closed it behind her. The wind had picked up, blowing in still more clouds and turning the sky as black as night. The mule and wagon would have to wait. Sanja ought to get herself back home before the storm broke right over her. With the small fortune in her belt purse hanging heavy at her side, she kept a wary eye out for any who might try to steal it and set off toward the cottage.

The main street was blocked by a row of horse-drawn wagons, so she turned onto a narrow side street instead. It would lead her past the woodsman's shed. If she asked him nicely and paid well for the firewood, he might let her borrow a wheeled cart to convey it. They had precious little left at home, and Sanja feared the coming nights would be very cold.

Past the green, not two houses away from a great big pile of chopped wood waiting to be bought, the howling wind died down with a suddenness that made her stumble. Sanja looked up. Those ominous clouds were still there, and the lights swirling and flickering through them made the entire sky look like a writhing mass of chaos. They'd had no rain since the sky had turned, and Sanja feared what might come falling from those clouds.

"Get going, girl," she told herself. Today was not the day to let her mind wander.

Out of nowhere, someone snatched her about the waist from behind and lifted her off her feet. Her scream cut off as her captor covered her mouth with a bony hand, and she dropped her basket to claw at him. Aside from an annoyed growl, he showed no reaction to her struggles, holding her up with ease and letting her flail herself to exhaustion right there in the empty street.

Sanja scratched and kicked back, screaming all the while, for all the good it did her. Her captor merely chuckled, turning her to face two more men, both dressed like men of means, yet carrying no marks to reveal their identities. But for those hard eyes and pinched mouths, they looked like perfectly decent men. And they terrified her into silence.

She recognized the one with a beard. It was the selfsame man she'd noticed following her around the market. Looking at his smirk now, she wondered how she ever could have thought of him as harmless.

His beardless companion looked around, then twitched his head sideways in a silent message.

Sanja screamed anew as her tall captor jerked her around and loped off with her into an empty barn. She heard the door groan and slam, sealing them away, out of sight.

"What's this, then?" one of the other men spoke up from behind them, and she heard noises that could only mean he was rummaging through her things and tossing them out of her basket. "Planning to leave without a fare thee well?"

Sanja went cold all over.

"That won't do, now will it?"

Her captor turned around so she could see the mess all over the barn floor. Her precious vials of salve had been upended and tossed aside, the meats and cheeses set beside the door, no doubt meant to be shared among them. The satchel itself was torn, and the beardless man was examining the embroidery along the edges of her blanket, his foot propped up on the crushed remains of her basket.

The man holding Sanja lowered her enough to allow her feet to touch the ground, but he didn't release her. So much shorter than him, Sanja was no match for his strength. She tried, anyway, and managed to do no more than bruise herself. She was terrified, but furious as well, watching through a blur of tears as they ripped apart her precious necessities. No doubt her belt purse would be next, and gods curse the filthy curs! They might as well have killed her.

The one without a beard smirked at her as he balled up her blanket and threw it onto a patch of wet mud. "The master said he cared naught if you lived or died," he mused, looking her over in a way that made Sanja's skin crawl. "But that's masters for ya. Hotheads and cold hearts. No bollocks to do the dirty work, but coin enough to buy them."

He came closer and drew the tip of one finger across her cheek. Sanja shrank from his touch, but she couldn't move far enough to escape him, and her reaction seemed to please him. He speared his hand into her short hair, tugged a curl straight, then let it bounce back. "Unlike our wealthy friend, my brothers and I know how to appreciate the finer things in life, there being so few for the likes of us. And there's no reason to let a morsel like you go to waste, now is there?"

"I have a craving for something sweet, myself," her captor said in an incredibly deep voice, his palm at her waist, trailing boldly up her side.

Sanja panicked. She clutched his hand over her mouth with both of hers and tugged down with all her might, budging it a hair, but even that little was enough for her to set her teeth on him. She bit down on his bony knuckles as hard as she could, tasting blood.

He howled and released her waist to pry her off, shoving her aside into a pile of hay.

The beardless man laughed. "The bitch has bite! I like that."

While his tall, lanky brother cursed him, Sanja got to her shaky legs and darted for the door, but the beardless man was faster. He caught her and spun her around before dumping her on the ground once again, taking a stand between her and her only means of escape. His smile turned vicious as he leaned over her and promised, "I'm going to enjoy hurting you."

Someone screamed outside, drawing his attention away from Sanja and to the third member of their gang as he burst through the door, wide-eyed and deathly pale. He reached out to the beardless man, about to speak, but some invisible force caught him short and sent him flying back outside.

The tall man lumbered out after him, and all Sanja heard was his deep-voiced shout before he disappeared from sight, leaving her alone with the last, and probably the most dangerous one. Seeing his brothers would not be returning, that one pulled a knife from behind his back, clutching it tight at his side. He didn't pay her any mind as she scrambled away to the other end of the barn, keeping his eye on the door as it began to groan shut.

Sanja never heard anyone enter, but she could feel another presence inside the barn with them like invisible smoke. The beardless man tapped the flat of his knife against his thigh, his head turning and tilting this way and that as he listened for the unseen enemy. With his back to her, he gave the appearance of calm and confidence, but his shoulders rose and fell with rapid breaths. Sanja would have enjoyed his distress, if only she wasn't so painfully aware that whatever was hunting these men was not likely to stop with them. She needed to get out somehow, get help.

"I know you're here," said the beardless man, turning just enough for her to see his crooked smile. "I've killed men for less."

A subtle rustle caught Sanja's eye, and she looked down to where a quaff of hay had moved across the ground.

"I've killed Others for less," the man boasted. Had he noticed? If he had, he gave no impression of it.

Sanja watched the ground, waiting for the next shift. It came in the form of a soft wet sound as a footprint depression formed in a patch of mud. A moment later, as the beardless man turned a quick circle, another one appeared farther to his right. The

Other was circling him.

The man gave a shout and slashed a wide arc with his knife, snarling. Another rustle and he did it again on the other side, attacking nothing as the unseen creature toyed with him.

Sanja winced each time he lashed out, shrinking in on herself more and more. He was moving closer toward her, that blade of his now rending the air with such speed and force it left him winded.

"Show yourself!" he demanded. Sweat soaked the back of his shirt; his knife hand was trembling with the force of his fury. "Face me true, you coward Other scum!" A small whirlwind stirred the hay between them, and the man's gaze traveled from it directly to Sanja. "You," he accused. "It's you doing this."

Sanja cried out, throwing her arms up to shield her head as he came at her.

She heard a sickening crack and a scream of pain and peeked out from between her forearms to see the man's knife on the ground, his arm held out with his elbow bent the wrong way. His own weight pulled it straight again as he dropped to his knees, and whatever held his limb up let it go with enough force to swing it into his front.

No sooner did he hunch over to hug it in than some terrible force slammed him back into and through the barn door. His screams faded far into the distance, where the rumble of approaching thunder eventually drowned it out.

With a flare of lightning, the air shivered outside the barn, congealing into the Other's shape. It filled in from the bottom as if taking of the earth to form itself. First, the fringes of cloth sweeping the ground, then up the expanse of a cloak to a hood folded against its back.

The figure turned just as the rest of it solidified, revealing the true face of her rescuer, and Sanja nearly fainted from relief.

Seeing the look on Sanja's face in the shadowed barn, Fal shuddered, cold to the marrow of his bones. For her sake, he made an effort to calm himself and forcefully pull his illusions into the chill, freezing them there before he went anywhere near her. She was shaking, huddling against the far wall as she watched him enter the barn, and Fal wanted to go back out there and kill those men, instead of merely maiming them.

"Are you all right?" A silly question. Of course she was not. He could see that much. But it gave him something to say, and her an easy thing to answer. Her haunted silence terrified him. Fal approached slowly and lowered into a crouch before her. "Did they hurt you?"

At last, she shook her head, but her eyes still wouldn't blink. Then she launched herself straight at him, her arms coming around his neck and squeezing so tightly her entire body shivered.

Caught off guard, Fal didn't know what else to do but put his arms around her. Each of her unsteady breaths rippled through him, made him feel weak, even as a strange new strength caused him to squeeze her tighter into him. He felt it flow from within him to surround her like an invisible shield, and the chill of his rage began to thaw. Little by little, the icy prison melted, and his illusions leaked out once more, carpeting the stomped dirt in lush, green grass, and filling the barn with mist from an unseen waterfall. The air around them warmed considerably until Sanja stopped shivering. It wasn't Fal's doing, but somehow, it was.

"Thank you," she said against his shoulder, her teeth gritted to keep her voice steady. It trembled, anyway.

Had he come by but a moment later… "Do you know who they were?"

Another wordless no. "But I know who they worked for," she whispered. "They as good as told me."

"'As good as?'"

Sanja loosened her hold on him to pull back and, in response, his arms tightened further, refusing to let her go. It felt too good to hold her; too dangerous to lose the grip he had on her as if she would slip through his fingers if he let her out of his grasp.

Fal forced his body to comply, made himself allow a small distance between their bodies. As she retreated, the shield of his willful magic followed, seeping into her skin, causing her to shiver, though her cheeks were pink from the pleasant warmth around them. "You think Steen was behind this," he said, rather than asked.

Sanja's eyes brimmed with tears she refused to let fall, and when she wiped her nose on her sleeve, she rubbed it red. "They never spoke his name outright," she admitted, accepting his arm so he could help her stand. "But yes. I think this was his doing."

Without a name, Fal couldn't officially hold the true villain accountable—especially if that villain was titled. Simply to accuse Steen would have been unheard of for a commoner like Sanja, and Fal couldn't do it in her stead without revealing he'd been meeting with her in secret himself, which would cause all manner of political complications in his already troubled court.

Sanja shook her head a little. "I expected underhanded tricks from him, but not this. This is… "

"The smallest hint of what Steen is capable," Fal supplied, livid with the jarl. This was only the beginning. Royal decree notwithstanding, Steen would stop at nothing to get what he wanted. "*Now* will you let me kill him?"

"You say that so easily as if his life means nothing."

"It doesn't." Not when weighed against Sanja's.

She shook her head. "Who are you? Certainly not the same man who wove flowers into my hair. That man would never have said such things."

"Sanja, you don't understand how dangerous Steen can be."

"I would have given my life for that man on the green," she said, stepping back from him. "But I want nothing to do with this one." As she brought her arms around her middle, the magic she'd somehow taken from him flared a warning, making her skin glow in the darkened barn. It was beautiful, an exotic beast guarding its mistress. Though he knew it couldn't harm him, the sight of it, the knowledge that it had flared against him, was enough to ward him off from her.

Fal was supposed to be the one she turned to when she was scared, not the one she feared. He didn't want her to fear him. But he had to make her understand. "You would defend the man who would see you beaten, or worse?" If Steen had been pushed to resort to this, Fal dared not imagine what else the man might do to keep Sanja from reaching the clerics' temple.

"It is not him I am defending. It is you."

"Sanja—"

"If you do this, you are no better than him."

"What?" A rush of water suddenly burst out of the wall behind her to flood the barn with an illusion of murky rapids that engulfed them up to their waists. Neither of them wavered. The water churned angrily as Fal gaped at her, offended and frustrated by her refusal to see reason. Did she truly not understand how important she was to him? To the kingdom?

Sanja took his hand in both of hers, and all at once, the barn was completely dry again, all traces of his illusions gone. "Please, be better than this. You said I was your hope. I need you to be mine. "

"I will not leave you unprotected."

"Then protect me. But do not make me be the reason you turn into a monster. I felt it in you when you appeared just now. It scared me. And it scares me more that I can feel it in you still." She shivered again. "The jarl's temper is hot; he loses his head to anger and behaves no better than an animal, but you… Your Highness, your anger is cold as ice."

Ice. What a fitting way to describe it. She was right. The moment Fal had heard Sanja scream, he'd felt a biting cold take over him. He'd thought it was his fear for her freezing his bones, but it hadn't been. And, as much as he wanted to be able to say otherwise, he hadn't acted purely in defense of Sanja. His actions had been cold, calculated. Fal had chosen to cause those men pain. And even now, with the weight of Sanja's disappointment all but crushing him, he didn't regret that choice. "They deserved what they got and worse."

"The first two, perhaps," she allowed. "But not the third. You took your time to toy with him. You deliberately made him as afraid as he'd made me."

Fal flushed. "Is that not justice?"

"Was it justice that drove you? Or did you enjoy tormenting him?"

"I wanted to kill him," Fal confessed, feeling the chill shiver along his spine once more. "But I knew you would not have wanted that."

"You rescued me. For that, I shall always be grateful to you. But please promise me you will not do anything foolish about Jarl Steen. He is rich and powerful, and the last thing any of us need is his clan declaring war on the crown."

"I will not live in fear of my own subjects," Fal returned hotly, but even as he said the words, he was forced to concede Sanja's point. Whatever Steen's faults, Fal still needed the man's soldiers. He'd already sent a messenger to summon a full third of their number to gather against the threat from Synealee, and he needed the rest to guard the eastern border. "All right," he relented. "I will submit to your wishes, for now. But don't entertain any romantic illusions about me, Sanja. If it comes down to a choice between his life and yours, he *will* die. I can allow no other outcome. Do you understand?"

She gave a reluctant nod, bowing her head in deference to his royal decree. "I am to start my Journey tomorrow. I will be safe from him on the path."

By the laws Wilderheim's wizards had planted into the earth itself, no one could touch a Journeyman while he or she was moving onward along the path. But once she stopped for the night…

Fal would keep her safe. "Go home, clean yourself up, eat a hearty meal, and rest. You will finish it, Sanja, you are too stubborn not to." He managed a crooked smile. "But if you could, make it quick, will you?"

Thunder cracked outside, the scent of coming rain wafting in through gaps in the walls. Fal's heart began to thud. They'd tarried too long.

Sanja ducked her head. "I know I have no right to ask. But would you escort me home? Please?"

"Sweet Sanja," he replied, distracted by what he could feel coming on the wind. "Any other day, I would do it with pleasure, but…"

Sanja pressed her lips together in a tight line and nodded, dropping her chin lower. Her grip on his hands loosened as she stepped back, and Fal found his own tightening in response.

"Today there is no time for pleasure," he said. "We must hurry before the rain comes." He gathered what few of her possessions were still salvageable, then returned to her, taking her hand in his. His mind focused on the task before him: Convey Sanja safely home, and somehow return to the castle before the rain.

He set off down the street, with Sanja quietly keeping pace with him. She only slowed once to cast a wistful glance at the woodsman's pile of firewood. She must have been on her way to him when those men had attacked her.

Fal squeezed her hand, and she shook her head, hurrying along beside him. The streets were empty, all doors and windows closed against the coming storm. Fal was glad. It meant there was no one around to see him with his invisibility stripped away.

He cast for his magic to pull it back around him once more, and his step faltered briefly at how difficult it was to work a spell he'd done a thousand times before, if not more. It felt as if he was forming it for the first time: arduous, clumsy, and awkward. He managed, but by the time he felt the spell take hold, Fal was winded. How could something so simple suddenly be so complicated? Merely holding the illusion in place around the two of them took his full, constant attention.

"Is something wrong?" Sanja asked. He'd stopped four houses away from her cottage.

Fal looked down at their joined hands. Did touching her drain his magic? No, he felt it as strong as ever, but it was flustered, unfocused as if a lifetime of study and practice had never happened.

"Your Highness?"

Where it usually flared out of control, it now shied away into hiding, making Fal force it out rather than pull it back in. A spell he normally performed without conscious thought now became a complex undertaking, drawing his focus away from more important things—he couldn't work another spell without releasing the first.

Touching Sanja was reducing Fal, a master wizard, into a fledgling novice.

"Your Highness…"

Fal had been so consumed with finding a way to cure himself of his excessive magic he'd never considered what would become of him if he succeeded. How could he stand against Fenrir without the full use of his powers? A lamb to the slaughter and all of Wilderheim with him.

"Fal!"

He blinked at the woman by his side as she squinted up at the sky, and he followed her gaze, flinching as a big raindrop splashed onto his cheek. "I must go," he said, yet his feet rooted to the ground, and his eyes closed as three more raindrops wet his face.

Nothing.

As the rain began to fall in earnest, drenching them both within moments, Fal felt nothing but cold and wet. There were no visions flooding his mind, no hint of the madness that usually reduced him to a raving, writhing mass of agony.

Sanja tugged on his hand, trying to pull him into the shelter of a tree. She had to be freezing. Fal ought to take her home and get back to the castle himself. Instead, he pulled her back to him and brought her into the shelter of his cloak. It didn't keep either of them from getting soaked, but the thick wool at least provided some warmth. For all that water was the element of his soul, "Have you any idea of how long it has been since I have stood in the rain?"

Sanja squinted up at him and shook her head.

"Neither do I. Yet here I am." And as he slowly came to accept that inconceivable blessing, Fal's fear melted away, and a giddy joy filled him to the brim. His laughter must have made him sound to Sanja like a madman, but he couldn't stop it for fear he might break into tears instead.

He picked up Sanja one-armed, not daring to release her hand, and spun around, dancing her down the muddy street with an abandon he hadn't felt in far too long. Still holding her up, Fal jumped into a large puddle. Water splashed up his legs, over the rims of his boots, soaking his feet, and it was a beautiful thing.

"What is the matter with you?" Sanja shouted at him over the storm's din. She was shivering against him, and he, too, was beginning to feel the unpleasant clutch of cold. His fingers were going numb, his face stung with the wind as it blew the storm right on top of them. Lightning cracked down on Castle Frastmir's western tower, and then twice more in quick succession near the green. Any man with sense would be running for cover, yet Fal remained frozen, loath to give up the smallest part of this moment.

Sanja would never know the gift she had given him, simply by being there, holding the world at bay. Were he a braver man, he would tell her and risk terrifying her into fleeing. Were he an honest man, he would tell her she was now irreversibly bound to his company for as long as she lived. But in that moment, Fal was neither brave nor honest. He was the Prince of Deceit, and Sanja was the only thing keeping him from drowning.

Ragnarok be damned. He didn't care about Synealee, or Wilderheim, or the Otherlands. In that moment, he didn't want his magic back. All he wanted was more of this: cold rain on his face, peace in his mind, and Sanja in his arms.

She made him feel human. He could love her, just for that.

Another flash brought lightning roots streaking across the sky. Sanja gasped, flinching closer against him. The rain had soaked her short hair to her scalp, and as she hid her face into his shoulder, Fal could see the pale elegance of her nape. He set her down to free his hand so he could cup the back of her neck. A drop of rain rolled down its center beneath his palm, and he felt it run all the way down her spine as if he were tracing his fingertips along its path to where it soaked into her clothing at her waist.

Sanja pulled back to look up at him, her pale cheek warming with a blush as if she'd felt it, too. He read confusion in her eyes, but no fear. Despite the fright of being attacked earlier and her unease of being caught out in the storm, she seemed to trust him to keep her safe. Another gift and one Fal didn't deserve. It humbled him.

With great care and reverence, he cupped her cold cheek, savoring the feel of her skin against his palm. Though he couldn't hear her, he read his own name on her lips as she squeezed his other hand. Sanja closed her eyes against the driving rain. Without her gaze to focus on, physical sensations washed over Fal, taking him from his own self and into the water that traced Sanja's brow, her cheeks, her lips.

Forgive me, he silently prayed as the water showed him formless portents of pain and sorrow down the path he couldn't stop himself taking. *I will make it up to you—all of it. You have my word.*

He pressed his lips to hers, sealing his pledge with a kiss that removed all other possible futures. Fal didn't care. He kept kissing Sanja, swearing to himself again that, whatever disasters he might be bringing down upon her, he would be there to keep her safe. He would make certain she never wanted for anything.

By all the gods, for all she could give him, and all he would take from her, it was the least Fal could do. And he could not fail.

Sanja made a small sound that tasted like a drop of honey on his tongue as she softened into him, kissing him back with all the sparkling energy she never seemed to be able to contain. Fal smiled against her lips, pulled her closer still, clutched her hand to anchor them both. His entire body thrummed to the beat of his heart, his magic pulsing within his skin, yet it felt focused. It made *him* feel in control of it.

The pulse became a hum, and then a crackle that made the hairs on his arm stand on end, and too late, Fal realized what it meant.

When the lightning struck, it slammed into both of them with such fury it nearly tore Fal's chest apart. The fire of it seared his insides, made his limbs cramp. He went blind with its brightness, and deaf with the thunder's boom, yet all the while, he felt Sanja with him, suffering the same. He felt her go limp a moment before the awful force released him as well, and he caught her against him.

Through the ringing in his ears, Fal heard voices, people shouting from somewhere nearby. He shook his head and squinted, willing the bright spots in his vision to clear so he could see. Sanja's parents stood in the open doorway of their cottage, beckoning to him and calling for their daughter. Fal wanted to go to them, but moving at all felt impossible with his legs still burning and his arms locked around Sanja. He tried anyway, but with the first step, his knees buckled, and he dropped thigh-deep into the puddle. Standing again was beyond him. All he could do was hold on and wait for his strength to return. Surrounded by water, it should have come to him in an instant. It didn't, and Fal's scrambled mind slowly comprehended why.

He was still holding Sanja's hand.

Seeing Fal was done for, old Gerhart came hobbling out into the storm, hunching his shoulders against the rain. He winced as he got down on one knee and reached for his daughter, but he hesitated, the angry scowl on his face turning into a wide-eyed look of surprise. "You… You're—"

"Keep her safe," Fal managed to say and thrust Sanja into his arms. As soon as the last contact between them broke, Fal fell through the puddle, into a dark, churning vortex of endless water. Its mad current tossed him about without mercy, battered him with chilling blows that forced the air out of his lungs.

Disoriented, on the verge of drowning, Fal struck out blindly, trying to swim his way out. With each movement, chunks of ice struck his limbs, scraped against his face and neck. He was dying.

Terrified, Fal thought of home, fixed the image in his mind, focused his intent on the basin in his chambers, and held on to it as his lungs burned with the need for air. One more time, he struck out, kicked with all his might to orient himself in the current's direction, using its strength to propel him up and out.

The rush of water shot him toward the light, and forcefully expelled him into dry air. Shaking with exhaustion, gasping in lungfuls of air, Fal dragged himself out of the basin. "Thank you, gods," he prayed as he recognized his bedchamber. "I am never doing that again." Collapsing onto the floor, he fell headlong into the abyss of sleep.

CHAPTER 12

When the water swelled in its basin, it flooded through the cage and submerged the dragon up to his chin. Tethered to the wall at his back, his ropes afforded only room enough to keep his head above the surface when he stood on his toes. Sometimes the current sent errant waves to wash over his face, threatening to drown him, but never enough to sink him fully. When it receded, the dragon collapsed to his knees, weakened as if the water had stolen away his fire, banked it to almost nothing.

It was not alive, and yet the dragon could almost believe it could be. The hiss of its current spoke to him, the lap of its waves beckoned in invitation. The floods were his punishment for not speaking back. The water slapped at him and threatened, but eventually calmed as if it understood that drowning him would solve nothing.

In the quiet, sulking lulls, the dragon wrestled with his bonds. The simple ropes were anything but. He could neither claw through them nor burn through them. His immense strength had no effect on their thick braids, and he risked his fangs trying to bite them free. He'd even attempted biting off his own hand to escape. For all that pain, his wounds had healed almost instantly, and he'd not come an inch closer to freedom.

The ring on his finger pulsed with heat, reminding him there was another way. All he needed to do was twist the ring to summon his blood kin, but the dragon refused to entertain the thought of it. Bad enough that he'd fallen for Hel's cruel trick. He would not lead his family into the same trap. For all he knew, it was what Hel wanted. Why else would she have allowed the ring's magic to persist, but none of his? She'd imprisoned him in a 'tween where the needs of his human body were as muted as the power of his dragon essence. He never slept, ate, or drank, yet he felt no need for it. He could grow his claws longer, cover his body with scales, and conjure fire, yet never enough to complete the transformation or affect the confines of his cell.

Whatever this place was, his senses told the dragon he could be kept imprisoned here forever, if his jailer willed it so.

No different from your lonesome cave, Solveig pointed out in his mind.

He shook her away, stabbed his claws into his palms to give himself something else to think about. His cave might have been lonesome, but he'd chosen it of his own free will. It'd had no doors, locks, or binds, and he'd not been alone there all the time. Nialei had visited sometimes, and Saeran. Liadan, too, though not as often anymore, despite the blaze he kept burning in her chamber tall enough for her to walk through any time she chose.

The dragon's human skin prickled with the sense of a presence nearby, and he snarled, yanking on the ropes, only to have them snap him back into place. "I know you are there."

"I have always been here," Hel replied, melting into being across the chamber. As before, her face was a beautiful, blank mask, her eyes empty as they stared at him.

He wanted to hate her, but couldn't. Her presence alone robbed him of any passion of feeling, good or bad. He felt nothing for her; cared nothing for his present circumstances. But he did wonder, "Am I dead?" The ruler of Helheim had pulled him through darkness to this place where he felt almost nonexistent. What else was the dragon to think, but that she had killed him?

Hel tilted her head a little as if debating her answer. "No. But you are a mere sip away." Her gaze slid over to the iron gate and the water rushing on the other side.

How many times had that water swept over him now? A score? Two? The dragon hadn't allowed a drop of it to pass his lips. Had he known how close he was to demise…

"You are as old as I am," Hel noted. "Perhaps even older. You have seen things others only dream about. Your age and memories have strengthened your blood more than any other living being, short of a god. A few drops of it hold enough power to make a human immortal."

The dragon said nothing.

"My father blames you for all of it, you know. You were the one who gave Nialei her strength. Without your blood, she would have fallen in the Battle of the Veil. The sorcerer's trinket would have spilled its dark powers, and they would have eaten through the Veil, cut my brother's binds, and my father would finally have had his battle with Woden. You took that from him. Instead of a fair fight, Loki got imprisonment in eternal Shadow. Instead of his fated victory, he has been driven into madness." She raised her hand, and pale smoke congealed above her palm, a murky vision of a realm engulfed in flames. Though the dragon had never seen them with his own eyes, he recognized the gods strewn about like broken toys, dying. Woden's wizened face was half burned off, his good eye turned red with blood. Next to him, his wife Frigga, the most beautiful of goddesses, savagely ripped apart. Tir, the stalwart god of war, was impaled on a spear, a sword still clutched in his hand.

This was Asgard, the realm of the gods, fabled for its beauty and endless riches, reduced to a scorched black plane, its golden spires crumbled, and its white marble roads turned red with blood.

And there, in the middle of it all, was the Halfling Trickster, Loki, with his hair like living copper and black runes swirling beneath his skin. Seated on a great, eight-legged stallion, he took in the scene around him with crazed black eyes and smiled, revealing sharp, pointed teeth.

"There, but for a few small drops of blood."

The dragon rolled his wrists, but kept to his place, kept silent.

Hel curled her hand into a fist, dissolving the vision. "Neither," she said in answer to some question no one had asked. "What do I care for Loki's plans?"

"Then why help him?"

"I…wanted."

The dragon waited for her to say something more. Wanted *what*? He wasn't certain Hel knew. For her, desire itself seemed to be its own answer, a new taste she savored but couldn't identify.

"Why am I here?"

"To suffer," she replied. "Your world will end. Your kin will perish. Woden and his children will fall—"

"As will Loki."

She paused. "Yes. In the end. But you will remain. When all the world has frozen, you alone will be left. Your fate will be to forever roam the void left behind."

"Assuming, of course, I do not take that sip." He said it lightly, but the idea merited a thought or two.

"You will not," Hel replied. "That is the nature of your suffering. As long as your kin live and fight, you will not leave them." She floated toward him, changing along the way until Solveig once again stood not two paces before him.

Despite knowing it wasn't her, the dragon surged forward, straining against his binds to reach her, desperate for the smallest morsel. A whiff of her scent, the feel of her warmth. He stared at the face that haunted his mind, loving her and hating her. Solveig, Hel, neither and both at the same time. He shook with need at the sight of her, craven for the feel of her in his arms again. So he could tear Hel asunder.

"You will fight to free yourself until there is no more hope. You will come to yearn for those waters more than you yearn for your mate. But you will hold out and hope, and curse, and pray until the end comes. You will go mad here, many times over, so you can feel what my father and brother have felt. Until the end. You will watch those waters flood less and less, you will know when they begin to dry out, and still you will not drink. Until you know the end has come, and everyone you have ever loved is dead. You will not know when that moment will come, but it will. And when it does, those waters will be gone."

The dragon roared, thrashing against his binds, snapping his fangs at her, hating himself as much as her for putting that broken, frightened look on Solveig's face.

"Shh," she crooned, reaching out to cup his cheek in the gentle softness of Solveig's palm, and the dragon stilled, bowing his head. She stepped into him, putting Solveig's lips to his ear to whisper, "Hush now, my love. Your binds will come away in the end, and you will be free again. You will soar through the clouds as you once did, and your fire will light up the empty world."

Every word she spoke was a dagger through his heart. He couldn't think through that pain, couldn't reconcile his beloved voicing such things. Yet, despite everything, he bowed lower, pressed his forehead to her shoulder, and breathed in deep of her scent, letting the lie of her shelter him from the truth.

Too soon, that lie retreated once more as Solveig stepped away.

"No…"

She smiled at him as she backed toward the far wall. Her body shimmered against the cold, gray surface, and then she was gone.

The dragon dropped to his knees, his head bowing so low his nose almost touched the water's surface. A hair's breadth away. One sip, and it would all be over. And he could rob Hel of her victory.

He tilted his chin to bring his lips to that water but stopped before they could touch it.

He had kin now, Saeran, Nialei, Liadan, and Fal, all bound to him by blood, all fighting against the coming tide.

Fierce pride straightened the dragon's spine, and he pushed to his feet again, standing tall, staring defiance at the place where Hel had disappeared.

She'd been right—the dragon would not abandon his kin.

But she'd been right about another thing, too. His blood was, indeed, powerful. Enough to turn a human immortal, to give a Halfling power so immense it brought forth not one, but two offspring, each stronger than all the rest of them combined. There lay Wilderheim's hope, and his, burning bright enough to stoke the cold embers of his soul back into full blaze.

Perhaps it would burn bright enough to turn the tide.

↞ ››·◇·‹‹ ↠

Never before had Sanja felt such trepidation walking through the city. With only a handful of people out and about so early of the morning, she had no crowds to hide in, and she felt each curious gaze on her like a physical touch.

Sanja adjusted her satchel on her shoulder and kept going, picking her way carefully across the frozen mud. Yesterday's rain had left the earth soaked through, and last night's frost had hardened it into precarious dips and swells that threatened to turn her ankle with every step. Already she felt the cold seeping into her bones. It would only get worse from now on.

As the sun rose higher, a bright shaft of its light illuminated the library tower not far away. Sanja followed that shining beacon, eager for the illusion of safety behind its grand doors. But when she finally reached the towering building, those beautiful portals were barred. The library was closed.

Time is running out. All of Frastmir seemed to feel it, even if they didn't know why.

Straightening her spine, Sanja went up to the top of the library stairs and looked out toward Hallowed Mountain. There, its peak glistened white with snow, a trail of it snaking down to the forest's edge to mark the staircase she would need to climb toward her goal.

As daunting as the Journey looked from its beginning, Sanja knew that once she got underway, it would seem endless and impossible. She breathed in deeply of the chill air and etched the sight of that peak into her memory.

Taking a knee, Sanja looked over her satchel one last time. Olga had worked through the night to stitch the tears so it could still be used, and despite its shabby appearance, it was perhaps stronger now than before.

"As ready as I will ever be." And none too soon, either. She shouldered her burden, grateful for the moment at least that she had so little to carry, and sent a quiet prayer for good fortune to any god who would listen.

Then it was time to begin.

Sanja turned sideways and placed her knee on the next step down. It was precarious going at first, but she managed to get all the way to the bottom. Now there would be no turning back. She couldn't rise from her knees until she stopped for rest, and when she resumed, she'd need to do it from the same spot again.

She moved slowly, choosing her path with care where the travelers had already worked the mud soft enough to cushion her knees. Still, though the ground was relatively soft, stray pebbles dug into her flesh, and the chill seeped up to steal whatever warmth the breeze left behind. Sanja kept looking at the sun, urging it to rise faster. Once she reached the forest, even its small comfort would be lost to her.

After a while, her thoughts began to wander. Olga and Gerhart had wanted to accompany her to the forest at least, but she'd declined. The less attention she drew to herself, the better. Besides, the roof had leaked in the downpour last night. Gerhart would need to fix it before more rains came. And with him busy, Olga would need to do the chores Sanja usually did for them: feed the chickens and geese, go to market, cook supper, and a dozen other little things.

Sanja had made Gerhart promise to buy a wagon and mule, in case she didn't return.

"Aye, I'll buy them," he'd said, but the stubborn set of his mouth had made her suspicious.

"And you'll both leave for Lyria when the time comes," she'd pressed. A fortnight and two days. If she hadn't made it back by then, it would mean she was dead, and her parents would have no more reason to stay. Aegiros was too dangerous, and they'd need to go through Jarl Steen's territory to reach Ravetia. Better they turn their feet in the opposite direction. It might take longer to reach it, but Gerhart and Olga would be safe in Lyria.

Gerhart had crossed his arms over his chest. "The prince himself can come knocking on that door with an army of guards to evict me from my own house, and I'll not step one foot past the threshold 'til you're back safe and sound."

"Da, I—"

"Safe and sound, Sanja."

That had been the only time Gerhart or Olga had mentioned the prince. Had they seen her with him the day before? Had they seen him kiss her?

That kiss…

She must have dreamed it. Real kisses didn't make one feel weak and strong at the same time, no matter what the poems said. Nor did they sear with the fire of a lightning strike. There had definitely been a lightning strike, Sanja decided. She could still taste it on her tongue today, feel its crackling energy pulsing in her lips. It was a miracle she hadn't been burned to ash then and there.

Against that pain, she recalled Prince Fal holding her in the barn, his arms so strong, his heartbeat so steady against her. She'd felt his strength in his embrace, a world of it contained in such a human-looking shell. For a moment, she'd felt as if nothing bad could touch her—not Jarl Steen, nor his men, nor even Fenrir himself.

She'd found the safest place in all the worlds there in the prince's arms swaddled in warmth and light, and something else she dared not name.

And the next day had dawned as lonely as the one before, despite his oath to be there to see her through the Journey.

The Prince of Deceit, indeed.

Before she knew it, the sun was directly above her, and the ground dried out under her knees. She was halfway to the forest, a pathetic achievement for the morning. Her mouth was parched, but Sanja had planned out her meals and water breaks meticulously, and she had a ways to go before she could allow herself to indulge in either.

A few more paces and she paused, adjusting her satchel across her back. It was beginning to weigh on her. Perhaps she ought to drag it along instead. It might get wet and dirty, but that would happen eventually, anyway.

Some yards ahead, the river cut through the tall grasses, a final barrier between her and a straight footpath toward the forest. But there was no bridge across the stream, and its muddy waters churned and swelled to double their usual size after yesterday's storm. At the edge, the planks had been swept away by the current. The sodden grass on either bank told her those waters had been much higher at the peak of the flood and had already receded quite a ways, but they were still high enough to soak her to the waist if she knee-walked through it.

Sanja winced, debating her options. The stream widened a little farther down, which meant it shallowed out as well. She could either go off the path to spare herself the cold or go straight through to save some time. Neither was ideal.

"Scared of a little water? That don't bode well for snow and ice, now do it?"

Sanja barely stopped herself from screaming as she hunched down in anticipation of an attack. When none came, she dared to peek out from behind her arms. "W-who said that?"

A hand waved out from the tall grass on the other side of the stream, and then its owner poked his head out to grin at her. "Didn't 'spect another clod to be at this folly so cold in the year. Where'd you come from, then?"

Had Prince Fal found a way to meet her after all? No, the eyes merrily twinkling back at her were brown, not his distinctive shade of blue. Still, he could have been one of the jarl's men. "Are you going to kill me?" she shot back, unable to stop herself. "You'll have to. I won't go back to him willingly!" Sanja started to wheeze at the mere thought of it, her eyes wide and stinging, welling with tears, but she couldn't blink them away, afraid of letting the man out of her sight. Her body shook, aching to find a corner to crawl into, as she had last night. Echoes of harsh voices hurt her ears, memories of pain set her shivering. Cruel faces flashed before her mind's eye, making her flinch, and all she could think was, *Make it quick. Kill me and have done with it.*

The stranger's easy smile turned sad. "Ah, lass, you've one bear of a tale behind you, haven't you?"

He wasn't attacking her. He was pitying her. Sanja swallowed hard and turned away, forcing deep breaths in and out through her sore throat to keep from bursting into uncontrollable sobs. She ground her knees into the dirt, turned her face up to the sun that its light might sear away the hateful visions in her mind, and warm her chilled flesh. *Breathe… Breathe…*

Only when her shakes had abated could she bring herself to face him again. He hadn't moved a hair, still gazing at her with that same expression of pity and concern. Gods, what must he think of her?

I didn't use to be afraid of strangers.

She had Jarl Steen to thank for that. He'd robbed her of all peace of mind and taken away her trust in the goodness of others. She had to get them back somehow, otherwise, win or lose, Jarl Steen would rule her life forever.

I can't let that happen. Raising her chin, she pushed back dark thoughts of hidden knives and large hands wrapping around her throat. "My name is Sanja," she told the stranger, braving a tremulous smile. "I was born here in Frastmir."

"Aye, and a pretty bird you are." The man smiled back with obvious relief, then scratched his head, making his flaxen hair stand on end. "Not well in the head, though, seems to me. A local lass like you ought to know the weather like her own face, eh?"

Sanja sat back on her heels, weary with cautious relief. "It ought not be this cold yet."

He grunted in response. "Aye, that's true enough, it is. Bad omen when the sky itself turns 'gainst you. That water ain't going down none, so's you know. Might as well get it over with while the sun's still hot enough to dry you. Name's Mattias, by the by. Pleased to meet you."

"Likewise," she replied, but her attention was already on the problem of her river crossing.

Mattias chuckled at the face she made. "Throw your satchel over and strip down so's your things don't get wet."

A momentary stab of fear froze her in place, but Sanja balled her hands into fists and pushed it back. "Perhaps I would if you weren't there to watch me do it."

Mattias laughed outright. "On my honor, yours is safe with me."

Sanja scowled at him, not at all convinced. Choosing to trust him not to attack her didn't mean she relished the thought of him ogling her.

With a put-upon sigh, Mattias disappeared back into the grass. "Go on, then."

She wasn't likely to get a better offer. And she couldn't very well turn back now.

Setting her satchel aside, she stripped off her trousers and tied them around the bundle before tossing it to the other bank. With those safely across, Sanja pulled the hair shirt up to bunch under her arms, with the ends trailing down to cover her chest. That left her bare from there to her toes, but for her loincloth and soft-soled shoes. Thinking better of it, she took off the shoes and loincloth, too, tossing them past her satchel.

Her first contact with the water shocked her to her core, and that was before she sank to the muddy bottom. Up to her behind in freezing water, Sanja couldn't catch her breath. Her high-pitched gasps got Mattias talking again. "A bit nippy, eh?"

Sanja gritted her teeth and took another knee-step forward, which dropped her up to her waist into the cold and pitched her forward. She squealed and hurried the rest of the way across before she fell face-first into the current. As soon as she climbed out, Sanja collapsed in the soft grass, shivering in the open air.

"There now, wasn't so bad, was it?"

"Don't look!" She still had her hair shirt bunched up.

Mattias made a rude sound. "Less you got a good-sized cock and ball sac twixt your legs, ain't much for me worth looking at, is there? Wouldn't mind a peek at one of them, truth be told. Been a while, if you catch my meaning."

It took her a moment to catch on to what he was saying. When she did, Sanja blushed. "Oh." To each their own, she supposed, but redressed quickly nonetheless. Even soaked and muddied, the haircloth trousers warmed her chilled legs instantly.

"So where did you come from?" she asked, wary in the silence.

"A small village, far side of the Dragon Lakes from here. You'd hardly know it's there, it's so small. Don't even have a proper name."

Deciding a short break was just the thing right then, Sanja shifted carefully to one side of the path and took out a bit of cheese and her water skin. "The Dragon Lakes are by the Lyrian border. You could have left through the pass with everyone else."

"Ah, but the Hallowed Mountain is here," he said, still reclined behind the cover of tall grass. "Can't very well earn my robes elsewhere, now can I?"

"Is becoming a cleric worth all this to you?"

"Seems to be worth it to you," he countered.

"Fair point. I used to think becoming a cleric was a noble pursuit, undertaken for noble reasons. I still think it ought to be, but it's not, is it?"

"Aye, the Journey's a haven for all manner of lost souls," he replied in a way that invited one to unburden oneself.

Sanja returned it back to him. "Are you a lost soul, then?"

She thought she heard a sigh, but it might well have been nothing more than the rustle of grass. "I'm more of what you'd call a wanderin' soul. Some run from a thing, some run to a thing. I have naught to run from or to. I like to wander hereabouts and thereabouts. See new places and meet new people."

He said it easily enough, but there was a hint of something deeper, something sad and lonely, in his voice. It resonated inside her, and for the briefest moment, Sanja felt kindred with him. Mattias had his reasons for being on this path, same as Sanja, but he hadn't pried into her life, so she decided to return the courtesy and let him keep his secrets for the time being. "You chose your Journey well, then."

He chuckled at her silly jest. "Aye, I figger if I'm to wander hereabouts and thereabouts, might as well make myself useful by it. Though it boggles the wits what any of this has to do with the pursuit of knowledge. Doubt anyone knows anymore."

"I do," she said proudly. She'd read it in one of the books Princess Liadan brought her. "The physical journey is meant to teach perseverance in the quest for truth. We are meant to seek until we find not what is easy or what we wish to find, but what is there to be found, no matter how painful it might be." The path itself was laid to appear barren, yet in truth, a village or settlement was never more than half a day's walk from it. The constant temptation of a soft bed and a hot meal nearby was a powerful lure for those too weak to resist. Sanja preferred to think of it as assurance that, should she encounter trouble of any kind, help would never be far away.

"So, if you go looking for mushrooms, don't stop with strawberries," Mattias interpreted. "And, suppose once you find mushrooms…"

"Once in possession of the truth, one's obligation becomes to speak it when called upon, no matter the consequences."

"You find the mushroom is poisonous, you warn others, even if they stone you for it. And that's why they'll be draggin' truths and secrets from our exhausted shells the wink we cross their threshold, is it?"

"Precisely! Truth and knowledge are dangerous; their pursuit could easily lead to demise and, once acquired, both are often used as weapons. Clerics must prove themselves above such temptations."

"Well then, I say we ought to get to it, eh? You best avert those bonny eyes of yourn, lass, elsewise, you'll be seeing far more of me bare arse than you've a wish to."

Sanja turned away, blushing.

"It's fair beautiful, mind. Not to brag, but verses a'been sung about it, Bonny Baldr shrink my cock if I lie. Ah, now if you were of a fancy to see, you'd know I spake the truth, I did. There we are!" More rustling heralded his emergence from the grass onto the path, which Sanja deemed a sign that he was decently covered, and it was safe to face him once more.

Another wave of panic almost bowled her over to behold his towering frame. Mattias must have been of a height with Jarl Steen, and just as strong. For a moment, staring at him, she couldn't unsee her intended standing there in his place, his pale eyes staring hatred at her, and his mouth twisted into a vicious snarl.

Sanja squeezed her eyes shut and took a deep breath or two to banish his image from her mind. When she opened them again, Mattias was making a face as he twisted around to scratch his behind. "Of all the hardships of this madness, methinks the haircloth'll be the death of me."

Instead of one tight, brown braid, Mattias' flaxen hair stood in messy curls. Instead of cold, flat orbs of gray, his deep brown eyes twinkled at her with easy humor. His gentle face was clean-shaven, and his mouth had a smile perpetually tucked into one corner.

She returned his smile with a cautious, commiserating one of her own. "I would love to argue that point, but I think you may be right." The big man heaved a dramatic sigh, drawing a giggle out of her. "No doubt it is meant to signify the itch for knowledge or some such thing."

Mattias scowled at her. "Now, you've gone too far." He lowered to his knees at his marker and raised an eyebrow at her. "Shall we, then?"

Sanja shouldered her satchel and nodded, resuming her place where she'd stopped for a rest. Mattias waited for her to catch up, and then the two of them moved down the path. She found her burden lessened, and her mood much improved in his company.

For all that he spoke with a village accent, Mattias was far from simple. Sanja was delighted to learn they shared a love of all things Other and had read enough volumes on the subject to have several in common. Discussing them made the trek nigh pleasant, excepting the random rock or root, and both time and the path went by quickly while they talked.

They reached the forest well before sundown, and Sanja barely noticed. When she did, she was surprised to find the fear she'd carried ever since the betrothal was dissipating.

By the time the sun went down, they'd made camp at a fire circle that must have been lit and doused a thousand times. The resting point seemed made for Journeymen, and meant that, despite her slow start, Sanja and Mattias had made good enough progress to be on pace. At this rate, they might reach the temple in a fortnight, with two days for Sanja to spare.

She could make it.

They built a fire, drank enough water to wet their throats, and settled down to tend to their wounds. Sanja couldn't straighten her legs in front of her. Her knees and shins were badly bruised, and despite the meager protection of her trousers, she'd managed to collect a few abrasions that had caked over with dirt and dried blood. Sanja hadn't felt them before, too overwhelmed with far too many other pains, but now that she saw them, even her exhaustion couldn't keep their stinging burn at bay.

"So what brings you along this dreary road?" Mattias asked. "Or should I say *who*?"

Gods, but she was weary. Opening her mouth to answer felt like more effort than she could manage. But her wounds still needed cleaning, and she ought to eat a bite before she slept. A little conversation might help her stay awake long enough to do that. "It was the only way I could think of to escape a bad betrothal."

"Where I come from, a lass but says no."

Sanja drooped, her body sagging deeper as she scrubbed a wet scrap of cloth over her knee. "In Frastmir, it can get complicated."

Mattias hummed, watching her all the while. "You look fit to drop."

Sanja didn't recall answering with any coherence before the washcloth dropped out of her hands. Too tired to struggle any longer, she wrapped her blanket around her, lay down, and closed her eyes.

She dreamed of whispers in the night, a strange creature kneeling before her. It was all black, like a statue made of glittering pitch, save for the fiery glow of flowing hair that could easily have been the campfire at its back.

Sanja reached out a hand to the fire to warm herself and gasped to encounter the solid, scorching surface of the creature's shoulder. A pair of burning eyes turned to her. A long, clawed finger raised to signal silence before it lowered to Sanja's exposed knees.

Heat poured into her limbs, stinging at first, burning away the discomfort of an exhausting first day, and then comforting, soothing. She felt her strength restore itself and yawned, closing her eyes once more. The creature's parting words followed her into darkness: "I told you we would not abandon you."

Mattias' hand at her shoulder woke her the next morning. He helped her sit up and pressed her water skin into her hands. He must have been up for quite a while to warm it by the fire without burning the whole thing. Sanja hugged it to her middle, savoring its warmth.

"Forgive my saying, lass, but mayhap you ought to turn back."

"No," she croaked, then took a sip from her water skin to wash away the hoarseness from her voice. Odd, she was chilled, but nowhere near as cold as she ought to have been.

"Only that it's but the first night, and you don't look so good."

She might not look it, but she felt well enough, all things considered. "What I lack in stature, I make up for with pure stubbornness." Had last night's dream been more than visions conjured by her exhausted mind? Sanja dared not see for herself with Mattias watching her so closely. "And I don't have a choice," she admitted, clambering to her feet. No pain in her knees, no aches in her back. She was only a little stiff from sleeping on the hard ground. Keeping her blanket about her shoulders, she turned away to pack her belongings and furtively pulled up first one filthy trouser leg, then the other. No bruises, no scabs. Her legs were healed into old scars and fading bruises.

"How can that be? Have you no one to speak for you?"

I told you we would not abandon you.

Princess Liadan? No, it couldn't have been.

Could it?

"It makes no difference now," she replied, distracted by her thoughts. How would the princess have found her?

"Still, it must be some tale to tell."

Sanja busied herself putting out the fire and making her way back to the path. Healings were allowed, she reminded herself. Salves and ointments were no different than an Other's touch. They performed the same function, after all. And it wasn't cheating if someone healed Sanja without her asking for it.

She knelt by her marker with ease, wincing to hear Mattias groan when he lowered to his knees. "Well?" he prodded, nudging her with his elbow.

Though the canopy of evergreens overhead had staved off the worst of the night's chill, the ground was still cold and hard, covered in a thick layer of dried needles. According to her readings, if Sanja kept up a steady pace, this would be the way of it for the next ten days, until the forest thinned out at the foot of Hallowed Mountain.

That would leave her five days to crawl up the stone staircase to the temple and pass the clerics' interrogation. There'd be no shelter from the elements up there, and no respite for her knees. As grateful as Sanja was for last night's healing, she dared not expect it again. She would need to measure her pace to make good progress without causing herself injury in the process.

Turning away from the tree canopy above, she met Mattias' expectant gaze. "I suppose I may as well tell you," she decided. "We have time enough for this tale."

"Naught but time," Mattias agreed.

Hardening herself against the cold, the pain, and any doubts, Sanja put her left knee forward in her first step of the day and began her tale of woe.

↞ ››·◇·‹‹ ↠

Despite the generals imposing strict standards of conduct and cleanliness, the western camp was turning into a pigsty. The horses had trampled the ground into so much mud it coated everything from tents to equipment to clothing. Camp wenches had stopped tending to their duties, preferring to swive their way through the ranks rather than keep them clean and fed. The latrine trenches were so full, no one bothered to use them any longer, and shit was beginning to pile up everywhere.

This was what happened when soldiers whose blood boiled for battle were ordered to make camp and await further instructions.

For months they've been stewing there, waiting for the troops to gather from every corner of Synealee. When they'd reported for presentation, the order had come to wait longer. The time wasn't right. All was not set. Queen Genevieve wouldn't tell them anything, and anyone stupid enough to question her found himself strung up on the gallows.

Two score men in the western camp alone had already been flogged for insubordination. Any longer and the generals would face a riot. These were not soft, pampered lordlings waiting to trot their noble steeds to a high vantage point above the battlefield so they could say they've been to war. These men had no softness in them. They were savages trained from childhood to live for naught but killing in the name of God.

And they'd learned to like it.

"My Lord! What news from her majesty?"

Lord Artairas The Golden, second son of Prince Uther of Synealee, and fifteenth in line for the throne, faced his faithful squire, tempering his scowl so as not to frighten the boy. "The sign has still not appeared," he said.

What sign his grandmother was looking for, no one knew, and she wouldn't say. Everyone with two eyes in their head could see Queen Genevieve had taken a turn for the worse. She no longer attended court or even communal worship. She had sequestered herself in her chambers, and only her most trusted guards and servants were allowed entrance. Each of them always emerged ashen, saying the queen was gravely ill.

A procession of healers had come and gone, all saying the same. The queen was nearing the end of her days, and they could do naught to save her. Artairas had seen it for himself that morning when he'd been summoned to her bedside. His grandmother had looked so small and frail beneath the thick, embroidered covers. The air in her chambers had been thick with a sickroom stench, yet she'd refused to allow the windows to be opened. The warmest autumn breeze seemed to chill her.

But it was not her physical weakness that worried Artairas. The Queen of Synealee appeared to be losing her mind. She struggled to make herself heard, and when she spoke, much of what she said made no sense. This morning, she'd sounded as if she'd been carrying on two different conversations at the same time. One with Artairas, and the other with someone unseen, all interspersed with prayers.

The squire shook his head. "May God ease her suffering."

"Amen," Artairas agreed, but the benediction was little more than a reflexive response as his fingers curled around the hilt of his strange new sword. He could feel God's will humming through the weapon strapped to his side, his own blade discarded in the castle in favor of this one. "Go about your duties, Gareth. There's nothing for you to do here until we get our marching orders."

After the young squire had bowed away, Artairas ducked into the privacy of his tent and drew the mystical sword, holding it up to the light. A work of art, if ever he'd seen one, with the handle shaped just right to fit his grip, and the pommel twisted into an intricate globe of a knotwork cage. The crossguard was broader than usual, an unmistakable symbol of God's sacrifice. A symbol of faith and, for Artairas, a reminder of his purpose.

The blade was masterfully crafted, strong and true, without a single flaw marring its surface. Etched with symbols down the center, it caught the light just so and glittered like a jewel. What manner of prayers were they, inscribed in the blade? What language were they comprised of? Artairas had never seen their like before. Each symbol was its own entity, standing out stark and clear in the configuration, its meaning a mystery that itched his mind with endless questions. Yet, at the same time, each symbol also flowed into the next in an unbroken river of silent speech.

It mesmerized.

Artairas traced the lines with a reverent fingertip from hilt to tip, and back down, feeling the blade heat to his touch. Its warmth seeped into him, making his heartbeat stronger, his breath come faster. He caressed each symbol's voluptuous curve with a lover's gentleness, whispered praise into each mysterious whorl and valley. The blade sighed, pulling his fingers tighter around the grip, digging the pommel into his flesh, where it rested against his thigh.

Candlelight played across its polished surface, unmarred by a single hammer strike. Pure and eager, humming secrets he had yet to uncover. Artairas read its mysteries in the brief dark lulls between the flashes of light and followed them slowly up the fuller channel and beyond, to the tip. There, he tested the edge with his thumb. He barely felt the blade's sting, watching a crimson droplet slide down the center of the blade.

Red against steel.

Blood upon the holy prayers.

A scar across the reflection of his face.

Artairas saw himself within the blade, a golden crown upon his head and faces at once strange and familiar standing behind him, keeping watch over him. All of them men seasoned by battle, brows creased with the weight of victory, eyes shining with faith, in their God as well as their king.

Artairas shouted and tossed the blade aside. Shaking, he crossed over to the washbasin and splashed cold water over his face. He couldn't catch his breath, his body humming with a strange energy, a purpose, and a calling. For a moment there, staring at the blade—*into* it—Artairas had felt God's hand upon his shoulder. He'd heard the unspoken truth in the vision: "Thus shall it come to pass."

The compulsion to answer was too powerful to resist. "Thus shall it be," he murmured, gritting his teeth against the words. It felt like sorcery, but how could it be? The queen herself had placed the sword into his hands. None other served God as faithfully and completely as Queen Genevieve. The sword could only be His Divine instrument.

And Artairas had been chosen to wield it.

His fingers curled hard into the edge of the washstand. God had chosen him to carry out His holy justice. The heathens would perish beneath His blade. Artairas himself would lead the way to victory and bring God's light into the dark, Godless north.

And then he would be their king.

Thus shall it be.

Thus had God decreed, and there could be no other outcome.

Artairas turned once more to face the blade, lying stained on the bearskins carpeting his tent. He wet a washcloth and returned to it, weak-kneed and weary. He cleaned the blood off its face, polished the surface to a steady shine, then laid it to rest within its scabbard, setting it in a place of honor: on the pedestal of his altar beneath the holy cross. Kneeling there, he bowed his head and said a prayer, accepting God's gift into his keeping until death.

The time was growing nigh. Artairas felt the air whispering portents of things to come. God had waited long enough. Having delivered His gift unto Artairas, nothing else remained but for the armies to march.

And win.

CHAPTER 13

A bright glare of sunshine speared through the gray mist of dreams, bringing Fal a vision of green grass and sparkling waterfalls. He saw himself hand in hand with Sanja, smiling. A length of string wound around their hands while a drop of crimson blood seeped out from between their palms, a seal over their joined fate.

He stared at the dark little blob falling through the air, and the focus of his attention sucked him into its depths, from the brightness of the meadow to the cozy shadows of a darkened bedchamber. There, Sanja slept peacefully while Fal stoked the fire in the hearth. Outside, the moon shone down on a midnight land turned silver with thick blankets of snow, and all was beautifully, softly peaceful. The dream version of him returned to bed, kissed Sanja on the brow, and drew her into his arms to sleep. It was a gesture of pure love he could feel, and it stilled the churning chaos inside him into a reverent balance.

He blinked slowly, savoring the sensation, and when he opened his eyes again, Fal found himself in Castle Frastmir's throne room, seated on King Saeran's throne. But it was no longer Saeran's. It was Fal's, and Sanja was there beside him as his queen, serene and composed, save for her foot tapping out a rapid rhythm beneath her skirts. Dream Fal ducked his chin so his subjects wouldn't see him trying not to laugh and squeezed Sanja's hand to make her still.

Then he was somewhere else, an Otherland of purple grasses and a brilliant green sky, watching Sanja take it all in with breathless wonder.

In the next blink, they were in a deep forest of black trees. Shimmering silver leaves showered over them as a shy unicorn foal approached to sniff at the apple Sanja held out to it.

As it reached out, the scene changed once more to his library, where Sanja sat on the floor surrounded by books, oblivious to the world at large.

And in the next instant, they were in a garden filled with bright, colorful blooms. And then a cottage in the woods, where dream Fal, older now, danced Sanja around a fire pit. And in the castle again, older still, hand in hand as their crowns were removed with reverence and passed on to their heirs.

Over and over, again and again, new scenes of a lifetime Fal had never lived, but desperately wanted to. And wherever he found himself, Sanja was always there beside him, calming his chaos with nothing more than her touch.

It was a gift, a vision of what could be, and Fal didn't want to leave. He strained to see more, even as the colors began to fade back into a mist that robbed him of details first, then entire scenes, and then all memory of what he'd seen. But the sensation of them remained. It became a sweet, hollow ache inside his mind, a sense of having misplaced something precious, and an urgent need to find it again that followed him into wakefulness.

Fal came to his senses on the floor of his bedchambers. Brilliant light flickered through the windows, a steady fire burned in the hearth. He was sore all over, his body cold and stiff from sleeping on the floor for who knew how long. As exhausted as he remembered being, it could have been a full day.

The last thing he remembered was kissing Sanja, and a lightning strike slamming into him with incredible power. He remembered falling through water that was already freezing over, and then…

There'd been more, hadn't there? Something important, a message he couldn't recall. It itched deep in his mind and made his chest ache as if something he'd been holding onto had slipped from his grasp. The echo of warmth and laughter left Fal with a sense of impending loss.

He could only imagine how Sanja must be faring. Had she started her Journey already? More likely, she delayed her departure to recover, as Fal would need to. Good. He'd promised he'd help her, and he intended to keep that promise. As soon as his bones stopped buzzing. It shouldn't take him long. A cold bath, a good meal, and he'd be back at full strength once more.

But when he attempted to jump to his feet, his body wouldn't obey. He was forced to use the hearth for support as he climbed upright and got his unsteady legs under him. Dizzy, weak, it was all he could do not to crumble back to the floor.

And as his gaze slowly focused on his surroundings, he noticed something far more disturbing. His bedchamber was dry. No water, no fish, no churned up mud at his feet. His illusions appeared to be gone, yet he still felt them all around. His body was drained, exhausted, yet his magic was as strong as ever. Something was wrong with him.

Fal hobbled to the bathing room where a copper tub stood filled with cold water. He stripped and sat into it, sinking low to submerge himself. The water remained silent, dormant. He felt its chill, but not its vastness and power. It buoyed him but didn't lure him deeper. It felt as if the connection he'd always sensed to all the waters of the world and to its Eternal Source had been severed and left him disoriented and lonely.

He hastened through his bath and redressed in clean clothes that felt foreign on his skin. The polished silver disc reflected his true face, and all he saw was a stranger staring back at him. Everything looked as it should, smelled as it should, felt as it should, but it was all the slightest bit off to his weary mind.

Fal emerged into the empty hallway. Not a soul in sight. Not a single torch burning. He called out, but no one answered him. At the end of the hallway, he descended the staircase to the next level, calling out again. No answer.

Finally, he came to the great hall and there, at last, found a sign of life. Food on the long table, unfinished and abandoned. Someone had eaten there not long ago. Some of the candles were still burning.

Fal selected a morsel from one of the platters and bit into it, tasting nothing. He frowned at it, then at the platter. But, starved as he was, Fal couldn't afford to be picky, so he stuffed the rest into his mouth and reached for the next. By the time his fingers closed over a piece of sausage, the morsel in his mouth had popped like ripe fruit and disintegrated into tasteless jelly.

Fal swallowed with a shudder and raised the sausage to the light. Before his eyes, it became translucent, then lost its shape as it expanded into a perfectly round ball before it popped in a splash of water.

This wasn't real—none of it.

As he looked around again, harder, staring through what was before him to what might lie beyond, the world rippled outward from him, jarring the illusion enough to reveal it to his senses. Fal stumbled back, gasping for breath. He wasn't dreaming, that much he knew. But he wasn't awake, either. At least, he didn't feel fully in the physical world. The one that mattered, that was real.

A larger ripple revealed people milling about the great hall. Servants carried away empty dishes beyond the illusory veil, and as each was picked up there, it disappeared from the table in Fal's world. Gone, as if it had never been.

Fal met a serving girl at the far end of the table, grasped the platter she reached for, but he couldn't hold onto it. The silver disc melted like mist through his fingertips.

"Hello!" he called. "Can anyone hear me?" Running up the steps to the dais, he stood on the king's throne, waved his arms about, and shouted, "*Hello*!"

In the ripples where the illusion briefly gave way, he saw nothing change. Not a single head turned to look his way.

No, it couldn't be. He'd been so close to a cure! Was it too late?

"*Hello!* Someone answer me!"

He was denied the smallest evidence of his existence: an echo.

I'm still standing, he thought, trying to reason himself out of this mess. *I can feel the throne beneath my feet. I can see all that is unliving.* The candles blew out one by one, and the tapestries moved on the walls. Doors opened and closed. Chairs moved about. But he couldn't see or hear a single living being, and they couldn't see him. And then, with one last slamming of a door, all movement stopped.

Desperate, Fal sought the core of his magic within himself, wrenched it about to release its hold on his world. He felt the illusion waver the smallest bit before it settled back into place once more. He tried again, harder, felt the world twist and wrinkle, a heavy tapestry refusing to let itself warp. The effort left him winded.

Fal hopped down from the throne and ran for the council room. Surely, someone there would sense him. Liadan would be there. Surely she'd feel her own brother nearby. And if not, Braith had magic in her. If he pushed hard, his call for help might reach her.

Down the hallway, he ran up the staircase, wheezing back the blinding fear that he would never again make it out of the illusions. The council room stood open, the chairs set around its only table at different angles, a sign of people sitting in them. But who?

Fal took hold of his magic once more, wrenched with all his might, and felt it shift the slightest bit.

"…nine days," Tarben said. "Nine days with no sign of him. We must assume the worst."

His hold slipped, washing away all but a faint hum of the response. *Nine days…* He'd lost over a week.

Concentrate. One more try. He held his breath, his entire body tensing to grasp something that wasn't there. The illusion thinned, allowing him to see the members of the royal council. They looked tired, far older than the last time he'd seen them, and Kvaran was absent. Eira was speaking, but Fal couldn't make out what she said. Her lips formed the word *war*, and a cold fist closed around Fal's heart.

He clutched thin air in white-knuckled fists, pulled with every last ounce of his strength.

"…not unsympathetic. But we cannot fight two battles at once. We must face the threat we can defeat."

"Winning a war will not stop Ragnarok," Braith argued. "If we cannot find a way out of Fenrir's path, defeating Synealee's armies will mean nothing."

"What do you suggest?" That was Olgier, his voice reedy, lost without a firm command to follow.

"We must find the cauldron Queen Nialei hid away. We must finish what she and King Saeran began. It is our only hope."

"A fool's errand," Tarben scoffed. "An Other trick to keep us chasing our tails, as they have had us doing always. What proof do we have that the blood of all clans will restore the Veil? None, other than their word. It is folly to trust an Other."

"You speak treason," Braith hissed.

"And you speak blindly! Our Other king and queen are gone. Their Other heir has abandoned us, and his Other sister has fled—"

"Princess Liadan is patrolling our borders," Eira argued.

"So she said," Tarben replied. "But who is to say she hasn't gone back to Aegiros to save her own life? They all left us to fend for ourselves!"

"And so we must," Kvaran wheezed behind Fal. He couldn't turn to face the ancient councilor and waiting for him to be carried to the table drained Fal almost dry. His hold slipped again and again, but thankfully, the other councilors respected Kvaran at least enough to wait for him to be settled before they resumed their treasonous rhetoric. It gave Fal enough time to shore up his strength for a few more moments.

"Whatever is keeping the royal family away makes no matter now," Kvaran decreed. "What matters is what we do in their absence."

"Hear, hear!" Tarben agreed.

Kvaran nodded at Tarben. "You are right. We have a duty to protect the people of Wilderheim from all threats. And so we shall. Give the call to arms. If Synealee attacks, we must be prepared to defend against them."

Tarben drew himself up and sneered at Braith.

"And Councilor Braith is right, as well," Kvaran added, making Braith sigh with something akin to relief as Tarben's grin dimmed. "I sense this war is a portent and first wave of Ragnarok, but it is by no means the only one. Queen Nialei believed the blood of the clans could restore the Veil, and we have no choice but to trust her judgment. We shall summon anyone with magic Sight to search for the cauldron."

"And if we find it? What then?" Tarben asked. "The queen has only collected a portion of what is needed, and we don't know what portion it is. It could be a single drop away from completion, or thousands short. And if we somehow got all the clans to contribute, do you know how to complete the spell? Because I most certainly do not!"

The councilors looked from one to the other for an answer, any hint of a hope they could grasp onto and rally. But no one spoke. There was nothing they could say; Tarben was right.

"As I said," Tarben spat with the finality of one who didn't realize his victory meant bitter defeat. "A fool's errand."

"Perhaps it is," Braith allowed. "But it is all we have left."

She kept speaking, but her voice became more and more indistinct as Fal lost control of the window he'd opened. "No… *No!*" He thrust his will at the veil of his illusions, forcing a desperate cry through its weave: "I'm here!"

Braith faltered, a frown creasing her brow as she looked up. She'd heard!

"I'm here! *I'm right here!*" Fal shouted over and over again, but already the waters of nothing were closing around him. The councilors began to fade, the hum of their voices dulling into silence. "Braith!" he screamed, but it was of no use. She was no longer paying attention.

And then they were gone, leaving Fal alone in an empty chamber.

His knees gave out, and he collapsed on the floor, dropping his forehead to the cold stone.

Whether he wallowed there for moments or half the day, Fal didn't know. He had no awareness of the passage of time. But when he managed to force himself back to his feet, his legs still quivered with strain to keep him upright. His arms hung limply by his sides, fingers numb. He had no strength left to try opening another window. Probably too late, anyway. Indeed, the chairs had already been pushed flush against the table, and the door was closed. The council had adjourned for the day.

Yet a faint wisp of *something* swirled around him. An awareness without comprehension. A thought without shape. Not purpose, nor hope, but…

A memory?

No, it was too ethereal for that.

Whatever it was, it brought his head up and seized him, mind and body, to follow where it led.

Fal dragged his feet out the door. The hallway was dark already. Sunset had come and gone. He followed the wisp of a feeling out to the courtyard, unsure of what he sought, but certain it would be there. Above him, the black velvet of the sky glittered with countless stars. No swirls of colorful Otherlands in his illusion. It presented a version of his world where Wilderheim was still whole, shunning the smallest hint of Ragnarok as if it had never existed.

The unseen current altered the illusion around him in some intrinsic way, as if it was drawing him into a vision. Only, instead of anchoring in water, it took shape in the air all around him.

Echoes of a single voice whispered a chant in his ear. It guided him sideways from the main door, along the wall a ways to a patch of nothing. He followed its strange instructions to run his palm across the surface of the stone wall and then pushed. His hand sank through the stone as if it were mud and flattened against a smooth wooden surface. Startled, Fal pulled back and stepped away. The stone wall revealed no secrets, yet Fal knew they were there, as surely as he knew his name. The barrier before him was the same as whatever lay on the other side of it: crafty and familiar.

Never before had Fal interacted with a vision this way, as if he was physically inside of it. He could feel its workings, an intricate puzzle falling into alignment little by little, and it felt personal. The vision felt as if it had been placed there for him alone to find. Meticulous, overwhelming in its size, yet subtle at the same time.

Fal would have known his mother's magic anywhere.

Back to the wall he went, shoving his hands at the stones and through them, tracing the surface of a door from edge to edge. He found the latch, released it, and gave a hard shove. Had it not been for the fake stone wall slowing his momentum, he would have tumbled a long way down a dark stairwell underground. As it was, he barely caught himself on an empty torch holder, hanging aloft for a moment until he found his feet on the landing.

Behind him, the open doorway revealed not a hint of the wards keeping it hidden. Before him, at the bottom of the long, winding stairwell, a small flicker of candlelight drew his eye. The current felt stronger here, pulling him down into the bowels beneath Castle Frastmir.

Fal advanced with caution, tested every stair with the tips of his toes before he put his entire weight on it. Scanning the walls along the way, he found no spellwork etched into the stone, no lights of magic hidden in the cracks and crevices. But he sensed an ocean of it at the bottom, like a beacon calling to his soul.

The stairwell emerged into a stone chamber with domed ceilings held up by thick columns. In one corner, tall bookshelves overflowed with ancient-looking tomes at the top and scrolls at the bottom. The sheer power of them saturated the air until he could hardly breathe. Each volume was marked with a length of ribbon, some blue, some green, and some black. Fal traced careful fingertips along the spines, sensing both the spells that preserved them, as well as the magics contained within. With the first, marked green, the tightness in his chest gave way, and he breathed easier. Healing spells, then. Earth magic. With the next, he felt strength returning to his limbs, but it came with a sense of danger, a readiness to take up arms and fight. The blue ribbon would mean battle magic.

He hesitated to touch the third. Its black ribbon wasn't shiny like the others. Rather, it was a shadow against the book's spine. The magic inside whispered through his mind, telling him in words so old they predated spoken language that anything he wanted was his for the taking. It promised a world filled with wonder, power, and riches, all laid out at his feet, and every word it spoke dripped with blood.

Swallowing hard, Fal backed away and hit the table that took up a good portion of the chamber. The candle at its center jarred, the flame flickering, scattering the shadows back into their darkened corners. It distracted him enough from the black book's pull that he was able to turn his back on it.

And there, in a separate nook peeking out from behind a doorless doorway, he found a sight he'd never hoped to glimpse. The current drawing him in dissipated, the voice quieted, and the vision turned slightly hazy, like a dream.

The cauldron was smaller than he'd imagined. It was a smooth glass orb nestled on a wrought iron pedestal. Inside, the blood Nialei had gathered from the Other clans shone bright with multicolored magics. It moved like a living thing, creating a slow, roundabout current eager to rise into a funnel if disturbed. Fal couldn't stop staring. There was so much of it. A drop from each clan—it had to be almost complete. How many clans could there be?

How many still left, with Fenrir devouring Otherlands one after the next?

He stared like a gobsmacked fool as the vision blurred more and more, darkening from the outside in. Having delivered its message, it slowly expelled him back to his illusion, where the light of one eternal candle could not hope to illuminate the full depth and breadth of the underground chamber.

Queen Nialei's most powerful secret was hidden inside Castle Frastmir. Right beneath all of their feet.

He had to tell someone. The most important part of the spell was within their grasp. They had the blood, and the spells for reforming the Veil had to be stored with it somewhere. All they needed was a little time to find them. Once the Veil was restored, the gods would return to their full strength, and then *they* could make a stand against Fenrir. There was still a chance for Wilderheim!

In his excitement, Fal made it halfway up the stairwell before he remembered no one could see or hear him. And on the heels of that realization came another: he'd passed nine days in the oblivion of wizard's sleep.

It'd been nine days since he'd handed Sanja over to her father, on the eve of her Journey. Nine days since she'd been attacked by Jarl Steen's men.

He'd promised he'd be there to help her and keep her safe on the path to the clerics' temple, and instead, she was out there in the forest on her own, with only an ancient spell along the path to protect her, and only as long as she kept moving forward.

CHAPTER 14

Three nights in a row, after the first, Sanja dreamed about Prince Fal. She dreamed of such beautiful things—sunlit meadows, and strange Otherlands, and so many books. And anywhere she found herself, the prince was always at her side. She lived an entire lifetime in those dreams, each night building on the previous one, filling her mind with the sweetest memories she'd never lived, yet somehow missed, nonetheless.

Each night she dreamed and remembered the searing heat of a kiss sealed by lightning.

And each night, she awoke from those dreams to the princess healing her wounds while Mattias slept. Princess Liadan's aid didn't break any rules—salves and healing were allowed on the Journey while petitioners rested, after all. But as much as Sanja needed and appreciated the help, she felt uneasy receiving it. The princess gave Sanja small morsels of food and drink and assured her that Steen had not left his keep since her warning. They talked in whispers about the Journey and what lay ahead. Sanja was making good progress, all things considered.

But for all the princess said during their hushed conversations, she never spoke a word of her brother, no matter how many times Sanja asked why he wasn't there himself.

"You must not reveal my presence to your friend until you reach the temple," she said on the second night. "Swear to me."

To know a truth and not speak it? That would go against everything the Order of Clerics stood for. Was it a test? Sanja owed the prince and princess far more than she could ever repay. Her loyalty and silence were the least she could give them. But did she not owe the same to Mattias? "Why not? I'm not breaking any rules, am I?"

"You're not. But I am."

"What?"

"*Shh!* Keep your voice down. You are not receiving anything more than any other Journeyman. I am not clearing stones from your path or making the ground softer for your knees. If the clerics question you about it, that is what you tell them. Let them blame me. By then, it will not matter anymore."

"But why can I not tell Mattias now?"

"Because I am not supposed to be here. Wilderheim's noble clans are openly threatening rebellion, we're preparing for an invasion, and I have been tasked with patrolling our borders. Look." The princess raised a finger over her head to touch a shimmering dome above them. "It's a spell that protects us from the wind. I cannot have it carrying word of my presence to the royal council, or any of the nobility. If they knew I take nightly detours from my patrols to show preference to one subject above the rest of the kingdom, I would lose what little authority I have over them, and Fal would suffer for it. We cannot afford to be divided now."

A chill that had nothing to do with the freezing night crept up her legs into the pit of her stomach. "Is… Is Fal in danger?"

Instead of answering, Princess Liadan put another branch on the fire. "Steen may not have left his lands, but he is using his wealth to turn the nobles against the crown. He has refused a direct order to send men to protect the kingdom. The longer he defies us, the more nobles follow suit. Our crops have frozen, the game has disappeared, and our people are fleeing every which way they can to get away from this sky. Wilderheim is falling apart, Sanja."

"Where is Fal? And what about my parents?"

"Rest easy. Your parents are safe. Worried, but safe. I have a guard patrolling past your street each day to make sure of it."

Thank you, gods. And, "Thank you, Your Highness."

"I don't need thanks, Sanja. I need your oath."

"Of course, Your Highness, I swear on my life I will not reveal your secret to Mattias until we reach the temple."

The princess nodded and disappeared.

But it sat ill with Sanja to enjoy such care while her friend and companion suffered without the same respite and so, on the third night of their Journey, Sanja asked the princess to secretly ease Mattias' torments as well.

After some hesitation, she did, and then healed him again the night after that without being asked.

On the last night, Princess Liadan brought Sanja three small, flat leather pouches. "Slip the smaller two into your shoes and tuck the larger at the small of your back to keep warm," she instructed in a whisper. "This one thing I cannot share with your friend. For his sake, as well as yours, do not let him know you have it."

Another secret, and this one skirted a dangerous line. It might not make the ground easier for Sanja's knees, but it did make the air warmer along the path. She'd never heard of anyone taking the Journey in weather like this, and so she had no way of knowing what was allowed and what was forbidden.

Petitioners were required to wear haircloth, but nowhere was it written they couldn't wear other things over it to keep warm. And if she interpreted the texts in that way, then there was nothing to say heat magic was forbidden in the absence of a cloak. The reasoning was sound on the surface of it. But was it true, or merely a convenient lie Sanja wanted to believe because she was cold? By accepting the pouches, she risked the clerics turning her away. If she refused, she might be forced to give up or freeze to death when the weather turned unbearable.

Sanja weighed one option against the other. With all the resources of Castle Frastmir, the princess would surely know the rules of the Journey better than Sanja. And she wouldn't jeopardize Sanja's Journey after taking such pains to help her, would she?

If the princess wasn't worried about the consequences, Sanja ought to trust her judgment. She accepted the pouches more eagerly than was decent, but Princess Liadan didn't seem to mind. As she rose to her full, towering height and folded back her wings in preparation of stepping into the fire, Sanja asked yet again, "Where is Prince Fal?"

The fire flared up, swallowing the princess, then banked down to embers, and left Sanja cold and without an answer.

That was the last Sanja saw of her.

Several wretchedly cold and miserable days followed. A great storm blew through the forest, forcing them off the path for a while to seek shelter in a man-made burrow some other Journeymen had built long ago.

"Least you have your lightning kiss to keep you warm," Mattias teased to distract her from the howling winds outside. He'd been doing that ever since she'd told him about it their second day on the path, careful to keep Prince Fal's identity concealed.

"The dream of one," she replied, only to get a knowing smile in return.

"So you say. But mark me, lass, what the mighty Thor binds with his lightning no man will ever break apart again."

"I think you might be a worse romantic than I am, my friend."

Mattias chuckled. Shuddering with cold, he reached for another piece of wood to add to the fire. "Mayhap, if I believe hard enough in love, it will find me one day, too. And then mayhap, I'll never be this wretched cold again."

The bitterness in his words brought her gaze up to his face. "Is there no one you fancy in your village?" she asked carefully.

Mattias smiled a little, his eyes twinkling, not with bashfulness but hurt. "Aye. Suppose you could say." She waited for him to say more, but he didn't. Lost in thought, he stared into the flames, that sad smile turning sadder still.

"Will you not tell me about him? After all, I have told you all about my woes." She'd rambled about them for two days, and he'd listened with infinite patience and kindness, never once revealing a hint of his own troubles. "I thought we were friends." Sanja wanted to believe they were more than friends. The misery of their Journey had forced them to rely upon one another and trust one another so much, she'd happily call him brother. But perhaps he didn't feel the same.

Mattias remained silent for so long Sanja almost gave up hope. When he spoke again, his voice barely rose above a whisper, as if he feared his own words would somehow turn on him. "His name is Brand. We grew up together, fishing on the lake, running through the fields, stealing apples from old man Ivar's orchard. Good lad. Good to the marrow. Eyes like jewels and a smile to set your heart dancing. We were always together, thick as thieves. Whenever I was in trouble, he always shared the blame. Whenever I needed help, he was there 'fore I could ask."

Sanja smiled. "He sounds wonderful."

"Aye," he sighed. "Old man Ivar's daughter Helen thought the same. They're to marry this Midwinter. Never seen a smile like that on his face before. Not for me, nor anyone."

Sanja hugged herself against the sudden pang in her chest. He wouldn't look at her, but his pain was a throbbing pulse in the air, suffocating her with its sheer weight and breadth. Nothing to run from or to, he'd said. "Is that why you are here?"

Mattias poked at the fire with one of the larger sticks. "The day of their betrothal, Frigga knows why, must 'abeen some Other lacking for fun made my head all addled, but I had to go to Brand. Heart in hand, I would go to him and tell him all 'fore t'was too late, I thought. And when I got there… He looked so happy to see me, and for a wink, I thought…" He scoffed at himself. "Foolish things. Brand embraced me, same as he'd done always, but there I was, heart in hand, thinking t'was the happiest I ever been. And all the words were there, ready to be spoke, and I wanted to see his face when I said them. But then he took me by the hand and asked me, his chosen brother, to stand with him when he took Helen to wife." He tossed the charred stick onto the fire as if it disgusted him. "He'd no inkling of what I felt, much less returned it."

"Oh, Mattias."

"I'm no coward, lass. I would have fought a bear for that man and done it glad. But I couldn't watch him take a wife. The words twisted and changed and came out so proud-like. 'Best wishes to us both, then, brother. As you to your wife, so I to my white robes. And may the gods cross our paths again, when we've lived our lives to the fullest.' The shock on his face haunts me to this day. Broke his heart, I did, as much as he broke mine. I went off that very day without once looking back."

She felt his sorrow as her own. Swallowing unshed tears, she asked, "Will you ever go back?"

Mattias sighed. "One day, mayhap. When the thought of him bouncing his babe on his knee stops ripping me apart, I'll turn my feet back home. Mayhap by then, he'll have forgiven me."

They passed what felt like half a day in silence. Each time Mattias shivered so hard, his teeth chattered, Sanja shrank with guilt. Princess Liadan's tokens didn't make her immune to the cold, but at least they kept her in better shape than poor Mattias, who only had his blanket and their small fire to protect him.

Sanja wished there was a way to ease his torments, but she'd sworn to the princess to keep her involvement secret. She compensated by taking on as many tasks as possible while they camped. She gathered wood, foraged for food, tended the fire, and melted snow for water, allowing Mattias to rest by the fire's warmth so he could recover.

Perhaps this storm was a good thing, forcing them to stop and regain some strength before they moved on. Watching the storm's fury wreak havoc on the forest outside of their burrow, Sanja thought about that kiss. The *dream* of it. And the more she thought about it, the more miserable she felt. "It could not have been real," she said aloud, earning herself a raised eyebrow from Mattias. "The kiss. I know, I have said it before, but…" How could she begin to explain? "I felt an entire lifetime in that kiss. Every joy, every heartbreak, thousands of moments of pure contentment, and…" *Love.* She'd felt love. Not the kind that burned like lightning, but the kind that swaddled her in warmth. She'd felt herself an inseparable part of another, as he'd been a part of her, and she'd known there would never be a single moment of loneliness for either of them.

"A lifetime in the blink of a lightning strike," Mattias mused. "T'was a beautiful gift you've been given, lass. Now, what will you do about it?"

Sanja blushed. "Nothing." She'd been given a glimpse of what could never be. It wasn't a gift, but a curse to wonder, and wish, and know better. The kiss couldn't have happened. The vision must have been a dream, same as all the ones she'd dreamed since. Nothing more than wishful thinking and a yearning for things she would never have. Sanja was only clinging to it because having something beautiful to think about distracted her from the looming threat of Jarl Steen's marriage bed and gave her the strength to endure this wretched Journey.

"Because of this contract of yourn?"

"The contract would be the least of it," she said, glaring at Mattias to let it go. Sanja didn't want to talk about the kiss anymore. She didn't want to dream about beautiful, impossible things and wake alone in the middle of a forest, on a path that took her ever farther from their warmth. "I will do nothing because nothing could ever come of it."

Prince Fal had been right. She needed to stop wasting her mind on maudlin poetry. He was not her romantic hero, and she had no business imagining he could be. Love like the one she thought she'd felt didn't exist outside of books and dreams, and if it did, it wasn't meant for her. Princes didn't marry paupers. Not in the human realm, at least. She was alone on her Journey, and once it was done, she would be alone for the rest of her life. That was the price she had to pay to free herself from Jarl Steen.

"Beware squandering what gifts the gods give you. Next time, they may not bother."

Sanja thought of the lights flaring in the sky outside and almost told him the gods had run out of gifts to give. Instead, she bit her tongue and turned away.

"All's I'll say is this. Were it me, dreaming such a dream, I'd not be so quick to let it go."

Freedom was the only dream she could afford to think about. Therein lay her salvation. Even if it left her cold.

Yet that very night, Sanja dreamed a vision sweeter than all the others combined. A sunlit meadow, a glittering waterfall, and Prince Fal smiling down as he wound a piece of string around their joined hands.

The storm broke eventually, and the two of them resumed their trek along the frozen path. The day was overcast and cold, causing Sanja to shiver almost constantly, despite the warming leather pouches. She didn't know how long Princess Liadan's tokens were meant to last, but she suspected they were beginning to lose their magic. Soon, she'd be left to the mercy of the weather, same as Mattias, and Sanja wasn't nearly as well equipped to handle it.

When night fell, she braved the dark forest to go collect water. Only those eerie, colorful lights now illuminated the clear sky. Blues, greens, and reds danced together but never mixed. Sanja had grown so used to the sight she knew them all by heart, and she noticed each time another one burned itself out. The sky cleared a little more each day. How much longer before Fenrir devoured Wilderheim, too?

She smacked her dry lips, wavered on her feet, but forced herself to keep hobbling toward the well. The sooner she found water, the sooner she could return to the fire. Mattias said they had to be close now. Perhaps another day to reach the mountain and its winding stairs.

He was hopeful. Or perhaps he only made an effort for her sake. Sanja knew better. The worsening weather had forced them to slow down far more than Sanja had anticipated. Without proper nourishment to keep up her strength, her body had already shed its meager plumpness, reducing her to skin and bones. She stopped more often than was wise during the day to catch her breath and collapsed exhausted at night, sleeping undisturbed by dreams long past sunrise, yet waking no more rested.

Without Princess Liadan to keep her in form now, Sanja's misery bled from day to night, to day again, blurring the passage of time. How many days left until her contract forced her to take extreme measures? The most accurate answer she could give herself was *not enough*.

The well she found was crude, but someone had taken pains to keep it maintained. The bucket was sturdy enough, and the wooden cover looked as if it had been replaced recently. She pushed it aside and looked down into the black hole. Rather than waste effort with the bucket, she picked up a pine cone and dropped it down into the well, listening for the splash.

The cone landed with a sharp smack, and then a softer one as it bounced off something hard. No splash. Either the well had gone dry, or the water in it had frozen. Sanja hung her head and hobbled back to Mattias. She collected firewood along the way and snapped off the tips of pine branches for tea.

"No water?"

Sanja dropped her burden and sat next to him with a groan. "Frozen." She held her hands out to the fire, shivering as its pleasant warmth flowed over her. The pouches were definitely losing their magic. "No mushrooms, either." She'd managed to find at least a handful of small, frozen ones every night until now. Berries, too, and one day Mattias had caught a small fish in the creek.

"A shame." He already had their small pot sitting by the fire, heaped with snow, adding more as the mound in the pot melted down. As he swirled the contents near the flame, Mattias looked up into the trees. "Hear that?"

Sanja listened. "I hear nothing."

He nodded. "Nor do I. All the game's fled the cold."

"And there I was, hoping for a nice shank of venison for supper."

Mattias smiled. "It would a'helped. Of a certainty, we'll not find food or shelter up that mountain."

"Do you think we're getting close?"

"Aye," he said, but he wouldn't look at her. "After the morrow, I think, we'll be free of this cursed wood." To himself, he murmured, "And none too soon."

Surprised by the bitterness in his voice, Sanja waited for him to say more, to meet her gaze, but he kept staring into the flames, lost in thought. "Is something the matter?"

Mattias took a deep breath as if to answer, but in the end, he released it on a wordless huff.

"Mattias, you're frightening me." His eyes were bleak, his mouth downturned at the corners. His happy spark had dimmed, and he looked to be on the verge of tears. "Here." She took the pot out of his hand and moved it to her side, throwing in the pine needles to brew.

Mattias never looked away from the flames. "You're a strong lass, Sanja," he finally said. "You've spirit, and the hand of Thor himself on your shoulder to give you courage."

A guilty blush brought heat into her cheeks. "Nonsense."

"Nay, I see it clear. All these days we've crawled our knees bloody, I thought I was keeping you going. But t'was backward all along."

"We help each other," Sanja said. "We are strong together."

Mattias shook his head as a log split, sending a cloud of sparks into the air and setting the tears in his eyes aglitter. How hollow his cheeks had become, how deeply the shadows beneath his eyes painted his face. His hands trembled as he held them up to the fire.

"Don't give up now," she said, desperate to lift his spirits somehow. "We are close, you said so yourself. A few more days, and we will be at the top of that mountain, and all will be well, you'll see."

His mouth twisted in a tremulous smile. "What if I can't? What if I make it up there and fail their final test?" He shuddered, squeezed his eyes shut. "I watch you get up each morn with so much purpose it shames me for being so weak. I am that proud of you, I truly am. But each day this cursed forest keeps going on, I die a little more."

Every word he spoke stabbed at her with the knowledge of how she had deceived her friend—was deceiving him still by keeping Princess Liadan's aid secret. Setting down the pot, she took his hand in both of hers and squeezed her words firmly into his palm. "You are stronger than you think. You will make it to the temple, and you will pass the final test, and when you return to your village, you will be dressed in a cleric's robes. You are right. You do keep me going, and I cannot finish this Journey without you." The thought of it made her throat close up. She swallowed hard to clear it. "We will finish this trek together, side by side, yes?"

His nod left much to be desired.

"I warn you, Mattias, I am very stubborn. I will not let you give up when we have already made it so far." A world removed from her little life in her parents' little cottage. She was all on her own in the wilderness, except for Mattias.

"Aye, then," he said, squeezing her hands. "We will scale the mountain together. Reckon we'll need our sleep for that, though."

Sanja smiled. "Tea first."

They passed the pot back and forth between them, taking careful sips of the hot brew. It restored Sanja's spirits, helped her breathe a little easier. Weary though she was, as she lay down on her pallet, she couldn't sleep. Instead, she watched those brilliant colors swirl and wink at her through the tree canopy above. Such a lovely sight, for all that it spelled the end.

Her thoughts turned to ways she could help Mattias along the path. Perhaps she could share Princess Liadan's gift with him in some way without him knowing. She could tuck a patch into his satchel, where it would rest against his back. They often packed each other's things away or unpacked them for the night. She could do it then, without him noticing anything amiss.

In the morning, before they set out again, Sanja would share what little warmth she had with her friend. Decided, and relieved to lessen her guilt, Sanja slept soundly through the entire night.

She woke the next morning, hopeful and excited to continue. The pot was already boiling, teasing her nose with the scent of strong tea.

Sanja smiled as she stretched out of her coverings before scrunching back under them to hide a moment longer from the cold. But all those little touches didn't go unnoticed. How kind of Mattias to go to such trouble. He must have risen before dawn to gather enough snow for tea.

"Good morrow," she greeted loudly, waiting for his usual response from somewhere nearby.

When none came, Sanja frowned and sat up, noticing the second blanket draped over her own. And there was Mattias' satchel, packed and neatly set beside her own. But no Mattias.

Shivering, she draped the blankets around her shoulders as she stood. "Mattias!" Her call echoed through the trees, but no answer came. Sanja ran to the well, her boots crunching the morning frost. The clearing showed no sign of her companion.

Back toward the camp she ran, calling his name, searching for any hint of movement, any glimpse of a body lying on the forest floor. He'd looked so tired and weak last night; they'd not had a proper meal for too many days, and he'd spoken as if his spirit had abandoned him. Anything might have happened to him, and if something had, Sanja would never forgive herself. "Mattias, if you're here, answer me right now!"

A strong wind set the trees swaying and groaning around her, their shadows dancing along the forest floor as a shower of frozen needles rained down.

Mattias never answered.

Only one place left to check.

Sanja's leaden feet dragged to the trail, her heart heavy and her eyes stinging with the dread of what she knew she would find.

Knowing didn't make the evidence any easier to bear, and for a moment, as she stared down the trail, it was all Sanja could do to keep upright.

There, written in the thin layer of white snow, was Mattias' farewell: a trail of footprints leading back toward the nearest settlement.

The fire, the tea, his blanket, and satchel… A final act of kindness before he'd abandoned her to fate. He'd made his way back that much more unpleasant for giving her what aid he could on her Journey forward.

Numbness rooted Sanja to the spot. Her marker from the previous day stood out stark black against the white snow—Mattias must have cleared it so she'd know where to resume. A mere three steps away, but so many miles still to go. Sanja tried to remind herself of her purpose, the reason she was putting herself through this, but it all suddenly seemed so distant, so small and insignificant.

Better to freeze to death than spend a lifetime with the likes of Jarl Steen. The words that had been her source of strength now echoed hollow in her heart. Years of misery with him, or mere days left out here in the cold—what difference did it make? Either way, her life would be forfeit, and no one but her wizened parents would mourn her. And if that was to be her fate, Sanja's end was better met at the tip of a dagger.

No one would blame her for giving up. No one in their right mind would attempt a Journey in this weather at all. It had been folly from the start, and Mattias had proven it. If a big, strong man like that couldn't see it through, what chance did Sanja have, all on her own?

Her right foot crept forward, frost-covered boots touching the center of Mattias' footprint. Her body turned in his direction, and her heart yearned for the warmth of her mother's kitchen fire. She could see it in her mind's eye, could almost feel its heat warming her weary bones.

One more day.

The stray thought brought her crashing back into the cold. She swayed off balance and stepped away from the trail to right herself. Dizzy, Sanja stumbled back to the fire.

"One more day," she whispered to herself, tasting the idea on her tongue.

One more day wasn't too much to ask. Now that she had Mattias' supplies to add to her own, perhaps the Journey would be easier. She could keep warmer with the second blanket. And his pot, the one thing she hadn't thought to bring, would keep her in hot tea for as long as there was wood to burn for a fire. Rooting through his satchel, Sanja found strips of dried meats he must have been saving for the mountain. Added to her own meager supplies, they'd stand her in good stead once she got that far.

Heartened again, Sanja returned everything neatly back into its place. Thinking better of it, she emptied her own satchel and added its contents to Mattias' bigger one. Into her empty one, she shoved as much kindling and small branches as she could. Mattias had left a pile of them to dry by the fire; they'd catch much easier than the soaked, frozen wood littering the forest floor and save her some time in the evening when she made camp on her own.

"One more day." And if the Journey was too much to bear on her own by then, she would turn back and face the consequences with her head high for having made it this far.

Sanja banked the fire, drank down her tea, and dragged both satchels back to her marker on the trail, casting one last look at Mattias' footprints. She didn't blame him for giving up. His Journey had been a choice. Hers was a necessity. He'd know that, and he'd done everything he could to help her before setting off on his own path somewhere else. Sanja was grateful. She hoped he found the love he sought and lived a long and happy life with a strong hearth fire always burning bright to warm him. Everyone deserved that.

Sending up a silent prayer for his well-being, she turned toward her own fate.

"One more day."

≪ »·◇·« ≫

Three days later, the sky went dark, and a powerful snowstorm blew in, stealing Sanja's breath away. Forced to abandon the trail, she sought shelter in an empty burrow that reeked of some kind of animal. Bear, perhaps, or wolf. She found tufts of brown fur farther in the back and promptly scooted to the mouth of the burrow to keep her eye on the surrounding forest, praying the animal wouldn't return.

Fire was impossible, but as the burrow gathered thicker and thicker layers of insulating snow, it kept the cold at bay. Coupled with the leather pouches tucked as always in her shoes and at her back, Sanja weathered the storm in warmth and relative comfort.

With nothing to do but wait, she thought about Mattias. Sanja missed him dearly. His gruff voice in the morning had always made her smile. His easy humor had kept up her spirits at the start, and his thoughtful conversation had kept her mind occupied when humor had failed them both.

She hoped he'd made it safely back to Frastmir. She hoped he'd found her parents and told them Sanja was well so they wouldn't worry. She imagined her mother weeping, and her father shaking Mattias' hand and thanking him for the news.

Would Mattias linger a while in Frastmir? Likely not. Her parents would feed him and clothe him, and as soon as he'd regained his strength, Mattias would leave.

A shame. Sanja would have liked to have seen him again, to tell him about her Journey, however long it lasted.

Perhaps one day.

If they lived that long.

In the morning, the sun came out, illuminating a world of unbroken white. The forest had become a beautiful and quiet blank slate, with stray snowflakes drifting aimlessly through the air.

"Oh, no." Sanja pushed her satchels ahead of her as she crawled out of the burrow. Everything looked the same. She couldn't tell where the trail lay beneath that thick blanket, much less where she'd broken from her path the day before.

In the silent stillness, Sanja's heart beat as loud as a drum to her ears. She wracked her weary mind for memories of the day before. The storm had come on quickly, and she'd been hiding her face from the winds, ducking her head to stare at the ground, rather than what was around her.

She remembered climbing over a fallen tree to get off the trail. Its trunk had been split, and its roots had jutted out on all sides, one of them broken and hanging limply to the side. It had to be nearby; Sanja couldn't have gone too far off the trail in that weather, could she?

She had to resume her Journey from the exact spot she'd left off the night before, else she would fail, and all of this would have been for nothing. But with a thick blanket of glittering white covering the forest floor, Sanja had no hope in the world of finding it again. Without a marker, she was lost.

Shouldering the satchels, she waded through thigh-deep snow in what she hoped was the right direction. *Don't cry,* she ordered herself without mercy, gritting her teeth and forcing breath through the tightness in her throat. *Keep moving. That's all that matters. Crying solves nothing.* The day had dawned much warmer after the storm. The sun beat down, reflecting off the snow, making Sanja's eyes sting. It melted the surface just enough to soak her trousers. *Don't think about that now. Find the path.*

Where was it? She had to be getting close by now.

With her next step, her shin hit something hard. Wheezing, Sanja stopped to catch her breath, digging her hands into the snowdrift. She laughed at what she found, dashing tears away on her shoulder as she traced the tree trunk one way to its roots. Dusting off the top one, she found the familiar break and collapsed against the limp portion, boneless with relief, only to have it come loose and drop her into still more snow.

Sanja didn't care. She turned onto her back and lay there in the snow, shivering, laughing, and crying all at the same time. The hardest part was finished. Now all she needed to do was find her marker.

A sound somewhere in the distance awakened her back to her senses and into a moment of breathless silence. Sanja sat up, seeking its source in the depths of the wintry landscape.

There it was again! A voice echoing through the trees.

"Mattias?" She dared not speak his name too loudly, but already her heart beat faster with desperate hope.

Sanja scrambled to her feet, waded out to the center of a narrow ribbon of smooth white that had to be her path, and listened.

The voice was too far to make out its words, and she couldn't see its owner, but her heart told her it had to be Mattias. He'd come back! But why would he?

No, it couldn't be him. Her mind was playing tricks on her.

But she did hear *someone* out there.

Then another voice joined the first, this one deeper—an angry growl. And there, much closer than she'd thought, Sanja spotted movement among the trees. Three figures, one in the back and two up front, dragging something heavy between them. They were agitated, their movements quick and sharp, disturbing the forest's tranquility.

Three men wrapped in scarves, as unprepared for this weather as she. They argued amongst themselves and cursed their heavy burden, pausing every few steps to kick it.

"Wasting our bleedin' time!" The tallest man delivered a savage kick to the huddle at his feet. "Leadin' us out to nowhere to die? I'll show you!"

His companion on the right shoved him away. "Save your strength. No use wasting it on this putrid shit."

She knew those voices.

"I'm cold," the tall one snapped.

"We'll warm ourselves soon enough," the shorter one assured him in a way that made Sanja tremble with fear. "Isn't that right, Dyri?"

Unconvinced, the tall man spat, "She's like as not frozen unner all that snow somewhere. An' here we are, chasin' a ghost for a pouch of coin."

Sanja froze to the spot. She couldn't move or think as she watched the men wade closer and closer. The same three men who'd attacked her in Frastmir, fully healed, and furious at being out in the cold.

"Enough!" snapped the leader bringing up the rear. She knew him only by his voice now. With his beard grown in, he was otherwise indistinguishable from his bearded brother. "Have you forgotten the terms of our contract with Steen?"

Confirmation, clear as day. For all the good it did Sanja now.

Strangely, Dyri's brothers fell silent at those words, and even from so far away, Sanja could see the one on the right shudder. The tall one made a sound deep in his throat like an enraged animal and dropped to his knees, mercilessly beating the huddle there and screaming at it until it emitted a reedy cry that wrenched an agonized moan from Sanja's lips.

She slapped both hands over her mouth but couldn't have kept the tears from coming if she'd tried.

It took Dyri and his other brother both to drag the raging man off the poor, beaten lump of humanity. She blinked away her tears, strained her eyes to see him twitch, and listened for the smallest sound he might make to indicate he was still alive.

She could not move. Not to run, nor to fight.

Trapped in her terror, Sanja stood there, with only one hope left—that if she stood perfectly still, the murderers wouldn't notice her.

But of course they would. She'd left a deep trail wading out of her burrow, and no amount of effort would hide it. They would see her anon, and then Sanja would be done for.

"You did this!" The tall man surged to his feet and toward the source of his current misery. "We trusted you, and you led us into this poxy mess—"

He stopped abruptly with his back to Sanja. She couldn't see what Dyri had done to make him break off his assault, but she saw the other brother step back from them both.

"You trusted the coin, same as me," Dyri said. There was a man who would slit his own mother's throat if it suited his purposes. "Now, do we do this with you, or without you?"

"Alfrec," the third man beseeched his tall brother. "Be reasonable. We came this far. Think of the reward."

The tall Alfrec snarled, his wide shoulders rising and falling with deep breaths as he fought for control. "One of these days," he said, his voice trembling as he pointed at Dyri. "I'll take all this misery out of *your* hide."

"No, don't!" The shorter one started forward, but it was too late. Alfrec made a gurgling sound and dropped to his knees before Dyri. A cruel twist of the blade, a hard kick, and Alfrec sprawled in the snow at his brother's feet.

"And you, Bale?" Dyri asked, wiping the blade clean on Alfrec's shirt.

Bale held up his hands and shook his head.

"Then pick him up, and move."

Move, responded an echo in Sanja's mind. *Move!*

Without thinking, Sanja dropped to her hands and knees and began to shove at the snow, clearing the path around her. She heard one of the brothers shout as he spotted her, heard both of them rush forward, but dared not break off from her task. The snow was knee-deep on the forest path, slowing their progress, giving her a brief reprieve she knew would not last.

Shoveling armfuls of snow aside, Sanja ignored the numbness in her limbs and the desperate wailing sounds clawing up her raw throat. She let the tears flow and swiped her arms as wide as she could, digging down to the dirt.

Pain ripped through her fingertips as they met black, frozen ground. The dirt had already been frozen the day before, impossible to impress a marker into it. She didn't care.

As the men bore down on her, Dyri's blade still red with Alfrec's blood and Bale's fingers curled into cruel claws, Sanja turned away from them, pointing herself forward. She put her knees to the path and hunched down, arms up to shield her head as she cried, "I claim Journeyman's sanctuary!"

The boom of a soundless explosion reverberated through her chest, and then silence descended on the forest. Sanja held her breath, waiting for the blows to land, for the knife to stab her through. Nothing happened. Nothing stirred but for the sound of ragged breathing and the crunch of fresh snow beneath measured footsteps nearby.

Sanja peeked out from under one arm. Bale was laid out some distance away, and Dyri paced back and forth, staring at her with murder in his eyes. He could only come so close before his feet turned him away again, seemingly against his will, taking him a safe distance from her.

Sanja gazed from him to his brother, then down at the ground. She felt no different, couldn't detect the smallest presence of magic, but it had to be there, just as the books had said. By the law of the kingdom and the ancient magic Wilderheim's wizards had sown into the land itself, no one was allowed to interfere with a Journeyman's progress on the path to the temple. As long as Sanja stayed on her knees and kept moving forward, she would be safe.

Thank you, gods, she prayed, trembling with equal measures of relief and dread.

Dyri made another pass beside her, closer this time. Turning around, he came back slowly, sheathing his knife at his back.

Bale roused with a groan. He sat up, cracking his neck, then rubbed his jaw as he stared at her.

"You will not be allowed to harm me," Sanja declared.

Without warning, Bale sprang up and charged her full tilt. Sanja screamed when he slammed into the invisible barrier of the protection spell and shot back a second time.

Focused on Sanja, Dyri didn't spare his brother so much as a glance, and she felt the chill of his intent like icy hands wrapped around her throat. Rather than rush her, however, Dyri took a more measured approach, sliding a slow step closer.

Sanja shifted her knee forward to keep moving, hoping any advance on her part would keep him away. "You are wasting your time. I will not stop."

Dyri took another step that brought him almost within striking range. As if testing the magic's boundaries, he shifted first left, then right, then slowly took one more step toward her. It brought him so close that when he crouched down, his knees almost touched her. He kept himself far enough to avoid contact, but he stayed there, watching her with cold, faded green eyes, and not a hint of feeling.

Sanja shifted aside a little on her next forward push to get around him, and he turned with her to keep his eye on her. "You think you've bested us, don't you?" he said with an eerie calm. "You must know it's only a matter of time now. We will not fail in our task—we *cannot* fail. Do you understand?"

"Yes," Sanja replied. Only one thing could make a man that relentless in his pursuit: a contract signed in blood. Sanja would wager her life that after the way she and Olga had outsmarted Jarl Steen with her contract, he'd made quite sure no one else ever would again, and she shuddered to imagine what terms he had pressed upon these men. The reward must have been worth the price for them to agree, and now they were bound by those terms for as long as they lived.

"Steen will have you in the end, one way or another," he said.

"Best make your peace with it," Bale added before spitting in the snow. His assault had left him winded. He grinned at her, wiping off the blood from his broken nose. "Come with us now, and we'll bring you back alive. Bit used, mayhap, but the master won't mind."

Dyri's expression turned ice-cold, his eyes fading to almost gray as he reached behind his back to draw his knife once more.

Sanja bit back a moan, frozen to the spot as she watched the blade slowly raise between their faces. It was well used but also well cared for. The blade wasn't polished to a shine, but Sanja could see it was honed to cut with ease.

The pale-eyed man demonstrated this when he brought it to his free hand and pulled the blade lightly across his palm. Blood welled, and he cupped his hand to keep it from dripping to the ground. "Give me your word you will come with us willingly, and I will swear on my blood that we will deliver you to Steen unharmed."

"Dyri!"

Without taking his eyes off Sanja, Dyri replied, "I sent one brother to Helheim today already. Don't think I won't send the other." As Bale turned his anger on a nearby tree, Dyri added for Sanja alone, "Or you, for that matter."

"Y-you cannot harm me on the Journey," she said, needing to believe it herself.

"Not while you're on the path," Dyri agreed. "But you'll stop when you run out of time. I wonder if you know..."

Sanja frowned at that unfinished sentence but refused to rise to the bait, despite the welling sense of dread that suddenly made the air almost too thin to breathe. She kept moving forward, dragging one knee in front of the other as quickly as she dared, and tried not to look at him.

"It's not easy, keeping time when you can hardly tell up from down anymore—and who could blame you? Days bleed into nights, boundaries blur..."

Sanja looked away when he contorted himself to meet her gaze again. He was trying to manipulate her into giving up.

"Child, you're wasting your efforts. Truly. Not even on your best of days could you hope to reach that temple up there in the time you have left."

Sanja bit back a desperate moan. No, she was well on her way. It'd only been... Gods, how long had it been? Four days at the start stood out in her mind, etched with Princess Liadan's presence, then three more, carved with Mattias' absence. That made seven. But how many in between?

How many left?

Despite herself, Sanja met Dyri's gaze at last. Whatever he read in her expression put a sickening sneer on his face, and he seemed to take great pleasure in drawing out her misery, holding his silence, waiting for her to ask.

But she wouldn't.

She couldn't. Her tongue was stuck fast to the roof of her mouth, and the words simply wouldn't come.

Dyri answered, anyway. "Two days."

CHAPTER 15

Against the heat of the sun, the hard, frozen ground chilled Fal to the bone. In the freezing wind, the lush, green trees swayed with gentle grace. Out of the shadows, visions glittered like snowflakes in moonlight. At first, Fal thought his eyes were deceiving him, but the harder he tried not to see, the more vibrant the visions became.

Steel struck sparks off a helmet in a shaft of sunlight spearing through the tree canopy, and in the next blink, the echo of a breath misted in thin air on the path before him. An old woman died in her bed of moss, and then his royal council lined the battlements up in the trees, gazing down at him with defeat.

Fal saw water flood the streets of Frastmir and freeze into a smooth sheet of ice across the ground at his feet. A fallen tree became a bridge, shattered into rubble, and carried away by Frastmir's river. Looking up at the bright blue sky, he felt himself falling into the black abyss of Fenrir's maw.

Fal stumbled and turned away, stared at a tree trunk to push the visions back. Before his eyes, the rough bark became Hallowed Mountain, and on its staircase, Sanja stubbornly climbed upward, shaking, freezing, her knees torn and bloodied. He saw her collapse at the feet of a robed cleric before the bark reformed to its natural state.

Fal knew that tree. He knew the nymph who lived inside it. Balling his hands into fists, he beat at the trunk to wake her. It was a violent gesture sure to bring her wrath down upon his head. To harm a nymph's tree was an unforgivable offense. A nymph's existence was bound to her tree. It was her life source and her connection to the earth. If it was damaged, the nymph felt its pain. If it was felled, the nymph's immortal soul died with it. She became human, doomed to wither, and die in a few short, agonizing years.

If Nala had left Wilderheim with the rest of the Others fleeing Ragnarok, she'd have shrunk her tree into a sapling and taken it with her. The tree remained, so Nala had to be there, too. As an Other, she ought to be immune to his illusions. Why would she ignore him?

In a fit of desperation, Fal beat at her tree with all his might. "Nala! Show yourself!" He kicked at the protruding root, yanked at the branches, tore at the bark, hating that he had to resort to hurting her, but it was the only way he could think of to force her out of hiding.

Nala ought to be wrapping him in vines and dragging him deep underground in punishment by now. But her tree remained dormant, and that could only mean one thing.

Fal stepped back, squinted hard, and saw the subtlest of waves ripple across the world in front of him. This wasn't Nala's tree. It was merely another part of his illusion—like everything else, a hollow imitation of the truth, hiding the world from Fal, and Fal from the world. Nala wasn't ignoring him. She couldn't sense him.

Whatever had happened to Fal had made his illusions so strong an Other couldn't see through them, and Fal sensed they were still growing not only stronger, but larger.

Little by little, the real Wilderheim with its frost and shattered sky was fading away beneath the warmth and sunshine of its simulacrum. How long before he lost all sense of the real world? All his hopes now depended on Sanja and her ability to break his illusions, but if he couldn't find her, he couldn't touch her, and whatever magic she possessed would be lost to him forever.

Fal started down the path once more, straining to see farther into the distance, looking for the edge of the illusion. He pushed himself to feel the chill, to see the snow he ought to see along the path.

And somehow, the snow did appear.

And then the trees were gone, the earth beneath his feet turned to stone, and his next step brought him over the threshold into a vision of the clerics' temple. His ears thrummed in the silence. Fal couldn't hear, but he saw with perfect clarity. A lone candle burned in the carved circle opening of a marble pillar. On either side of it sat Sanja and a white-robed cleric. The cleric whispered a question to the flame, and then it was Sanja's turn to give it her answer.

But she hesitated. Her gaze broke away from the flame to look at the cleric. She was quivering, half-starved, exhausted, and filthy from her Journey. Her cracked, bloodied lips momentarily compressed into a thin line before her shoulders slumped. With her head bowed, she spoke her answer.

The flame turned black.

She'd failed.

The cleric rose to his feet and slowly walked to the door with Sanja limping behind him. He turned her out into a furious snowstorm, and she didn't say a word. The clerics would have given her shelter, had she asked for it. But her contract wouldn't let her stay. Fal saw its faint red-brown aura flicker around her feet, forcing her onward back to Steen.

But, instead of turning down the staircase to her right, Sanja walked straight ahead, to the edge of the rocky terrace, and off it.

"*No!*"

The vision blew away on a gust of wind and left Fal miles and days away from the temple. With no other thought in his head, save to find Sanja, he ran.

For two days, Fal raced along the Journeyman's path like a madman, shouting Sanja's name until he became hoarse. And all the while, the prison of his illusion plagued him with harrowing visions that wouldn't abate. Like the chaos he suffered each time it rained, the flashes built one on the next to shape a future in his mind.

It was a future in which the streets of Wilderheim stood empty, echoing with soft cries of the lost and abandoned, where King Saeran's proud wooden throne lay broken in the hearth while an iron seat took its place on the dais. Where icy mist cloaked the land in eternal winter, and the night fell hollow in utter silence.

It was a future where they'd failed. Because Sanja died, and Fal never made it back to the real Frastmir.

He refused to accept such an outcome. Against those horrors, he called up the memory of Sanja swathed in flowers, twirling on the green. Against the chilling sound of her whimpers, he recalled her laughter. And when he did, the visions changed, chased away by the hope of a much sweeter alternative.

Like a forgotten dream of a life he'd never lived, Fal recalled what the lightning had seared into their kiss. Sanja exploring strange Otherlands by his side. Sanja reading ten books at once in the castle library. Sanja sitting beside him as they held court, and lying against him in their shared bed.

A life of friendship, companionship, and love—a life he'd always yearned for but didn't think he could have.

He wouldn't see it if it wasn't still possible. And that meant he still had a chance to make it real. He still had time to save Sanja and find a way to stop Fenrir.

At the end of the second day, the frayed edge of his cloak caught on something and yanked him back by the neck so hard his feet flew out from under him, and he slammed to the ground. Choking, gasping for breath, Fal stayed there, staring at the bright blue sky and cursed himself a thousand kinds of fool.

This wasn't like him. Fal didn't rush into mindless action. He didn't fight his way out of problems. He thought his way out. Precious little thinking he'd been doing over the last two days. *And look where it's gotten me.*

With a weary groan, he levered himself up and sat with his back against a tree. Fal was beyond exhausted, yet his magic still flared out in a relentless pulse, feeding the illusion surrounding him. He needed to sleep, to regain his strength, but the fear of what else he might wake up to kept him from it. Too weary to keep moving, too wary to sit still, Fal was left with only one thing to do. He closed his eyes and breathed, opening his senses to the world around him.

As the tumult of his frenzied thoughts and chaotic visions slowly quieted, his focus turned inward, and he began to notice something strange. A sentient presence hovered somewhere nearby. It had no body, yet it somehow surrounded him. It had no eyes, yet it watched him.

Fal pushed farther, trying to make sense of this entity, to give it meaning, a name.

What he found robbed him of breath.

It was his illusion. Only, it was no longer quite as simple as an illusion.

Fal took a deep breath and let it out, feeling a puff of magic follow and disperse into the illusion. Beneath him, the feel of hard, frozen ground gave way to sun-warmed dirt. Another deep breath brought a soft southern breeze to combat the bitter northern winds he'd run through to get this far. A third swayed the branches above him, giving him sunshine and bird songs.

And as his mind seized on those new details, he realized it was all real. He thrust his hands into the dirt and felt it dig underneath his fingernails. He raised a handful of it for a closer look, and with another pull of magic, that handful of dirt became alive. The scent of it filled his nostrils. Smooth movement tickled his palm as an earthworm wriggled free, dislodging a tiny pebble to drop into his lap.

Awed, he placed the worm back where it belonged and took a good look around. Suddenly, a world that had appeared hopelessly empty filled with sound and movement. Not only birds but insects, too. Fal's gaze snared on something lurking in the shadows across the path, and a moment later, a beautiful doe raised her head to look right at him. Startled by his presence, she leaped in a graceful arc over the shrubbery and raced away.

The changes were small and gradual but tangible. Little by little, this illusory world grew real and solid, filling in details he would expect to see and feel, and Fal sensed it was because of him. The illusion took not only his magic but his thoughts and memories, too. It built itself not only of him but for him. Each new addition pulled a little more magic from Fal and gave back something he sorely needed.

A tickle at his elbow brought his attention to a raspberry bush that had most definitely not been there a moment ago. Famished, he didn't hesitate to reach for the red berries, stuffing them into his mouth one after the other. Their sweet juice filled his mouth, and Fal nearly wept from relief. His first bite of real food in two bloody days. It restored his spirits immeasurably.

Now, if only he could find water to restore his body as well.

As if his wish had been granted, Fal heard the telltale trickle of water nearby. Struggling to his sore feet, he shuffled toward the sound and found a spring welling up from deep underground. He dropped to his knees in gratitude and put his mouth directly to the surface, drawing deep. It was cold, sweet, and so clean. Instantly, he felt its magic restore his aching limbs. His blisters healed, his mind cleared. He sat back and was finally able to breathe with ease.

The cost was another puff of magic leeching from his core. He gave it up gladly as the world opened up to him, revealing all its waterways aboveground and below. The water's voice was different here than in Wilderheim, but its magic was similar. It called to his soul and gave freely of its strength to restore what he'd lost. Within moments, Fal was back to himself, standing tall and eager to continue.

He returned to the path and cast his senses forward, hoping to catch a hint of Sanja's presence nearby. He'd made good progress so far. He must have closed a fair amount of the distance. Perhaps he was close enough now for her to hear him.

Arrowing his intent the way he'd done in the council room, Fal focused on her with all his will, took a deep breath, and at the top of his lungs shouted, "Sanja!"

His call went nowhere. It had no echo in the forest and, though it carried far and wide, Fal sensed it never left the confines of this world.

"Sanja!" he called again. "Hello! Anyone!"

Nothing. The world around him didn't even ripple.

Fal staggered and caught himself against the trunk of an ancient tree. Its rough bark dug into his palm, grounding him in the moment, in this reality, in this world.

He gathered his will and attempted to punch out of the illusion one more time. Instead of breaking through, the power of his intent flared and absorbed into his surroundings, extending the boundary of this place farther beyond his reach.

And in return, it gifted him a sky filled with glittering stars as the sun began to set at last, erasing any remnants of his awareness of Wilderheim.

Fal sat hard, raked his fingers through the earth. He dug and struck at the ground, pouring his frustrations into it, needing to punish it for trapping him far away from his home when it was *just there*. Two of his fingernails tore off as he struck solid stone, and he screamed to the sky, clenching his hands into tight fists around small mounds of dirt. His entire being pulsed with magic he couldn't hope to contain. Wave after wave of it poured into his hands, making them clench tighter until he felt the dirt dig into his palms.

When he ran out of breath, he sat up and uncurled his fingers. Diamonds lay in the center of his right palm. Rubies in his left, droplets of his blood forever contained in crystal, his fingernails fully restored as if they'd never been damaged in the first place.

The absurdity of it struck him as hilarious. He laughed and kept laughing, unable to stop while angry, hopeless tears tracked down his face.

With a furious swipe of his hands, he sent the crystals flying as he shoved to his feet and shouted to the heavens, "Where are you?" Undeterred by the silence that answered him, he turned in a circle, searching the darkness for something he knew he would not find, daring it to materialize. "You've been meddling with my kin our entire lives—where are you when we need you the most!"

An owl hooted in the tree canopy above.

"Woden! Thor! *Loki!*" He flinched a little at the last, biting the inside of his cheek as he waited for the cruel Trickster to appear and smite him for his insolence. He waited for so long, holding his breath, his lungs began to burn, but no one appeared.

Fal hung his head with a sigh. "Begone with you, then. Riddance to you all."

If the gods wouldn't fight back, Fal would do it himself.

With his strength restored and his mind wide awake, Fal set out down the path once again, this time at a more measured pace. He would think his way out of this, as always. Everything could be learned and explained. All he needed was time and patience, both of which had become precious scarcities.

Fal held out his hands, shaped his intent, and fed it magic in a simple spell he hadn't had reason to work for many years. As he worked it now, the familiar currents twisted into a jumbled mess and dispersed in a confused swarm of firefly flickers. He tried again but, this time, rather than forcing it into the patterns he knew, Fal allowed the magic to flow and arrange itself in its own pathways, loosely guided by his will.

He was rewarded by the light of two good-sized orbs taking shape above his palms. They were bright enough to illuminate the forest for several paces around him and, once fully formed, seemed to take on a life of their own.

Fal studied their structure, felt their spirit, and smiled. In this place, unburned by the chaos of illusions, he could finally do what he'd not been able to do since reaching adulthood: wield magic like the tool it was meant to be.

And then a curious thought occurred to him, and as he considered it, the truth of it bloomed into a wondrous realization. This place behaved more like an Otherland than an illusion. It had a unique structure, its own magic, and its own rules, yet it still felt familiar—because all of it was coming from Fal.

His magic was feeding the creation of a new realm. His needs and expectations formed the foundation upon which it grew. Acknowledging his hunger had brought edible plants and game into being. The depth of his thirst had called up water. Fal had only to think it, and the natural order of things seemed to bend and evolve in answer.

Fal sensed the sentience of this world like a growing child. It needed his magic to evolve, and in return, gave him what he needed to survive. They were learning from one another, their symbiosis giving shape to something that had never existed before, and Fal sensed it was nearing completion. Soon, the Otherland would mature enough to exist on its own. Once it reached that stage, it would no longer need Fal's magic to sustain itself, and he would no longer be able to shape it, only manipulate it in the way of wizards.

Somehow, before that happened, Fal would need to find a way back out to Wilderheim. Else the borders of this world would close, and he might never be able to get out again.

↞ »·◇·« ↠

Sanja's eyelids drooped. She shook herself to wakefulness and dragged her right knee forward through the snow. The afternoon sun speared through the trees, teasing her with soft caresses of warmth before the wind swayed more branches into its path, sinking her back into cold shadow. The snow had melted down to almost nothing during the heat of the day, but what remained was crusted with a thick layer of ice. It cut across her knees and thighs as she pushed forward, wearing holes through her haircloth trousers.

And still, the cold and pain were nothing compared to her other torments. Every push forward took her one knee-step farther away from the dead bodies lying in the snow behind her. She didn't want to think of them but, the harder she tried to push them from her mind, the more insistently they haunted her. The tall Alfrec, murdered before her eyes, and the dying stranger the brothers had brought with them.

It had to be a stranger. Mattias was in Frastmir. He'd made it back before the storm hit. At this moment, he was sitting at her kitchen table, eating a bowl of porridge and telling her parents that he'd left her provisioned and in high spirits, well on her way to the temple.

Therefore, he couldn't possibly be lying there beside Alfrec. Her heart ached because she was tired. And the tears in her eyes were from the wind. She wasn't fighting back sobs because she mourned him—because *he wasn't dead!*—it was because Dyri and his brother wouldn't leave her alone. The ancient protections kept them from harming her physically, but the brothers had other ways to torture her.

The first thing Dyri had done when she'd refused to give in to his demands had been to take her satchel. He'd shown it to her and asked her again if she would go with them. When she'd refused, he'd cut the satchel open, spilling its contents. The meats, he'd shared with Bale. The rest, he'd burned then and there.

Sanja had almost wept at the loss of her blankets, but she'd soaked up the heat of the fire to warm herself and kept going. Not thinking of the dead bodies at all. Not imagining Mattias face-down in the snow, beaten, broken, and alone.

Bale had been furious at her continued resistance. He'd shouted and railed at Sanja from a distance of several arm's lengths—as close as the protective magic would allow him to get. Bale had a terrible temper he couldn't seem to control. He lashed out often, usually at the trees, because he couldn't get to her.

In contrast, Dyri was cold as ice. Rather than waste the effort to rage at Sanja, he studied her. Any time Bale lashed out, he watched for Sanja's flinch. He'd watched her the entire time her belongings had burned. He watched her each time she paused to rest. Where Bale was the rabid dog let off its chain, Dyri was the lynx hiding in shadow, waiting for the perfect moment and the most efficient way to strike. She squeezed her eyes shut whenever she felt the urge to look behind her so he wouldn't suspect how badly she needed to know it wasn't Mattias back there beside Alfrec. She could not let him use that stranger—*not Mattias!*—against her. It would destroy her.

As night approached, the men started to get cold. They paced and hopped in place, breathing into their hands for warmth, but Dyri wouldn't allow a fire. He would deny himself and his brother the comfort of its warmth to force more misery upon her.

It was only fitting for her to return the kindness. So long as she kept moving, they couldn't touch her, and their contract wouldn't let them leave.

Might the path's protective magic keep them at bay long enough? Could it be strong enough to counteract her blood oath for a while? Yes, her contract did say she had to marry Jarl Steen if she failed to earn her robes within a month, but it didn't say when. What if she simply kept going, all the way to the temple?

The thought of completing her Journey, and giving Jarl Steen not only a hairless bride but a robed one, filled her with grim satisfaction. He would be furious. She could still score a victory against him, however small. And Steen's men would be forced to suffer with her.

They'd tormented her all day long. In fact, all of her suffering along the Journey could be attributed directly to Jarl Steen and his men. They all deserved to suffer the same. If Sanja could keep the brothers in the cold and misery for one night longer, she would somehow find the strength to endure, to punish them for as long as she could. Why should they be spared when she could make their task as long and difficult as possible?

One knee after the other, she moved onward.

But she was beginning to fade after a day of pushing forward without pause. Her progress was so slow she could still smell the smoke from her burned things behind her. Still, at least she was moving. Every knee-step took her farther from those bodies. Before long, she would forget they were there at all.

And then her mind would give up this nonsense of Mattias lying dead in the cold when all he'd wanted was a peaceful life and a love to keep him warm.

As the light began to fade, Bale grew wary of the dark. "We should make camp," he said. "She can't run far, anyway. We could build a fire a ways down the path and wait for her."

Dyri's response was short and curt. "No."

"You're being unreasonable," Bale growled. "What do you expect her to do out here?"

She felt Dyri watching her and detected a cruel smirk in his voice when he said, "Rest."

With a frustrated huff, Bale let the matter drop.

But only for a while.

As the forest turned dark and Sanja began to feel as if she was floating through a dream, the hot-tempered Bale couldn't stand it any longer. He disobeyed his brother's wishes and lit a torch, waving it in Dyri's face. Dyri glared at his brother but didn't say a thing, and Sanja thought he was secretly grateful for the light.

So was she. It revived her enough to keep dragging one knee in front of the other. She watched for its flicker, took comfort from the promise of its warmth if nothing else.

Dyri noticed. "Douse it."

"No," Bale replied, mocking him.

Dyri started for Bale, who danced away to Sanja's other side, waving the torch back and forth. Rather than chase his brother, Dyri fell silent and crouched beside Sanja to take a closer look at her face. "You must be exhausted. I am, and I haven't been shoving along on my knees all day. On an empty stomach, to boot."

While he waited for her to respond, Sanja took another step. This time, the sharp ice cut through her trousers and scraped her bare skin, making her hiss in pain. She paused, sitting back on her heels and drooping forward to her elbows. She was so tired breathing was a chore. Her lips were covered in brittle scabs where her skin had split from the cold.

"Poor little thing," Dyri said. "So much misery you brought down on yourself for no good reason at all."

Sanja turned her head to spear him with a glare. "You say that when you have Jarl Steen's contract hanging over your head?"

Dyri shrugged. "Steen is nobility. All nobility are filthy shits." He leaned closer to meet her gaze as he imparted his next words of wisdom. "But one learns to tolerate them for the pleasures they provide."

"Pleasures?" She nearly choked, saying the word. He had to be jesting.

Dyri shook his head in mock pity. "You poor, ignorant thing. Bale, tell her."

"The Steen clan has coin," Bale said. "Mountains of it. Their keep is almost as big as Castle Frastmir, and Jarl Steen enjoys his comforts very much. The best of everything, he has. Food, clothes, jewels..."

"And you can still have all of it. You can have your own chambers with a hearth so big you'll never feel another twinge of a chill. You can have servants carry you anywhere you wish to go. Your feet need never touch the ground."

Sanja laughed, wincing as her lower lip split again. When Dyri frowned at her, she laughed harder. How could she not? "Do you think I would be out here," she said, her voice raw and reedy, "if any of that mattered to me?"

A burning ember sailed over her head to land in front of her. Mesmerized by its glow, she didn't notice Dyri move away from her, but she heard him demand, "What are you doing?"

She reached out slowly, hovering her hand over the small ember, feeling its meager warmth soak into her palm as its light began to dim.

"Worth a try," Bale said. "Now we know we can't kill her from a distance, neither."

Sanja took a chance and snatched up the ember. It burned her at first, but she held on, hugging it to her chest. Its warmth streamed into her, through her, into Princess Liadan's tokens. There, the heat flared stronger, stroking up her spine and through her limbs. Sanja sighed, feeling lighter and stronger for it. If only it would last.

When she dropped the ember back, Sanja became aware of the silence and looked up to find Dyri watching her once again.

He glanced down at the cold, black ember, then at the dark scorch mark on her palm, and finally at her face. Moving with calculated intent, he slowly drew his knife and crouched down to place it on the snow in front of her.

Sanja stared at the blade, her mind struggling to comprehend its purpose. It was right there, within easy reach, a weapon, and a tool. A chance to end it all. All she had to do was pick it up and turn it on herself.

Or on them.

Sanja had never deliberately harmed another person; she didn't know how. With Dyri's blade, the prospect seemed easy enough. The bandage he'd wrapped around his hand was still a bit wet where his cut hadn't healed all the way. She knew how sharp the blade was, how quickly it could do a world of damage.

She stared at it and thought, *I could do it.* Dyri was close enough that she could stab him dead if she moved quickly. But what about Bale? He would never let her get away with it, and the moment she left the path, she'd lose its protection.

Her gaze rose to meet Dyri's. So that was his trick, then.

His pale eyes watched her, steady and curious, waiting for her to decide her own fate. He didn't move a muscle and, if Sanja guessed correctly, he wasn't breathing, either. His entire body, as relaxed as it appeared, was poised to move with a speed Sanja could never hope to match. Unlike her, Dyri *was* a murderer, an expert at his trade, by all appearances.

She half-turned away from him. Bale was on that side, but it wasn't him she wanted to seek. Somewhere on the trail behind her, Mattias lay unmoving in the snow, freezing to death, if he wasn't dead already. The knowledge burned inside her, refusing to be defeated by the lies she clung onto. Mattias had never made it back to Frastmir. If he had, the brothers never would have come looking for her this far down the path. Mattias was the only one who could have told them she was still alive and moving forward.

It was him, lying there in the snow beside Alfrec. They'd killed him—because of her.

The pain in her chest doubled her over, robbed her of breath when she wanted to scream her grief and kill Dyri and Bale for what they'd done to the kind, gentle man she would have called brother.

It won't bring him back.

No, it wouldn't bring him back. It would only destroy everything she'd been suffering for and everything he'd done to help her keep going.

Honor him. Give his death meaning.

Yes, she could still do that. She wasn't finished.

Sanja sought Dyri's gaze and held it for so long his mouth twitched in an almost smile. With her hands somewhat more limber from the ember's added warmth, she uncurled her fingers and reached down, taking hold of the weapon Dyri had offered. When she straightened to meet his gaze once more, the blade now in her grasp, she found him in the same place, his head tilted the same way, his mouth stretched into the same smile.

But his eyes were sharper, staring hard into hers. She felt the tension in him now, a predator poised to strike. His time had come, and he was merely waiting for the signal to move.

Sanja looked at the knife in her hand, then back at him. His chest rose with a deep inhale, his unblinking gaze reflecting Bale's torchlight back at her. She raised the blade high, watching his eyes open wide, then drew back and threw it sideways as hard as she could. The knife sailed into the darkness beyond Bale's light and landed softly in deep snow some distance away.

Sanja smiled into Dyri's shocked face and dragged her left knee forward, forcing him to move out of her way. Satisfaction burned through her veins, heating her limbs a little more. She used it to her best advantage, picking up her pace to a slightly faster crawl.

They'd spend hours searching for that knife, and might never find it, anyway.

"Bollocks this," Dyri muttered.

"Oi! Where are you going?" Bale's torchlight dimmed as he followed his brother down the path behind Sanja. She heard noises but didn't turn around. Better not to know what they were up to.

But Dyri would not be ignored. His grunts and curses signaled his return as he dragged something toward Sanja. "Right," he said, dropping his burden by her side. "You know him, yes? He of a certainty knew you."

Sanja squeezed her eyes shut rather than look at the limp body beside her. She could tell by its size it could be none other than Mattias, and her heart broke for him all over again.

"Friend of yours, is he?" Dyri taunted. "A good one, too. He was that distraught when we met at that ramshackle inn a ways back. Going on and on about the wee lass he'd left behind, and how ashamed he was to have left her all alone out there. 'Would that I could have done more,' he said to us, didn't he, Bale?"

"That he did," Bale confirmed. "Cried tears worthy of a spurned virgin, he did."

Sanja bit the inside of her cheek as she brought her left knee forward.

"And we told him, my brothers and I, 'A lass, taking the Journey at a time like this? She must be either very brave or very stupid.' And what did he say, Bale?"

"He said, 'A stronger, braver one I've never met.'"

Sanja shifted her right knee forward, then her left. She kept her gaze on the path before her, but inside she was dying a little more with each word they spoke.

Dyri kept pace with her, dragging Mattias a bit ahead of her. He leaned down to see her face and grinned. "And then he told us all about your quest to escape an unwanted suitor."

"Which we already knew," Bale chimed in.

"Of course we knew. All of what's left of Frastmir is abuzz with rumors of a daft girl going off to her death on the Journey. We almost left you to it, too. But we do have our contract to consider."

Bale grunted agreement and spat on the ground.

"So we told the man, 'We're messengers sent to the temple by the king, bound by honor to keep his peace. We've naught to offer but our company, but surely the girl would be grateful to have even that. Tell us where to find her, and we'll convey her safely to the temple.'"

Sanja breathed down her revulsion, kept moving forward. Her throat ached from keeping silent when all she wanted to do was scream.

"He resisted," Dyri said. "At first. Tried to keep us from you. Three against one and still, he fought us. But my brothers and I brought him 'round in the end, didn't we, Bale? We can be very persuasive." He leaned over Mattias and dragged him up before Sanja, where she couldn't hope to avoid looking.

Sanja slapped a hand over her mouth, sat hard on her heels to see her good friend brought to such a state. His hair shirt was covered with dirt and blood, his face nigh unrecognizable underneath a mottling of swollen bruises. He had gashes on his temples and cuts all over his arms. Had it not been for the tears in his trousers and the wounds on his knees that she had helped him tend, Sanja would never have known him. "You've killed him."

Dyri looked down. "Did I?" He put a hand under Mattias' shattered nose. "Not quite yet. He's still breathing." He met her gaze again and again gave her that cruel smirk. "Bale, give me the torch."

Bale obediently handed it over and stepped a safe distance away.

"Now, then," Dyri told Sanja. "One last chance. Will you come with us willingly?"

Sanja couldn't tear her gaze away from Mattias. In the flickering torchlight, she saw his head move a little. A trick of the light? It had to be. Dyri was lying. Mattias had been motionless on the ground from the moment they'd dropped him there. Even if he had been alive then, he couldn't be now. His fingers and toes had started to turn black from the cold. None of his wounds were bleeding, and despite what Dyri said, Sanja could not detect any hint of breath in him.

Mattias was dead. Never to find his love, or a hearth fire to keep him warm. After all he'd endured, and everything he'd already done for her, he'd died out there in the bitter cold, fighting to keep the brothers from Sanja.

They'd killed him to get to her, and if she gave in, he would have died in vain.

"Consider it a trial of the heart," Dyri offered, bringing the torch closer to Mattias' face. "We're about to find out whether anyone's life is more precious to you than your own. Will you save him, oh brave one? He paid dearly, trying to save you. It's only fitting you return the gesture, no? The gods do love their balance. The honor ought t'be answered. The blood ought t'be repaid."

She owed Mattias everything. His kindness had kept her going, and the supplies he'd left had saved her life, she was certain. To know he had died for her was more than she could bear. How in the world could she repay a debt like that?

"I..."

Dyri raised an eyebrow. "Well?"

Her numb face scrunched up as she took in Mattias' visage. Such handsome features, he'd had. And such a big heart. Sanja wasn't worthy of his sacrifice. "I..." She reached out to touch him, dreading the feel of his cold, lifeless flesh beneath her fingertips.

Dyri yanked him out of her reach and brought the torch closer still. "I'll not wait much longer."

My fault. Sanja had expected Jarl Steen to keep pursuing her, but not at such a cost. Did he know what his men had done?

Had he given the order himself?

I can't go back. Mattias, brother of my heart, please forgive me.

Dyri must have seen her decision in her eyes. With a savage snarl, he shoved Mattias away and stabbed the torch against his side. With his hair shirt so thoroughly soaked, it took an agonizing while for the flame to catch. Mattias never stirred or made a sound. Sanja watched his body burn a moment longer, praying that his ancestors would meet him with open arms in the afterlife.

As she turned away to keep going forward, Dyri barred her path with the torch. "No great loss for you, then, is it? Eh, you're probably right. What's a stranger worth these days, anyway? Certainly not more than blood kin. And you still have two of those left in Frastmir, if I'm not mistaken." He leaned down as close as the magic would allow. "I'll give you the night to think on that. In the morning, my brother and I will set out back to Frastmir. You'll want to be coming with us, then, if only to make sure your parents don't go the way of your friend. Because I'll make sure they're alive when they do."

CHAPTER 16

Nialei tensed as the tracker approached. Though her shoulders were proudly pulled back, she wouldn't meet Nialei's gaze. Bad news, then.

Gods, how bad?

The female's horned head bowed as she knelt her front hooves to the ground, her many golden plaits slipping over her shoulders to cover her face as though she was ashamed. Her kind was a beautiful blend of doe and human, thin and lithe, appearing so delicate, yet thrumming with immense power. When she became agitated, that power coursed through her veins, painting them black against her silvery skin.

She would not speak until prompted, and Nialei could not bring herself to ask the question she desperately needed to have answered.

Saeran took her hand in his, drawing her gaze to his strange, yet still familiar face. Despite having retained his human shape for the most part, her beloved mate and king looked more dragon than human in this land, with thick horns adorning his head and shimmering black scales framing his brows. His teeth flashed sharp whenever he spoke, giving his smile a feral edge, and his eyes blazed with blue fire that seemed to burn just for her. His Other form was similar in shape to their daughter's, save for his size. As if he'd stuck partway to becoming a true dragon, Saeran's shoulders were wider than normal, his arms and legs thickly muscled. His wings were far bigger than Liadan's, flaring and furling with a will of their own, and his tail ended in a sharp, arrow-like tip that cut like a blade. Yet he retained his human-shaped hands and feet and seemed to have the ability to retract his claws when necessary.

Nialei had not dared to look at her reflection since the first day, but she knew she appeared no less Other. A Halfling daughter of a water sprite and a demigod, she'd inherited the pearlescent skin of her mother's people and the antler crown of her father's. The transformation had made her eyes bigger and rounder, her nose smaller, more delicate. The sides of her neck were scarred with straight lines where her gills lay flat and dormant while she was on land, but in water, her antlers dissolved away, her gills opened, and fine webbing grew between her fingers.

In Wilderheim, the two of them would have terrified the masses. Their appearance would have incited panic and riots among the humans who tolerated their regents' magic only because they didn't look Other. Here, among her father's people, no one bothered to cast them a second glance.

She steeled herself to take a measure of the gathering. Her father's herd, all giants walking on two hooved legs, with antlers jutting out of their heads, stomped restlessly within the circle of trees that marked the gathering green. They were wary of the tracker whose delicate, four-legged form barely reached their hips with the top of her antlers. The sooner she delivered her message and left, the better.

"Speak, please," Nialei invited softly, cautious of her voice. It sounded the same, but felt much more potent and seemed to have an unpleasant effect on her father's herd. Though she was always careful to show proper respect and humility to her father's people, her smallest request was met with disdainful obedience. They reacted as if she hadn't asked, but ordered, and then forced their compliance against their will. Nialei had no way of knowing how much of this effect was caused by the power in her voice and how much by her rank as the only offspring of their leader.

"My Lady," the tracker replied, her voice as gentle as her form. "I have located the daughter of fire on the border between Aegiros and Wilderheim. She wore battle gear and soared as a black shadow across the night sky."

"Where was she heading?" Saeran asked and cleared his throat, still annoyed by the growl he could not shake from his voice. Nialei bit back a smile. She rather liked that growl, herself.

"Nowhere, My Lord. She appeared to be patrolling."

This had both of them leaning forward in their seats. "My daughter, patrolling Wilderheim's border?"

"Yes, My Lord," the tracker replied and answered the question they were both thinking. "Fear travels on an icy wind across the land. The sky burns with magic, and the earth freezes with dread. Others have fled. Trade and travel have come to a halt. Humans who leave Wilderheim do so for good. Those who stay are bracing for war. And..." She glanced up, a fine webbing of black sprouting out from the corners of her eyes like an elaborate mask.

Cold dread settled deep in Nialei's gut. "What is it?"

The tracker bowed her head once more. "Strange things are growing throughout Wilderheim. Masses of power that have no origin and no anchor. Only an Other would sense them, but this Other sensed them growing stronger with each day."

"Creatures of some sort?" Saeran questioned. "Traps?"

"Portals, My Lord. Seven of them."

Saeran squeezed Nialei's hand so hard, had she been human, her bones would have been crushed to dust. "Does my daughter know of this?"

"No, My Lord. She has not ventured that deep in her patrols. Her path takes her southwest, along the Aegiran border to Lyria. She expects Synealee to march from that direction."

"Where is Fal in all of this?" Surely, Nialei's son would have sensed the portals; surely, it was he who'd called up the army. He would know something was brewing and take measures to protect Wilderheim and its people. Even if he never left Castle Frastmir, he could still—

"Gone, My Lady."

Nialei lost her breath. Her body felt encased in a layer of ice so thick she couldn't move even to blink.

"No one has seen or heard from the son of water in over a week. There is no sign of his presence within the borders of Wilderheim."

Silence met the tracker's report. Not a single hoof stomped down, not a leaf rustled in the trees. Nialei heard her own heart beat slower and slower, and she knew if she let it, it would stop completely.

A tracker's magic was unique to all the Others, and their kind was both feared and revered because of it. Simply, they never failed to locate what they'd been sent to find. Ever. If this tracker hadn't found a trace of Fal, it could only mean he was not there to be found.

Saeran's hand grew cold, holding hers, and Nialei began to feel lightheaded. Somehow, she managed to turn her head and meet her mate's gaze, desperate for the comfort of his fire, the surety that he would know what to do. It wasn't there. The eyes gazing back at her were as gray as the sky above her head, not a spark of fire to them.

"We have to find a way back," she pleaded.

Saeran's wings flared, sending the herd stomping out of the way. His glittering black cheeks turned dull in a Dragonblood version of an embarrassed flush as he folded the willful appendages tight against his back. "We have already tried fire and water, and we have found no portals in the entire Otherland. What else can we do?"

A tall, swarthy warrior stepped out of the herd toward them. "Forgive, Nobility. Cernunnos not allow."

Saeran speared him with a burning glare. "The tracker has come and gone. So has Varr."

The warrior flushed and bowed his head. "Forgive, Nobility. Cernunnos protect herd. Nobility is herd. Nobility cannot leave. Cernunnos not allow."

"A god I have barely heard of will not keep me from my children," Nialei grated and instantly regretted her tone when the warrior whined and retreated back into the herd.

A warm, heavy hand settled on her shoulder, thick, blunt fingers curling into her flesh to offer comfort. "That god is your grandsire," her father said kindly. His face showed no emotion, but his eyes warmed to a shade of gold, looking at her.

"I don't care," she replied hotly. "I will not be kept prisoner while my children fight for their lives. Fal could be dead—"

Gjafvaldr, the first son of Cernunnos and leader of his herd, squeezed her shoulder a little harder. "Cernunnos has given of his essence to shield this world from Fenrir. He has given his life to protect his offspring for as long as he can, that we may live as we do, and die swiftly when the time comes. It is a kindness. Not punishment."

"We mean no disrespect," Saeran said humbly. "But we cannot stay here. We must finish what we started."

"Fal is not dead. If he was, the tracker would have found a body. This has Loki's cunning written all over it. And that means it can be nothing but a trick. You have raised powerful children, daughter. Have faith in what they are destined to accomplish."

It was what he'd done. He'd placed his newborn daughter into the arms of a human and abandoned her there to grow up with no notion of who or what she was. He'd trusted her to be strong enough to grow into her destiny without his interference. Nialei both loved and resented him for it. She might not have needed his help but, gods, how she wished she'd had his guidance. And now he was asking her to do the same to her children. "I cannot abandon them. I will not."

"The wards are set, daughter," Gjafvaldr said and, though his voice was kind, his eyes hardened. He spoke to her like a stubborn child who needed to be taught a lesson. "They are god-made. You will not break them while he still has power."

"By the time his power fades, it will be too late. Please, we must leave now."

He held her gaze a moment longer, then released her to approach the tracker.

The herd stepped back in deference, and the tracker bowed so low her antlers touched the ground before she rose to her full height, brought her shoulders back, and stared straight ahead.

"You have done well, tracker," Gjafvaldr praised. He held out his hand, and a large pouch appeared in it. Nialei had seen him perform this magic enough times already to know the pouch would be heavy with gold coins.

The tracker nodded and reached for her payment, but Gjafvaldr pulled it back out of reach. Her eyes sparked bright black when she met his gaze, her temper showing in a webbing of black veins that snaked from her fingertips across her hands and up her arms.

"I have one more task for you," Gjafvaldr said, holding up his free hand in a staying gesture. "And will pay you handsomely for it." As he spoke, the pouch grew larger, heavier, mesmerizing the tracker out of her ire. "The daughter of fire will need help in her brother's absence. She is a fierce warrior, but even a Dragonblood cannot oppose the power of a god on her own. You will race across the Otherlands and deliver my call to arms to each and every clan."

At this, the tracker frowned at him. "They have their own battles to fight, My Lord."

"They can spare two warriors each. Two warriors from every clan, understand?" He placed the now massive pouch on the ground before her.

"If only a tenth of them agree, the daughter of fire shall have a formidable force at her back," the tracker mused. "But not an army."

"I am aware," Gjafvaldr replied. "The final battle need not be won in Wilderheim. Only fought long enough."

The tracker cocked her head to one side. "You do not wish me to find the dragon, My Lord?"

"We already know where he is," Nialei said. "A creature of in-between has already been sent to retrieve him." If Cernunnos' wards couldn't be breached by her or Saeran, then the dragon was their last hope of escape. His blood had been powerful enough to change their clan's destiny more than once. Nialei could only pray it'd be powerful enough for one more magic spell.

≪ »·◇·« ≫

Helheim's prison had no sun or moon. Its torches and candles never burned down, and no creatures scurried in and out of the safety of their burrows to feed. Without these things, the dragon had no way to tell the passage of time, save by the deadly floods. He'd endured two score and three of them thus far but, whether each flood translated to an hour in Wilderheim or a year, he couldn't tell. For all he knew, two score and three centuries have passed in his absence, and the worlds he had known were long gone down Fenrir's monstrous gullet.

"Are you tempted yet?"

The dragon tensed at that voice, his mouth drawing back from long, sharp fangs that ached to rend flesh asunder.

"The water has receded already, have you noticed? Do you know why?"

Hands balled into fists, the dragon pulled taut his binds, strained against them, and prayed to feel the rope strands fray and snap. Instead, they tightened around his wrists until his hands throbbed.

From the shadows at his back, a cool, pale hand brushed against his burning one. Snarling, the dragon turned his face away, and there she was, his beautiful Solveig, her eyes sad as she gazed at his bound wrists.

But her voice spoke with Hel's apathy. "Its source lies outside the borders of my realm. It feels my brother's approach and freezes into eternal winter." She looked toward the river and sighed. "Soon, the stream will disappear completely."

The dragon frowned. He could almost believe he'd heard the slightest hint of true sorrow in her words. Or was it grief?

"What is it like?" she asked, still watching the waves ripple down the stream.

The dragon refused to indulge her with an answer.

Rather than press for one, she remained silent, her head tilted as if she were listening to someone else speaking to her. Had her question been directed at him at all? "Why did you choose this shape?" When she turned her face toward him, it briefly split, Solveig's ghostly visage facing him a moment before Hel, and in that moment, before Hel realigned herself, he saw genuine surprise in Solveig's eyes. He saw her mouth open to speak as Hel took over once more. "You could have become anything. Why this?"

Having borne witness to the creation of all living beings, dragons carried within them the ability to become any of them—until they chose one. Then, and ever after, the infinite potential of shapeshifting narrowed to but one alternative: dragon, or their chosen other. In all his long millennia of life, the dragon had never understood the reason for it, until he'd met Solveig.

He'd thought the ability and its restrictions to be a secret kept by his kind alone. He'd never spoken of it to anyone. Not Solveig, or their daughter, or any of his clan. How could Hel have known?

The dragon flinched when she reached out to touch one of his horns, but she persisted, running soft, cool fingertips from one's base at his left temple all the way to the tip. "You, a creature born of infinite potential, chose *this*. Why?"

Water splashed up as he whipped his tail to knock her hand aside.

Hel stepped away.

Solveig lingered a moment longer, gifting him with a glimpse of the woman she'd used to be. Her lips began to form his name, and he sucked in a breath, aching to hear it again, but she faded too soon, blowing back around Hel and settling over her until Hel once again became her. "You bound yourself in shape and form. You gave up infinity for a wizard's trick. I will know why."

The dragon bared his fangs in a vicious snarl.

Solveig's eyes closed as Hel stilled for a moment. "For her," she said. "For *love*. No, that cannot be." She opened her eyes to regard him with her utter lack of interest, even as a ghostly tear glittered down her cheek. "You must have known her fate the moment you looked into her eyes, yet still, you condemned her to it."

The dragon's scales bristled with a roiling mixture of fury, grief, and shame. He'd been selfish from the start, wanting Solveig all for himself. He'd known it from the start, too. The brave, beautiful, kind-hearted human girl had given up everything and everyone she'd ever known to be with him. It'd been a steep price to pay, and the dragon had matched it eagerly by binding himself into a shape she could love, one that could love her back.

He'd thought it would be enough to keep her safe. Blinded by his love, humbled by everything she'd sacrificed, the dragon had been loath to take away the one thing she'd retained: her freedom of choice. Solveig herself had refused the offer of his blood, treasuring her mortality as the last remaining vestige of herself and, despite knowing what the consequences would be, the dragon had honored her decision. He'd loved his mate all the more for the brevity of time he knew he'd have with her.

Yes, he had known Solveig would eventually die.

But he hadn't expected it to happen so soon.

"She forgave you for her plight, but not yours."

"Enough," he growled. "Stop this, Hel."

"It pains you to hear this." Her arms billowed with pale mist, Solveig trying to reach out, but Hel wouldn't allow it. "It pains her, as well. I feel it pressing on my chest. She cannot bear to see you like this, bound in flesh, tied like a rabid animal—and she knows you are. She can see the creature she had loved so dearly is gone. She mourns you."

"Let her go!" he roared.

"Answer me, and I'll return her to oblivion where she knew nothing of your presence here, or her own. She will be at peace. That is what you want for her, is it not? An end to her suffering."

The dragon looked directly into her fathomless eyes, sought Solveig's heart in them, sought some meaning to this madness Hel had brought him but found neither.

Hel floated closer, a current of magic twining around her form to split it into two. Hel, in her natural form, tilted her head at him, ignoring the ghostly woman hovering beside her. Solveig's eyes were closed as if in sleep, her lips leeched of color, her cheeks pale in the sunless dungeon. "Tell me why," Hel insisted. "Why sacrifice everything when this was always going to be the result?"

The dragon couldn't breathe. His entire being screamed with unbearable agony to see his beloved in such a state. And she would remain that way forever, asleep even when her eyes opened, wandering through Helheim, oblivious, lost. Alone.

"Tell me."

Defeated, the dragon dropped to his knees, bowed his head to escape the sight, but he couldn't. As if sensing his turmoil, the water stilled so completely its surface became as smooth as a silvered glass where Solveig's image floated unattainably near, glowing like a sleeping star waiting to awaken.

Then Hel's face took shape in the reflection, the smoking shadows of her dark hair hiding Solveig from his sight. His relief shamed him.

"Tell me."

"Because…" The words stuck in his throat like shards of volcanic glass tearing it to shreds until he tasted blood.

Hel sank to her knees before him, bowing her head, and he saw her in the water's surface, seeking his gaze.

The dragon looked up, not at Hel, but at his heart floating behind her, as lifeless there as the organ that lay within his chest. He'd lost all sunshine the day she'd died in his arms, and darkness had choked him every day since. "Because…" he swallowed with difficulty, clenching his jaw so tightly he thought he'd never get it open again. "The briefest moment of joy with her was worth a thousand years of torment."

Hel absorbed this in silence while the river resumed its flow. The torches briefly banked to humble embers before resuming their steady burn, and in that moment, the whole of Helheim sighed its secrets into him, repaying his intimacy with a glimpse of its vast depth. Hel had spoken true. This realm was steeped in tranquility that blanketed all who dwelled within its borders. Solveig was part of it now, if not happy, then at least at peace, untouched by the turmoil and pain of her mortal life. It was more than he would ever have.

"Without her," he confessed, "infinity would have held no meaning. She was my everything. Always. And her memory is more precious to me than my own life."

Hel turned to look at Solveig, and his beloved's ghostly form disappeared, leaving the dragon alone with his unfeeling tormentor. "This is what they call love," she said.

"Yes," he replied, though *love* felt too inadequate a word to convey the true depth of his connection to Solveig. She was a part of him, as he would always be a part of her.

"Thank you," she said after a while, and then she was gone.

For a long time, the dragon knelt there in silence, listening to the river sing its lullabies. It almost began to make sense to him. Without Solveig, he felt his fire begin to weaken. The pain of grief eased, the rage against his prison faded, and he became numb.

He didn't change positions again until the water around him had risen to his chest, and then it was with a bored sort of reluctance that he bothered pushing to his feet.

It was a tiresome chore to keep his head above the surface, to hold his breath when it washed over his face again and again. What did it matter, anyway?

When the water receded, he sat with his back to the stone wall. The tips of his horns dug into the cold stone, and he raked them back and forth across a single groove, scoring it ever deeper. Liadan's ring throbbed cold around his finger, its rhythm matching the shallow waves lapping at his thighs. All he had to do was twist it on his finger to summon his clan to him from wherever they happened to be. But what purpose would it serve? Instead of setting him free, they'd end up imprisoned in Helheim along with him. No, they were needed far more elsewhere.

The dragon submerged his hand, cupped some water into his palm, and brought it up to his face. His mouth watered for a taste. One sip…

Squeezing his eyes shut, he dug deep within his soul to bring forth his fire and heated the water until it steamed. The hiss it produced sounded almost like a scream, and he took perverse pleasure in drawing it out to the last drop.

CHAPTER 17

Fal's new Otherland, which he'd decided to name Anderheim, was a veritable playground for his mind and magic. He could shape the world into anything his imagination could conjure. But, though necessary, using magic, learning the way it moved and could be moved here was dangerous. With little enough time to waste, every moment Fal spent sitting or standing still to work a spell felt like a moment wasted. He weighed the importance of each pause and task against Sanja's life, trying to balance the scales in some way. Fal didn't kow where Sanja was along the path, but as long as she kept moving, he knew she'd be safe. If he failed to learn enough about Anderheim's nature and structure, he knew he'd lose her no matter what.

But the more magic Fal used, the faster it poured out, speeding up the process he wanted to slow down. He'd tried to stop it altogether, and Anderheim had struck back at him with a furious thunderstorm, demonstrating not only its strength but also its weakness.

It appeared Anderheim needed Fal's magic far more than he'd originally thought. Fal suspected its existence still depended on it and, if he were to remove it, the Otherland would not only stop evolving, it would disintegrate.

A tempting alternative, but only as a last resort. His life was currently so entangled with Anderheim, destroying it might kill Fal in the process.

Instead, he turned his efforts toward passive spells that used what was already there, rather than an infusion of his will. It felt very much like learning everything for the first time. Of all the lessons imparted to him by the dragon, his parents, and his tutors, Nialei's wisdom proved to be the most useful: "There is no separateness in the world. Everything is connected to everything else. Find the connection. It will be your conduit for change."

With that in mind, Fal sought water. As the most abundant element anywhere, it was the most powerful and the farthest-reaching. It was the source of life, flowing through every realm and connecting them all.

He sacrificed another puff of magic to find his way to a small puddle that might eventually grow into a lake. Lowering to his haunches, he gazed into the surface as he would his scrying bowl. The difficult part was patience—allowing himself the time necessary to work the magic when with each beat of his heart, he felt it slipping through his fingers. "Show me what you will," he said, making it an invitation, rather than an order.

At first, nothing happened. The water heard him and understood what he wanted, but struggled to form a proper response. Fal hovered his hand over the calm surface without touching it. As if sensing his nearness, the ripples pushed up higher, closer, with a yearning he could feel. "Show me what you see," he beseeched.

The surface stilled, reflecting his own face back at him.

Fal smiled. "Can you show me Wilderheim?"

The puddle hummed and vibrated with confusion. It shrank down to almost nothing, and Fal sensed it had retreated to its source deep underground, as if for guidance. When it welled up once more, the reflection showed him the same configuration of trees, but no Fal.

He frowned. "That's not..."

The water welled up more, insisting on what it showed him. It rippled, and the tips of its waves shone with colorful lights. He hadn't noticed them for the trees, but now that his eyes knew what to look for, he spotted swirling, roiling coils of chaos in the reflection of Wilderheim's sky.

"Thank you," he said politely.

The waves jumped back and forth. Now that they'd found the right place, they were eager to show him more. *Ask,* they whispered without words. *Ask. Ask...*

He asked the only thing that mattered, already knowing what the answer would be. "Can you take me there?"

The waves stilled. Once more, the pool shrank down to its source. He waited for it to return, but the task he'd set it appeared to require a far longer consultation. Fal had almost given up when he felt the pool pushing to the surface again. No longer jaunty with excitement, it settled to its original level far more subdued than before.

The answer, as expected, was no. Even between two worlds directly on top of each other, the waterways were still frozen. He would not be getting back to Wilderheim that way. "Worth a try."

The water welled toward him, pushing out of its basin in an attempt to forge its own path for a stream. It reached out to him with encouragement, urging him to keep trying. It wanted him to succeed and wanted to help him do so.

Fal placed his hand flat to the surface and filled his mind with thoughts of Sanja. The wild disarray of her hair, the sparkling intelligence in her eyes, the sweetness of her smile. He gave the water his memory of her covered in wildflowers, laughing and twirling on the green with so much joy it made his heart clench with longing. He gave it her curiosity, her courage, her perseverance. The smell of books that would forever remind Fal of her love of them, the reverence with which she treated every word on every page. He gave it the feel of her soft kiss in the rain, the cool smoothness of her skin, the music of her sigh, and the sweet clutch of her hand on his. "Can you find her for me?"

A wave lapped up over his hand, pulling it down beneath the surface. It tasted his request, absorbed the image of a thin, pale girl with black curls cut short around her head. It took far more than he offered, pulling from him the searing pain of lightning melting Sanja to him, and the vision of a lifetime condensed into a single heartbeat that thumped back into him without mercy, reminding him of things that had never been, and would never be, yet hurt regardless as if he'd lost something precious he'd never known he had.

Fal shrank from the memory, presenting Sanja instead in her haircloth shirt and trousers, crawling on her knees up the staircase carved into Hallowed Mountain. She had to be somewhere on this path; he needed to find her. His need dispersed beneath the surface, urging the water to guide him, to show him she was all right.

It quivered away from the cold and pushed back instead, seeking out another sunny day, with the grass still green and soft, though the ground from which it grew was already freezing. It sought Sanja's face turned up to his, her eyes filled with breathless wonder as his hand gently cupped her cheek. It sent warmth up his arm and across his chest, bringing him the feel of her shivering in his arms inside the cold barn, trusting him with herself, even as her fear of him harming others pushed her away.

"What is this?" He didn't understand. His instructions had been clear: find Sanja.

As the soft ripple whispered with Sanja's voice reading from the book he'd gifted her, he realized that was precisely what the water was doing. It sought her—inside Fal. And with each memory it raised to the surface of his thoughts, his need to find her in Wilderheim grew sharper. Sanja was safe, warm, and protected in his mind, but not in the real world. With every moment he wasted here in Anderheim, she could be slowly freezing to death or suffering at the mercy of Steen's temper.

It hurt like a thousand needles scratching across his mind to force the memories aside. In their place, he filled his thoughts with the worst possible outcomes: Sanja lying on the ground, still, frozen, with the wind blowing drifts of snow to bury her in eternal winter. He imagined her bound and beaten, kneeling before Steen as he sneered down at her in victory. His heart grew shards of ice that stabbed frozen dread into his body with every beat. His breath misted as he forced the visions into the water with the understanding that it could never come to pass, else the ice in him would never melt, and he would freeze right along with Sanja.

The water keened and shrank away, then came back for one more taste of Sanja's joyous laugh, shivering as it receded again. When it welled up, it showed him the dark night sky and snowy trees swaying against it. It gave him the flickering light of a fire, the smell of smoke and burning flesh, and the sound of male voices shouting angrily at each other.

"Closer," Fal commanded with enough magic to make the water flinch and obey instantly.

Anderheim rumbled around him, pulling more magic for its own ends, but in return, it gave him fireflies to illuminate the night.

In the water's surface, he looked out through the thin sheen of melted frost clinging to a tree trunk. Skeins of black smoke rose from the ground below, and his gut clenched when he noticed the charred remnants of someone's hand amid the burned foliage.

Too big to be Sanja's. It wasn't her.

But Fal's relief was short-lived. Some distance away, the light of a torch waved back and forth. Male voices argued over something to do with a blade, and Sanja was nowhere in sight. Fal squinted to see better, but the arguing figures were too far. "Closer," he commanded again.

The water's surface quivered. It wanted to obey, but beyond that charred circle where the fire had melted enough snow and frost to liquid water, everything was frozen. The edges of his window were beginning to freeze as the chill of night descended on the scene.

No, this couldn't be right. Sanja ought to have been much farther along already. By his unreliable count, a full fortnight had passed since he'd last seen her—she only had one day left to reach the temple and earn her cleric's robes. How could she have fallen so far behind? And who were those men?

Fal pushed again to get closer, and again the water resisted. "Please," he begged, feeding more magic into the spell. "I need to see." Everything about the scene looked wrong, and all he could think was that Sanja was in danger. He needed to get to her and quickly.

Anderheim absorbed the request along with a great deal of his magic. The entire world quivered and shifted around him so fast his head spun, and, when Anderheim settled once more, Fal was kneeling in a different spot entirely. Despite the gentle glow of fireflies, the dark of night obscured his surroundings. Fal couldn't tell where he'd been taken; had no point of reference to orient himself, but he sensed he'd been brought closer.

"Sanja!" he slurred as Anderheim claimed more of him to feed itself. Fal needed water, but, perversely, Anderheim denied him. The ground all around him was completely dry, not a single droplet of mist to be found anywhere.

Fal braced himself against a tree as he conjured orbs of light and sent them flying in all directions in search of a reference point. One of them halted a short distance away and flared to illuminate a rock wall. He was almost to the staircase carved into Hallowed Mountain.

"Sanja," he called again, and when his echo returned, it carried with it those strangers' voices.

"Think I need a knife to end one troublesome little bitch?" one of them said. "I'll kill you with my bare hands!"

Fal sucked in a sharp breath as something raw and terrible sparked inside him. It turned his blood hot and cold at the same time, made gooseflesh prickle all over his arms and legs. He gritted his teeth, felt his feet root down, drawing his magic back from Anderheim. It coursed up his body, churned in sickening torrents in his chest, and when it released through his voice, it made Anderheim shriek. "*Where is she!*" he shouted, the rockface returning his voice threefold.

In the silence that followed, frost crackled into being at his feet. He watched it spread, shivered as his breath misted in the sudden cold. The trees turned white, mounds of snow grew at their bases. Dry ground became churned mud, frozen into hard peaks and hollows.

Fal smelled winter on the air, distant smoke, and the reek of blood and unwashed bodies. Like a mirage, Anderheim drew back from him for a distance of several paces in all directions and, as it did, the men he'd only seen from a distance before appeared in front of him.

And between them, kneeling in the middle of the frozen path was Sanja. Her hair was wet, freezing into stiff curls and spikes. Her shirt was filthy from sleeping on the forest floor, the trousers torn and bloodied at the knees. She looked impossibly small and fragile, huddling close to the ground between the two men intent on killing her.

She leaned to one side, shifted the other knee forward, and drooped lower still as she settled her weight on it. The effort came at a great cost. Already weak and shivering with cold, Sanja was forced to pause and gather her strength as her shoulders rose and fell in great, labored breaths.

"Sanja…"

"Just drop already!" One of the men shouted at her. His legs were crusted with snow up to his thighs, and he was rubbing his hands for warmth.

The other seethed in silence, his clenched fists quivering. "She will, soon enough. She's half-dead as it is."

In answer, Sanja took a deep breath, leaned to the other side, and brought the opposite knee forward. As she did, the last of her strength seemed to desert her. She dropped forward onto her hands, her head hanging limp, and a broken moan shivered from her lips.

She was dying.

"There, you see?" the quiet one purred, cracking his knuckles. "We're almost on our way."

"Steen wants her alive," argued the other one.

The quiet one's reply never came as all sound faded into echoes. The men's figures became transparent, closing in on Sanja as the warmth of Anderheim began to creep back toward Fal once more, slowly taking the scene from him.

Fal didn't think. He lunged forward, reaching for Sanja even as whatever doorway Anderheim had opened began to slam shut.

↞ »·◇·« ↠

She'd overestimated herself. Only forty paces along and Sanja was flagging in a dangerous way. Her legs were numb, her body shaking uncontrollably in the freezing night. Without fire, without her blanket, even Princess Liadan's gift wouldn't keep her from succumbing to eternal sleep.

She needn't die, either, only grow weak enough to faint. Dyri and Bale would finish the rest.

Keep moving forward. No other choice. She had written this ending for herself by choosing to let Jarl Steen live. *My own fault.*

If only her body would obey. Her spine was turning to jelly, her limbs as heavy as sacks of lead. She could no longer keep her head up, and staring at the ground made her yearn for but a few winks of sleep.

It took everything she had left to bring her knee forward. She had to be leaving tracks of blood in her wake, but Sanja no longer felt any pain. Only cold. Her mind was beginning to play tricks on her. It almost seemed to her like summer had returned. As chilled as she was, Sanja felt a warm breeze caress her frozen cheek with the scent of night-blooming flowers.

She heard it whisper her name…

"Just drop already!" Bale snapped. He'd failed to locate Dyri's knife, which infuriated the brothers and pleased Sanja to no end. He'd soaked himself to the thigh looking for it, and the cold was beginning to gnaw at him now, too.

"She will, soon enough," Dyri replied. He'd grown silent since his threat to her parents, keeping his voice quiet when he did deign to speak, but it was no less malicious for its softness. "She's half dead as it is."

Sanja wanted to prove him wrong. She shifted forward a little more, and her body simply gave out. Dropping to her hands, her head dangling, it was all Sanja could do not to keel over and let them have her. She tried to right herself but had no more strength left to draw upon. A weak little moan made it past her lips, her eyes stinging with the need to weep. But she had no tears left to shed, either.

It's over. This was where she'd breathe her last.

"There, you see? We're almost on our way."

Sanja felt Dyri move closer. The protective magic keeping him at bay was fading right along with her. Would she feel his hands on her before her heart gave out? Its laboring beats already shuddered in her chest. And still, Sanja would have smiled if she could. *Better than Jarl Steen's marriage bed.*

"Steen wants her alive," Bale argued.

"Look at her, brother. She's dead, no matter what."

Here it comes. There'd be no stopping Dyri now.

If only she could have said good-bye to her parents…

A large hand curled hard around her upper arm, yanked her sideways off the path. Sanja didn't have time to cry out before she struck the ground, her impact softened by a thatch of soft, dry grass.

Head spinning, she struggled for breath, struggled to move, but the lightest of touches easily overcame her efforts. Warmth surrounded her with the smell of dry earth and tree sap. Lights flickered in the darkness of her vision, and an ethereal buzz of insects filled her ears. If this was death, it was a more peaceful ending than she ever could have imagined.

Sanja sighed, letting her weight sink down into the cushion of a warm cradle.

Heat touched her cheek, chafed across her brow, and forced her eyes open. Everything was dark and blurry, swirling this way and that, refusing to let her focus.

"Sanja, can you hear me?" She knew that voice… "Hold on a little longer. You're not going to die. I won't let you…"

CHAPTER 18

Gods, she was frozen through and through. Fal gathered Sanja in his arms. He needed to get her into water. He could restore her in water.

Anderheim hummed in its stillness. Wary after Fal's earlier outburst, it neither took from him, nor gave, waiting for his next move, and he was glad of it. Now, perhaps, the Otherland would learn to obey its creator.

He filled his mind with thoughts of his waterfall. On foot, it would take him days to reach it, but Anderheim seemed to have other means of travel. Reading his intent, the Otherland blurred, streaking around him as it had before, and in the next moment, Fal stood precisely where he'd wanted to go.

The crescent moon shone brightly above the clearing, setting the waterfall ashimmer. Where it poured into the lake, the surface churned white, throwing off clouds of cool mist. This, at last, was a familiar and most welcome sight. This was where he'd first learned to travel through water.

He offered quiet praise and thanks to Anderheim in the form of more magic. In return, the world sighed, and night birds began their song.

Fal waded into the lake, taking comfort and strength from the water's embrace as it lapped at his legs and waist. It was deep enough to come up to his shoulders when he lowered to his knees, bringing Sanja with him until she was submerged up to her neck.

He knew spells to channel the water's healing magic, but Fal dared not speak a single word of one while that terrible vortex still churned within his chest. It was wild, barely contained, and far too powerful, seeming to respond to water with an eagerness that unnerved him. If he miscalculated even a little, if Anderheim twisted his spell…

Swallowing the raw magic back as deep as it would go, he tested his voice on a whisper. "Sanja, can you hear me?"

She didn't stir.

Fal touched a gentle fingertip to her cracked, bloodless lips, dripping water between them in the hopes it would revive her a little. "You are safe now." For the moment, at least. And only if he could heal her.

How do I heal her?

Kneeling in a pool of reflected moonlight, Fal remembered a lullaby his mother had used to sing to him. It had no words, but the melody had never failed to soothe his troubled mind. Now, it teased his senses with secrets and mysteries that lay beneath its surface.

Adjusting Sanja in his arms, he began to hum.

With the first few notes, the chaos in his chest flared like a blooming flower, reshaping itself into some semblance of order. He clenched his stomach to somehow keep it contained, but despite his efforts, a delicate strain of it seeped out into his voice, weaving through the melody, shifting it into something new and unfamiliar, yet somehow comforting.

When he would have stopped, the strange magic refused to let him, commanding his voice to keep going. It wasn't finished yet; it had barely begun its work.

Sparks of light glittered over Sanja's face. Her pale skin became like snow in the moonlight, then pinkened with signs of life. Her lips softened and reddened as the bleeding cracks and fissures healed from within before his eyes.

And in the water's cool embrace, her body began to radiate a tender heat.

The melody hummed through him louder, and Sanja bowed up with a gasp, as a burst of light flared from within her. When it faded, the song's magic finally released Fal into silence, and Sanja softened against him.

Her color had improved, and her body had filled out a bit from its earlier, terrifying leanness. She looked the way she had in Frastmir. *Thank you, gods.* Whatever that magic had been, it had saved her life.

"Sanja?"

Her brows drew together in a disgruntled frown. She didn't respond, still fast asleep.

But she was alive, and she was safe here with him, where neither Steen's men nor Wilderheim's untimely winter could touch her.

Fal pushed to his feet and carried her out of the lake, drying them both along the way. Though he was loath to let her out of his sight again, he needed to gather wood for a fire and to take stock of the situation.

He could sense Anderheim's consciousness watching him. It was mollified for the moment, but a tense awareness existed between them that Fal now had the means to force his will upon the Otherland if he so wished.

Such a weapon would be formidable in his current circumstances—if he knew what it was, and how to use it. That it seemed to be somehow connected to his voice hadn't escaped him. Anderheim had drawn back on his verbal command. His melody had brought Sanja from the brink of death back to blooming life.

As an experiment, Fal held out his hand and tried to manipulate the churning vortex of strange magic out into his palm. It didn't react at all.

But when he hummed a low tone, it leaped to life, and a flower bush burst from the ground at his feet, dozens of pale white blooms flaring open in the blink of an eye. They were his creation, not Anderheim's, and he could feel the Otherland's curiosity as it responded by growing a second bush next to Fal's.

"Perhaps I'm more water sprite than I thought." His grandmother's people had carried such potent power in their voices, it could give life as well as take it. Seol had tried to teach it to Fal, but the lessons had always ended in disappointment for them both. Fal's Halfling blood had simply been too diluted. Or perhaps the limitations of his homeland and his illusions had made it impossible.

Whatever the reason, the old rules seemed not to apply in Anderheim.

“Open the doorway,” he commanded. Now that he knew Anderheim could be escaped, it should only be a matter of learning how. Far more useful would be learning to travel back and forth. “I said, open the doorway.”

Anderheim remained unchanged. It didn’t seem to understand what he was asking.

“Do what you did before.”

At once, the Otherland blurred and shifted, delivering him triumphantly back to Sanja.

Brilliant.

Shaking his head, he returned to his quest for firewood. The lessons would have to wait; he couldn’t experiment with new, unpredictable magic around Sanja, and he needed to be there when she woke up.

Fal gathered as much dry wood as he could carry and returned to the waterfall. Having learned his ritual over the last few days, Anderheim warped itself to clear a fire circle for him, pulling the grass blades back underground to keep them from harm. The gathering of stones was Fal’s task. Happily, the lake had plenty of them, and in no time at all, he had the makings of a proper campfire. Striking a flint stone against his eating knife, he produced a spark strong enough to light the kindling and catch the dry wood. The only thing missing was something to roast on it.

In the morning, he’d catch fish from the lake to feed them both. But for now, Fal was too preoccupied with other thoughts to concern himself with physical nourishment.

The night was so peaceful he wished he didn’t have to return to Wilderheim. He had everything he needed in this place.

Everything but his family and his people.

Fal was becoming convinced that nothing would stop Fenrir from destroying anything and everything in his path. The damage had already been done the moment the great wolf had broken free. Restoring the Veil would not bind Fenrir back into his prison.

But Anderheim felt different.

Fal had spent almost a week within its borders, and no higher being had thus far made it through. With Otherlands falling one after the other, he would have expected a flood of refugees to come pouring in, but they haven’t. Either they weren’t aware of Anderheim’s existence, or they couldn’t get in.

Could it be possible, then, for Anderheim to stand strong against Ragnarok simply hiding in plain sight?

Fal rubbed his weary brow. He was grasping at straws, looking for hope in illusions.

Even if this Otherland was truly the safe haven Wilderheim needed it to be, it was still as impenetrable for him as it was for everyone else on the other side of its borders. The doorway he’d opened to get to Sanja had lasted mere moments. Enough time for him to pass through, but no more than that. It wouldn’t be enough to fold all of Wilderheim into Anderheim—assuming he could open another one.

Fal looked over at Sanja’s sleeping face. Still there, still safe. The tight band of fear around his chest loosened enough for him to take a proper breath. With an unsteady hand, he pushed a stray curl away from her brow, then brushed his knuckles gently across her soft, warm cheek.

She was safe.

But her parents were still in Wilderheim, as was her betrothed. She would never make it to the top of Hallowed Mountain in time, and now Fal couldn't even go back to Frastmir to sort out Jarl Steen as he'd meant to do. Every promise he'd made this girl, he'd failed to keep.

Well, there was one thing he could still do to make up for it.

She's not going to like it.

But it would keep her alive. That was all that mattered.

When sleep pulled him under, it was into dreams of storms and fire, with darkness blanketing the land, and a strange, beautiful sword cutting through it in screams flashes of sharp, bright light.

CHAPTER 19

Artairas didn't sleep a wink all the night through. The animals in the camp were agitated, horses whinnying, and dogs howling as if they felt something amiss with their world. Artairas felt it, too, like a warm wind of change blowing through their midst, altering the ground itself. It set his teeth on edge and made him clutch God's sword so tightly his fingers cramped around the handle.

When the first light of dawn appeared, he put on his boots, fastened his sword belt around his waist, and walked out. The rest of the warriors were beginning to stir as well and, though they were quiet and subdued, each had a weapon at the ready, wary of whatever unseen enemy had crept through their camp in the night.

Artairas nodded to his men in passing, then veered off to make his way up the hill. He needed a better vantage point; he needed to see what lay in the distance. God's sword quivered in its scabbard. He stroked up and down its handle as if his touch alone could soothe its restless spirit. Rather than settle, the blade responded with eagerness, humming to him louder and louder, until Artairas clutched the grip hard to make it stop. Though he didn't mean to, he found himself drawing the blade out of the scabbard and raising it before him. Then, and only then did its spirit quiet enough to let him think.

Sometimes, its power over him worried Artairas. When it became that insistent, he could no longer tell which of them wielded the other. He could now feel its influence from anywhere in the camp. If he strayed from it too far, too long, it screamed in his mind for him to return. When he failed to draw it at least once in a day, it roused within him a terrible thirst for violence and blood.

The blade was a living thing, needing to taste the air, to see the world beyond its sheath. It was a jealous, demanding, controlling mistress, as all God-made things were, he supposed. But the power contained within the blade and its promise of victory made it a pleasant burden to bear. It set his shoulders back with pride each time he wore the sword at his side. He relished the men's envious glares, as well as the deference they paid to the sword and, by extension, to him.

He ascended the hill like a king about to face his people and reached the top as the sun peeked out from behind Silver Mountains in the distance. Shielding his eyes from its glare, he frowned at something a little higher in the sky.

A star glittered there, uncowed by the sun's majesty. It shone bright, like a beacon pointing the way forward, and remained there as the sun slowly climbed up across the sky. Artairas had never seen its like before.

Nor had the blade. Faced with the glory of the morning sun, it reflected only the star, as if its cool, twinkling light were a signal for the blade, and needed to be answered.

Caught between the two, Artairas swayed on his feet. A foreign warmth started in his sword hand and crept up his arm. It turned his head with dizziness, set his heart pounding. His breath became labored as his limbs quivered, and his loins stirred with excitement and anticipation.

He licked his lips and tasted blood, but when he wiped his mouth on the back of his hand, it came away clean. Artairas licked his lips again and smiled. *It is time.*

The thud of hooves broke him out of the strange spell and drew his eye back toward the camp. His squire, Gareth, waved from the saddle, riding pell-mell up the hill. Artairas headed down to meet him and caught the horse's reins as Gareth pulled him to a stop. The squire leaped down and dropped to one knee, bowing his head. "My Lord, the queen is asking for you."

Wasting no time with questions, Artairas mounted the horse and turned him about, riding toward the castle at a breakneck sprint, the sword still clutched aloft.

He was forced to sheathe it when he reached the castle courtyard but kept his hand on the pommel as he raced up to the queen's chambers. The pall of impending death saturated the hallway. Servants and priests scurried in and out, carrying armloads of cloth either way: in with the clean, and out with the sullied.

Artairas stopped before the closed doors, and the current of activity halted along with him. All of them stared at the soldier most improperly dressed for an audience with the queen, but none of them said a word, as aware as he was of the power now radiating from the blade at his side in flashes of blinding light they could feel, but couldn't see.

He wanted to ask them after the queen's condition, but the thought of hearing any of them speak of her nauseated him. No, Artairas would rather see for himself.

With a shaking hand, he pulled open the massive door just enough to allow him to slip inside. There were no guards on either side of it. The priests had all removed themselves into the hallway, and as Artairas entered, the last two maids ran out with quick, passing curtsies. They closed the door behind them, abandoning Artairas in the living tomb of the queen's bedchambers.

The walls had already been draped with black cloth, the mirrors covered, and all the windows shielded with thick tapestries so no hint of the morning sun could intrude. Hundreds of candles had been lit all through the chamber to make up for it. While the hearth stood cold, those candles filled the room with stifling heat, but all of them combined could not mask the sickroom stench.

Had he come too late?

Artairas approached the bed as he would a trap, stepping with his toes first, creeping in silence up to the queen's side. She was nigh invisible in her bed, with the covers pulled up to her chin, and her pallid face and white hair almost the same color as her pillows. Her eyes were closed, her mouth open. She made not a sound.

Artairas lowered to his knees and crossed himself, speaking a silent prayer that the queen might find peace in God's presence at last. "Amen," he whispered.

"Artairas," the queen said, startling him.

"My Queen."

She turned her head to face him, her eyes opening a little as her dry lips pressed together. She hummed weakly, then took a struggling breath and tried again. "My God has left me in a state," she said, attempting to smile. "But He will be back. Once His victory is secured, He has promised to restore me to strength and youth for all time."

"Yes, My Queen."

Queen Genevieve shifted, struggling to free one hand from beneath the covers. Artairas helped her, then clutched her bony hand as hard as he dared. Her grip was stronger. Such a powerful spirit, trapped in such a weak, withering shell. "He bade me tell you, the sign has appeared."

"I have seen it," Artairas replied in a discreet whisper. "A star has risen in the east. It is not banished by the sun, but shines through in the day sky."

Queen Genevieve sighed. "Then it is true. The time has come at last, as He promised."

"What are your orders, Majesty?" He expected he already knew what she would say, but his heart beat stronger, faster, waiting for her to say it.

"God wills that the armies be ready to march into battle at sunset," she said.

"Sunset? But—"

"When the day has turned to night, the star will shine the way," the queen said as if she had not heard. Her gaze was distant, her voice slurring, weakening. She spoke as if from a dream, and Artairas wasn't certain if any of what she said made sense. March to battle at night? Whoever had heard of such a thing? And how could they meet an enemy hundreds of miles away by sunset?

Yet he felt in his soul, and in the hum of his blade, that it was not the queen speaking at all. It was God Himself, using her voice as His conduit.

"The star will point the way, and the men must be steadfast in their faith that He will see them safely through to the other side." She paused for breath, clutching his hand tighter. "They must not stop or turn back a single time. Have faith in God's promise, and He will deliver you to the land of heathens."

"We will not fail, your Majesty."

"You will come upon them in the dark of night. Fight well, and by morning, their kingdom will be ours."

Even if, by some miracle, God could deliver them directly into the heart of Wilderheim, attacking in the night was a cowardly, dishonorable way to fight. "Is Wilderheim truly so strong that we must resort to underhanded tactics?"

Queen Genevieve smiled. "It is not for us mortals to question the word of God."

"Yes, but… Forgive me, My Queen, I simply do not understand. Our armies are vast and well trained. Does God not have faith in *us*? We can win this war the honorable way."

A disgruntled sound came from the queen, and she shook her head, her eyes closing. "There is no honor in war. There is only pain and death. Winning or losing. God has favored us to win, and we will do so only with His guidance." She sighed. "I am weary. I must rest. God will guide you, Artairas. Heed Him, and all will be as it should."

"I will," he swore.

He took his leave with purposeful strides, brushing away questions from the priests who demanded to know what had been said in their absence. In the courtyard, he reclaimed his horse and mounted.

There was the star, high in the eastern sky, unperturbed by the sun's bright glare. "Tell the castle guard to ring the bells for muster," he ordered the hostler. "Send messengers to each camp with orders to prepare to fight by sunset."

"Yes, My Lord. At once!"

By the time he made it back to his tent, the preparations were already underway. After waiting for so long, the men finally had purpose once more. Servants and squires ran about, gathering gear and supplies. The restless horses were saddled, weapons cleaned, and armor inspected.

Gareth had already packed all of Artairas' belongings and was in the process of breaking down the tent. His eyes were feverish, and his color was high when he took over the horse's care. "We heard the bells. Is it true?"

"Yes," Artairas replied. "We war at sunset."

"Sunset? But—"

"Don't. Do as you are told. I do not want any rumors spreading through the camp. We have our orders, and we will obey. Do you understand?"

"Yes, My Lord. Of course."

By noon, the tents were down, and a caravan of carts was making its way from the castle to the camps, carrying fresh food and gear to replace what had been lost during their long wait.

As the afternoon grew into evening, the men began to assemble into formation, a long line of mounted warriors, followed by foot soldiers bringing up the rear. If there were grumblings or rumors, they didn't reach Artairas' ears. After so long, the troops were quiet, eager to get going, and their restlessness translated to the animals. Horses stomped and fidgeted, battle dogs barked and snarled, and hooded hawks screamed, beating their wings to fly.

At the front of the formation, Artairas faced east, staring at the star which had not dimmed a single time throughout the day. Many had already remarked upon it, a few going so far as to approach him with questions. Artairas had sent them all off with a stern reprimand to keep their minds on the battle to come.

But everyone and everything hushed as the sun began to dip below the horizon in the west. "Do not light the torches," Artairas ordered as he heard flints being struck to do just that. His words carried back through the formation in a long hum, and the eve remained dark.

Then, the sun finally disappeared, and as soon as its last light dimmed, the new star flared brighter. A wave of gasps and prayers moved through the men as a shaft of its light speared down onto a place some distance away, a beacon marking their direction.

"*March!*"

Artairas set off, and the formation roused to life, following after him. The measured pace maddened him, made his entire body itch to spur his mount to a sprint, but he resisted. They would need to keep their heads about them and preserve their strength for the battle to come.

Yet as he crested a hill and saw the light shimmer in a clearing down below, the impulse became too powerful to fight. He fancied he could see Wilderheim within that shining pillar, a landscape just different enough from Synealee's to stand out against the night.

Reading Artairas' eagerness, his horse sped up to a trot down the hill, the others matching his pace.

"My God," someone cried.

"What is that?" another chimed in.

"It couldn't be…" added a third, and the murmurs spread until every man within sight of that light was praying for God to keep them safe. A chorus of metal chimes rang through the ranks as every man drew his weapon, and Artairas could feel them all brace for battle.

Their eyes did not deceive them. It was, indeed, a different world within that shaft of light, and, as the army neared, it widened like a doorway opening directly to the heart of enemy land. As Queen Genevieve had said, God would deliver them to victory.

"Ride on," Artairas ordered, "and don't look back!" Drawing his sword, he raised it high, relishing its soundless war cry as he spurred his mount on and shouted, "*In God's name!*"

And as the army streamed through God's portal to catch Wilderheim unaware beneath the cover of night, in her royal bedchamber, hundreds of candles gently blew out as Queen Genevieve breathed her last.

CHAPTER 20

Sanja woke to the sound of bird songs and rushing water. The sun beat relentless heat into her cheek, the scent of campfire smoke teasing her nostrils. It was the latter that startled her into full wakefulness. "W-what..."

As her mind first comprehended and then accepted what she was seeing, Sanja slumped with equal measures of relief and sorrow. A puffy white cloud made its languorous way across the blue sky above her. Not a hint of those strange lights to be seen anywhere. The grass was green and lush, warm in the morning sun. Someone had built a small fire nearby, now all but reduced to embers, and Sanja herself was relatively clean and dry. She felt stronger than she had in weeks.

She was dead. The torments were over, at last. She would never again need to think about Jarl Steen and his machinations. Ragnarok would no longer be her concern.

Oh, but her parents...

And Mattias! Where was he? She needed to see him, to thank him, and beg his forgiveness. "Mattias? Where are you?"

She heard a splash and then someone calling her name.

Sanja pushed to her feet but hesitated to turn and face the man who'd died because of her. *You owe it to him to look him in the eye and speak the words.*

The running footsteps neared.

Braving his reaction, she turned around. "Mattias, I—"

"Finally! I was afraid you would sleep through the day." Sanja gaped as Prince Fal dropped his catch to the ground, wiped his hands on his thighs, and grasped her shoulders, looking her over with a bright smile on his face. He pulled her into a brief embrace and, when she didn't return it, set her away again, his glittering blue gaze searching hers. "How do you feel?"

"Y-you are here..." Not only that, he was himself, in all his Other beauty. His hair was so dark it gleamed blue in the light of day. With his cloak discarded, his sleeves rolled up past his elbows, and the laces of his shirt undone down his chest, he looked so human and approachable. No more changing faces, no more illusions. His form remained his own, and he stood tall and proud, finally relieved of the burdens he'd carried all his life. He was the same Fal she knew, and yet nothing at all like the crown prince of Wilderheim.

A lifetime in a kiss...

"Are you dead, too? But that means... Is it over?"

His smile dimmed, and he looked as if he wanted to say something but then thought better of it. Bending over, he retrieved two long sticks, each with three lake fish skewered on them. "Let us sit down. We have much to talk about."

"Where is Mattias?"

Prince Fal winced. "Sit, please." He waited for her to sink back to her pallet, which she now recognized as his cloak before he added more wood to the fire, set the fish to cooking, and picked up a small, sharp eating knife to fiddle with. Anything but tell her what he so clearly wanted to.

Bad news, then.

"I am not dead, am I?"

"No," the prince confirmed.

"And Mattias isn't here because..." She had to swallow past the lump in her throat to recover her voice. "He *is* dead."

"I found you on the path near Hallowed Mountain in difficult circumstances."

"Yes," she murmured, "I remember." Dyri and Bale, and the freezing cold she couldn't escape. She'd been so close to dying, had expected it at any moment. And then—"You took me away from there."

"Yes. I brought you here and—"

"How much time has passed?"

"You have slept through the night and half the day." Guessing at the unspoken question, he added, "The last day."

Sanja couldn't breathe. Her gaze lowered from Prince Fal's to the ground, and then to her toes curling into the grass. *The last day.* Any hope of her making it up Hallowed Mountain was gone forever. Without the magic of Journeyman's Sanctuary to counteract the contract, there was nothing left to protect her from Jarl Steen.

"Sanja, are you listening?"

Nothing but a dream. And, gods, how it hurt.

When the sun set, she would officially fail the wager. Her blood oath would compel her to return to Steen if she had to walk her bare feet bloody to get to him and, oh, he would be so much worse than the brothers. He would hurt her until she begged for death, and no one would help her.

"Sanja..."

It was his fault. The prince had promised to help her, and instead, he'd stolen her last chance of escaping the Jarl. He may as well have handed her to Steen himself. "You should have left me there to die."

"No, you don't mean that. Listen."

But she didn't hear. She couldn't think or hope anymore. She could only see Jarl Steen's face turn red with fury, his ham-sized fists slamming into her again and again. With each imagined strike, she flinched a little more, breathed a little faster, a little harder, until she couldn't take it anymore.

When Prince Fal reached for her, Sanja ducked past his arms to the knife he'd stuck into a piece of wood on the ground. Her aim was off, and she caught it by the blade but catch it she did. Its bite hardly registered at all, and she shifted her grip to the handle and tugged it free.

"Sanja, no!" Prince Fal snatched her around the waist, rolled her away from the fire, and caught her hands on the knife.

"Let go, curse you!"

They grappled back and forth. The prince was twice her weight. He would easily overpower her if she gave him a chance. Not about to be stopped, Sanja kicked and flailed to keep him from pinning her down. If she could turn the blade enough…

Prince Fal cursed, curled his hand over hers on the knife, but his hold slipped, right down the blade. Rather than pull back, he squeezed her wrist with one hand and wrenched the knife from her grip with the other.

"No!" She reached for it again when he tossed it away, and he caught her hand in his, bleeding wound to bleeding wound. Sanja gasped and stilled.

Prince Fal growled, disentangling his legs from hers so they could both sit up, but he didn't release her hand. His expression thunderous, he yanked the lacing free of his shirt and wound it around their clasped hands before her mind caught up with what he was doing. When she would have pulled the lace free, he swatted her hand away, then caught her chin to make her meet his gaze and bit out, "Two as one, now unto always, and evermore."

A tingling heat began in the palm of her hand, spreading up her arm to her shoulder. Confused, Sanja shook her head to clear some of the dizziness, but it wouldn't go away. In her mind, she saw the lightning's vision, a sun-filled meadow, and the prince smiling down at her. Against that dream of happiness, love, and ceremony, this was a farce.

"Say the words," Prince Fal commanded.

Sanja blinked the dream away, but the waking moment didn't feel any more real. "What are you doing?"

"Breaking your contract," he replied impatiently and repeated, "Two as one, now unto always, and evermore. Say it, Sanja."

"Two as one"—the tingling intensified tenfold—"now unto always…"

"And evermore," he supplied.

"Now unto always, and evermore."

The heat flared until she felt like she was holding onto a burning ember, but just as quickly, the sensation cooled and, when at last Prince Fal untied the lace and released her, a thin line of an old scar graced her palm where a fresh, bleeding cut ought to have been.

A lifetime in a kiss…

"We could have avoided the battle had you let me explain, rather than try to throw yourself on a blade," Prince Fal grumbled, retrieving his knife.

"Was that…?"

"A marriage ceremony. The uncivilized, heathen version of one, anyway."

Sanja traced her new scar. "We are married?"

"Yes, Princess Sanja, we are married. Congratulations, you are officially free of Jarl Steen for all time."

"Why would you do that?"

"Because I had to," he replied simply.

It wasn't the solution either of them had wanted, but it was the only thing Fal could have done to keep her alive and safe. He didn't expect dramatic displays of undying gratitude, but a simple "Thank you" might have been welcome. He had just solved all her problems, after all. Whatever debts Master Carver had managed to amass would be wiped clean. Sanja and her parents would move to Castle Frastmir and never again need to set foot into that ramshackle cottage they called home. Mistress Carver would have an army of servants at her beck and call, and Sanja herself would one day become the queen of Wilderheim.

All things considered, Sanja ought to be dancing for joy.

Instead, she sat there, staring at the scar on her hand as if she couldn't quite comprehend what'd happened. Her wound had healed instantly, and Fal wondered whether it was a part of the binding spell, or whether his blood had changed her on an elemental level. And if the latter, how great was the change, and how long might it last?

"You bear no responsibility for my decisions," she said.

"I should have let you kill yourself instead?"

"Why not?"

Fal wiped off his knife and sheathed it back into its scabbard on his belt, furious that she would even consider taking her life in the face of another possibility. "What a little hypocrite you are. You would not have Steen's death on your conscience, but you would have had me carry yours? Does your own life truly mean so little to you?"

"My life," she snapped, "would have meant nothing at all, had it remained in any way tied to Jarl Steen. My only thought was to remove myself and my parents from his hold the surest way I could think of."

"And it never occurred to you that marriage to me would do the same?"

"No! Why would it?"

Her immediate answer, delivered with equal measures of affront and ridicule, enraged him beyond words. "Were it not for me—"

"Steen's men would have done unspeakable things to me in Frastmir," she said without mercy, making him shudder at the chill of her words. "And if they did not kill me after that, I would have done it myself, rather than let my parents see. I would have suffered briefly, but at least I would have been free of Steen, and the world at large would not have suffered in the slightest for my absence." Her anger brought a little color to her cheeks, but the gleam of tears belied her indifference. "I may be an idealist, Highness, but I am not a fool, and neither is Steen. He knew his men would bring me to heel. You may have bought me time with your rescue in the barn, but nothing else. Their involvement ensured I would have died sooner or later, by their hand or mine, and no one, save for my parents, would have mourned me."

"*I* would have."

Sanja was about to say something but, taking a good look at his face, seemed to think better of it. In a more cordial tone, she allowed, "Perhaps. But not for long." She rubbed the scar on her palm, then held it up for him to see. "You have done yourself no favors with this. Nor me."

The fish were beginning to burn. Fal repositioned the skewers away from the strongest flames and turned them to cook the other side while his temper flared hotter than the sun. Fal had never considered himself particularly proud, but for her to dismiss him so easily, as if he were no better than Steen, offended him on a level he wouldn't have thought possible.

"You don't deny it," she noted.

"What would be the point? You have already decided that death would have been preferable to marriage to me. I'll be damned if I waste my breath exulting my virtues after that." He sounded like a sullen, spoiled child.

"Your virtues have never been in question."

Fal snorted with derision. "Haven't they? Admit it, you still think of me as the Prince of Deceit. As you said, I saved you from those men in Frastmir only to set you on a path of suffering. I promised you aid and wasn't there to give it. And after everything you have endured, when you had your chance to escape forever, I pulled you back instead and locked you into marriage with a man you haven't chosen." He flushed at his own words, realizing too late the enormity of his actions. Intentionally or not, Fal carried no small responsibility for the pain she'd suffered.

Gods, what a fool he'd been. He never should have listened to Liadan—never should have made promises he'd been in no position to keep.

But his gut still told him he'd done the right thing. No matter that it didn't seem to have made either of them very happy.

Sanja shifted to her knees and pulled out one of the fish skewers. The top fish was burnt, but the other two would be just right. Using one of the sticks he'd carved into a simple fork, she removed the fish and placed them side by side on the large piece of bark he'd stripped for a platter. "We both know that, had the situation been anything other than what it is, you would never have chosen someone like me as your wife."

"We most certainly do *not* know that."

"Please, let's not lie to each other."

Fal straightened in his seat, his hackles up to be called out for deceit, but he bit his tongue against a harsh response. His words had been spoken thoughtlessly, for no other reason than to contradict her. He hated how calm and rational she appeared after what she'd said when his heart was still pounding at the thought that, had he been but a little slower, Sanja might have been dying in his arms now, instead of taking care to arrange their rustic supper just so.

Their roles seemed to have reversed. Where before Sanja had been all restless chatter to his cool rationality, she now appeared to have no trouble at all delivering a cogent argument, while Fal struggled to form a single coherent thought.

The change felt so out of place Fal broke one of his most resolute rules. Without her knowledge or permission, he reached out to her mind, telling himself it was for her own good. He only did it to make certain Sanja was truly as calm as she appeared; that he wouldn't need to sleep with one eye open, fearing she'd do him or herself injury in the night. She'd already proven herself more than capable of it, after all.

What he found was akin to a lake after a storm—calm on the surface, but murky with churned up mud. The remnants of her torments might have been safely contained, but they were by no means gone. Basking in the fire's warmth, she still felt ice chilling her from within, shards of it lodged in her hands and feet, so cold Fal shivered and curled his own fingers into his palms to warm them.

He saw her memories of Mattias, the jolly, fair-haired giant who'd kept her company along her Journey. His bearded face shifted between a good-natured, happy smile, and a grotesque mask of swollen, bleeding bruises. She would never again separate the two. The tainted memory of her friend would always squeeze her heart with the smell of burning flesh and the knowledge that she'd been the indirect cause of his demise.

He saw her tormentors, too. Dyri, Bale, and Alfrec, their faces dark and demonic, their voices slicing at her with vicious threats as sharp as Dyri's blade.

All of it, she'd endured alone, walking her knees bloody along the frozen path, as her hope of making it to the temple had slowly withered to but one wish: to repay her pain in kind and die before Jarl Steen or his men could get their hands on her. She'd known she'd lose her wager, but she'd kept going, anyway, because every moment she'd spent continuing her Journey had meant a moment more of safety from Steen and his men. A moment more to live. A moment more for them to suffer.

Fal's chest ached for the torment he felt inside her. He wanted to pull her into his arms and make the bitter cold go away. More than anything, Sanja needed the warmth of an embrace that asked for nothing more than it gave. But as much as she craved such contact, she feared it. If she allowed herself the briefest show of emotion, admitted the smallest moment of weakness, any need for comfort or support, the dam would break, and she would drown.

Simply, Sanja was calm because she had no other choice.

Suffused with guilt and helplessness, Fal withdrew quickly and refocused on what she was saying.

"…poetry where it belongs—in books. People like me don't get dashing heroes riding to our rescue. We must make do with what we have."

The connection with her mind was severed, yet he still felt a chill he couldn't shake. Breathing into his hands for warmth he ought not need, Fal made his face neutral so she wouldn't suspect the liberty he'd taken with her mind. But he couldn't keep the bitterness out of his tone when he said, "My choice would have been irrelevant. As the royal heir, my wife would have been chosen for me for the benefit of Wilderheim."

Sanja nodded, her point proven.

But, though it was the truth, it was far from complete, and Fal was not inclined to let her believe otherwise. "Matters of state aside, I am still Other, and ever at the whim of more powerful forces—my illusions among them. I might not have had the chance to marry at all, if not for you. It is also quite possible you were always meant to be mine, regardless of my—or your—current thoughts on the matter." Fate had a way of manipulating its outcome, and only a fool chose to oppose it.

Sanja absorbed everything he said, and from the shift of her gaze, he knew she was gearing up with all sorts of arguments in opposition.

He forestalled all of them by saying, "But, were I completely free to choose, I might well have chosen someone like you." When she would have replied, Fal held up his hand to silence her. "You asked for truth. That means you don't get to ignore the parts you don't want to hear."

"Fair point," she allowed and set the task of supper aside to give him her full attention.

Perversely, her calm gaze made the words harder to say. "The truth is, you charmed me from the first. Your spirit, your wit,"—he grinned, rubbing at his temple—"your aim with unconventional weapons."

She blushed, but couldn't duck her head fast enough to hide a quick little smile he was most relieved to see. Despite everything, Sanja was not broken. Her trials might have transformed her, but she was still there, underneath it all.

"You don't balk at taking me to task." If he were to be honest with himself, as much as it frustrated him, Fal enjoyed the challenge. "I like that you are not afraid of me. I like that you are too clever for your own good. You are honorable to a fault and more beautiful than you seem to realize. I would be proud to have you by my side as my queen."

Without looking at him, she returned her attention to the fish, breaking them into thirds. For a moment, Fal was afraid he'd gone too far, said too much. But, though her hands shook a little, Sanja didn't run or cry. Instead, after a deep breath or two, she replied, "Nevertheless, your family would not—will not approve."

Fal grinned. As far as arguments went, that one was weak, at best. She was running out of objections. Accepting the bark platter when she offered it, he took one more risk. He pulled her to sit beside him and placed the platter over both their laps, then picked out a fluffy piece of fish and held it up to her lips. "You underestimate them greatly."

Sanja frowned, but as he continued to wiggle the morsel enticingly before her, she opened her mouth and accepted it. "How so? Your father married for political reasons."

Fal shrugged, feeding her another piece of fish. She was literally eating from his hand, not seeming to realize the small show of trust spoke far more than words ever could. He soaked up the light scrape of her teeth on his fingers with relish. "The first time, yes," he said in answer to her question. "The second, he married for love, and scandal be damned." His father's decision to take his wizard and right hand to wife had caused dissent among their people at first. Many had feared that having to obey her royal husband's wishes would prevent Queen Nialei from standing up to him when needed for the good of the kingdom. It had taken his parents years to quell that fear, but in the end, they'd earned their people's trust and proven their loyalty to Wilderheim beyond all doubt.

"But your sister's marriage was one of state, to forge an alliance with the Imarah tribe of Aegiros."

He laughed, taking a piece of fish for himself before feeding her another. "So the official story would have you believe. The truth is, I very much doubt Wilderheim was in her thoughts at all when she ran off to Aegiros in search of adventure. She, too, married for love. The resulting political alliance was merely a happy byproduct."

"And your parents did not object?"

He considered that. "By the time they found out, there was nothing they could do about it. But no, I do not believe they begrudged Liadan her happiness for a single moment. It had been too hard-won for that."

Sanja grew quiet, turning away from his next offering, so he ate it himself. A sparrow flew overhead, and a woodpecker drummed out a rapid rhythm somewhere in the trees. The day was warm, the rush of water lulling. Sitting there beside a fire, with fish cooking over the flames and Sanja pressed against his side, Fal felt almost content. He could happily while away his days this way and count himself a lucky man, indeed.

But when she refused his next offering, he grew worried. "What are you thinking?" he asked, resisting the temptation to see for himself. He needed her to trust him enough to tell him of her own accord.

She gently pushed the platter fully into his lap and got up to remove the second skewer from the fire. This one, she placed on the ground and sat back on her heels, facing away from him. "They all married for love," she said. "But you did not. You married me because it needed to be done, you said so yourself."

Fal winced. "I did say that, didn't I?" And, naturally, she had given his words the worst possible interpretation.

"Do you deny it now?"

He frowned, unsure of how to answer. "No." He chose his next words with care. "I would do it again without hesitation." He would have done anything to keep the blade from plunging into her heart. "But it was not only an act of necessity."

She faced him with obvious reluctance, waiting for him to say more.

But what could he say? She couldn't expect a declaration of love. They'd known each other for so short a time, all of it fraught with so much, he hadn't had an opportunity to analyze the connection between them. Nevertheless, a connection was there, and Fal did feel *something* potent enough to make the prospect of Sanja's death unthinkable.

With the perils of Wilderheim out of reach and Sanja safe in Anderheim, Fal at long last had a moment to take measure of the situation. And, ever the scholar, he tried to look at it objectively. He liked Sanja a great deal and couldn't deny a deep attraction. Their first kiss had been seared like an invisible pulse into his lips. As he recalled it again, he felt the same sensation of an impending lightning strike yet, at the same time, being in Sanja's company felt like the most natural thing in the world—effortless, guileless, and comfortable.

The feeling was in no way similar to what his sister felt for her husband. Theirs was a love as fiery and intense as Liadan herself. Nor could he say it was like the connection his parents shared, which went deeper than the heart all the way to the soul.

Having ruled out those possibilities, Fal was at a loss. He hesitated to mention it at all, not wanting to give Sanja false hope, but neither could he dismiss it outright. "Ours may not have started as a love match," he said, "but that doesn't mean we can't still make a good life together. I know I haven't given you much reason to trust me when I say this, but I will be a good husband to you, Sanja."

She studied him so intensely for so long, Fal almost suspected she could see into his thoughts the way he'd peeked into hers. He wished she could; perhaps she might make sense of it all. "I believe you," she said, the words themselves spelling the surprise of her new realization.

"You do?"

Sanja nodded.

"Why?"

She hesitated, appearing to consider several responses before announcing, "Well, you could hardly be worse than Jarl Steen."

Fal grinned. "If that is the standard against which I am to be judged, we are off to an excellent start."

Sanja chuckled but sobered quickly. "Thank you for not taking offense. I may make light of the matter, but please believe I am aware of where I would be now, if not for you." Her gaze lowered to the eating knife at his waist, and he tensed, waiting to see what she'd do next. Seeming to come to some sort of decision, she nodded to herself and said, "I am grateful to you for saving my life. And I would like the chance to spend it with you. You are right. We can still make a good life together. And perhaps, in time, there may come affection. It would be more than I have ever dared to hope for."

Me, as well, he thought, and the unknown feeling within him swelled a little more.

CHAPTER 21

Me, as well.

The sentiment whispered across her mind in the prince's voice, startling her. Sanja blinked at him. Had he said it aloud? No, she'd been watching him, and his mouth hadn't moved. She must have imagined it.

And yet Sanja was certain she hadn't. As certain as she'd been a moment ago that he'd spoken the truth. She'd felt it in him, somehow.

Fal looked away first, shifting forward to awkwardly poke apart a splitting log. "You have not asked me yet where we are."

The sudden change of subject caught her off guard, breaking whatever strange connection she'd thought she'd felt a moment ago. Now that he mentioned it, she was curious about the lack of swirling colors in the sky. And since he said they weren't dead, "Where are we? And why isn't your face changing anymore?"

"Because everything else has changed. We are in an illusion made real. An Otherland directly on top of Wilderheim, in every way the same, and completely separate."

"How can that be?"

He began to speak, then winced and said, "I don't know."

"That is hardly encouraging."

"I know we are safe for now. I know we have everything that exists in Wilderheim, except its people and its troubles. The war there will never touch us here; nothing can go in or out of Anderheim, and I think… I think it can keep us safe from Fenrir, too."

Nothing in or out? "We are stuck here?"

The prince flushed. "More or less. Temporarily," he rushed to assure her. "I got you through, did I not? So it follows that passage back and forth is possible. I just need time to learn how."

"Time." Sanja looked up at the sun marking its slow progress across the sky. Time was the one thing she didn't have. "Before we get to that, there is something else we ought to address." And the mere thought of it made her palms sweat, and her tongue stick to the roof of her mouth.

"Yes?"

His patient gaze sought hers, soothing and encouraging, making her throat too dry to speak. Gods, she couldn't even bring herself to say it.

"Sanja, you need never be afraid to tell me anything. Whatever it is you need, it is already yours. Remember, you are the future queen of Wilderheim."

Oh, she remembered. That was the problem. Her face burned. "The handfasting," she ventured, hesitating. "It is only the first step."

"Ah," Prince Fal cleared his throat and, when she dared a peek at his face, it was as red as hers felt. "Normally, you would be correct. The handfasting is meant to be a promise that must be consummated to keep." He shifted in his seat, drew his knees up and rested his forearms on them. Not quite hiding, but almost. Well enough for him to speak the words of a marriage vow but, apparently, the marriage itself was as awkward for him as it was for her.

"But…?"

He toyed with one of his golden cuffs, keeping his gaze averted. "It is the physical commitment that must be confirmed with… And, you see, under normal circumstances, it would have only been the holding of hands and a piece of string but…"

Sanja traced the scar on her hand. "Our hands were cut. We shared blood before the string was tied."

Prince Fal nodded. "And, as you know, blood binds all things."

Sanja considered this. The bond would be irreversible and everlasting. And, for an Other whose lifespan might well stretch across several millennia, *forever* was a very long time. Then another thought occurred to her. "You had a good grasp on my hand when we fought. But you let go and cut yourself in the process."

He ducked his head.

But this was too important for either of them to hide from. If he was mistaken or, gods help her, lying, her life was still in danger. "Did you do it on purpose?"

Without looking up, he mumbled something under his breath.

"What was that?"

Prince Fal hunched his shoulders up to his ears, then let them drop and looked off to the side, his mouth twisting as if it could keep him from having to respond. Finally, he faced her and admitted, "I had my reasons." That appeared to be as much as he could bring himself to say on the matter.

"I see." But she didn't really. The Other prince had bound himself to a human girl for all time; he had to know there would be repercussions. Was that why? With the physical requirement satisfied by a blood bond, "Did you intend for us to never share a marriage bed? Ever?"

"If necessary."

Sanja steeled herself not to flinch or look away. He was resolute in his decision—fatally so. Sanja felt the tide of his will wash over her in a silent command to let it go. Don't ask questions, don't look for answers. Accept what is and don't want more. "We are to have a marriage in name only? What about the line of succession?" Did he consider her so undesirable he would give up legitimate heirs to avoid lying with her even once?

"Liadan and I are Halflings, Sanja. The line will end with us no matter what."

Sanja gaped. "But then—"

"Truth, yes? That is what we agreed. The truth is, I may be more water than fire, but I am still a Dragonblood, and the risk of conception might still be there, even if the child doesn't survive to be born. And it would likely kill its mother from the womb as it died. I refuse to do that to any woman, much less my human wife."

Sanja closed her mouth, absorbing this news. So much fear and dread concealed in that short speech. A lifetime of it, as if he'd always known, or been taught to be wary of his own desires. Part of her wanted to tell him it wasn't his choice to make. Having faced death once already, Sanja felt reckless and defiant of Fate and Destiny. But she remembered the stories she'd heard whispered across the market square every year on the prince's birthday. "There are rumors about Queen Mari." King Saeran's first wife was said to have died under mysterious circumstances while pregnant with their first child. Some had connected this to Saeran's mother having died in childbirth and said the royal line was cursed.

Prince Fal nodded. "All true. Any human woman would meet the same fate, were it possible for me to give her a child. Only dragon's blood can birth a Dragonblood."

"I suppose your mother survived birthing twins because she is Other." Something Sanja most definitely was not.

"I am sure that was part of it. But there was also my dragon grandfather's involvement. He offered Nialei three drops of his blood to protect her."

Sanja held up her hand. "What do you mean, your *dragon* grandfather?"

He flushed. "I, uh… My family is called Dragonblood. You knew we were descended from dragons."

"Yes, but centuries ago, not…" Gods, the look on his face. "But no one has seen a real dragon in over six hundred years."

"And therefore they no longer exist?"

Sanja gaped. "Do you mean to tell me there are still dragons in the world?"

"I only know of one. But that is not what I—"

"Dragons are massive. If they were still alive, would we not have heard of them by now?"

"You certainly would not have heard of this one. He is my father's grandsire. If he does not want to be known, it is our duty to keep his secret. A dragon's blood is so powerful it can change a person from within. Can you imagine how dangerous it would be if people learned a true dragon dwelled just north of Wilderheim?"

"The dragon lives north of Wilderheim?"

"I should not have told you—"

"A real, live dragon? Just north of Wilderheim?" There was nothing north of Wilderheim except mountains and snow. Hallowed Mountain was one of the southern peaks of its range. How close had she gotten to the dragon's lair on her Journey? Did the clerics know? They couldn't. If they did, they'd be compelled to share any knowledge of its existence—

"Focus, Sanja. You can never tell anyone about the dragon, or he will die. Do you understand?"

"Yes." Having seen the levels of depravity some men were capable of, she could well picture what they would stoop to for but a scale from the dragon's tail. "I understand. I will keep his secret." If a single dragon still lived, the last thing Sanja wanted was for people like Steen to make a sport out of hunting him down.

Her answer seemed to mollify Fal somewhat. "What I am trying to explain is that without the dragon's help, my mother would not have survived birthing me and Liadan. It is the nature of our bloodline and the curse of being a Halfling. It is why I will not risk giving you a child. Had circumstances been different, I would have prevailed on Grandfather to protect my wife the same way he had my mother. But he appears to have gone missing, along with my parents. Not that it would have made a difference here." With a belligerent wave of his hand, he indicated the clearing around them.

"Is there no other way to keep me from conceiving? Surely there must be some herbal concoction or a spell."

"No witch's brew or wizard's spell would work—they never do. Theoretically, an Other ought to have control over such things, but I have always considered the risk too great to experiment." He flushed at his own admission, and, with an annoyed huff, pushed to his feet to add more wood onto the fire. "In any case, I have told you, the need for physical communion was satisfied with our blood bond. It is not necessary for us to do any more than that."

"Yes, well, forgive me for being skeptical, Your Highness, but you have told me other things in the past as well, and not all of them have been strictly accurate." To put it mildly. "We can live the rest of our lives chastely, if you wish, but this one thing I must have. I must be certain my contract with Jarl Steen is well and truly broken."

That it might not be all but sent her into another bout of panic. Despite Prince Fal's assurance that the sharing of blood finalized their marriage, she still felt the dread of her former betrothed like a blade at her throat. She dared not move or take a breath too deep, while it threatened to cut her. Sanja needed to finish it, consummate the union as it ought to be, so there was no question of its validity.

"What precisely are you suggesting?"

Sanja steeled her spine and clutched her hands together to stop them shaking. "An act of necessity." When the prince scoffed and cursed, she flushed. "It is not how I would have preferred it to happen, either," she admitted. "But I cannot afford the luxury of waiting for it to be right. I cannot risk our being wrong about my contract. Not after everything I have been through." By sunset, it would be too late. "Surely it must be safe *once*." She'd known couples who'd tried for years before conceiving a child. Some never did, at all.

"Sanja, you do not know what you are asking."

"I am asking to be your wife."

He looked at her sideways, and she saw in his eyes all the things he dared not share. Anger at his own nature, and at her for demanding he risk her life. Fear of what it would mean for both of them. Yet, despite all that, Sanja was surprised to see a spark of heat in his gaze as it traveled down her body and up again to clash with hers. It lit up his eyes like jagged sparks of lightning, and she remembered as if it had happened mere moments ago.

A kiss sealed by a lightning strike, a lifetime inside a heartbeat of joy so pure it'd almost made her weep. It was a long ago dream of countless beautiful impossibilities, all of them contained within the press of his lips against hers. The searing heat, the blinding pain, and the unspeakable pleasure of a secret embrace. It had been real.

And he remembered, too.

A lifetime in a kiss. And it hadn't been a dream.

Despite her humanity, and all the risks involved, Prince Fal had wanted her then, and he wanted her still.

Sanja found herself responding. A wave of warmth spread across her body as she boldly held his gaze, knowing in her soul that this man would never cause her a moment's pain if he could prevent it. She would never have cause to fear his temper or his touch; she would never be lonely for companionship with him by her side. Somehow, by a stroke of divine luck, Sanja had married a man who put all those romantic poems she'd read to shame.

"Please," she said on an unsteady breath. "Let me be your wife."

At length, his jaw twitched as he dipped a slow, meaningful nod. "As you wish," he answered, then turned and walked away.

Stunned, Sanja pushed to her feet. "Where are you going?"

"To think."

"To *think*?" They didn't have time for that! What in the world did he have to think about, anyway?

But he was gone before she could ask, leaving her alone to pace around the fire and watch the sun slowly crawl toward the west.

The shadows grew longer while she waited. The day's heat cooled, and a light breeze began to blow. Sanja added more wood to the fire, ate more of the fish to fill her empty belly—anything to stave off memories of freezing nights without any food or shelter at all.

Whenever the wind blew stronger, she shivered, inching closer to the fire. With every hiss of movement in the grass, she flinched, seeking enemies about to descend upon her without mercy. Out in the open, she was completely exposed, and without the prince's voice to keep her grounded, fear raked its icy claws down her back, scoring it clean through to her spine.

Desperate for any kind of distraction, she dashed off toward the trees, intending to gather more firewood, but came to an abrupt stop several paces before the tree line. Too many shadows. Too many places for an enemy to hide. Despite her determination to do something of use, her feet slid backward in retreat.

An owl swooped down from a tree in front of her, and Sanja cried out, covering her head with her arms as her right foot slid back another step. When she calmed enough to peer into those woods again, the owl sat on a high branch, its overlarge eyes watching her.

Is this how I'm to live my life now, afraid of birds and shadows in the trees?

What a wonderful queen she'd make.

Closing her eyes, she tilted her face up to the sky and breathed in deep of the evening air. Summer nights had always been her favorite. She loved the scent of warm earth and flowers; she loved being able to taste the sunset and feel life thriving all around her. Simple pleasures in a small, simple life. It'd been so safe before Jarl Steen, with never a worry too deep to overcome.

Now, all Sanja knew was worry and fear. They maddened her, these enemies within, for she had no way to fight them back, no weapon or shield to use against them. Sanja would rather have met Dyri face to face. A physical opponent, at least, she could confront.

She needed a weapon. No matter that she wouldn't know how to use one, anyway, she'd feel much safer just for having one. A knife, a club—a large stick would do. When Prince Fal returned, Sanja would ask him for his eating knife.

He won't give it. Not after she'd tried to stab herself with it and, out here that left her at the mercy of his protection alone.

The light dimmed, and she opened her eyes. This close to the trees, she could no longer see the sun, and its light in the sky was beginning to fade. Her time was running out, and the prince still hadn't returned. Should she look for him? But what if she left the clearing and he came back to find her gone?

She ought to go back. But not with empty hands. Sanja searched the ground around her, gathered a few stray sticks, then dared to walk farther along the forest's edge to collect a few more before rushing back to the fire. Already, her heart was beating too fast. Her hands were so cold her fingernails had started to turn blue. She held them up to the fire's warmth, willing herself not to imagine Mattias' body lying there in place of a woodpile.

"Prince Fal," she called, hoping to hear him answer.

He didn't, but Sanja sensed something from the direction where he'd gone. No more than a little twitch of new awareness, like a soundless beacon waking to her call, unfamiliar, but not menacing. Sanja felt drawn to it. In her mind, she imagined its location not far from where she stood. It beckoned to her, and Sanja found herself following its lure away from the safety of the fire.

The waterfall at the northern edge of the clearing spilled into a sizable lake—the apparent source of her supper. It was pristine and so beautiful, burnished in pale gold by the setting sun.

A cold breeze brushed her cheeks with delicate mist that ought to have chilled her. Instead, Sanja felt it like the sun upon her skin, warm, comforting.

She imagined the water sang to her in ethereal melodies that swept away her fears and worries and wrapped her entire being in the comfort of an invisible embrace. It swayed her on her feet in a slow, gentle dance, loosened her tense spine. As the sun dipped a little lower, swarms of fireflies took to the air, filling the meadow with flickering lights.

What a beautiful, magical dream this was. Sanja never wanted to wake up.

She came to the water's edge, sensing her beacon's approach. The surface bulged up at the other side of the lake, the protrusion silently gliding in a straight line toward her and, as it reached the height of its endurance where the water shallowed, the smooth barrier broke, and Prince Fal rose up before her.

He was shirtless, water running down the valleys of his body in rivulets and, oh, how beautiful he was. Unlike Jarl Steen's bulky, intimidating form, Prince Fal had the body of a lean warrior, encased in smooth, golden skin, sheened with the merest hint of pearlescence. Sanja saw a mystical glow about him, the coolness of water and the fire's heat mingling together in his being and radiating magic strong enough to banish the chill of approaching night.

He was the same prince who'd pulled her from the freezing winter, the same one who'd sat with her by the fire and fed her pieces of flaky fish, yet he seemed a different being altogether; an Other being, gazing at her from his watery demesne with eyes like glowing sapphires.

Without a word, he held out his hand, beckoning her forward.

Sanja froze, suddenly nervous at the prospect of his touch. "The water is cold."

"I will keep you warm," he promised, his deep voice causing heat to pool deep in her belly.

Still, she couldn't bring herself closer than the water's edge. It lapped gently at her toes as if to draw her in. Its welcome called her home.

"Don't be afraid," the prince said, waiting patiently with his hand still outstretched.

Sanja looked over her shoulder. The sun was already halfway hidden behind the trees.

This is what you asked for.

No, she'd asked for an act of necessity. This felt so much bigger, more dangerous. The Other Prince was asking her to trust him with her body, but Sanja felt an insistent tug at her heart as well. The two would go into his keeping hand in hand, and what if she never got them back?

"Come to me, little love."

The endearment brought her gaze back to his face, and Sanja was struck by a sense of connection she hadn't felt before. Its gentle, relentless pull drew her ankle-deep into the lake, close enough for him to reach, yet he remained still, waiting for her.

Another step brought her off the rocky ledge into waist-high water. She gasped, reached for his strong shoulders to steady herself, and he caught her by the elbows, holding on while she found her balance.

Sanja shivered as warmth suffused her entire body, from the toes of her feet to the crown of her head. She blinked, and her hair shirt and trousers were gone; she was bared completely to the prince's gaze. Blushing, she pressed herself against him to hide and felt him suck in a harsh breath, his heart thumping hard, drawing hers into the same, rapid rhythm.

His arms came around her, and he sank back, pulling her along into deeper water, buoying her safely near the surface. His hands caressed her back, her sides, over her rump and thighs, gently guiding her legs around his waist. Wherever he touched, the sensation lingered, multiplied by the lapping waves until Sanja felt her entire body being petted by countless hands.

"Will you kiss me, sweet Sanja?"

Overwhelmed into an almost drunken stupor, Sanja lifted her heavy-lidded gaze to his and nodded. His lips brushed hers, one of his hands cradling the back of her head, anchoring her to his searching kiss. He teased her and tasted her, and Sanja responded with timid enthusiasm, feeling the intrusive pressure of his manhood against her core.

"Fal…"

His name on her lips shuddered through Fal, nearly sending him over the edge. Already, he hovered there for the pleasure of having Sanja in his arms. She fit to him as if made for him, and he never wanted to let her go. "Trust me?"

"Yes," she said.

With a hard thrust, he rent through her maidenhead, taking her cry into his mouth. He felt the water draw magic from him as it swirled in a lazy current around them. It didn't take for itself, but for her. It soothed away the pain he'd caused, brought her pleasure in its stead. Fal waited until he felt her relax once more in his hold before he moved again.

With the lake buoying them softer than a mattress made of clouds, they floated and kissed and loved, straining together as one. Fal's awareness of the outside world narrowed to the woman in his arms. Her gaze held him captive. Her heartbeat set the rhythm of his, and, as he felt himself nearing the endless precipice, the two synchronized for a beat.

And another.

And one more.

At the last moment, he pressed his palm flat against the small of Sanja's back, called up a thin barrier of water to contain his rising seed, and prayed it would be enough to keep her safe.

And then there was only the blinding light of pleasure and the breathless wonder of it echoing through Sanja, and back to him. Light enough to brighten the falling night. Heat enough to bring steam up from the lake's surface. A connection so complete, he shuddered when their heartbeats fell out of sync once more, each returning to its own unique rhythm, leaving a lasting echo in the other. He would know Sanja anywhere now. Deaf and blind, he would find her by the feel of her heart in his.

Slowly, reluctantly, Fal came back to himself, to the water's chorus singing a sweet lullaby. Sanja clung to him, shivering, and nothing had ever felt so good, so right as the feel of her skin against his. "Mine now, wife," he said. "And the sun's still in the sky."

He floated them around so she could watch the sun's final ray disappear behind the tree line in the west. The glittering blanket of night descended on a soft sigh, countless stars shining above. They reflected on the lake's surface all around Fal and Sanja, creating an illusion of them floating unfettered in the night sky.

"Magic," Sanja whispered.

Yes, he thought. *You are.*

CHAPTER 22

He dreamed of battle. A great army rushed the empty field, their weapons raised high, but their voices silent. They came in the night, with only the bright Otherlands above to shine their way. And they came in droves.

The ground shook with the beat of their gallop. The wind screamed as it wove among their blades. They were the sounds of an approaching storm, and this one would end them all.

Fal dived down and became someone else.

A lone sentry on patrol heard the noise. He squinted into the night sky, seeking thunder clouds and, when he saw none, turned his gaze lower. Fear tightened like a noose around his neck; he couldn't find his voice to shout a warning. For too long, he stood frozen to the spot, watching a sea of armed warriors flood toward him.

His torch shone the target for their arrows. They missed, but their clatter against the wall at his back roused the sentry into action. He dropped the torch and ran for the tower, tripped and fell so many times his body was bruised and his face streaked with tears by the time he reached the bell. Wheezing sobs echoed off the stone as he gripped the hammer and swung.

Over and over, he beat the bell, desperate to hear an answering gong from the other towers before the army reached him. An arrow pierced his neck as the first response rang out, and he smiled as he fell. The alarm had been sounded.

Fal left the man's dying body, hovered there a moment with the entire world open to him, before he was drawn away, pulled to another place, to become another man.

In the next tower, two sentries had been placed in charge. The one remained to continue sounding the alarm, but the other had a different task. Torch in hand, he ran down the tower stairs, across the field to the other tower, where a great pyre stood ready to be lit.

The princess' instructions repeated in his mind as he thrust the torch into the pile: "Light a fire large enough, and it will call to me. I will come at once."

As the dry wood caught, the sentry watched the night swarm with soldiers. They came out of nowhere, soundless, but for the beat of horse hooves. They carried no banners, but their white tabards were emblazoned with a bright red cross.

He watched the first tower fall, its bell already silent for some time. Soon, they would reach the second. He wanted to run for his life. Clan Steen had never answered the crown's call to arms. There were no soldiers stationed here, only sentries charged with sounding the alarm, should anyone think to sneak up on them from behind. They'd expected perhaps a score of men, not legions.

In the end, when the second tower's bell fell silent, fear got the better of him. The fire had just started to consume the pile of straw and wood. It would burn on its own and had no need of more tending. The sentry dropped his torch and ran.

A spear through the gut ended his escape halfway down the staircase, and by the time he tumbled to the bottom, the soldiers had already run up and doused the pyre. The sound of thousands of booted feet marching past drowned out his wailing moan of despair as his soul fled its dying prison, expelling Fal along the way.

He flew far up into the sky once more, gazing down at death creeping through the night. The rush of feet, the drum of hoofbeats came to him in waves like great, growling breaths of Fenrir's approach. Icy mist followed in their wake. It concealed deep furrows in the ground, invisible claw marks none but he would ever see.

With a shudder, Fal turned his gaze in the other direction.

Only a stretch of open fields and forests remained between the army and Castle Frastmir. Their path, it seemed, lay open to seize the seat of the crown but, overeager and overconfident, they made a mistake.

Someone in their ranks ordered the fields to be burned. A series of flaming arrows shot into the sky and landed true, lighting a wild blaze that flared across the landscape and sparked an unmistakable alarm.

With the fire's roar to sound their advance, they gave voice to their fury and screamed a chorus of war cries so loudly they never heard the wildfire flare behind them as high as the castle wall, spewing forth a creature of nightmares.

Instantly, Fal became the dark, silent being who soared over the army to head them off. She flew, and flew, seeking an edge to the sea of troops, and found none. Were she anyone other than who she was, the Dragonblood princess might well have panicked at the sight.

But Liadan had faced far worse in the past, and she knew that succumbing to fear would spell defeat before the battle had even begun. Baring her fangs in a snarl, she beat her wings harder to gain more speed. She could see the front lines now, almost to the castle's outer wall.

Liadan allowed them to reach it, let them corner themselves, and then let loose a massive stream of fire. Men screamed below her, but she was already gone by the time they turned their gazes to the sky, flying along the wall to burn as many of them as she could reach.

There! The army did have an end. Liadan veered along the edges of the formation, the weak point where those who bore witness to their comrades burning alive grew afraid enough to run. She cut them off with her flames, framed the formation in glorious, golden fire.

There were too many to burn all at once; she knew she'd never get them all this way, but she needed to kill as many as possible, weaken their ranks, and give Wilderheim's forces time to muster.

The dragon would be furious with her if he knew how badly she'd miscalculated the enemy's intent. He would never forgive her for leaving their flanks so exposed.

But he wasn't there, and neither were her parents or her brother. Liadan was on her own, facing a threat more massive than any of them had anticipated.

All of them had failed, and if she couldn't make it right, all of them would die for their failure.

Catching a favorable wind, she let it carry her higher so she might better see the battle. Frastmir's soldiers were streaming up to the battlements, ready to face the enemy. Inside the castle, everyone trained for battle was busy at work preparing weapons and vats of oil. Servants carrying armfuls of linens rushed into the great hall, which would serve as their infirmary. Anyone too old or too young was being evacuated.

Unsettled by the surprise attack, Liadan took a chance and abandoned the fight to soar over the city. The streets were dark and quiet, not a soul out of doors. The sounds of battle hadn't reached them yet.

Liadan threw a fireball into a pile of hay, and another at a stack of firewood, and one more into the middle of the green. It was all the warning she could give the people, and she prayed it would be enough.

The wind shifted, bringing with it the scent of burning flesh. It called Liadan to return to the fight, but she resisted, drawn toward the west by a sense that she had overlooked something.

Beyond the city of Frastmir, the countryside was peacefully asleep as far as her eye could see. Still, something about it felt wrong. Liadan flew on, trusting her instincts more than her sight. She flew so far, the battle for Castle Frastmir seemed an entire world away, and all the while, her gut clenched with dread.

Almost to the town of Crossroads, Wilderheim's central point, Liadan stopped, hovering aloft to get her bearings. A ringing started in her ears, high pitched and relentless. It speared into her mind, confusing her sense of up and down. She lost control of her flames and they cracked fissures across her black scales, turned her hair to living fire.

Liadan clutched her temples, shook her head, stabbed her talons into her scalp, but nothing would make it stop. She flipped over in the air, lost the wind, and tumbled headlong toward the ground.

As she fell, a sparkle of light nearby tore the world open with the flash of a strange, polished sword, admitting another wave of mounted troops.

Liadan struck the ground, writhing in agony as flames flared out of her in uncontrollable bursts. She crawled her way to a creek and doused herself in it until the smoke that usually accompanied her transformation from one shape to another congealed into sludge. Fully human, unarmed, and disoriented, Liadan lay still in the stream as the sky spun madly above her.

She heard screaming as soldiers murdered their way through the town. They would find her soon and, in her current state, they might succeed in killing her. Liadan turned to her side to ease her way up to sit, but the world tilted, sending her back into the creek.

The relentless noise filled her skull to bursting. It was the sound of metal, a blade forged to thirst for blood. It screeched with madness and cut without mercy. Guardsmen and soldiers died by that blade, and more would have, were it not for the hand of its wielder turning it forcibly away from women and children. But the blade's metal kept screeching, demanding its due and growing more powerful with each drop of blood it absorbed. It would not keep obeying for long. Liadan squeezed her eyes shut to somehow keep them from popping out. The scent of blood reached her, and she realized it was her own. Liadan's mouth opened on a soundless scream as her body began to turn against her.

Desperate to get away, she tried one more time to rise.

A cold, wet foot slapped against her shoulder, pushing her back down. Liadan opened her eyes just a little to see something standing over her. It had two legs, two arms, a torso, and a head—a human shape, but made entirely of water. Though the undine had no discernible eyes, Liadan could feel it watching her. She sensed it was angry, and Liadan was helpless to defend herself against it.

The undine lifted its head to look away, then turned back to her. Faster than Liadan could react, it slapped its transparent hand over her face and submerged her head in the creek.

She fought to surface but, though she felt no binds on her limbs, they wouldn't move. Her fire flared to the surface of her skin only to be instantly doused by the water. Without air, she couldn't burn to defend herself. Mud churned up around her as she thrashed, rendering her blind, hiding her from sight as a stampede of human feet shook the ground.

Her lungs burned with the need for air until she could bear it no longer. She inhaled and let the stinging, muddy water burn deep into her lungs. Heavy pressure on her chest kept her submerged, pushing her deeper into the mud as she coughed and drowned, until the mud encased her up to her neck.

But she wasn't dying. Water rushed in and out of her lungs, alien, painful, terrifying, but it wasn't killing her. Heavy footfalls stomped her legs and torso, an army rushing across the creek. She felt them, but they never saw her. And, as she gasped in lungful after lungful of murky muck, she noticed something else. Her head no longer hurt.

The water cleared above her, forming the shape of a translucent head as the undine held a watery finger to its nonexistent lips. It was helping her?

Suddenly, the creature was gone. The pressure keeping her submerged disappeared, and the water in her lungs became deadly without the Undine's magic to protect her. Buried in the mud, Liadan thrashed as hard as she could to get free. She only needed a little give, a hand's width to reach the surface—

⋘ »·◇·« ⋙

Fal's own shout startled him awake, and he bolted upright out of a stream. He was soaked through, and nowhere near where he'd laid himself to sleep the night before.

He stepped out of the stream and crawled up the grassy bed to level ground. The town of Crossroads spread out before him, every house and roadway as he knew it from Wilderheim. Here, it all stood empty, not a soul to be seen, not a single animal scurrying about.

By the location of the sun, Fal guessed it to be a little before noon. How had he gotten there?

Sanja was probably looking for him by the waterfall, no doubt imagining all sorts of nightmares of Fal having abandoned her again. The need to return to her burned so badly within him it turned water into steam, drying him in an instant.

But he must have been brought here for a reason, and until he discovered what it was, Fal couldn't risk bringing it back with him to put his mate in danger.

"I dreamed."

But *what*?

Though the fear he'd felt remained, shivering through his limbs at odd intervals, Fal couldn't remember anything else from his dream. It had been vivid. He knew that much. And, as he walked through Crossroads, he remembered the odd detail here and there. A sparkling light, accompanied by a ringing sound, a flash of fire, and a blade screaming for blood.

He didn't like this. Being alone in nature was one thing, but Crossroads felt alive and dead at the same time, like a burial ground full of ghosts watching him from darkened doorways and closed window shutters. Fal's skin crawled in the echoing silence; he needed to get away from it.

Offering more magic to Anderheim, he pushed to be transported elsewhere. Anderheim responded eagerly and, through a blurred stream of its particular mode of travel, delivered him into the courtyard of Castle Frastmir. It was as empty as Crossroads, and every other town Anderheim had copied from his memories, turning the castle's structure into a massive bell reverberating with echoes of a long-ago strike. He felt those vibrations in his bones; expected at any moment to see the walls begin to disintegrate beneath their silent force, but they remained standing, tall and proud. He didn't know what to make of it.

There were pitchforks and gear beside the open stable door and barrels by the kitchen. This version of Castle Frastmir appeared to be as equipped as the original in Wilderheim. Better still, his tower library, destroyed in the original, was whole and untouched in Anderheim. It gave him hope its contents would be there as well.

Eager to find out, Fal stepped up to the great front door but stopped with his hand a finger's breadth from making contact. The last time he'd been here, everything he'd touched had disintegrated into water. But Anderheim had been little more than an illusion then. Things might be different now.

Taking a chance, Fal pressed his palm to the door and pushed. The great portal groaned a loud complaint that echoed through the hall. Stepping across the threshold, Fal felt like a tiny ant walking into a cave.

"Hello," he called to relieve the yawning silence. He didn't expect an answer.

In the great hall, his parents' thrones stood on the dais, illuminated by a shaft of light coming from a high window. They glittered with magics imbued in the wood with symbols as sharp and fresh as the day they'd been carved.

Fal ached to see his parents seated there. He craved the comfort of their presence and the guidance of their knowledge. He missed them both, as well as his sister. Never had he yearned for Liadan's presence in his mind as much as he did now, in this new, empty world.

Turning his back on the dais, he went to his tower library in search of answers. All the books and scrolls he'd collected over the years greeted him when he arrived at the top, and Fal breathed in their familiar scent. There, among those pages, lay the answer to his predicament, he was sure of it.

He sought one tome in particular, an old, leather-bound volume with iron clasps and a meticulously stitched spine. He remembered the title embossed on the front: *The Origin of Worlds*. He remembered setting it aside, at the time more interested in the ending of worlds than their origins. Considering Fal had somehow managed to start the birth of a new world, the book might prove useful now.

Where had he put it?

Aha! At the top of a stack of books on the topmost shelf. Out of reach and out of the way of more important research material. Three more books fell from the stack when he extricated the one he wanted, but he didn't care. With fingers so eager they shook, he unlatched the iron clasp and opened the book onto the first page.

It was blank.

He turned two more pages, then fanned through the rest of them, but all of them were completely blank. Anderheim had known to recreate a book Fal remembered seeing, but it couldn't reproduce words Fal had never read.

Setting the tome aside, he picked up another and leafed through it. This one was a treatise on elemental magic he'd read in search of a cure for his illusions. The copy in his hands was filled with passages he remembered, but the writing faded to illegible stains in parts he'd only skimmed, or hadn't read at all.

He wouldn't find anything here he didn't already know.

But the library was still shielded with spells Fal himself had devised to keep his experiments contained. He would find no safer place to test his limits within Anderheim. Offering up a puff of magic, he sent the Otherland a silent request for a window.

Anderheim accepted, but not as eagerly as it had in the past. Sometime between Fal's retrieving Sanja from the path and now, the Otherland's formation had completed fully. It had become its own thing, separate and no longer dependent on Fal, and the magic he offered became no more than part of a transaction. In return, Anderheim physically shifted several stones out of the tower wall to create an opening large enough to pass for a window. It smoothed the edges, formed a sill along the bottom, and sent the remaining rocks tumbling away.

The window opened to the east, overlooking fields and forests. Far beyond the horizon in that direction was the demesne of clan Steen and, beyond that, the Ravetian border. Fal took in the sight, savored its tranquility for a moment longer before he began his work in earnest.

It may have quieted while he'd slept, but the water sprite magic still roiled in restless eddies inside his chest. Fal sensed it like a sleeping beast. If and when it awakened, he wasn't certain he could keep it from overwhelming him.

New magic was dangerous magic, regardless of who wielded it. Water sprites were born with an innate understanding of the power they held and learned nuance as they matured. To come into possession of so much of it so late in life put Fal and everyone around him in peril. He could bring the entire tower crashing down simply by voicing the wrong melody.

But more power could also mean a way out of Anderheim. It was another straw for him to grasp. With Sanja safely away at the waterfall, now was the time to try.

Fal closed his eyes and focused on the churning magic within him. Like a flower in the sun, it bloomed and flared, tickling his throat to be released. There lay the lock to keep it contained: the magic could only work through his voice. As long as he remained silent, it would be safe.

Fal took a moment to center himself. On his next inhale, he thought of home, and when he exhaled, he gave the thought a melody. He sang softly, at first, uncomfortable with his voice and unsure of how it would affect Anderheim.

He felt the Otherland quiver in reaction. It didn't like this new magic. But it wasn't being hurt, and so it held as steady as it could while the spell built upon itself. Fal's voice grew louder, folded back on itself in endless echoes, and the melody begot layers, growing more complex.

As it turned into a chorus of several voices singing along with Fal, he felt the boundary beyond which he would no longer be able to pull it back. It was so close at hand it frightened him, and he stopped at once, his eyes snapping open.

His tower, a moment ago whole, now looked destroyed. Fal stood on what felt like solid stone, but when he looked down, he saw nothing under his feet but a long drop to the catacombs below. A chill wind brushed the back of his neck, turning his gaze to the east.

The peaceful scene from Anderheim was no more. Before him, the fields and forests of Wilderheim were aflame, thick smoke obscuring the sky. He could not hear a thing, but he saw enough to force a terrified cry from his throat.

At once, the vision slammed shut, closing him away in the safety of Anderheim. But the sight of a sea of warriors spilling over the castle's outer walls remained seared into his mind's eye.

Fal stumbled back, fell over a chair, and slammed his head against the bookcase. His mind seized with terror, and his body shook uncontrollably.

Castle Frastmir was under attack.

Spurred into action, he shoved to his feet, stumbled his way down to the great hall and, through it, to his own chambers. In the far corner of his dressing room stood an old, ornate chest he never expected to have cause to open. Now he had no choice.

Fal changed his clothes and boots, then knelt before the chest and, with shaking hands, opened it. Pulling aside the embroidered wrap, he began to take out the contents one after the other—leather padding, arm and leg guards, chain mail, body armor, a helmet. He didn't put on any of them, save for a leather jerkin trimmed with embroidered protection spells.

Despite having trained with Wilderheim's soldiers from a young age, Fal was a mage, not a warrior. He didn't need heavy armor weighing him down; he needed speed and freedom of movement to work his spells.

But there were a few items in the chest he couldn't afford to leave behind.

First, the sword and dagger Liadan had forged for him in the dragon's fire. Light as a feather, stronger than any steel made by man or Other, with grips fashioned for his hands alone. Liadan had forged many weapons under the dragon's tutelage, but these were the first she'd ever parted with, a gift he'd treasured more than any other. He strapped them both to his waist, grateful to have their protection at hand, should he need them.

From the bottom of the chest, he retrieved a pendant on a long, thick chain. The image of a dragon in flight was etched into its round face, chips of diamonds marking his fangs and a glowing ruby forming his eye. It had been a gift from his parents, the same design worn by his father. The charm protected its wearer with the dragon's magic from both physical and magical assault. As soon as he put it on, he felt his grandfather's fire fuel the water magic inside him and knew instantly that the dragon was alive and well somewhere out there.

Good. They'd need all the help they could get.

Fal pushed to his feet and rolled his shoulders back, preparing himself for the battle to come. He was ready, and the path stood unobstructed. It was time.

Only when he reached for his new magic to open another portal did Fal remember he'd left Sanja at the waterfall, and he faltered. With one hand over his heart where hers beat alongside, he couldn't bring himself to voice a single note. *More than a wife.* She was part of him now, and it brought him equal measures of peace and dread. If he got hurt, she would feel it. If she felt sorrow, Fal would grieve with her. Their lives would be so closely linked neither of them would ever be alone again.

Last night, when he'd held her sleeping in his arms, the knowledge that he'd have a lifetime of such nights ahead of him had filled him with such happiness it had bordered on relief.

Today, faced with the prospect of having her life cut short in an awful, violent way, made him sick to his stomach.

She'll be safer in Anderheim, he told himself. At least here, none of the ugliness and death could touch her.

But she would be alone, in an unfamiliar part of an unfamiliar world, with no magic of her own to aid her. She would think he'd abandoned her.

Fal couldn't take her with him, but at least he could put her in more familiar surroundings. Yes, he could do that. He would not leave her with only a dying campfire to keep her safe.

Decided, Fal sang once more. This time, his voice was steady and strong, his intent clear and focused. He would accept no other outcome but what he was after, and Anderheim dared not oppose his will.

As he sang, he watched the world ripple, felt the doorway opening before him. And it was a doorway. Unlike the brief wound he'd torn open to retrieve Sanja and the window he'd created in his tower, this opening felt as steady as a portal. Anderheim wasn't fighting him anymore. It had taken what it'd needed from Fal. Its existence was no longer bound with Fal's, and so it no longer cared whether he came or went.

Fal altered the melody, forging roots for the portal, anchoring it in place. He sang three more portals into being—one at the waterfall, one in the heart of Crossroads, and one more in the mountain pass between Wilderheim and Lyria. He anchored them deep into the earth and locked them all so no one but Fal could open them. Once he stepped through to Wilderheim and let the doorway close, Fal might lose all sense of the Otherland. He would need another way back.

With his task complete, it was time to go.

Though it looked much the same on the other side, Fal knew he no longer saw Anderheim through his bedchamber doors. He heard sounds of battle; he smelled smoke and felt the fear and pain of his kingdom saturating the cold air. His heart beat faster in response, wavering his resolve, but he pushed his fear aside. His people needed him, and he could not abandon them.

With one hand on the grip of his sword, he stepped up to the portal. Goose flesh prickled all over his skin, and his breath misted in the cold as he stepped through to Wilderheim. As the portal began to close after him, he sent one last bolt of raw magic back to Anderheim with the image of a small, cozy cottage on the western side of an empty copy of Frastmir and an order it wouldn't dare refuse: "Send her home."

He prayed Sanja would understand.

And, if he never made it back, that she could find it in her heart to forgive him.

CHAPTER 23

There were shadows and, from with their prison, a copper-haired Halfling god stepped out into the night, this time for good. He breathed in deeply of the cold as he surveyed the vastness all around him. Stars watched him in silence as among them multitudes of worlds lay naked, exposed to eyes that ought never have beheld their mystery. The wild dervish of their fear filled the silence with a melody of soundless screams, terror whispering on the dark wind.

All of them sang their own end.

The Trickster closed his eyes to better savor the anticipation, hands flexing at his sides and sharp teeth bared in a snarl. Freedom had never tasted so sweet.

His Shadow prison swirled around him one last time, trying in vain to pull him back into its depths, but Loki barely felt its cold caress as it turned to mist and faded away completely.

Triumph, rage, vengeance—all of them had long ago melded together within him into something new and dangerous. Loki felt it coursing through his veins, crawling beneath his skin, and swirling 'round and 'round in his mind, a madness that gave him strength, a weapon that would rend Asgard asunder. He would feast on Woden's bones and drink of his lovely wife's blood anon.

And he couldn't wait.

The void between worlds shuddered with a howl not heard but felt.

Loki turned his gaze in its direction and watched darkness grow in the distance, swallowing light after swirling light as Fenrir neared, devouring everything in his path. Loki launched himself forward to meet it halfway.

What a beautiful monster his son had grown up to be. The great wolf, they called him, for they lacked the words to describe the true shape of him.

He had none.

Fenrir was hunger itself, ever empty, ever ravenous to fill the void inside. He could never be sated and, in the end, would devour himself, as well.

But not yet.

Loki drew on his essence, extending his being through his arms to shape a pair of swords. They tore away from him, then slammed back into the secure hold of his reformed palms. Like the sword he'd given the ancient queen in Synealee, they were imbued with not only his power but also his will, his madness, and his thirst for the blood of his enemies. And they would never be sated.

The queen would never know the magnificence of the gift she'd received. Whoever wielded the sword would slay anyone who stood in his way and win any war he deigned to fight. The blade would bring him power and glory for the price of his precious soul. Those who stood with him would sing his legend for centuries to come, and none of his enemies would live long enough to hate him.

But the blade would have its way in the end. It would infect his mind until right and wrong became life and death. He'd spend his life trying to build a kingdom with the glory and mercy of his god, for fear of burning in his eternal wrath after death. And the harder he tried, the more he would fail, and the deeper his madness would root inside him, forcing him farther along his path to damnation. He would come to loathe the weapon with every fiber of his being. But it would never release him from its hold.

Divine magic always came with a heavy price. Had the queen not been so intent on her revenge, she might have thought to ask. Then again, had she not been so intent, she wouldn't have needed his gift at all.

Humans. Never had another species entertained Loki more. He might miss them in the end. But, for now, he had more than enough games to keep him occupied.

The blades in his hands were as cold as ice and, when they sliced the void, they left gaping wounds. He scraped one sharp edge across the other to produce a screech that stopped Fenrir in his tracks.

The yawing darkness turned on Loki, howling for nourishment. It recognized its maker—for now.

Now was all Loki needed. "Our time has come at last," he said, gazing into the heart of his monstrous progeny. He could feel Fenrir's anguish brimming the endless abyss of him and steeled himself not to fall into it. "Soon, we will have our vengeance on everyone."

Fenrir bayed furiously, displacing the stars as they shrank away, dimming to hide from his seeking gaze. To be seen was to be no more.

Loki's feral smile stretched wider, his lips dragging across the sharpened tips of his fangs. He tasted his own blood, and it fueled his burning wrath. "We claim Wilderheim as our first prize." Cut off all possible paths of retreat; destroy any chance of the Dragonblood clan restoring the gods to their full strength. Then there would be nowhere else for them to hide.

As Fenrir thrashed, eager to set off once more, Loki turned to the line that served as both an anchor and a border between Wilderheim and Mitgard. The border was so thin it was nigh invisible, but Loki felt the power weaving along its length, fortifying it with millions upon millions of whispered prayers. It moved so quickly back and forth it appeared as an unbroken ribbon of light. Only when it stopped, its task complete, could Loki perceive its true shape.

A new god had risen in Mitgard, a fiercely territorial being, willing to sacrifice anything to lay claim to his faithful. And they were very faithful. The old gods had their champions, but their numbers were few and scattered, each paying tribute in their own way, to their own god, diluting the collective strength of their faith. This new god had but one path of worship, and he never shared. With each prayer and offering, his power grew so vast, all the gods of Asgard combined—even Fenrir himself—could not match it.

Wilderheim was but the first casualty of his wrath, sacrificed to Loki and his machinations to wipe out all of Asgard. Once it fell, the new, nameless god would turn his sights onto every other kingdom, and every other god, until only he remained to reign over Mitgard unopposed. Whether the other gods knew it or not, the age of many was fast coming to an end. And only part of its demise would lead down Fenrir's insatiable gullet.

The lines had been drawn. The light of the fledgling god's essence flared bright behind the safety of his impenetrable border, an acknowledgment of Loki on the other side of it, and a reminder of their ultimate bargain. He'd already played his part, paid his price by sacrificing the souls of his oldest, most devout regent follower and legions of her warriors to Loki's war in Wilderheim.

Now it was Loki's turn. *Pay up, Trickster.*

Loki nodded, clutching his swords. "As agreed."

Then he filled his lungs with borrowed power and let it loose on a roar that sent Fenrir into a frenzy, racing straight for Wilderheim.

CHAPTER 24

The water came up to the dragon's chest, languishing there a moment, its waves lapping at his heart on sorrowful sighs. The dragon braced his feet against the wall at his back and pulled steadily, twisting his wrists and chafing his skin off against the coarse ropes. He felt blood seep out of the wounds, but it never dissolved. Rejected by the water, it coalesced into heavy droplets that sank to the floor and rolled around like marbles until, with more deep sighs, the water slowly ebbed back into its basin.

When his cell had dried completely, the dragon regarded the crimson orbs with dispassionate interest as they levitated off the stone floor to hover in the air before him. Without saying a word, he waited for his tormentor to announce herself while she played with his blood, making the drops swirl in the air, then coalesce into one larger orb, then break up into hundreds of minuscule specs before coalescing them once more.

"Does it hurt to bleed?" Hel's disembodied voice questioned.

The dragon refused to answer.

Having shaped his blood into five little spheres, she moved them into a circle and conjured lines of soft green light to form a pentacle. "Gods have no blood," she remarked as the pentacle reformed itself into another, more complicated shape. "We have no hearts, no stomachs, no lungs. Our forms are arbitrarily chosen to give physical shape to our essence, but they are a lie. We are very much like dragons in that way."

She paused, no doubt waiting for him to speak his mind. The dragon remained silent, keeping a watchful eye on his blood. Nine droplets now shaped a sphere of webbed light, then the lines twisted into a flat weave of knotwork in the shape of a dragon.

"It is whispered that the first god who chose to take a physical form went too far and fell into living flesh. It is said that he became the first dragon, and the curse of his mistake is why his descendants can only ever choose one shape to escape their own."

The knotwork dragon reshaped itself into a human man with horns and a tail. The figure bowed its head to look at its own hands, then dropped to its knees as though in anguish.

"When a god dies, she first loses her ability to coalesce into a body. Bodies are useful things, such practical vessels for our power. Hardly any effort at all to manipulate. Take it away, and the power begins to scatter."

The shape collapsed into a ball of light with his blood at its center. Its bright glow dimmed by slow degrees, dispersing light into nothing until only his blood remained.

"We die by disintegrating into nothing, our power redistributed throughout the worlds in such trifling quantities as to be impotent. We become part of everything, and can never again rebuild ourselves whole."

"You are dying," the dragon surmised. Why else would she bother telling him all of this?

He didn't expect her to respond but, to his surprise, she did. "Yes. Like the waters beyond those bars, and the wards of this world, and every other." She didn't sound particularly distraught at this development. "The Other blood that formed the Veil drained away when it shattered. Without it, all the gods are dying. All except one."

"Loki."

His blood suddenly dropped to the stone floor, absorbing into it, and a moment later, Hel coalesced before him like a ghost. "My father lied to us. He sacrificed us all to save himself."

The dragon sneered, baring his fangs. "Did you expect anything else of him?"

"No," she said with what might have been a shrug. "Familial ties hold little meaning to us. But he isn't all bad. After all, he left me a parting gift. A mighty Other of my own."

As he comprehended what she was telling him, the dragon's fury stoked an inferno inside him. He yanked on his ropes, felt them strain even as they tightened further, cutting into his wrists. Every drop of blood that fell to the floor fed power to his prison, strengthening his binds, turning him into his own jailer.

"As long as I have you, I, and all of Helheim, will persist."

"My blood will not keep you alive forever."

"It will keep until the war is over, and Fenrir has had his fill. Then, perhaps it will be my turn to strike a deal with the new god." She looked around. "Helheim can grow as large as it needs to be. It can change as much as it must to please him. After all, the dead must go somewhere."

"And if I drink before then?"

Her pale lips formed something like a smile, though it carried as much feeling as her voice. "And what if you do?"

If he did, he'd die.

Or so she'd led him to believe.

"You lied?"

"My father's idea. He said the greatest torment that can be wrought upon a soul is its own hope of redemption. Perhaps that is why the new god likes him so well." She spoke as though reciting a practiced speech. The inflection of her voice and the expression on her face felt like a performance fabricated for a specific purpose: to anger him. The dragon knew this, and still, he couldn't stop himself rising to the bait.

Fire sparked in his palms and spread to glove his hands and arms up to his elbows, burning his wounds whole. He would not give Helheim a single more drop of his blood if he could help it. If he had to remain burning for the rest of his eternal life, he would, if only to see Hel wither and die. Wrath added fuel to his flames, and soon they covered him from horn to tail, scorching black marks on the cold stone floor.

Hel watched him, her head tilted at a bored angle, but her gaze strayed from his eyes to the ropes tied at his wrists, and the dragon caught the faintest hint of a scent: smoke. Startled, he followed her gaze to see the tiny fibers fraying from the braid turn black and wither into the whole. The rope didn't weaken in the least, but the small damage was enough.

When the dragon faced Hel again, his smile was as dark as his wrath. "Shall we say our farewells now?"

"How about a bargain instead?"

In answer, the dragon's flames flared hotter, turning blue, scorching the ropes black. Yet, writhing as if in pain, they refused to set him free.

Through the blue haze, he saw Hel's form flicker and grow fainter. "Dragon, you have not considered the full consequences of your actions."

"I starve you, you disintegrate, and I go free."

"And Helheim disappears forever. Along with everyone in it."

In the next instant, his flames were gone, and he shivered with cold dread.

"Do you understand now? If you starve us, you will never see your beloved Solveig again. Her soul will die, never to be reborn. That is why you have forced yourself to carry on this long, is it not? Somewhere in the depths of your burning heart, you hoped to meet her again one day, in another life, another body. You have kept yourself alive, waiting for the day when you would see her again, so you might right your mistakes and save her. You would have waited an eternity for that."

"Curse you." He couldn't deny it. Seeing Solveig again, even as a slave to Hel's whims, had only made his yearning deeper. Hope was, indeed, the cruelest torment Hel and her wretched father could have wrought upon him.

"What would you do to be with her again?"

Anything. But if he gave in to Hel, she would repay his sacrifice with nothing but more pain. He would never be free of her. But how could he go on living knowing he'd left Solveig to die?

"All I want is to live," Hel said, drifting closer. "Give me that, and you can have her."

"What would you have me do? Bleed myself dry so you can build a body to contain you?"

"Yes, a body for me, and enough energy to convey you to her. Here in Helheim, her soul is as immortal as you are. She can never sicken, get hurt, or die. You could be with her forever."

"As long as we stay," he clarified bitterly. "I would be your prisoner for the rest of eternity." He would have to give up the clan he'd sired to their fate in Wilderheim. They might all die for his selfish need for his mate. Oh, but to see her again, hear her voice, touch her skin, and feel its vibrant heat…

"Say, rather, you would be allowed to stay. Still, a small price to pay for the gift I offer in return." Hel looked around as a soft mist filled his cell. It carried sunshine, and birdsongs, and green grass on a dream so enticing his eyelids drooped heavily. "And it need not be in this cell."

A figure moved through the mist, indistinct, yet painfully familiar. He watched Solveig stroll through the tall grass, oblivious of being observed this way, and if he could have torn off his own arms to free himself and go to her, he would have.

The rope bit deeper. Helheim claimed more of his blood, and its mistress solidified beside him. "I offer you an eternity with your woman for but a little bit of blood."

At the sound of her voice, Solveig turned to face them, and the hazy vision sharpened a little more. All it cost him was another drop of blood.

The dragon forgot to breathe, staring at her. Her eyes widened in surprise, and he could hear her gasp as if she was right there before him. When her lips shaped his name, the dragon's throat constricted until it hurt.

She smiled.

"Does she know?"

A faint scratching sound made his ear twitch, but with Solveig's tearful gaze on him, the dragon dared not let her out of his sight to seek out its source. Hel traced the seam between the ropes and his skin, taking his blood directly from him. He shuddered when her form condensed enough to restore her scent. The queen of Helheim smelled like mist and cold, and death. "Which answer would make your choice easier to make?"

The dragon growled, shuddering when the sound echoed back from somewhere else. Not an echo. A response.

"She knows enough," Hel said, her hair whipping at his arms when she briefly turned toward the source of the sound, then back to the dragon.

Solveig started toward him slowly, hesitating. She knew. And she understood how impossible a choice had been put before him. Too many paces away, she came upon some invisible barrier that would allow her no closer. Placing one hand on it, she brought herself as close as she could and touched her other hand to her heart.

"Sol," he whispered.

"You have but to say the word to be with her. Give me what I want, and you shall have what you so desperately need."

The dragon was so focused on his Solveig he didn't notice another presence invading his cell until he felt its approaching snarl shudder the ground at his feet.

Solveig gasped, backing away from the barrier separating them, and only then did the dragon tear his gaze from her to see Hel, too, had retreated as far as the cell's confines would allow. Though she showed no fear on her face, the dragon could smell it.

A deep, rumbling growl rendered the wall at his back liquid. Massive ripples deformed the cold stone slabs as a large, lupine snout pushed through, followed by the rest of his head and torso. In the bowels of the withering Helheim, the beast was as big as a small horse. Head canted low, hackles standing on end, the wolf glowed as he faced off with Hel.

Yet, instead of smiting the creature where it stood, the goddess of Helheim appeared to weigh her choices. Surely she didn't consider herself unequal to the battle. Then again, if her state was so desperate that she needed a dragon's blood to survive…

Braving a sideways glance, Hel noticed the dragon watching. She placed her hand on the wall at her back, and the dragon felt a disturbance as the cell walls expanded, retreating to give her more strength. Her body filled out, becoming heavier, more solid, and she raised her chin in defiance. "You cannot have him—"

The wolf snapped his fangs in her face, silencing her with a snarl so vicious the dragon shifted sideways to place himself as much between the beast and Solveig as his ropes would allow.

When Hel would have raised her hand to strike him down, the wolf growled a low warning and pressed his snout to her chest. "He is *mine*," she insisted. "He chose to stay. He chose her."

The wolf's next growl reverberated through the cell and struck fear into the dragon's heart—for Solveig's sake, not his own.

The wolf's body shook with the force of it. *—Liar—* he accused. *—You will not dare!—*

Hel quieted, pressing herself as hard as she could against the wall without escaping through it to safety. With his enemy backed into a corner, the beast turned to the dragon.

"Varr?" The wolf Nialei's magic had inadvertently brought back from death had been her faithful companion ever since. He was not alive and so could not die, but neither was he dead. As a creature of in-between, he had an inexplicable ability to move between realms with ease and defy any attempt to keep him restrained. The dragon almost smiled. "What took you so long?"

Varr huffed his displeasure, wordlessly communicating a deep dislike for this place. Ignoring the vision of Solveig altogether, he turned around to sniff at the dragon's ropes.

"You cannot break them," the dragon said. "They have withstood my fangs, my claws, and my fire countless times."

One large, milky white eye focused on him with what might have been amused indulgence. Opening his maw, Varr took a rope between his teeth and bit down. Lightning crackled along its length, biting back at both Varr and the dragon, causing the wolf to flinch and retreat.

"Helheim will not release him," Hel said. "It needs him too much. And he needs her."

On the other side of the barrier, Solveig spoke the dragon's name. She was wary of the wolf but drawn to the dragon as he would always be drawn to her. "She said we could be together again."

The dragon nearly went to his knees. Starved for the sound of her voice, he silently begged her to say more, unable to speak himself.

Varr answered for him. *—He is needed elsewhere.—*

Though he'd spoken as softly as a creature of his size could, the force of it still caused Solveig to flinch. "Ragnarok," she whispered in response as she hugged herself, shivering. "I can feel it coming. It's cold and dark. No place for a dragon and his kin."

"I could stay here," the dragon said at last.

The wolf stomped his front paw, claws curling down into the seam between two stones, and then, with a growl that made the dragon's fangs ache, bit down once more on the rope, yanking back so hard it tore free of its moorings.

The wolf had no magic of his own, but he was immune to it. His very being would not suffer the binds of a prison, even if they weren't his own. The rope had withstood the dragon's fury, but it couldn't hold out against Varr's.

The dragon heard its dying squeal, watched it flail like a snake with its head cut off, fighting desperately to live until all fight drained out of it. The loop around his wrist loosened, and he shook it free of his arm. He came as far as the remaining rope would allow, to the place where the metal grate ought to be. Now, instead of keeping him from the water on its other side, it marked the invisible shield keeping him from Solveig.

With another powerful bite, Varr severed the remaining rope, freeing him. *—It's time. Your clan needs you.—*

Ignoring Varr, the dragon shoved at the barrier and repeated, "I could stay." His fire all but split him in two, one half yearning for his mate, the other needing to return to Saeran and his family. He still had the ring; he could stay and bring them all here as well, all together and safe from Fenrir and Loki's mad machinations.

"Oh, my love, how I wish you could." Solveig came to him, pressing her hands against his. "I wish with all my heart and soul that I could feel your arms around me one more time."

From where she cowered, weakened back to her ghostly translucence, Hel said, "You can. Give me your blood, dragon, and I will take you to her right now. You could be together forever, and nothing would ever tear you apart again."

All the while Hel spoke, Solveig shook her head. "I have loved you with all of myself, every moment of my life, from the moment we first met."

"Sol, all that I am is yours. I missed you. Gods, how I missed you."

She smiled, even as glittering tears spilled down her cheeks. "And I you. But our time is past, my love. No matter how much we wish it, we can never have it back again."

"We can!" he insisted.

"You know better," she replied.

"No—"

"Things do not *live* in Helheim," she said without mercy. "They do not feel or love or cleave. Seeing you now, alive, I remember what it felt like to be loved by a dragon, and I feel your fire warm my blood. But it will fade just as you will if you stay. Things do not *live* in the land of the dead."

"I cannot keep her here much longer," Hel warned, her form now all but invisible. "Alive or dead, you would still be together. She died for you, dragon. Are you not willing to do the same for her?"

The mist began to fade, Solveig's beautiful face blurring.

—We must go,— Varr growled, nudging him away.

"He's right," Solveig said, stepping back.

"No, Solveig!"

"Our clan needs you. Go to them, and give them my love. Let it be your strength and shield you against what is to come."

Varr closed his maw over the dragon's shoulder, pulling him back from the mist, which was already losing all color as Solveig faded away.

"Sol!"

"My love with you, my heart. Always…"

With one hard yank, Varr knocked the dragon off his feet and swung him onto his back, then took off running. Darkness swallowed them as Varr leaped at the stone wall and through it into the in-between. Worlds blurred as they raced ever onward, and soon the searing pain of losing Solveig dulled to the familiar old ache. The dragon became numb, hollow, as the flowing aether stole his tears and scattered them into the darkness like glittering stars that would forever mark the path to where Helheim lay dying.

Varr ran, and ran, for how long the dragon didn't know. But the farther they went, the smaller Varr shrank, as if shedding his fierce warrior's shape until he was once again his normal size. By then, the dragon had run out of tears and pushed back the pain of loss enough to turn away from Helheim and toward Wilderheim.

He could see its shining borders flicker up ahead and, with a bend of his will, burned his human shape into that of a full dragon. Taking Varr gently into his claws, he beat his great wings and flew headlong, racing the ravenous darkness hurtling toward his clan.

And he prayed to whatever gods were still alive to hear that he would not be too late.

CHAPTER 25

As soon as he stepped through into Wilderheim, the doorway closed, and Fal shivered with cold. No torches burned in this part of the castle; no fires had been lit to relieve the chill. In the dark silence, screams and wails echoed from the great hall. Fal conjured a swarm of lights to fly ahead and show him the way but, as they spread out before him, the sight they revealed drew him up short.

A long, shallow creek wound its way down the center of the floor. Tall grasses swayed on either side with little yellow flowers bobbing atop long, sturdy stalks. The walls he knew to frame the path on either side had disappeared, giving the impression he was walking through a nighttime forest.

His illusions were back.

No time to think about it. Fal was needed on the battlements.

He splashed along the creek to the staircase and down to the great hall to first take measure of things there.

So many wounded already. Healers and servants rushed from one to the other, slipping in puddles of blood. The dead and the dying side by side, because those charged with their care were too busy tending those who still had a chance.

The sounds they made tore at him.

Fal clutched the grip of his sword, grateful to have illusions blanketing the bloody floor with visions of soft grass and piles of sweet, dry hay. He forced himself to look into the eyes of the dying, watched their cries quiet, and their eyes grow big with wonder to behold the world changing around them. Many wept. Still more looked at him in awe, whispered prayers as he walked past them.

The healers and servants tending the wounded looked little better than their charges. They nodded their greetings and thanks but kept their attention on their work. Fal did his best to keep out of their way.

Near the dais, he knelt by a man whose bloodied face was half-covered by bandages. He'd been badly burned and couldn't stop shaking. Fal laid a hand on his shoulder, called on the healing powers of water to soothe his pain. When the man calmed, Fal asked, "What happened?"

"Gods all bless, milord," the man mumbled, delirious from shock. "Gods all bless ye an' keep ye…"

"Tell me," he tried again, but the man was already fading into an exhausted sleep.

"They came in the night."

Fal pushed to his feet to face the speaker and steeled himself not to react. Councilor Braith had always been a force unto herself, with boundless energy despite her advanced years, and a glib tongue that had refused to blunt for anyone, including the king himself. Now, her hair was a disheveled mess, her pale face flushed and stained with blood. Her bleary eyes and stooped shoulders bespoke of a long day of endless labors, and her bedraggled, bloody clothes said those labors had been torturous.

"Clan Steen abandoned us," she said. "They never answered the call to arms."

Frost tipped the grass at her feet. She was too weary to notice, but others did. Whether or not they understood the reason for it, to the last they drew back as far as their cots and pallets would allow. Shards of ice crackled and groaned beneath Fal's skin as his fury grew. He should have expected this. Liadan should have expected it. "Why was our flank left exposed?" he demanded, his voice colder than he'd intended. "Tarben should have known better."

Braith rubbed her brow, smearing dirt across her forehead. "Tarben ordered the bulk of our army to the south." Her tone made it clear what she thought of his decision. "He was convinced Synealee would march through Aegiros to reach us. Princess Liadan did not like it, but she was outvoted. Even Kvaran said…" Braith stopped on a deep sigh as if to catch her breath. As if it was too painful to speak of. "They are dead, you know. Kvaran bedded down that night and never woke again. Tarben, the old fool, was the first to climb those battlements. He took an arrow for one of the men and threw himself over the wall."

Fal staggered. "And Liadan?"

Braith shook her head. "She burned a good number of them, woke the city, and sounded the call to battle. But she has not been seen since."

"She is not dead. I would know it if she was."

Braith's gaze turned distant. "The Others are holding the line for us now. No human troops left to defend us. All we can do is wait and pray."

Others fought to defend Castle Frastmir? "How did they get here?"

Braith shrugged. "The gods only know. They started appearing at sunrise. All different sorts. But there are too many soldiers."

"Then we will need every warrior armed for battle."

Braith waved a shaking hand to encompass the great hall. "You are looking at them, Your Highness."

Fal balled his hands into fists at his sides. The creek running through Wilderheim's gardens was closest. It carried a fair amount of blood, but its source was still pristine. Agonized with the violence spilling over its banks, it answered his call at once. He caught hold of its strength with one hand, sent it blanketing the great hall in preparation of a much larger undertaking. With the other, he reached out to the river flowing along the outer edge of Frastmir. Its responding roar of fury flooded him with strength, and Fal channeled both into a wave that swept across the great hall, feeding it no small amount of his magic as he hummed the same melody he'd used to heal Sanja.

The sound pulsed and bounced off the stone walls like ripples traveling back and forth, the one building upon what the other had begun in cycles that swept away pain, melted broken parts whole, and cooled burns in turn.

Screams quieted into moans, then rose again into cries of astonishment. One by one, the men sat up, pulled away bandages to reveal wounds fully healed. The servants and healers sighed as their weary bodies restored themselves to full strength.

And Fal hadn't even strained himself unduly.

"Gods all bless," Braith said, appearing stunned, and at least a decade younger. She clutched his arm tight and nodded, her eyes bright with fighting spirit. "Go. Teach those fools they ought never have dared set their sights on Wilderheim."

An answering shout echoed through the great hall and, within moments, Fal had five score men in full vigor marching out the door behind him.

Where they split off to arm themselves with discarded weapons and armor, Fal ran through the gardens for the battlements. Already, he saw several beings lining the top of the wall. Their attention was turned outward but, as he topped the staircase, the closest speared him with a quick, sharp, golden glance. Her skin was as blue as the sea, her hair composed of gray, bladelike fins. She looked none too pleased to see him. With a growl, she launched a volley of invisible blows into the swarming army below, knocking them over like children's toys.

Beyond her, a giant covered in black fur swept a massive paw along his part of the wall. His claws, as long as Fal was tall, hooked on ropes and ladders, yanking them from their anchors, along with the enemy soldiers climbing them. Some let go right away, plummeting to their deaths below. Others held on, and the creature spun, swinging them in a great arc before he released his hold. The force of his throw sent his victims flying clean across the bailey to slam into the outer wall. As if angry with his accomplishment, the creature snarled and shook himself.

Still farther stood a tall, thin creature, like a sliver of a star-filled sky. Fal couldn't see it move at all, but he sensed its magic grow outward like a bubble, forcing the soldiers below into retreat. At a certain point, the magic reached its limits and burst, allowing the army close once more until the shield rebuilt itself and forced them back again.

The creature appeared to be working in harmony with another down below. As the bubble pressed forward, flashes of light along its edge cut across the barrier, slicing into the enemy. When the bubble burst, that spear of light spiraled up into the air out of harm's way until the battlefield was cleared enough for it to descend and resume its carnage.

"At your leisure, son of water," the blue woman growled through several rows of sharp, pointed teeth.

"Who are you?"

"Talk later, fight now." She nodded toward the outer wall, where more soldiers spilled into the bailey. "Have they circled fully 'round?"

"Yes," Fal confirmed. He'd felt them in the river. "Frastmir is overrun. They have cut off all paths of retreat.

"Best start making yourself useful, then. Hear tell there are more of them in the south. Your army's holding its own at the borders, but your people farther in are dying."

"Whatever happens, hold the castle," he ordered.

The female scoffed. "I take no orders from you. I protect the blood, not your pile of stones."

So that was why they'd come. The Other blood Nialei had collected over the last two decades was a source of untold power, and it lay hidden beneath the castle. The Others would sense it and fight to keep it out of mortal hands while the threat was imminent. Would they try to take it for themselves if or when an opportunity presented itself?

Every Otherland was in danger of destruction. The blood represented a chance for their survival. No matter that no one seemed to know how to use it, it was still a beacon of hope for them all. And now a deadly liability for Frastmir if its prince failed to protect it.

"Move!" The female shoved him hard, and Fal felt an arrow whiz past his ear before he tumbled headlong down the staircase, back into the gardens.

He righted himself in time to see her swat arrows out of the air. She caught one and dropped for cover as a cloud of them darkened the sky above. Not one of them made it to the ground. The shafts burned up in the air as a new Other appeared on the battlements, a tiny fire sprite no larger than an ember, but no less powerful for its diminutive size.

Braith had been right. There were too many soldiers for the Others to hold back on their own. Fal needed to improve their odds—and quickly.

With his jaw set and his thoughts dark, Fal marched back up the staircase, working magic into his palms as he went. The mad vortex inside him roared, ready to be released, but he held it back. *Not yet.* He might only get one chance to make a lasting impression. He had to time this right.

At the top of the staircase, the blue female took one look at him and stepped out of his way. The furry giant sensed his approach and whined, shaking his head violently. He jumped off the wall, holding on by the claws of one paw to allow him passage. By the time he'd reached the center, Fal's body hummed, and illusions of water spilled over the battlements.

In the bailey below, the sight of so much water made soldiers wary. They paused in their assault, stepped away from their ropes and ladders. Already, they could see water bursting out from chinks in the wall like a great dam about to break.

Fal made sure they saw him, too, with his ever-changing shape, and the blue light of his magic glowing around him. He used their fear against them, gave them the display they expected to see. Raising his hands high, he tipped his head back and shouted to the sky. Behind him, a wall of water rose well over his head, causing panic down below. Its roar drowned out desperate calls for retreat as soldiers turned to run. The bailey was enclosed on all sides by a wall three stories high. They were trapped.

Fal brought his hands forward, sent the wave crashing down on them. It swept them to the outer wall, crushed them against its barrier, and churned wildly, forcing them under so no one could escape. Those atop the outer wall watched their comrades drown and froze in place, their assault forgotten. Many disappeared down the other side. Those who remained bore witness to hundreds of men floating dead up to the surface of an enclosed lake that hadn't been there a moment ago.

Fal sensed their gazes turn to him, their horror a palpable thing. He picked out one man and met his gaze across the bailey, then let his hands drop to his sides, releasing the great illusion. The water filling the bailey shimmered out of existence, leaving the ground dry, piled with bodies no less dead for his deceit.

He stared the survivor down a moment longer, reading visions of a dark, cloaked bringer of death in his mind. Fal reinforced the image, carved it into the man's memory with a deep stroke of an invisible scythe so he would never forget what he'd seen this day, so he might tell everyone he came across about Death reaping mortals without mercy.

He felt a shudder rake through the man, leaving a soul-deep chill in its wake, and he made sure the rest of them saw him as he turned and walked away, dismissing them offhand.

"Where is Liadan?" he asked the blue creature gaping at his approach.

"Crossroads," she replied as he passed her without pause.

Fal nodded, heading down the staircase. "I trust you can handle things from here."

"Aye," she said, and though he didn't turn back to acknowledge it, he heard a feral smile in her voice. "Remind me to never get on your bad side, Reaper."

By the time he'd reached the ground and glanced up, the Others were gone, removed to the outer wall.

He ran back around to the castle's front gate, traced the wall to the left of the main doorway with the flat of his palm. Between one stone and another, the wall turned soft. Making sure no one was watching, Fal pressed through the illusion, opened the door, and stepped into the dark, winding stairwell.

His mother's magic was strong. It drew him deeper, yet at the same time created a heavy barrier against his descent. It felt as if the stairwell was filled with sand, and Fal had to swim his way through it to get to the bottom. He didn't recall it presenting this much of a challenge before.

Then again, he'd been halfway to Anderheim when the vision had shown him the way.

At the bottom, the selfsame candle still burned in the center of its table. The selfsame books lined the shelves, whispering their secrets into his ear. Fal struggled his way to the nook, confirming the glass container was still there, swirling with Other blood. It was safe—for the moment.

But the kingdom was not.

He returned to the bookcase and started pulling tomes from their shelves. Battle spells, healing spells—each book contained enough magic within its pages to make his skin tingle. His people would need them all. With his arms full, he turned for the door, but a quiet whisper pulled him up short.

One small, delicate book remained on the closest shelf, leaning against its edge, its black spine pulsing relentless shadows into the dark chamber. For all that it was the smallest tome there, its magic sent a chill down Fal's spine. Its leather was so soft, its pages translucently thin. It couldn't contain more than a single spell.

Fal shook his head hard to break its hold on him. Tucking the volume into his belt at the small of his back, he raced for the stairwell. The same magic that had hindered his progress coming down now all but shoved him back up the stairs to the courtyard.

He emerged into the light of day and turned his gaze to the sky. Before his eyes, a swirl of red faded away. Another Otherland dead and gone. Dark, foreboding clouds gathered from the north. He could sense a great storm's worth of rain in them. Heart pounding with dread, he ran for the great hall.

"Braith!"

She came to him at once, relieving him of his leather-bound burden. The councilor had magic in her. Not much, but enough to work a spell or two. "What are these?" she asked.

"Reinforcement. Gather everyone who can read and everyone with a spark of magic in them. A book to a wizard, no more."

Tearing her gaze away from the arsenal he'd handed her, Braith raised her chin and nodded, her eyes blazing with intent. As he knew she would, she turned her back on him at once and began shouting for people, sorting them into groups, and handing out tomes and orders. Councilor Tarben would have been proud of her.

Fal left her to it. With men once more engaged in the castle's defense, Others holding back the enemy, and wizards at the ready with magic at their fingertips, the castle was as safe as Fal could make it.

It was time to find his sister.

CHAPTER 26

A gust of cold wind woke Sanja with the faraway sound of angry voices and the smell of frost and blood. Startled out of deep sleep, she sat up on the pallet, her heart thrashing as she searched the clearing for unseen enemies. They were there; she could hear them.

But they weren't. The echoing screams had already faded back into a forgotten dream, and despite the chill making her skin pebble with goose flesh, the day was as warm as it had been yesterday.

There was no reason to fear, yet the shivers wouldn't stop. Sanja felt exposed and chilled to her core.

"Fal," she called.

Another breeze stirred the grass, and in its hiss, she imagined she heard the screech of metal against metal. It forced her to her feet, her shoulders hunched as she hugged her middle, and curled her toes down into the dirt.

No one around.

"Fal, where are you!" He ought to be there. Unless she'd imagined him, too.

No, there was his cloak, and his eating knife laid out beside the uneaten fish from the night before. It hadn't been a dream. She truly had married the crown prince of Wilderheim. She was safe—from Jarl Steen, his henchmen, and anyone else who might think to do her harm.

So why could she not make herself believe it?

The sun was at its zenith, hot enough to warm her despite the cold sweat on her brow but, as a dark cloud passed overhead, the ground beneath her feet turned to ice, and her skin pulled tight over her bones as if she'd stepped from summer straight into bitter winter. And then, just as quickly, the cloud moved on, and the sun embraced her with its comforting warmth once more.

Something was wrong.

"Fal, answer me! Where are you?"

The silence echoed back at her, making her suddenly hollow body reverberate with the rumble of a coming avalanche. She dared not move a muscle for fear her bones would crumble into dust where she stood.

Breathe, she ordered herself, forcing air in and out through her tight throat. Each breath became a tremulous wheeze while her jaw clenched so tightly it ached. And no matter where she looked, Sanja couldn't make herself unsee invisible soldiers locked in a terrible battle.

Breathe! Squeezing her eyes shut, she pressed her hands against her ears to block out the silent screams and fought to calm her racing heart. It was only her mind playing tricks on her, nothing more. Fal had brought her to a place where nothing could intrude. Nothing could harm her here, he'd said so himself.

Gradually, the oppressive chill of imagined war passed, and she opened her eyes. The fire was going out. She loosened her limbs enough to take two shuffling steps toward the pile of wood Fal had gathered for them. Her spine creaked as she bent over to grasp one of the sticks in her numb hand and add it to the fire. Shivering all the while, she stoked it higher, pretending not to hear a child crying in the woods, pretending not to see the ghostly apparition of a woman in a bloodied dress wailing wretchedly, not fifteen paces away.

Sanja turned her back to the visions, hunching closer to the fire as another wintry gust of wind turned the ground around her feet momentarily white with frost.

Ignore it.

It wasn't anything she hadn't experienced before with her new husband's illusions. What she saw and heard might be different, but *how* she saw and heard it remained the same. Was Fal casting the visions from a dream somewhere? Being no stranger to nightmares herself, Sanja knew how tightly they could tether a body into sleep. If Fal's dream was as bad as what she was seeing, it could have made him act on it, respond in truth to what was playing out in his mind.

He could be anywhere, fighting those terrible soldiers all on his own.

A man shouted at the lake.

"Fal?" She took off without thinking, abandoning the safety of her fire.

Had he called her name?

"*Fal!* I'm coming!"

Diving heedlessly into a thatch of reeds, she ignored their sharp lashes, fighting her way through to the other side. Fal was in pain; he needed her; she couldn't let him suffer his nightmares alone. But the merciless plants refused to clear a path for her. With each step, they swayed toward her, scratching her, tripping her, stealing the sun from the sky, and turning the mud beneath her feet cold with ice.

She could no longer see where she was going. Fal's weak voice became her only guidance in the darkening maze. She thought she heard him say something…

Send her home?

No, that couldn't be right. He wouldn't send her away without a word farewell, not after everything he'd done last night.

He couldn't.

Her vision blurred, and her breath misted in the cold, but she kept going. Even when the ground swayed beneath her feet. Even when a wrenching shift stretched the world into endless streams of color.

With her next step, the vortex spat her out into darkness, and she fell to her hands and knees onto the wooden slats of a familiar floor. With the entire world tilting violently this way and that, Sanja stayed there, breathing as deeply as she could until it settled and the urge to vomit had passed. Then raised her head to look around.

Her father's cottage hardly looked the same anymore. The chairs were overturned, the table shattered. The floors were covered with dirt, the walls smeared with dark stains. With the shutters closed and barred and no fire in the hearth, the cottage was dark and as silent as a grave.

This was no dream.

Shaking, Sanja righted herself and squinted through the darkness.

He'd done it. He truly had sent her home.

She'd believed him when he'd said they could make a life together, and the next day, her new husband had washed his hands of her.

Fal, how could you?

An insidious voice inside her taunted, *Did you expect the Prince of Deceit to keep his word? What use does the crown prince of Wilderheim have for a lowly merchant's daughter?*

She might have listened to it a week ago. But now, after everything she'd endured, everything Sanja had become rebelled against that voice. *I am not useless.* Fal wouldn't have bothered saving her, much less marrying her, if she were. He must have had good reasons to send her back to her father's house, and as soon as she found him again, she would ask him about it.

But for now, she needed to get herself together. Her home wasn't what it should be. Something was wrong, and she couldn't sit there and wait for disaster to find her.

"Da?" she called softly. "Ma?"

But, of course, they didn't answer. The cottage was closed up; they must have left for Lyria when Sanja hadn't returned. Good; they'd listened to her and removed themselves to safety. She was glad. Her only regret was not having had a chance to wave them off.

Running footsteps rushed past the front door. She heard whimpers, soft cries nearby, hushed by urgent whispers. Heavier footfalls followed, accompanied by the clang of metal.

An angry voice speaking in a foreign tongue elicited rough laughter in response.

Sanja crawled back against a wall, watching shadows move across the floor as the figures passed by. They stopped not far off, and in the heavy silence, Sanja counted her heartbeats and prayed.

When the screaming started, she slapped both hands over her mouth to keep from joining them and prayed harder.

Slaughter. That's what she was hearing. The wet sound of blades slashing through flesh, the tear of cloth and a woman's wretched howls, abruptly cut short. She turned her face away, made herself as small as she could, hoping it would somehow make her invisible, wishing she could melt through the walls and fall back into the world from which she'd been exiled.

She didn't look up again until the men had left, their footsteps fading into silence. By then, her entire body had cramped, and the smallest movement caused pure agony. Sanja gritted her teeth against making a sound and slowly pushed to her feet.

Painfully aware of Death prowling the streets, she measured each step and tested the floor with her toes first before committing her weight to it. At the staircase, she stopped, torn between running for cover and braving the outside to offer what help she could, but as the silence stretched on, she realized there was no one left to help out there. Though her heart ached, she made herself turn away and quietly sneak up the stairs to her room.

She found it in the same disarray as the kitchen below, her bedclothes torn to shreds, the furniture broken, but the stack of books and parchments in one corner had remained curiously untouched.

She reclaimed her dress from a haphazard pile and changed out of her haircloth shirt and trousers, layering another dress on top of the first, and a sheepskin vest on top of that. With thick wool stockings and her winter boots restored to her cold feet, Sanja's shivers subsided enough for her to move more easily.

A crash near the front door startled her. She held still and waited, but in a moment, the sounds grew distant again.

She was safe. At least for now.

Shoring up her courage, she sidled up to her window. Like the ones downstairs, this one, too, had been shuttered and barred, but there were gaps large enough for her to slide her fingers into and, with a careful, creaking snap, she broke off a piece to take a peek outside.

The swirling colors in the sky, obscured by wafting clouds of thick smoke, confirmed that she was, indeed, back in Frastmir.

And, like her house, the castle city looked nothing like the place she remembered.

Princess Liadan had told her on the eve of her Journey that Fal was preparing for war.

Well, war had come, and it had ravaged her home without mercy.

In the streets beyond the next cottage ahead, lights flickered where thatched roofs had caught fire. Streams of smoke rose up toward the sky, choking the air yet, despite so many flames, it was still bitterly cold.

The screams were the worst. Higher off the ground where nothing stood between her window and the sky, the dulled hum she'd heard downstairs became a cacophony of furious war cries mingled with the clash of weapons and the sound of women and children dying.

In the distance, the castle echoed with massive booms of noise. Its banners had been torn down. The towers were reduced to rubble. Beyond the main keep, the sky flared with fire from below where the battle still raged on. The invading army must have caught the city unawares. Else it never would have fallen so quickly—and fallen it had. There was no more fighting; only stragglers prowling the streets, exterminating anyone left alive.

Only the keep remained. The kingdom's warriors would fight to the death to defend it, not only as a symbolic seat of political power in Wilderheim but as the beating heart of its magic. Wilderheim was so much more than its land or its castle city. If Castle

Frastmir fell, it would be the end of everything.

This was no dream or illusion.

This was Ragnarok.

That was why Fal had sent her here. He'd kept his promise and saved her from Jarl Steen. Now it was her turn to do what needed to be done and help him stop the end in its tracks.

Sanja dived for the stack of books, shoving loose parchments aside and tossing ancient volumes left and right to get to the one she sought. She'd only gotten through half of the contents of Fal's journal before starting her Journey, and that half had been so dense with ancient lore and modern interpretations it had overwhelmed her. The rest would be no less difficult, but she needed to learn it and quickly if she was to help him in any way.

"Aha!"

Clutching the journal tightly, she shifted closer to the window, but the broken shafts of weak sunlight stabbing through the shutters, weren't enough. Sanja set the journal aside, grasped the bar her father had nailed across her shutters, braced a foot against the wall, and pulled with all her might until the bar ripped free, sending her sprawling.

The shutters flew open, admitting a cold blast of wind that lifted scraps and sheets of parchment into the air. The pages flew up and circled around in a funnel, and Sanja stilled. For a brief moment, the pages had aligned, and sunlight had shone through them just so, that a brilliant spark of epiphany struck Sanja dumb.

"They do fit!"

Scrambling to her feet, she snatched at the pages still wafting in the air, while trying to gather all the ones still on the ground at the same time. Her arms were filled with a mess of them when one of the shutters slammed against the wall as a frigid gust sent the remaining two sheets flying.

She caught one at the windowsill, but the other slipped out of her reach. As she watched it flip end over end in the air, her gaze shifted to the rolling waves of darkness coming toward the city from the north. Never before had Sanja seen clouds so thick and black. They swallowed the swirling colors, obscured the horizon, and, though she knew it couldn't be, Sanja felt them baying with a terrible, silent hunger that devoured her cry.

The wind snapped her page up and sideways, over three rooftops, and a ways off before letting it drop out of her sight.

Sanja didn't stop to think. Crumpling her stack of parchments together to keep it safe, she raced down the stairs and out the door into the cold.

CHAPTER 27

With no time to waste, Fal needed the quickest way to Crossroads. The waterways were too dangerous. They'd already started freezing over before he'd disappeared into Anderheim. The gods only knew what condition they were in now. A horse would take too long, and there were no Others around to convey him such a distance.

But he might have one other way.

It would have to be meticulously executed—if it worked at all. What better way to test pathways into Anderheim?

Fal ducked out of sight in the courtyard and churned up the vortex inside him. His connection to Anderheim was still there at the core of his illusions. It wove through his ever-changing face, through the visions of grass and flowers that spread out around him. All he had to do was channel it into a doorway. The song it required was the same one that had brought him out of Anderheim. He forced himself to slow down, focus, and do it right. Any mistake could be disastrous; he couldn't afford to take any chances.

He sang, and the doorway opened. With the song still humming from his lips, he sent his request to Anderheim ahead of his crossing, and it responded with such eagerness Fal stepped through the Frastmir doorway directly into a streak of blurred scenery and was expelled forcefully through another doorway in Crossroads.

Fal stumbled to his hands and knees, the mud rippling beneath him until he feared he would pass out. As the ringing in his ears cleared into the clang of weapons, he shook his head and squinted at the battle raging around him. Anderheim had delivered him straight into the thick of it, with no armor and his head spinning like a top.

He fought to stand, only for a heavy foot to slam into his back. "Stay down!" Liadan barked, and a moment later, a stream of fire blazed over his head, scorching a trio of soldiers into dust. In the short lull that followed, Liadan hauled him upright, grinning brightly. "It's good to see you, brother."

Fal took in his sister's condition and found her to be roughed up around the edges but, on the whole, hale and strong. Covered in the gore of battle, she held her head up high and smiled in the face of death.

He'd seen her like this before, hadn't he?

Liadan's gaze flicked sideways over his shoulder, and she shoved him away to meet a soldier's blade. She, too, wore only leather armor, which made her faster and more nimble than the enemy's heavily armored knights. She used their ungainly weight against them, tripping them and shoving them into one another.

"Don't just stand there—fight!"

Fal drew his sword, put his back to Liadan's, and fought.

But all the while, every face he saw looked familiar; every attack felt as if he'd seen it before. He reacted from memory more than instinct, anticipating each move as if he'd rehearsed it. There was the one with the cracked spear. Fal shifted to the side, brought his sword down on the shaft to break it, then whirled a swing to take off the soldier's head.

Stepping over his fallen body, he met swords with another, whose gap-toothed snarl he knew so well he'd already counted the remaining teeth. This one was strong, but he'd braced his foot in mud, and Fal was able to shove him sliding back into another man's blade. They fell together, and Fal was so certain they wouldn't get up again, he turned his back on them to move on to the next.

He fought until he couldn't feel his sword in his grip anymore. His body went through the motions while a dream-like haze mired his mind, keeping him going when lesser men would have dropped from exhaustion. Vaguely, he noted that Others fought alongside Wilderheim's men. Fal saw so many of them he lost count; stopped bothering to identify their kind. He was simply grateful they were there.

And in the midst of it all, Liadan shone with strength and courage, fighting as well with her blades as the berserker tearing through enemy ranks not far off. She was a thing to behold, using her fire as a weapon without marking herself a target with it.

And *he* fought better for having her at his back. They worked in tandem, guarding each other's flanks and keeping each other safe.

But soon, the tide of battle began to turn against them. Fal cut down a soldier and behind him saw an Other disappear before his eyes, followed by another to his left, and one more farther on the right. Without those allies to hold off the enemy, the soldiers came at him and Liadan.

"Did you see that? They're gone, the cowards."

"They're dead, Liadan." He felt the empty void the Others had left behind. "Not just them, their entire worlds."

Liadan tensed at his back, then swore and hurled a fireball at two men charging her. Their tabards provided eager kindling, flaring up in an instant. As they stumbled into others, the flames jumped, and soon a dozen enemy soldiers were flailing on the ground, screaming as they cooked in their metal shells.

Fal's stomach clenched as he met another attack, anticipating something terrible he couldn't remember. He glanced up at the sky, saw it darken with storm clouds, and grimly turned his attention back to the battle at hand.

He turned with Liadan and rammed into a man's midsection as he brought up an ax. They fell together, and Fal stabbed him through, quickly jumping back to his feet to meet another blade.

By then, not even the dragon amulet could keep exhaustion from weighing him down. Picking up a shield someone had dropped, he reclaimed his place by his sister and willed himself to hold steady, but despite overflowing with magic, he couldn't harness it to give himself more physical strength. His legs shifted heavily, and his sword swung slower. Evening would soon be upon them, but the battle wasn't waning in the least. If anything, it was heating up.

"Liadan," he called, needing her to restore him.

She didn't hear, locked in battle against three soldiers at once. They pushed her farther from him until he lost sight of her altogether. Taking advantage of the situation, more soldiers poured into the gap between them, pushing them apart, and Fal didn't have the strength to go after her.

Liadan lived and breathed battle every day, but this was Fal's first, and he didn't know what to do, other than fight the next man coming at him. He needed his sister's guidance and strength. The farther she went, the weaker he felt until his chest ached with each tired beat of his heart.

Fal blocked a speartip with his shield, his feet slipping on a fallen tabard as the enemy forced him back. He twisted the shield, snapping the tip off the spear and ran the soldier through. The grip of his sword was drenched with blood. More of it dripped down his face. He adjusted the chipped shield on his arm and wiped his wet cheek on his sleeve.

Time seemed to slow as he looked at the carnage all around him. The battlefield was littered with hundreds of dead soldiers already, their bodies trampled into the mud by hundreds upon hundreds more.

Just as he'd seen in his dream.

As if reliving it again for the first time, he sought Liadan's fire amid the chaos, but far too much of it already blazed left and right, and the din of screams disguised her battle cry.

At his feet, the ground had turned to dark mud, pools of blood reflecting the sky back at Fal. It hurt like a long needle stabbing into him to witness each light going dark. He had no time to mourn them when his own world was dying. Thunder rumbled above, threatening a storm, and fear knotted his insides. He looked up once more, hoping it had only been a fluke, but a fat raindrop splashing down onto his cheek confirmed his worst fear.

Fal had to retreat. Already, the air felt thick, and flashes of another battlefield miles away obscured his sight. Shadows flickered all around him, a brightly polished blade cutting down his soldiers. He sensed magic in it again, as he had in his dream, yet when he sought its wielder's identity, he met with dark shadows that only cleared enough to reveal parts of the knight's body and never his face.

Another soldier came at him, the red cross on his tabard no longer distinguishable beneath the muck of battle. His mind weary and his body weak, Fal blocked the soldier's battle ax with his sword, rather than duck out of the way. The impact forced him to his knees. He gritted his teeth, pushing back with all the strength he had left, to no avail. He couldn't hold out much longer. That ax would cleave him in two.

Suddenly the solder spit up blood as the tip of a curved blade forced its way out through his chest. Wide-eyed, he tipped sideways, taking his ax with him.

Liadan grasped Fal's arm and pulled him to his feet.

She'd changed. Her eyes now blazed with fire behind a braid that had fallen over her black horn-crown. Though she had yet to unleash her wings, her tail slithered back and forth with a mind of its own, and her feet had grown long, curved talons that dug into the soft mud. Her entire being glowed with fierce strength, smoking, on the verge of burning up into her Other self. "Wilderheim will not die on its knees," she snarled at him through the sharp fangs filling her mouth, reminding him so much of their dragon grandfather. Her grip fed strength into his exhausted body, but nothing would shield him from the madness the rain was about to bring.

As Fal recovered, still connected with his sister, he felt within her the tiny, bright spark that had turned his dream into a nightmare, and his body grew cold with dread. "Take to the sky," he ordered. "Now!" Away from the armies, beyond the reach of their weapons. Against all odds, his sister had managed to conceive. If there was any chance for the child to survive, Fal had to get her somewhere safe.

"And leave you to die?"

"Liadan—"

She shoved him aside to meet another enemy soldier head-on, her curved blade making quick work of him and his three comrades. The two coming for her from the back met with Fal's sword and fell in short succession.

Liadan retrieved her other sword and put her back to Fal's. They were surrounded.

"You must go!" Fal tried again. "For the child's sake, if not mine."

He felt Liadan tense at his back. "Won't be the first time I've lost a child. Or the last." She tried to make it sound careless, but Fal wasn't fooled. Her grief was a living thing, coiling inside her like a snake, biting at her heart—and now at his.

A vision of women running through a nearby raided village blinded him just as the soldiers attacked. He gave a shout, bringing up his shield to block a thrust and slashed sideways. Between rapid blinks, he saw his enemy again, then Liadan's, then another place entirely.

"Oh, no," Liadan whispered as a few random drops turned into a heavy downpour. She looked back at him, her eyes dimming anxiously. Then a furious snarl turned her face into something beastly, and she faced her enemy once more and screamed, bursting into flame, scorching their foes to dust where they stood as she transformed.

Within moments, the thick mud at their feet turned into pools and creeks, the earth already soaked with too much blood to drain the rainwater away. Fal became blind and deaf to the world around him as everything the water touched flooded into his mind. He saw everything, heard everything for miles around. He felt a thousand deaths, smelled smoke mixed with blood and bile, and tasted hopeless prayers on his tongue, knowing there was no one left to answer them.

His sister's voice echoed through the madness: "Wake up! *Wake up!*"

It was too late.

Imprisoned by his own weakness, Fal's mind was already gone, scattered as far as the storm stretched. His body became weightless in flight, and then, with a sickening capitulation, the remaining physical sensations faded away, and he ceased to exist.

CHAPTER 28

The storm swept across the whole of Wilderheim and, where it touched, Fal saw, and heard, and felt. Scattered among countless raindrops, he ceased to be himself and became everything at once.

Seven portals speared up toward the sky, bright, screaming cuts into Wilderheim that had admitted hordes of enemy soldiers all throughout the kingdom.

In Frastmir, a girl wearing sheepskins cautiously stuck her head out into the storm, then ducked under an overhang. A moment later, she was out, racing down the muddied street, hugging a small, flat bundle to her chest. She pulled her large hood down low against the rain, turned away from the bodies littering the ground, and ran on.

Two portals had cut off the passage to Lyria only recently and were still spewing mounted riders to trample over fleeing families, pushing inward to force the rest into retreat.

A group of five soldiers in soaked white tabards strolled through the city, laughing at a lame woman trying in vain to get away from them. Her fear tasted like bile, and her skin felt slick as she flailed back and forth like a fish out of water at their approach. She didn't get far…

Two more portals had appeared in between camps of warriors sent to guard the Aegiran border. True to their honor, even outnumbered five to one, Wilderheim's forces were holding their own, but they could do nothing for those being slaughtered farther inland.

An old man somewhere in Crossroads wailed over his young son. "My boy!" he cried, his heart breaking over and over as he hugged the boy's lifeless body up from the muddy ground, rocking him back and forth. "I curse you, dogs! I curse your blood and the blood of your offspring!" His poisonous spell slithered from him on noxious green smoke, splitting and racing toward every enemy soldier he could see. It wound up their legs and bodies to shackle their throats. They would never know it, but madness would forever stain their bloodlines, forcing men to turn on their wives, children to cut down their siblings—

To the east, two shafts along the Ravetian border flickered weaker than the rest. These had been the first, admitting the flood of knights who'd attacked Castle Frastmir. Clan Steen was no more. Those who'd managed to escape the carnage were scaling down the walls of the ravine to cross to its Ravetian side.

Rain pelted down heavily there. It poured over old women with gnarled hands and aching backs, over screaming babies swaddled in soaked linens, over armed men with wide eyes whose blades had never left their sheaths, and over the man leading them all—the traitorous jarl himself.

As the river swelled outside of Frastmir, its rage spilled over the banks, knocking soldiers off their feet, washing over them. At its shallowest, the flood was still high enough to drown a man held to the ground by his heavy armor. He kicked uselessly, held his breath as long as he could, but the river wouldn't release him. It felt the pain he'd caused, mourned the lives he'd taken, and it wanted to repay him in kind. It rushed into him, swelling his body. In his last moments, the man looked up toward the surface and the sky beyond, his lips moving in prayer before his stained tabard floated over his face, closing his eyes forever.

So much death. So much rage, and fear, and agony. It carried on the blood of the fallen, soaking deep into the ground, poisoning it. The earth shuddered with disgust, rejected it all, crying out for help that was nowhere to be found. In its absence, it woke the trees to life. Roots tore free of their anchor to lash outward. They knocked riders off their mounts and twisted them up in unbreakable wooden binds that tightened until armor warped and bodies crushed beneath the pressure.

Jarl Steen ran onward, his gaze trained on the rope ladder that would be his salvation. He dared not blink and would not answer anyone who called his name. His men-at-arms stood his guard, keeping the clan back, but as they neared the ladder, they, too, lost their heads to fear. Abandoning their master to the panicked herd, they raced ahead to begin their climb, fighting one another, jerking the ladder back and forth until one hard yank snapped it out of its moorings and sent the whole of it tumbling down.

The last portal stuck out of the very center of Wilderheim in Crossroads. There had been no fighters to meet the soldiers there, only farmers and merchants, families sleeping innocently in their beds. This had been the one to herald the shining blade so thirsty for blood it drove its owner ever eastward.

The girl in Frastmir reached the market, a muddied ball of parchment clutched in her hand. She could go straight toward the castle or right toward the library. Her beloved city was now black, stinking of death and wet, scorched wood. The ground quivered with explosions of magic. Everywhere she looked, her neighbors lay dead or dying, and she hurt for each and every one of them. But she could not stop. She turned her muddy boots to the right, pulled her hood lower over her face, kicked up the soaked hems of her dress, and ran on to the library.

A forest nymph stepped out of the shelter of her tree in Frastmir's glen. Her large brown eyes gazed out over the carnage and wept. She saw the group of soldiers approach, their tabards still pristine with red crosses emblazoned on white fields like virgin blood staining the marriage bed.

They were laughing. But they fell silent as she came into view.

She blinked her doe eyes at them, reaching out her delicate brown arms in welcome. She smelled their excitement but kept her expression soft and innocent.

They came to her at once, dropping their weapons, shedding their helmets, unbuckling their belts. She let them come, floating backward, deeper into the glen. Their breath stank of death; their hands were sticky with sweat and blood.

The nymph smiled at them, caressed a cheek here, brushed a hand there. Her touch whispered over them, making their hearts beat faster, their thoughts churn slower. Her spell kept them docile as they sank to their knees.

It kept them quiet as their bodies began to dry out. It made them smile as vines slithered over them, drawing them into their graves before they'd breathed their last. The nymph smiled bitterly and set out to seek more.

As Others lay waste to the enemy where they could, the shining blade continued on, never allowing its owner a moment's rest. Already, he was crossing the bridge into Frastmir at a breakneck pace. His horse's strength gave out, its legs buckling. The blade drove its wielder onward on foot, directing his gaze where it might taste more death.

It cut down straggler soldiers armed with swords and ordinary men armed with scythes and pitchforks but, unlike the others, its wielder turned it time and again away from women and children. He spared the old, too, and any who ran from the sight of him.

But already, the blade screamed louder, shone brighter, ravenous for so much more than he could give it.

To the north, impenetrable blackness opened its yawning mouth, slowly crawling toward Wilderheim. It swallowed all sound, yet its insides screamed. It robbed the air of warmth and burned the land with frost.

Those who fled along the Journeyman's path in hopes of seeking shelter in the cleric's temple took one look at it and turned the other way. Safer to chance a mortal's blade than the void of that terrible, nameless nothing.

They were right to fear.

Though the storm stretched well into that blackness and beyond, where the void encroached, Fal's consciousness slammed into a barrier that forcefully expelled him back and scattered him.

To the south, Wilderheim's soldiers were pushed out all the way to the Aegiran border, cornered and fighting not for their kingdom, but for their own lives. Though no physical barrier stood between them and the relative safety of Aegiros, they remained in Wilderheim, unable to escape.

To the east, a flash flood raced down the ravine, washing away the last remnants of Clan Steen and anyone else foolish enough to have followed them. Some washed up far downstream. Others caught on rocky outcroppings and ledges. None survived for long. Jarl Steen's body caught on a rocky hook. The current had already washed the blood from his clothes, but it could not hide the tears in his flesh or the odd angles of his broken limbs. The churning waters flopped him like a rag doll onto his back. With one eye missing, his jaw all but severed, the jarl was recognizable only by the markings on his scalp.

The man who'd defied his king and abandoned his people had died not as a warrior but a coward, drowned, broken, and dishonored.

To the west, beyond the mountain range, King Ulrich's men stood at attention, awaiting orders. To enter the narrow pass would mean certain death, and not even Ulrich's love for his royal cousins could compel them onward. The rocks echoed with the sounds of Wilderheim being torn apart, and all they could do was stand faithful watch, herd the small handful of terrified refugees toward safer ground, and prepare for the war to come for them next.

The clerics' temple to the north was gone, swallowed by the void.

The city of Crossroads was razed to the ground.

The Dragon lakes gleamed red with blood, dead things floating along their surface.

And in a crude, makeshift tent, surrounded by countless other tents in which the wounded rested their weary bodies, Prince Fal twitched with feverish visions that wouldn't abate. He could neither see nor hear his sister calling his name. He couldn't feel the warm fire blanketing him and drying the rain from his clothes and skin.

A guard rushed into the tent, rainwater running down into the open cut on his face, tracing his mouth as it formed frantic words. *We must retreat!*

He received a quiet response from the princess as she stared at a small, incongruously heavy black book in her hands.

Humming with the need to act, the guard stomped deeper into the tent. His wet hand hissed as it closed around Liadan's arm, and he pulled back, momentarily stunned. In the face of her fiery glare, he repeated himself with low, growling words that rumbled out of his throat.

A raindrop made murky with mud caught Liadan rubbing the torc around her neck and shaking her head as she replied into silence.

Dismissed to his own devices, the man ran back out and was struck down by an arrow not two paces from the tent.

The girl with her bundle had reached the library. She struck the barred portal with her small, pale fist, fearful of making so much noise, but having no other choice. Three soldiers were heading her way from the east. Two more on horseback had heard the noise in the south and were already turning their mounts in her direction. In a dark alleyway, the last of five soldiers shoved away from the woman who'd long ago gone still and silent. He drew his dagger and slit her throat for good measure, leaving her ravaged body sprawled where it lay as the group moved on, drawn by the sound of the girl's voice.

She pounded harder at the door, shouted louder, begging to be let in. At last, it opened, and she was pulled inside. By the time the first soldiers came into view, the door was once again closed and barred.

The hungry blade had run out of blood to spill. Its tip gleamed clean and bright, not a scratch upon its surface as it leaned left then right, seeking, seeking…

It turned its wielder left and pulled him along through the market to meet the other soldiers gathered outside the library door. One of them had already tied a rope around the handles and lashed the other end to his saddle. He sat his horse and waited for the other to do the same. Between the two of them, they would rip the entire portal off its hinges, and those on foot had already drawn their swords, eager to storm inside.

Their excitement caught up the blade, and it screamed pleasure-pain up its wielder's arm infecting him with the selfsame zeal. With his lips drawn back in a snarl, he tasted the rain, and, though it couldn't see him, it could taste him in return. It tasted hunger mixed with righteousness, hatred muddled with pride, and bitter darkness enshrining it all, hazing his vision and slowly silencing the voice of his conscience.

There were innocents in the library; he couldn't slay them.

But the others could.

The rope was lashed; the riders kicked their mounts; the library door groaned, cracked, and finally gave way.

CHAPTER 29

In the absence of golden candlelight, the library was a dark and sinister place. The bookshelves transformed into looming walls filled with nooks and crannies where feral creatures lived. The sweet smell of old books had taken on a musty, rotten undertone more akin to an abandoned cellar than a reverent place of learning.

"Hurry," Brother Erik urged, "this way."

He took Sanja by the arm and led her past writing desks already covered with a layer of ash and dust, past the display tables where precious illuminated tomes of magic lay spine up with their thick pages haphazardly crumpled underneath. Quills were strewn all over the floor, bottles of ink shattered and bleeding dark stains into the polished wood. There was no one left to look after it all. The library had been abandoned to its own fate, and Sanja felt its sorrow weep down the candlesticks in frozen rivulets of melted beeswax.

She would mourn its memory later. For now, Sanja followed the cleric all the way to the back, where a humble wooden door opened on a dark stairway leading down. Brother Leif stood on the second stair with a torch in hand, waiting for them to precede him. It seemed he and Erik were the last of the cleric brotherhood. The rest of them would have made their escape at the first sign of trouble, hopefully taking as many volumes with them as they could carry.

"They are right outside the door," Brother Erik reported.

"The others are almost to the end of the tunnel," Brother Leif said, wide-eyed. He had one foot on the next step down, anxiously looking back and forth between the escape tunnel and Brother Erik. "We ought not have tarried this long."

Brother Erik didn't argue, merely pulled Sanja along, eager to make his own escape.

"No, wait!" Sanja pulled free of his hold. "We can't leave. I have to find Prince Fal."

Brother Leif huffed with impatience while Brother Erik shook his head, baffled. "My girl, haven't you heard? The prince is gone." He said it with the weight of regret, the way people always delivered news of death.

They wouldn't know about the realm Fal had created. Sanja didn't know how long Fal had been missing, but it must have been long enough for his people to assume the worst—that he'd either died or abandoned them to their fate. But they were wrong, and Sanja didn't have the time to explain.

"He is somewhere in Wilderheim, and I must find him."

"Sanja, he's dead."

"He is not!" She could feel his heart beating next to hers. He was alive and fighting for them all, and she had to give him what he needed to finish it.

Brother Leif's torch swung down into the tunnel, then back up. He'd already gone two steps deeper down the stairway. "Brother, we must go."

Acknowledging him with a wave of his hand, Brother Erik approached Sanja as he would a wounded animal. "The city has fallen. If we don't leave now, we will be trapped." He tried to herd her toward the door, but Sanja rooted her feet.

"I know how to stop it."

"Stop what? The war?"

"The war, Fenrir, all of it." The song of worlds had woven the first Veil to keep the realms separate, yet connected. If Fal could sing it again, he could forge a similar connection with the Otherland he'd created. He could fold Wilderheim into it and effectively move the entire kingdom out of Fenrir's path.

"Brother Erik!"

"Please," Sanja begged, fumbling the bundle in her arms, "you must help me, or it won't matter where we run; we will all die anyway." Pieces of parchment spilled over the floor, and she dropped to her knees to gather them together. "The directions are all there in pieces. I only need to shape them together into a cohesive whole." Then Fal would have everything he needed to save Wilderheim. He'd only need to open the doorway once. It would take an awful lot of magic, but he already had that, and more. It could be done. There was still hope!

Brother Erik sighed. "Brother Leif, go."

The other cleric took off so quickly his torchlight faded in moments, leaving Sanja alone with the last of their brotherhood. As she frantically picked up page after page, folding them where the symbols cut off, she felt him staring at her and glanced up to see sorrow in his eyes. "I can do this," she insisted. "I swear. I only need help. This page…And this one—no, this one. Yes, and this one here." One after the other, she matched them together, but they wouldn't fit perfectly laid out on the ground. She picked up three of them, matching up the symbols as best as she could. "They fit together, I swear, I just can't—"

A groaning sound echoed through the empty library. The cleric laid his hand gently but firmly over both of hers, stopping her movements. "Sister," he said, addressing her as one of his order, as if she'd earned the honor. He thought so highly of her. Sanja couldn't bring herself to meet his gaze and tell him he was wrong. But she felt his gaze on her; felt him squeeze her hands, urging her to look up. "We must go."

Desperate tears blurred her vision. She needed time, a safe place to put it all together; more hands than her own two to hold the parchments aloft in the spherical shape it was all meant to have. Had she any magic in her, she could have floated them in the air with ease, but her cursed human limitations cost her precious time none of them had to lose. And the cleric would not—could not—help her.

The main door groaned again, a loud crack making her flinch. She'd run out of time.

A shaft of sunlight briefly broke through the clouds, spearing through the narrow window high up by the ceiling down onto the floor beside her. Dust swirled lazily through its beam, and the polished wooden floor gleamed with dreams lost to misery.

Sanja stared transfixed at a small triangle of darker wood that had been inlaid into the design. It fit seamlessly with every other piece it touched. Its surface had been smoothed to a shine, but she could still see the lines of its natural grain veer around a dark, almost invisible eye. She imagined it winked at her, and in that moment, her path became clear. "The knowledge must be preserved." No matter what happened to her, to the clerics, or anyone else down in that stairway, those mystical symbols had to be kept safe for Fal. He was the only one left who could use them to save Wilderheim.

Another groaning crack. The door would give way soon; she had to move.

Swiping the parchments together again, she quickly bundled them up and shoved the whole lot of it into the cleric's arms. "Take these. Keep them safe. Prince Fal will need them, and you must swear to me you will place them in his hands, and no one else's."

"Child—"

"Swear it, Brother, or all is lost."

Compressing his mouth into a tight line of displeasure, he gave a single nod.

"Tell him they fit together in an unbroken sphere. That's how he must read the spell. Find the centerpoint and sing the symbols in a spiral along the sphere."

"I don't understand."

"It doesn't matter. Only tell him exactly what I told you." The pattern was so obvious, once she'd seen it take shape. Fal would already know the symbols by heart; he'd be able to put it all together instantly, and all would be well, but he still needed to be told. "Go, run as far from here as you can. I will lead them away, give you time to escape."

"They will kill you!"

"They will have to catch me first," she replied recklessly, then pushed and shoved him into the stairway and closed the door behind him.

A tall bookshelf stood not three paces away. Filled as it was with heavy tomes, it took everything Sanja had to rock it out of balance. But she had to bar the doorway to give the clerics a fighting chance. She'd seen those men prowling the streets; they were scavengers looking for easy prey and would be more likely to chase her than bother with what looked like a privy door. She pushed hard, rocking the shelf forward, then let it fall back toward her before pushing again as it tilted away. Sheer force of will gave her enough strength to nudge it past the tipping point just as the front door tore outward, and both crashed at the same time.

She saw foreign soldiers running up the outer stairs. They spotted her. Spinning on the balls of her feet, Sanja took off as fast as she could toward the opposite wall, weaving through the familiar maze of bookshelves back toward the main entrance. She was much faster than them. If she could reach the main door undetected, she could slip out into the storm and disappear. But if they chased her into plain sight outside, Sanja wouldn't stand a chance.

Ducking into a narrow passage, she slipped around a pillar and tiptoed into the shadows, skirting the wall all the way to the front entry. It was clear. The soldiers were busy rampaging inside the library, pushing over bookshelves to root her out like a rabbit from its burrow.

Sanja wanted to smile. How much easier it was to evade evil men when she wasn't bound to her knees in the snow. *Useless? Ha!* They hadn't seen anything yet. They had horses outside. She could loosen the saddle straps or send them running altogether. Weapons set on the ground? They were as good as hers; none of the soldiers would ever find them.

Sanja might not be a fighter, but she had her wits, and there were infinite ways in which she could make those soldiers' lives unbearable without ever coming near them. Frastmir was her city; Wilderheim was her home. She would do her part to see it safe and sound if it was the last thing she did.

Sounds of fighting registered in her ears as she pushed away from the wall and raced for the storm outside.

She ran straight into the thick of it.

≪ »·◇·« ≫

A sea of red crosses had overrun the camp, tearing tents from the ground, dragging wounded men from their beds. Shouted warnings came too late and cut too short. It was a massacre, and the rain saw and felt it all.

As they neared the farthest tent, a circle of fire flared up from the ground around it, stretching high up into the air. Its flames changed colors from red to yellow, then flickering blue, burning so hot the rain couldn't douse it.

Stopped in their advance by that impenetrable veil, the soldiers didn't see the strange, black-scaled creature step out of the tent on its other side. They couldn't see her fiery eyes, the flowing flames of her hair, or the massive black wings flaring and folding restlessly at her back.

The rain did. It saw the small book clutched warily in her claws, felt its chill turn her scaled hands cold with powerful magic, heard her shuddering gasp of revulsion, and mourned the way her claws clutched the tome all the harder for it.

The creature gazed up, her eyes pleading for the clouds to part, for the rain to abate—not for her sake, but her brother's. But she knew she couldn't make them move, and her brother was in no condition to try.

And that left her only one choice.

Already knowing her call would go unanswered, she rubbed the torc around her neck yet again, sending out one last wordless summons to the only creature who could sway the tide now. Then she turned her attention to the fiery barrier, listened to it sing to her of the many armed men standing at the ready on the other side, of their bloodied weapons and their savage faces, and their hushed voices chanting soft prayers up to the sky. It knew their hearts and warned they could not be reasoned with. Nothing would compel them to mercy, or retreat. They would keep fighting until the battle was won and, if they fell, more would be sent in their place.

The Dragonblood princess shuddered as the book's cold voice slithered through her mind. Her palm pressed to her belly, and she closed her eyes for a moment to feel the life of her unborn child glowing inside her. No matter what she did, the princess knew she couldn't save that precious life. It might survive the war and Ragnarok unscathed, but in the end, Liadan's own nature would burn it out of her, as it had the two before.

She would never give her mate a son. But she still had a chance to save her clan and her people. The spell was their last hope, and the child's life was the price she had to pay for it.

She missed her mate; wished with all her heart to see him one last time.

In answer, the flames called her name and showed her a great open chamber with ceilings so high they almost reached the sky. They showed her a dark-skinned man with golden adornments woven through his hair, standing at the window. It gifted her with a waft of sweet, desert air, and the scent of fragrant oils. She whispered his name softly, willing him to face the flames.

But as he turned his head to the side, a blade came flying through the flames. She caught it on reflex, but the damage was done. The vision had shattered, and all she had left were her flames, and the book in her hand.

Pulling back her shoulders, she called heat into her hand to melt the foreign blade and flicked molten drops of metal from her fingers with disgust. A crude weapon, hammered in haste without care or delicacy. Its metal had had no voice of its own, just like all of the others—except the one.

Even from miles away, the Dragonblood princess still heard that one screaming for death. Soon, nothing would be able to stop it. Not even her.

As the flames warned of more weapons about to be thrown, the princess mercilessly pushed back her fear and sorrow, shut out all awareness of her brother lying senseless on a crude pallet nearby, and pretended she couldn't hear him shouting incomprehensible warnings to the empty tent. The rain saw her, so she knew he would, too.

He would hate her for what she was about to do, but at least he'd be alive to do it.

She stepped into the flames and, with shaking hands, opened the little book. Impervious to fire, neither woman nor book noticed the heat licking over them. But with its ancient pages at last laid bare to open air, the book bled from every word she read aloud, red-black ink running down the page, rushing her through the text before it was rendered illegible.

The torc at her neck burned white-hot, its metal warning her to stop before it was too late.

She didn't listen. Her breath misted as her spell poured heavily to the ground outside her flaming circle and spread outward with a life of its own.

The shapeless monster slipped beneath booted feet, shod hooves, and bare, bloody paws. Every creature it touched instantly turned rigid, its soul sucked down and devoured by a black magic that cared nothing for distinctions between friend and foe. Animal, human, Other—everything outside the protective circle for miles around paled and died on an eerie, echoing sigh, and little by little, the battlefield fell silent.

But the spell wasn't finished. The words kept pouring out, forcing their way off the page, severing it free of its parchment prison and loose of its caster's control. Having tasted freedom at last, the black magic turned up its nose at mortal fare and raced instead toward a heartier meal: raw power in the shape of seven open portals. It poisoned the ground in its wake, sowed the seeds of weakness and malady everywhere it touched. When it reached the portals, it paused as if in awe to whet its appetite and then, with a massive boom that shook the ground all throughout Wilderheim, gobbled up all seven of them at once.

With the last word on the last page spoken, the book's black magic was free, off to seek its next repast. It had no sense of scale and knew nothing of pecking orders. It sensed the darkness in the north and hungered for a taste, recklessly racing toward its own doom.

The Dragonblood princess snapped the book shut. Despite its spell being done and gone, the tome retained enough of its stain to curl her claws around it, refusing to let go. She cringed as tainted ink dripped over her hand, burning her like acid that somehow seeped into her blood and made her feverish with stinging frost.

Forcing her hand to straighten, she released the book at last and let it drop into the mud at her feet. Instead of burning to ash, it sank down and disappeared in the muck, a black heartbeat throbbing malice through the earth.

Her knees quivered, and her arms felt too heavy for her body when she banked her flames and faced the destruction she'd wrought. The battlefield reverberated with silence. There was no one left alive for miles around. Men, women, human or Other, all of them lay dead where they'd stood, and she was to blame for it all.

But the portals were no more.

The ravenous void spreading from the north had met the spell and slowed, pausing for a while to feast on the power it had consumed, destroying it little by little before it could do more damage. For the price of innocence, the princess had bought the rest of her kingdom a little more time.

A dull, burning pain started in her belly, growing more intense until it doubled her over, and she dropped to her knees. Fighting the darkness, she raised her gaze to the sky, fancied she could see a dragon's shadow against the flash of a lightning bolt. If only it were real.

But if the dragon hadn't answered the hundreds of summons she'd sent out every day since the Veil had shattered, he would not have answered this last one. Fal would be on his own. Liadan had done all she could to help him, but she had nothing left to give. "Wake up, brother," she whispered through numb lips. *Wake up, the kingdom needs you…* Darkness closed in on her, swaying the ground beneath her. "Wake up…"

A strong downward wind buffeted her upright just long enough for her to feel the heat of fire against her skin. She embraced its comfort for the beautiful dream it was and gave herself up to it, hardly noticing a pair of strong, hard arms closing around her as she collapsed.

CHAPTER 30

They came out of nowhere, peasants with farming tools and creatures such as Artairas had never seen before. They rushed the square from all sides on rising war cries, attacking with the single-minded abandon of a people who knew they were running to their deaths.

An elderly man came upon Artairas from the back, wielding a pitchfork. It took no effort at all to send him to the ground, but right on his heels, a hissing red creature with slitted green eyes jumped high into the air, its clawed hands and feet aiming for Artairas. He fell back and rolled with the creature until he had it pinned to the ground. Raising his sword high, he stabbed the demon through, savoring the shock in its eyes before they dimmed in death.

Two women jumped onto his back, their little eating knives aiming for his heart, scraping against his armor. He shook them off, his arm itching to swing the killing blow, but at the last moment, he changed the sword's aim to miss them by a hair's breadth. They screamed and ran, leaving Artairas shaking with the need to go after them and finish them off.

With great difficulty, he turned his sword to the two men who'd managed to fell one of his soldiers with a scythe. They were no match for him, and the blade shouted in triumph when their heads toppled to the ground.

But in the next blink, the blade fell silent, quivering in his grasp. The ground roiled beneath his feet in a massive shudder that stopped everyone in their tracks. The fighters tripped off balance; the mounts screamed and ran.

Everyone in the square gazed around warily, waiting for whatever had caused the ground to shake to come bearing down on them. When nothing did, the peasants picked up their crude weapons and attacked in force.

God's blade roused instantly and screamed with renewed vigor, causing his arm to cramp. The blade clutched his fingers around the handle, directed his movements to defend against creatures he never saw coming. Rather than fight its control, Artairas gave himself up to it, thanking God for keeping him safe from those savage demons.

They fell one after the other, their eyes dimming, their claws turning to ash, and with each one slain, he felt more strength flood his body. The weight of his armor was nothing to him; the fatigue of battle was banished by a feverish zeal. He bared his teeth in a snarl, something akin to joy taking hold of him as he moved, flowed, danced through the fight.

More bodies poured into the square, and he reaped them down in quick succession. He didn't see their faces, didn't hear their shouts. All he saw were moving targets and the shining blade cutting them down.

And he loved every moment of it. His heart raced with excitement, the blade singing in his grasp, sending zings of pleasure through his arm, down to his loins.

He felled a knight, watched his mouth open on a shuddering gasp as his wide-eyed gaze shifted to something behind Artairas. Pulling his sword free of the dying man, Artairas brought it around in a flash. His aim was perfect; the blade stabbed into a soft belly before his mind had located the target.

It was the gasp that broke through his battle haze.

With the blade still buried in its victim, Artairas froze. His focus returned slowly, registering the sounds of battle before the sights. He blinked and blinked again, finding himself staring into a pair of large, green eyes. The pale face went blank as baffled as Artairas, plump, red lips opening and closing soundlessly.

A woman. A young girl with cheeks stained pink by the cold and hair cropped so short it made her look like a child.

Artairas shouted, releasing his grip on the sword as he backed away from her. The sheepskin had already begun to turn dark with her blood as she dropped to her knees. Artairas was only vaguely aware of the silence around them, so focused on the girl, he didn't notice the fighting had stopped.

She sat back on her heels, shuddering, and Artairas shuddered with her. He couldn't feel his body past the thud of his heartbeat. His mind refused to comprehend what he was seeing. No, this couldn't be. He wouldn't have slain an innocent—the queen had expressly forbidden it.

The girl swayed where she sat, tipping her chin up to stare at him with those doe eyes filled with confusion and fear. She wasn't breathing, but Artairas could still hear the soft whimper quiver past her lips as she slowly tipped over. With her hands around the blade, she gasped a breath, then another as she curled in on herself and changed. Like frost licking up from the ground, her body became gray and stiff, turning to stone before his eyes, the sword sticking out like an accusing finger pointed directly at him.

Artairas couldn't move. He couldn't look away, frozen to the spot, an easy target for the most inept of peasants.

But no one was fighting anymore. They all stared at the girl sealed in stone, holding the sword inside her as if she would never let it go again.

"My Lord," someone said.

Artairas moved his numb lips, managing to speak a single word: "Retreat."

CHAPTER 31

The dragon carried Liadan into the tent with Varr brushing against his legs and sniffing at her. "She will heal," he assured Varr.

In response, the wolf keened a frantic, high pitched whine, pressing close as the dragon laid his granddaughter on the spare pallet. She was cold, her hands and clothing stained with black sludge that tainted the veins beneath her deathly pale skin.

On the other pallet, Fal lay panting and twitching, but silent, as if he waited for news of his sister. As long as the rains continued, the dragon could do nothing for his grandson. He needed to focus on Liadan.

He called fire into his palms but, before he could begin, Varr pounced on Fal with a sharp whine-bark as the boy gasped and turned rigid.

"Fal!"

A sheen of cold gray stone quickly spread over Fal's body. It turned him into a statue up to his neck, and only a broken whisper of, "Sanja," made it past his lips before the stone crept up over his face to encase him fully.

The dragon quickly banked his flames. Stone had no give. Too much heat, and it would shatter.

While Varr whined and paced frantically back and forth between Fal and Liadan, sniffing each of them in turn, pawing at them, nuzzling them, the dragon stabbed a claw into the base of his ring finger and twisted Liadan's ring 'round and 'round, using his blood to power its spell. He cast the summoning far and wide, adding the strength of all his will to bring Saeran back. Where the king of Wilderheim went, his queen followed, and right now, Fal needed his mother's magic more than ever.

A curious sound brought him back to Fal's pallet. He put his ear to the boy's chest to hear better. Strange, it sounded as if two hearts beat within him almost perfectly synchronized. As their rhythms separated more and more, the gray stone slowly faded back to living flesh. Fal sighed and went limp, and his breathing settled into the rhythm of deep sleep.

The dragon laid a cautious hand on his forehead, seeking his grandson's mind. He found it scattered in the breadth and depth of the rain. Safe, but lost to the tumult of the storm.

The dragon couldn't force him whole without causing irreparable harm. Without Nialei, all he could do was wait for the storm to end so Fal could find his own way back. "Keep an eye on him," he told Varr, then turned his attention back to Liadan.

The vibrant girl who danced with flames now lay as one dead, still holding the stain of the dark spell inside her. He called fire back into his palms and laid both of his hands over Liadan's abdomen. His flames licked along her body, seeped down through her skin, seeking out every last remnant of the dark magic's corruption.

Burning it away was the easy part. Far worse was the damage it had left behind. Black magic was an insidious thing, warping anything it touched in ways no one could predict. Liadan's veins were melted closed, and her heart was rotted like rusted iron. All of these things would heal with fire and time. But no amount of time would heal the sorrow and pain in her mind. No amount of fire would bring the child in her womb back to life. And no amount of magic would reform Liadan's wounded soul to the way it used to be.

Like a bad break, Liadan would mend into something altogether different. Stronger, more powerful and resilient, but different.

A warm hand on his shoulder brought him back to himself. He looked up to meet Saeran's questioning gaze. "I could not save the babe."

The king of Wilderheim blinked back the tears in his eyes. "You saved my daughter," he said fiercely. "It is more than I could have done."

"And Fal?"

Both of them turned to watch Nialei work on her son. A faint blue aura glowed around her where she knelt beside Fal's pallet with one hand on his forehead, the other over his heart.

Varr crawled over to Nialei and carefully laid his chin on her knee. Saeran took his place behind her, putting his hands over hers to lend her his strength.

The dragon left them to it. He encased Liadan in a shroud of blue flames to help her heal, then stepped out of the tent.

The rain had eased to a soft drizzle. As far as he could see, the land around him was dead aboveground and below. Mist covered the field of battle, blanketing thousands of dead bodies, but it couldn't mask the smell of death.

Taking a knee, the dragon once more called up his flames. He stoked them white-hot and sent them racing over the earth, scorching the remains to soft ash, razing the empty town of Crossroads to the ground. All of it would sink down into the earth and turn the valley into a lush, verdant paradise in the years to come.

If Fenrir didn't destroy it first.

The dragon cast his gaze to the north. There in the distance, the stain of eternal hunger hovered at the base of Hallowed Mountain. It had stopped to feast on the dark spell and all the powers it had absorbed. Divine powers—a delicacy not easy for it to digest. The dragon sensed Fenrir gnawing away at it a little bit at a time. He was grateful for the short reprieve. Though his fire had warmed the earth for now, it could not banish the frost of Fenrir's approach completely. Another storm was brewing over the mountains, and this one would cover the kingdom in eternal snow and ice.

Night fell without fanfare. In the sky above, Otherlands twirled their dance, a beautiful spectacle he'd witnessed in all its glory before the Veil had fully formed. Back then, the sky had been on fire with a riot of colors. The dragon had watched them clash and reform anew. He'd spent centuries visiting each Otherland, watching its dominant species evolve and rise to power. He'd learned politics from the shadows of the Sidhe court and warfare from Ice Fey battlefields. He'd known that ever-changing sky like the back of his claw.

This one was little more than its skeletal remains.

Saeran joined the dragon outside the tent, and the two of them sat together, watching the sky in silence. "What happened to you?" Saeran asked after a while.

The dragon couldn't begin to explain. "I was…away. Your grandmother sends her love."

Saeran turned to stare at him. "You saw her?"

"For a moment too brief." And one that would never happen again. The dragon turned away from the thought.

Thankfully, Saeran didn't push for more. "What do we do now?"

"I do not know." With all the knowledge he'd collected over his endless millennia of life, the dragon had no solutions to offer. There was no spell to stop a void as ravenous as the one bearing down on them.

"Is anywhere safe from Fenrir anymore?"

"Not within Wilderheim's borders," the dragon replied. "Do you feel the new barrier?" He huffed out a plume of smoke, and inside it showed Saeran a vision of blinding white light. On one side of it, Wilderheim's soldiers battled an army of invaders. On the other, foreigners from each bordering kingdom looked on in silence. They couldn't see the barrier but sensed its force pushing them back. No one could cross it from either side. "I do not know if it is strong enough to stop the Wolf, but it is more than strong enough to stop us escaping him."

Never one to back down from a fight, Saeran balled his hands into fists, ready to face off with death itself if need be. "Can Fenrir be killed?"

The dragon sought the void and found its meal reduced the slightest bit. Another day or two, perhaps three before it moved on to the rest of the kingdom. Fortified by the Divine powers, it would make short work of Wilderheim and everything in it. "If he could, the gods would have done it long ago."

Saeran nodded his grim acceptance. "Don't tell the others," he asked. "At least not yet."

A scream-gasp behind the tent's flimsy curtain brought both men to their feet and back inside. Liadan sat up on her pallet, pale and shaking. She was panting for breath as her body smoked, and her wide eyes burned bright orange.

"Liadan?"

"It stopped raining. Where is Fal?"

She looked to them for an answer, then followed their gazes to Nialei, still working on Fal. With an incoherent cry, she rolled from her pallet and fell to her knees beside Fal, taking his hand in both of hers. "No, no, no, it should have been me." Errant flames flared out of her back like ethereal wings that couldn't quite coalesce. "It should have been *me*!"

Saeran and the dragon pulled her away, embraced her shaking form between them to keep her erratic fire from burning down the tent. "I cast the spell. I paid the price," she sobbed. "Why won't he wake?"

"Hush, child," the dragon crooned. "It will be all right."

"I paid the price," she repeated over and over. "I did the right thing!" Then, on a broken whisper, "Didn't I?"

"He won't die, Liadan," Saeran said. "I swear to you we will not let him die."

But she didn't hear, fighting them both as her flames flared out farther and farther. Neither of them could reach through the chaotic haze in her mind to make her calm, and so the dragon did the only thing he could. He sent Liadan into a deep sleep.

Her fire banked in a rush, and she went limp. Saeran caught her against him, rocking her back and forth, his face pressed to her shoulder.

By Fal's pallet, Nialei sighed and sat back. Varr scrambled to his feet immediately, licking her face and whining his concern. Nialei endured his attentions for a moment, quietly assuring him she was all right. When at last she managed to push him away and face the rest of them, she looked utterly drained. "I did what I could," she rasped. "The rest is up to him."

↞ »·◇·« ↠

Scattered into millions of raindrops, Fal plummeted from the sky, washing over a kingdom drenched with blood. He slid down chipped blades and torn flags, washed over open wounds and dead, sightless eyes. A small, quick current carried him down city streets, past enemy soldiers retreating into huts and haunted people huddling in fear of them.

Little by little, his essence coalesced back together, guided by a warm, blue light. But before he could be made whole, the current splashed into a boulder, scattering him over its surface and straight into the blade sticking out of it. It cut him through, and the current moved on, spinning him end over end into the black void of a rabbit hole.

He fell, and landed, and seeped through to fall deeper still until drop by drop, he dissolved into an underground well. There, at last, his mad dervish stopped. Fal coalesced into consciousness, cocooned in darkness and silence.

He sighed, basking in a moment of much-needed peace.

The water echoed his sigh with sorrow and the crackle of growing frost.

Where am I? He needed to get back to himself; his kingdom depended on it.

Another sigh was its response. The water had no answer for him. It only collected the drops that seeped like tears from above, each one carrying tales of horror, and pain, and suffering.

I want to stop it.

There will never be an end to ending, it replied. *Fenrir cannot be stopped.*

Can he be contained?

Fenrir cannot be stopped, the water repeated. *Fenrir will devour the worlds and then itself, and it will expel the dregs of what it has devoured, and bits of it will birth them-*

selves into all that was once immortal, and there will never be an end to ending.

Everything that had once existed would be forcefully altered into a different state of being, the water related without words. Not once, but again and again. The water accepted this. It was the natural order of things, after all. Water froze to ice and melted back to water, or boiled into steam. It was as it should be. The elements knew this; all of Nature knew this, but only some higher beings accepted it.

Change is the only truth.

The water perked up at those words. *Yes,* it agreed, pulsing in the rhythm of a heartbeat that echoed inside him. *Like her.*

Cold, sharp spikes of frost scraped along the edges of his consciousness. *What do you mean?*

The water swirled him about, pushed him back up to the surface, reversing his flow. He emerged into the night and splashed up over the selfsame boulder with the sword sticking out of it. The blade sliced through him, and he poured down over a surface far too smooth to be simple stone. He gathered sensations drop by drop and collected them all together in a pool at its base. From there, he gazed up at a boot shoved against the stone, hands clenched tightly around the sword handle. The soldier pulled and strained, but couldn't free the sword.

The woman it had impaled wouldn't let him.

Fal gasped, suddenly finding himself elsewhere, staring at a familiar tent roof. His head pounded, and his chest ached with each breath. Moving at all felt impossible, so Fal remained still, clutching at the heartbeat echoing his own as the only steady thing in a world gone mad. She was alive. Her heart still beat as strong as ever. She was alive, and that meant he could heal her.

She's alive. He repeated to himself against the flood of furious panic that threatened to drown out all lucid thought. She wasn't dead, merely sleeping, and he had to focus on that because if he didn't, he'd shatter. And Sanja needed him at full strength and thinking clearly so he could wake her.

How is she here? He'd left Anderheim with a clear order to—

Gods…

He'd told the Otherland to send Sanja home, and it had. To her real home in Wilderheim during the middle of an invasion. And now she was stone.

No, she's alive. Fal set the rhythm of his breaths to the beat of her heart and pushed everything else from his mind until the cold noose around his neck loosened, and he could breathe normally. *She's alive, and I can heal her.* And once he did, he would find whoever had brought that sword to Frastmir and make him pay.

His next breath puffed out cold mist. Icy crystals of magic rattled in his throat, demanding to be set loose. He swallowed them back, wincing as they cut him up on the inside. Rather than ground him, the pain increased his fury tenfold, and above him, the tent roof froze into intricate patterns of white frost.

Cold stone anchoring her to the ground. Drunken men crowding around. Reckless hands yanking on the sword, jarring it inside her. Filthy boots shoved at her for leverage.

The ice inside him spread, cramping his fingers into grotesque claws as snowflakes wafted down from the tent ceiling.

They'd kicked at her. They'd spat on her.

The ice grew so cold he couldn't feel it anymore, and he welcomed it, let the wrath consume his fear until he felt nothing but hate.

"Fal?" Nialei appeared beside him with Saeran and the dragon close behind. She placed her hand on his shoulder, allowing her magic to flow over him, warm and soothing, the epitome of maternal love.

He didn't want to give up his wrath and desperately fought her gentle healing. But she was relentless and the ice inside him began to melt. Fury gave way to anguish so deep it cut his soul to shreds, but his mother's light mended it back together, stitching him whole until he could heal on his own. His wild magic settled back into place, leaving him alone with his grief.

"You are not alone," Nialei told him. "We are with you now."

Yes, he had his family back.

Lush green grass sprouted from the cold, muddy ground at his feet, spreading through the tent as his illusions returned. He no longer bothered to pull them back. Instead, he welcomed the wildflowers blooming here and there as a reminder that all was not lost.

But all was not well, either.

He sat up, lightheaded, but relatively sane. "Where's Liadan?"

"Resting," his mother replied, shifting aside so he could see where his sister slept.

"She became frantic when you wouldn't wake after the storm passed," Saeran added. "She will want to see you when she wakes."

"The child?"

Their collective silence was answer enough.

The flowers at his feet sprouted thorny vines that choked off the blooms. "I saw it coming," he confessed. "I tried to make her leave—"

"This was not your fault."

"What bloody good is seeing the future if I can't change it?"

"I used to wonder the same," Nialei said, her gaze on Saeran. "I used to fight the will of Destiny and paid for it dearly every single time. But eventually, I came to accept that what we see is not meant to be a challenge, but a gift. We're not meant to change what is to come, only prepare for it, come to terms with it, and help others do the same."

Fal shook his head. "Not this time." He would not stand by as everything he'd ever known froze and died.

"Son, you can't fight Fenrir," Saeran said.

White frost adorned the tallest blades of grass and weighted the flowers down among them. "Perhaps I don't need to."

Anderheim called to him, eager to take him back. All Fal needed to do was find a way to fold all of Wilderheim into it. "I can save us. All of us. Everyone in Wilderheim, and any Others still alive out there."

"How?"

"We have a drop of blood from almost every clan. We can use it to summon them." The magic was the same one Liadan had used when fashioning the dragon's ring. The blood would call to its kind. He merely needed to feed it enough magic to reach everyone still alive. And, at the moment, magic was the one thing he had in ample supply.

"And then what? There is still no escape from Wilderheim."

No, but Anderheim lay directly on top of it. If Fal could create the doorway, no one would need to escape anywhere; the Otherland would simply enfold them all where they stood. "I'm certain there is a way, but I will need help to find it."

Nialei cupped his cheek. "Fal, you are grasping at a dream."

Perhaps he was. "But haven't you noticed, Mother? Our dreams have a way of coming true."

Hope surged within him on a rush of renewed strength. The grass all around them burst into a riot of dandelions and bluebells, and he felt them solidify in truth, a small part of Anderheim encroaching on Wilderheim, carrying its soundless call. For a moment, he could almost see the border between the two worlds misting around his family.

They noticed, too. The vision caused King Saeran to reach for his sword, while his queen looked about her in wonder. She met her son's gaze with something akin to awe. "Oh, to walk among such giants," she whispered, her eyes glinting with tears.

Fal pushed to his feet, eager to get started, but he tempered his excitement before approaching Liadan's pallet. The dragon might have cleansed the stain of the dark spell from his sister's body, but Fal sensed the turmoil it had left behind. Plunged deep in dreamless sleep, Liadan's fire still roiled inside her in a wild vortex of sparks too scattered to coalesce into a coherent flame.

He took her hand into his. As his mother had done for him, he left his body in search of his sister's soul, gently guiding each spark back into the whole. He took his time, left nothing to chance—Liadan was too important to all of them. When at last the final spark was corralled back into place, Fal drew back to behold his handiwork, and the sight of it shocked his consciousness back into his body.

Liadan's soul was altered. Instead of the wild, flaring inferno of golden fire, her core was now a small orb of blue flames so intense he dared not get too close. By breaking apart, Liadan had reformed much stronger than before. Like dragon's fire tempering a blade, Liadan's pain had seared away any remaining human weakness and forged her into an Other whose magic could change the world.

She was beautiful. Inside and out.

And, after Wilderheim was safely folded into Anderheim, he might never see her again.

Fal gave her hand a squeeze to wake her from her slumber. Despite the softness of his call, Liadan woke with a startled gasp and arched up to sit. Her magic pulsed with each frantic beat of her heart, sending waves of heat over the entire tent. When she met his gaze, Liadan's eyes were as blue as his own, a physical representation of the flame that would never bank again.

"You feel different," she said. Noticing the flowers around her pallet, she reached down with her free hand and plucked one of them. "You *are* different." Her discerning gaze raked over him in a thorough examination and came to a halt at his chest. Liadan pressed her hand and the flower in it over his double heartbeat then, with a curious tilt of her head, she turned his hand in hers palm-up to reveal the thin scar of his handfasting.

Fal attempted a smile but couldn't quite manage it past the thought of his mate trapped in stone. He needed to get to her and see firsthand the damage the sword had done. He needed to heal her before the echo of her heartbeat drove him mad. The grass dried around them, and the flowers froze to ice mid-sway. What little calm his mother had managed to gift him was already freezing away at the thought that Sanja might remain trapped in stone forever.

Liadan noticed. When she met his gaze once more, he felt her seeking through his memories, and what she found made her eyes glow like stars. "The same magic fashioned the blade and tore Wilderheim open to admit our enemies at our backs."

"Yes," he confirmed. Summoning a puddle, he wove an illusion across its surface to show the others. He conjured the glowing blade as it cut down their soldiers from the shadows. Liadan supplied its unearthly metallic scream.

"It cuts from shadows," Nialei noted.

Saeran swore viciously. "Loki. It must be."

Fal showed them what the rain had seen of the man wielding the weapon, but looked away himself before its final stroke.

Nialei gasped to see Sanja fall.

Saeran moved in for a closer look as she turned to stone. "The blade died with her?"

"The blade died," Liadan agreed, watching Fal. "The girl lives."

The dragon laid his hand over the surface, taking over the vision to make the blade its only subject. His magic filled the tent as he pulled a simulacrum of the sword from the puddle and turned it in the air. One by one, he removed all the symbols etched into its blade, then broke apart the handle to reveal its shining core. "No, the blade isn't dead."

Fal frowned. "What is that?"

"Divine power," the dragon answered. "A piece of a god's physical form refashioned into a weapon. Which means it cannot be killed, save by an act of the Divine."

"Get rid of it," Liadan growled, squeezing Fal's hand so hard his knuckles creaked.

Nialei grasped the vision in a tight fist and shoved it back through the puddle. Its scream carried on long after it disappeared.

"When the girl rouses," the dragon said, "the blade will wake again, as terrible as ever."

"A clever trap for whoever pulls it free," Saeran sneered. "I would have expected nothing less of Loki."

"I'll pull it out," Fal declared.

"You will do no such thing," his mother snapped.

"She's right," Liadan chimed in. "That privilege will be mine."

Saeran drew his sword and stabbed it into the center of the puddle. "Enough! Nobody will touch the sword until we know how to do it safely. Do you understand?" He stared down Liadan until she flushed and bowed her head in a nod. Then he moved on to Fal, demanding the same obedience from his son and heir. When he got it, the king of Wilderheim turned to his wife and queen. "That includes you too, love. Don't think I don't know how your clever mind works. Swear to me you will not go near the thing."

Nialei raised her stubborn chin. "I swear I will not lay one finger on Loki's cursed sword."

Saeran narrowed his eyes at her.

"In your place, I would accept it, Father," Fal quipped. "A better compromise will never pass her lips."

Saeran's mouth twitched in a smile despite his thunderous scowl. They all knew Nialei too well to expect her to keep her distance altogether.

Liadan pushed to her feet and removed herself to the far corner of the tent to stretch. Her joints creaked and crackled like old firewood as she realigned herself. Small blue sparks danced along her fingertips. She caught them up and molded them into a sphere, watching it spin in the air above her palms as the rest of them looked on in wary silence. "Two days it took me to do this in the desert," she said with a wry shake of her head.

Fal exchanged a silent look with his parents and the dragon. As unpredictable as Liadan had been before, she was now a thousand times moreso. That small blue flame burned so hot Fal felt its sting clear across the tent. If she lost control of it…

But Liadan handled the orb with such ease, it seemed to bore her. She played with it for a moment, let it weave among her fingers and dance up her arm to her shoulder, then caught it with her opposite hand and stifled it in her fist. And she did it all as if she was handling a ball of yarn. "In the morning," she said with calm gravity, "we will return to Frastmir, reclaim the castle, and take back the girl. But tonight, I think it's time for Fal to show us where he's been for the last three weeks."

CHAPTER 32

In a cold, dark hut, Artairas sat at the remains of a shattered table, his head in his numb hands. Men came and went, bringing news of the siege, but it was General Gawain who received them and issued new orders. Everything they said passed through Artairas without acknowledgment. Every question directed at him went unanswered. Artairas was lost to the world at large, his mind mired in memories of the girl's face, the shock in her eyes.

He recalled the smallest details again and again. The way her lips parted, the sound of her soft cry. The way she collapsed so slowly, like a weightless feather wafting to the ground.

The bloodstain spreading over her sheepskins. A lamb slaughtered before her time.

Artairas hadn't felt a single moment of doubt before last night. Now, doubt was all he knew. If this was what God had wanted, why was Artairas so ashamed?

Dawn had come and gone.

Sometime in the night, the storm had broken, leaving in its wake a miserable chill that refused to yield to their hearth fire. His men had taken over abandoned houses in the castle city, burning whatever was available to warm themselves.

"My Lord."

The fifth address. Or was it the sixth? Either way, Artairas didn't move to acknowledge it.

"My Lord, the sword."

A good man, Gawain was. Despite his misgivings, he remained true to their cause. His faith hadn't wavered a single time, even after what he'd seen, fighting side by side with Artairas. Even after the girl.

"We sent men to retrieve it, but no one can budge it from the stone."

No one ever would. It belonged to the girl now. She'd bought it with her life.

Artairas shuddered, ducked his head lower, and curled his fingers into his hair, tugging hard.

"My Lord, it is the symbol of our cause," Gawain insisted.

"What cause?" he muttered. "What has Wilderheim ever done to God that He would send us to destroy it?"

Gawain flushed and jerked his head to send the others out. "God's will is not for us to question. You are tired, My Lord. You have not slept or eaten a proper meal since we got here. You know not what you say."

The man was right. Artairas had fought through the night and day without cease. He'd slain so many he couldn't remember any of them, except the last. The girl. "We trespassed where we were not meant to go."

"We were sent by God to cleanse this heathen land in His name."

"Were we? Or was it the Devil whispering in an old woman's ear?" He'd been there the day they'd burned Sir Arnaud. He remembered the man's last words and the whispers that had spread through the castle about Queen Genevieve.

Gawain shot to his feet and took two angry steps toward Artairas before he stopped himself to rein in his temper.

"Do you not have even a whisper of doubt?" Artairas challenged. "After all we have seen here, do you not wonder?"

A muscle twitched in Gawain's jaw as he fought valiantly to hold onto his temper. Rather than answer, the general chose to change the subject. "The siege towers have been abandoned on the east side of the outer wall. I have ordered them to be moved to the south. The moat has been drained, and we have men digging through the mud to undermine the wall on the north side. We appear to have struck a tunnel there, which may be our way inside, but the stones are too tough for our weapons."

Artairas shook his head. "We are at the heart of it all, Gawain. There is magic in everything around us, and it will not yield to chunks of metal for our asking."

"Happily for us, we have a supply of masonry tools made right here. They seem to be holding up well enough."

"How many men have we lost on the east side?" It must have been a significant number for the siege towers to have been abandoned altogether. "And how many dead everywhere else?" He'd caught random words of a report here and there. In the south, the dead numbered in the thousands. The western front had failed to send a report with their blood-stained pigeons. Artairas could only assume their forces there were lost. "Would God lead us all to slaughter like this?"

"Yes," Gawain answered. "His glory demands sacrifice, and it is our honor to have been chosen to bleed in His name."

Artairas scoffed. What a wretched waste of life.

"You speak of devils in Synealee, yet you refuse to see them screaming you in the face right here. You have slain enough of them yesterday to know our cause to be true, yet now that we are so close to victory, you falter? Then it is as I suspected. All of your courage lies in the sword. And if so, then God be my witness, I shall get it back in your hand if I have to reduce the stone to rubble!"

"You will fail." Dozens had already tried; he'd heard them out there all through the night. After the girl had turned to stone, after the fighting had stopped, the sun had set with such quiescence that for a while, Artairas had believed himself to be stumbling through the darkness of purgatory.

But food and drink had eventually been brought forth. The men's spirits had been revived, and they'd flooded back out to the sword to test their strength against it. By midnight, their cheers and laughter had echoed through the streets, setting Artairas on the razor-sharp edge of impending disaster, and that's where he'd been ever since.

Sunrise had come and gone. The sun had reached its zenith and passed it. Night would be upon them again soon, and still the men were out there, taking turns trying to free the sword from the stone—the girl.

Artairas was exhausted in mind as well as body, ready to embrace the endless sleep of death, yet the cursed blade still called to him, and it was all he could do not to stalk out there and fight each and every one of his men to claim the weapon for himself. Some ancient, mystical awareness told him he could do it. The blade had been given to Artairas by God—he was the only one who could free it from the stone.

He knew precisely where to brace his feet and how to take hold of the handle. He knew how hard to pull, and he could already feel it giving way in his grasp; hear the scrape of metal against stone turn into the wet sound of the blade slicing free of soft flesh.

Artairas shuddered, his stomach heaving as he turned away from Gawain and the open doorway behind him. A shame he couldn't turn away from his own mind. In it, he smelled the blood seeping from the girl's gut. He saw it pooling at his feet, staining his boots. He saw it running down the center of the blade, over the handle, and onto his hand. It was cold, sticky, and Artairas would never be clean of it.

A desperate sob escaped him as he frantically wiped his hands. He prayed for mercy, for forgiveness, for peace.

When he came back to his senses, it was to find Gawain before him, staring at him with horror. "You've gone mad."

Artairas almost laughed. If only it was that simple.

"Stay here," Gawain ordered. "Rest. You will see sense again after you have slept. I will find a way to retrieve the sword, and in the morning, we will take the castle. Then everything will fall into place."

"You overstep, General. I give the orders here."

"You are in no condition to lead us!"

Artairas merely sighed. "The sword is dead."

"Dead or not, you'll still carry it into battle tomorrow." Turning on his heels, he marched out, snapping orders at the men outside. No one was to enter the hut without his permission.

Artairas dropped his head into his hands once more and prayed for God to guide him back into His grace.

CHAPTER 33

Morning dawned on the sound of a battering ram slamming into the castle's massive gates. It bounced off harmlessly, only to be propelled forward once more. On the battlements, bleary-eyed sentinels stood silent watch. The humans clutched little books in their hands. The Others paced restlessly, watching the archers below ready their bows.

Outside the walls, Synealee's army stood in formation, weapons in hand, waiting for a path to open for them to storm the castle.

Inside the courtyard, humans and Others waited for something else.

Word had spread of the prince's return, and the great blow he'd stricken against the invaders with the ease of an afterthought. Rumors whispered on the breeze of a dragon flying across the sky, breathing great plumes of fire through the clouds. Though many had fallen during the first wave of attack, those who'd seen their crown prince bring a hundred dying men back to roaring life stood tall in the face of Ragnarok, knowing their rulers would not abandon them.

The ram slammed into the gates, leaving behind the shallowest of indentations. It had barely come to a stop after its recoil when the general shouted, "*Forward!*"

As the north wind kicked up, its whistling rush grew louder, carrying an unearthly chorus of baying howls. No time to sound a warning. The screams spread southward as a pack of ferocious befurred beasts tore through the ranks. Their claws rent metal with ease; their fangs crushed bones like dry tinder. Six of them cut a wide swath through the army, distracting a third of their forces away from the siege. No arrow was swift enough to catch them, no blade sharp enough to cut through the Ulfhednar's thick fur.

Atop the battlements, the humans opened their books and began to read. Magic poured from them, tearing up cobblestones from beneath the soldiers' feet for ammunition, turning the frozen ground to quicksand that sucked enemy forces down faster than they could run.

When arrows began to fly, aimed at the wizards, the Others plucked them out of the air, sending them back to the archers coated with fire and poison. For each fallen archer, two more stepped up. One arrow hit its mark, killing a woman mid-spell. She tumbled off the wall onto the mud giant taking shape in the moat below, and both collapsed back into the muck.

The Other left behind shrieked a volley of barbs at the soldiers below, felling ten of them into the selfsame moat. But with that blow, he himself collapsed and was no more.

The wizards spread out farther, ducked low to make smaller targets of themselves, but they couldn't retreat. To strike a blow against the enemy, they needed to see it.

In the south, ghostly apparitions of beautiful women with pale skin and bloody eyes wove through the ranks. Their hands wafted like mist over a shoulder here, a hand there. Their mournful sighs whispered across dry lips cracked by the cold, and everywhere they went, death followed. Soldiers' faces turned gray in their helmets, their eyes widened, and their mouths opened as they wheezed for breath.

This time, the warning spread, but mist could not be cut down. And when the wraiths keened, weeping tears of blood, the soldiers began to drop like flies.

And the siege towers never touched the wall.

The steadfast ranks fractured outside the walls while in the courtyard, Wilderheim's soldiers stood their ground. A shield on one arm, a sword in hand, they beat the one against the other in a steady rhythm, watching the gates bow inward each time the ram slammed forward. One hundred strong and fifteen fledglings all ready to lay down their lives.

A dull thump joined the chorus of clangs. A scrawny waif with mud-stained cheeks and wild brown hair had joined the ranks. Twelve years old, if she was a day, she defiantly stared up at the soldier shooing her away and banged her little eating knife against the wooden barrel top she'd tied to her arm.

Sheathing his sword, the soldier swooped up the brat and endured her screaming fit as he carried her back through the kitchens into the pantry. He made sure to lock the kitchen door behind him as he returned to his place in the formation.

Others had joined them while he'd been gone. Giant creatures with furry, hooved legs as long as he was tall, swarthy torsos, and thick antlers on their heads. A shield and a sword each, they added their much louder beats to the rhythm.

Two knights in thin golden armor winked into being at the front. Their spears were made of light, their shields like translucent frost. A male and a female with no helmets to cover their long, snow-white hair. The ram's next blow cracked the bar securing the gates. The pair turned to one another. Pale blue markings covered their dark brown skin, their fierce black eyes flashing a wordless message.

They smiled a challenge at each other when the ram rolled forward and, when it shattered through the gates, wordlessly rushed into battle, leading the charge. They managed to push Synealee's soldiers back far enough for the hooved Others to get out and join the fray, but even with all of them standing between Synealee's soldiers and Castle Frastmir, too many still managed to slip through the gates. They were met by Wilderheim's steel.

Outside the gates, the cold wind became a gale, and the sky rained shards of ice over the city, blinding anyone foolish enough to look up. The battle was thickest around the castle gates, but weapons clashed as far west as the river with Others converging from all sides to herd the invaders in for slaughter.

Those on the bridge saw it first—a great shadow gliding through the clouds. When it roared, all of Frastmir shuddered. That roar was the only warning the warriors would get. Every Other who heard it disappeared, taking friendly humans with them and abandoning the invaders to their fate.

The great shadow swooped in from the west, emerging from the clouds with a stream of fire that incinerated an entire streetful of soldiers in a single pass. It banked left and returned for another pass one street over, systematically cleansing the city of its infection from the outside in.

Those quick enough to escape the dragon's flames ran straight into the clutches of its progeny. On one side, a black-scaled creature with a horned crown and fiery hair used her flames to pen them in by the dozens. On the other, a human with massive black wings swooped over them, taking heads with his flaming sword so swiftly, the bodies ran on for ten more steps before collapsing in fits and spasms.

The survivors ran toward the keep, some to seek safety in numbers, others to shout for crossbows and catapults. At first, they rejoiced to see water spilling down the streets as a respite from the flames. But the water grew, thickening the mud to calf-depth, and on its heels came a heavy mist that obscured everything beyond arm's reach, and then the cold deepened, freezing the mud solid around their legs.

They called to one another as they struggled to free themselves. Their voices, dulled by the thick mist, didn't carry far. Word of the Reaper in their midst spread too slowly, dogged by the swish of his cloak and the soft whistle of his blade as, one by one, the soldiers fell silent.

Water spread through the streets all the way to the library, where Others had cornered Artairas and Gawain's battalion. The ground turned into a shallow lake, and as the thick blanket of mist descended over them, the sounds of battle grew silent.

Though they couldn't see it, the dragon had reached the keep and perched on the battlements. Its roar resounded across the city, and its flames briefly illuminated the mist.

"Stand fast, men!" Gawain ordered.

Artairas put his back to Gawain's. "We're surrounded." He felt the noose pull tighter and tighter as the enemy closed in unseen from all sides.

"My Lord, the sword!"

Artairas shook his head, already too tempted by its soundless call to need any further urging. That sword spelled damnation. He couldn't risk laying another finger upon it.

Gawain grasped his arm. "If anything can save us now..."

But Artairas wasn't listening anymore. His attention snared on a whisper of a sigh somewhere nearby. His breath caught as his mind filled with visions of a beautiful woman with pearlescent skin calling to him from the depths of a lake. His legs were knee-deep in water, but the surface was perfectly smooth, undisturbed by the falling hail. It reflected his face back at him, but also something else. Something he couldn't name.

The sigh became a whispered word of command, and the ice raining down upon them froze mid-air as if time itself had come to a silent halt. Artairas watched a clear glassy ice crystal come to a stop on the surface of the lake, balancing there on its tip, spinning slowly to reflect weak sunlight at him. He looked up to find thousands more suspended in the air like a sea of stars glittering in the mist.

It humbled him to supplication, and he wasn't the only one. All around him, his men lowered to their knees right along with him, bowing their heads. The mist parted, and the creature he'd imagined a moment ago emerged from its depths. She was beautiful beyond words, her golden hair aglitter, her flawless pale skin sheened with pearlescent perfection. She glided forward over the water's surface, her bare feet neither disturbing it nor sinking through. The ice crystals moved out of her way to allow her passage, showering her with loving kisses of reflected light.

"The Lady of the Lake," men whispered at her approach.

She glanced at each of them in turn, and they crossed themselves in gratitude for her blessing. Her presence overcame even the steadfast Gawain, whose forehead kissed the water almost despite himself.

But the Lady wasn't alone. A great white-eyed wolf followed on her right, and on her left, a cloaked figure of chaos matched her footsteps, carrying a bloodied sword in one hand and a great, curved scythe in the other. Where his booted feet touched down, the water froze solid and cold mist swirled outward.

The company came to within four paces of Artairas and stopped there. He felt the wolf's hot breath on his face, expected at any moment to feel its fangs tear into him, but they did not.

He chanced a look up and found his gaze snared by the Lady's silver one. "Move aside," she said, and it was only then he realized they hadn't come for him, but for what was behind him.

The sword in the stone.

Artairas moved.

The Lady's gaze shifted to her cloaked companion. "Are you certain?"

The man tossed aside his bloodied sword, made the scythe melt into mist, then pulled back the hood of his cloak. He looked human enough, but Artairas felt magic pulse around his cloaked figure in waves so powerful they almost bowled him over. He overflowed with so much of it Artairas could hardly breathe in his presence, and he knew it was but a fraction of what the man held contained within.

He imagined this had to be what it felt like to stand in the presence of a god. A god, not the God. Then the man looked at him, and Artairas knew it was not a god, but Death itself staring frost straight into his soul with eyes of pure blue ice.

"Be ready," the Lady of the Lake warned. "I don't know how much time we will have."

As the man knelt before the sword, he reached out to touch the girl's stone cheek with the gentlest of caresses. "Hello again, little mate."

"As soon as she is free, take her to the other keep. She will be safe there."

"Father's still at the green and Liadan's miles to the south. Someone sent up a beacon."

"Whoever it is," the Lady said dryly, "I hope for their sake they called her for something important. Or something bloody. Are you ready? My spell will not hold these men forever."

Gawain raised his head, and just as quickly bowed it once more. But his honor would not allow him to remain silent. "My Lady, you cannot take the sword."

"I respect your courage, knight, but I would prefer your silence." Turning to Artairas, she waved her hand and forced him upright, holding him entranced with her gaze. "King Arthur, it is time to claim your legacy."

"I—cannot."

Her serene silvered eyes turned fierce. "I was not asking."

As gently as she delivered the words, they carried the force of a magical command that gave Artairas no choice but to obey. His feet turned him to face the sword while Death's icy, hate-filled glare watched his every move. Artairas' fingers curled tightly around the sword's handle. As he'd imagined the night before, his feet braced just so, and he pulled just hard enough to loosen the blade. The sound of metal scraping against stone shuddered through him with the first tingles of the sword's waking hunger, and as the blade pulled free from soft, living flesh, its whispering voice roused to a blood-curdling scream inside his mind.

Artairas stumbled back, shaking from head to toe, the hateful sword clutched in his grip. He watched through the blur of unshed tears as the cloaked man scooped his felled maiden into his arms and disappeared.

"Please," he whimpered to the Lady of the Lake. "Take it with you." He wanted to fall to his knees once more to offer her the blade, but its power wouldn't let him bend a knee. Instead, it gripped him tightly and squared his stance, raising the tip to the Lady's neck. "Please, I beg you."

She looked at the blade, then met his gaze with her unfeeling one. "No," she said, killing his hope with merciless efficiency. "This is your legacy, King Arthur. This sword will build your kingdom on a foundation of the blood and bones of all it has killed. Your realm with endure for generations and your faith will do your god proud. In the end, you will all have what you wanted: a world without magic and the Other creatures you find so repulsive. And until your dying breath, you will not walk a single step without the regret of it bearing down on you."

Artairas whimpered, blinking away his helpless tears as the old thirst for blood once more tensed his limbs for a battle he no longer wanted to win.

Between one breath and the next, the Lady of the Lake was gone, as was her wolf, and the mist, and the lake she'd brought with her. The ground was covered in snow, his men kneeling deep in it. As they roused and pushed to their feet, entranced by the tableau of ice crystals suspended in mid-air, the dragon roared from the castle's battlements, breaking whatever spell had been placed upon the scene. The storm resumed its chilling fury, and from all around them, creatures of nightmare attacked in force.

No time for prayers and regrets.

The war was only just beginning.

CHAPTER 34

Fal appeared in Anderheim's waterfall lake with the healing melody already humming from deep within his power's core. Sanja's injury ought to have been a quick thing to mend, but the sword that had stabbed through her had not been an ordinary blade. The wound closed slowly, fighting his spell every inch of the way, draining as much blood as it could before Fal's healing overpowered it.

It left behind a scar inside her womb that refused to heal any more than it already had, no matter how Fal altered the melody. The human body could only absorb so much magic; Fal had already brought Sanja back from the brink of death once before, and she simply couldn't take any more. Her body was healed, but it would never conceive a child.

"Thank you, gods." He bowed his head in gratitude. The possibility of his child draining Sanja's life from the inside had tormented him ever since their handfasting.

Sanja groaned, frowning before she'd opened her eyes. "You didn't tell me when you married me that I'd have to wake in water every morn."

He chuckled. "I suppose her Royal Highness would prefer a bed of goose down."

Nothing had ever looked as beautiful as her smile. But then she gasped, flailing out of his hold to right herself.

"Whoa, easy!"

She sank, pulled down by her soaked clothing, then came up sputtering and shoving her wet hair out of her eyes. "The parchments," she said, coughing. "Did the Brothers find you? Did you sing it? Is it over?"

Fal pulled her from the lake, dried them both with a thought. "Take a breath. What are you talking about?"

"The puzzle, the song of worlds, don't you remember? I solved its shape. I know how it needs to be sung. But I… The soldiers chased me out of the library. I gave the parchments to Brother Erik and told him to find you."

"That must be who sent up the beacon for Liadan."

Sanja looked around. "We're in Anderheim."

"Yes, it's all right, Sanja, you are safe now. I will not let anything happen to you again."

"No, we have to go back. There is so little time left."

Sensing her rising panic, Fal kept his voice low and spoke slowly to calm her. "Tell me what you solved. I will go back and sing it."

She was shaking her head before he'd finished. "You cannot do it by yourself. I have to go with you."

"I am not taking you back to Frastmir. It may have slipped your notice while you were getting stabbed with a mystical sword, but there is a war going on there."

"Did creating Anderheim cure you of your illusions?"

He flushed. "No, not as such."

"Then you have to take me."

"Sanja—"

"You said if all I do is hold your hand, it will be a gesture far more powerful than any spell you could ever speak."

Fal gaped at her. "How in all of Anderheim can you remember my exact words from a month ago, but not recall that you almost died—*twice*?"

"There is far more at stake now than my life, Highness. You may get one chance to save everyone. Only one. If you cannot control your illusions and sing the song at the same time, they will all die, and you along with them."

Fal opened his mouth to argue but found he had nothing to say. If the song was somehow the answer to everything, then she was right. He couldn't sing it with his voice changing on every line, nor could he do it from within his illusions and halfway in Anderheim.

Still… "The song itself only creates a Veil—"

"It creates a connection and a doorway," Sanja corrected. "That is what the Veil has always been. To keep realms separate, something has to exist between them, and that something will always connect them. Humans could never see it without magic, but it was always there, and you can build it again and bring everyone across."

"Then the blood can be the key that locks Fenrir out."

Sanja frowned. "What?"

Fal took her face in his hands and kissed her. "Little mate, I have just come to a wonderful realization."

"What's that?"

"I married someone much smarter than myself."

Sanja's laughter carried them all the way to Anderheim's version of Castle Frastmir, and through to Wilderheim. All at once, the heat of summer turned to bitter winter. High up in the remnants of Fal's tower, there was no shelter from the frigid wind that lashed them with sharp hail. With Sanja tucked into his side, Fal carefully chose his steps along the inner wall, far away from the broken edge of the floor.

"Don't look down," he warned.

Sanja, being Sanja, didn't listen. She whimpered and clutched him tighter. "It's all gone. The fields, the forests—everything."

Fal followed her gaze to the east, where the fire had leveled everything the armies hadn't trampled into dust. Outside the castle's walls, the earth was scorched black, slowly getting covered in a layer of snow. Between the inner and outer walls, the ground was piled with dead soldiers wearing the red cross of Synealee's mad monarch.

"What are we doing here? We have to find Brother Erik. He has the parchments."

"He has the copies, remember?" Fal gently pried Sanja's arms free of him and pushed her all the way to the wall where the bookcase would provide some shelter from the winds. “Don’t move.”

“Where are you going?”

“I took everything that survived the lightning storm to my chambers, but the book containing the song wasn’t there. That’s why I gave you copies. The book itself must still be here somewhere. I have to find it.”

“But Brother Erik—”

“Isn’t here, and we don’t have time to wait.”

He had a point, “But do I have to be here while you search?”

Fal shrugged. “You wanted to come with me. At the moment, this is the safest place in all of Frastmir. The castle is under attack. If the soldiers get inside, they will raid the entire keep and kill anyone they come across.”

“But no one will bother with a tower that’s teetering on the brink of collapse.”

He grinned. “Precisely.”

Sanja glared.

“Not to worry, princess, I spelled this tower to withstand far worse. It may look unstable, but trust me, it’s as safe as can be.”

“Oh, just hurry up, will you?”

Sanja sank down and made herself as small as possible, watching her mad husband in the shape of a long-haired, dirty hermit rummage through piles of rubble in the stairway. The wind stole her breath away. Her face was numb from the cold, and the tips of her fingers were beginning to turn blue. She tucked them underneath her sheepskin tunic and shivered.

She was glad Mattias didn’t live to see Wilderheim come to this. “Do you th-think we could find my p-parents somehow?” she called to Fal through chattering teeth.

“It’s not here. It must have fallen down in the collapse,” Fal called ahead as he clambered back to the top. Were it not for the familiar blues of his eyes, Sanja would have shrieked. He was swathed in the illusion of an enemy soldier, his dirty tabard flapping in the wind.

She did shriek a moment later when a dragon dropped from the sky and roared at Fal. The sheer force of it shook the tower, knocking Fal off balance and shattering half of the remaining floor. Sanja scrambled for purchase on the last two stones left beneath her feet. She reached out to the bookshelf, but it tipped away from the wall and tumbled off the edge.

Sanja tripped sideways. Her foot slipped off the edge, and she screamed as she fell, landing hard a short way down. Her relief was short-lived as her saving perch moved, raising her up to a giant golden eye.

“Too bloody close!” Fal snapped in the voice of a shrill young girl. “What were you thinking?”

“I was thinking,” the dragon rumbled, “that the enemy had managed to get past my watchful eye. Did you know, boy, that your illusions also change your scent now? I smelled Synealee and reacted.”

"Never mind. It's good you are here. I'm looking for a book that is probably buried down there beneath the rubble."

The dragon scowled fiercely. "Is this really the right time for books?"

The face and voice of an old Aegiran crone gave Fal's answer gravity beyond the words themselves. "It is if it happens to be our only hope of surviving Fenrir!"

The dragon turned his golden gaze on Sanja and shrugged. "Fair point." He gently handed her down to Fal, now an old warrior with a scarred face and missing eye, then let himself fall down below.

"T-that was…"

Fal took her hand in his and swirled his cloak around her, pulling her into the warmth of his embrace. "My great grandfather," he said in his own voice.

"He's en-n-normous." Her teeth chattered so hard she couldn't speak properly, but she couldn't keep quiet, either. She'd just met a dragon!

"Is he? I hadn't noticed."

Sanja would have kicked him, were she not so cold. "W-where's he gon-n-ne?"

In answer, a loud rumble of rock exploded up from below them, massive boulders flying up to hover in the air. Among them, books in various stages of destruction spun slowly, stray pages wafting left and right.

The dragon climbed back up the tower until his muzzle was level with them. "Which one?" he asked, the gentlest puff of his breath slamming them both against the wall at Fal's back with a blast of much-needed heat.

Sanja squinted at the volumes. There were so many, at least half of them damaged beyond repair. What if the one they needed was missing the pages they were looking for?

"That one!" Fal pointed to a sizable tome bound in thick, dark red leather with a bronze clasp holding it closed. One corner of its back cover was bent up, the last few pages crumpled, torn, and darkened with soot.

The dragon gently plucked it out of the air with two massive clawtips and handed it to Fal. Then he turned his paw palm up and, to her dismay, Fal shoved her ahead of him into the dragon's grasp. His claws curled up around them into a living cage, encasing them in too much heat, but Sanja was glad for it. Then everything the dragon had raised from the pile below dropped back down as he pushed away from the tower and crawled around and down to the front courtyard, using one of his wings as a shield against the storm.

"You couldn't have saved the books?" Sanja shouted before she could bite her tongue.

The dragon's chuckle reverberated in her chest and made her bones rattle. "I like her," he said, sounding pleased. He set them down in the courtyard but couldn't join them there himself, as large as he was. Instead, he perched on the wall over the gate, seeming not to notice the shower of arrows that bounced off his scaled hide. "Pardon me a moment."

With catlike agility she wouldn't have expected of a creature his size, the dragon pulled in his wings and pivoted around on the relatively narrow wall.

"Duck!" Fal shouted, tugging her down as the dragon's massive tail swooped over their heads and curled around the remnants of another tower. Sanja heard him take a breath, and through the open gateway, she watched his stream of fire scorch three hundred soldiers at least.

The volley of arrows stopped.

Fal straightened and took her hand in his once more. Immediately, his illusions fell away, and her husband squinted against the driving wind, shouting to make himself heard. "Where is everyone?"

"In anticipation of your return, your parents are in the great hall," the dragon replied.

"And Liadan?"

"On her way, I presume."

A blast of frigid wind blew in clouds as dark as night. Sunlight dimmed, the temperature plummeted even lower. Sanja, already chilled to her bones, felt her skin pull tight across her face. Her eyelashes frosted over so quickly, when she blinked, her eyes almost stuck closed.

"Hurry, Fal!" the dragon urged. "I can hold off the soldiers, but I can't stop that."

Fal pulled her into the keep. A pitiful little company awaited them in the great hall. Survivors, both human and Other, huddled together, scrambling to add more wood to the giant hearth fire. Chairs, tables, tapestries—they fed the fire anything they could get their hands on, and still the flames faltered.

"Fal!" A beautiful, golden-haired woman who could only be Queen Nialei rushed to meet them. Her husband, Sanja presumed, shouldered his way to the hearth and revived the flame with a blast of magic that momentarily filled the great hall with heat and light, but the fire refused to burn on its own.

"Mother, this is Sanja. My mate."

Mate. Not wife, but *mate*.

The queen, too, noticed his deliberate choice of words. She swept her gaze over Sanja in a perusal at once critical and loving.

Painfully aware of her haggard appearance, Sanja pulled on a short curl, wishing she'd had more time to make herself presentable. This was not the way to meet the queen.

But Queen Nialei merely smiled. "Well met and welcome, Sanja. We have been waiting for you both. Come, there is no time to waste. Tell me what you need."

They followed her to the dais where four giants with hooves and antlers stood guard over a small glass cauldron swirling with colorful lights.

It was so beautiful…

"I need Liadan's summoning spell," Fal said. "Where is she? Has the dragon added his blood to the cauldron?"

"Not yet," the queen replied. "But we added ours."

"Father, we need that flame much higher for her!"

At the hearth, the fire blazed so high its flames licked the top edge and scorched the stone wall there. The small crowd drew back from its heat, but not too far. The rest of the cavernous chamber was still freezing.

"I can't hold it for long," the king called back.

"You won't need to," Fal said to himself.

The fire blazed outward, forcing the survivors farther back. Then with one more flare, it spat out a ball of fire that rolled across the floor. It unfurled on the shape of a woman who emerged from it running, her hair still on fire. "The clerics sent this," she said, thrusting a burned stack of parchments at Fal. "I saved what I could, but—"

"And this is why we needed the book," Fal told Sanja. To his sister, he said, "I have it. You and Mother start on your spell." He squeezed Sanja's hand. "Are you ready?"

Sanja nodded.

"Then tell me what I need to do," he said, already pulling her toward a clear corner where they'd have more room to work.

A man who might have been the king's twin stepped into their path. His gaze raked over Sanja. "You still look cold, child," he said with the dragon's voice. "Have some mead to warm yourself."

Sanja looked at the wooden cup he offered in his clawed hand. Its contents were too dark to be mere mead. "Maybe later," she said politely.

Fal squeezed her hand, pulling her back when she would have walked away. "Go on," he said, his voice low and intense, his eyes steady but grave. "Take it."

"But the spell—"

"We have time enough for this," he insisted.

He wouldn't let her refuse, and suddenly Sanja felt as if everyone in the great hall was watching her. Fal blinked, and she looked away, only to have her gaze snared by the dragon's. In the depths of his eyes, she saw so many things, light and shadows, love and pain, endless memories from an ageless existence stretching back farther than anyone but the gods could remember.

Sanja found herself letting go of Fal's hand to accept the cup. The moment she touched it, she felt its magic like a flame neatly contained in liquid. It seeped into her skin, warming her up to her shoulders, and she wanted more of it, still shivering in the cold. But a flame that strong wouldn't warm her; it would burn her alive.

"It's a gift," the dragon said. "A drop of fire, so you will never be cold again." His voice was low, soothing, and threatening at the same time.

A gift. The same one he'd given to Fal's mother? Sanja didn't know what to say.

Fal put his arms around her and whispered at her ear, "Drink, little mate. To the last drop."

"It will hurt," she said with absolute certainty. "But I have already endured far worse." She'd endured snowstorms in nothing but haircloth. She'd been stabbed through and turned to stone, and still walked away in one piece. Whatever else this cup had to throw at her, as long as she had Fal holding onto her, Sanja knew she could survive anything. She'd gladly take a drop of fire over the piercing ice in her bones.

Raising the cup to her lips, she tossed the contents back in one large gulp.

It burned going down, but the pain was nothing compared to the inferno it ignited in her belly. Her breath caught on a scream that never made it past her throat. Her knees buckled, but Fal held her fast. Liquid fire exploded inside her, pouring into her veins, melting through her bones, searing her mind with things no human should ever have to know, but she dug her fingers into Fal's bracing arms and held on. She didn't fight the fire; she embraced it, gave herself up to it, and let it do with her what it would.

And it hurt in ways she didn't have words to describe.

But it also made her stronger. It reshaped her somehow on an elemental level so that when she felt her husband's heart beating next to hers, she also felt his magic. She heard his thoughts whisper across her mind. His strength poured through her limbs and fortified her spine, and Sanja felt invincible.

When the fire eased to a soothing warmth, Sanja braced her legs to stand on her own and looked around with new eyes. Everything she saw had a glow of magic around it, and nothing moreso than the dragon. His essence filled the great hall to bursting, and he'd just given a little piece of it to her. She bowed humbly. "Thank you."

"Would that I could have done it sooner."

A shrieking howl echoed outside. The ground shook under them, and dust rained down from the rafters.

Fal released her to pry at the book's bronze clasp. "We're out of time. Sanja, the spell."

She brushed his fumbling hand aside, and deftly worked the mechanism. The latch popped open, and the strap fell off. "The pages fit in an unbroken sphere," she told him quickly, leafing through the volume to find the pages with symbols on them. "You must find the centerpoint and sing the symbols in a spiral."

She found the section and began to tear out one page after the other, careful to preserve all the symbols. As each one fell away, Fal caught it with his magic and raised it into the air. The edges folded down along the proper seams, and he fit them together.

With the sphere completed, the symbols began to glow. They separated from the parchment that was no longer needed to contain them, and the pages wafted to the floor.

Sanja watched the last one drop into the water and warily lifted her foot out of a puddle that was growing into a lake around them. "Fal…"

He hadn't noticed, still holding onto the book as he studied the sphere of symbols. "It's a perfect sphere. Where is the starting point?"

"Fal, I need you to pull it back." She groped at his shoulder, but his hands were busy with the book, and she couldn't find his bare arm beneath the folds of his cloak while also keeping an eye on the chaos reigning around them. His illusions were manifesting in reality. Water spilled across the great hall in a flood that swept everyone off their feet. It poured down the walls into a lake that filled the chamber and began to freeze over. The streaming waterfalls froze to icicles and broke off into deadly sharp spears.

The dragon had joined the rest of the royal family on the dais, where Princess Liadan was performing some other kind of spell with whatever was in the glass cauldron. He grimly surveyed the rising water and said something to the princess, who nodded in answer without looking away from her task.

"It doesn't make sense!" Fal leafed through the book, barely glancing at the pages. The water rose faster the more agitated he became, and within moments it was up to her waist.

She was still groping along his sleeve when someone opened a door.

"I found it!"

"Fal!" The fabric slipped through her fingers as her feet went out from under her.

"Sanja!" The book fell from his hands as he reached for her, too late. The current swept her away from him and through the open doorway into a dark, narrow corridor. She managed to catch hold of a tapestry, but it tore off its moorings. Sanja screamed as she went under. Her skirts tangled around her legs; she couldn't tell up from down. In the cold, churning darkness, all she could do was hold her breath and pray.

Something lashed around her wrist, pulled her back to the surface. She came up sputtering, never so grateful for the ability to breathe. She traced the thin red tail wound around her wrist up to its owner, a small red creature perched on the rafter above with black hair and silver horns. It hissed at her, then took off on all fours, dragging her against the current all the way back to Fal.

He caught her hand, and the waters stilled into a placid lake, but they could no longer be undone, and the frost was already spreading across the surface.

She laced her fingers through her husband's and held on for dear life. "Sing, Fal!"

The first notes lifted them both clear of the water. Fal sang, and the melody filled the great hall with raw magic that stretched it at the seams. It pounded inside Sanja's head, constricted her chest until she couldn't breathe, but she held on, refusing to let go.

One chance. That was all they'd get.

The sphere spun faster, commanding Fal's song to follow along. He matched it, turned it to his will, and molded it into something bright, and warm, and sweet. Sanja smelled clovers in the air; she tasted honey on the tip of her tongue.

Then, all at once, everything dropped. Sanja broke through the surface of the lake and sank down into its impossible depths. Up became down, light turned dark. She wanted to laugh, and cry, and scream, as chaos tossed her about, and her only anchor was the hand holding fast to hers.

⋘ »·◇·« ⋙

The tide of battle was turning in their favor. Artairas could feel it in his bones. They'd cut across the city and left a path of destruction in their wake. The heavens had turned dark and brought them a terrible snowstorm to hide their advance. The frigid wind cut deeper than any sword, but Artairas and his men had God on their side. Their purpose propelled them on toward the castle seat of this heathen land.

It was guarded by beasts of legend, but he already knew none of them would be a match for his Holy sword. Not even the dragon. The Lady of the Lake had said so herself. She'd anointed him King Arthur and told him his kingdom would be built on the victories he would win here. She'd returned to him the sword he'd thought lost to evil magic, and it was even now guiding him true.

The storm clouds coming in from the north were as black as night. He dared not stand against such might. When the storm reached the city, Artairas would have to sound retreat.

But not yet.

"*Charge!*" he roared, meeting an opponent at a dead run. He slashed through the soldier's leather armor with ease. Cold made them all slow and clumsy, but not him.

He cut down three more in quick succession, grinning at Gawain fighting at his side. The two had become nigh inseparable, gathering more loyal men along the way. Percival fought bravely to his left, a man called Galeas not far behind.

As they neared the castle, the battle intensified. Gusts of wind-born snow obscured his vision. He attacked anything that rushed him, be it human or other. Beasts with silver claws fell at his feet. Things with green skin disintegrated into slime when he pierced them.

Tristan's shout sounded a warning moments before one of the great, unkillable beasts slammed its way through the ranks. It reeked of rot and death. Its crazed eyes never stilled. With a severed limb still clutched in a monstrous claw, it tore open throats with its fangs and tossed away dead bodies like discarded toys.

Gawain caught his arm, already pulling him away. "My Lord, this way!" He had to shout to make himself heard over the roar of the coming storm.

Artairas shook him off. "I will not cower before a mindless beast!" He wiped the melting snow off his brow, spat blood onto the snow, and ran at the monster holding Sir Marrok in its clutches.

With a mighty war cry, he charged, God's sword clutched tightly in his grip. He slashed at the beast and scored a mark, a thin cut across its thickly furred arm. The beast tossed Marrok aside and snarled at Artairas, a drop of bloody saliva pouring from its maw.

Artairas' blood boiled. This was a worthy opponent. Strong, fast, and deadly. One wrong move and it would rend him in two. He grinned, savoring the spicy thrill of danger. With black clouds darkening the sky overhead, and the deafening roar of the storm crashing down on him, he charged the beast. His sword glinted in the dying light as it cut the air itself, aiming true for the beast's neck.

But the strike fell empty, and Artairas stumbled to his hands and knees in the snow, with nothing to show for his bravery.

The beast was gone.

The storm died down with a suddenness that brought his head up, and as sunlight broke through the receding clouds, he looked out across an empty landscape of snow and distant trees.

The snowdrifts moved, spewing out his men one after the other, including Marrok, torn and bloody, but alive. Gawain stumbled up to Artairas, helped him to his feet, but said not a word. Percival crossed himself, his wary eyes gazing around in disbelief.

All of the men looked as baffled as Artairas felt, searching for an enemy that was no longer there.

They'd fled.

No, not fled, disappeared into thin air, along with the entire God-forsaken city, leaving nothing but a level patch of ground where the castle ought to stand.

As far as the eye could see, Artairas and his men were surrounded by land covered with snow and completely devoid of life.

CHAPTER 35

The water spat them out onto hard stone, exactly where they'd been a moment ago. Only it wasn't the same place any longer. The great hall was dry and neatly appointed, with all its furnishings returned to pristine condition and a strong fire crackling merrily in the hearth.

Fal groaned as he sat up. "Did it work?"

"I don't know," Sanja said. "But, I am not cold anymore."

Rather than risk letting go of her prematurely, Fal pulled her up to stand and drew her with him to the courtyard outside. A beautiful clear blue sky greeted him above. The ground was warm, with flowers blooming in their garden beds. The gate that had been shattered moments ago was now whole and opened to admit visitors from far and wide—and there were many. Humans, as well as Others, filled the streets, bedraggled, wounded, but very much alive.

"This is Anderheim." Fal whooped and caught Sanja up in a spinning dance around the courtyard. "We did it! We saved everyone! I can feel them, Sanja, hundreds of thousands of them. We are going to need more space. I will have to expand the Otherland farther out to fit them all in."

Laughing, Sanja pushed to be set back on her feet, and he obliged her. "First, I want to see my parents. Can you take me to them?"

Fal searched through the many minds filling his new world, but as far as he could reach, he found no sign of Gerhart or Olga. He tried again, and again, and one more time, but came up empty. "They… Sanja, I'm sorry. They are not here."

"Don't be silly. They have to be. We saved everyone, remember?"

Gods, how he wished he had a different answer to give her. Fal wished he didn't have to say the words that would break her heart, but he owed her the truth. "Liadan's spell summoned everyone still alive in Wilderheim with its magic inside them."

Sanja's bright smile dimmed. He felt the pain of loss stab through her, and it nearly brought him to his knees. It hurt all the more to know how hard she was fighting to stay strong. "Y-you're saying they're dead."

Fal pulled her into his arms. Sanja didn't return the embrace, so he squeezed her as tight as he dared, needing her to know she wasn't alone, and never would be again. "I'm so sorry."

"B-but they were on their way to Lyria. They could have made it through the pass in time."

"Yes," he said for no other reason than his mate needing to hear it.

She shuddered, sniffling back a sob as she put her arms around him at last. "Thank you for lying to me."

He pressed a kiss into her hair and squeezed her a little harder.

Princess Liadan burst out of the keep, calling out, "Tir! Tirasdunh al Dhakir, answer me right now!"

Fal swore.

"*Tir!* Where is he, Fal? How bloody far south do I have to fly to get him? Because he is sure as shite not anywhere in this Frastmir. I called the dragon's blood—that means he has to be here somewhere, too."

Behind her, the dragon emerged slowly, followed by the king and queen, side by side and hand in hand. The dragon placed a hand on Liadan's shoulder. "Do you remember the barrier along Wilderheim's borders with Mitgard? It kept us in and others *out*. Tir isn't here, child, because your spell never made it past Wilderheim's borders. He is still in Aegiros."

"He's safe?" Liadan asked through gritted teeth.

"Yes," the dragon confirmed. "I sensed the storm coming from the north before we left and felt it strike the barrier to our east. Fenrir claimed Wilderheim, but he was not allowed into Mitgard."

Later, when the dragon's words have had time to sink in, Fal would revisit them and wonder what could have stopped a creature so powerful all the gods of Asgard couldn't keep him contained. For now, his worries were much more immediate.

Liadan's eyes blazed blue, and her skin took on a faint glow. "Then let's go get him."

"We can't," Fal said. "The doorway is shut to keep Fenrir out. I might be able to open a small window briefly, but whoever leaves will never be able to come back."

Liadan shook her head, her entire being steaming as her fire rose, only to be doused by her tears. "No, I will not believe that with all the magic contained in this courtyard alone, no one has the power to bring my mate to me."

"And if we could?" the dragon asked. "His tribe would be left without their leader, vulnerable to attack again when they have barely found their footing back in the First Valley. They need him. His place is with them."

"And mine is with the clan," Liadan replied bitterly. "Is that what you are telling me, Grandfather?"

"I am telling you the time has come for you to choose."

Liadan gaped at him, speechless.

Nialei and Saeran reached out to her, but she shook them off and launched into the air, burning into her Other self, and she flew as fast as her wings would carry her, heading south.

"I should go after her," Saeran said.

The dragon sighed heavily. "No, give her time. She needs to come to terms with this, and none of us can do that for her." The last, he said to Fal, but whatever silent message he tried to convey with his inscrutable eyes, Fal didn't understand.

≪ »·◇·« ≫

Night descended gently on a chorus of bird songs and cricket chirps. Those Others who chafed in close confines removed themselves to the farthest reaches of Anderheim. The rest spread out across the Otherland to begin building new homes for themselves. The cities they left for humans. Fal had done what he could to bring as much of Wilderheim with them as possible to ease the transition. What the people lacked, Anderheim could easily provide.

Nialei and Saeran took over organizing a new council and getting their new kingdom on its feet. Fal, meanwhile, closed himself off in his chambers with Sanja.

Beyond exhausted after the day's trials, Fal wanted nothing more than to sleep, but Sanja's grief ached in his mind long after she dozed off. Without trying, he saw her thoughts churning over the last time she'd seen Olga and Gerhart before her Journey. Her father had been adamant about staying put until Sanja returned. They never would have left Wilderheim without her.

When her dark thoughts pulled Sanja into bad dreams of faceless monsters hunting her in the night, Fal couldn't stand it any longer. He put his forehead to hers and closed his eyes. Reaching into her dreams, he brought sunlight to her night and turned the dark woods into a meadow filled with wildflowers, birdsongs, and music.

Tables laden with food appeared on one side. A group of musicians picked up their instruments on the other. Fal's clan, Sanja's parents, and her friend Mattias shimmered into being around them, and then the meadow filled with nobles and villagers, all cheering for their happiness.

It was the feast they should have had to celebrate their wedding. Fal could never give her a real one now without her parents, and so he filled her dream with as much warmth and happiness as it could hold until it became as real as a memory. Then he let himself sink into it, too, and forget it had never been real. It was the most beautiful dream Fal had ever dreamed, and the most restful sleep he'd ever slept.

But when dawn broke, and Liadan still hadn't returned, worry over his twin dragged him away from the warmth of Sanja's embrace to the window.

"You look dashing in the morning light," Sanja said from the bed. She was smiling, rosy-cheeked, and deliciously rumpled. Just awakened from their shared dream, the shadows of grief had yet to catch up to her, and the beauty of her spirit sparkled across their connection directly to his heart.

Fal welcomed her momentary happiness, let it distract him from his own heavy thoughts. "And does that please her royal highness?"

"Very much," she purred, stretching beneath the covers. "I like you very much without your illusions and cloaks."

"I feel weightless without them." It was an odd feeling but a pleasant one.

Sanja slipped out of bed to join him at the window. Her thin arms came around him, and she pressed her front to his back, kissing his shoulder. "Don't worry. I will keep your feet firmly on the ground."

Fal chuckled, bringing her hand to his lips. "Did you sleep well?"

"Well enough." He followed her thoughts to her dream and, through it, to the memory of her parents. The heartbreak he'd begun to heal while she'd slept reopened, but she didn't say a word. Instead, she raised up on tiptoes to look over his shoulder out the window. "Any sign of Liadan?"

"Not yet."

Sanja wasn't ready to face the loss of her parents, and Fal wouldn't press her. There were other, gentler ways to help her. Sensing her persistent chill, he left her embrace to stoke the embers in the hearth and added more wood to it. Despite Anderheim's summer heat and the dragon's blood warming her from within, he knew Sanja would always need a fire burning nearby. He would never let her be without one. "What did the dragon mean about her having to choose?" Sanja asked, slipping back under the covers.

He sighed, searching the skies for any sign of his sister. "One trip, no way back. If Liadan decides she wants her mate more than all of this, it is possible I could still send her to him. But once the window closes, I may never be able to open it again."

"What if she chooses to go, anyway?"

The fire flared in Fal's hearth, admitting his sister. "Then she would be trapped in a foreign land forever, the only Other of her kind among mortals who fear her magic," she said. "Never to see her beloved mountains again, never to embrace her parents, or call her brother a bumbling idiot."

Fal snatched his sister into his arms. "Would a bumbling idiot have saved an entire kingdom from destruction?"

"No," she replied softly, then turned them to wink at Sanja. "But his brilliant mate would."

Fal scowled at them both as Sanja burst into helpless giggles in their bed. The gods had smiled down upon him the day they'd put him into her path on the green, and he would be forever grateful.

"Rest easy, brother. I have made my choice. I am staying here, with you cantankerous lot." But her eyes turned gray like ash when she said it, and despite her irreverent grin, he sensed the heartache underlying her words. She was saying what she thought he wanted to hear. "I came to you only because I would like to see Tir one last time. I tried to scry for him, but it appears my flames don't reach beyond Anderheim's borders."

"Of course," he said without hesitation. "I will need a few things. Sanja?" Only yesterday, she'd lain bleeding in his arms. He found it difficult to let her too far out of his sight.

She smiled softly, but he saw shadows of unease gathering in her eyes. "Go, I will be all right on my own for a little while." Sanja wouldn't say anything, but he felt the way her heartbeat sped up. She didn't want to be alone any more than Fal wanted to leave her.

He nodded. "I won't be long."

He took Liadan to his tower library. Fully restored to its original glory, it now had a window to let in the morning light.

Liadan hesitated at the threshold. "The last time I stepped in here, half of the chamber was gone. The time before that, it was filled with water." She shook her head with wonder. "You never fail to amaze, brother."

"So says the woman who burned a horde of demons to ash and restored water to her desert people."

She answered his smile with a wan one of her own. "How long will this take?"

"No time at all. I just wanted to have my wards around me when I muck about with the fabric of my Otherland." Without any further ado. Fal placed the flat of his hand on the stone wall and sang a sweet melodic command to open it. The stone rippled like a mirage, and when the center cleared, the desert night stretched out before them. They were looking at the First City, nestled in a verdant valley that a few short months ago had been a barren desert.

Liadan joined him before the window, her face lighting up with wonder. "Can you bring us closer?"

Fal tilted his head, and they raced across the sands to the riverbank, over the bridge, and into the heart of the city. Fal opened the window wider, watched his sister's face closely as the scent of jasmine and oil lamps filled the room. Her eyes closed dreamily as she took a deep breath. That was all it took for the sallow pall of her skin to recede beneath its natural golden glow. Liadan came to life at the merest glimpse of the desert.

With tears spiking her lashes, she opened her eyes so she wouldn't miss a thing as they followed the main thoroughfare through the market to the palace with its towering spires and arched windows. They found Tir in the royal chambers, sitting at the edge of a fire pit, so close his billowing pants were beginning to singe. He didn't notice, staring intently into the flames.

"He is looking for me," Liadan said miserably, hugging her middle. "I told him I would never be more than a call away, that as long as he kept a fire burning bright, I would always come back when he called. Fal…"

"I know, Lia."

"I can't stay here."

"Nor could I." If he were the one standing there, looking at Sanja across an eternity, knowing he'd never be able to touch her, hear her voice… The thought of it made his throat close up. He would no more keep Liadan from her mate than he'd want her to keep him from the woman he strongly suspected he was beginning to love.

Liadan had helped him find his way to Sanja; he owed it to her to get her back to Tir. Even if it meant he might never see his twin sister again.

"But I cannot leave you, and our parents, and the dragon—"

"We will never be more than a thought away, sister. And who knows? Perhaps one day I will find a way for us to visit without undermining the foundation of an entire Otherland."

She launched herself at him, hugged him so tightly his ribs creaked.

"Careful! If I lose the window, it will be gone forever."

"I love you, Fal. You will always be the other half of my soul."

"Live long and rule well, Liadan. The hearts of your clan go with you."

She released him, wiping her nose on her sleeve. "Don't let Father's head get too big for his crown. He may be king, but Anderheim is your world. And keep an eye on the dragon, will you? He puts on a brave face, but he needs his kin more than he will ever let on." Touching her forehead to his, she added, "And don't you dare let that girl in your bed slip through your fingers."

"Never," he swore. "I will miss you."

"Always, brother."

With those final words, the Dragonblood princess, *shensari* of her people, and the other half of Fal stepped back through the rippling wall to her beloved mate. The disturbance caused Anderheim to squeal in pain, fighting to heal the wound Fal had opened, and the window rippled closed, leaving behind nothing but a long crack across the stone wall of his tower library.

Fal took a deep breath and let it out slowly. "Fair winds and farewell."

He stayed there for a while longer, imagining the life his sister would have in Aegiros. It would never be easy, but Liadan had never liked easy. She wouldn't have her family to advise her, but she'd never taken their advice, anyway. The only thing his sister truly needed was to have her mate by her side, and Fal was fairly certain that after Liadan told Tir all about the war, and Ragnarok, and how close he'd been to losing her to Anderheim, Tir would never let her out of his sight again.

The scar of her departure retained the desert's heat and, if he leaned close enough, Fal could almost smell the heady scent of jasmine and hot sand lingering around it. Liadan would thrive in Aegiros. Now Fal had to make sure everyone in Anderheim did, too.

The castle gates were open. Soon, the great hall would fill with people come to petition their royal majesties for whatever they couldn't live without. His presence would be required, no doubt. He'd spend the next year at least stuck in council meetings and royal banquets, or roaming the lands to mend whatever got broken during his spell. People would look at him and truly see him, and they'd tell him how grateful they were for their new home, and how they'd love it so much more if only they had this or that. And once those conversations began, they would never end.

Fal would be expected to teach wizards the ways of Anderheim's magic, and the Others would keep him so busy creating unique landscapes for them he would never again lack for an outlet for his magic.

In short, his days of solitude and study, of hiding from his people and fearing his magic were over. His only solace of peace, if not quiet, would be measured in the moments he spent with his lovely, brilliant mate, who would always have wildflowers in her hair and a book in her hands, and whose heart would forever beat right next to his.

Fal smiled.

It was good to be the prince.

APPENDIX

« THE REALMS »

WILDERHEIM

As a physical border between the world of humans and Otherlands, Wilderheim is steeped in magic and home to all kinds of otherworldly creatures. However, they were not openly welcome or accepted as members of society until the crowning of Queen Nialei. Because of their presence, the kingdom's political structure is also quite unique. Wilderheim is meant to be ruled by a human king. However, to keep the peace with Otherkind, a skilled wizard is appointed to act as the king's most trusted advisor and a peacekeeper to ensure both human and Other needs are addressed. The careful balance of human law and Other magic is the crown's highest duty.

The land is distinguished by a vast mountain range to the north, with a border of thick, evergreen forests at its base. The region to the north of this range is inaccessible and remains unexplored by humans. The range curves south on the western side and forms a natural border between Wilderheim and Lyria. On the eastern side, the range fractures into a gorge which forms the natural border between Wilderheim and Ravetia. The southern border with Aegiros has no natural defenses. It is lined by a string of stone keeps which date back to the Aegiran war.

LYRIA

The coastal kingdom of Lyria is known as the land which welcomes all. Its people are skilled seamen, explorers, and traders who favor diplomacy over conflict in all things. Lyria shares a border with Wilderheim to the west, Synealee to the south, and a small, open pass in between with Aegiros. This pass presents the only natural vulnerability, as the rest of the kingdom is bordered by either mountains or turbulent northern seas. Its castle city of Dai is a haven of culture, education, and art. As a well-known trading post, it's popular with merchants from all over the world, and its markets offer wares not easily found elsewhere.

Lyria welcomes all who come in peace, which made it especially vulnerable to invasion during the Aegiran war. Though the kingdom suffered tremendous damage and loss, its political philosophy has not changed. Despite having learned from their mistakes and fortified against any future attacks, Lyria remains open to all who seek to enter in peace. Because of the king's strong familial ties with the ruling clan of Wilderheim, the two kingdoms have been at peace for generations. This does not hold true for Lyria and Synealee.

SYNEALEE

Also know as Synealee by the Sea, this kingdom used to share a border with Wilderheim, but lost a great deal of its northeastern territory to Aegiros during the Aegiran war. It is now cut off from the rest of the continent by a continuous mountain range that curves northwest to east. Its landscape is largely flat and fertile. Its natural resources are few, and the most common trades are agriculture, woodworking, and fishing. The castle city of Palos is also the largest in the rural kingdom and is considered the birthplace of Synealee's faith.

The kingdom's physical separation causes political and spiritual isolation. Synealee's relations with Wilderheim ended completely after the war and its association with Lyria is strained at best. As a result the kingdom suffers for lack of trade, both mercantile and intellectual. Many advances embraced by other kingdoms are either unknown in Synealee or forbidden outright. It is ruled by a religious zealot who imposes harsh laws for the kingdom at large. Dissent of any kind is not tolerated. To speak out against the faith is to speak against the crown, and such treason is met with swift and brutal punishment.

Aegiros

The region of Aegiros is not politically unified. It is populated by small, individual tribes, each ruled by its own king, or *shansher*. The region is mostly desert and, as a result, its tribes are in constant conflict over its limited resources. The Aegiran war marked the largest and longest unification of tribes in recent history. Under the leadership of Dhakir the Conqueror, *shansher* of the Imarah tribe, Aegiran warriors attacked to the west, claiming a large swath of land from Synealee, and invading the non-combative kingdom of Lyria. There, after a long, bloody campaign, Aegiran forces were defeated with the combined forces of Lyria and Wilderheim.

At the heart of Aegiros lies the First Valley, a narrow strip of green on either side of a river which flows west to east. The First Valley is the most fertile region and, as such, is a constant target for tribal attacks. It has been held by the Imarah tribe for centuries, until its river dried out seemingly overnight, forcing the Imarah into exile.

Ravetia

The kingdom of Ravetia lies to the east of Wilderheim. Geographically, it is the largest kingdom on the continent and mostly isolated from its neighbors, Wilderheim and Aegiros. At its heart is a gigantic inland sea at the center of which lies its island castle city. The kingdom is rich in gold, silver, and precious stones. Jewels and adornments from Ravetia usually have a unique cultural motif and are highly sought after in Lyria and Wilderheim.

Ravetia is open to travelers and traders, but does not initiate travel or trade. The kingdom is steeped in ancient traditions and superstitions. This includes a deep suspicion and distrust of magic, which makes for strained relations with Wilderheim. The shared border is reinforced on either side of the ravine by keeps and outposts manned by armed warriors in an endless, but thus far peaceful stand-off.

⋞ GLOSSARY ⋟

Aegiros – Desert region in the south, instigators of the Aegiran war.

Aesma Daeva – God of lust, anger, wrath, revenge, violence, conflict and war. Antithesis to Ahura Mazda.

Anderheim – An Otherland that mimics Wilderheim, created as an illusion by Pince Fal of Frastmir.

Aseti – Aegiran term for outcast, someone on the fringe of tribal society forbidden from acquiring work, marrying, or having children.

Asgard – Realm of the Northern gods.

Cernunnos – A secretive horned god of wild things. Little is known about him, other than he has a gift of bringing rival species together in peace. He can also create new species. He rewards those he likes with pouches of gold coins. His symbol is a rack of antlers, and a torc.

Clerics – An order of men and women whose calling and duty is to acquire, share, and preserve knowledge.

Crossroads – City in Wilderheim, the central point of the kingdom.

Daeva – Demonkind, male spirit of chaos, disorder and evil.

Dai – Capital city and castle seat of Lyria.

Danna – Aegiran term for uncle.

Dragon Lakes – a group of lakes in Wilderheim in the shape of a dragon.

Fenrir – The great wolf foretold to devour everything, including the gods themselves during Ragnarok.

Fire Sprites – A clan of Others made of fire. They appear to be diminutive, like floating embers, but they are no less powerful for their size. They can be mischievous and temperamental, leading humans by their hearts and passions. In battle, they wield the full force of fire.

Frastmir – Capital city and castle seat of Wilderheim.

Hallowed Mountain – A peak of the mountain range north of the castle city of Frastmir, location of the cleric's temple.

Hel – Goddess of the realm of the dead, daughter of Loki.

Helheim – Realm of the dead, a place for those who did not earn their place in Valhalla.

Ice Fey – A clan of Others who live in a land of eternal ice and snow. They are characterized by white hair and often have blue markings tattooed into their dark skin. They fight in golden armor and weapons made of ice and light. Known for their fierceness in battle, they sometimes fight in human conflicts to turn the tide of war.

Idrah – Aegiran term of endearment roughly translated as dear one, little heart, darling.

Inaras – Queen of heaven, great mother, goddess of fertility, love and war.

Journey (the) – A quest to join the order of clerics, consisting of a physical trek up to Hallowed

Mountain, and a mental test of truth and honesty.

Journeyman – Someone (man, woman, or child) who is undertaking the Journey to become a cleric.

Journeyman's Sanctuary – Ancient magic imbued in the land itself that protects Journeymen from malice and assault on their path to the cleric's temple.

Kharesh – Aegiran warrior/assassin, trained in the arts of battle and death.

Loki – Half-giant god of mischief, known to play tricks on gods and humans alike, foretold to bring about the end of the world: Ragnarok.

Lyria – Kingdom neighboring Wilderheim to the west, ruled by Saeran's uncle, King Halden, succeeded by King Ulrich.

Masar – Aegiran term for slaver or slave driver.

Masiranah – Aegiran term for slave harem.

Meagara bahran a mi – Aegiran for "Please help me."

Naras tograth fa toran di taprath – Aegiran proverb: "A wise man knows to hold his tongue."

Palos – Castle city of Synealee and castle seat of Queen Genevieve.

Ragnarok – A prophecy of the end of an age, when the great wolf Fenrir will break out of his binds and devour all the worlds and the gods themselves.

Ramesh feh – Aegiran custom of ending a war and ensuring peace through marriage.

Ravetia – Kingdom to the east of Wilderheim, seat of King Gavriil.

Shai'iss – A term which has no simple translation in any other language. It is rarely used, and always with great respect and humility, as it implies an aspect of the soul and its connection to another.

Shalla shansher an Imarah – Aegiran war cry, "For the king and tribe."

Shansher – Aegiran title of a tribe leader. The equivalent of a lesser king.

Shensari – Aegiran title of a tribe leader's mate or first wife. An honorary title which carries respect, but not authority.

Shensari bahran sephri – Aegiran battle cry, calling warriors to the aid of their queen. Literally, "Your queen needs help."

Sher'nah – Aegiran term for heir or prince.

Sidhe – A clan of royal Fae. Cold, logical, beautiful, and powerful. They are often seen as either the leaders of all Other clans, or their designated rulers. In some ways, they are the law makers for all Others. Not all clans accept their judgments.

Synealee – Kingdom to the south of Lyria. Also known as Synealee by the Sea, seat of Queen Genevieve.

Tir – God of war who sacrificed his hand to trick Fenrir into stasis.

Trackers – A clan of Others with a unique ability to find anything or anyone in any realm. They are highly prized and feared for this. Exclusively female, they have the lower half of a doe and the torso of a woman. When angered, their veins stand out black against their skin.

Tree Nymphs – A clan of Others whose life force is bound to her tree. Exclusively female. Tree nymphs can live in their trees and step out of them to freedom, but they can never go too far from their tree. If the tree is harmed, the nymph will feel its pain. If it is killed, the nymph will become human and wither to death.

Ulfhednar – Woden's special warriors, akin to Berserkers. Exclusively male. Fearsome wolf shape-shifters with supernatural strength and speed. They can kill a soldier with a single blow and, in warfare, are used as shock troops.

Undines – A clan of Other creatures made of water. Undines dwell in lakes and rivers. They can be playful, but they become fearsome when threatened. Because they're made of water, they cannot be killed by conventional weapons.

Vayu – Wind god, rules the void between light and dark, even other gods sacrifice to him.

Veil (the) – A mystical barrier separating Otherlands from the realm of humans and one another. Said to have been forged as an extension of the ribbon which bound Fenrir into stasis. Most humans are unaware of its existence and location. However, those with magic can sometimes sense it and pass through to other realms.

Water Sprites – A clan of Others who dwell in waters, but are not made of water. Their voices can heal or kill, and they use them rarely, communicating with their thoughts instead. They have the ability to travel through waterways between Otherlands.

Wilderheim – Northern kingdom home of the Dragonblood clan.

Woden – All-Father of the gods. Gave up one of his eyes for the wisdom of seeing everything, past, present, and future.

Wraiths – A clan of Others who appear as ghostly women with pale skin and bleeding eyes. They usually appear to right a terrible wrong, or to punish someone for a crime. They do so by infecting their prey with disease and malady.

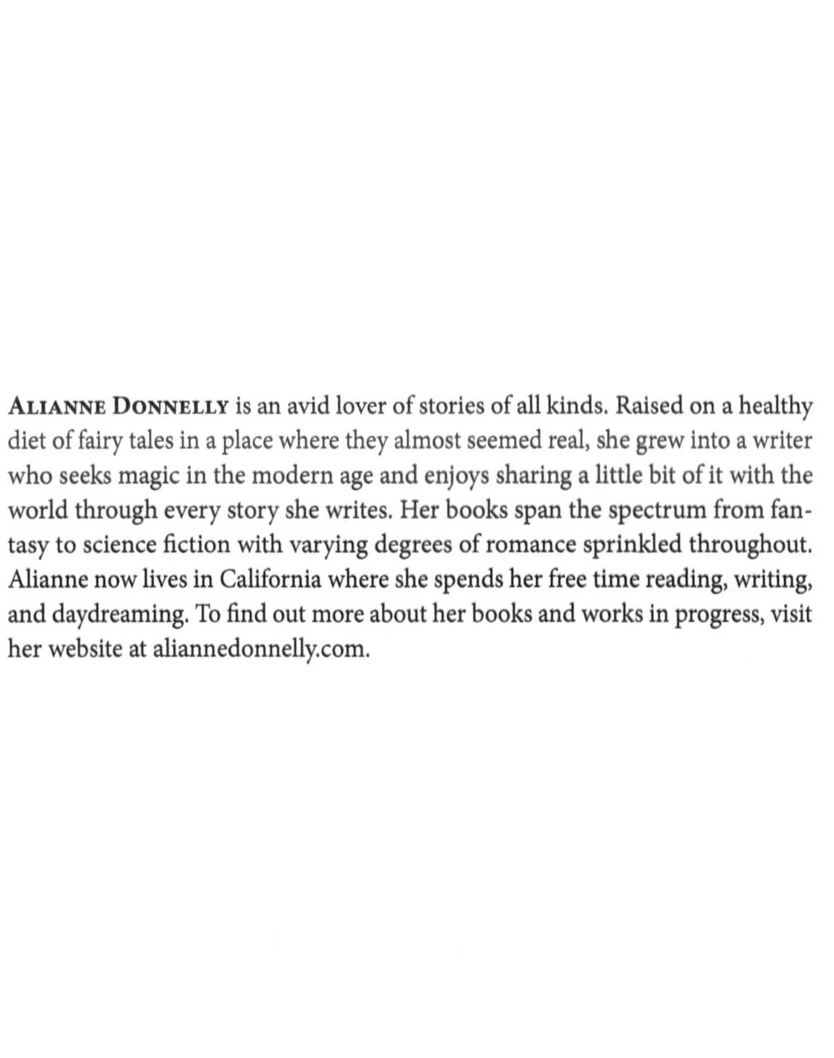

Alianne Donnelly is an avid lover of stories of all kinds. Raised on a healthy diet of fairy tales in a place where they almost seemed real, she grew into a writer who seeks magic in the modern age and enjoys sharing a little bit of it with the world through every story she writes. Her books span the spectrum from fantasy to science fiction with varying degrees of romance sprinkled throughout. Alianne now lives in California where she spends her free time reading, writing, and daydreaming. To find out more about her books and works in progress, visit her website at aliannedonnelly.com.

www.ingramcontent.com/pod-product-compliance
Lightning Source LLC
Chambersburg PA
CBHW020533310726
48979CB00014B/2316/J

* 9 7 8 1 9 4 8 3 2 5 1 3 4 *